The Wars Of The Shannons

Book #3 Of The Shannon Series

By Allan Cole & Chris Bunch

For
Kathryn, Karen, Philip & Betty
And Making His Dedication Debut:
Ryan Ito Cole

Patrick aimed... hearing down the line the SNAPCRACK ripple *of other muskets going off, and the holler came with it, the high-pitched ululation some said came from hogcalling but nobody knew for sure, and all Patrick knew was it scared him to the marrow, so he knew it'd have to set a Yankee back.*

The musket surged against his shoulder, and he realized he'd fired, no idea if he'd put the ball into the gunport as Billy had suggested or maybe let it go at the moon. He couldn't have missed, could he?

The damned gunboat was even closer now. He couldn't hear much, and was fumbling to reload, and Billy was pulling the musket away, shouting about givin' somebody else a chance, and he slid back down the slope as the cannon muzzle came back out the port, fresh-loaded, and again the gates of hell opened. He heard screams, and they weren't battle cries.

Smoke from the cannon fire rose around the gunboat, and down Forrest's battleline. Patrick saw men muscle the little sixpounders up, and they cracked/cracked/cracked and Patrick saw wood splinter and fly, and saw men shout and fall on the Conestoga.

Then Billy had shot and it was his turn, and he loaded, and aimed, and was hollering as loud as anybody, and by heaven this time his musketball did go through the port, he knew it did, and Billy was shouting as loud as he was, a shriek of "damnyoudamnyoudamnyou... "

He couldn't have heard, his eyes must have told his ears to respond to something, but he thought he heard the Conestoga's engines chuffing louder. Certainly he saw one side-wheel churn water, and the Federal gunboat was turning, back the way it had come.

They'd won! A handful of men with muskets, and a few little cannon had driven off the Terror of the Cumberland. Why hell. He heard cheers.

Damn.

About The Authors

International bestselling authors and screenwriters Allan Cole and the late Chris Bunch were collaborators for nearly twenty years. Together, and separately, they published over forty novels and sold more than 150 TV and movie screenplays. Their most noteworthy collaboration produced the eight-book Sten series, hailed as "landmark science fiction" by Publishers Weekly, among others. Especially notable are their novels about America's wars. Those books include, The Wars Of The Shannons, A Daughter Of Liberty, A Reckoning For Kings and Freedom Bird.

For details about the books, as well as Allan's life and work, see his homepage at http://www.acole.com. For information about Chris, see his Wikipedia entry at http://en.wikipedia.org/wiki/Chris_Bunch. Both authors are also featured in the International Movie Data Base (IMDB.com)And be sure to read about the authors' hilarious years as Hollywood screenwriters in Allan's popular blog, My Hollywood MisAdventures at http://allan-cole.blogspot.com/

The Shannon Series:
A Reckoning For Kings
A Daughter Of Liberty
The Wars Of The Shannons

Part One

"And all to leave what with his toil he won to that unfeathered thing, a two-legged thing, a son. " -John Dryden (1631-1700)

"All would live long, but none would be old." - Benjamin Franklin

CHAPTER ONE

VICKSBURG – LATE JUNE, 1855

PATRICK SHANNON SAT crosslegged on the roof of the Texas deck, staring up at the pilot house. The Eclipse was an hour below Vicksburg. Ahead was Great Grandmother Shannon, and - his father had told him - Shannons from every corner of America. But this was not to be a celebration: Diana Shannon was dying and she wanted to see the clan she had created before passing away. Patrick hoped and prayed this woman, whom he could barely believe had actually seen George Washington, would still be alive when they arrived. He also hoped she was still capable of solving problems and bringing justice, as she had been doing for years.

Patrick Shannon, grandson of James Emmett, had serious problems - problems, he believed, which could only be solved by running away. Perhaps to sea. Perhaps north. Perhaps to become a soldier. Almost anything that would take the boy away from his father's lonely, haunted, dying plantation in Virginia. At this moment, Patrick was considering yet another career.

In the Eclipse's pilot house was the 12 year-old boy's newest hero. Said hero stood, resplendent in his brass-buttoned blue coat and plug hat, behind the open window of the pilot house. One hand was negligently draped on the packet's great wheel, the other held a long cheroot.

Patrick Shannon imagined himself pilot of the great steam packet Eclipse. Not the Eclipse whose deck he sat on, but a new Eclipse, one that was longer, wider, faster - much faster - and with more gilt and crystal. He would paint his own symbol on each of the paddle houses. Maybe a shamrock, or his initials. The captain be damned. Patrick would be the best pilot on the river. If the captain would not let him do what he wanted... why, he'd find another boat. He'd have a uniform and the respect of anyone who boarded the steamer. And if anyone gave him any lip, why, he'd pull the steamboat over - no matter if there was a landing, an island or a swamp - and put that person off. Let them walk.

He liked the idea of his stepmother wading through quicksand, alligators all around her. Would he put his father ashore with her? Not unless he objected too much. Even then... he'd just put him down with the deck passengers. Let him ride upriver with the servants and peckernecks.

His thoughts were broken by a voice from the promenade below. "Patrick! Get down from there!" It was Pamela. His stepmother. He pretended not to hear. The voice came cracking again. "Patrick Shannon. I am speaking to you. Do I have to fetch your father?"

Patrick rose, his mood shattered. He leaned against the rail and looked down. He didn't want to, but he had no choice. His eyes met Pamela's, and he saw the gloating look on her face and the little smug smile.

Pamela Shannon was a dark-eyed Southern beauty, with six-inch curls dangling under a bonnet the size of a small sail. From Italian leather toe to Paris parasol, she was dressed entirely in pink. Patrick supposed she was pretty. His father said so. The way other men panted around her, he guessed maybe his father was right. To Patrick she was about as welcome as a water moccasin. Less so - at least you could skin a snake.

"Where have you been? Your father has been looking all over for you."

"Here," was all Patrick said. He knew she was lying. The only thing his father ever fretted about was horseflesh, cards and keeping Pamela happy.

"I don't believe that for a moment," she retorted. "You can fool your father. But not me. Now, tell me what low account mischief you've been up to."

"I told you," Patrick blurted, "I've been right here all along." His voice was harsh and full of hate.

"Don't you sass me, Patrick Shannon."

"I'm not sassin'."

"There you go again. Contradicting me."

"Well, I sure as shoot don't know what else to do," Patrick exploded. "If tellin' the truth is contradictin', then I guess that's what I'm doin'."

His stepmother's hard eyes gleamed - she had him now. Patrick's stomach gave a lurch. Pamela was egging him on, pushing him until he made a fatal misstep which she could report in gloating detail to his father. Her lips contorted for a blasphemous hiss sure to send him boiling over. At that moment, an older woman and her young daughter strolled into view. It was plain from their stares they had overheard some of the exchange.

Pamela was sudden total sweetness. "Now, you get away from that rail, Patrick, dear, before you fall," she gushed. "I swear, you'll worry your poor father and me to death."

She pretended to see the women for the first time. An artful blush tinged her cheeks. "Boys just seem to be impossible to handle at his age," she shyly confessed to the older woman. "One scrape after the other. I don't suppose I'll ever get used to it."

The matron nodded in sympathy. "Take a switch to him. That's the only thing I know of that works."

Pamela giggled, shaking her pretty curls. "Oh, I suppose you're right... but I just don't think I could bring myself to actually lay a hand on the poor child."

"He'll thank you for it someday," the older woman said. She looked up at Patrick. "Do as you are told, young man," she said. "Away from the rail or I'll hunt up a fresh switch for her myself."

Patrick got, using the command for his escape. He heard Pamela walking away with the two women, chattering about her young savage of a stepson in that sweet thing, butter wouldn't melt, voice.

As he walked past the pilot house, the pilot leaned out and grinned. "My maw's hair curled if I even looked at a boat from shore. Guess she thought I was gettin' ready to run."

Patrick gaped; Zeus had actually noticed him. "What... what'd you do? Sir?"

"Guess she was right. First chance, I hooked it." The pilot struck a lucifer against the wheel and relit his cigar. "You're a Shannon, aren't you, boy?"

"Y... Yessir."

"Thought I saw the names on the purser's list. Have a gander. Up there on the bluff. That's Mrs. Shannon's place."

Patrick craned through the summer haze. Even at this distance, it looked to be a magnificent house - multiple-sided, like a geometry shape. A... hex... no... octagon. Three - Patrick guessed - storied, with a dome at its top. When he dreamed of Great Grandmother

Allan Cole & Chris Bunch

Shannon's house he knew it had to be wonderful. But just what kind of wonderful he could not decide. Wonderful like some of the houses he'd seen in Virginia styled like Greek temples. Maybe her house would be like the engravings in Mister Irving's books: a great castle of the Moors. A new possibility would be like the houses he'd seen in New Orleans, all filigree and iron work.

But, he decided, what he was looking at was perfectly satisfactory. That great octagonal marvel up there, and its lush grounds would be the kind of house the head of the Shannons would build. The grounds around it, cabins, outbuildings and gardens, were as manicured as any rich Virginian's. White-painted steps with handrails wound down the bluff to a small landing. There were two or three skiffs tied up - Patrick heard they were called yawls on the Mississippi.

The yawls would help. Patrick had learned - especially in the last few years since his father had remarried - that getting out of the house, away from the plantation onto the nearby river was a good way to keep out of trouble. When he was nine, and his father had been momentarily flush, he'd been given a small boat, complete with mast, sail and oars. Even in the worst of times, Patrick could ease his mind by grabbing a book from his father's library, a fishing rod or the cutdown fowling piece he'd been given in another period of good times and heading for the water. Away from the trouble, he could drift, fish, be a pirate, read and eat - under the transom he kept a small box of salt and a small iron spider. Sometimes he'd taken Nehemiah with him... and then he forced his mind back to his previous concern.

He was about to ask the pilot what he'd done after running away to get where he was now. But the man's eyes were fixed on the river. The cheroot went overside. The man's free hand got busy on his bell pulls. The boy looked to spy what danger loomed. Just in front, the river rilled. If this was a creek, that might mean a rock. But there couldn't be rocks big enough this far from shore to threaten the boat. Could there?

One of the great paddlewheels - each one forty feet in diameter - slowed, then churned backward. The Eclipse turned in its course. More bells, and the wheel's buckets spun in the other direction,

Allan Cole & Chris Bunch

lifting great gouts of brown water into the air. Maybe there was a reef of some kind. Like those he'd read about in the Pacific, just waiting to rip a ship apart.

No, he thought, I won't be a pilot; or at least not for awhile. Maybe later. Maybe, after I'm captain of my own clipper, I'd get tired of going around the Horn. That sounded better than his other idea, which was to join the army. Which was best? A good-looking uniform, and being able to tell everybody how you led a cavalry charge against... against whoever the dragoons would be fighting? Guess the Mexicans will never dare American army men anymore, so it'd have to be somebody else. He was pretty sure it had to be a clipper ship, bringing back silks and tea and things like that. Then he would go back to the plantation. That would show Her. He would not bring Pamela silk or anything. Just ride up with his carriage, pulled by a matched set of bays. Let them all look at him, and think about how they had their chance. Maybe he'd let his father take the reins for a turn around the plantation. Or maybe, better yet, he would never go back. Just let them read about his triumphs.

He went downstairs, toward the stern. The cabin was all glitter and color, stretching almost the full length of the Eclipse's boiler deck. Glass chandeliers hung overhead. At nightfall they were filled with lard oil and lit. Transoms over each stateroom door lit the sleeping chambers. At one end of the richly carpeted cabin was a statuette of President Jackson, when he'd been a general; at the other a noble-looking Henry Clay. From the piano to the tableware to the furniture, everything was of the finest.

The menu offered everything from roasts to mutton to chicken to game, plus a cold board. The meals were included in the cost of passage. First class ate very well, as did the ship's officers and clerks. This wasn't true, Patrick had noticed, for the roustabouts and mostly black crewmen. When the cabin passengers had finished eating, their scraps were piled together and fed to the workers. It was called the "grub pile." Some of the passengers thought it funny to stand on the deck above and watch the scuffle. It made Patrick sick. His father would have whipped a man who suggested the Shannon slaves be treated like that.

The cabin was fairly empty - most of the passengers were preparing for the landing in Vicksburg. The big game had broken up and only one of the players was still sitting at the table. The sleek, impeccably-dressed man relaxed, a perpetual half-smile on his face, dealing himself a hand of Patience. The game had started after leaving New Orleans, near Red Church. After supper, three planters ruminating over rum punches were joined by this man. He'd stood around. Somehow the conversation led to the pleasures of studying the History of the Four Kings. Cards and gold had materialized and the play had begun. Patrick's father had stood near the table, wanting to get in. But within an hour, he reported to Pamela more than $20,000 had been on the table. One hand had seen a raise of $1,000 - in gold.

"Too rich for my blood," he'd muttered, and walked away.

Patrick had barely noted the game. After stuffing himself beyond reason at the supper table, he staggered out on deck, just as dark settled down. The Mississippi was a river of lights. Each packet was an illuminated palace, and the palaces stretched far down the river. Probably clear to New Orleans, Patrick thought. And here, coming toward them, were more steamers heading downriver. Lights dancing reflections on the dark, rolling waters. Everyone in America, and all their goods and produce must be afloat this night, the boy had thought. The passenger packets here, here and there.

A cotton packet coming downriver. All that could be seen was the pilot on the Texas and the lofty smokestacks and the twin gangplanks at the prow. From beam to beam, bow to stern, the boat was a mass of bales. They passed a floating grocery, a flatboat that had been converted to better purposes. A few skiffs were tied up to it, and Patrick heard shouts and the screech of fiddle music. The grocery evidently sold more than dry goods.

Further upstream there was a floating blacksmith's shop, the forge still glowing into the night and the sound of the smith's hammer. It was most odd, Patrick thought. Through the flatboat's open door he could see the tiny figure of the smith crashing his hammer against the anvil. And then, seconds later, while the smith's arm was lifted overhead, would come the clang of metal against metal.

12

A bit later the river grew a huge square of darkness. An island - but the island had small lights ahead of it, and a gleam at its rear - a tow of barges full of Pittsburgh coal. The towboat was a steamer, pushing at the rear of the line. Barges were lashed to either side of its bow, and more barges stacked in front, three across and four long. The open span of water in front of the towboat roiled. A man told him this was called a "duckpond" tow. The first barges were cushions, to keep the towboat from staving in the other barges.

Patrick thought about missing a step in the dark and tumbling into that "duckpond..." and the churning paddles of the steamer going over him. He shivered. No. The boy didn't understand how any captain could navigate that monster. The man explained the skill was called "drifting." The towboat would put its wheels in reverse, and let the river slide the entire tow around a bend.

He wished another boat would challenge the Eclipse to a race. Then there would be something to see - if the captain accepted the dare, that is; which he would: Steamboat racing was good for business. The fastest packet charged the highest prices and travelers would seek out its runners to book passage and merchants would pay prime rates to get their goods on the manifest. Good for business - unless there was a wreck or an explosion from the deliberately over-stressed boilers. The illustrated papers regularly showed ghastly woodcuts of parboiled Americans. Patrick heard somewhere that more than four thousand people had died in steamboat catastrophes.

At Baton Rouge the Eclipse pulled against the levee to load/unload passengers and freight. It also took a coal barge under tow. Like the other fast packets, the Eclipse would load from the barge as it steamed upriver. When the barge was empty, it and its roustabouts would be cut loose to drift downriver to load for another customer. The barges somehow never showed up in the engravings Patrick had seen.

There was something different about Baton Rouge, just as there had been in New Orleans. Different from around his father's plantation or even the city of Richmond, where the Shannon family had enshipped for New Orleans. Not just the polyglot of languages and men and women dressed as the boy had never seen in Virginia. He suddenly realized: those cities were alive. This was the West!

Even the air breathed different, easier, in spite of the river's hanging damp.

People seemed like they were going somewhere. As if there were only so many hours in the day, and much to be done. And there was much to be done - cargoes waiting in New Orleans were stacked many yards deep in front of the mile-long row of waiting steamboats. White businessmen and clerks scuttled through the maze - as did the blacks.

Patrick grew up hearing everyone from his father onward swear that "the only thing the niggers know is come day, go day, God send Sunday." A black foreman would stand on a pile of merchandise handing out tickets. Black roustabouts would clamor for them, and then rush toward a steamboat. Huge bales of cotton would be rushed off the boats toward a stacking point. Patrick saw one steamer early in the morning - a cotton packet - loaded to the Texas. At noon the packet was bare of its cargo. Six thousand bales of cotton, and four thousand sacks of seed had come off. Someone said the stevedores were all freemen.

But that was only one of the oddities he'd witnessed. Patrick felt as if he had suddenly been propelled into a entirely new world, as alien as any of Mister Irving's or Mr. Dumas', and as inviting.

Now, the man playing Patience noted Patrick, and his smile broadened. He drew in his cards. Shuffled them twice, his wrists flat on the green baize table. He offered Patrick the cut. The boy shook his head - no. The man cut the cards elaborately, laid the deck on the table, and passed his hands over it. Then he dealt. Four cards snapped down, face up. All of them were aces. The fifth was a king. The man scooped up the hand, reshuffled, and dealt out his solitary game of Patience, half-smile unchanged.

Patrick went out on deck, fairly sure in whose pockets the planters' gold was reposing. He stared out across the water. On the far bank, a shantyboat was tied up. He could see a woman hanging clothes on its deck. Closer to him, turning in an eddy, was a ramshackle dinghy. Its planking was battered and in many colors, all peeling. In the boat was a boy about Patrick's age. He held a long pole and a line ran from the pole down into the water. The boy wore only a ragged pair of pants. The fisherman heard the crash of the paddles and saw the Eclipse. He came to his feet - Patrick admired his ability to stay up in the rocking the boat, waving. The ship's whistle blasted a return greeting, almost deafening Patrick. He waved as well. I could live like that. Live on the water. Be able to watch the ships go past. Maybe go with them someday.

Most of Patrick's childhood had been spent alone. His mother died when he was three. Her name was Beth and Patrick had almost no memory of her. What he had - warmth, a soft voice, someone singing - might well have been memories from the slave, Molly, who was his mammy. His father, Edward, never seemed to know what to make of Patrick. At times he would seem to be very fond of his son. But the affection did not last for very long. Edward acted as if Patrick made him nervous, and would quickly make an excuse to be busy elsewhere.

The children on the nearest plantation - its house nearly ten miles distant - were years older than Patrick. Seven miles further was the home of the only boy about his age. Patrick tried to make friends with him - but that young man seemed interested only in horses or how many birds he, his father or his brother had shot out of the sky - birds left to rot where they fell.

Patrick spent a great deal of time in his father's library. It was large - James Emmett Shannon had begun it - but disorganized. Patrick's grandfather had not been much of a reader. But a library was a symbol of the gentry, like imported claret and champagne, clothes from London, blooded stock, silver flatware and china service. Edward believed the same: reading was not only a mark of the Shannons, but one thing that divided a gentleman from the "others." It would not be uncommon for a visitor to the plantation to find Edward in the library, deep in his Latin Plutarch, and for that visitor to remark on Edward's remarkable learning.

A darkling suspicion made Patrick put a pinprick on the open page of Plutarch. Weeks later, after another visitor had come and gone, Patrick examined the book. It was open to the same, pricked page.

Patrick's playmates were black, the sons and daughters of the plantation slaves. Their parents would be in the fields, and the children put under the care of one old black woman. The children called Patrick the "white pun'kin." They were as quick to push him in a creek, fully dressed, as any of their own. Patrick thought the servant children had more fun than white youngsters. White boys and girls would stand around, making faces, teasing and pulling hair. Somebody would want to have a fight. Somebody might suggest throwin' rocks at the niggers. It was stupid.

Also, none of them ever seemed to read. Nobody ever seemed to want to be a pirate or Natty Bumppo. About the only game they liked was playing soldier. But Patrick tired of always having to be the evil British redcoat thrashed by brave Virginia soldiers. Patrick struck back one time, and told his peers about the novels of Walter Scott. We could play knight. That sounded fairly good, so the group shambled to a pasture, found fence poles for lances and tried to convince some plough horses to be chargers. The game lasted until one boy had a rib cracked by a lance, and Patrick was whipped.

The adults were no better when they came a-visiting. If the visitors were a man and his wife, they would talk endlessly about what was going on in London, or "The Continent." As far as Patrick could tell none of them had ever been out of Virginia, so the information came second or third hand from merchants. Certainly his father had never been to Europe. Still worse - and Patrick was not sure why - was when two or three white men would arrive. There would be a great deal of shouting and drinking and loud boasts of past feats - especially dueling.

Edward Shannon was as expert with a pistol as he was in taking offense. Several men had paid dearly for either not knowing, or disbelieving his reputation. After the visitors were well in their cups, Patrick would be called down and required to spout a lesson won from the latest drunken tutor. Late at night the laughing would get louder. Then he'd hear the men shambling down toward the slave quarters. The next day the slaves would be very quiet. No one would talk about what had happened and Patrick didn't press the question. No, all in all, the blacks were a lot more fun. Real fishing for real fish, with doughballs, cheese or hellgrammites, many hooks on a trotline. That caught fish - fish the black families would have for dinner, Patrick with them, unless his father got snooty and wanted him to eat with him; silent deadly meals of boiled food, just the two of them at the long, linen-draped table.

But the problem was having somebody to talk to. When Patrick started discussing how, when he grew up he would be a soldier, or a sailor or a pirate, the slave children's' faces would go blank. They had nothing to say. In desperation, Patrick started telling them about the books he'd been reading. They were very interested in Washington Irving's Moors - most of them had heard their parents called that by a master. They lost interest in the Moors when Patrick said they were the same folks Stephen Decatur beat up in Algeria. But they were glad the American Navy had won - nobody ought to do that to Americans. Knights in armor were fine - especially when Patrick told them about Edward, the Black Prince. "He was a nigger? Like us?" Patrick didn't know. But he said yes. When he found out the man's nickname came from his armor, he let the lie stand.

His closest friend was Nehemiah, Molly's son. He taught Nehemiah to read. Patrick didn't know - at least for sure - this was against the law. He certainly didn't know this violation of the "Black Codes" was a capital offense in some states. But he knew not to talk about it around white folks. Nehemiah was quick to learn. At first Patrick thought himself an excellent teacher. Then he suspicioned perhaps Nehemiah's mother could also figure. There were a lot of things, he realized vaguely, no black, no matter how young, would ever tell the white pun'kin.

Things changed when Patrick was ten. Something went wrong, and he didn't know what. Plantation land he'd once played on had been sold off to meet his father's mounting debts. Then his father began courting. The object of his affection was Pamela Weatherby. Her father's plantation was two days ride from the Shannons'. She was introduced to Edward by another neighbor - Fitz Maguire. Patrick had always despised Maguire, even though he was related - Patrick was not sure exactly how - to his Great Grandmother Shannon in Vicksburg. Fitz was like Edward, except to extremes. Unlike Edward, however, Maguire was successful. At least he was still buying land and at a bargain price he would tell everyone. He was constantly advising Edward he was too soft on his slaves. "Find an overseer with rice plantation experience. He'll make the niggers

17

hum." Patrick wondered why Maguire would introduce Pamela to his father. Far as he knew, men mostly sought out their own women or were introduced by parents.

Patrick hated Pamela on first sight. They met in his father's house. The boy was dressed in his Sunday best: boots blackened, hair slicked with water. He'd been carefully coached as well as groomed for the meeting. Patrick gave a little bow, and said he was pleased to meet her. He'd tried not to look at the dazzling display of breasts spilling from her low-cut gown.

"Oh, what a darling child," Pamela gushed. "You didn't tell me he was so handsome, Edward."

She flung herself on Patrick - kissing, pinching, and smothering him in heavy perfume. He thought he'd throw up. "Oh, you poor, motherless boy," Pamela said, shedding a single tear. "Look how thin, you are." She pinched at his flesh. "And your clothes..." She plucked at his best jacket. "So shabby."

Then she whipped out a hanky, dabbed spit on it with her tongue and wiped at a spot on his cheek. "Why, Edward Shannon, you should be ashamed of yourself. Who's been looking after this child?"

Patrick saw a silly grin on his father's face. He tried to pull away. Pamela yanked him back, pressing her soft body against his, as she petted and fretted.

"It's kind of hard on a man without a wife," Edward had said. "Nobody but the servants to mind him. It's not the same... without a white woman about."

What was his father saying? They were both doing just fine. Why was he poor mouthin' to this... this... he wasn't sure what she was? But he wished she'd get her claws out of him. He couldn't breathe, she was squishing him so.

"I think I'm goin' to be sick," Patrick said. He wasn't lying. If she didn't let loose right this minute he was going to do something terrible down the front of her dress.

"Oh," Pamela said. In a blink she was across the room, hovering in Fitz Maguire's protective shadow.

Patrick's father felt his forehead for fever. "Can I go to bed?" Patrick whined. He was feeling worse.

"Poor thing," Pamela said, voice dripping sympathy.

Over his father's shoulder, Patrick saw Pamela grin at Maguire - like she thought it was funny Patrick was sick. Maguire winked at her and squeezed her rump. What was going on? He saw Pamela squirm into the squeeze... liking it.

That's when Patrick threw up. He was put to bed without delay.

Some weeks later, Edward took Patrick riding. They dismounted near a stream, and Edward haltingly told his son he had proposed to Miss Weatherby - and she had accepted. "We've been too long," he said, "without the gentling touch of our better side."

Thank God Edward continued talking - because Patrick probably would have blurted something. Even as it was he said, "But... why Her?" He'd already begun capitalizing the pronoun when he thought of Pamela.

"Because... I'm in love, son. You'll understand. When you get older." Edward completely mistook Patrick's look of utter disgust. "Patrick, your mother was a wonderful woman. I shall treasure her memory forever. But there comes a time when a man wearies of walking alone. When he needs a companion. Think on it, son. You'll get used to the idea." Patrick knew he never would.

Despite his feelings, it wasn't Patrick who declared war. That honor went to Pamela. She threw down the gauntlet shortly after the wedding - it was Fitz Maguire who'd given away the bride. While the newlyweds were off on their honeymoon, Patrick became guilt-stricken. He remembered his father's words about being lonely after the death of Patrick's mother. What kind of a son was Patrick to be so unfeeling? If Pamela made his father happy, Patrick would be lower than a skunk to get in the way. He determined to make his peace with Pamela. When she and his father returned, Patrick steeled himself and went to Pamela to apologize. He'd been a rude, selfish fool of a boy, he'd tell her, for acting so cold and hateful after that first meeting.

Patrick found her alone fussing over a bit of embroidery in her sewing room.

"There you are," Pamela said before Patrick had even gotten the first word out. "I think it's about time you and I had a little talk. To begin with-"

19

"Yes'm. That's why I was..."

"Stop that right now!" Pamela's voice had snapped.

Patrick goggled. "Stop what?"

"When I am speaking, young man, I do not wish to be interrupted. Especially not by some spoiled ruffian child who has his father fooled into thinking he's merely high spirited. Do I make myself clear?"

Patrick was floored. "You got no call to talk to me like that," he managed.

"What are you going to do about it? I am your father's new wife. It's me he will be listening to from now on. Me who will be advising him." She leaned forward, eyes blazing with such furious hatred, Patrick's heart lurched. He could see she'd stomp him like a bug if she had the chance. "Listen to me, you little bastard. You're the only child now. A hateful only child. If you get in my way, I'll see that your father disowns you. Do you hear?"

Patrick was too stunned to speak.

"Just remember," she went on, "the last person your father speaks to every night is me." She gave an obscene laugh and patted her flat belly. "In fact, I'm working on the disowning part right now. Keep a close watch on this Patrick. I'll have a little brother in there for you any day now. Do we understand one another?" Again, silence from Patrick. "I'm speaking to you. Answer."

"Yeah... I guess we do," Patrick said, then stormed out before she could respond.

Patrick sought comfort from his only friend - Nehemiah. It took awhile to find him - Pamela had already turned the place upside down. All the household slaves were banned to the fields, traded for her own pet servants. Nehemiah was chopping cotton with the rest of the gang. Very slowly. Advance a step. Bring the hoe down. Wait for a long moment. Another step along the row. Nehemiah, once a dart of energy, worked like he was middle aged.

When the overseer wasn't watching, Patrick went up to his friend. "Let's light out for the creek," he said. "Bet the fish are real hungry."

Nehemiah looked up. Patrick thought he saw a flicker just for a moment, then a great dull look blanketed his friend's eyes. "Can't, massa," was all he said. He started chopping cotton again.

"Whatcha mean, you can't? Course you can." Patrick hadn't caught the "massa." "Come on. It'll be fun."

Nehemiah kept working, ignoring him. The stored up anger rose in Patrick's breast.

He grabbed the hoe from Nehemiah's hands, and threw it down. "What's wrong with you?"

His friend kept his head down. "I'm not allowed to play no more," he'd muttered. "Not with you, anyways."

"Who said?" Patrick was shouting now. Nehemiah shook his head, refusing to answer. But he didn't have to... it was Pamela. "Don't listen to her," Patrick pleaded.

"I gotta listen. Massa."

"Quit callin' me that. I'm Patrick. Not massa."

"Yes... massa."

The kettle Pamela had set to flame boiled over and Patrick struck out blindly. But even as his fist was crashing forward, he tried desperately to stop. But the blow landed.

Nehemiah's eyes glittered. Then he regained control. "Nigger's sorry, for wha'ever massa say he done," he finally said.

There was nothing Patrick could say or do. He got back on his horse and kicked it away. Nehemiah watched him, then, again so slowly, shuffled back to work.

Patrick knew he had to apologize - but could not figure how. He never got the chance. Four months after the marriage, Edward sold twenty slaves south. "A business deal in Jamestown didn't pan out," he explained. Cards? Horses? Patrick didn't know. Among the slaves were Molly and Nehemiah.

Patrick retreated even farther into himself and his books. His father, besotted with his new wife, and charmed by that snake, Fitz Maguire, didn't seem to notice. They were a permanent threesome, although the boy thought, when his father's back was turned, the other two seemed to be sharing a private joke. Sometimes at night, he heard shouted arguments between Edward and Pamela, and never knew the reason. At least the arrival of the dreaded baby hadn't been announced.

He felt - and did not know why - something was about to happen. Just as you could feel the sticky, sweltering silence before a storm. Patrick had no idea what was going to happen - but he determined he would not be there to witness it. He would run. Run to sea, run to the army, run to the north, run to the west. It didn't matter.

Then the letter came from Vicksburg. Great Grandmother Shannon was ill and had called the family together. Edward was suddenly king of the world. This, he told his son, was the answer. With the inheritance Diana Shannon would settle on him, their problems would be answered. "It'll be like old times, son. Nicer things for Christmas. We'll be able to send you to the university. Get you the law degree that'll make you rich. I'll be able to buy back the land. And... show Fitz his help wasn't in vain."

Help? What did that mean?

Patrick discarded the question. Vicksburg. A chance to meet his great grandmother. Maybe ask her advice, although she would probably be no more help than any other grown person. Most important, there would be other Shannons there. One of his cousins was a clipper ship captain. Another was living in California. A gold miner, he hoped.

He would sound them out. They'd never suspect his purpose. But before they left Vicksburg, Patrick would have determined in which direction he would run.

CHAPTER TWO

VICKSBURG

THE TEN-MILE carriage ride to Grandmother Shannon's house seemed longer than the entire journey from New Orleans. The late June heat lay close to the ground and in the shady places the moisture rose from the rich black soil in a mist alive with battalions of mosquitoes. He brushed beneath Spanish moss, which felt like breaking through a spider's web, the touch lingering in the skin's memory long after a body passed.

Patrick had a boy's tolerance for these things, delighting in the little yelps and moans coming from that great bitch-woman, Pamela. "They're eating me alive, Edward! Make them stop!" "Don't fret. We'll be there soon." "Oh, and my poor skin. I swear, I feel like I'm being poached." Patrick smiled, conjuring up a vision of Pamela being put into a big poaching dish by the old black cook back home.

Just before they reached the house the carriage track dipped into a little shady hollow. There was a break in the trees, and Patrick could see the river far below and the private dock poking from the bottom of the bluff. As they climbed out of the hollow, a delicious late afternoon breeze crept down the hill, laden with the scent of wild orange. The road led through a tunnel of trees that widened into a view of the strange-shaped house he had seen from the river. It was sparkling white, and its odd shape promised any number of crannies to explore. The dome made him wish he had a spyglass to watch the river traffic pass. Woods crept up almost to the house's entrance on one side; on the other were magnificent magnolias and white oaks leading toward the river. There were fruit trees of all kinds, including peach, which still bore small white blossoms. A garden planted with roses and camellias hugged the front, with a spray of tall red flowers on either side - poinsettias, he learned later, all the way from Mexico.

People came crowding out of the house to greet them. Patrick was so dazzled he only noticed a woman with a Yankee accent. She was round and small and when Patrick mumbled his name she burst into tears and threw her arms around him. It was Kitty, the woman who had cared for his great grandmother for many years.

Patrick was so tired he didn't much mind Kitty blubbering over him. Besides, she was soft and smelled like fresh bread and Patrick was suddenly taken ravenous. Pamela and Edward were rushed off in one direction with promises of supper served in their room. It was apparent Edward Shannon and his family were the first to arrive.

Kitty whispered that he needn't wait and led him straight through the house. Its inside was as marvelous as the exterior, with everything from Oriental geegaws to paintings to odd sketches that must've been made by one of the Shannons to illustrate his travels. There was even an old sword on the wall. Patrick wondered if it was old enough to come from the War of Independence. Later, he learned his great-grandmother's second husband, John Maguire, had actually carried it in two wars.

Kitty pulled him into the kitchen where she made a thick ham sandwich, poured out a big cold glass of buttermilk, and set the pitcher before him for refills. She chattered away while he ate - asking questions about the trip and listening attentively to his answers. He tried not to talk through his food, but he was so blamed hungry it was hard to mind his table manners.

It was near dark by the time he was done. Kitty took him up the stairs to his room, which was at the end of a long hallway. Inside was a steaming bath in a big tub on a pallet. The bed was turned down and the sheets looked so clean and cool, Patrick wasn't sure he'd make it to the bath.

"You tuck yourself in for the night," Kitty said. "If you need anything, come down to my room and ask. It's just off the kitchen. In the morning, I'll take you to see Mrs. Shannon."

Patrick was suddenly terror-stricken. What if he made a fool of himself in front of his great-grandmother? He had heard so many stories about her that he had an unformed image in his mind of some kind of queen - like Elizabeth of England or Catherine of Russia. What if he never had a chance? What if Great-Grandmother Shannon took one look at Pamela and turned all three of them out?

Kitty must have guessed some of what was on his mind. She laid a small soothing hand on his arm and looked him full in the face with wide, searching eyes. "Mrs. Shannon's been waiting a long time for this, young Patrick," she said. "You know she's very ill, don't you?" Patrick nodded. "I'm not sure she would have lived this long if you weren't coming," Kitty continued. "So have no fear on her account. Just be a good boy and take a bath before you sleep so you're nice and clean and don't ruin your great grandmother's sheets."

Patrick lied nicely and promised he would. When she shut the door, he waited no more than a second or so and then leaped on the bed, fully clothed, expecting to fall instantly asleep. But his conscience needled him and he tossed and turned for long minutes. Finally, he flung himself out of the bed, yanked off his shirt and marched to the tub. He dipped up a big handful of water and splashed his face, even sprinkling a few drops on his upper body. Feeling like a saint, he dried himself vigorously with a rough towel and fell back on the bed. He slept the untroubled sleep of a boy who was as good as his word.

It was not an empress who greeted them the following morning, but a frail little bundle who was hard to make out amid all her bedding. First Edward and then Pamela stepped forward to kiss her. They spoke awhile in tones reverent for being in such close company with death. She lay there, an unbelievably tiny matriarch, with a shock of white hair tied back with a blue ribbon. She wore a white gown, picked out with little bird-like forms the same color as the ribbon.

Patrick would remember her face for the rest of his life. It was smooth for someone so old; his father said she was ninety two. Her skin was the color of fine ivory and was stretched across regal bones. Once when she smiled at something Kitty said, he saw delicate white teeth flash, which surprised him. There were other details, too. Like her hands, which were small and well-formed, except for a few twists and knots for character. The skin was delicate and he could see the blue blush of veins running just beneath the surface. Also, he thought her voice quite remarkable after he had listened closely for a while. It seemed weak at first, but then you caught the strong, underlying timbre. She had a stubborn tilt to her jaw, and a frown that could have put a Roman legion to flight.

The bedroom was large and smelled faintly of some flowery perfume. There was a great ancient trunk at the foot of the bed, made of horsehair and bound up with cracked leather straps with big copper buckles. Light shone through two glass doors that opened onto a verandah. On a mantel there was an oddly new clock - the kind you could set the time on and a bell would chime to remind a body of an errand. It had a bright tick-tick-tick that marked the uncomfortable minutes his father and Pamela were trying to fill. An open door led into a sitting room, where he saw a table laid with a breakfast of tea, biscuits, jam, and a pitcher of orange juice.

His father and Pamela continued their mumbling. Patrick couldn't hear all that was being said, but everyone was being so nice, it set his teeth on edge. Patrick thought he saw Diana's eyes flare when Pamela addressed her once as "Mother Shannon." Maybe it was just wishful thinking. He kept on waiting for his great grandmother to call him forward, but for some reason she didn't seem to notice he was there. Finally, he heard her give a weary sigh. She begged their pardon and waved a frail little hand in dismissal. Patrick was disappointed, but he instantly forgave her - she appeared so... tired.

As they were withdrawing from the room she seemed to notice him for the first time. "You must be Patrick," she said, her voice suddenly light and gentle. "Will you stay with an old woman awhile?" She patted the bed.

Despite the gentle tone, the look in her eyes made the request seem a command. As he stepped forward he heard the door close and they were alone. He sat gingerly on the edge of the bed, leery that his weight might disturb old, aching bones. But a sudden transformation came over her as he sat. She seemed to drop decades when the door shut, and she sat straight up, plumped the pillows behind her, made herself comfortable, then turned the full force of her personality on him.

Her eyes were young and sparkling blue. The pale cheeks took on a lovely, pink hue and she laid a small hand on one of his. It was amazingly warm, and he could feel the strength of her grip and the heavy beat of her pulse.

Allan Cole & Chris Bunch

"I wanted to tell you how much I've enjoyed your letters, Patrick dear," she said.

He flushed and mumbled a "Yes'm," feeling guilty because his letters had been few and mostly abrupt scrawls.

"When last you wrote, you were reading Mr. Dumas, I believe. The Count of Monte Cristo, was it not? What did you think?"

Now, Patrick felt on steady terrain. "It was wonderful, Great-Grandmother Sh-"

"Just call me Grandmother Shannon, dear," she admonished. "The other is too long, and I am much too old to wait for people to get it out."

"Yes'm. Anyway, that's a book a fellow can really tuck into. And read again and again."

"All of it?"

"Well... the first half, really. The rest kinda dribbles on and is sort of silly with all those years he went missing and got mysterious. It was like two books, with the second one not so good. But the first part, when he's in prison with that old man, who teaches him all he knows..."

His voice trailed off as he realized he was prattling on like a baby. Grandmother Shannon, however, gave his hand a squeeze that told him she was enjoying his observations. "What are you on to now?"

He said he liked some of Mr. Dickens, and Typee, by Mr. Melville, and all he could set his hands on of Mr. Poe. Hawthorne was all right, but in his opinion he lacked fire. Not like James Fenimore Cooper. Now, there was a writer! Hawkeye and frightened settlers. Indians creeping through the forest to take a man's scalp.

"Have you read no women?" she asked. "Like Harriet Beecher Stowe, as a for-instance?"

The mention of this great blasphemer's name rocked him. No such book would ever be allowed in his father's house. Patrick had a secret yen to read it, but was afraid to say so. So he ducked behind shyness for shelter and shook his head no.

"You should," Grandmother Shannon said. "As for Mr. Cooper, he is fine for a stirring yarn. But that is all they are: yarns. With little truth to them."

He gaped: The Great Mister Cooper in error? That was a blow. But his great grandmother should know - according to his father she had lived on the frontier for many years. He waited, breathless... Would she tell him anything of her adventures?

Instead, she asked: "Are you a terror, Patrick?" The question stunned him, and he flushed, mumbling he didn't think so. "James Emmett was a terror," she said. "From the moment he was born... he was a terror. And a terror he remained. But he was a good shot. He was also good at hiding from Indians - a valuable talent in Cherry Valley in those days. We all became skilled at that."

Patrick's mind was swimming: His grandfather a good shot when he was a boy! Hiding from Indians! This was thrilling news. He assured his great-grandmother he was an excellent shot himself, although he wanted some teaching on hiding and tracking and such things. But if she needed something shot, then Patrick was her man. She only had to point it out.

Then he forgot all this in a flash as she started telling him a tale of his grandfather when he was a boy on the frontier. He laughed, and she told him other things: the pranks, the scrapes, the hidings he got, the ones he escaped. And she told a few of his great-uncle Farrell Shannon's adventures, which didn't have the same style but were grand just the same. He'd never met either man - they'd died long before he was born - but as she talked they came alive and trooped about her room as if they were boys his own age. Near the end she told him about Brian, and how her stepson was slain while James Emmett was still in her belly. Patrick nearly lapsed into tears at this story, but held them back in manly disdain.

But he couldn't fool his great grandmother. She squeezed his hand and said tears were God's blessing to the Irish. They came as easily as the temper, and might serve to wash away anger's sin.

It was the first of many tale-telling sessions in that room. Before she was done, Patrick would hear the entire history of the Shannon clan in this country, from the old pikeman who admonished his great-grandfather Emmett to read if he did nothing else with his life, to the origins of all the cousins who would soon arrive in Vicksburg.

As the days unfolded he would learn the story of how she met Emmett, who had deserted the army at Valley Forge for the sake of his motherless children languishing on the New York frontier. How she escaped indenture to join him on his wilderness trek, and how they fell in love and were wed by an old Indian. Then, just short of his goal, Emmett was killed by raiders and Diana was left alone at sixteen to raise his sons and the child who was his grandfather. He would hear how Diana had conquered odds and survived bloody Indian raids so the Shannon family could grow and prosper. How she turned a shack in Cherry Valley into a prosperous inn, and then journeyed to Philadelphia with her sons to conquer that city as well.

Finally, she told him how - after many years alone - she had agreed to marry John Maguire in the guttering flames of war-ravaged Washington. John had been a plantation owner, grown bitter at the southern legacy of slavery. Bolstered by her love he had found the courage to risk the wrath of his family and earned the hatred of his sons and their descendants by freeing his slaves, picking up stakes and traveling to Vicksburg with Diana. Here, Diana had prospered even more, creating a healthy financial foundation for all the Shannons to come.

All she had accomplished and dared, Patrick realized many years later, was because of a promise she had made to Emmett. In a wooded glen she had shouldered the burden of the Shannons and carried it for nearly eighty years.

There was much tragedy in her story, but the grand arc of it was glorious: achievement despite all setbacks and against all odds.

After a time she fell silent, as if a great weariness had overtaken her. He looked about, wondering how he could creep away and leave her in peace. But the little hand squeezed at his again and the light grew back in her eyes. "Would you run a small errand for me, Patrick, dear?"

He said he would, that as a runner of errands he had no match, once he fixed his mind to it. She laughed a little, then coughed slightly and touched her chest. "I'm feeling a trifle congestive, dear. There is a medicine a friend of mine makes that relieves the symptoms wonderfully. Will you fetch it for me?"

Patrick said he would, so fast a shadow wouldn't touch his feet.

"Just out back," she said, "you'll see a road along the bluff. It curves into the wood about a mile and then comes to a farm. That's

29

where you'll find my friend, Daniel. Mr. Daniel Cuffe. Give him my respects and ask if he would be so kind as to make up a packet of his special restorative tea... Would you do that for me?"

"Yes'm," he said, and almost bolted from the room so anxious was he to somehow repay her for the stories he had heard and the many more he hoped she would tell.

He got no more than two steps, however, when he turned back shyly. He hesitated, then crossed to her bed. He dared a small peck on her cheek, but a slender arm drew him in and he felt her frail body hugging him close and her heart thundering against the fragile bones of her chest.

She let him go, turning slightly to wipe at an eye. Then she smiled weakly and waved him away. Her eyes closed in drifting sleep. He tiptoed from the room and closed the door softly behind him.

Diana opened her eyes when she heard the door shut. She had only pretended weariness, an art she had practiced since the seizure many months before. The whole thing had started as a means to cover her initial humiliation when she had awakened after weeks of unconsciousness. It was an illness she knew would prove fatal when it struck again. It took her long helpless weeks to recover from the initial effects of the stroke. She knew her mind was as sharp as ever, but she would be suddenly overcome by a great sucking lethargy, drawing her down, down, until she couldn't speak or move. There was no pain, just a feeling of uselessness that she, of all people, could not bear.

She covered by pretending to sleep until the feeling passed. Actually she slept hardly at all, and even then in snatches. With her eyes closed, people left her to her own thoughts.

Diana did not complain, even to herself. She had never expected to live this long. When John died, after twenty years of shared happiness, she had expected to follow him soon. Not for some glorious meeting beyond - Diana did not relent in her doubts of any sort of an afterlife as the Reaper approached. Actually, as she grew older she had became more impatient with notions of religion.

In many ways she'd seemed to grow stronger after her second husband's death. Her business senses sharpened, her insights grew deeper. When she reached eighty, she thought... well, it must come soon now and she made suitable arrangements. But eighty passed, and then some. Ninety she hardly noticed at all, although she reworked her will. Then the illness struck and she knew her run was finally over. As she lay there helpless in her bed, she began forming plans that were about to culminate in this gathering of the main threads of her family; all the while fearing she would never recover to put them into play.

She remembered keenly the moment the symptoms fled. There was no one about, not even Kitty, who was off to town on business. Suddenly she felt alert. She slipped out of bed, still weak from the long confinement. She wobbled to the verandah doors and flung them open. The air was so cool upon her flesh, it felt like the waters of the little brook where she and Emmett had first made love. She drank the air in and it was so rich and sweet that you could taste it, like a fine wine. But just as she thought all was normal again, the lethargy crept up on her and she barely had strength to get back to the safety of her pillows.

At that moment she thought of Patrick. She had never seen her great-grandson's face, the result of her love for Emmett. And what of the others: all those Shannons spread across the land? It was no old woman's conceit that their very existence was due to her. She longed to see how things had worked out. If not well, she supposed she would be a little sorry. But it would not spoil her last moments.

Diana knew her many failures easily matched her victories. After ninety years, however, only she was left alive to keep the score. And it did not look so bleak from such a great distance. Still, she needed to see for herself.

So she'd lain in her bed and plotted and word went by packet and train and telegraph key to all the Shannons to gather at her home on the high buff-colored bluffs overlooking the Mississippi. That Patrick was the first to arrive was a happy accident. Diana felt a little guilty for playing her game of feigning tiredness and then sleep on the child. But it was necessary.

31

After the rest of the family arrived she would have her lawyer, Mr. Levy, drop the cannon shell regarding a new will. Exactly what she would do after that depended on the boy. This was why she had sent him off... not on an errand, as she'd claimed, but to be tested. If he passed, she would be pleased, of course, but not so pleased that she wouldn't pose a few more. Except these wouldn't be tests so much as an education, Diana Shannon style.

The schooling had to be quick, because she had almost no time left. All she could hope was a little would stick enough to serve him the rest of his life.

The boy was absolutely marvelous. She'd fallen in love the instant he'd come into the room. Even at twelve he was so much like Emmett she could barely keep her eyes off him. You could see the shoulders starting to get their breadth, the deep chest filling in, the shock of thick, dark hair, and the dark brows over eyes so blue you thought it was the sea you were gazing into.

Her heart had thundered so loudly, she'd found it difficult to pay much attention to her grandson Edward, or to that woman he'd married... Pamela. She could tell Patrick disliked his stepmother. Poor Edward. He was the unsurprising product of one of her life's great disappointments - James Emmett, her only natural-born son. For a short time she'd thought Edward might be saved when he'd married Patrick's mother. She'd been a sensible woman, just beginning to influence her husband when she died. Obviously, from the news Diana'd had over the years and the foolish, grasping visits her grandson paid on and off, none of it had taken. Then he had wed Pamela, which had seemed to end whatever hope he might have had.

Patrick was another matter. From what she'd heard, the child had been difficult, which was understandable. It would have been hard for any youngster to accept a new mother after many years with only a father for company. Diana had written to Patrick since he was very young and laughed at the infrequent replies in a hand that matured from little scrawls to something steadier and almost legible. She'd watched his mind mature as well in those notes. He seemed to have an odd, catch-as-catch-can education, not unlike herself nearly eight decades ago. His self schooling appeared to be a broth of boys'

Allan Cole & Chris Bunch

adventures, mixed with great literature, with a little Plutarch and Paine stirred in.

Now she had urgent business to tend to that might or might not center on her great-grandson. She had a small empire to dispense, either to split into many parts or to remain under the single banner of the Shannon she might choose to head it. If the latter, the family fortune might serve to buffer the people she left behind.

The money itself meant little to her. She was so much a woman of her revolutionary generation that inherited wealth seemed a bit distasteful. It tended to give folks an opinion of themselves above their real value, shoring up a class system she had fought against her entire life.

The opposite, however, was the current rage: money above all else, prospects of instant wealth which required no sweat of brawn or brain. The new American dream was a heady liquor that clouded the eye and numbed the senses. Diana thought the country had become a nation of compulsive travelers, all looking for accommodations at the same time. Like the weary traveler, nobody seemed to care a whit for any but his own immediate needs.

She heard a bird call from the window and thought it might be a whippoorwill. Her old friend Ann Walsh would have known, although Ann would have wanted to look it up in a book rather than dare the woods. It was tame in these parts at present, but there were still cougar about, and bear, snakes and swarms of alligators in the swamps and krills. It hadn't been like that when she'd first came to Vicksburg. In fact, there hadn't even been a Vicksburg then.

The place was called Walnut Hill. The modern town was born out of a squabble over land. Mr. Vicks, who'd laid out the lots that were to become the Vicksburg of today, had died leaving ten children and no will. The resulting battle had lasted nearly twenty years and was finally settled in the family's favor, hence the city's name, by a judge almost as wise in the ways of the law as he'd been to choose one of the Vicks women for his mate.

Diana was now attempting to avert a similar battle for the Shannons.

None of the people in the area's history were particularly far-seeing to believe there was a rich life to be made here. The town lay at the confluence of two rivers, the Mississippi and the Yazoo. No traffic could pass the high bluffs if those who held the heights said nay and backed it up with shot and shell. A further blessing was the soil and climate that made all growth startlingly quick. Crops would flourish nearly year-round. It was this twin gift that had helped make her life with John so complete. The river with its commerce became her drink, the bountiful soil, John's meat.

She and John Maguire came to Vicksburg as man and wife two years after the war with England ended. Those whose fortunes or place in history depended on it claimed a great victory in that war. They crowed like young bucks who had just breached an unwary tavern maid, strutting about waving the bloody sheets as triumphant banners. The real victory was a dry parchment scratched out at Ghent, and it could have been won many times before at less cost. Perhaps the war had been what the nation needed, Diana thought - some great feat to prove to the world its worth. Still, truth suffered.

She'd witnessed many of the events and knew the men involved, as well as their wives and families - from the president, down. The alleged victors, however, had recast any fact that discredited them and ordered up statues for the town squares. All who opposed them were branded cowards or worse. It was Diana's view that out of this had risen a new political system that Adams couldn't see but Monroe swiftly caught: perception mattered more than truth. Truth satisfied few, but perception could be bent to please any number of people. If someone still claimed blindness, you could help him see by bribing him with a post office, a printing or military contract, or with a position skimming the tariffs at a customs shed. Most sought after of all were banks, which offered presidential cronies a whole tangle of opportunity for graft.

After the war, Diana had determined to get a little happiness for herself and John in the remaining years of their lives. This required a bit of selfishness. The Shannon family had to rely on its resources and Diana had to relinquish some control.

Her stepson Farrell had not mellowed with age and was all but useless, even an obstruction. But he had also become more dependent on his wife, Connie. After so many years of following Diana's orders, there was not much difficulty or danger in handing the reins of the Philadelphia portion of her business to her. Over the years Connie had proven more able than even Diana had hoped. They had communicated constantly by letter, but even with this delay, Connie would often arrive at the same conclusion as her mother-in-law and acted before the missive arrived. Connie had also been wise in her choice of managers, and was as fussy as a shepherd over the care, feeding, and education of the Shannons. This was fortunate. Times had not become simpler. If anything, they were riskier and more complex: what was wisdom one day became foolishness the next.

As Diana expected, the war's end triggered a crash. In New York alone thirteen thousand were paupered. People reeled from the tentative unity they had been forced to forge during the war. They buried themselves in their own troubles and cast blame on outsiders. What followed set the course of events to this very day, with the same issues chewed into mush and the same bits of grit to test the teeth. Some people became newly religious, but it was the mean sort, where charity was only issued with absolute doctrine, and those few pious ones with any claim to intelligence insisted that a new order would arise from the current pain. They said the bad times were a sign America had a divine mission to spread Republicanism and peace to the world. Meanwhile, factories went empty, fields unplowed. Whole city streets were turned into pawnshops and secondhand stores filled with stolen goods. Diana thought the South had become an even a greater wasteland than before, squandering its cotton money on imported goods and refusing to build industry to match the burgeoning North.

Meanwhile, disease and hard winters held the nation in a terrible grip. Churches split and split again, each preaching different truths from the same gospel. Presbyterians praised slavery in the South and damned it in the North. Old alliances were destroyed and new ones formed, only to crack and be reassembled anew. Powerful men were broken on these racks, while others turned their misfortune into glorious cash.

There were booms in the middle of all this. But all of them contained fatal flaws. Industry burst across the land, with thousands of factories built, canals dug, new states and territories opened. But

35

cities were stinkpots, where a factory girl might be required to invest savings equal to a week's pay for a promised steady job, then be fired as soon as the trial period ended and a new girl brought in with fresh funds. Immigrants, fleeing great lost causes in Europe, swamped the system. Some brought valued skills - masons, mechanics, farmers, and breeders. Others brought odd ideas, some frightening because they questioned the entire system.

Many were so ignorant - such as Diana's peasant Irish cousins, who came by the thousands - they served mainly as a never empty pool of cheap labor. The population burst upward, from twelve million to over thirty, with nearly a third foreign born. And all the while the beckoning western frontier kept retreating until there was only an ocean left. Now the Union itself stretched to the Sandwich Islands and beyond.

Diana had been a businesswoman for nearly eighty years. She'd made her first dollar when all was a wilderness and a king still claimed the land. As her time came to an end, she felt well-qualified to judge. And as one of the few surviving members of the first generation of Americans, she somehow felt duty-bound to do so. To her disappointment, her conclusion was that the America she was about to depart was certainly not the America she and her revolutionary sisters and brothers had envisioned when they were attending the birth.

When Diana arrived in Vicksburg she saw great opportunity in the river that flowed past the bluffs where she and John were building their home. She'd gambled a portion of her fortune on the route that goods from the newly-opened West would take. The gamble paid off handsomely and now steam boats regularly cruised the Mississippi, carrying those goods to New Orleans and places beyond. The packets reigned supreme for more than forty years, and they still might have a little in them until enough railroads were built to snatch the rest away.

John loved to farm, and he was good at it, growing corn and beans and all kinds of good things that always had a market no matter what the fortunes were of other crops like cotton and tobacco. Diana left this to him, while she concentrated on the river. Diana had a wonderful time, becoming a partner in many enterprises, but avoided risk by being sole owner of few. Many years ago, for example, when she still ran her small empire from Philadelphia, she helped men and women build salt works on the other side of the Appalachians, freeing them from the tyranny of the Eastern traders. After her arrival in Mississippi, she had helped these same folk to expand their business with new boilers, then provided equipment to turn the salt into soda.

Now, she sent shipments of oil of vitriol upriver to the salt manufacturers. They mixed the oil with the salt, fired it, and it came back again in a new form. She sent this East, via New Orleans, where it was transformed into all sorts of marvelous things, the least of which were Epsom Salts or sparkling soda water with a refreshing bite that was delicious plain or mixed with fruit syrup.

Despite her concerns for the nation, the many problems it faced had lately taken on an unreal hue to Diana. She would be gone soon, and people would work it out or they wouldn't. In a way, Diana was past caring, because she had survived everyone she'd known and loved from her generation... and most of the next.

Dolly Madison had died, the ward of Congress, beggared by her only son. In her last days she was only known as a great hostess from gentler times, not as the heroine Diana had seen that terrible day the British came to burn down the President's House.

Her stepson Farrell had died in his bed, a little mad at the end, babbling obscenities and cursing the priest who was trying to comfort him.

Connie had lived until just ten years ago, vibrant and startlingly funny to the end. Her youngest daughter, Susan, had taken over and was coming to Vicksburg with the other Shannons.

Everyone, including Diana, expected James Emmett would die in a duel over a whore or a hand of cards. Her son worked harder at enjoying life than any man she had ever met. But surprisingly, he and his wife had died in a visit to New Orleans not long before Patrick was born. Cholera, not a jealous husband's bullet, had taken him before his time.

With such a parent, Edward had not much hope. Diana knew he had all the failings of his father, but wasn't sure if he had any of

James Emmett's graces, such as the laugh that could disarm a regiment of debt collectors.

Patrick had inherited that laugh. Would the boy also develop James Emmett's sense of fun? She wished she could have recognized it more when James was small and thought of a way to direct it.

Yes, that would be nice, Diana, dear, she told herself. But it is too late for regrets. Hadn't John, her lovely John, taught her how senseless it was to take all the burden upon herself?

He used to tell her in her bleakest moods if she had failed - which he strongly doubted - it was because she had dared too much. And was that really such an awful thing? Then he would kiss her, and caress her, and...Diana laughed aloud. She felt a stirring in her loins, and it was funny to be ninety two and still feel it and funnier still to think of all the turmoil it had caused in her mind for so many years. Men were not alone in their silly obsessions. How much had she gone through for what amounted to a little dimple her maker had pinched in the clay below her navel?

She was honestly weary now. The curtain moved in a soft breeze. She would sleep a bit. In a little while, Patrick would be back and she would need all the energy she could muster.

As she fell asleep, his face rose up in her mind. What a handsome lad! Wouldn't Emmett have been proud?

*

CHAPTER THREE

VICKSBURG

PATRICK EASILY FOUND the road to Daniel Cuffe's house. It followed the edge of the wooded bluff, and he caught brief snatches of the river through the trees.

The morning air had a bite to it, blowing up from the water, carrying the rich scent of Mississippi mud. To his left he saw sprawling farm land with distant figures at work. All was in morning shadow, so he couldn't make out the figures for awhile. He knew this was his great grandmother's land and these must be tenant farmers. Then the road curved out of the glare of the sun. Now he could see the farms and the people more clearly. The first thing that jolted him was the equipment they were working with. No short handled hoes for Grandmother Shannon's land! Everything was new, with complex gears, wheels, and sturdy blades of designs he had seen only in magazines. The second thing he noticed was the hands were Negroes. He hadn't know his great-grandmother owned slaves. He'd heard his father warn Pamela not to bring up racial matters in Grandmother Shannon's presence. She was an old eccentric, his father said. She didn't see the many benefits for owner and slave alike. Watching the slaves work the fields bothered him, although he couldn't say why. He put it from his head and walked on.

Mr. Cuffe's place was a tidy farm, with neat rows of corn, melon and beans. At the end of the road Patrick saw a small white house picked out in forest green, and behind it a sturdy barn. He saw no one about. Must be in at breakfast, he thought, and wondered if he'd be offered a plate. Some catfish and bacon would set nicely on the pone and syrup Kitty had fed him. And maybe some coffee. He giggled. A fellow named Cuffe just had to have some coffee beans about.

As he got close to the place, he saw a Negro working at a compost heap with a pitchfork. The man was about his father's age and was working away with a fever. Patrick was amazed Negroes worked with such a will in these parts, especially with no white men to keep 'em at it. It sure was different from his father's plantation, where they were constantly hiring and firing overseers to get the hands to work - especially since Pamela came.

Patrick was heading for the door when the man saw him, stuck the fork in the ground, wiped his brow, and asked if he could help. Patrick almost jumped out of his skin. It wasn't the accent, which was pure Mississippi and clear as any white man's. It was the man's manner. Polite, oh, yes. But it was White polite, easy, confident. And his eyes were direct and didn't go ducking down with a lot of head bobbing. He just asked if he could help Patrick, with no "Massa" or even a "Suh" at the tag end to show respect. Pamela would of had him whipped.

"I'm looking for Mr. Cuffe... please," Patrick said. He didn't know why he added the "please," but there was such a dignified look about the man, it came naturally.

"I'm Mr. Cuffe," the Negro said. "Y'all must be the boy Mrs. Shannon's been frettin' to see. Patrick, right? Pleased to meet ya', son."

Daniel Cuffe wiped a hand on his trousers and stuck it out for a shake. Patrick knew his jaw was dragging on the ground, and his eyes must be as wide as a farm cat closing in on a pail of milk. But he couldn't help himself. Mr. Cuffe, a slave! No. Not a slave. Grandmother Shannon said he was her old friend. So he must be free. And those other black folks he saw in the fields... free as well. Now, didn't that beat all.

He let his hand be taken and shook, but before Mr. Cuffe let go, he gripped the big black paw hard and gave him a shake back.

If Mr. Cuffe noted anything amiss, he didn't let on. "Now, if I'm guessin' correct like," Mr. Cuffe said, "Mrs. Shannon pointed y'all down this road. What can I do for that fine old woman?"

Patrick gulped and told him about the restorative tea. Mr. Cuffe said he had put some leaves up the other day and to come on in and visit while he poked around in the cupboard for it.

The house was spanking clean, despite a swarm of little kids who were tormenting their momma for a snack. Mrs. Cuffe was a big woman with skin as black as a stove, all shining and healthy pretty, and she had a big friendly smile that would charm a squirrel right out of a tree and into a boiling pot. Despite her size, and the number of children underfoot, she had a wonderful figure, with a waist that pinched in above the firm flare of her hips. She shook Patrick's hand

40

and told him to sit while she hustled up a little bite from the kitchen. She shooed the kids out of the living room and Patrick settled down on a big stuffed chair across from the perch Mr. Cuffe took on a bench that ran beneath the front window.

"She just made a pie," Mr. Cuffe said. "Peach pie. I've been sniffin' at it all mornin' and tryin' to get up the gall to ask for some." He grinned wolfishly and patted his belly. "Ain't company a treasure," he said. He settled back with a sigh and commenced the visit.

Patrick sauntered home, the packet of tea in his pocket and his belly full of pie, coffee, and good cheer.

What an amazing fellow that Mr. Cuffe was, as amazing as his history. His father, Paul, had been the headman to John Maguire, Grandmother Shannon's second husband. His mother, Adele, had been a kitchen slave whom Mr. Maguire had rescued from a neighboring plantation. Now, don't that beat all? Patrick had never thought of the word - rescue - under such circumstances, but it seemed to fit when Mr. Cuffe said it.

John Maguire set all his slaves free, which was incredible to start with. It was more amazing, even for a boy Patrick's age, considering planters in Virginia made more money breeding slaves for sale down in these parts than they did growing cotton, and most especially when he thought about Pamela's "friend" and John Maguire's grandson, Fitz. Mr. Cuffe said some of the freed slaves came to Vicksburg with John Maguire and his great-grandmother, along with some other people - mostly white - from Philadelphia, to help get things started. Some had moved on. Some had set up business in and around town. And some had settled on the plots of land Grandmother Shannon owned.

They were tenants, to be sure, but free, and Mr. Cuffe said that after John Maguire died, Grandmother Shannon took just enough of the crops to cover her expenses. She'd also promised to give them all title to the land when she died. Mr. Cuffe owned his place outright. His father had bought it, and he had added to it over the years.

Before he met him, Patrick thought Mr. Cuffe's name a little strange. Now he felt like a fool for not seeing it before. He once knew of a slave with a similar handle, but hadn't thought much of it.

Mr. Cuffe said it was an African name. Since he had volunteered that much, Patrick wasn't too shy to ask how he got such a thing to put after his first name, Daniel.

Mr. Cuffe said it was like this: His father, being a slave and all, only owned the name Paul for his own. And he was satisfied with that, just as Adele kinda liked Adele standing by its lonesome. But this wouldn't do when they had kids. Being free, they figured the children ought to have a second name like everybody else in America. Adele thought Shannon, or even Maguire, ought to do. Paul didn't like that. He respected them both, but they were white just the same. In the end Grandmother Shannon settled it. The way she saw it, their people were stolen from Africa, so they should at least get some kind of African name back. Paul liked that. But Adele was such a religious woman, she thought African would be fine for a last name, but each of the kids ought to have a Christian name as well.

Patrick still didn't see where "Cuffe" came in, but he was patient and waited for the telling.

Mr. Cuffe was the first born. Soon as Adele popped him out and Grandmother Shannon had slapped some breath in him and cleaned him up, she called Paul in to see. "My mother said he stuck his nose in the door - a little fearful, because that kind of thing was real new to him, and all the shoutin' while I was bein' birthed scared him. Anyway, he saw my momma was all right. Then he asked what day was it? Mrs. Shannon allowed it was Friday. So, he said, that settled it. His last name's Cuffe. And all the kids from now on, their last name will be Cuffe as well."

Patrick frowned. What did Cuffe have to do with Friday? "Why, it means Friday, son. Cuffe is African for Friday."

A great light flared in Patrick's head. He laughed a little, then explained quickly before Mr. Cuffe took offense. He told him about the slave he knew of named Cuffe. Or, maybe it was Cuffee, or Cuff - which was all the same thing, it now appeared - it didn't matter. What was funny was that there was another man on the plantation whose name was "Friday," and the master and mistress never knew it meant the same thing.

Mr. Cuffe saw the humor in this, but then topped it. "You read Mr. Defoe?"

"You mean the fellow who wrote Robinson Crusoe?"

"Surely. Now, tell me. What was the black fellow's name in that book?"

"Why, everybody knows it was... Oh, I see. Friday. Right?"

"It was Friday. At least that's what Mr. Crusoe thought, which means old man Defoe. But what do you suppose his real name was? His African name?"

There could be no other answer: Cuffe. Friday, was Cuffe. Cuffe, was Friday. Did that beat all? Patrick laughed until he almost threw up the second piece of pie. When he was older - and he met a lot of black people with similar names, both front and back - he realized the joke had been sitting there waiting to be told for a hundred and fifty years.

Mr. Cuffe knew all kinds of stories, and Patrick was sorry when the visit was over. He wanted come back real soon. Yes, all in all, Patrick thought Mr. Cuffe was a pretty good fellow.

When he told Grandmother Shannon this, he didn't notice she waited just a moment after he said it. Then she smiled and her eyes were misty and she patted his hand, although he couldn't say why.

He didn't know she had been fearfully waiting for him to add, "For a Negro."

Now wasn't that nice, Diana thought, as the boy slipped out, walking softly so as not to wake her. Without even speaking to Daniel she knew the boy had passed her first test, probably the hardest of all. The whole visit had been prearranged, and Daniel would come soon to tell her exactly what Patrick had done under circumstances very difficult for a plantation child.

It also had become clear there was more gold in this mine than she had thought. After Patrick told her of the visit and the wonderful and humorous tales Daniel had spun, he had suddenly grown silent. And it wasn't a shy shyness, but a mournful thing with broken, fluttering wings.

The source of his pain took a while to get out, but get it she finally did. He told her about Molly, the woman who'd been his wet

43

nurse, and how to this day, when the word mother was spoken, he thought of her.

Diana stirred, remembering the fate of Sandra, the slave Nate Hatch kept to wet nurse Diana. Molly had suffered the same fate as Sandra. The woman whose breast Patrick had suckled was sold along with many other slaves after Pamela had come along and his father had fallen deeper in debt.

Then he told her about Nehemiah - the boy who had almost been a brother, although he was a slave as well, and the shameful treatment Patrick had handed out to him. He said he would never forgive himself. Diana badly wanted to hug him, comfort the pain and tell him everything was fine. But this would be a lie of the worst sort and do no service. Instead she told him the wrong he'd committed was grave, as grave as his father's for selling the people, as grave as Pamela's for pressing it.

"Keep that pain close to you, Patrick," she said. "Hold it tight to the guilt and do not let it go. If you keep it safe, it will protect you from committing the sin again, if nothing else. And I promise someday you will take it out and look at it and see something you had never thought to see before. Remember those people when you do that. And you'll never be the same again."

She wanted to tell him so much more. She wanted to tell him that everyone's soul in the nation was damned for what was being done. Did he know in these parts "Gone to Virginia," meant a slave buying trip? That black people were purchased from breeding plantations and then marched hundreds of miles across the mountains and through the swamps and forests? They were "seasoned" during the journey, which meant those who survived the malaria and exposure to the elements were deemed doubly fit. The column would march with little raggedy children in front, women straggling behind, and then the men, kept closely guarded so that they could not overpower their tormentors.

It was continually amazing. Here she was, in 1855, supposedly a modern, civilized world. Yet slavery sat like an ugly boil on the face of this "civilization," yellow, and quivering, and no one had the nerve to burst it. For a long while she thought emancipation would be achieved. It had almost been in the nation's grasp several times.

Every president had wrestled with slavery, in one manner or another. In all of them, courage had failed. There were fortunes at stake, she knew. But what of it? The men who founded the country, from Washington on, were as great cowards as any who followed. Washington had warned of foreign entanglements, she thought. What kind of legacy was that? Better the Father of the Country had said, "Beware of slavery." Of course, that would have meant a personal example - freeing his own slaves. So men kept drawing the line, saying slavery here, but no farther, then redrawing it again. The agreements were as empty as any treaty with the poor Indians. Diana often thought at the heart of it slavery excused the treatment of the Indian - or any man or woman authority wanted to deny.

Diana had known she would find slaves by the scores when she and John came to Vicksburg. She despised the institution, but she had grown up with it about her - although not on such a grand scale. She had been a slave herself - for that was what indenture was all about. Perhaps that was why she had set the course she had. Once free, she would be at no one's mercy ever again. No man would be her master.

To her dismay, slavery became the permanent future of Mississippi when cotton came. The planters and the men who wanted to be just like planters found new soil to bankrupt. Now there was so much cotton about it was nearly worthless at market. No need to curse Egypt for joining the party.

As a businesswoman, Diana found slavery to be as stupid as it was reprehensible. The cost and waste was enormous. A wheat farmer could tend several hundreds of acres with only his family to help. They took what they needed for themselves and sold the rest. Even a medium-sized cotton planter, however, needed at least fifty field hands. He had to feed them, cover their nakedness, and care for the sick. If cotton prices were even borderline, the planter would have to add to his immense debt to keep going. The debt he carried - held by a Northern bank - might be three times the value of his holdings. The planter could hire his skilled slaves out to the townsfolk. But this created problems of its own. A hireling - even a slave - had set hours. When the job was done the worker was left to his own devices. This meant large groups of slaves might gather to

45

have a little fun. Prospects of revolt, rape, and crime danced in the head of the local whites when they saw all those people laughing and smiling and courting.

She and John had added these facts to the arguments they hurled about to stop the spread of bondage. The amazing thing was so many people agreed. Mississippi was made up of folk from all over the world. There were as many New Englanders as Virginians, as well as Germans and Italians and Jews from all over Europe. All of them - from native born men and women of the North, to the new immigrants - were practical, hard-headed people.

At gut level there was a strong streak of morality that was offended by the sight of another person in chains. So with support from them and others, the state's constitution banned the slave market. This did not mean slavery was forbidden, but at least the market places were. It was a small step, and although there was great pressure now to take even that back, at one time she and John had shared a glass of wine to toast this little victory; and dreamed of the time when the rest would be achieved.

The difficulty, Diana knew, was so many other things were tied in. One man might say no to slavery, but he also didn't want tariffs. Or maybe he wanted his county to have as much say in Congress as a county in the North. There were a host of other issues - such as crime, which had birthed "law and order" parties. Law and order, however, had become code words, meaning protection against troublesome black folks. All these groups meant splintered power.

The planters were in the minority, but it was a minority of single purpose, which made it vast. If all else failed the planters had one remaining thing to rely on: Patriotism; but not to the Union, for this barely existed. In the South and a large part of the West the United States was an empty conceit. Loyalty was to the state. Fire on Virginia and you would have war. Fire on Washington, and everyone would talk war, but you would have to burn it to the ground before matters moved beyond discussion.

Diana told Patrick only a little of this. She knew if she preached, insisted on a view he was too young to grasp, he would turn away. But if he could see one person's plight, or act of courage, the seed

Allan Cole & Chris Bunch

would be planted. And if he had only a little of what she thought he had, the seed would flourish.

So she told him about Sandra. She told him of the bravery of Moses and Aaron, the two runaways who stayed with her in the wild days in Cherry Valley. And the free blacks of Philadelphia who dared the Yellow Fever to help their white brothers and sisters and how they were so shamefully rewarded, but continued on just the same, unable to escape the tug of human misery.

Patrick was spellbound at her story of the Negro couple who lent her a mule when she fled the advancing British troops in Washington, with only a pistol in her pocket to stave off peril.

To her all of those people were Shannons, from the wet nurse to Mr. Cuffe at the farm. We all come from circumstance so brutal, she thought, it beggars the mind when words are sought for the telling.

We are all willing to do any labor, no matter how filthy or mean. There is no risk we would not take just to lift our head and look another in the eye and never call him Master.

This was the legacy of the Shannons, her gift to Patrick. She hoped he could see how great was its worth.

CHAPTER FOUR

VICKSBURG

THE NEXT SHANNON to materialize was a disappointment at first. This was Captain Joshua Barney Shannon, the renowned clipper ship captain. But where Patrick had expected a barrel-chested heavy-bearded man with a couple of saber scars from his bloody-handed quelling of a mutiny, Captain Barney looked more like a sketch he'd seen in a book of the poet Byron. He had full lips, not unfamiliar with smiling, and a sensitive expression. At least he did stand over six feet and wore a silk coat that must've come from China and carried a gold-handled cane. However, Joshua redeemed himself in Patrick's eyes by greeting him civilly, and telling the boy to have a look inside the valise the seaman carried.

Patrick followed orders. Just inside the bag was a great, gleaming revolver. The kind soldiers carried and, he'd read, the kind ships' officers used to stop mutinies and send sailors up the mast in a hurricane. It looked to be nearly a yard long. About the only hand guns Patrick had seen were single shot target pistols, his father's dueling pieces or the huge dragoon pistols some of his father's friends sported with their militia uniforms. Virginia was civilized, after all. Bright copper percussion caps gleamed on the cylinder's nipples. The pistol was fully-loaded. "Look under the cannon, Patrick. It won't go off."

Nestled beneath the .36 Navy Colt's Patrick found a metal tube, brass gleaming as brightly as on the revolver's caps. A telescope.

"That's it, Patrick. Hard pressed figuring what'd be a proper gift, young man your age. But I bethought myself. When I was growing, I had... let's say an interest in what other people did. When they didn't know anyone's eyes were on them. Put a proper name on it, I fancied myself a bit of a spy. Got too close a couple times, and got rocked for busyin' myself with what was none of mine. But probably that was just me, growing up loose as a sailor's boy whose father was seldom to home. I'm sure you never think of things like that, do you boy? Spend time learning your lessons and practicing good works?" Joshua's face was unreadable.

"Uh...I dunno, sir. But I don't think that's what my father'd say."

"Pity, that. Well, use that glass as you see fit. Watching these packets on the river. Or wild creatures. Whatever your mind turns to. Be careful with it. Dutch lenses it's got. Supposed to be water-tight. Wouldn't put it to too much of a test, though." Joshua picked up his valise. "Since you appear to be the official welcoming committee, how many Shannons do we have to deal with, so far?"

"Just me. And my father. And... and his wife."

"Wife, eh? Not stepmother?"

"Nossir. More are supposed to come in tomorrow. I get to take the carriage in to town and pick them up."

"Could be you'll have an extra passenger. Your cousin, Michael, came out from Frisco with me. Would've been here now, but down in New Orleans he went out to the quadroon ball at Pontchartrain... and found congenial company. But he'll be along. Eventually. Supposin' you run ahead, now. Looks to be a long climb up to the house. If Grandmother Shannon is up, you can announce me."

Patrick, looking alternately at his wonderful telescope and his now equally-wonderful cousin, started off. "One more thing, Patrick. I'm no temperance apostle, Marblehead man or no. Some refreshment against this heat'd be found welcome. If you'd pass the word? And, once I've settled into quarters, come by and visit. You can tell me the news from Virginia."

Patrick was on his way.

He flew up the stairs to Grandmother Shannon's room. He was too excited to wonder whether she might be resting or even if he would be welcome. As he hit the top of the stairs he saw Kitty ushering Mr. Cuffe into his great-grandmother's room. He was about to go back down the stairs when he heard his name spoken. Curiosity drew him closer.

Patrick was relieved when he heard Mr. Cuffe singing his praises. Then he heard his great grandmother speak. She was thanking Mr. Cuffe for helping her with some kind of test. What in the world? Then he understood: his great grandmother hadn't trusted him... the visit with Mr. Cuffe was as big a humbug as a pewter penny. Everything had been arranged and they had played Patrick for a fool.

Allan Cole & Chris Bunch

He stormed down the stairs, flung the door open and slammed it behind him as he went off to find a nice gloomy place to nurse his injured feelings. He found solace in the root cellar. On one side a hatch opened into the garden and he could hear Kitty talking to a maid while she was hanging up clothes. On the other was a set of stairs leading into the kitchen. He heard Kitty's voice stop and the two women walk into the kitchen, where they resumed their talk.

Patrick spent long moments thinking thoughts of idle murder. What had been done to him was betrayal of the worst kind from two people he had come to admire. Maybe he ought not to blame Mr. Cuffe. He was only helping out his friend. Although Patrick had thought he had won a friend of his own in Mr. Cuffe. Oh, well, maybe he had. After all Grandmother Shannon would come first in Mr. Cuffe's mind, seeing as they had been friends long. But he had misjudged his great grandmother. He should have known never to trust any adult.

Patrick was terribly hurt. He grew impatient with his self confinement. He was restless, wanting to strike out at something or someone.

Then his pulse gave a bump as Pamela's voice drifted down to him. "Have you seen Patrick about, Kitty?"

"No, Mrs. Shannon," Kitty said. "I think he's down by the river. Shall I send someone to fetch him?"

"Oh, what's the use?" Pamela whined. "I love that child more than life itself.... but, sometimes he's such a trial. I blame Edward for spoiling him."

"He seems like a lovely boy to me," Kitty said. "If you had an errand for him, I'm sure he's just forgotten. No different than any other youngster."

"You would say that," Pamela laughed. Patrick could hear the falseness in the laugh, but he was sure no one else would catch it. "After all, you and Grandmother Shannon absolutely dote on the boy..."

Patrick could bear no more. He slipped out of the root cellar into the garden. His heart was pumping hard and his nerves were tingling. Maybe he'd go drown himself in the river. Maybe he'd burn down the house. Maybe he'd... Then he saw the washline where

Kitty and the maid had been working. From one end to the other, stacked two deep, hung a flowery array of clothing... all of them Pamela's. Patrick had helped haul the damn things clear from Virginia - his father was watching the pennies where muscular assistance was required. Here, Patrick, fetch that bag. Oh, and Patrick, throw that other over your shoulder while you're at it. They treated him like a mule. No, worse than a mule. A mule won't budge if you put too much on him. And he'll kick the life out of you if you get too close.

All of his anger now centered on Pamela, represented by the clothing hanging wet and dripping on the line. Dripping into what? Mud. Oh, really! Then he saw a pig. More of a shoat, actually. Wasn't very big. The shoat was minding its own business, rooting around near the clothesline, looking for some scraps.

Patrick glanced about: there was no one to see. He found a nice, sharp little rock. A zinger if he ever saw one. He wound up and let fly. Rock hit pig. Pig squealed. Pig ran like it was turpentined. Pig through clothes. Clothes followed pig. Mud followed clothes. He watched the pig and the entire line of mucked up clothing disappear into the woods.

That'd show Pamela what's what!

Feeling better, he started to stalk away. Then he saw something he hadn't noticed before. Someone was sitting up on the second story verandah. The one outside his... Oh! It was Grandmother Shannon. She was looking right at him. Then he saw her turn and slowly walk into her room. Well, that busted it. She'd tell. Although his father had almost never given Patrick a licking, he was sure to get one now. He didn't mind that so much: Even when he was licked, his father never put his heart into it.

It was that Woman. Her. Pamela. She'd have something over him. A real big something. So what? What could they do to him? He was going to run anyway, but he still didn't know where. Then he thought of Joshua.

What Patrick needed at this moment was some good tips on the sea. He set off to hunt up his cousin.

"So you think you're for the sea, eh? Pirates, cutlasses, the bounding main and that?"

Patrick was in no mood to have another adult play games. Joshua caught his expression.

"I wasn't trifling, Patrick. M'pologies. When I was not much younger than you, I was planning to run to be a pirate. Problem was, even then, pirating'd fallen on hard times. Never recovered, I guess, from poor Blackbeard getting his head lopped off. Real pirating, I discovered to my considerable dismay, is only a sound trade if you're partial to the South China Sea, dusky complexions, junks and bamboo cannon. Mostly your treasure works out to be rice. Unhulled rice. But you seem serious. Must say, I've heard it said that a man who'd go to sea for pleasure'd go to hell for a pastime."

Joshua lay sprawled on his bed, his vest unbuttoned, but still dressed except for his hat and coat. A decanter, pitcher of water and glass were on the stand beside him. "Have you talked to your father about this?"

"No."

"Didn't think so."

"What did your parents say when you told them you were going to sea?" Patrick asked.

Joshua explained. On his side of the family there wasn't a real problem, since they all appeared webfooted. His father, Luke, had been a seaman since he was a boy, once even impressed into the British Navy and somewhere around Washington when the capital was burnt, way back in 1814. That, Joshua said, was when he evidently got the idea for what he'd name his firstborn, after "the only man in that damned war, and I'm quoting him directly, boy, who seemed to have much sand in his craw."

Not that the sea or seafaring was ever the highroad to glory or riches for the family. Luke returned to the sea after the war, and disappeared. "Mother wrote everybody, trying to find out what happened. Finally Grandmother Shannon got involved. We received a letter from the consul in Hamburg... Father had been killed. Stabbed."

"How? Why?" Patrick wondered.

"Nobody knew. A brawl, a robber, a shipmate with a grudge. Nobody had asked. The thing you learn, early on, a sailor is not thought much different than a black man. Got about as many rights, and about as much indifference when they find your body floating face-down."

Joshua smiled mirthlessly and went on. Luke's brother, David, who Diana had wangled a midshipman's birth in the Navy, also stayed at sea. Any ship headed for new places, and David would be volunteering. But one day the most prosaic of accidents happened - his ship was being paid off and put up in ordinary. Someone was careless, and the top hamper crashed down to the deck far below, crushing David's leg and ending his time at sea.

"Damned fool never learns," Joshua went on. "He's still in the Navy, up in Washington, in a damned bureau helping make charts of the world's winds. But he'll go nevermore to sea. That's the way it is, sailorin'. It settles into your system just as bad as if you were a Hong Kong coolie on the pipe." Joshua drained his glass and refilled it. "Not that anything I'm saying is even marking on your slate, if you're bound to the sea."

He peered at Patrick. "Here's the way it sets: First, you have two choices. You come in the cabin door when you're a bit older, with some education, and you'll be an officer. But if... just to suppose... you lit out today and got signed on, you'd be coming through the hawsehole. Need training before you're even an ordinary seaman. That's a damned sight harder."

"But you did it."

"I did. And I'll tell you how. On the North Atlantic run. By God, I was the first to turn out every watch. Somebody wanted something, I did it. Didn't matter if it was blowing full gale, the masts were ice and the mate thought a gasket up on the topsail wasn't Bristol. Studied everything I could. The weather. What charts there were. Learned navigation. Watched other people make mistakes, and promised I wouldn't make them. Most of which I turned around and did worse. Learned when to fight. Learned when not to fight. Learned a heaver, a belaying pin, a slung shot or a set of brass knuckles is good. Learned a bowie knife or pistol's better, sometimes. Learned to live on... even like, I suppose, what they feed

Allan Cole & Chris Bunch

you. For instance... I know you read about wormy biscuit and rancid salt pork. You figure you'll be tough enough. Prob'ly right. I've been so hungry I went hunting rats down in the hold, when I was a boy. It's what becomes your favorite food that's off-putting. Sea pie. Cut up salt pork, onions and potatoes. The cook throws a crust on it. Sounds bad? I've seen sailors wait in line, five minutes before mealtime. Seen men fight over whether they got a smaller portion than a messmate.

"Another thing I learned was to drive men. Americans... lascars... squareheads... even Finns. And to have a Finn aboard is to test the Fates, I'll tell you. The men'd turn out when I called, or spend the next watch nursing a sore jaw. Sailors don't seem to think like anyone else.

"Had a skipper once. On a tea-clipper. Damn good man. Cap'n Howland. Saw him cry, once, when a man went overboard. Saw him turn back to look and lose passage time. He was a bible thumper - but every man jack got his grog every day. Crew thought he was useless. He never went for'rd, unless it was to hand out Bibles. Only person he'd talk to was the first mate. And he played pure hell getting seamen to sign aboard. Another thing I learned to live with landsmen calling me 'Bully.' Newspapers saying if a man didn't jump when I said Frog he'd go overboard and I'd be laughing."

Joshua paused. Drank. "I made a good run to Frisco this last time. Near record. You know what welcome I got? Lynch mob at the dock because four men went off the main yard when a pampero struck above Valparaiso. I didn't turn back to look, not that there would've been aught good anyway. Bent on more sail. And now Bully Shannon is Killer Shannon. Not that it'll matter to the owners. Fast passage with most of your cargo intact... you could be related to Lucifer on your mother's side and they'd give you another ship. I assume you want to be a clipper ship skipper? Like me?"

"Maybe."

"Better change your plans. Because there aren't any clippers being built any more. Those that haven't wrecked are looking hard for cargoes. And crew. You look at Frisco Bay. Nothing but ships. You could most likely walk across to Pelican Island without getting your feet wet. Tied up, yards crossed or just abandoned. Rotting with

54

no cargoes and no one to sail on them. Not that there won't be ships time to come. But I'll wager they'll be steam-run. Maybe sidewheelers like the packet you came upriver on. Maybe stern-wheelers. More likely, screw-propelled like the one that Britisher Brunel was experimenting with some years back. Sailoring will be different. You better know more about when a safety valve pops and what kind of coal burns best than holding the weather gauge. But it'll still be sailoring. If that's what you want... there isn't a damned thing that can stop you. But get all the education you can before you do. That's all the advice I've got in me. At least just now."

"Joshua?"

"What, boy?"

"If it's so awful... why do you keep sailing?"

Joshua grinned, and started to speak. Then he stopped and thought for a long time. He was looking past Patrick, out the window. "One reason could be that a sailor - no matter that he cannot read, cannot write and has no goals beyond a meal, a drink and a doxy - is part of something bigger. He is not a Virginian. Or a Massachusetts lad, even though that may be his home. Not even an American. Staring at a horizon that appears to go on forever maybe brings you something. Something I think a lot more of us could use. Be damned if there shouldn't be a better way to learn it than before the mast."

Joshua came back to himself. "I am afraid I have said little to steer you toward a more sensible life."

"Nossir. That was... very interesting."

"One more thing. This is a suggestion, son. Anything Grandmother Shannon tells you...remember it well. Even if it makes no sense right now. Years gone, it might. Because that old woman is by far the best of us all."

Determined to avoid facing the business over the washline "accident" as long as possible, Patrick crept down the hallway to his room. He was closing the door when Kitty called his name. Well, here it came. She said his great grandmother wanted to speak with him. Patrick searched her face for any sign that she knew, but he found only kindness there. Reluctantly he trailed behind her.

His great grandmother was sitting up in the bed waiting for him, her eyes clear and her hand steady as she motioned for him to sit beside her. The sullen anger returned. Patrick pretended not to see, and instead plunked himself on the edge of the old horsehair trunk.

"That wasn't a very nice thing you did, Patrick, dear," she said.

The anger flared hotter and he stared at her, his eyes burning defiance. But he didn't say a word back.

"Kitty and Nina worked all morning washing Pamela's clothes, you know. Now they have to do it all again."

Some of the heat lessened. He was sorry for that. He should have known she wouldn't lift finger to help if you held a gun on her. Still... the defiant look returned. Grandmother Shannon was going to chew him out good and then call in Pamela to tell. Very well, if that was to be his fate, he was ready.

He straightened his shoulders, imagining the approach of the firing squad. He'd go out game.

"I suppose each of us learned a lesson today," his great grandmother continued. "And I want to tell you how sorry I am that I played a trick on you. Please do not blame Mr. Cuffe. He is a good man, and he and his wife really did enjoy your company. They were not pretending. Honestly."

Patrick stared and stared. Did that mean she wasn't going to tell?

"So, where are we now?" she went on. "I tested you. And you tested me... Are we even?"

That got him, especially as she held out her hand for a shake. He took it and was surprised again at the strength in her small fingers. Tears welled and he swallowed hard to fight them back. No one had ever apologized to Patrick Shannon before.

"Even," he said, voice gruff.

She chattered on then - lightly, not about anything in particular. Then she asked him if he would get something for her out of the trunk. He got up from it and lifted the lid.

It was filled to the brim with all kinds of things poking out. Small objects wrapped in cloth. Old bits of clothing. Some interesting looking wooden boxes with tricky catches. A faded doll dressed in old-fashioned clothing, but, completely outfitted: down to slippers and earrings and gloves. He wondered what it was for. On the very top of the pile was a folded up piece of lace, a little yellow, like aging ivory, and picked out with small designs.

"Yes, that's what I need," she said.

He lifted the lace and caught a glimpse of a thick sheaf of fancy legal parchment underneath. As he carried the lace to her bed, he felt something small but oddly heavy inside. Without thinking he sat close to her on the edge of the bed.

She unwrapped the lace carefully, talking as she did so. "Did you know I was once a seamstress, Patrick? This was one of my very first attempts when I was a girl. I kept it because it brings back memories."

The lace was fully unwrapped now. Patrick peered over to see the object it had hidden. The thing didn't look like much. A small, leather sack so old it was black and cracking at the seams. There was a rawhide thong keeping it shut. It looked as stiff as a piece of wire as she delicately drew the bag open. She turned it upside down, and something fell into her hand. She handed it to him.

It was an old rifle ball. He looked up at her, puzzled. "Your great grandfather gave that to me," she said. "I suppose it was our wedding ring. Although, these days I guess they would say what happened between us was not a real marriage. There was no one about to witness any bans, much less post them. But we wanted to be married right away. We could not wait. We had been on the run and an Indian and his family took us in."

She cast her mind back remembering Abraham Duval and the crucifix of the tortured Christ on the farmhouse wall. "It was that Indian who married us. More as a witness to the promises we made to each other, if anything. But we meant the pledge as much as if he had been a priest. Perhaps more so. I was... fifteen, or sixteen... I forget."

Patrick realized she had been only a few years older than he when this happened. For a moment he thought he could see that young girl in her eyes, but then he lost her as Diana continued.

"Abraham - that was the man's name - told Emmett he should give me something to seal the bargain. Neither of us had anything to

Allan Cole & Chris Bunch

give. "The bullet had to do." She stopped and smiled at him. "So, I think you'll agree this thing is more than just a lump of lead."

Yes, it was, Patrick thought. A vow of eternity pledged on a bullet was better than any oath from any pirate he had ever read about. "Then he was killed," he blurted.

"Yes... The next day."

"I guess you were right to be in a hurry," Patrick said. And then he thought she might take this as cold and unfeeling. But his great grandmother just nodded. "Then you went to Cherry Valley?"

"Yes. I went on... In his place."

"Were you afraid?"

Diana felt the flutter in her heart as she recalled her feelings as she approached Emmett's place and saw the Brian and Farrell run out of the thicket. "Yes, I was," was all she said.

They both let it lie there, silent for a while. Then she hoisted up the bullet. "I want you to have this when I'm gone," she said. "I'd give it to you now, but it's been with me all these years and I don't think I could let it go. Even though I keep it in the chest now." She shrugged, trying to fill the gaps.

Patrick felt very sad when she said this. "I don't deserve it," he said.

"Why do you say that?"

"This is important," he answered. His voice was fierce, trying to explain. "You shouldn't give it to somebody like me. I'm..." He wanted to say, "useless," but that wasn't it. Or maybe it was.

"Do you know what is going on here?" she asked, suddenly. "Why all the family is gathering?"

He supposed he did. She was... dying. But he couldn't say that.

She pointed at the legal parchment. "It's about my will," she said. "Not really, but that is what everyone thinks it's about. You will see what I mean a little later when Mr. Levy arrives."

He nodded. The will business was all Pamela could talk about. His father would inherit everything, which meant Pamela could spend it. Patrick had not much use for money. He'd always figured he go adventuring for a long time, then save his money until he was old... maybe forty. Then he'd buy stuff that was really useful. Like tons and tons of books! Now, there would be a treasure.

Allan Cole & Chris Bunch

He told his great grandmother this, and she smiled and said she agreed with him with all her heart. "I want you to help me, Patrick, dear," she said. "No tricks this time, I promise." They both laughed.

She said him she wanted his view of all the Shannons who were coming. She wanted him to talk to each one, and see what they did and how they acted, then report back to her.

"You want me to be a spy?" he said, elated.

His great grandmother misunderstood and was even a bit shocked. "No! I'd never ask..." Then she saw the crestfallen look on his face and stopped. "That's it exactly," she said. "Although I didn't see that was the word for it right away. So. Will you be my spy, Patrick Shannon?"

He said he'd be glad to, and not an enemy would get by him. He would stick like paint to anybody who looked even a bit suspicious.

They made the bargain.

Diana felt the weariness suddenly descend on her. She patted the child's hand and said maybe he'd better go so she could rest. As he rose from the bed she saw him stare at the bullet one more time, perhaps a little sorry that he had refused it. She called to him just as he was exiting the room. She asked him to put it away again in the trunk.

He did, and as he closed the lid she spoke: "We have only known each other for a short time, but already I value your opinion, with one exception."

She indicated the trunk, but he knew she meant the musket ball in its little sack. "You are the very best person to have it, Patrick, dear. Of this, I am convinced. And it would be a great comfort to me that when I'm gone it is in your keeping. To keep and pass on to your own children..."

She felt herself drifting away, but she saw the huge grin on the boy's face as she fell asleep, and knew she had been understood.

CHAPTER FIVE

VICKSBURG

THE TRICKLE OF Shannons turned into a steady stream. Patrick never knew he had so many relations, or heard folks talk so much. They talked and talked, never letting a body get a word in of his own. He was also feeling tenderized from all the loving pinches and pokes he had suffered from his relatives. "You must be Patrick," a cousin would coo, drawing a squad or so more of other female kin. "So, handsome," another one would say. And, "couldn't you just eat him up," Then the pinching would start.

Others would wander over and praise him for being the size God made him, squeeze his muscles until he thought his arm would fall off, and give him a little punch in the ribs, remarking on his agility as he tried to dodge away. Why he was so popular among all these folks, he had no idea. He only wished he could shrink up and creep away.

Not that all Shannons were like that. The biggest exception was Cousin Michael, the Californian, who'd arrived a few days after Joshua. He showed up wearing a low gray beaver hat, beaver short coat with black facing, silk shirt, a black silk brocaded vest with a heavy watch chain across it, and nankeen trousers bloused into high, very shiny riding boots. He rode a blood horse with expensive English saddlery.

Patrick thought he must be richer than any of the Virginia gentry he'd ever seen, even Fitz Maguire. Michael was always friendly, always smiling around the twisted, evil-smelling cheroots he smoked incessantly. Except for his eyes, which were cold blue and steady. Patrick was reminded of the gambler he'd seen aboard the Eclipse, and determined he must find out more about his cousin the ex-dragoon war hero.

He was also fascinated by his cousin Susan Dolan, from Philadelphia, but not by anything immediately apparent. At first sight Susan was a small, pretty woman in her 40's. She oversaw Great Grandmother's varied concerns in Philadelphia, and, Patrick thought immediately, probably did it very well.

Her husband, Ian, was a bit more obviously interesting. He was not much bigger than Susan, but far more solid, with curly hair and cheery red face. He was also immensely strong - Patrick had goggled a bit seeing Ian unload their luggage from the carriage that brought them out from Vicksburg, hoisting a trunk on one shoulder, and lifting two large valises in his other fist. He was also Irish-Irish, having emigrated from Dublin not many years ago.

Patrick was intrigued - so this was what the family roots looked like. But the biggest reason for his curiosity was Pamela's snarl, after learning of Susan's arrival: "I'll vow this Yankee thinks she'll get a big piece of your grandmother's fortune. You mind her when you take charge, Edward. She's a damned abolitionist if I ever saw one."

Patrick had heard a visiting preacher describe northern anti-slavery people as: "vicious women lacking decency, husbands or children and men - if they can be termed that - from foreign shores who will force mixed-race breeding on our Southern flowers and let the coons pleasure themselves on our properties."

Although the boy was confused about the whole issue, he didn't care if Susan Dolan had tiny horns and a forked tail. If Pamela didn't cotton to her, his cousin was all right in his book.

His step-mother was behaving even worse than usual. The woman would hastily agree with a Shannon that Patrick was quite a fellow. Pity, she would coo, he had a habit of taking advantage - but that, Pamela would quickly add, would change once he went out into the world and had to make his own way. Another smile would follow, and Patrick was reminded of that great stuffed pike with its rows of teeth and glittering marble of an eye that had hung in the Eclipse's dining room. In private it was the same whispered threats and hands that could somehow bruise at just a touch. Patrick tried to stay away from Pamela and concentrate on Grandmother Shannon's assignment.

Spying was harder work than he thought, and not so glamorous either. He had already gathered a heap of stuff to tell his great-grandmother, but he thought maybe he ought to sift it over some to get his bearings before he went to report. Patrick realized this was a weak excuse, but he forgave himself, snitched something to eat out of the kitchen and looked for a nice place to rest before they hunted him down for more torment.

He found it at an old-fashioned springhouse, set near a dry krill and hidden by a small grove of trees. The place was long abandoned and the front door had rotted through and hung open on twisted hinges. It was two stories high and had wide eaves to help keep in the cool. Forty or fifty little swallows' homes were tucked under those eaves. It was getting onto dusk and the air above the little glen was filled with buzzing insects. The swallows were darting back and forth through the clouds, gobbling up bugs. Patrick watched for more than an hour. Then the fire flies started coming out and the swallows were going frantic at all those fat, sweet bodies, calling out for their friends to look over here if they really wanted to tuck into something fine. He was concentrating so hard that he didn't hear the man come up behind him. Even then, he was so intent studying the birds that he wasn't startled when addressed.

"Pardon me," came the soft voice, "I didn't know anyone else was about." The boy looked up to see a slender man, blonde and fair-skinned with touches of red on his nose and cheeks where the sun had nipped at the flesh. His clothes and accent were pure Yankee, but there was no mistaking the man's resemblance to all the other people yammering away around his great grandmother's house. He was Shannon, through and through.

"You must be Patrick," the man said - four words he had heard so often in the past few hours he had sworn if one more person said it he would scream like a wild Indian. Then he remembered the task his great-grandmother had set him at.

"Yessir," he said, not real enthusiastic.

"I'm Russell Conners," the man said, surprising him for the first time. The second surprise came as the man stuck out his hand - not to poke or pinch, but to shake hello like normal folks.

Puzzled, Patrick shook back. The puzzlement ended a second later. "I'm from Isaac and Ruth's side of the family," Russell said - explaining the last name. "Cousin to Susan."

Patrick realized the man must be the Philadelphia lawyer Pamela had been going on about. Funny, he didn't look like the slick beast she had described. Only a gentle soul with a disarming smile. Patrick quickly forgave the interruption. He was almost sorry when Russell apologized again for spoiling his peaceful moments and

Allan Cole & Chris Bunch

turned to leave. He was about to go back to watching his feathered friends when Russell asked him a question.

"They're awfully pretty. Do you suppose they're some kind of swallow?"

"Purple Martins," Patrick blurted. "Which is a kind of swallow. You can tell that right off from those long, narrow wings and the forked tail. But they're kinda blue-black, which is why they got the name, I guess. Least the males are that color. The ladies ain't so grand. You can see..." Patrick indicated some drabber examples swooping through the air.

"You know a lot about birds," Russell said, sounding impressed.

Patrick shrugged. "Not a lot," he said. "Least, no more than most. But I'm kind of curious about those Martins. They got them back home, too. And they all live in those little houses. See?" He pointed at the nests in the eaves.

"What's so interesting about them?" Russell asked. He squatted down next to Patrick, but the boy was warming to the subject and didn't mind anymore.

"See how they're gobbling up the bugs?" Russell watched the birds feed a moment, then nodded. "Back home, some, uh... hands... told me their kin used to build little swallow nests like those soon as they got, uh...settled. They'd no sooner get to the plantation and get a shack of their own, then they'd plant a little garden - if they were allowed - and then build the little bird houses. I asked them why their folks used to do that, and they said they didn't know. They thought it was some kind of African superstition, or something."

"What do you think, Patrick?" Russell asked.

"I don't know, either," Patrick confessed. "Although I'm gettin' an idea. I heard the Indians in these parts used to do the same thing. Build homes for the Purple Martins to live in. Choctaws are from these parts, you know?" Russell nodded that he did, but he didn't interrupt. "When I heard we were coming here, I thought maybe I'd see some of those Indians. Maybe even get to talk to a couple. But Mister Cuffe says they've run them all off to the territories. So, now I'll never know if I'm right or not."

"You didn't say what your theory was," Russell prodded. Patrick preened a bit. He hadn't considered his thoughts to be worthy of being called a "theory." But maybe Russell was right, and it was.

"I think it was to eat the bugs," Patrick said. "You know... If they built a bunch of houses, saving the Purple Martins all that work, why the birds would be so grateful they'd stick around and gobble up bugs that would ordinarily eat up the folks' crops."

Patrick flushed, sure that now he'd hung himself out. The adult squatting beside him would laugh and call him a young fool. Instead, Russell nodded and said that made sense. Maybe they ought to look in Grandmother Shannon's library for a copy of Mr. Audubon and see what he had to say about Purple Martins as insect eaters to the Indians.

"She doesn't have one," Patrick said quickly. "I already checked. Besides, I don't hold with Mr. Audubon much. I think he's a humbug."

Russell lifted an eyebrow. Patrick explained. A book seller came calling to his father's place some time back. Among other things, he was peddling a subscription to Mister Audubon's books. One complete set would run more than a thousand dollars. But his father was all ready to buy. He just had to have it for the library, even though it cost so much and didn't come all at once, but book by book, as new volumes were published.

"I talked him out of it," Patrick said, remembering a little sadly the time when his father used to listen to his opinion. "I was flipping though the sample the salesman brought, and I spied this big picture of a red-eyed bird. It was real pretty. Anyway, right beneath this bird was a big spider, spinning a web. And it was a great spider, too. Mr. Audubon is a painting fool, I tell you."

"What was wrong with it?"

"It was a jumping spider," Patrick said, smiling with great satisfaction and looking at Russell, expecting a laugh. Instead, the man seemed puzzled. "So?"

"Don't you get it? A jumping spider. Why any... I mean... jumping spiders don't make webs."

Now, Russell got it. He gave Patrick a good laugh, too. Years later, Patrick would remember the conversation and only shrink a

Allan Cole & Chris Bunch

little at his - in this slight instance - correct, but certainly naive opinion of Mr. Audubon's worth. But he would also remember Russell's laugh as if it were only yesterday. There was real enjoyment in it. It stood in odd contrast to Russell's shy and wholly unremarkable manner.

"First birds," Russell said. "Now, spiders. You sure are full of information on Mother Nature."

"Oh, only just a little," Patrick said.

It only took a speck of coaxing and he was rambling on about wolf spiders, who did not hunt in packs as their name might imply. And he told Russell what he knew of the Indians from the Mississippi area, which he said wasn't very much, but interesting just the same. They talked for an hour or more. At least, Patrick talked and Russell listened. He was a good listener, interrupting only to prod out more information, and then letting the boy go on.

That night a tap came on his bedroom door. He was just about asleep, so it took him awhile to shuffle to the door. When he opened it, there was no one about. At Patrick's feet was a book. He opened it and saw a note from Russell, saying he hoped the book would help with his theory. The book was by William Bartram of Philadelphia, the most famous naturalist in America.

Patrick had planned on asking his great-grandmother if she had ever met the great man. The title of the book was: Travels through North and South Carolina, Georgia, East and West Florida, the Cherokee country, the extensive territories of the Muscogulges, or Creek confederacy, and the country of the Choctaws...

Russell Conners had just made a very good friend.

Allan Cole & Chris Bunch

CHAPTER SIX

VICKSBURG

DIANA LAY BACK in her bed, weary from all the talking and last-minute planning with Mr. Levy, but invigorated by thoughts of the action about to commence. In her mind she could see the family gathering in the dining room, taking their places around the big table or in the chairs Kitty had set up along the walls. They'd be chattering just now about inconsequential things. Pretending indifference to what Mr. Levy was about to announce. The will, however, would be uppermost in their minds.

She thought most would be merely curious; confident Diana would do well by them, or figuring it was none of their business what she did with her estate. She was sure a small number would be dismayed. Diana was interested in what Patrick would make of their reactions. In the case of his own father, she doubted if he would say.

As for her estate, Diana was deliberately rocking the ground under the Shannons. For the few she was concerned about it would be a quake rivaling the great temblor that had struck in this region in 1811, when the waters of the Mississippi, it was said, suddenly reversed course and flowed north for more than three hours.

How people behaved after Mr. Levy's announcement would determine what she would do. But even in her final decision, Diana wanted to be very careful. It would be a great bother for her to witness from the peacefulness of her grave a decades-long legal mess, such as the founder of Vicksburg left behind.

There was a tap at the door and Kitty entered. From the twinkle in her eye Diana knew the stage had been set and the curtain was about to be drawn.

Before they entered the room, Pamela had a hushed fight with Edward. Patrick saw nothing unusual about this, because Pamela always got het up when anything special was in the wind. The approach of a holiday, birthday, party or a treasured outing to town always seemed to get her into a temper. At first, Patrick had laid it to her mean streak. She was just out to spoil a body's good time. Then he saw it was a meanness many levels below mean. She wanted to be the center of attention no matter what was to occur, and a good tantrum was one way of assuring it.

As they stood outside the room waiting to enter there was some of that meanness in her fierce whispers. And a bit more, besides. Patrick noted her tight grip on his father's arm to keep him from straying. Her face was all screwed up and hateful as she talked, then it would go to a big smile and a nod hello when someone passed. Pamela was one angry woman. And it was all over seating arrangements. "I asked that... that... that lawyer where we were supposed to sit and do you know what he told me?"

Patrick and his father knew she didn't want an answer so stayed wisely buttoned up for the storm. "He said we could sit where we pleased! I never heard of such a thing. Why, you're the most important Shannon in the room, darling, everyone knows that." She gave his father's arm a squeeze as she said darling. The squeeze was not gentle.

"So, I told him although I did not much care where everyone else sat, that you should sit right up near the head of the table next to him. It's only proper.

"I mean, when dear Diana... uh... passes on... you'll be in charge, Edward. We don't want any quarrels with people. Matters of inheritance bring out the ugly side of folk. That's a fact. There's no denying it. In my opinion, if we want to avoid future ugliness, then we should be very concerned about appearances from this moment on. The head of the clan should sit at or near the head of the table. But, that... that..."

Patrick knew she was going to remark on Mr. Levy being a Jew. He didn't like it much, although he thought Mr. Levy was probably the first Jew he had ever met, so he did not have an opinion one way or another. His great-grandmother thought highly of the lawyer and she had praised all the Jews she had known. Patrick was willing to give them the benefit of the doubt, if any existed, and if there was one, he sure hadn't heard of it.

But Pamela stumbled out of her hateful dilemma by saying "lawyer" again with as cutting an edge to it as she could manage without a nice, juicy slur attached. "... said Grandmother Shannon was specific about there being nothing formal in the seating

67

arrangements, so that's the way it should remain. Now, what do you think of that?"

His father said if that's what his grandmother wanted, that's the way it would be, begging your pardon, darling. Pamela's lips drew into that thin line she got when she was being defied. She said if that was the case, then they should all sit together to show "family solidarity."

His father said it was fine by him. It wasn't with Patrick and he said so. He lied and said he promised to sit with his Cousin Joshua, and he didn't want any one's feelings hurt. So, he was sorry, but Pamela knew how seriously Patrick took his promises. Why, if he promised a fellow the moon, and then learned it couldn't be got at, Patrick would build a ladder that would reach. Everyone knew this about him, and it was no time to go back on his word now. Like Pamela said, appearances were real important, and... Her face got red and he shut up fast.

Pamela said he'd mind her and sit where she told him, but the door opened and Patrick ducked away and crowded close to Joshua so she couldn't grab a place. A minute later he was in his seat - near the head of the table, but quite by accident. He gloated a little that Pamela and his father wound up in two little chairs against a distant wall.

See what her temper got? Hah!

Mr. Levy trailed in with Russell. They were both lawyers and must have had a touch in common, because they were laughing about something or other. Patrick looked close at Mr. Levy to see if there was anything odd about him.... being a Jew and all. He was a tall man, in his late sixties and he had a dark, hawk face that might have been fierce, but there were laugh lines every place a frown might have stuck if he'd have been a different sort of fellow. Otherwise he looked like any other lawyer, with dark coat, shoes rather than boots and a buttoned vest with a heavy watch chain tucked across his belly.

Mr. Levy ambled to the head of the table and rustled some papers that were waiting. The paper shuffling continued until everyone was seated, and curiosity overtook jaw flapping. Mr. Levy cleared his throat and started right in. "We have all met," he said, "so if you'll forgive me, I'll dispense with the usual pleasantries. Also, each of you has spoken with Mrs. Shannon, so I'm sure you know how pleased she is you were able to come from so far and the great comfort she takes in having so many members of her loving family about in these, her last days."

There were a few feeble objections about his use of the phrase "last days," but Patrick noticed that folks had accepted this with varying degrees of sorrow. Joshua's chin got a little firmer, if that was possible. Susan touched the corner of one eye with a handkerchief. His own father's eyes widened some, but whether in alarm or anticipation, Patrick couldn't say. Pamela humbly bowed her head, as if to the Lord God Above, but he caught the little play of a smile on her lips.

Mr. Levy took no notice. Instead, he raised a sheaf of parchment - exactly like the kind Patrick had seen in his great grandmother's trunk - for his audience to see. "Diana Shannon's last will and testament," he intoned. Pamela bent forward eagerly. Instead of reading, Mr. Levy laid the documents down, right firmly, too. Patrick wondered what was coming.

"This will," he said, "no longer applies." No one actually gasped, but the intake of air around the room was definitely heavy. Mr. Levy didn't stop there. "Mrs. Shannon has believed for some time that she'd like to see her estate - which as you all know is as large as it is various - under one person's control."

Patrick saw his father give a reflexive nod. He knew his father thought Mr. Levy meant him. The boy wondered if he was the only one that caught the word "person," which did not necessarily have any particular sex attached. He looked at his Cousin Susan. From the blank expression on her face, she hadn't caught it either. Maybe he was just reading into something that wasn't there. He reminded himself he was only twelve going on thirteen, so what did he know of adult affairs?

Then Mr. Levy dropped the bombshell like it was fired by a fancy howitzer, and Patrick saw if he wasn't right, he was close as dammit.

"Mrs. Shannon tells me she hasn't determined yet who that person ought to be. In the next few days she plans to speak with each

Allan Cole & Chris Bunch

of you, and - in consultation with myself - come to a final decision. She hopes all of you will be patient with her and understand that she isn't doing this to inconvenience anyone. She is attempting to plan ahead much farther than the immediate future. The decision is highly personal, and she begs your forbearance."

Mr. Levy looked around blandly. Whether he saw the great furrows growing across his father's brow, Patrick couldn't say. But no one could miss how pale Pamela had become, or the twist in her mouth that looked like someone had stuffed a lemon in it and slapped her on the back so she just had to suck. Patrick loved it.

He glanced about to see if anyone else was having as much fun. But they were all looking at Patrick.

What in the world? The expressions ranged from nodding warmth to speculation. Why, no one could think this shift in plans had anything to do with him, could they? What for? He was just a kid. He saw Pamela whispering to his father and looking over at him. What was going on?

Mr. Levy called the meeting to a close. People crowded up to the lawyer, asking if there was anything they could to do to help - not in regards to the will, mind you, but any business details that might assist Grandmother Shannon and Mr. Levy. So pointedly was the subject of the new will avoided, Patrick thought this had to be the uppermost thing in their minds.

Pamela grabbed his father and they slipped off. She didn't even hurl one of her famous looks at Patrick. The absence was worrisome.

The steamboat whistle brought Diana back from her musings. Far out across the river she saw the plume of white steam above the riverboat churning downstream toward Natchez. One of her captains sending a greeting. She tried to see which boat it was - the Shotwell? The Kentucky? She couldn't quite make out the name blazoned on the box. There must be a haze on the water.

Of course, Diana, she thought amusedly, there's no possibility 92 year old eyes might have a bit of trouble, is there? Eyes that once looked down the sights of a long rifle at an attacking enemy. It reminded her of Daniel Boone, who hunted into his eighties and beyond – but had to stick a bit of paper with spittle to his rifle's sights to target a deer for supper. It was said that he never missed.

Oh, my, it's not the eyes that go first, Diana dear, but the wandering mind. Shaking herself to the present, she returned her consideration to the two men who had just left.

On the surface, they appeared completely different. Joshua, the church-going Godfearing ship's captain from New England, devoted to his family and children, and Michael the rakehell Californian. But to her, they were remarkably similar. She'd begun her interview by asking bluntly what they thought of their Cousin Edward. Joshua had blandly returned he seemed gentlemanly enough, but hardly different from a hundred other Virginians. Michael had a similarly empty, but courteous response. Diana had really little interest in their opinions on Edward, and was using the gambit to see what they made of Patrick.

Michael begged off, saying he'd spent little time with the boy thus far. Diana half-smiled, but was not surprised that he might have divined her possible plan. Gamblers, like seamstress-speculators, needed minds as agile as the muscles of a German gymnast. Joshua also chose his words with care, saying he was not sure how much help he could be, either: "I've been trying to remember myself at that age. But that might also be a waste. I was an entirely obstreperous child who most likely should have been drowned in the millpond. I am aware of your possible plans, Grandmother. The best I could offer is, if the boy appeared when I was signing on a crew... I would consider letting him sign the articles. Which, I should warn you, is most likely to happen.

"Patrick spent some time inquiring, in such an innocent manner, about life at sea. It was more than the curiosity of a romantic lad, but more like someone who is thinking of running away."

"I've wondered about that," Diana said. "If it happens, it happens. Although his feelings are an interesting commentary on... other matters of concern."

Neither man inquired about those other matters. Joshua sought another subject, then, a bit nervously, asked if he could broach a delicate matter. Diana told him to proceed. In a near blurt, he'd said he truly hoped the one person Lawyer Levy had mentioned as a possible single heir would not be him. He felt incapable of assuming the mantle. Diana answered honestly, but obliquely, saying that indeed, the Captain was among those she was considering, and if she decided to revise her will, his objections would be taken into consideration. She went on to say she was mostly interested, this afternoon, in what the two of them felt would lie ahead for the country. Both men assembled their thoughts, and Joshua was the first to speak.

He foresaw America reaching across the sea, becoming the trader to the world. He felt Diana, since he could not bear speaking of a Shannon empire without her, would be best advised to close down her holdings in Philadelphia and Vicksburg, and concentrate on New York and San Francisco. A continental railway would be built in the next few years, and the nation would be linked. "We can feed the world or, if it wants to fight instead, hammer iron for their swords. The North will be the world's forgery, the West its larder."

"And the South?"

"The South will wither like the Ottoman Empire," Joshua said, his voice harsh and bitter. "There is something in the nature of this region, Grandmother. Something self-destroying. They say they want our ships in their ports, but they let those ports go to silt. They complain to ship's captains about having to send their cotton north to make into cloth - but if someone wishes to open a weaving factory they're looked at as if they're lepers. Southerners say there is a plot by the North to break them from the West. So there well might be. So why are there no railways being planned whose railheads would be in the South? Or almost none, at any rate?"

For the first time, Michael entered the conversation. "Grandmother... if I'm not intruding? Joshua, since you are playing at Nostradamus, what do you think the South will be like in, say, ten or fifteen years?"

"Possibly... Egypt. A nearly deserted land, with peasants scrabbling in the ruins. Except the South has no monuments that will stand, unmaintained, for one-millionth the life of the Great Pyramid. Until they are re-colonized by the North."

"There has been talk," Diana said, "of nullification once more. Secession, even." Suddenly she felt years younger. These two

Shannons were alive. They thought and reasoned, unlike the insensate beasts she'd dealt with in Vicksburg, full of prattle about French gowns or English manners, or the latest invisible offense that could lead to two men with pistols or sabers at dawn on DeSoto Peninsula.

"There is talk," Joshua agreed. "I have heard it myself. But it will not happen. Even these fools are capable of looking at their own circumstances. A nation must feed, clothe, defend itself and provide work for its citizenry. What is there to eat? Cotton? And cotton cannot be worn in bolls, dangling from a loincloth. Defense? There are no shipyards in the South I am aware of. Almost all bottoms are registered in the North. For an army, will they accept the local fancy-dress militia? Jobs? Doing what? Picking yet more cotton? No. If the Southern states would withdraw from the Union, they must form an alliance with another country. Actually, become a colony of that country."

"That would not be permitted," Michael said. "The North would be forced to go to war. The presence of a European power would be intolerable."

"So how are your talents at crystal gazing, Michael, dear," Diana said. "Do you agree the West will continue to boom?"

"Most likely. At least the northern part of the state, from Monterey to Oregon. Below that is little except desert. I have heard - Joshua would know whether this is true - there is one good harbor in the South called San Diego. Little else. A few pueblos with fleas. Rancheros being thimblerigged by Yanquis. That part of the state will never amount to anything. San Francisco, however, and the region around it will grow. One caution, however. If you plan any investment, you will need an excellent lawyer."

"Such as your cousin, Russell?"

"I understand him to be most competent. But... no. He should be given some assistants. Preferably ones who know our politics. And carry guns."

"You exaggerate, Michael."

"I do not. California is currently a state of thieves. The Americanos have stolen everything from the Mexicans, and are now busy fleecing each other. Two years ago, our secretary of state killed

Allan Cole & Chris Bunch

a newspaper editor in a duel, because he ridiculed another politician. And no one, least of all the governor, thought anything of it." Diana knew this was as common an occurrence in Vicksburg, but she didn't interrupt. "Give us a chance to hang a few dozen more of these blatant felons," Michael said, "or at least guarantee them a safe future at the public trough... and California will be the place."

Diana felt her energy beginning to ebb, but she had a few more questions to ask before she could rest. "Michael, dear. You have not said what interest you have in my estate."

"I have none, Grandmother. What would it give me?" Michael asked. "To say I am rich? I have been rich. And poor again. One day I shall most likely be rich once more. At the moment... my wants and needs are either provided for or I can easily acquire the means for them. The responsibility? People in Philadelphia or Vicksburg or elsewhere whose faces I have never seen, whose names I do not know? That is not for me. I tried it once, when I wore the uniform. The experience became... distasteful. At the moment what I would desire most is a new face and identity, at least until the present... difficulty in San Francisco clears up."

"Can you stay footloose your entire life?"

"No. I suppose not. I hope when I reach that point I am aware of the change, and still in possession of enough of my faculties to do something about it."

"One final question, dear. No one exactly has told me what trade you follow, out in San Francisco."

"I am what might be called a speculator."

"Speculator covers a great deal. I myself have speculated." Diana wouldn't let him wriggle off.

"My area of interest has been somewhat more... ephemeral. In areas of leisure, around men of means."

"A gambler?"

"That, too, at times. But currently I have been interested in real estate. And, to my downfall, politics. Next time, I shall ensure that my candidate is honest."

"That he stays for hire, dear?"

"Exactly, Grandmother Shannon." He stood, and Joshua shortly after him.

Allan Cole & Chris Bunch

"Once more, I thank you for coming to see me, and for your honesty. And for other things as well."

After Joshua and Michael bowed out, Diana allowed herself a broad smile. Regardless of how the division of the estate went, she was becoming convinced of her success in fulfilling that unspoken promise she'd made over a solitary grave many years ago. The Shannons would continue.

"I was warned before I reached Kansas the whole territory was a powder keg ready to be touched off," Russell said. "The fellow told me only half the truth. It's a powder keg, that's for sure, Grandmother Shannon. But the fuse is already burning... I think when it goes off the whole country is going to go with it."

Diana listened intently to Russell's account of his journey to Lawrence, Kansas, where he had been tending a client's legal needs when he got word to come Vicksburg. He had visited with her several times over the past few years and Diana had learned to trust the young man's opinion. As he talked, however, she kept an eye on Susan, who was just as wrapped up in Russell's description. When he spoke of larger events coming from the North - Susan would give a reflexive nod, confirming his view.

"Long before I reached there," he continued, "the turmoil in Kansas was all people were talking about. There was nothing one-way, or quiet about the talk. It got so fights and near killings on the packet were commonplace. The closer I got the hotter things were. I don't mean border ruffians, or Jayhawkers or Kickapoo Rangers, but common folk as well. The taverns and inns are full of men drinking and brooding and spoiling for a fight."

The whole business of the dispute over the Nebraska and Kansas territories was as confused a morass as even Diana had witnessed. It boiled down to a series of skirmishes and full-pitched battles between the North and South. California could enter the Union immediately if the debt of the previous Republic of Texas was assumed by the federal government. The Northern bankers liked the smell of guarantees and fat government interest rates in that. Strict fugitive slave laws applying to all states greased it more. That had been back in 1850 and Diana knew it was a mistake when she heard of the plan. If the South wanted to keep its filthy institution, rubbing the noses of the Northern masses in the mess was no way to go about it.

Russell told her about the people of Kansas. The majority were either New Englanders, or stolid German farmers who despised slavery. But the South would not be thwarted in its efforts to add to its power in the Senate. Thousands of ardent slavers poured across the Missouri border. When the vote came the previous March, the renegades stole the election and a pro slavery government was established. A second affront followed when President Pierce recognized the fraudulent government. Then the price of wheat hit $2.55 a bushel and the anti-slavery settlers knew their desirable land would be stolen as well. Guns and men were flowing across the border to beef up both sides.

"I wouldn't be surprised if we heard tomorrow that war had already broken out in Kansas," Russell said. "These are hard people. And I don't mean just the ruffians, but the common folk as well. They plow the land and hold off mounted Indians at the same time. I don't think they've met the mortal yet who strikes fear into them." Diana knew the breed. She knew them very well.

Susan said the situation in Philadelphia and the other cities of the North was nearly as fierce. "The laborers hate the Negro as much as the slavers," she said. "And I'm ashamed to say our new Irish cousins are the worst. They see every free black as a man taking their wages. But it's not so simple as that, so if the Southerners think they'll get some support there, they'll be handed their hat and kicked where it smarts most. Patriotism is on everyone's lips. The rich say the planters are humiliating them before the civilized world. The machinists believe the factories will be stolen by the South if it gets any more power. And the immigrants fear they will be run out of the country to God knows where because they have no homes to return to, for that is why they fled." From the hot look in her eyes, Diana could see that Susan believed these things as well. Her granddaughter was a committed abolitionist, as well as an ardent worker for feminist causes.

So, it had come full circle, Diana thought. The war that had never been fought finally seemed due. And this time there did not

76

seem to be a great enemy from without to divert attention. She wanted to tell them she had seen times as bad, or worse. It was possible to survive, just as it was possible nothing might happen at all. Crisis is an ordinary word, she wanted to say. Because there are always so many about. The natural state of things is war, she thought, with bits of uneasy peace between. Diana almost spoke this aloud, but she saw their flushed faces, plans and opinions roiling about behind outraged, stormy eyes. She realized if she said this, she might be handing them a gift of despair, rather than hope. Instead she let her eyes close for a moment or two, so they would lapse into silence and wonder if they should go. It was a lovely device to shift a topic to another plane. Then she opened them and asked what they thought of what Mr. Levy had to say.

Russell was first. He said he believed the drift of the remarks was that for some reason her grandson, Edward, might be out of favor. Or at least, Diana might think him incapable of managing her estate. He looked for Diana to interrupt him, but she just nodded for him to go on. "I might be embarrassing myself by believing you were thinking I might be the person to do the job," he said. "If this is so, it would be a grave mistake, and I hope you put it out of your mind."

Diana raised her eyebrows: Why?

"Because I'm a Yankee, Grandmother Shannon. From the view of people around here I'm even worse than that. They'll see me as a slick Philadelphia lawyer, out to fleece them of what is rightfully theirs. If you put me in charge, the whole thing will collapse. Besides, I really don't think I have the knowledge or experience, even if there wouldn't be any trouble."

"What would you advise, then, dear?"

"Susan should be the one," he said. "No one knows business better than she does. No one is better with people. I think Susan is a match for any of them."

Diana turned to Susan. Her granddaughter was shaking her head violently, as determined as her mother, Connie. "I don't agree, Grandmother Shannon," she said. "It's true I have a good business head. I won't deny it. I had good teachers." She smiled, remembering her mother and gave Diana a pat of thanks. "But what I

77

know is the city. And I know trade, but only as it relates to the city. I am not that comfortable with country people, especially these horrible people down here. One last thing. I'm a woman, and there is no way a Southern man - like Edward, for instance - would listen for one minute to what I had to say. If you take that course, I fear immediate failure."

Again, Diana asked: "What would you suggest?"

"What about Mr. Levy?" Susan said. "He's trustworthy and as loyal to the family as if he were a Shannon himself."

"Good thought," Russell said. "He's been your manager for years, now. Why not confer responsibility on him? Put the estate in trust, with him overseeing affairs."

"He's nearly seventy," Diana said. "If he died a few months after me, what would happen then?" Silence. With no hope of it being broken. "Think on it awhile," Diana finally said. "Discuss it amongst yourselves. I am open to any opinion or option."

She meant those as her closing words and they were taken as such. There came a scraping of chairs, a few kisses and embraces and they all took their leave.

Russell hesitated at the door. "Would you mind very much, Grandmother Shannon," he said, "if I went over things with Mr. Levy? Perhaps that might jostle the weak thing I call a brain." She smiled at his slight jest and said to do as he pleased.

So peaceful were her thoughts after the interview, that the instant he left she felt asleep.

Patrick ambled down the hallway towards his father's room. His face was pure innocence, but his heart was full of mischief. Just before the room there was a big closet he had investigated before. He glanced quickly about, saw no one lurking, and slipped inside. He heard the low rumble of his father's voice and Pamela's sharp whine coming clearly through the wall. The closet held plenty of soft things to make into a bed, and his father's outdoor coat hung just over his head. Patrick pictured Her at the makeup table, coaxing another layer of cream into her skin. His father would be stalking back and forth listening to a flurry of complaints, answering only when the attacks could not be avoided.

"I just don't see why you won't speak to your grandmother," Pamela was saying. "My God. She's only an old woman who has obviously lost her senses. This thing has to be set straight before it goes too far."

"Now, Pamela," his father said. "there is no reason for alarm. My grandmother has her odd ways and she likes to shake things up a little for her amusement."

"I saw no humor in it," Pamela said. "Neither did anyone else. Everyone has been up and down those stairs sniffing at the money since Mr. Levy left. Even that slick lawyer cousin of yours. And that other one. Susan. The abolitionist! And the gambler. And... And... that sailor. He smells like fish!"

Patrick wished his Uncle Joshua could hear. He'd march her off a gangplank, or have her whipped with a cat, or something equally as awful.

"You are about to be disinherited," Pamela continued. "Don't you see that? Or aren't you man enough to stick up for your rights?"

"Now, Pamela..."

"Perhaps you can live like a beggar, but I hardly think I should be expected to share that fate. Have you no pride?"

"Listen to me, dear," his father said. Patrick almost cheered when he heard the firmness in his voice. "I will repeat. I am the only son of James Emmett Shannon, who was the only son of Emmett Shannon and my grandmother. We are speaking of blood here. Direct descent. My grandmother may be many things all of us find a bit eccentric. But she is a traditionalist.

"My grandmother is from another century. She's strange, but she certainly is a woman of her times. Everyone had odd ideas then. You should have heard my father talk about it. A generation of Revolutionists, he called them. But one thing you can be sure of, is it would be impossible for her to turn her back on me."

"I don't know... " Pamela said, her voice wavering.

"It's only a game she's playing," his father insisted.

"Then why didn't you go see her?"

"Because, my love, everyone else was trooping up there just like you said. Did you ever see such greedy bastards... Excuse the language, my sweet. But you must see that I can't appear as if I'm

79

part of that crowd. My grandmother and I have a special relationship. Over the years, who is the one who always wrote to her? Me. Who was the one who would travel clear across the country just to see if she was in good health? Me. No one else has ever shown that kind of interest. And she appreciates it. Besides, any talk we have should seem natural. She and I have spoken together many times since our arrival. Running up and down the stairs with the rest would only look suspicious."

"Maybe you're right."

"Of course I am. Besides, look how well she's getting on with Patrick. She dotes on the child, I tell you. I've never seen her taken by anyone so much."

"Yes, I did notice that," Pamela said. But it came so flatly Patrick wondered why his father didn't catch the hatred in her tone.

"Well, then. If she disinherits me, she has to cheat her great grandson. And you know she won't do that!"

"I guess you are doing the best thing for both of us, dear," Pamela said, relenting. Or was Patrick only imagining that? No, the woman was a bitch, through and through. "Still, it won't hurt to make absolutely sure," Pamela said. "I think we should get some advice."

Patrick wondered how this would be accomplished. He listened closely to see if there would be some hint. But the arguing had faded. Now all he could hear was her disgusting billing and cooing as she tried to work her witch's spell on his father.

"Don't you think it's time we tried again to start a little friend for Patrick?" he heard her say. This not only worried Patrick, but made him mad as well. He'd rather have a wart then a friend Pamela grew. There were more nuzzling sounds. Then he heard Pamela say something like: "Damnit!" He wasn't sure, but it seemed like he had just gotten another reprieve as far as a baby half-brother went. Victory!

He heard his father mumbling apologies. Some angry noises from guess who? The bed gave a great creak. Bootsteps thundered for the exit. His father was making a break for it. Patrick almost cheered aloud.

Oops.

Allan Cole & Chris Bunch

He looked up at the coat hanging overhead. If his father was going out, he'd be needing it.

Three breaths later, Patrick was out of the closet and sprinting for the stairs. He leaped down a half a dozen or more, then did a quick turn. Back up he went. Leisurely. Minding his own business, and all. He forced a bright smile and cheery greeting on his face as his father came toward him, the coat hanging over one shoulder.

But he just got a pat on the head, and his father headed down the stairs without a word.

CHAPTER SEVEN

VICKSBURG

THEY CLOPPED ALONG the road to Vicksburg at a brisk pace. The track was hard-packed and the wheels moved smoothly, with hardly a jounce to spoil Patrick's reverie. Russell handled the reins easily, which was a surprise to his nephew, who had been told that all Yankees were clumsy brutes when it came to horseflesh.

Russell still had "city" written all over him. He talked faster than Patrick was used to and when he set his mind on business he got right down to it, with none of the delays of his country cousins. He told Patrick over breakfast he was off to Vicksburg to speak with Mr. Levy, and would Patrick like to keep him company? Patrick said it was fine by him and expected the first nudge along about noon. But no sooner had his cousin wiped his mouth, than he was all for getting out the little carriage and hitching up a horse.

If there was one thing Patrick liked less than being prodded, it was being prodded before his eyes had come unstuck. He almost said so, but then remembered the book Russell had given him and decided bad temper would be mean repayment. So he got at it with a will and they were soon on their way.

Patrick wasn't much on talk this early, so the greatest part of the journey had already passed before a few questions he had been harboring came awake and started nagging at him. The first one was the hardest, however. He wasn't sure how to go at it. Then he looked over at Russell, saw the friendly look on his face, and took heart.

"Uh... Russell, you said you were kin to Susan. Right?"

"That's what they tell me," Russell said. "If they lied, it sure was a fancy one."

That's what Patrick was after, but Russell came out with it so easily that it shook him back into silence.

"What do you have on your mind, Patrick?" his cousin prodded. "Spit it out. If I have anything to hide, I'll warn you off and no hard feelings. Bargain?"

Patrick nodded. "Everybody says you and Susan are cousins. And you said you were cousins. But..."

"I'll help you out," Russell said, taking amused pity. "This is sort of scandalous, so keep it to yourself, okay?"

The Wars Of The Shannons

Patrick swore that if a hundred Indians descended on them this minute - all of them determined to sweat it out of him with scalping knives and anthills - not a word of Russell's secret would escape his lips.

"All the original people are dead now," Russell said. "So I don't think it really matters. You see, my mother's name was July Shannon. One of Susan's sisters."

Apparently, he went on to explain, it was not only Farrell's sons who had run wild; one of his daughters had gotten into difficulty as well. July was so close to her brother David that when he went to sea, she was as broken up as if they had been twins. The sorrow turned into a stubborn streak and one day she took off with a notions drummer. The family was frantic - Farrell over her great sin; Connie, because July was so young. They called in Grandmother Shannon for assistance, and a few months later July was found- abandoned in Boston. She was so ragged, hungry and scared that she gave no one any fight at all when they took her home. There was one big problem.

Russell patted his stomach. "Me," he said.

Patrick gaped. He had never met a bastard before. "Folks were just as narrow-minded about those things as now days," Russell said. "So, although no one in the family cared that much - they were all just glad she was back and safe - they thought a little disguising of the facts was in order. They made up a kid brother to my grandfather Isaac. Which made me a Conners. Then they invented a tragedy to put me in Farrell and Connie's care. And I was raised up as a poor orphan cousin." He grinned at Patrick. "So what do you think of that?"

Patrick frowned. "That means Susan..."

"Is my aunt, not my cousin. Make sense now?"

Patrick laughed. It made sense while he was telling it, but now that it was out he was back where he started.

"You're still my cousin, right?"

"Right. Is that okay with you?"

"I like it just fine," Patrick said. And he meant it.

The next question was only a tad less awkward: how did a nice fellow like Russell Conners become a Philadelphia shyster? He had been raised to distrust Yankees, especially of the lawyer variety. Patrick didn't put it that way, but Russell didn't miss what was behind his question and laughed. "I keep my horns in my valise," he said, "along with a couple of books covering the fine points of cheating noble southern gentlemen."

Patrick blushed and said he was just curious how Russell had taken up the law to begin with.

"I guess you could say I got into it purely by accident," Russell said. "When I was about seventeen or eighteen, I got the Shannon wandering disease. Most of us are afflicted by it, and in fact, some of us never recover. Tell the truth, I'm still not over it. Which is why I tend to travel at the slightest excuse to the most god-awful places. I tell myself it's for my clients, but that really isn't true. I could make a better living hiring someone to go west for me, and sit back in my office and rake in the dollars, instead of letting business go all to hell while I take off to see what's really happening in the world."

"But what did you do back then?" Patrick wanted to know. "Back when you got the wanderlust for the first time? Did you run away? Did they find you and drag you back and punish you by making you go to lawyer school? Is that what happened?"

"Not exactly," Russell said. Dry. "When the wander fever struck me, my mother got together with Grandmother Shannon and they both decided I ought to see for myself what life was about. So they put me in charge of a shipment bound for the frontier. It was an easy trip, with a only a few adventures. At Cincinnati, however, everything went sour. The captain of the boat I had hired was a smiling, genial fellow when the arrangements were first made. But soon as we got amongst his own people, he revealed himself to be a scoundrel.

"He was out to steal the cargo from under me. He hired a crusty old gent for his lawyer, who looked like a fool to me. I believed I had the case won. That all I had to do was to show the proper documents to a judge or jury, tell the truth as I saw it, and any reasonable fellow would rule in my favor."

"But they cheated you and you lost," Patrick blurted out.
"That's right."
"Then you shot the captain and had to go on the run, right?"

"Nothing like that. Why would I want to shoot a man over a boatload of tools and bolts of cloth and other such foolishness?"

Patrick had to admit his cousin had a point. But he wished Russell wouldn't be so reasonable. That way the story would be more exciting.

"So, there I was," Russell said, "stuck in Cincinnati with my first failure. I thought I was such a big man, but I'd lost the cargo that had been entrusted to me. I could see no way that I could return home and admit my failure."

"Absolutely," Patrick said. "First a body'd want to poke around the frontier. See what it was all about. If you're gonna be in trouble, might as well make the most of it."

He was pleased to learn this was exactly what happened to Russell. With one small switch - the old lawyer who had hornswoggled him took pity, and hired him as his clerk. They traveled the wilderness circuit for nearly three years.

"There was not a thing about law the old man didn't know," Russell said. "More important, he knew people. When to go around them, when to confront them, when to ignore them, and when to kick your horse in the ribs and run like blazes. I learned a lot from that old man. Then one day he told me it was time I struck out for myself. Said I should hang up my shingle and go into practice. But I had different ideas. I thought it would be better to go home and get myself into law school. A few years later The Great State of Pennsylvania finally agreed with my old mentor and said I was qualified to practice the law. And that, as they say, was that."

Patrick stared at him, wondering why his cousin had insisted on doing things the hard way, the dull way. Russell saw this running through his head. He laughed.

"I grew up a bit during that time," he said by way of explanation. Patrick shrugged. The mysteries of adulthood again...

By this time they'd reached Vicksburg and the conversation petered out. They left the horse and carriage at a stable and walked to Mr. Levy's place of business in a shabby wooden building above a newspaper called the Vicksburg Gazetteer.

Patrick spotted all kinds of interesting-looking people and shops as they climbed the outside staircase and was more than a little disappointed when they entered Mr. Levy's office. He knew he was facing several hours of boring lawyer talk, while out there things were happening - important things. But with only a little ill grace, he resigned himself to his fate, shook Mr. Levy's hand, answered his polite questions, and then suffered to sit in a corner on a hard chair while Russell and Mr. Levy got down to it.

There was some preliminary jawing about personal matters, then the two men shuffled through some documents and got wrapped up in a discussion over what old terms versus proposed new ones ought to be considered in his great grandmother's will. About the only things that drifted through Patrick's bored haze was that the old will basically split up his great-grandmother's estate into many parts, with each part going to a specific person, and that certain other people would be receiving small cash settlements instead of a piece of the business. He heard his father's name mentioned once or twice, then his own. He perked up at that and then saw that both men were looking at him.

What had he done? Scratch too loudly or something? But it was only Russell, worried he might be having a dull time. Patrick admitted he'd experienced more exciting moments, but assured them he was fine. Of course, if they had some chore they wanted done, like counting the apples in a hogshead, they only had to ask and Patrick would count until his brains fell out.

The two men laughed, and Russell fished some silver out of his pocket and suggested he get a bite to eat, adding if there were any money left over, and he saw something that might appeal to a boy, he was welcome to treat himself. Patrick didn't argue. He grabbed the money and was out the door like the arrow fired from Ulysses' great bow.

Patrick headed instantly for Vicksburg-Under-The-Hill. He found Washington Street, and headed west. At Chiney Street, he'd turn south. The street was crowded with pretty women and bearded, well-dressed men. Some were strolling, some smoking pipes or cigars, others sitting under the covered walk on either side of the street studying newspapers. Or arguing. Nobody seemed to be working. Patrick guessed there must be a lot of independently wealthy people in Vicksburg.

He was close to the Washington Hotel - and his downhill. The path to perdition was easy and paved, he thought, just like the preachers say. Then he spotted something: drawn up in front of the hotel was a carriage - a carriage belonging to Grandmother Shannon. He'd seen it earlier at her house when he'd hitched up the smaller wagon. If someone had wanted to come into town, why didn't they ride with Russell? He was about to go see what was up, when out of the hotel stepped his father, Pamela, and... Fitz Maguire! What was he doing in Vicksburg? If that bastard Maguire had business here, why hadn't he traveled out with them? This was getting very strange, he thought, as his feet scuttled him sideways behind a group of men absorbed in a game of draughts.

He slid from there into a doorway and peered out. Maguire was talking rapidly and quietly. Pamela and Edward listened intently. Pamela was the first to understand, it appeared, since she was the first to nod agreement. She gave Edward a swift peck and squeezed Maguire's arm. The two men started away, but Fitz looked back. Patrick saw Pamela give him that swift you-and-I-have-a-secret flicker of a smile the boy found so maddening. But what secret could she and Maguire be sharing? Then she went back into the hotel. Maguire and Edward strolled toward the corner, and turned down Chiney. Toward Vicksburg-Under-The-Hill.

This was real spying, Patrick thought. If nobody had said anything about Maguire, there Must Be A Conspiracy! Maybe, his mind jumped, this had something to do with the will everyone was so concerned about. Maguire was, after all, the son of Grandmother Shannon's second husband, and she'd told Patrick John Maguire's decision to free his slaves and abandon the state had caused much animosity among his sons. Patrick couldn't figure what they had to be mad about. Their father had given them their inheritance, hadn't he?

He trailed the two men, keeping about a half a block behind them. At the bottom of the hill, Edward and Maguire walked along the waterfront.

Patrick wasn't so intent on his spying that he didn't have an eye for what was going on around him. For once, reality was better than expectation. If Vicksburg-Under-The-Hill couldn't give Sodom a good solid run for the prize, it wasn't from lack of trying. Every building looked to be devoted to some kind of pleasure. Pleasure the church-goers up above probably would shrink at considering - and then find their way to under cover of darkness.

Here was a flatboat that'd been pulled up on dry land, and converted into a raucous tavern. There was music, screeching fiddles, a blare of battered horns, a jangle of tambourines and someone singing. Patrick stumbled over a man, started to apologize, and realized there was no need. The drunk, unless Patrick had stumbled over a corpse instead of an inebriate, would not have moved if a packet had steamed over him.

Two men flailed at each other in mid-street. They were on their knees in the mud. Wagoneers shouted, but the two fighters were in their own pugilistic world. Every now and then, one would land a blow with little effect. Three men were singing, tankards of Monongahela whiskey in their hands - "You Never Miss Your Sainted Mother Till She's Dead and Gone to Heaven."

Here came four women. Maybe their clothes weren't as clean as they should be, and a little tattered and pinned together. But Patrick had never seen so much bare flesh in his life, from the scooped out bosoms to the high-hemmed dresses, which were slit almost to their knees. One of them smiled and winked as she went past. Patrick nodded, and then rocked back as the blast of whisky fumes and perfume hit him. This lady - Patrick guessed she was what he'd heard called a strumpet - smelled worse than even Pamela.

A man stumbled out of a tavern, bottle in one hand, pistol in the other. He began shouting, punctuating his comments with gunfire: "I'm a ring-tailed squealer! BANG! I'm a reg'lar screamer from the ol' Massassip! WHOOP! I'm th' very infant that refused his milk before its eyes wuz open, and called out for a bottle of old Rye! I love the women and I'm chockful o' fight! BANG! I'm half wild horse and half cock-eyed alligator and th' rest o' me is crooked snags an' red-hot snappin' turkle! I can hit like fourth-proof lightnin' an' ever' lick I make lets in an acre o' sunshine! BANG! I can out-

Allan Cole & Chris Bunch

run, out-jump, out-shoot, out-brag, out-drink an' out-fight, rough-an'
tumble, no holts barred, ary man both sides th' river from Pittsburgh
to New Orleans an' back agin to San Louie! BANG! C'mon you
flatters, you bargers, you steamers, you milk-white mechanics an'
see how tough I am to chaw! BANG! Cock-a-doodle-do!"

No one but Patrick paid the slightest attention.

He ducked behind an upended rain barrel when his father and
Maguire stopped. They were outside a brightly-painted and bannered
building that looked much cleaner than most of its fellows - THE
ALHAMBRA. A gambling hell, Patrick chanced. They were
approached by three of the most singularly evil men he'd ever seen.
Maguire was introducing them to his father as if they were Fitz's
best friends. The man who appeared to be their leader was a giant.
He towered over both Virginians as if they were children. But he
was an emaciated giant: rail-thin, long of countenance and beard. He
wore black from beaver to boots. The lace on his white shirt
threatened to spill over and bury his coat lapels. Patrick could see the
flash of a red vest. The giant looked as if he could be an undertaker.
In this part of the world, Patrick thought, that could be the case, and
the man looked capable of providing all services from choosing the
victim, assisting him through his final miseries to disposal of the late
lamented.

A man down the street shouted "Mornin', Judge," and the giant
smiled - gold glinting - tipped his hat, and returned to whatever was
being discussed. His two henchmen were almost as striking. One of
them, gross, bearded and wearing filthy buckskins might have been
one of those mountain man like he'd read about. The other man was
a ferret, and as dirty as the bearded one. This Judge - and what kind
of judge would be on these streets, Patrick wondered - listened first
to Maguire's proposal, if that was what was being made. He had
some questions for Edward, then seemed to consider.

Finally he laughed a loud but utterly humorless laugh, and
shook first Maguire and then Edward's hands. The ferrety sort's eyes
flickered about, as if some bargain that would not bear the light of
day or the scrutiny of honest men had been struck.

Even though there was no way the Weasel could have known
him, Patrick ducked further back behind the barrel. He suddenly

realized the barrel was not empty. There was someone else in it, unmoving and curled at its bottom. Patrick had just learned a lesson: you could tell the difference between Dead Drunk and Dead. He swallowed quickly and found a parked wagon for his new concealment.

His father, Maguire and the others were not in sight. They must have gone inside the gambling house. The boy pondered what he should do next. Could he perhaps, slip around back? Get inside, near enough to find out what was going on? No. Hell, he thought. If I were a few years older, no one would notice or care. Maybe I can find a vantage point. Wait until they come out.

He looked about Vicksburg-Under-The-Hill. Not too far away was a two-story building, with SALOON & BOARDING HOUSE on its upper story and, below it, a black-painted sign in lettering quite hard to make out: DEUTSCHES GASTHAUS. House? Gast - guest? He'd never eaten Dutcher's food. Just inside would make an excellent place to wait. He was starting for the gasthouse, when he heard a whistle. Patrick looked up. Hanging off the balcony of the building next to him was a girl. She seemed not much older than he was. Real pretty, even if her hair needed combing. And surely her mother would drag her inside if she knew the girl wasn't wearing anything but her shift.

"Uh... Good afternoon, ma'am," he said.

The girl giggled. "A little gentleman. What are you doing, little gentleman?"

"Just... looking around. I've never been in Vicksburg before."

"Are y' a goldfinch?"

"I beg your pardon?"

"Did y' come out wi' any cash?"

"Well... my cousin gave me a little."

"Whyn't y' come up? Packet'll be in, hour or so. Real in'restin'. Help me pass th' time til it do."

That, to Patrick, sounded a real proposition. From her room, he would have a fair view of The Alhambra. It was time, anyway, for his own adventure.

He was looking for the stairs up, when a hand fell on his shoulder. Patrick jumped like a horse who'd had ginger pushed up his vent. He whirled. Oh, God.

Michael stood there, nearly omnipresent cigarillo in one hand and a bit of a smile on his face. Now he was for it. "Que paso, Patrick? This is an odd part of the world to encounter you in."

"Well, I was..." and Patrick flat had no story.

"Yes. You unquestionably were." Michael looked up at the balcony. "M'pologies, m'lady. But my friend here can broaden his horizons without encountering a fireship. He'll take his entertainment elsewhere."

The sweet girl exploded. She called Patrick a fancy boy - whatever that was. A bastard cub. The cully's catamite. And more. Michael, however, received the brunt of the name-calling. He made no response, other than to tip his hat politely, take Patrick by the elbow, and steer him down the street. "You do not need that, cousin."

"I was just going to use her room. To watch... watch something."

"As that young lady back there might put it, I am neither a nigmenog nor cork-brained. Although, before we continue the discussion, I should advise you that what you most likely hoped would happen up there would not."

Patrick tried to look innocent - but Michael just laughed.

"I suspect just behind the door you would have found have been her cock bawd lurking. Her pimp. Who would have tapped you just so... back of this ear... with a slung shot if he were in a bad mood or a sock full of buckshot if he were feeling kindly, and you would awaken much later in the gutter stripped to the skin. And even if the procurer were not dancing attendance, the girl would offer you a drink of the finest whisky. You probably would not notice she but touched her glass to her lips. Once again, some hours later, you would wake in that same gutter, in the same condition. Except that the hammers of hell would be playing in your skull. Having myself climbed too many stairs, met too many pimps behind doors and woke in more than my share of sewers, you may take my predictions as gospel. And that is all I propose to say on the subject of soiled doves.

"To return to the original subject. Were you down here, Under-The-Hill, looking for anything in particular? Or just general adventure?"

"I was... following my father." Patrick wondered why he'd told this man, almost a stranger. As soon as he blurted it, however, he decided to leave out any mention of Maguire. The explanation would be long - and humiliating.

"Tsk. At least it is still daylight. But even so, a Virginia gentleman down here, is far beyond his reach. Unless your father is more of a rakehell than I suspect."

"I don't know what that word means, sir."

"Ask Joshua. Where is Edward now?" Patrick turned and pointed back down the street at The Alhambra. "Hum. The situation grows more interesting. That is where one Sturdevant is said to enrich himself. 'Judge' Sturdevant, he would have it. I have not yet enjoyed the Judge's hospitality, although I have heard much about it. Perhaps this might be the time."

Michael considered a moment. "Patrick, who are you in town with?"

"Cousin Russell."

"Get back above the hill. Busy yourself doing whatever it was he gave you permission to do. I shall make you a bargain. If you do not mention what I have said, nor anything else that happened since you came down Chiney, neither shall I."

"Nossir. I won't. Is my father in some kind of trouble?"

"I hope not."

"What are you going to do?"

The half-smile was back on Michael's face. "Nothing in particular. Visit some places. Meet some people. Have a drink of bourbon. On your way, boy. I have business."

For once, Patrick followed orders.

The next morning, Patrick burst from bed, dressed and hurried downstairs. What had happened in Vicksburg? Neither Michael nor his father had returned home by the time Patrick was chased to bed.

In the dining room Michael was filling a plate at the sideboard. His cousin was washed, bright-eyed, fresh-shaven, and wearing clean linen. Joshua was sitting at the table, in the middle of a solid breakfast of sturgeon, eggs, and rolls. "The late life," Joshua observed, "appears to agree with you, Michael."

"Because my heart is pure," he answered. "Good morning, Patrick. Have you eaten yet?"

"Nossir."

Michael heaped ham, applebread, and honey on a plate, then took a glass of fresh spring milk. But he shook his head when a servant offered him the plate of eggs. "Not that pure, I am afraid."

Patrick's father came through the door. His eyes were red, he had not shaved and was wearing the same clothes as the previous day. The boy thought he smelled like a gutter in Vicksburg-Under-The-Hill.

"Good morning, father."

A growl came in return. Edward shambled to the sideboard and poured coffee.

"Buenos Dias, Edward," Michael offered.

Edward went to the end of the sideboard and splashed brandy from a decanter into his cup. His hand was shaking. Without another word he went out.

"Cut me dead, as I am a Christian," Michael observed.

"What occurred last night?" Joshua asked.

"Let us just say... " Michael stopped, glanced over at Patrick. "... that we agree with the old saw about pitchers and ears. Shall we repast in the garden, Joshua?"

The two men left with their plates and utensils. Like a rifle ball, Patrick shot away. Starving he may have been, but this tale needed the hearing. Into the kitchen, down into the root cellar, and to the hatch leading out into the garden. He had time to prop the hatch open a crack before he heard the footsteps of Joshua and Michael.

"I am not sure," Joshua said, "that if the matter is of this great an import I should be even asking."

"It is important, but quite indirectly. What happened... wait. Before, or even if, I tell my tale, I must ask you what is your opinion of our good cousin Edward? Quite honestly."

93

A silence, then: "To be brutally direct," Joshua answered, "and to use the phrase of a poor, uneducated Irisher of my acquaintance, I do not find him to be worth a hill of shit."

"Much my sentiments. So I may proceed."

Michael did so, telling Joshua how he'd seen Edward enter The Alhambra, and had gone in after him. He made no mention, the boy was pleased to hear, of Patrick being Under-The-Hill. "I held at the bar, keeping my drink before my face, until my eyes were familiar with the darkness. Over to one side of the room, bucking the tiger, was Edward, one Judge Sturdevant who is The Alhambra's proprietor, and two of his blacklegs."

The faro game, Michael continued, had been going on long enough for the tiger to show its teeth. At first Edward would have been permitted to win a few hands and drink a few juleps. But now the flow of money had reversed itself.

"Of course the game was crooked," Joshua said.

"Of course. In faro, the cards are dealt from a box. Sturdevant was using a screw box, a mechanism any dunce may use to make himself a King Gambler. A small button narrows or widens the slit the cards are dealt through. This is used with a crooked deck where the cards are sanded. An imbecile could learn the skill in an hour," Michael went on. "At a suitable moment, I wandered over and was most surprised to encounter my noble cousin in this place. I, of course, was asked to join in the game.

"I protested a weak memory, telling them I have trouble remembering whether the first card is Soda or Hock, let alone the other conventions. But poker, now. That was a game. It was a pity, I continued, no one in Frisco appreciated poker and its subtleties. Thought it took too much time for the action. Indeed, when they did play, they still used the old, twenty-card deck. I was eager for a game, especially with a full deck and the new rules."

"Why did you want to change the game?"

"Because the only way to win at faro, when the dealer's got a screw box is with cold steel. And the lookout up on his stool had an eight-bore shotgun. Sturdevant protested, but agreed. At first, he tried to continue his rather bullish approach by ringing in a marked

94

deck, marked so blatantly a blind man could read it. Pretty soon the buck was mine.

"Damn this losing deck of cards, I swore. I pulled a boy in from the street, gave him some coins, told him to purchase a deck of cards from a gambling den I'd noticed further down the street. With the new, unmarked deck, Sturdevant was at sea. So instead of having his lazy man's key to victory, he was forced to fall back on his assets. It appeared a long time since he had been forced to rig an honest deck. He gave it his best. Pickup, holding out cards, all the rest. I started throwing Edward some good hands. Even then, the damnation eejiot didn't play them right.

"But finally Sturdevant was ready to deal the hand that would destroy Edward. He would give him a very good hand - but he himself would have a better one. Unfortunately, he set the deck down within my reach while he poured himself another julep. I had already stacked the bottom of that deck, so I cut to where I'd crimped the card I wished to be on top and it was if I was dealing.

"Sturdevant got a very good hand. Better than the one I had given Edward. I also gave the plugs acceptable cards - I did not want them to fold out, and have time to consider mischief. Edward bet them like he had them. The plugs hung in there, as did I. By the time the raising and re-raising was finished the Judge had shoved Edward's markers, his losings, and a large amount of his own gold were in the center of the table. Edward stayed in the hand by scribbling further markers. I suspect his wife and plantation were on two of the slips. It was a large pot. In San Francisco, even, it would be considered slightly out of the ordinary.

"Edward made the last bet. Everyone else just called. Full of victory, our cousin laid out his hand. A king-high straight. He reached for the pot. The Judge grinned - as ghastly an excuse for a smile as any skull - and displayed his own cards. A spade flush. And then I showed him my hand. Four aces and the mistigris."

"Was that not a little... blatant?"

"It was. Sturdevant actually acquired some color in his sallow cheeks. One of his bully boys was about to accuse me of cheating, I think. Sturdevant snarled him to silence. Since we were the only patrons of The Alhambra, the faro lookout had come down from his

Allan Cole & Chris Bunch

perch to watch the fleecing. His shotgun lifted. I saw the barkeep reach under the counter. With a wave of his hand, Sturdevant brought them to heel. He announced that with this upset, the game was finished. However, he suggested, in a tone that did not seem to allow me to hear mother calling, that he and I play one final hand. Showdown.

All the cards face up, dealt one by one. I thought that acceptable. However, I informed Sturdevant my cousin appeared somewhat hornswoggled with drink. That he should leave. Sturdevant thought that excellent, not preferring witnesses for what would follow."

"How," Joshua wondered, "did you ever convince our fool of a cousin to leave?"

"I merely used what I have heard you describe as your quarterdeck voice to inform him he and I would be meeting in a few minutes at the bar of the Prentiss House."

"Weren't you worried about Edward being jackrolled as he stumbled out?"

"Not particularly. I even thought a mild larruping might do him good. Besides, at this point, he had little to steal. At any rate, he staggered out. I gathered the cards, shuffled them once, and gave them to Judge Sturdevant. I asked what he thought to be an acceptable bet. He said what was in the previous pot. I agreed. But I made him to match the stakes in gold. Sturdevant went to work, doing everything except walking widdershins around that deck. Then he offered me the deck and told me to deal. No cut. I took the cards in one hand, sipped my wine, and dealt. Judge Sturdevant received a pair of deuces."

"What was in your hand?"

"Coincidence struck most strongly last night at The Alhambra. Once again, I had four aces and the joker."

"Damnation, Michael. You like to sail close to the wind!"

"Perhaps. But the man had irked me. That ended the game. After some... discussion, I withdrew to the Prentiss House, where I evidently made an error. I returned Edward his winnings, told him he had been playing with a cheat, and that he was incompetent to play Patience and should learn his lesson. I may have been under a slight

Allan Cole & Chris Bunch

amount of tension which kept me from practicing my usual taciturnity."

"That is quite a tale," Patrick heard Joshua say. "Quite a tale indeed. I surely hope Grandmother Shannon is aware of the fellow's failings."

"I am hoping, Joshua, these mysterious conferences with young Russell are what I think them to be."

"Russell. Yes. That would be an excellent choice. For a lawyer, he appears honest. And intelligent."

"Shall we adjourn to the stables? A ride through the country might prove refreshing. We can continue our discussion."

"Damn you, I'll do it. But tell me, should we not consider the probability this Judge Sturdevant will have a certain lust for vengeance, and be willing to wreak it on anyone with the surname of Shannon? Perhaps we ought to exercise a certain preparedness. Particularly if any of us travel into Vicksburg."

"You are a cautious man, Captain Joshua, and your advice is worth heeding."

That was the end of the conversation. Patrick was only partly relieved there had been no mention of Fitz Maguire. Where had the man gotten off to? Strange...

He had much to think on.

CHAPTER EIGHT

VICKSBURG

PATRICK FILLED IN the events for Diana since they had last spoken, particularly his conversation with Russell and their visit with Mr. Levy in Vicksburg. He reported with such step-by-step inconsequential detail, Diana was sure he was holding something back. However, she didn't think mischief was at the bottom of it. The boy had seen something in Vicksburg that disturbed him. Of this, she was sure. The only thing certain was the boy had come to admire Russell, although the fact his cousin had willingly and intentionally taken the hard way to reach his goal plainly stumped the child, whose models of behavior had thus far consisted entirely of short-sighted men and women. So, despite his dodging about the subject of Vicksburg and what had occurred there, Diana was satisfied. His attitude towards Russell fit in well with her tentative plans. When he had finally finished his report, she decided to prod him a little.

"What do you think of your cousin Susan?"

Patrick brightened at the mention of her name. "I think I can give her a clean bill of lading right off, Grandmother Shannon," he said. "No need to worry yourself about her."

"Oh, I'm not, Patrick, dear," Diana said. "Especially now that you've set my mind at ease. However, don't you think it would be poor procedure to leave her out? If everyone isn't questioned - and thoroughly - then how can we be absolutely sure of our facts?"

Patrick thought about this, then grinned and said from here on out no detail would escape him, or clue go uncovered no matter how small.

They heard footsteps outside the door, and then Kitty's gentle tapping. She entered with a badly shaken Mr. Levy at her heels.

"There's been a fire at my office, Mrs. Shannon," he said. "Everything has been destroyed."

Diana calmly took this in. She knew Mr. Levy hadn't come for sympathy. The question was the possible cost to both of them.

"But it is your habit to keep originals in the fire proof safe at the bank, Mr. Levy," she pointed out. "So, except for the property - and the building was worth much less than the land - how great a loss could it be? Was someone hurt?"

"No, but we can only thank God for that," he said. "The cause was arson. No question of it!"

"Against you, Mr. Levy?" Diana was shocked.

"Absolutely not. Forgive me if I've alarmed you. The newspaper office downstairs was the obvious target. Probably some scurrilous editorial attracted the wrath of low criminals. Their office was wrecked, then set alight. My main concern is all the business records. We may incur some loss of profits until I can get everything in order again."

Diana repeated that under the circumstances there was no cause for great alarm. "Hire someone to engage new offices, Mr. Levy," she said. "And to sort things out. Where I'm bound, a little profit or a loss won't mean a thing. Unless you disagree, I think we should concentrate on the immediate business at hand: The disposition of my estate. Do you have the original of the last will?"

"I haven't checked with the bank as yet," Mr. Levy answered. "But I believe so."

"If not," she said, "I have its holographic sister in my chest." She pointed at the great horsehair trunk.

As his great-grandmother and Mr. Levy drew deeper into discussion regarding the potential losses from the fire, Patrick slipped quietly out of the room.

"I've lost patience with your excuses for your lack of spine, Edward Shannon," Pamela was saying. "I have listened to you for all this time. Promises and more promises. Always lies. Always hiding disaster."

Patrick huddled in the closet, trying to make out exactly which lies his father was being accused of this time. He wasn't quite sure what was upsetting Her so much. That it might involve money was not too difficult to guess.

"Well, this is too much. You're to receive only five thousand dollars! After all you've done for her, that is your repayment! And if that wasn't insult enough, did you see how much that Philadelphia lawyer was going to get?"

99

Allan Cole & Chris Bunch

Her voice grew muffled as she walked to the adjacent parlor, apparently dogging his father. However, Patrick was certain they were speaking of his great grandmother's will - the old one, obviously, for the new one hadn't even been drawn up, yet.

"What a low-sneak that Russell Conners is," Pamela was saying, her voice ringing through clearly again. "Coming down here time after time behind our backs. Cozying up to that silly old woman. Getting her to do his bidding."

His father had barely said a word, so great was Pamela's anger. But when she mentioned Russell, Patrick heard a low rumbling he couldn't make out, although the tone was descriptive enough. Patrick desperately wished his father could get his loyalties straight. Michael had done him a favor, and Russell had done nothing at all. Pamela, however...

"It's that Susan Dolan who put him up to it," Pamela said. "Everyone knows she's his aunt, and not his cousin at all. I tell you, that abolitionist bitch has been conspiring against us for years."

More mutterings, but no argument from his father. Then: "From now on, Edward Shannon, we'll do things my way," Pamela barked. "Is that understood?"

Patrick ducked out of the closet and fled before he could hear his father's humiliating answer.

"Good evening, Patrick."

"Good evening, sir. Might I come in for a moment?"

Michael bowed the boy into the room. "How may I be of service to you?"

Patrick didn't waste any more time on preliminaries: "You didn't peach on me."

"Nor you on me," his cousin said. "I guess we should congratulate each other for being honest rogues together." Michael walked to the desk, which had a towel cast across it. He sat down and removed the towel. Patrick gaped - on the desk were three pistols, an evil-looking knife, and a walnut box with cleaning implements, gunpowder and balls.

Michael saw his reaction and smiled. "Since I did not know it was you, I thought it best not to panic my visitor if it were a less bloodthirsty relative."

Patrick had never seen weapons like these. The knife was a slender bowie, with about an eight inch blade; its handle was styled like a coffin, with silver and some multi-shaded, pearl-appearing substance on the sides.

Michael passed it to him. "This is what a proper San Francisco gentleman wears as part of his walking-out dress. The silver and abalone shell keeps it from being a plebeian's murder weapon. It was built by an excellent mechanic named Joseph Kious. Who, when you extract him from the bottle and opium pipe, is possibly our most gifted artist of cutlery." Michael's sardonic smile deepened. "As yet we Californios have not turned our eye to more cultural pastimes."

"Everybody in San Francisco goes about wearing these?"

"The knife, possibly. The others are less common, although too many caballeros think themselves naked without a pistol. These are peculiar to one of my trades." The three pistols were a small, elaborately scrolled .36 Bentley revolver and two ornate derringers, each with a barrel about an inch long, but almost half an inch in diameter, trimmed in silver and gold with ivory grips.

Michael loaded all three, and tucked the tiny pocket pistols into pouches specially sewn inside each sleeve of his short coat. "These," he observed, "are for use when all else fails, much as a politician uses patriotism." He took four brass percussion caps from a pillbox and forced them onto the nipples of the revolver's cylinder. "Always leave the charge under the hammer unprimed, if you are ever unfortunate enough to have to carry a gun for a living. I have seen very minor errors ensure a man never having to worry about progeny."

He went to the closet and took out a brocaded vest. He put the bowie into a sewn-in sheath on the left, the revolver into a holster on the right. "In San Francisco, I would now be ready to join the company of gentlemen. However, I prefer the company of the gentleman I am with. Be seated. I assume you came here for some other purpose than to admire the art of the gunsmith."

"I heard you were a soldier," Patrick said hesitantly. "In the war. And I wanted to know what it's like. If you don't mind telling me. Sir."

Allan Cole & Chris Bunch

"Never can see myself as sir around family. Let us try Michael... Might I ask if you have a reason? Or are you just interested in gore and stupidity? I thought, from what your Cousin Joshua said, you had your heart set on the sea."

"I'm not sure."

"Allow me to be the first to advise you that soldiering as a career is about as intelligent a choice as, say, trying to walk the Sea of Galilee before you find out where the rocks are situated."

Patrick was disgusted. "You're like Joshua. He spent most of his time tellin' how terrible it was bein' a sailor. Don't grown people like what they do? Besides... if I was a dragoon, I wouldn't be afraid... I don't think."

Michael smiled, a bit sadly. "Oh the dragoon bold he knows no care/As he rides along with his uncropp'd hair/Something something he lightly throws/As on the weekly scout he goes. Yes. Being afraid has nothing to do with my decrying the military. Although something you will learn, if you are ever so despised of God you participate in battle, there is nothing ennobling about, say, a horse or mule that's been gut-shot, thrashing about in the dirt and rolling his intestines around him like you wind kite-string. Nor talking to your best compadre and suddenly his brains are splattered on your uniform. And you know it will be a week or maybe never before you can have a wash. You shall not hear further details of battle from me, since I have learned attempting to dissuade people from blood and slaughter by telling them about it produces an exactly opposite reaction and, not uncommonly, the thought that if the teller of the tale could withstand such horror, the listener could be twice the man, and he promptly seeks an enlistment sergeant. I will merely mention that a dragoon is more likely to die of a fever than in a heroic charge. I will only give you one image, which you may wish to dwell on later, a daguerreotype of the mind that says all I have to say on soldiering."

Michael poured a glass of water and lit a cigarillo. He lifted the glass, sipped, scowled, went to the closet, took out a flask, seasoned the glass's contents and drank. "Much better... I wager you have seen the engravings of what dragoons look like? In serried squadrons, each squadron's mounts the same color? A hat with chinstrap?

Allan Cole & Chris Bunch

Piping on your uniform? Sashes and bright stripes? I shall tell you, quite exactly, what I looked like when I rode into California with the most heroic dragoons. First, I rode a mule. Best animal I ever mounted. I cried when she died and we carved her up for dinner steaks. I carried a rusty musketoon, which is a sawed-barrel muzzle-loader intended for no logical purpose under heaven. Worthless. Utterly worthless. A knife, a revolver, and a shotgun I had won playing dice in Santa Fe. I wore corduroy pants, a blue flannel shirt worn outside. My beard was untrimmed. I resembled Methuselah more than slightly, I suspect. I had a greasy slouched hat I used for a drinking cup and a quirt. Great high boots like a teamster. Do you have that image in your mind?"

Patrick did, and shuddered. Michael must have looked like one of the peckerwoods he had seen aimlessly wandering through the back trails near his plantation. Except better armed.

"Awful, is it not? Yet I was regarded as being very well dressed by the others. I still had the seat to my britches and soles on my boots. That is all I have to say on the soldiering. Is there any other rain I may conjure up for your parade?"

Patrick thought for awhile. "On the packet... there was this man... I saw him shuffle a deck of cards twice. Cut the cards and then dealt five cards. They were four aces and a king."

"Shuffled twice? A rank amateur. Fetch me that deck from the top of my carpetbag." As Patrick followed instructions, Michael had another drink. "So, becoming a gambler is also on your mind. And no doubt you expect me to shriek about the evil of it all, and probably find a spinster cousin downstairs with a bible to preach over you until you see the error of your ways. Which, needless to say, I shall not do. Gambling can be a productive career. Exciting at times, even. Now, this deck is sealed. Quite safe. Although if you know the proper people, you can have a very individual deck of cards prepared that appears as virginal as the English queen your state was named for.

"I shuffle the cards once, to break up the suits. Now you shuffle them until the spots come off, if you wish. No. Not like that," as Patrick complied, fairly clumsily. "Keep your hands flat on the table, and never expose the bottom card. A small advantage to your

Allan Cole & Chris Bunch

opponent, but an advantage just the same. Let only the corner of each card meet with its fellow in your other hand. Mix them up well, and merge the two. Continue until you are satisfied."

As Patrick shuffled - trying his best to do it as Michael instructed and as he'd seen the man on the Eclipse do, Patrick took the flask and walked to the window. "I've done it, Michael."

"The deck, please." Patrick's cousin took the deck, squared it in his fingers and shuffled once. "Did the man on the packet offer you the cut?"

"He did. But I didn't touch the deck."

"Cut, then." Patrick did. "Now, watch closely. Damn. I smell something. Is my cigarillo still burning?"

Patrick glanced at the ash tray. "Nossir."

"Examine what I did while your eyes were elsewhere. I shall do it slowly. I picked up your cut, and, when you turned away, I put the cut halves of the deck back exactly as they were before. Always watch the hands of the man dealing. And if he holds the deck such as this - three fingers along the long end of the deck, index finger curled around the top - you could do worse than grab your money and hurtle toward the nearest exit. Now, I deal. Four aces and a king, you say. Ace... ace... king...ace...and the other ace. Am I not the luckiest hombre in the hall?"

Patrick was excited at such artistry. "How did you do it? Will you show me?"

"If you wish. But you will not be able to do it at once. The way I learned was with the aid of a small mirror." He saw the puzzled look on Patrick's face. "Yes, a mirror. I positioned it just in front of my hands. Then I practiced. When I could not see myself cheating any more, I went looking for a game."

"How long did you practice?"

"Four hours a day. For three and a half years." Patrick was downcast. "Nothing worthwhile comes easily," Michael observed. "But now let us talk about gambling itself. Which is what? Cards? Horses? The purchase of property with the idea it may be resold at a profit? Grandmother Shannon buying a load of coal in the North thinking that there is an unmet demand in, say, New Orleans? To me, it is a thin line - one that I sometimes cannot see at all - between

Allan Cole & Chris Bunch

what is known as gambling and just making your way through life without sinking."

Patrick felt overwhelmed. The real reason he had come to Michael's room was to see if there was any way he could thank the gambler for pulling his ungrateful, weak father's fat from the fire. But Patrick was not supposed to know what had happened at The Alhambra. So he just thanked Michael for his time and got up. "One final thing. I said that gambling was a profession, such as lawyering. There is an exception." He indicated the vest and its lethal implements. "Unfortunately the worst a lawyer might face when he defeats an opponent is angry words, a horsewhip or at worst a challenge to a duel. But people tend to take their gambling losses more seriously. Learn the cards if this is the career you wish. But also study violence. Because a .36 Colt's beats a royal flush every time."

As soon as Kitty let Edward into her room he went straight to Diana's bed to kiss her cheek. She heard an owl hoot in the nearby wood, trying to flush its prey into the moonlight.

"Are you well, Grandmother Shannon?" he asked.

She assured him she was and asked him why he hadn't been to see her since his arrival. Diana knew the reason but wanted to see how her grandson handled himself.

"I've been fearful of adding my presence to all the people, uh... coming up here to visit," he fumbled. "I didn't want to add further strain... Uh... I hope you didn't think my absence was a rudeness."

Diana told him no, she saw no rudeness. As she saw tension falling away with this answer, she said casually, "You seem to have married a most unusual woman, Edward, dear. She has a mind of her own. I expect she keeps you on your toes."

Edward made a weak noise, indicating humor, and said, Yes, she did. Pamela has a fine mind, he said. And he had learned to pay attention to her views.

"She reminds me a lot of you, Grandmother Shannon," he said with another hoarse laugh. "Perhaps that's why I was so taken by her when we met."

"Yes... Is that why you finally came to see me, dear?" she asked. "Was Pamela concerned I might be experiencing some silly slight?"

Her grandson's fumbling attempts to answer - yes, and no and maybe, then back to yes again - confirmed her view. Diana almost continued toying with him, then took pity, if only for Patrick's sake. She asked how his plantation was faring.

Edward flushed and insisted all was more than well. Diana kept silent as he spun a story of all his plans. Cotton prices were doing poorly just now, but it was a temporary weakness and that knowledgeable, experienced men knew they had only to weather a short spell of low prices. Enormous profits were sure to follow. He intended to buy more land soon and put it to the plow as soon as the market signaled a rise.

"Do you have sufficient funds, dear? For all that expansion, I mean?" Diana was feeling testy again.

The question produced more flushing and stammering. She could see he wanted to grasp at the opening she had given him. Edward was always financially embarrassed, always seeking a loan. She could see the turmoil in his mind, the indecision. He was powerfully tempted to ask for money. But if he did, what would that mean for his prospects as the new head of the clan?

Finally he gritted out that his funds were sufficient for his plans, and that if for some reason they weren't enough, he had good credit.

"That's nice, dear," Diana said. "Tell me, what did you think of Mr. Levy's announcement?" she asked, unable to resist. "Regarding my will."

"If you mean, your decision to place one Shannon at the head of your enterprises, I believe it is the wisest course. Depending on your choice of manager, naturally."

"Naturally."

"It would be a pity to see a life's work divided up into many lesser parts," he continued. "Almost as great a pity to see it all crumble due to poor management."

"I couldn't agree more."

"Have you made your choice yet?" Edward asked.

Diana was startled at his bluntness but a little pleased he had finally shown some courage. "No, I haven't," she said. "Do you have any suggestions, dear?"

"I won't lie to you, Grandmother Shannon," he said. "I think I'm the best man for the job. I am more familiar with southern sensibilities. I know the people here well. I've paid much attention to your advice in my many visits with you over the years. And learned a great deal from it. Most of all, I am truly a Shannon. I would be loyal to the family above all else. I would have no other choice. It's in my blood. Last of all, there is Patrick. If I inherit, then he would inherit from me. Passing the torch of your wisdom along over the generations to follow. So, that is why, Grandmother Shannon, I believe I must be your first choice."

He was staring at her, his eyes burning, caught up in the drama of his own pretty speech. Wasn't it strange that Edward - the weakest link in the lengthy Shannon chain - should be the only one to seek her fortune for himself? Diana wasn't surprised, but it made her a little sad. Yes, she had been correct in her planning. Above all else, she must shelter Patrick as best as possible from his father's influence.

Diana patted her grandson's hand. Soothing. "There's a lot to be said for your views, Edward, dear," she said. "And I promise to think on it."

She hoped it wasn't too terrible a lie.

Patrick had the light off in his room and his telescope out. For once it wasn't mischief he was about. He was studying the stars, sweeping the gift from Joshua across the constellations. Country boy that he was, he could identify many of them.

Suddenly he caught a flash of white just beneath his view and dropped the brass telescope downward. It was a figure dressed in flowing white.

Pamela! And who was that beside her?

With great disappointment, he saw it was Russell. Russell! Patrick was in a fury - not at his cousin, but at that... bitchwoman. What chance did a poor citified lawyer have against the likes of her? He was such an innocent. Pamela would weave a silky cage about him like that female spider who kept the tiny male imprisoned until she desired him. He wanted to shout a warning. But what good would that do? Just make everyone mad. Besides, maybe he was mistaken. Not about Pamela. Oh, no. He was never wrong when She was involved. But maybe Russell could resist her. His heart sank as he saw Pamela loop her arm through Russell's and lead him toward the wood. He lost sight of them as they passed through a curtain of Spanish moss.

He was about to turn away in despair when he saw a spark of light. Not a firefly: it was too large. The scope came up again. He saw Michael step out of the shadow of the building, a cigar glowing in his mouth. He was looking after Pamela and Russell.

After a moment he shook his head and flipped the cigar away in a long, gleaming arc against the night. Then he turned back toward the house. Slowly and, Patrick thought, a little sadly.

Allan Cole & Chris Bunch

CHAPTER NINE

VICKSBURG

A THUNDERSHOWER BROKE at breakfast. It rained for nearly three hours, underscoring Patrick's heavy gloom. His mood remained when the storm ended - despite the clear skies and heavy scent of flowers in the air. All he could think about was Pamela's deadly game. After she and Russell disappeared, he watched for their return for more than an hour. He took small consolation there were many routes back to his great grandmother's house that did not cross his view.

He looked closely at Russell as his cousin came down for breakfast but could see no sign of anything amiss. Still, when Russell asked if he would like to take a walk across the meadow and see what manner of life the rain had stirred up, Patrick lied, saying he had an appointment with Mister Cuffe.

Pamela came down before Russell left. She was all cloying and sticky sweet with him, but that was her way when she'd set her sights on something, so that was no proof. Russell was reacting warmly. But Patrick couldn't tell if there was any real intimacy about it. Then his father came down to take Pamela away for a quiet conference, and Russell strolled off on his walk, leaving Patrick in a torment of confusion. From the conversation he overheard between Pamela and his father, it was obvious she believed there was a possibility Russell would win out when the final details of the will were announced.

If that happened, would she dump his father and marry Russell? On one hand, Patrick would be finally rid of her; on the other, he wouldn't wish the woman on any man, much less his cousin Russell.

What about Fitz Maguire? Why was he in town? That he was in league with Pamela took no genius to decipher. Patrick saw him as a vulture hovering over his great-grandmother's undug grave. Anything his father got, Maguire would want to pocket. In a way he had a right to some of it. Hadn't his father borrowed from the man shamelessly, always promising his inheritance would more than repay the debt? Perhaps Maguire was here to keep watch on funds he considered rightfully his.

Patrick badly wanted to talk to someone, but shame kept him from it. So he kept to the habit he had acquired since Pamela had entered his life - the habit of gut-grinding silence. Eventually he left to spend a few hours with Mister Cuffe, mostly to lessen the lie to Russell; but his new friend's cheery outlook wearied him. Then he remembered his promise to his great-grandmother regarding Susan and he decided to look her up.

Susan was in the parlor with her husband, poring over a stack of accounts spread out on the table. She looked up and smiled when he walked in. "Patrick! Come on over here. If there ever was a lady in distress, you see her before you. Come on. I can use your help." She pushed everything aside and patted the chair next to her for him to sit. "Oh, Lord forgive me, I despise this," she said. She caught his startled look and laughed. "Did you think I was going to ask you to help with the books?"

Patrick grinned. "Yes, ma'am."

"I wouldn't do that to my favorite cousin," she said. "What I had in mind was a bit of distraction. If you came to your dear cousin and wanted to talk, why, I'd be a most impolite woman if I didn't put my work aside. Besides, this is a chore I wouldn't wish on my worst enemy."

"That's the reason she enlisted the likes of me," her husband laughed.

"But I thought you were good at it," Patrick said.

"Sure, I've a talent for it. I blame that on my father." She was speaking of his great-uncle, Farrell, a genius with figures, it was said. "But I've always considered it a curse."

"When someone is good at a thing, that doesn't mean she necessarily likes it," Ian said. "Now, when you look at me, you see a lucky paddy before you. Strong back, weak mind. No head for figures. Or liking, either. So there's no confusion about me. Show me a pallet of bricks and a little mortar and I'm in heaven."

Patrick thought this was pretty funny. Ian was certainly muscular enough for the strong back business. But if he was hiding a weak mind, he was a mighty good actor. "If you don't like it," Patrick asked his cousin, "why do you do it?"

110

"Because I love starvation less," Susan said. "Besides, I like to get a good cut of cloth to dress my Ian in. So I can admire his manly figure." She pretended to give Ian a pinch, but he warded her off with a tut-tut, and keep your filthy ways to yourself, lass, or I'll have the priest after you.

Their friendly banter made Patrick laugh. The affection he felt for his cousin kindled brighter. She reminded him of his great-grandmother. Before he'd met her, he had imagined his Philadelphia cousin would be a smooth, citified woman with a long, patrician nose fixed in position so she could always look down on her many social inferiors. An older, town version of Pamela. Instead, Susan was as warm as a kitchen hearth in winter, always bubbling with goodwill. She looked completely natural next to her husband with his broad, ruddy features and great horny hams for hands.

He could almost imagine them on a Sunday promenade in Philadelphia: Susan in her best white frock; Ian swelling out of his dark suit and ambling along in that rolling gait of his. The scene kept slipping away, since Patrick had never seen a place the likes of Philadelphia. So he asked them about life in the city and was mildly surprised when they reflected for a moment and said although they liked it fine - couldn't see any other sort of existence, as a matter of fact - they didn't think he would believe it so grand.

"The country is a better life for a boy," Ian said. "In a town there's always a great shadow of authority lying about just waiting to fall across a lad when he's contemplating fun. Then it's a cane alongside your head, a boot in the arse, and maybe a few days behind bars if you give the policeman any argument."

"Are there many police in Philadelphia?" Patrick asked.

"Not as many as the powers that be would like," Susan sniffed. "But if you are poor and Irish, there's plenty to go around."

"It wouldn't be quite so harsh," Ian said, "if there were any paddys on the force. They might not be so quick with the stick and the kick when dealin' with their brothers. But I wouldn't count on that. In my experience, a policeman is a policeman the world over. Although I'd prefer to be beaten by a Catholic than a Protestant. It saves time gettin' a priest to you if he's struck you a bit too hard."

111

Allan Cole & Chris Bunch

Ian laughed at his own joke, so Patrick joined in, although he was uncertain about Ian's bleak humor.

"But you should come to visit, Patrick. You really should," Susan said. "Philadelphia is a marvel for visitors. And you'd always have a place to stay with us."

"If you take a liking to the city," Ian said, "you can make our house permanently yours as well."

Patrick thanked them, a little confused. This was the first time he had received such an invitation. It was sincere, meant for him and him alone. It made him feel oddly adult. The next moment his world expanded vastly as he realized that more than a thousand miles away - across forests and mountains and raging rivers - he had a safe haven he had never known before.

"A visit would be lovely," Susan said. "There's so much to see. The gardens and the water works. All the fancy shops and inns and hotels. At night, it's all lit up. You can't imagine what it's like when all the gas lamps are lit and everything is a glitter. The theaters are fine as well, although not so grand as Broadway in New York."

"Oh, I don't know," Ian said. "I think his heart strings might play to a lively strum if he tagged along with me. We could take in Venus Rising From The Sea, or Psyche Going To The Bath." He made with a wicked chuckle, which drew an admonishing slap on the thigh from Susan.

She turned to Patrick with a mock frown on her features. "Our young Patrick would be shocked by all that naked flesh," she said.

Patrick's interest was powerfully stirred, although he tried to hide it. Ian explained the entertainment hid under dubious claims of "Art" to display a marvelous array of scantily clad women and men.

Susan and Ian went on for quite a time, describing the wonders of their city. Patrick thought it all very exciting, and said so. He also wanted to know why they thought anyone would prefer another sort of life. Susan sighed and said Philadelphia was fine, indeed, if you were well-to-do. "But it's no place for the poor," she said. "Especially for the Irish poor. I'm not saying the lot of the Negro isn't terrible, as well. Possibly it's worse; living in dank cellars down by Sixth and Small Streets. But since the potato famine the Irish immigrants have filled our city to the brim."

Ian nodded. "I grew up in Dublin," he said. "With a trade. So it wasn't so terrible for me. But most of our Irish brothers and sisters have always lived in the country. Cities are fearful places for an Irishman. We were all village folk before the British came. We view the city as a place where our oppressors dwell. Quite rightly, too."

"Why did they stay in the city, then?" Patrick asked. "I mean, coming from the farm and all, you'd a thought that's where everybody would've headed when they landed in America."

"I haven't the slightest notion," Ian said. "I'm a bricklayer. A city lad." Ian smiled at a memory. "But, I'll tell you my own thoughts when the ship I was on sailed into Boston Harbor. I'd never seen so many people running about in such a hurry. Not an idler among 'em. Every man - common or grand - seemed like he was blessed with a good purpose that might put a few coins in his pocket by end of day. If you'd a seen Ireland when I left, you'd know how happy such a sight made me. And I figured, if you can make it here, Ian Dolan, nothing can stop you."

"That's all very romantic, Ian," Susan said, "and I love you for it. But it's plain to see you have more heart than brains." She turned to Patrick. "I saw the immigrants get off the ferry down at the Schuylkill," she said. "You never witnessed such a ragged crowd. What they had, they wore on their backs. Most of them had not a penny to put in their pockets, and they were short of pockets as well. But there was work in the factories. And the railroads, and the wharves. A person could heave coal, or dig a great ditch of a canal. The wages to this day are very low, but to a poor man or woman, any amount seems a princely sum. No, Ian, my love. They didn't move on because they hadn't funds to do it."

Patrick thought his cousin was probably more correct, although he couldn't help favoring Ian's view. He felt sorry for his Irish immigrant cousins. "But, if there are so many of us," he said, "why don't we just... I don't know... stick together and make them stop?"

Susan and Ian caught his use of "we" and gave one another a quick smile. Patrick felt a glow in his belly when he saw the signal passed. He had just officially joined the Irish race.

Allan Cole & Chris Bunch

"Most of us are poor, Patrick. Poor and ignorant. And we're Catholic - which makes us children of the devil himself to our Protestant neighbors."

Susan told him the new Irish immigrants became the white slaves of the factories, of ship builders, mine owners, and canal diggers, and any attempt to rise above their station was quickly squashed. Laws were passed requiring the Bible - the King James version - to be read daily in the public schools.

"We fought it for years," Susan said, "until there was nothing to be done but build schools of our own."

Susan told him the Irish were driven underground and now there was a whole world - an Irish Catholic world - living side by side with Protestant Americans.

"We made our own jobs," Ian said. "Or, the church did, at least. We built churches and meeting houses, and schools, and all sorts of things - all of good brick and thick mortar. That way we can make sure there's plenty of work to go around to keep our brains and bellies full."

"I thought we had gone far," Susan said. "For a moment I was fooled into thinking the city was changing. But it couldn't have changed that much. They've just elected a Know Nothing as mayor - Richard Conrad. I don't believe there was ever a man who so despised all people from foreign shores. He's all for 'Law and Order.' In Philadelphia that means down with the Irish!"

She gave Patrick a long look. "If you ever hear a high-sounding name put upon a thing, Patrick," she said, "shy away from it as fast as you can. When they say: 'We're from the Star Spangled Banner Party, and we want your support'- know it's not the rights of man they're fighting for but the right to keep a man down."

Suddenly Pamela's voice lashed out: "What kind of black notions are you filling this boy's mind with?" They whirled to see her standing in the doorway.

"We... were... just talkin'," Patrick stammered, bewildered at her furious assault.

"I wasn't speaking to you, young man," Pamela snarled.

"Honestly, Pamela, we were only having an innocent chat," Susan said. She and Ian were as stunned as Patrick.

114

Pamela stormed up to them. "Innocent? You don't know the meaning of the word, you conniving abolitionist slut."

Ian started to rise. "Here, now," he sputtered. "There's no call to-"

Susan pulled him back down. "I'll deal with this," she said. She looked at Pamela, eyes steady. "What is the reason for this abuse?"

"You know very well what you are doing," Pamela gritted out. "You're trying to turn that boy into one of your kind. And I'll tell you right now that I'd be dealing out more than words for abuse if I were home. By God I'd have you horsewhipped and run out of town."

"You really must stop, Pamela," Susan said, fighting to keep her temper. "This is not the time or place for a silly quarrel. Grandmother Shannon is-"

"Don't run hiding behind her," Pamela shouted. "I know what you're up to with her as well, poisoning her mind against her own grandson. Don't you think for a minute I don't know what has been going on here. A damned Yankee conspiracy, if I ever saw one."

Patrick groaned. "Please, Pamela," he said. "Nothin' was goin' on. They were only being nice to me."

"I'll wager they were," Pamela said. "But you just see how nice they'd be if they didn't smell money. I can't believe you sat here listening to their filth. You were raised better than that, kissing up to these nigger lovers."

"That word certainly comes easily to those pure lips," Susan said. "It tells me much about your own breeding."

"Don't you malign my family," Pamela said. "I'll have you know we're among the finest families in Virginia. Certainly better than the immigrant filth whose company you favor."

At this moment, Edward's voice broke through. "What in the world is going on here?" He came into the room in a hurry. "What is all the shouting about?"

Pamela turned to him, hissing, stabbing an accusing finger at Susan. "I caught her in the act. Spewing filth at your son!"

Edward put a soothing hand on her shoulder. "Come on now," he said. "This isn't good. We're family."

Pamela shook his hand off. "Oh, so you're sticking up for them, are you? And here I am protecting your own child."

"Really now, dear," Edward said. "I'm not sticking up for anyone. I only want to avoid unpleasantness. Now come away with me. We can't go on like this in my grandmother's house."

He took her gently by the arm, and Patrick was relieved that she was letting his father draw her away.

"Very, well. If that's how you feel," she said. "I'll go." She turned at the door to hurl one more stone. "But don't think I'm done with you, Susan Dolan. I'll give you fair warning that this fight isn't over with yet." And she was gone.

Patrick heard her storming up the stairs, his father behind her. His stomach was roiling, and he thought he was going to get sick. He looked up at Susan and Ian, but found only deep concern and pity in their eyes.

"I'm sorry," he blurted. "I'm so sorry." He ran from the room before they could say something nice, and make him burst into tears.

Later, Patrick crept back into the parlor to apologize again. He'd also thought about their invitation for him to visit them in Philadelphia. Maybe that would be a solution to his problems. If they let him stay, he'd finally be free of Pamela. But to his disappointment there was no one about, and he feared that he wouldn't have the nerve to ask the next time he saw them.

He heard voices in the other room. He looked through the doorway and saw Michael talking to Russell. Russell was saying he was off to Vicksburg to visit with Mr. Levy again. After that he might look about to see what kind of night life the town offered.

Michael muttered a reply Patrick couldn't make out, but it sounded similar to the warning he'd received when he'd followed his father and Maguire, although tempered a great deal.

Russell shrugged and Patrick heard him say he'd be careful.

The lawyer started to leave, but was stopped by his California cousin. Patrick saw Michael reach into his coat and withdraw his revolver.

Russell refused at first, but Michael pressed him. Finally he took the pistol and placed it in his pocket. He gave it a reassuring path and made his good-byes.

Patrick slipped away to his room to brood. The house was filled with dark tension. Something was going to happen, and he was too fearful to imagine what that something might be.

CHAPTER TEN

VICKSBURG

IT WAS LATE, but Patrick was still awake. He had spent a long time lost in thought.

It had been wrong to think Russell could be ensnared by Her. No friend of his would fail to see what Pamela was made of. Tomorrow he would seek out Russell for that walk in the meadow, and try to muster the courage to explain Pamela.

He was about to snuff out the light and pull the covers over his head, when he heard the shot. He was out of bed instantly and to the window. City folk might think the crack no more than a limb snapping, but he knew better. There was another CRACK! This one from the road.

Patrick went out the window, nightshirt tails flying, and shinnied down the drainpipe. He heard a cry for help. Russell!

He flew through the darkness, without any idea of what he was doing or what he would do when he got there. Footsteps pounded close behind him, and then a hand had him by the shoulder, pitching him away into brush. It was Michael, still fully dressed, a derringer in one hand, his knife in the other.

"Stay here, boy! And stay down!"

Patrick had about as much intention of doing that as becoming a priest. He was up and then had to duck back as two more men ran toward him. Joshua, great pistol in hand, was in front. Behind him, ridiculous in a long flapping nightshirt, was his father. In one hand he carried a flickering oil lantern, in the other a sword - the Revolutionary War short sword that had belonged to Major Maguire.

Patrick remembered that the path wound down to the road. He knew these grounds better than any adult and darted away - in a direct line to the lane. Ahead he saw the glow of lamps and then two spurts of flame as guns were fired. Then he was out of the woods and could see clearly.

A carriage was skewed across the road, the horse rearing in panic. Light sputtered from the carriage lamps, and a pole lantern guttered in the dirt. The night became a succession of stroboscopic plates as the lanterns flared and flickered:

Russell, crouched behind the carriage, pistol aimed.

A body sprawled in front of the carriage.

Closer in, a tall, skeletal apparition, aiming a long gun.

A shouting white blur toward the skeleton. A flash as steel swung down.

A clear image, as the white blur became his father, still clinging to the sword, which had slashed deep into the tall man's back. The skeleton folded on itself and went down.

A patch of darkness, like a great looming bush, gouting fire. A shout of pain.

The plates stopped.

In the dimness Patrick could see two figures jump to their feet and crash into the night. Joshua was in the middle of the road, aiming carefully. The Navy Colt roared three times, and there came a yelp from the darkness.

Joshua was the first to move. He hurried to the carriage as Russell, dazed, got up. "Are you wounded?"

"No. No, I think... I'm uninjured. They... it was as if they were waiting for me. Thank God Michael gave me the pistol. One of them had hold of the reins. I shouted him away. I had the pistol, and fired full into... into his face. Jesus Christ. Jesus Christ." He was suddenly sick.

Michael came forward from where the bush had been, his knife in one hand. The blade shone from something other than the knife maker's polish; he bent and wiped it. That bush, Patrick realized, had actually been a huge man, whose face was marked by a dirty bandage. He had seen the man before.

The other three Shannons went to Edward. Michael picked up the lantern his cousin had dropped and illuminated the corpse's face. Patrick walked to where his father stood, staring down at the man he had slain. The skeletal figure was Judge Sturdevant.

Russell swallowed quickly, but held his control. "My God. If I'd seen him clear... I would never have had the presence to reach for a pistol. The band must have been intent on robbery."

"Not robbery," Michael told him. "Revenge. He's a gambler. His name was Judge Sturdevant."

"You know him?"

"I worsted him in an unpleasant encounter some nights ago. Below-The-Hill. He must have planned this, and mistaken you for me in the darkness." Michael turned. "Cousin Edward," he said, and Patrick noted that this was one of the few times Michael had addressed his father so, "you did well. This was a snake that needed killing years gone."

For the first time since he could remember, Patrick felt pride for his father. In his nightshirt, with only that silly old dress sword, he had taken on a murderer. Patrick hugged him. Edward seemed not to notice either Michael's congratulations or his son's presence. He just stared down at Sturdevant, his face a blank. "God damn him. God damn him. This was not..." his voice trailed away.

Michael picked up the bloody sword and clapped Edward on the back to bring him out of his evident shock. "Swear at the late Judge if it makes you feel better, cousin. But he is not hearing. At this moment, he is far below us and concerned with other matters. He should have been ripped from its mother's womb before coming into this world.

"Joshua, if you will help me roll that body in the roadway into the ditch, we'll see to the cleaning of this killing ground at daybreak. See if the bastard you wounded escaped or, hopefully, bled to death. It would not do for some innocent traveler to come on this scene and think he was witness to an Indian massacre. Then, to the house. Grandmother Shannon can spare some of her best brandy."

As they returned home, Patrick felt close to his father - perhaps he'd been too harsh in his judgment. He looked up and smiled, but Edward's face still held no expression. Abruptly Patrick thought that all he had read in the romances were empty lies, tales told by men who had never really seen sudden death. Both Joshua and Michael, men who had blood on their hands, were lost in their own thoughts. Perhaps the Judge had deserved death, but it was not as easy to pull a trigger as Cooper and the rest wrote. It was as if a bit of you died, as well.

He broke away and ran for the house.

The news of the attack shook Diana profoundly. She had laid the first shots to hunters poaching on her property. Anger stirred, and then she realized she'd heard pistol fire as well. She came further awake as she heard heavy bodies crashing through the woods, and shouts: first Edward's, then Michael's. This was followed by more shots.

She dragged her aching body from the bed to hobble out on the verandah to find nothing but empty night. She could hear the rumble of men's voices, anxious, but not desperate as before.

She saw Patrick break out of the darkness and race across the lawn to the house. Mid-dash he spotted her on the balcony and shouted something she couldn't make out. Diana waved him closer, instead he continued his sprint and a moment later was thundering into her room - Kitty in his wake, pulling a robe over her night dress.

"They tried to murder Russell," he shouted.

The statement was such an unexpected blow that Diana reeled back. Patrick and Kitty rushed to help her into the bed. Then she calmed herself. It didn't take long. Over her long life, many things in many different guises had crept out at her from the night.

Diana settled the boy beside her to explain. It came all out a-tumble. Highwaymen! Stalking Russell all the way from Vicksburg... a premature attack... first Patrick, then the rest of the Shannon men pouring out to the rescue... He tried to tell her the blow-by-blow details of the fight, but she pushed him past his excitement to what she really wanted to know: Russell was unscathed, as were the other Shannons. But the chieftain of the bandits was dead in the woods just beyond her garden. Of this, Diana had no concern at all.

Diana sent Kitty and Patrick off to help the men clean up, then lay against her pillows to think. All her planning had almost died out there amongst the trees. And Patrick dashing out like that. He might have been killed as well. Things were moving too quickly. It was time to get it all settled before events overwhelmed her.

She slipped out of her bed to the big horsehair trunk. Out came the document she had been laboring on. She found pen and paper and an hour or so later it was complete: Diana Shannon's last will and testament, scrawled in her own hand.

She would call the family together tomorrow and make her announcement. Some might be terribly displeased - Edward, for one.

Oh, well, sorry for you, Edward Shannon. And your darling wife. Don't you see, it's only your child I care about?

The completed will went back into the trunk, tied up with a red ribbon. It sat upon her copy of the old will, which was bound in green ribbon, for luck. Before she closed the lid she hesitated; it might be wise to destroy the document now that it was out of date and of no use. But she did not. Before anything else, she must speak to Patrick. She hoped he would understand.

Patrick listened closely as his great grandmother explained what she had in mind. She went over every detail so that it would all be quite clear.

She asked him several times if he understood, and each time he said yes, he did. He was careful not to reveal that he hated every word she was saying.

He wanted to tell her, Please, I want nothing. Give me the bullet, if you insist, but nothing more. He had seen what money did to people who dreamed of it and if this was the stuff of dreams, he feared what actually having money would accomplish.

He didn't want to be greedy and grasping and so quick to betray a friend, or someone he loved. Patrick was terrified that money bred a deadly plague, spreading to whomever came in contact. This was a real fortune his great grandmother was giving, not a boy's fantasy of pirate gold.

But he kept his fears to himself. Because underneath it all, his great grandmother was speaking of her death. Every word read from the will confirmed it and brought it closer. He wanted to grab time by the hair and drag its ugly maw back from his great grandmother's throat. She should live forever. He should be able to grow up, and always have her there by his side.

She showed him the two wills. One was tied in red: the people downstairs were waiting to hear its contents. The old will - bound in green - was for safety's sake, she said, although he got nothing special in it, and his father got much less. Patrick watched her put them both back in the trunk, one on top of the other. Red ribbon over green.

Allan Cole & Chris Bunch

Diana could see the boy was troubled. She knew the reasons: her death... fear of responsibility. But he would grow beyond it and understand one day.

She sat on her bed and reached under the pillow to withdraw the little pouch containing the bullet. "I want you to have this now, Patrick, dear," she said. "Please don't argue. Humor an old woman. I won't live to see what happens to the rest of it. To tell the truth, although it makes a large pile, I'm not so sure how important it all is. In my mind, from the moment Emmett handed the bullet to me as a wedding pledge, there was more value in that bit of lead than all the gold I had ever dreamed of. I know it's silly of me, but I believe that still."

Patrick took the amulet from her hand and hung it by the thong about his neck. She leaned close to him and tucked it out of sight inside his shirt. She could smell his musty boy's odor, saw the speck of dirt he had missed when he had washed up to be clean for his visit with her. And she could smell the strong lye soap as well. She could hear his heart fluttering, saw the moistness in his eyes.

So she drew him close to kiss away the pain. His young arms went around her to hold her tight, and from the unconscious strength of his embrace, she could feel the man growing in him.

They clung together for a moment. The old woman and the boy.

Finally, Diana drew back and settled into her pillows. The family was anxiously waiting, but she didn't care. Let them wait - she was the one short on time.

She thought over the family history, wondering which story she ought to tell him. Patrick was waiting in his usual position at the edge of her bed. She thought of the fate that awaited him, and wondered how he would fare. No matter how much she gave, there was no way she could protect him completely. Pamela, for instance. His stepmother was enough to sour any boy on all feminine-kind. He would be lucky, indeed, if she didn't affect his judgment the rest of his days. But there was nothing she could do about that.

So what story should she tell? Would he want to hear of the famous men? Of the heroes? Boys liked tales about men of great deeds. No, she didn't think so. If anything, she ought to warn him about those people. Tell him that the dazzle of a general's sword can blind a man to his fate. He should know about common folk. The ones who toted the guns or bound up the wounds or took the shot. But, which people in particular? Then it came to her. Just possibly, it might leaven some of Pamela's influence.

And so Diana told him about the women in her life. All the women, from the very beginning.

She told him about her mother, whom she never knew. Her wet nurse, Sandra; and Abigail Fahey, that marvel of a woman whose words she remembered to this day. Why, between Gramer Fahey and herself, they spanned nearly two hundred years. Wasn't that something? She had never thought of it before.

She went on. Ruth, and her daughter, Mary. Mrs. Dickson, who lost her pretty hair to Indians. And the other women of Cherry Valley, who could shoot as well as they could nurse.

Irene Jones in New York, who had once been a circus acrobat and introduced her to Michael Walsh. Which led to Philadelphia and his wife, Anne, that dear thing, who had taken a rough country lass under her wing. And gave her courage to make her fortune.

On and on.

The plague that struck Philadelphia.

Mrs. Leclerc, the mulatto seamstress from the Sugar Islands, who would have overcome her fear and sacrificed her life if Diana had allowed it.

Anne stricken. How she rallied, only to die and leave her husband mad with grief.

Kitty's mother, Mrs. Kenrick. Lydia Clarkson, the mayor's wife.

All the farm women who came to the city's rescue at Diana's urging. The fancy women who sometimes put their feet up in her kitchen and chatted with those same ladies.

And Dolly Madison.

She went on at length about Dolly. From the death of her first husband and son. The tale of her mother, Mrs. Payne, who took in boarders while her husband hid in his room. And Dolly's brave stand years later at the President's House with redcoats coming toward Washington... while her husband hid no one knew where.

Georgia Powers, the black woman who gave Diana a mule to flee the British troops advancing on the capitol. Mrs. Whitlock of Ohio and her daughters, Rosemary and Clarissa and how they waited for the redcoats with loaded guns.

A tumble of female folk came pouring out. All of them she could remember. The poor girl pregnant and dying in Virginia from the clap her husband had given her as a wedding gift... Sarah Carter was her name.

Charming Adele, who later bore Daniel Cuffe.

Connie. And Connie's daughters: April through Susan.

Finally, she was done. She hunted about to see if there was anyone she had left out.

Oh, yes. There was herself. She hadn't told him about Diana Shannon.

But... What was there to tell?

Diana sat before them, her white hair brushed to a glow by Kitty. Gold earrings dangling. A plain black ribbon about her throat.

She wore a simple but elegantly tailored red frock, with only a single emerald pin set in gold for decoration. Kitty had performed a hasty makeover of the frock to hide the weight Diana had lost in her illness. As she sewed, Diana had darkened her lashes just a touch and put a blush on her cheeks that she didn't feel.

Now she was ready. Her family gathered about the table with her at the head. The will lay before her, its red ribbon untied.

A few stared at it.

Pamela, who constantly licked dry lips. Edward, face drawn, eyes hollow in torment. Diana thought at first it was only the suspense over the will. Then she saw there was more behind it. Cold eyes stabbed at his wife. For what reasons, Diana could only wonder.

Patrick... eyes as wide as a young deer, pale. She saw him shiver. Easy, child. It will be over in a moment.

Russell and Susan. Ian. Joshua and Michael. Looking only at her, a little fearful. Of her weakness, she thought.

"Before I start," she said, her voice coming so abruptly, a few of them jumped, "I would like to tell you the real value of what this contains. And its source.

"All of you see a fortune here, I'm sure. Perhaps it is. Some of you desire this fortune above all else. Some of you have no care for it at all. A few may even see it as a monument to a lifetime of effort and want to preserve it always."

She patted the document. "I got this by stealing some money from my master, whom I fled; thus robbing him of myself, as well. I put it together with a horse and cart I cheated a farmer out of. Its sum, plus Emmett's land - which I lied to keep - was the foundation of this treasure chest, whose contents I have listed in my will. So, be warned, it comes tainted. Do not desire it so greatly that you are willing to assume my sins. Nor should you be too disdainful. There's no little sweat in it. And much blood as well."

She looked at Patrick, who gave her a thin smile. She repaid the smile with a broad wink and saw the grin grow into a laugh he almost couldn't contain.

Diana opened the document and looked in its leaves to tell the Shannons their fate. All her lands in Vicksburg went to the tenant farmers. A great sum of money was also divided up for Mr. Cuffe, Kitty, and many others who had helped her through the years. She listed the contents of the house, most of which also went to old friends and faithful servants. Everything else - the house, fortune and empire - went to Patrick, to be held in trust until he was of age. The trust holder was Russell Conners, who would manage all operations and control all proceeds in Patrick's name.

Pamela could barely stifle her moan.

Diana went on. She had spoken to everyone, she said, and believed she understood their needs. All of them would be handled, but only within reason. She nodded at Edward when she said this. She was going to suggest to Russell that twenty thousand dollars be considered as a settlement. As her new manager, however, it was up to him to decide. Meanwhile, she said, business would continue as usual after her death. She was sure Russell - whom she held in great affection - would see no Shannon ever went without.

She saw the young man give a reflexive nod. His face was expressionless, but she saw his shoulders sag for a moment, then shift, as if assuming a large weight. She looked at Edward again. His eyes said he believed himself betrayed. Poor child. Perhaps he would

126

Allan Cole & Chris Bunch

see someday that if he had gotten his wish, he would have paupered the family and himself within a few years. He might be unhappy now, but at least he was relatively safe.

Suddenly Diana felt so weary she could weep. Kitty must have noticed, because she came up from behind and put a soft hand on a shoulder.

People started to rise, to come to her. But Diana raised a hand to stop them, thanked them quietly for their love and attention, and excused herself until tomorrow, when Mr. Levy would arrive. She rose without assistance and went to the door. Abruptly the weariness dropped from her and she felt deliciously light and young, and there was almost a dance to her steps. She favored Patrick with another broad wink and exited the room.

She climbed the stairs with no effort at all, thinking, that was well done. Not everyone was happy, but then no one ever was. If universal happiness was required in a decision, none would ever be made.

She heard Kitty behind her, puffing to keep up. She went into her room, happy and chattering nonsense as Kitty helped her undress and get into bed.

Diana had not a care in her head. If Dolly had come calling that minute, saying, "There's an assembly at Mrs. Cogley's Emporium, and why don't you come with me, Diana, dear? For I love a dance and Mother won't let me, so why can't I watch you instead?" Diana would have been out the door in a flash, her dancing slippers tucked into her purse.

She told Kitty this, but Kitty just giggled and shook her head. "My mother said you never went to an assembly unless forced, Mrs. Shannon," she said. "She said it was her opinion you hated to dance."

"She was wrong," Diana said. "I've always loved to dance."

"If you say so, Missus," Kitty said.

"I do. And don't argue," Diana said. "Bring me a glass of brandy, please. And pour one for yourself. Haven't I just read my own will? It feels like a birthday, except instead of the beginning, I'm celebrating the end."

Patrick watched his great-grandmother leave and thought she looked happy. He didn't begrudge it, although he would have preferred a different reason. She looked almost beautiful, when at the door she had turned her face toward him and he saw the high-color in her face and the sparkle to her eyes. She gave him another great wink. Then was gone.

People gathered around him, to congratulate him and slap him on the back and say how wise Grandmother Shannon had been to choose thus. Some of them even meant it. Pamela had burst from the room, face screwed up in an awful fury, his father trailing behind - but angry, not hangdog. And there was a deep crease in his forehead Patrick had never noticed before. Across the table, Russell caught his eye and gave him a little grin of sympathy.

Patrick wanted to slip away from everyone so he could think in peace. At last Russell came over and asked if he would like to go for a walk? Before he could answer, they heard Kitty cry out from the top of the stairs.

Grandmother Shannon was dead.

Patrick was numb. Chaos and tears rained about him.

But all he knew was that his great-grandmother was gone. And in all his life ahead - even if it were a long one - he would never again meet her like.

CHAPTER ELEVEN

VICKSBURG

PATRICK HEARD THE great clock inside the house toll the hour... three in the morning. It barely registered in his mind. His hand kept reaching to his neck, touching the old leather bag with the musketball inside - he'd found a bootlace to replace the ancient rawhide. His thoughts came in jagged spurts and wild flights of meaninglessness. Sometimes there was nothing but blankness. He remembered crying, sitting on the floor of his room. Now he was on the front steps, not remembering how he got there or why. Why did people have to die? Did they go somewhere... or just stop? He had a shattering vision of himself as Grandmother Shannon. Old. All his friends gone before. If you believed in something, maybe you would want to join... no. Maybe there is nothing. Patrick shuddered. He never wanted to die.

He wandered out into the night with no destination. There were lights on in many of the bedrooms behind him. He was not the only Shannon unable to sleep. Near the wood he heard voices. He turned away - he did not wish to speak to anyone.

The voices grew louder, one a man's, the other a woman's. The woman's voice shrilled, and Patrick knew it for Pamela's. There was the sound of a blow and Pamela burst out of the wood. Her bodice caught on a branch, and she ripped it free and ran toward the house. She did not see Patrick.

Halfway there, she began screaming.

Patrick's mind jolted. What... what had happened? Pamela darted inside. Then he saw Russell come out of the wood.

"What did you do?" Patrick shouted. "You better run!"

Russell was panting. He turned as if to obey Patrick's shout, then stopped. He shook his head as if to say, to where?

The octagonal house was a blaze of light and sound.

"Go on," Patrick shouted. "I don't know what you did... but my father..."

Edward was in the doorway, blinking into the night. He held a pistol in his hand.

"Here he comes! Run!"

But Russell just stood there, waiting. Patrick knew what would happen next... and it must not. He pelted for the house to get Joshua or Michael.

Edward came down the steps toward him. "Where is he, Patrick?"

Patrick ignored the question and ducked around him toward the door. He saw Russell not running, not even standing near the edge of the wood, but walking slowly forward - toward his father.

Edward saw Russell's outline. "You bastard! You attacked my wife!"

Allan Cole & Chris Bunch

The pistol came up, and Patrick's father brought the hammer back to full cock and aimed. It was too late for Joshua, Michael, or anything. Patrick could not turn away.

There was a cold, hard voice from above him. "If you pull the trigger, Edward, there will be two corpses this night."

His father looked up. Patrick came off the steps and did the same. Michael knelt in his bedroom window, revolver aimed and steadied against the sill.

"He tried to... rape Pamela."

"Uncock the pistol, Edward. And lower your hand to your side. Now!"

As his father obeyed, Patrick had a flickering memory of what Michael had told Joshua about a "quarterdeck voice." Michael slid out the window, onto the roof and braced for a jump.

"Don't do it, Michael. I have him."

Joshua was on the steps, also armed. Keeping his weapon aimed, he walked to Edward and took the pistol from him. "Are you mad or drunk, you stupid son of a bitch?"

"You heard me. This God Damned Philadelphia lawyer went after Pamela! She's upstairs in hysterics."

"I doubt the truth of that."

"Are you—"

"Shut up! Russell. What actually happened?"

Michael came out of the house, pushing through a throng of other Shannons. "You people. Inside. We'll deal with this."

Reluctant, puzzled, the family obeyed, except for Ian, who with Michael joined the other men.

"Nothing occurred," Russell said. "At least not what Edward believes."

"You are a lying Yankee dog," his father hissed. "And if it weren't for these bastards who claim to be of the same blood as I am, you would be lying dead now. A Southern woman's honor has been violated. I demand justice!"

"Justice, except in your shitty swamps, is not shooting an unarmed man in cold blood. No matter what his offense," Joshua snapped.

Allan Cole & Chris Bunch

Patrick saw a cunning expression cross his father's face. "In a society of men, shooting a rapist as he stands is no crime. But very well. You want justice..." His hand cracked across Russell's face. The young man staggered but did not go down. He recovered both stance and coolness.

"I assume you consider that a challenge?" Russell said.

"I do, sir."

"I suppose it would change nothing if I proved what I have been accused of a lie?"

"It would not, sir." Patrick's father was quite under control, now that he was on familiar ground - the exactly prescribed code duello. "I believe and trust my wife absolutely. So even if the attack did not occur, you are now impugning her honesty."

"I thought as much. One question, Edward. Is this little charade a plot between you and Pamela, or are you just going to be the assassin and cats' paw?"

"I do not have to listen to this."

"But you will. Kill me, and that certainly creates an opportunity for you, does it not? Since the boy is far from his majority, that should give you ample years for looting." This was the first anyone had seen Russell angry.

"I will listen to no more," his father said. "Even though you are not a gentleman, I am treating you as one. Any communications between us should be between our seconds." Patrick's father turned to the others. "Gentlemen, which of you will be my second?"

Michael'd had quite enough. "No one here will be a party to filicide. Ian, take this poor excuse for a human inside and out of my sight. Because at the moment I think the most logical solution would be a knife in his throat and pitch him into the river beyond."

"I will not be restrained! Very well. If none of you are willing to assist me on the field of honor, I know a man in Vicksburg who shall."

Patrick knew instantly his father was talking about Fitz Maguire. Did this all fit together? The meeting Under-The-Hill with Sturdevant and his murderers? The fire at Mr. Levy's office? Was that to hide a theft? Was that how Pamela had seen the old will? But then why had his father saved Russell by killing Sturdevant? Or was

131

Maguire the master puppeteer for everyone? Quite suddenly Patrick knew the answer. Her. Not just Maguire. Her! He wanted to say something, to shout something. But he knew no one would listen. All of them would think him an hysterical child.

"You, sir," Edward went on, "should be ashamed to live under the false name of Shannon. I shall be on the DeSoto Peninsula at sunrise. If you have any honor, you shall join me in the satisfaction of this matter. If not, I promise, regardless of the pusillanimity of these others, I shall hunt you down and shoot you like the dog you are."

"Ian!"

The bricklayer's arms circled Patrick's father as if he were a child and lifted him away.

Michael realized he was still holding his pistol ready. He half-cocked it over the unprimed chamber and shoved the weapon into a pocket.

"Now. With that lunatic away from the scene, what happens next? Can Edward be calmed? And his wife made to tell the truth? I am assuming, Russell, to avoid complete confusion, that you are telling the truth and are innocent."

"I did not assault the woman."

Michael looked at Russell closely. "A lawyerly choice of words. But acceptable."

"Trying to talk reason to that Virginian," Joshua said, "would be like reading admiralty law to a drunk mutineer. Nor will that bitch change her story, unless I badly misread her."

"I thought not. Very well. Russell, pack a bag. Joshua and I will escort you into Vicksburg and get you safely on the first packet to anywhere."

"No. I will fight him."

"Like hell you will! Get out of town. Let tempers cool Let people return to their homes. I will remain here, and work with that lawyer to straighten matters as best can be done."

"I said no."

Patrick could restrain himself no further. "Russell! My father's been in duels before. He's killed two men."

As if for the first time, the men seemed aware of the boy.

132

"Patrick," Michael started, "you do not belong in this."

Joshua stopped him. "He does not. None of us do. But this bears on him more than any of us. He was in from the outset. Let him remain."

"I guess we must," Michael agreed reluctantly. "Russell, you heard what the boy said. You can't stay."

"But I have to. Grandmother Shannon was quite clear as to how her estate was to be managed. If I flee, letting that lie spread about, how long do you think it will be before that will is challenged? They'll say the woman was 'obviously of unsound mind,' letting a rapist, self-convicted by his flight, administer anything. But that is not important. I will not live the rest of my life hearing this lie, everywhere I go."

"Who the hell cares what they think of you in Vicksburg?" Joshua snapped.

"Vicksburg... then Virginia... then I am sure the story will appear in Philadelphia and then New York. No. I am ruined, unless this is dealt with right now."

"To blazes with being ruined. I've been ruined a dozen times over," Michael said. "Who cares what people whisper about you when you are absent?"

"I do. I must." Patrick thought of his cousin's confession of his bastard birth. Russell had made light of it. But now, it was apparent how deeply it affected him.

"I was born into a family of lunatics," Michael said, without jest. "You would prefer to be a bloody corpse than a man with a stain on his reputation."

"You all assume that Edward will kill me. That is not graven in stone. I am not a bad pistol shot, myself. And certainly, in the heat of anger, his aim could be clouded."

"Russell, you are a mewling infant in these matters. For the first shot, perhaps. But this matter will not be settled by a single exchange. I have read the so-called laws these imbeciles duel by. No apology shall be accepted until shots have been exchanged. Three times, for this is, as that shit-arse said, a matter of either a woman's honor or of blood."

"It will not go three rounds."

"I give up. Joshua, can you appeal to his reason?" The ship captain slowly shook his head.

Michael was silent for a long time. "I feel as if I am in the final act of a tragedy," he finally said. "Foolishness, the gods, and the weakness of men have put us all on an unchangeable course." He squared his shoulders. "Very well. If that is how it must be. Russell, I shall accompany you at dawn. Joshua, would you do the same? Because if there are any surprises awaiting us... I propose to settle them in a very direct fashion."

"I shall."

"Patrick, upstairs and in your room. I know you will not sleep, but I do not want you wandering about... The same for you, Russell." Michael started for the house. "And pride compasseth them about as a chain," he said softly, almost to himself. "And violence covers them as a garment."

Patrick sat at the top of the stairs leading down to the Shannon's small dock. It was about eight o'clock, and the morning sun blazed down through the haze over the Mississippi. But his mind was seeing another part of the river at an earlier hour. He saw a low, sandy peninsula, studded with brush, ten miles away across the river from Vicksburg. The light was pearl gray through the dawn fog. He had read books about dueling. Once he'd found the descriptions fascinating, very romantic. Now, in his mind, they sounded like exact prescriptions for murder.

Three carriages would be drawn up, back from the field itself, one at each end of the ground, one in the center. A Shannon carriage. Maguire's rented rig. The center one would belong to a surgeon.

At one end of the field would stand his father. At the other would be Russell. On arrival, they would have been escorted to the center of the field by their seconds, Maguire and Michael. An attempt to reconcile their differences must be made. Patrick desperately hoped that was as far as the reality had gone. Now he prayed they would be returning - the matter somehow settled without bloodshed. He hoped, but did not believe it for a moment. Once the settlement was rejected, the details would be arranged.

Allan Cole & Chris Bunch

There were three areas - how close the men would stand to each other and whether they be permitted to advance after each exchange. The distance could be as great as forty paces, as little as eight. And the number of lawful shots would be discussed. Three or more would be the most likely, as Michael had predicted. It could be continued until a serious hit was sustained. Patrick had heard of some duels fought with pistols, the duellists closing at each step and finally settling matters with bowie knives. That would not happen - his father would consider that barbaric.

Finally the firing orders would be agreed on: who was to give the command and who would count. These rules were absolute. Anyone violating them, or attempting to halt the affair before the principals might be shot by one of the seconds. Next, a large, flat box would be produced - walnut, with red plush linings. It would be opened reverently - at least by Maguire. Inside would be two twelve-inch-barreled single-shot pistols, each in its own nest. The weapons would be silver, worked metal, and highly-polished wood. Around them in the case would be ball, shot, loading implements and basic gunsmith tools. It would not do for a weapon not to function and spoil this grand ceremony.

The weapons would be loaded carefully, powder measured carefully, each ball inspected for roundness. Each would be wrapped in a bit of linen and then rammed home. Percussion caps would be fitted on each nipple. The weapons would have hair triggers. Experienced duellists preferred them. For the novice, they were likely to be death - the slightest touch on that metal bar, whether it was pointed up, down, or at his opponent, and the weapon would discharge, leaving the novice unarmed to face a carefully-aimed shot.

His father and Russell would be given their weapons. The seconds would withdraw eight yards from the line of fire. Behind them, the surgeon. Each man would stand sideways - to reduce the size of the target he was offering. The pistols would be raised, pointed straight up. Someone would shout: "Gentlemen, are you ready?"

A nod from both Russell and Patrick's father. The next command would be to fire, and a count of three. The duellists had

135

but that count to shoot. A slow count would favor someone being struck. A rushed count might guarantee both men shooting too quickly, and remaining unharmed.

"Fire! One, two—"Somehow Edward made a mistake, and, as he lowered his pistol to take aim, it discharged harmlessly into the nearby ground. Russell waited. Then, to show his true nobility, he turned his own weapon to the side and pulled the trigger or fired it into the air.

No. His father did not make that kind of mistake.

"Fire! One, two,--" Edward's pistol came down, and he touched the trigger. The cap was faulty and the pistol misfired. Russell's shot came a moment later, and hit Edward in the arm. He fell, bleeding. It was a serious strike, and both men agreed their quarrel had been settled. Edward had been taken to the surgeon's office, and even now the Shannons were returning.

Pamela, even now, was waiting back in Grandmother Shannon's house. Probably praying, to whatever she prayed to, that her scheme would pay off as she had planned.

Both men missed, on their first firing.

"Are you satisfied?"

Edward shouted "No." The pistols were loaded once more and the duellists took their stance.

"Gentlemen, are you ready?"

"Fire! One—" Edward's aim was unsteady. He missed. Russell fired - and the ball crashed into Edward's heart.

Patrick flinched. But that would not happen, he somehow knew absolutely. The duel would not go three exchanges. Only one.

"Fire! One, two—" Before Russell could touch the trigger, Edward fired. The ball went deep into Russell's chest. He screamed, his hand reflexively flung the pistol away, he tottered and fell, blood on his white shirt seeping into the dust.

Patrick forced his mind back to this place and this moment. The brass telescope lay across his knees. He peered through it, down the lane that led to Vicksburg. Nothing. He was sitting on a small pack he'd made up from a burlap bag. Inside was a change of clothes, a bar of soap, and some papers. The writing on them was spidery,

Allan Cole & Chris Bunch

shaky - in the hand of an elderly woman. The papers were tied in a red ribbon.

Below him was the yawl. He'd grabbed some provisions and two fishing poles and put them in its locker. If his worst fears were true, and Russell lay dead in the dirt of DeSoto Peninsula... they would never see him again.

He would be downriver. New Orleans. Natchez. He knew not, nor cared. The last will, naming him heir apparent would travel with him - until the first time he needed tinder for his cooking fire. He had left the old will bound in green. To hell with them. Let this be broken up among the people who know how to use each part of it best. Leave his father and that murdering bitch with their pittance. Even if a miracle happened, and Russell was the victor, Patrick could not listen to a man responsible for the death of his father. He'd return the final will; let him do with it as he chose. And still run.

Damn Vicksburg and damn all those who clawed about a dead woman's bones. Let the Shannons do as they wished.

Thinking of Grandmother Shannon, he looked down the lane once more. It was hard to see. Water must have condensed on the telescope lenses. Patrick wiped his eyes, and looked once more. There, far down the lane, came a single carriage. There were horsemen behind it. The group disappeared behind trees.

Patrick, not breathing, waited until they came into sight once more. His chest hurt. His mouth was dry. The telescope had excellent lenses. Even at this distance, he could make out the sole occupant of the carriage.

Edward Shannon. His father.

Part Two

"... What a strange time it was. Who knew his neighbor? Who was a traitor and who a patriot? The hero of today was the suspected of tomorrow. There were traitors in the most secret chambers. Generals, senators, and secretaries looked at each other with suspicious eyes. It is a great wonder that the city of Washington was not betrayed, burned, destroyed a half-dozen times." - *M. E. W. Sherwood On spying in Washington, D.C. when it was a Civil War camp.*

"All we ask is to be let alone." *Jefferson Davis*

CHAPTER TWELVE

WASHINGTON D.C. - JULY 21, 1861

THE OMNIBUS SWAYED down Pennsylvania Avenue. Heavy iron wheels ground through gravel and juddered over painful ruts. The passengers cursed the driver for being drunk on Sunday and early morning pedestrians dodged the shower of sewage thrown up by the horses' hooves.

A dainty carriage swept off Sixth Street, driven by a black child in smart, if much-patched livery. He was rubbing sleepy eyes and didn't see the omnibus swerve toward him. In the carriage's back seat one passenger squealed alarm. The other barked: "Mind the bus, Hercules!"

The child looked up, then froze in terror as tons of wood and metal and muscle and flesh bore down. Just in time... just as the horse began to panic... slender arms in transparent lemon yellow sleeves reached across. Slim hands in white kid gloves grabbed... and pulled... hard. The carriage scooted to a stop and the omnibus crashed by.

Pamela Shannon glared at the stuporous driver and turned up her pretty nose at the men leering out the windows. When the bus was gone she handed the reins back to the child. "I told you to mind the bus, Hercules."

"Yes'm, Mrs. Shannon."

"Well... get on with it, then. To Willard's, mind you. Not the Brown Hotel. I've no business with the Rebels on this day."

"No'm. I mean, yes'm."

Pamela sat and the carriage moved on. She tucked dark curls back under her sun bonnet and licked a finger to touch up her long lashes. She batted them experimentally over flashing black eyes then pinched some pink into her cheeks. Still ignoring her frightened friend, Pamela fetched her yellow parasol from the floor. She smoothed the light material of her summer dress and fingered the gold and pearl necklace at her throat, as if to assure herself of its safety. Finally, she turned. "Oh, Marcia. What a sight you are. I told you not to wear white, dear."

She whipped out a silk handkerchief and dabbed at nonexistent dirt on snow white crinoline. "I swear, I don't know what you did without me before I came to Washington."

"And I thank the Lord every night, you did," Marcia said. "Honestly, cousin, dear, I was at such a loss when mother died-"

"I know, Marcia, love," Pamela broke in. "You've told me before. And although it's very sweet of you to keep saying so, it does become boring with so much repetition." Marcia's sallow features slumped.

How tiresome, Pamela thought. I've wounded the little bitch's feelings again. Don't forget, she's young. God, was I that dumb at twenty? She turned her full charm on her homely cousin. "Pay no mind to me, Marcia. You know how I become when I'm agitated. I'm just fretting about getting down to Manassas."

Marcia perked up and turned adoring eyes on the vastly experienced widow of twenty six. "I don't believe you're afraid of anything, Pamela," she said.

"Of course, I am," Pamela snorted. "I fear many things. Unfortunately, they all involve that dreadful word, poverty."

Marcia giggled. Her laugh was the only pretty thing about her. When eligible beaus were afoot, Pamela encouraged that laugh. If her skinny cow of a cousin married money, Pamela's task could be eased. Right now the laugh irritated her. But she bit her tongue and settled little Miss 'Fraidy Cat Weatherby into her seat. Pamela's uncle, God rest his soul, must have been mad or drunk to wed the woman who bred such a weakling child. No, Pamela recalled, he was poor; afflicted with the curse of the Weatherbys, who were poorer even than her own family which barely made do on its Virginia plantation and twenty five slaves. Marcia's mother came from Maryland gentility. A decent sum was settled upon her when she wed, but Pamela's uncle squandered most of it before he died of drinker's liver. Plus, if Pamela knew her Southern men, whore's pox.

Pamela glanced over at her pale faced cousin. Perhaps that explained her looks. It was a well known fact pox weakened a man's seed. Look at Edward, the dearly departed Mister Shannon, damn his eyes. He had pleasured himself with harlots and slave wenches until he was limp as a boiled noodle. She was well rid of him. Pamela had a low branch hanging over the carriage track to her former home to thank for her widowhood. Drunk as a bargeman, Edward had ridden out one night to see his gambling chums.

Pamela laughed to herself. She'd told the lazy fool to get a nigger to cut that branch. "It will take someone's head off one day," she'd warned.

As usual Edward ignored her advice and Pamela's warning had proved a prophecy. She only regretted the horse. It had been a fine, young Virginia mare, but never the same after the incident. It was certainly no good for the hunt - blood spooked it something fearful. Pamela had been forced to sell the animal for a third its worth.

"Mind the pig, Hercules," she snapped at the child driver.

Hercules was awake now and had spotted the marauding animal. Muttering a barely civil "yes'm," he deftly wheeled the carriage out of harm's way.

Pamela sniffed. "Hercules has certainly been surly of late," she said. "He's been that way ever since I set him free. See how my generosity is repaid? Now I'm saddled with an impertinent little scalawag getting white ideas. I hope those damned Yankees are satisfied."

Marcia glanced nervously at Hercules. She lowered her voice: "He's just a little upset, Pamela."

"Speak up Marcia," Pamela snapped. "You're going to have that boy thinking he's white, with feelings." She whipped around on Hercules. "Wake that horse up, nigger," she snarled. "I do want to get to Willard's sometime today." She turned back to Marcia. "Now, what were you saying, cousin, dear, about Hercules being upset?"

Marcia was rattled, but spoke up as demanded: "Well... You said he was free. But you didn't sign any papers making it so. Legally... that is."

"That's what I mean about him getting white ideas," Pamela said. "Legal papers! For a nigger! Who ever heard of such a thing? My word as a Southern lady ought to be good enough. Don't I have enough to do with my own legal problems... and all the money it's costing me? I swear, some people have no concern for other people's problems."

Allan Cole & Chris Bunch

She tapped Hercules on the shoulder with her parasol. "I told you that you are free, Hercules," she said. "And that is good enough. I warn you, if I hear you tell somebody different - especially a Yankee - I'll whip you until there isn't a shred of flesh on your back. Do you hear me?"

"Yes'm, Mrs. Shannon," Hercules said, with feeling.

Pamela smiled sweetly at Marcia. "You see. It only takes a firm hand."

"You wouldn't really... beat him... would you?" Marcia asked.

"Of course not. " Pamela said. "What do you think I am, a barbarian?" In his driver's perch, Hercules shuddered.

Two soldiers lurched out of an alley, voices raised in obscene argument over the remaining contents of a jug. Pamela was livid. "Drunken Yankee cowards," she hissed. Whenever she saw such things Pamela despaired for the Union. Especially now. Why weren't they with McDowell's army at Manassas? The general would need every one of the scum he called soldiers to defeat the flower of the South - which were now gathered to block his march on the new Confederate capital of Richmond.

A gangling white boy rushed out of a telegraph office, screaming that Yankee artillery had just opened fire on the Confederate forces. Pamela bent her head, shutting out Marcia's chatter. For just a moment she thought she could hear the thunder of the big guns some thirty miles away. Her heart hammered in time with the half-imagined volleying. She squirmed in the soft, leather seat of her carriage. All her dreams rested on the accuracy of those guns. God, I wish I were a man. I'd place those cannon so the rebels were bracketed and pound them until they looked like a waffle turned out of a scorched iron.

It mattered not a whit most of her family and friends would consider Pamela a traitor for these thoughts. Was she not herself a Virginia aristocrat, a hater of Yankees who'd cheated their Southern cousins of their just due? Had she not cursed along with them at the Satanist abolitionists who were bent on destroying the very foundation of plantation society?

Pamela laughed at the thought of their shocked, genteel faces. All of these things were correct. If she were forced to tell the truth -

142

heaven forbid - she'd say ideals and politics were all very well for a strong man with money. But Pamela was blessed with neither coin nor musculature. She was forced by rude circumstance - none of it the slightest fault of her own - to struggle against all odds to find a little happiness. If heaven smiled this day there would be a heap of Southern corpses on the field. The great Beauregard would be shamed into submission. It was a sight she was determined to see for herself.

First Manassas, then on to Richmond!

Pamela was bound for the battlefield to witness the South's certain defeat. Marcia had said her mission was not only dangerous, but impossible. She didn't have a pass to get by the sentries at the Long Bridge, and there was no hope for a lone woman to obtain one.

"Never fear, Marcia," Pamela had said. "I'll find a benefactor... for both of us."

"Me? Oh, Pamela, I could never do such a thing. You know how delicate my nerves are. Besides... it wouldn't be... respectable."

Marcia was negative to the point of hysteria. It had taken Pamela half the night to convince her cousin to accompany her. She'd finally had to threaten to seek other, "more pliant" quarters, leaving Marcia alone and burdened with the full cost of her rooms - which she was unable to pay. Marcia finally relented and even regained her humor, mostly because she was certain Pamela would fail to find a male escort to Manassas battlefield. Pamela did nothing to shake this false confidence. Marcia would see soon enough, when it was too late to renege on the promise.

There were few who could resist Pamela when she'd set her bonnet on a thing, especially men. At Willard's, Pamela was hoping her plans would lead to more than a view of the battle. She thought it was a unique opportunity to land the protector she'd been seeking since her arrival in Washington many months before. Pamela was determined on hooking a powerful well-connected gentleman to help press her cause in the federal capitol. She expected to find no end of candidates milling and swilling at Willard's as they prepared to set out to Manassas to toast certain victory over the Rebel forces.

Part of Pamela's bait to secure a male escort to Bull Run was the lavish picnic lunch she'd had packed. The hamper was full of

143

everything from cold roast canvasback duck to gooseberry cobbler and several jugs of the heady brandy punch of her own recipe. Her carriage, however, was the most important part of the bait she'd be dangling at Willard's - besides her lovely self. There was not a saddle horse or carriage available at any price in Washington this morning. Pamela was convinced the right man would be waiting at the hotel, stranded, frustrated and ready to be charmed by the woman with the flashing eyes, daring smile... and free passage to Bull Run.

Pamela wrinkled her nose as the wind stirred, bringing the stench of the great canal that cut through the capital. Her Yankee friends said the canal was typical of this city. Hailed early in the century as a grand project to link the wilderness that was Washington with the rest of the nation, it fell into disrepair before it was barely completed. Now, after the coming of the railroads, the canal was nothing more than an enormous ditch and of no use except as a breeding ground for noxious insects, disease, and animal corpses poaching under the summer sun. She vaguely recalled hearing that Diana Shannon, herself, had escaped the British by scurrying along that very canal when it was nothing more than a raw, dry ditch. Pity they hadn't caught her.

Pamela had spent months trying to ignore the canal's dreadful odor as she waged her legal war in the red brick court buildings lumped near the canal's banks. In the early days - before she'd gotten her bearings - Pamela had even suffered a clerk's hand on her breast under one of the sickly trees that sprouted from the pallid waters. She might have let it linger, except Pamela learned just in time the young cad was a liar and that his claimed connections were boasts as empty as an aeronaut's balloon. She'd slapped his face for taking advantage of a poor widow woman. No gentleman, she scolded, would toy with passions that honor demanded be kept locked with a sacred key. The youth had fled her wrath. Still, Pamela took no chances. A few words in the right places and the young man was forced to flee the city altogether.

Beyond the canal - and that distasteful trysting place - Pamela could see the fantastic red towers of the Smithsonian Institute with its pretty planted grounds. Like everything else in this city its beauty was spoiled by all the jumbled shacks, filthy alleys, rude boys and

Allan Cole & Chris Bunch

whores, who also occupied the island. Just past the institute was the oddly truncated spire that was the uncompleted monument to General Washington. This was a project - like many others - few believed would ever be finished. Work had been halted some years before when the subscription funds ran out. A congressman's wife told Pamela it was the Know Nothings who'd had it stopped, scorning it as a religious artifact.

Although Pamela joined in the jests and cynical comments about the city's many flaws, she secretly found herself much at home. Basically, it was a Southern city - squalid and lazy and unsanitary; but charming just the same. Fine homes and mannered society, mingled with squalor. Pennsylvania Avenue, for example, was an accurate mirror of the city at large.

On her right the street was lined with lovely poplars, their falling plumes dusting the ground with gray. There were stately homes here, rivaling any mansion built by the richest of planters, and grand hotels even Europeans grudgingly admired. They boasted broad grounds and fine gardens, filled with hyacinths, snowdrops, clematis and a wilderness of roses. Here and there were some of the best restaurants she'd ever visited, with menus offering everything from French cuisine, to spicy Southern delights and even (she dreaded to admit) some rather fine examples of Northern cookery.

The south side of the Avenue, on the other hand, was lined with shacks, stables, dingy buildings, chicken yards, shambling grog shops and the rickety apartments of whores.

This was not too unsettling a contrast for Pamela. She'd spent her whole life in lavishly appointed Virginia plantation houses, surrounded by the filth and jumble of plantation living, as well as the slave quarters. As for the whores, Southern cities were equally as afflicted with their breed, although, she had to admit, they tended to congregate in areas outside polite view. In Washington, she'd heard it whispered, some of the finest sexual establishments sat directly across from the President's Mansion, or down the hill from the Capitol Building. In the byways, the sluts openly accosted and groped the soldiers as they passed.

As for the main street itself, the cobbling might be poor and thin and deeply rutted on Pennsylvania Avenue, but any kind of paving

145

was a luxury to a country woman. She'd learned to put up with the dense traffic - made worse by the crush of defending troops that had descended on Washington. In half a day she could visit any number of interesting places and people. At night, it was a joy to take the carriage down residential streets to a dinner party or levee. Windows were lit with cheery gas light. Fine vehicles, drawn by steaming horses, stopped at lovely homes and fashionable people stepped out to join the festivities. Of course the carriage might encounter a noisy and foul smelling night soil cart, wending its way to spill its noxious load into the river. That was little real bother to Pamela, who'd been delighted to discover the simple joys of a water closet in her new rooms with Marcia.

There was entertainment aplenty: magic acts and minstrel shows, delightful plays at the Ford and Washington theaters, where famous actors like Joe Jefferson, Charlotte Cushman and the Booth brothers performed. There were wonderful soirees hosted by genteel people, who bitterly regretted the uncouth sort that great boor of a peasant, Lincoln had set loose on the city: westerners and plainsmen and women who smoked and spit and chawed and belched.

They said they could hardly wait for the Rebellion to end so the "nicer people" could return - meaning the plantation aristocrats. Since Pamela was one of those "nicer people," her presence was greatly welcomed. Ever since she'd begun loudly announcing her allegiance to the Union she'd found herself in greater demand. A Southern woman with Northern sensibilities was a prize at the dinner table. The flurry of invitations surprised even Pamela, who'd carefully plotted the lie before she'd coldly cut the traces to her Southern kin.

The greatest advantage the city offered, however, was in Washington women were allowed more freedom than any other community North or South. They could flit about the town at will without the privacy of custom. They had an important political role to play in the parlors and salons. The streets were always filled with their bright bonnets and white kid gloves clutching calling cards. Anywhere else they'd be cooking, knitting or tending mewling babes. It was a freedom of movement Pamela desperately needed to wage her war with the Shannon family. The Shannons were entirely responsible for Pamela's present misfortune... and exile.

Soon, Pamela Shannon fully intended to have her revenge

No one would argue the Widow Shannon was a woman of uncommon beauty and outward gentility. But there was feminine beauty aplenty in Washington, and much of it available for the taking... for the right price. Adding to Pamela's desirability, however, was the fact a duel had been fought over her - a duel, it was whispered that had led to the death of a handsome, young suitor.

Pamela never brought up the duel in public, but she didn't mind the whispers because she realized they added to her allure. Sometimes, however, when she sat among her unmarried acquaintances and listened to their twitterings over their girlish conquests, it was all she could do to keep from shouting out.

"Shut up, you silly little virgins!" she wanted to scream. "What do you have to boast about? I've had a man die for me!"

She never said such a thing, of course, for although Russell's' death at the hands of her late husband was a source of tremendous pride it was impolite to say so. People acted so strangely about death. In her view they were terrible hypocrites, who secretly delighted they were alive when they heard news of the demise of another.

Pamela believed her reaction to Russell's death on that Vicksburg dueling field was more honest. She'd felt a great sense of power - a thrilling crawl up her spine, only vaguely close to the satisfaction she'd felt when she'd successfully bent a lustful man to her will. Killing had always been the province of men; but although it was Edward who pulled the trigger and sent the bullet crashing into Russell's chest, it was Pamela who had controlled matters from the beginning. It might as well have been her standing there with the dueling pistol.

Russell's death had been a spur of the moment decision, and although the duel ultimately failed to achieve her purpose, she still believed the decision was a correct one. If it hadn't of been for that damned child of Edward's everything would have worked out just fine. Her only consolation was when the boy stole the will he'd taken off for parts unknown and hadn't been heard from since. She

147

doubted he'd survived. How could he? He'd only been twelve years old.

But the boy had his revenge, she had to admit. When the spoils had been divided that witch Susan and rest of the Shannon clan in Philadelphia had been left well-fixed - although it didn't take much to satisfy such a rude lot. For Pamela and Edward, however, it was a disaster. Edward had already gambled and whored away his own money, and had borrowed heavily on his expected inheritance. Even then Pamela hadn't figured all was lost. She'd made a bargain with her lover, Fitz Maguire, hadn't she?

Maguire hadn't been the first to bed her, but he'd certainly been the only man to this day who had her kicking her heels at the ceiling and screaming in passion. She'd been young and pliable in his skilled hands and learned many a trick in bed and out. It was Fitz who'd come up with the plan for her to marry Edward, and then whittle away at his fortune little by little. Their eventual goal was the small empire Diana Shannon and John Maguire had created.

"Won't you be jealous?" Pamela inquired when he'd announced the plan. "I'll be in his bed, instead of yours."

Fitz laughed and slapped her on her bare rump. "I'd only be jealous if he were a real man," Fitz said. "But if I know Edward - and I've seen him at work with the whores to know him well enough - he'll do little more than tickle you now and again. You'll be all the hotter for my loving when we meet."

Pamela pretended to cry, but the thought of slipping from Edward's bed back to Fitz's made her squirm in anticipation. Little by little, she'd let Fitz convince her. Their bargain was once they'd stripped Edward of everything, he would meet with some unfortunate accident to be arranged by Maguire. After a suitable time she and Fitz would wed and live on forever in great wealth, ease, and frequent sex.

Pamela cursed herself for being so young and such a fool. She'd gone along with his schemes, from encouraging Edward to borrow from Maguire against his property, to helping him set up a bit of arson at Diana's lawyer's office in Vicksburg to cover a surreptitious peek at the old woman's will. There'd even been a botched early attempt to kill Russell with thugs to remove him from the

148

Allan Cole & Chris Bunch

competition. But as soon as Fitz saw the extent of the disaster, he'd made empty promises and then disappeared for several years - living with foreigners, it was said.

He'd returned after Edward's fatal accident, but not to console and then wed the widow of his "best friend." Instead, he'd called in the notes he held on Edward's property and in a few weeks Pamela found herself beggared and thrown out of her own home. If she hadn't stolen all the silver, plate and anything else of transportable value, she would have been left without a dollar to her name. In all that time, he'd refused to see her or accept any of her humiliating letters begging his mercy and proclaiming her love.

Maguire, she'd heard, was in Richmond now, cozying up to Jeff Davis. It was unlikely she'd ever be able to personally make Fitz pay for humiliating and pauperizing her. But Pamela took great comfort that the South - and Maguire - were doomed. In her mind every bullet and shell fired at them by the filthy Germans and other foreign rabble who made up the Northern army had her own special mark on them: from Mrs. Pamela Shannon to Mr. Fitz Maguire, with love. On the loneliest nights when she cried herself to sleep in her cold bed, Pamela took comfort in dreams of blood bubbling from Maguire's lying lips.

Meanwhile, she'd honed the skills that temperament - and Maguire - had given her. She was an expert in the art of downcast eyes and upcast breasts. Pamela had been born into genteel poverty and into genteel poverty she had been plunged once again. It was a condition she was determined to escape. This time, however, it wouldn't be a man who led the way. She'd learned her lesson well; a lesson, she grudgingly conceded, old Diana Shannon had tumbled on at a much earlier age.

Men had all the power, plus the law on their side. But a smart woman, unencumbered by male domination, could find a path that slipped through the woods and out the other side.

Although Pamela was miles short of her goal, so far she had done marvelously well in her battle with the Shannons. Before Edward died, she'd pushed him into filing suit to overturn Diana's old will, the one that split her far-flung businesses among the Shannons. For a long while the suit seemed doomed. To Pamela's outrage, although Mr. Levy was a Jew, he was very influential in Vicksburg. The local courts had no intention of favoring a Virginia interloper like Edward, even if he was Diana's only full-blooded direct descendant. Then old man Levy died and Pamela saw her chance.

The first part was easy. Guided by Pamela in the background, Edward convinced a friendly judge to declare the suit a matter for Virginia courts. This created a jurisdictional war between Mississippi and Virginia. Shortly after Edward lost his head riding under the low branch, Pamela's maneuvering paid off and a Federal judge ruled since the late Diana Shannon's holdings were interstate, the estate belonged in the province of the Federal court system. The ruling came in the nick of time – just before the guns were fired at Fort Sumter and the rush to secession began.

The issue was now languishing – in Northern Federal Hands - in the little red-brick buildings near the foul-smelling canal that ran along Pennsylvania Avenue. But if Pamela didn't move quickly, and strongly, it would continue to languish there awaiting a decision on whether the suit was worthy to be tried and then entered on the court calendar. Once she had maneuvered it there, Pamela planned to play a waiting game. When the South lost the war - and she prayed nightly it would - the very least Pamela expected to win was all of Diana's land and warehouses in Vicksburg, as well as her Mississippi River shipping contracts.

She had never been fool enough to think the case would be won on its merits. It would be decided by politics. Hence her quick conversion to the Northern cause, and her quiet game to win favor with influential Yankees. Pamela had already stirred up sympathy. The only thing she was lacking was one powerful man to speak for her at the court, and she was sure she could rally that sympathy to carry her the rest of the way to victory.

She settled deeper into the soft leather of the carriage seat, allowing herself the luxury of a little day dreaming. Pamela thought about the man she was certain she'd meet at Willard's. She wondered if he'd be handsome. She wondered if he'd be married. Most of all, she wondered if he'd be as good in bed as Fitz Maguire.

Allan Cole & Chris Bunch

Chaos ruled at the Willard Hotel. Outside, the street was swarming with men dashing about with excited purpose. Some were loading into carriages, or clambering onto horses and dashing away like frock-coated demons to see the fight. Others were rushing to stock up on rations for the trip. Slaves huddled here and there, shrinking from the violent confusion, fearfully waiting their masters' orders. Dogs barked and fought and hawkers shouted above the fray, selling hastily produced buttons and badges proclaiming victory over the enemy at Manassas.

Pamela left Marcia with Hercules and the carriage. Brandishing her parasol like a sword, she stabbed through the forest of blue and black broadcloth suits. A few men reacted to her jabs and turned angry drunk faces at her. But when they saw the slender figure bearing the parasol, and those darks curls and flashing eyes, the anger turned to grins and they bowed her on her way, sweeping back their swallow-tailed coats in their most gentlemanly fashion.

Inside was even greater chaos. Men were shouting, children were crying and women fought to keep a clear space about their brood. All the men were drunk, swigging whiskey and brandy and juleps, or knocking back the strong cocktails that had recently become fashionable. They were expensive, twelve cents a drink, but the expense just seemed to add to their desire to down as many cocktails as possible.

To Pamela's horror, many of the men were army officers. It was all she could do to keep from confronting one of them, and calling him a drunken coward to his face. Why weren't they with McDowell? Did they think Southern men were as yellow as simpering Yankees? Her blood boiling, she thought of how Edward - poor, impotent Edward - would have bested any one of them with sword or pistol. In a fight, she thought, any Southern gentleman was worth ten or twenty of these scum. They were men born and bred to lead, with a habit of command from so many years of handling slaves.

Why, General Beauregard would drown these Yankees like rats in that stinky little creek they called Bull Run.

Pamela suddenly realized the turn her thoughts had taken, and clamped down hard on her emotions. It was necessary for the North to win. Otherwise she had little hope of besting the Shannons.

Besides, she thought Beauregard's reputation undeserved. He was claimed a hero by the South for his bloodless victory over the outnumbered forces at Fort Sumter.

Well, this time, he'd be facing men who shot back. She pressed through the crowd with renewed purpose, searching for such a man.

"I told you there'd be no luck here, Howard," the little squinty-eyed man was saying to his companion. "It's kind of like a territorial election - all buyers, no sellers."

"Be patient, Charles," the companion answered. "If I can't find a horse, a mule will do. And if there's no mule to be had, I'll pay someone for a patch of clear space on a wagon."

Pamela ignored Squinty Eyes and studied the companion. He was middle-aged and craggy handsome, with a strong chin and heavy brows. His torso seemed powerful under his blue, broadcloth coat, although she could see by the strain on his vest that he was fighting portliness. He had dark hair, shot with gray and a bold mustache. She moved closer, dodging a frantic waiter trying to fight his way out of Willard's packed Common Room.

"Howard, you're wasting good card-playing time. You've got about as much chance to get down to Manassas as a sharecropper at a debtor's auction. Come away with me and we'll find a good game. The boys of the Ninth Ohio will win this one with or without the presence of their brave congressman."

Now she knew who the man was - Congressman Howard Wright, a Republican from Ohio. Pamela quickly sorted through the mental index she'd built up while suffering through countless teas in hot rooms buzzing with dull feminine conversation. God, she hated women. No wonder men were so disdainful of her weak, boring sisters.

She steered her mind back to her prospective target. Wright was a notorious influence peddler, enriching himself in schemes ranging from condensed milk for the army to sales of post office positions.

152

He was married, but to a sick wife who had reportedly taken to her bed ten years before and had never emerged.

How safe, Pamela thought. There would be no strings, discretion would be guaranteed, and after years of chasing whores, he'd be immensely impressed with himself for winning the attention of a good woman.

"Of course the boys will win," Wright told Squinty Eyes. "But when they do, it will also be a large feather in my hat when I regale the voters with eyewitness tales of their brave deeds."

"What're you worried about the voters for, Howard? You've got yourself one of the easiest cider districts in the country."

"It takes more than free cider to keep a vote, Charles," Wright said. "Especially since I have my eye on this sweet little tannery out by Gray's Creek. Now, if I could get my hands on that... think what we could make with the prices the Army is paying for leather."

Pamela gave a gasp and stumbled against Wright. The man instinctively grabbed for her and she gave her hips a twist so his arms would go about her waist. She let her breasts crush against him for just a moment, then pulled back in woozy alarm.

"Oh, my gracious, sir," she gasped. "Please forgive me, but I..." She let it trail, placing slim fingers against her pretty brow and squeezing her eyes tight. "Dear, me... I feel..." She sagged and Wright came to life. He steadied her with a strong arm.

"Get her a chair, Charles. Quickly."

He helped her sit and sent Charles to fetch brandy, while she fanned herself with a perfumed hanky. "Don't trouble yourself, sir," Pamela protested, very weakly. "It was only the heat... and so much stale air. I'll be fine in a moment."

She plucked at her scooped bodice, presenting a view of creamy breast no gentleman would look upon under her distressed circumstances. Out of the corner of her eye she saw Wright's gaze dive deep and beg for a glimpse of nipple.

Squinty Eyes came with the brandy and Pamela sipped from the glass Wright held for her. Their faces were close and she arched her neck as she drank to let her perfume tease his senses. Then she pretended to compose herself, taking the glass in her own hand and sitting up straight.

153

Allan Cole & Chris Bunch

Pamela fussed with her hair. "What a sight I must be. You proved you were a gentleman, sir, by rescuing such an ugly woman."

"Ugly? My dear lady. Although I am a stranger, I really must protest your description of yourself. You are anything but ugly. Now tell me who you are with and I'll send Charles to track him down so you can go home."

Pamela pretended alarm. In her best honeyed Southern accent she protested - "Go home? Why, sir, that is the last thing on my mind. And as for company, all I have is my cousin, Marcia, out in my carriage. We simply must get down to Manassas. But I am a widow and my cousin is a spinster and we have no man to take us there... in our carriage."

She tilted her head, knowing from years of practice before a mirror, that her eyes would be as wide and helpless as a doe's.

In her softest, most musical drawl, she asked: "Whatever am I to do, sir?"

Wright gave her a broad grin. He slipped a card from his waistcoat pocket. "Allow me to introduce myself, madam," he said. "I'm Congressman Howard Wright from Ohio... Perhaps we can help each other."

Pamela let a girlish, puzzled look cross her features. She took the card, thinking: there's no perhaps about it at all, my dear.

The Widow Shannon had hooked her fish. Now, all she had to do was land him.

CHAPTER THIRTEEN

BULL RUN - JULY 21, 1861

AT THE LONG BRIDGE leading out of Washington a sentry waved them through after checking Wright's pass. "You'll find plenty of congressman gone on before you," the sentry said with what Pamela thought an impertinent grin.

The morning was tranquil and lovely as they crossed the silver Potomac. They bumped along the Warrenton Turnpike through the wooded Virginia hills toward Manassas. Pamela left Hercules to find his own way home and Wright drove the carriage at a brisk pace. They were silent for awhile as they enjoyed being out of the mad crush of the city. They passed deserted farms surrounded by ripening cornfields. Frightened black faces peered out from roadside slave cabins as the carriage jolted over a road plowed up by artillery and army wagons.

All along the turnpike were other sightseers off to watch the South get a good licking. Pamela saw gentlemen dressed in light summer clothing, carrying spyglasses of every variety. They all had rifles and revolvers close by, and in many carriages Pamela saw bright flashes amid the drab male colors - other ladies like herself bound for the battle. Everyone was in a holiday mood, breaking out delicacies and drink from heavily-laden picnic baskets, and hailing passing horsemen to offer refreshment to fellow adventurers. Pamela saw many famous faces among the party crowd, Republican leaders like Henry Wilson and Zach Chandler, and one of Wright's fellow Ohioans, Benjamin Wade. They'd all been ardent for this fight and had scorched the halls of Congress with demands to put the boot to the rebels.

She turned her attention to her protector-to-be. He was relaxing now they were well on their way and she could see by the play of emotions on his face - and the quick side looks at her - the congressman was beginning to consider his good fortune. Here he was, a middle-aged man, just past his prime, and yet he had the admiration and close company of a beautiful young widow. Only her drab little mouse of a cousin kept them from being completely alone - and Marcia was so silent as almost not to be noticed. Of course, he couldn't know Marcia was under strict orders to speak only when spoken to.

Pamela gave an elaborate stretch, as if to unkink road-weary muscles. It was a stretch guaranteed to display her figure to maximum effect. She pretended she didn't notice Wright watching her, and buried a laugh as the carriage caught a rut and heaved to the side. Wright rose part way in his seat to steady the horse and Pamela saw the thick bulge in his trousers. My, my, Mister Congressman Wright, sir. Whatever could you be thinking? Do you have plans for that thing which might possibly involve sweet, little innocent me?

"Oh, my heavens, Marcia," Pamela said aloud. "What has happened to our manners? We have a big strong man with us, who is sure to be absolutely famished from so much effort in our behalf."

Wright blushed as if she'd eavesdropped on his sinful thoughts. Then he said: "I'd be lying, Mrs. Shannon," he said, "if I didn't admit I was hungry."

Pamela clapped her hands in delight. "I have just the thing to fill the aching void, Mr. Wright," she said. "I have a dish of oysters on ice and you have the look about you, sir, as a man who dearly loves his... oysters."

Wright blushed again and mumbled he'd be pleased to eat an oyster or two. Marcia drew the dish from the hamper and passed it to Pamela. She flipped away the linen covering and lifted the dish out of its newspaper wrapping. There was a notice of a sale on the ragged page, announcing Madame Delaure had just received a new shipment of dresses, bonnets and Jovin's gloves from Paris. "READERS, THE UNION IS IN DANGER!" said the ad. "BUT BY BUYING YOUR WARDROBE AT LAMMONDS, YOU MAY SAVE IT!" The oysters sat plump and tempting on their bed of ice, nestled among patriotic advertisements.

The congressman reached, but Pamela shooed his hand away.

"Now, you just mind the road, Mr. Wright," she mock-scolded. "And let a woman do her proper work."

She deftly shucked an oyster, speared it with a straw and nudged Wright to open his mouth. She popped it in and while he chewed, shucked another.

"Pass up a little punch, Marcia, dear," Pamela said.

156

Marcia did as she was told, but very slowly. Pamela thought, She's like molasses in January. Then she saw Marcia's white, pinched features and realized her cousin was frightened. Pamela sighed, hoping she wouldn't have to deal with hysterics. Finally Marcia delivered the jug and a cup and Pamela poured a drink for the congressman.

He sucked it down almost as fast as he had the oysters and Pamela quickly refilled it. She held the cup so he could drink when he liked.

"If you don't mind my asking, Mrs. Shannon," Wright said, "why is it so urgent for such lovely ladies as yourselves to witness events, I fear will offend your delicate natures?"

"Oh, we women aren't so delicate as we'd like you gentlemen to believe," Pamela laughed. "I don't want to give away the secrets of my sex, but just because a woman is a lady, it doesn't mean she's as ignorant of the real world as she leads the men in her life to think."

Wright smiled, but there was a bitter curl to his lips. Pamela was pleased this shot had gone so easily home. As she had planned, he was comparing her to his long-malingering wife.

She delivered another oyster tidbit and a drink of the punch. "But, you asked for a reason, sir, " she continued, "and I won't have you think of me as anything less than frank - even if I am a woman."

Pamela had learned long ago that the more she mocked her own sex, the more the man in her company held her apart from the others. "You see, sir, I was raised with a sense of duty. It was a trait my late husband - a man who was a visionary, and paid dearly for it - encouraged."

"Some wrong was done to your husband?"

"Oh, you don't know the half of it, Mr. Wright, and I shall not bore you with my burden. Just let it be said my husband's belief in the sanctity of the Union - no matter how just our complaints - cost him dearly. It left me destitute as well, but-" Pamela gave a brave sniff. "But... I can carry on, sir. I can carry on."

She dabbed an eye with a dainty kerchief. "Never mind about that. As I said, I am a woman who was raised to duty. And I believe it my duty to help our soldiers preserve the Union my husband loved so dear. I cannot carry a gun... although I would do so, willingly...

157

but I can at least be close to our boys and see their suffering as they carry us forward to Richmond."

"Noble sentiments, indeed, Mrs. Shannon," Wright said, nodding his head. "When I report to my district of the events this day, I shall tell them of the brave Virginia woman whose principles require her to stand with the Blue, instead of the Gray."

"I pray it's over before we arrive," Marcia said in a small voice. "I just don't want to see anyone... suffer."

"Oh, there'll be suffering aplenty, Miss," Wright chuckled. "But it'll all be on the other side." His tone took on a pedantic air. "We have thirty five thousand of the Union's finest to assure us of that. Surely, Beauregard might have a nearly equal force, but it's well-known his troops are green and their morale is poor. For they know it is not only flesh and blood they face, but the whole industrial might of our brave nation."

He shook his head solemnly. "I pity my Southern cousins in those ranks," he said. "They have been lied to by their leaders. But soon, they shall see the truth... even if it comes at them with a bayonet."

They drew near a young man jogging along the road. He wore a thin black shirt, sturdy breeches, low cut shoes and white stockings. His costume was topped by a broad-brimmed straw hat. He was about sixteen, or seventeen. As they began to go by, Pamela saw he had a wrapped package under his arm.

The young man smiled and put a hand on the carriage door. "Mind if I hold on a spell, sir?" he called to Wright. "Just 'til I catch my wind."

"Hold on all you like young man," Wright boomed. Then, with a broad politician's grin: "Is that an Ohio accent I detect?

The youth got a good grip on the door and let the vehicle carry him along the road. He nodded. "Yessir. We have a farm over Youngstown way."

Wright beamed and introduced himself as one of Ohio's own, and a congressman to boot. The youth seemed impressed. "Are you off to join the fight?" Wright asked.

"Nossir," the youth answered. "I'd be proud to, but my mother won't let me. My brother and father have already taken up arms, you see."

"Then what is your mission?"

The boy indicated the package. "I've got some delicacies my mother cooked up and I'm takin' them to my brother. He's down at the fight."

Marcia's eyes widened. "You've come all the way from Ohio for that?" she gasped.

"Of course, not, silly," Pamela answered. "He's probably living-"

The youth interrupted:" "No disrespect, Miss, but I did come down from Ohio, just like the lady said. But when I got to Washington my brother's unit had already marched out. A sergeant said he'd hold the package for my brother, but I didn't think that'd set well with my mother. So I thought I go to Manassas and give it to him in person."

"Very noble of you, young man," Wright said. Pamela noticed he tended to overuse that phrase... along with brave. "Perhaps you'd like-"

Pamela broke in. "I think I saw something fall from your pocket," she said to the youth, pointing back down the road. "I hope it wasn't your wallet."

The young man's mouth fell open and he let go of the carriage and stopped in the road to pat his pockets. In a moment he was left far behind.

Wright started to pull up. "Maybe we ought to-"

"Oh, please," Pamela said. "I'd feel so bad if we were late. The boy will make out just fine." As she spoke Pamela grabbed a packet out of the picnic hamper. "Care for some nice roast chicken, Mr. Wright?"

The congressman was easily diverted. He smiled and reached. "Yes, thank you," he said.

Pamela passed a bit of gleaming white breast forward, and as the congressman gnawed she glanced back at the swiftly diminishing figure of the boy. Let him stick his pushy nose in someone else's business, she thought. Stupid Yankee plowboy. The trouble with

Allan Cole & Chris Bunch

those people is they'd been doing nigger's work so long they forgot how to behave in polite society.

The muffled pounding of artillery grew heavier as they neared the village of Fairfax. A shifting wind brought a sudden acrid odor of gunsmoke and terror. Pamela felt wonderfully alive, her blood boiling as if she had just dosed herself with an Indian tonic. Marcia huddled small in the seat, but Wright must have drunk from the same flask as Pamela for he laid the whip down smart on the horse's flanks. "We're almost there," he shouted.

Around the bend came a bewildering sight. A shambling mass of men and heavily laden wagons filled the road. To Pamela's horror, the loose column was heading away from the battle.

From the loud protests from the advancing civilians she could tell others were as angry as she. The anger grew hotter as they came closer and they could see the soldiers laughing, joking and calling out for presents.

Wright shouted at an officer on horseback. "What is happening here, sir?"

"Our time is up," the officer answered. "We were mustered out at Centreville. Now we're all going home."

"The fight is over so soon?" Pamela cried.

The officer and his men laughed. "No, pretty lady," a grizzled soldier answered. It ain't even begun yet."

"They why are you leaving?" Wright demanded.

"I told you, sir," the officer answered, his smile gone. "My unit's agreed upon time is up."

There were more shouts from the civilians' carriages and wagons, calling the soldiers cowards and worse. But the soldiers cursed back, quickened their pace, and were soon gone.

"They won't be so cocky when this day is over," Wright said, grimly. "Mark my words, there will be many a hero made in the hours ahead. Those men will all rue the day they fled such glory." He turned to Pamela. "I hope you don't think all Yankees are made of such weak stuff."

Pamela patted his hand. "Never fear," she said. "All of us have our fools and cowards to bear."

She held up the jug. "Would you like some more punch, Mr. Wright?"

"Don't mind if I do, Mrs. Shannon."

If she had been Mrs. Lincoln, herself, Pamela couldn't have asked for a better view of the battle. On the other side of Centreville - just past Cub Run Bridge - sentries directed them to the top of a hill overlooking Bull Run. They joined hundreds of other fun seekers who had spread out blankets and lavish lunches on the soft grass. The hill was thick with fancy carriages, frock-coated gentlemen and ladies dressed in gay summer finery.

It was quite like a concert at a park, Pamela thought as she directed Marcia to unload the hamper and lay out the food. Her cousin jumped every time a cannon fired, but her senses seemed to have dulled and she carried out Pamela's orders with slow obedience.

While the congressman, carrying one of Pamela's jugs, ambled over to get the news from a group of frock-coated men lolling under a splayed oak tree, Pamela fetched her binoculars. She praised herself for having foresight to bring along Edward's powerful lenses, and sniffed at a woman a few yards away who was straining to see the action with opera glasses. Even so, it was hard to tell exactly what was happening on the thick, wooded farmland spread out before her, for the plain was choked with dust and gunsmoke.

Pamela thought it all quite exciting as she swept the scene with powerful binoculars.

The view was entirely unexpected, not at like the carefully staged oil portraits of famous battles Pamela had seen. She saw complete confusion, with no heroic center where victory was sure to be biding its time. To her right was a chaotic boil like ants panicking in the face of an approaching storm. To her left was even greater confusion. Far in the distance she saw smoke and flames from appeared to be a burning house. Directly below her was the slender, muddy trickle that was Bull Run. There was a stone bridge crossing the water, and on either side thick, small woods bristling with thorn and vine.

She saw the comforting blue of Union uniforms moiling around the bridge. But on the opposite side she saw the opposing gray

Allan Cole & Chris Bunch

uniforms of her former Southern kin. Her glasses swept on, but all she saw was furious motion and juts of smoke, mixed in with gouts of fire and pink-flashing light reflecting off metal in the in the afternoon sun.

She heard Wright talking to another man. "I didn't see the General myself," the man said, "but my friend has a cousin who's his adjutant."

"And how was General McDowell's health?" Wright inquired.

"His spirits were high, sir," the man answered. "He ate his usual hearty breakfast after he'd ordered the attack. His digestion suffered a bit afterwards, I was told, but they said it was from a spoiled chop."

To her left Pamela was gratified to see a shell burst in thick brush and what appeared to be the figures of gray-uniformed men tumble out. Then she spotted a Southern officer on horseback trying to rally his men. She prayed for another shell, but it didn't come and in a moment the opportunity was gone as smoke and dust obscured the field.

"I arrived just after dawn," the man told Wright, "and we'd already been giving them hell for hours. They made a feint for our right flank just awhile ago, but our boys sent the curs scurrying for cover with their tails between their legs."

Pamela's glasses moved back to the Northern side of the river. She saw the odd gaudy uniforms of the New York Fire Zouaves, blue and scarlet with white turbans and baggy pants. Moving closer to the hill she saw many more civilian carriages and horses, surrounded by their sight-seeing owners. Mixed in were blue uniforms, making the whole scene seem like a big military party.

Pamela made out a small figure in a broad, straw hat, lugging heavy objects from a wagon. As he began to began to put the objects together and they took recognizable form, Pamela thought it might be Matthew Brady, the famous photographer who'd sworn to everyone who bought him a drink to get a pictorial record of the war. Brady was an ugly little Irishman, with his wild hair and sharp nose, but a favorite of many society ladies, who yearned to have their portrait done by such an artist of the glass.

"My guess is," Wright's new friend said, "McDowell will attack across the stone bridge soon. That's the quickest way to Richmond! And he's got a good man to do the job. General Daniel Tyler of the First Division."

"I'd better get down to see my boys in the Ninth Ohio then," Wright said. But Pamela could tell by his tone he was not enthusiastic about getting closer to the fighting.

She forced herself to lower the glasses. "Oh, but I'm sure there's time for a little dinner first," she said. "You only had a bite or two getting down here. You must keep up your strength. You're an important man, Mister Wright. You owe people to look after yourself."

Wright reddened and the man laughed, but there was no mockery in the laughter. "Go ahead, Congressman," the man urged. "These things have got a way of taking a lot of time."

Pamela took Wright's arm, clinging a little as if for safety, and led him back to where Marcia had spread out the picnic. There were soft blankets and a few old parlor pillows to sit upon. In the center was a pure, white linen cloth set on top of the blanket. There were three place settings, with fine china decorated with little blue buds, as well as gleaming crystal goblets for their drink. The cutlery had been burnished to a high gloss by Hercules and was laid upon embroidered napkins picked out in blue buds to match the china. But the most dazzling view was the lunch itself. Pamela was a poor cook, but knew how to get what she wanted. The talented old woman who came in to do their meals had long been terrorized into submission and faithfully copied the dishes Pamela spied at the fine hotels.

She had duck and Virginia ham and a cold joint of venison rubbed in garlic, pepper and cayenne and barbecued Texas style. Along with this were cold terrapin cutlets and shad kept chilled like the oysters in a dish of ice. To accompany this feast were Maryland beaten biscuits, pickled eggs, and beets and caramel tomatoes. For sweets she had gooseberry and apple tarts along with a molasses pecan pie. For drink there was wine, chilled hard cider... and more punch.

Allan Cole & Chris Bunch

Wright gazed with awe at this culinary tapestry. "I was hungrier than I thought," he said. "I'll just tarry a bit before I go see my boys."

He sat himself down and ate and drank with gusto. All around was the sound of thundering guns and the racket of musket fire. But the wind was blowing away from them so there were no unpleasant odors to spoil Wright's appetite as he devoured the duck and ham and still found room to tuck in the shad - which he praised as the finest he'd ever eaten. Pamela nibbled with small appetite, wanting to watch the fight, but intent on keeping the congressman's attention with flirtatious small talk.

Marcia didn't eat at all, but sat close to the carriage. She was humming little tunes to herself as if to drown out the sounds and Pamela thought about shushing her. But the humming was so quiet it was unlikely to disturb Wright and maybe it was better to let her amuse herself. Otherwise she might become hysterical and with the congressman en compagnie, as it were, it would be difficult to give her a good slap to recall her senses.

After a time Wright patted his slightly bulging waistcoat. "That was a fine meal, Mrs. Shannon," he said. "You must have made your husband a very happy man."

Pamela arched an eyebrow. "He was pleased with more than just my cooking, sir," she laughed, and added an artful blush for being so bold.

Wright laughed so hard he forgot himself and patted her on the knee. Pamela let his hand linger, as if she had also forgotten herself in all the excitement, then delicately shooed it away, allowing her blush to deepen.

From far off Pamela heard men shouting and what might have been a horse screaming. Wright recovered his manners, and gave a slight bow of his head to apologize for any impropriety. He drank his wine and Pamela refilled the glass to the brim. She was completely sure of herself and her target, so did not begrudge the investment she'd made in the drink and the picnic fixings.

Another battery of artillery joined the others, hammering the far side of the river.

Wright was staring at her now, battle forgotten for the moment. His eyes were wide and bright. Pamela made as if she didn't see his rudeness, and stretched to put a little pickled beet on her plate - once again making sure he had plenty of opportunity to examine her figure. She made certain the dress caught in her knees, tightening the fabric over her shapely thighs, and the hollow between.

Wright's voice was hoarse when he spoke next. "Perhaps...uh... when we return to Washington...I could... uh... help with that little legal matter that's troubling you."

Pamela had poured out her plight in some detail during their journey. She clapped her hands in maidenly delight. "Oh, would you? I promise I wouldn't be much trouble."

Wright leaned close. "My dear Mrs. Shannon," he said, "It would be impossible for you to ever be too much trouble."

"Oh, then I must give you my card," Pamela said, putting just the right tone of innocence to her eagerness. She lifted a card from her pocket and handed to him. As he took it she raised her fingertips slightly and they drew Wright's lips like a magnet. He kissed her hand, and she pulled away and pretended to cover embarrassment at such close contact by fussing with the linen.

He was eyeing her with a satisfied, predator's look. He thinks he's got me, Pamela thought, and all he has to do is circle until I weaken.

"If I am to advise you, we'll probably have to... meet... fairly often," he said.

"If it wouldn't be any trouble, Mr. Wright," Pamela's voice was tremulous – as if fearful of her bold reply.

"As I said, Mrs. Shannon," Wright murmured, "it would be impossible for a lady like you to be any trouble at all."

Pamela gave him a dewy-eyed look of gratitude, her only answer a sigh of deep-felt emotion.

Then the man Wright had spoken to earlier called: "I think we're getting ready for the attack!"

Wright leaped to his feet, crying: "I hope I'm not too late to visit my boys." His eyes were a little crazy and he was suddenly sweating profusely. He's almost as frightened as Marcia, she thought.

"You shouldn't go now," she said, "it's too dangerous."

"It's my duty, Mrs. Shannon," he insisted, but made no motion to go. Artillery thundered and he flinched now the sound had personal meaning.

"You must stay with me, Mr. Wright," Pamela pleaded, thinking he was a fool and a coward, but what she required at this moment was a coward and a fool. "Marcia and I wouldn't feel safe alone. Besides, isn't it also your duty to protect your health, so you can manage important affairs of state?"

There were excited shouts from the edge of the hill. Wright's friend called: "Come quick, it's started!" Forgetting her game, Pamela rushed to see. The congressman ran after her - it was too late for duty now.

Wright's friend was pointing down at the stone bridge. Pamela put her glasses on the action. There was a furious fight in progress, but through the clouds of smoke she could see small gray figures slowly falling back before an onrushing sea of blue.

"Tyler's cleared the bridge," she heard Wright's friend say. She saw more Yankee troops massing behind the attack. Suddenly they broke through and streamed over the bridge. They spread out into a long line that quickly thickened with more forces, then they surged forward. "Tyler's got 'em!" the man shouted. "Now, you'll see our mettle, you traitorous bastards."

Pamela thrilled as she heard the Union troops cheering and firing as they rolled up the enemy, battle flags unfurled in front of them. Never in her life had she imagined war would be like this. She wanted to be down there among the blue uniforms, firing her musket into the fleeing enemy, shouting "Onward to Victory! Onward to Richmond!"

Suddenly, volley after volley of artillery shells exploded among the advancing troops. Pamela's heart wrenched as smoke clouds billowed and burst. She wailed as the blue uniforms were hurled back. She saw officers trying to rally the men but it was no use, because the gray forces were charging. The Yankees stumbled back across the bridge, where a hasty defense was organized. Stunned, Pamela lowered the glasses. Wright was pale and his garrulous companion silent. The entire battlefield had erupted into action - especially along her front and right.

Allan Cole & Chris Bunch

Even without the glasses she could see the thickening of the gray forces... and the desperate state of the blue. "What's happened?" she cried.

"A small setback, Mrs. Shannon," Wright assured her. "The General will soon put it right." But his voice trembled.

"We have plenty of reinforcements," his friend said. "Soon as they get their back into it, we'll have the rebels on the run again." Pamela nodded numbly. Yes. Of course. The reinforcements will carry the day.

Reinforcements never came. Pamela didn't know how long she stood there, but her fingers lost their feeling holding the heavy binoculars and her eyes ached from effort. It seemed like hours, but that was impossible, for the sun still stood at late afternoon. Pamela had no idea what was happening, but Wright and the other man seemed distraught, so it could not have been going well.

The man took his watch from his pocket and checked the time. "It's nearly 3:30," he said. "The rebels can't hold much longer. They've been fighting for thirteen hours."

Pamela thought in that case the Yankees must be just as weary, but didn't say anything. Then she heard the most terrifying sound - a wild scream of thousands of voices.

She whipped the glasses up and saw gray figures charging forward all across the field. The screams were coming from the rebels. She'd heard Edward scream like that - a shrill halloo when he was on a foxhunt hot on the trail of his quarry. To her horror the screams had more effect on the Union forces than all the shot and shell that had rained on them.

The blue lines wavered, then began to fall back. It seemed orderly, at first, but then gray closed with blue and blue ranks broke!

"My God, where are the reinforcements?" Wright shouted.

Then the Union troops were pouring back across the river, some falling, some crawling, but most running for their lives. There were clumps of blue covered with gore left in their wake. The rebels followed, screaming their wild yell.

"We have to get out of here," Wright cried, "or we'll be overrun."

Allan Cole & Chris Bunch

Pamela was so furious she paid him no mind. She'd pinned her fortunes to the Union, but she should have known a Southern man wouldn't fall so easily, especially against a yellow-bellied Yankee or these low foreigners who'd fled their own homelands to reach these shores.

Where would the Yankees run now? Canada?

Then she realized she was standing against a tide, as the civilians panicked at the sight of the oncoming Rebels and fled.

She saw Wright was gone. At first she'd thought he'd run as well, then saw him caught in the tangle of traffic fleeing the hill. Marcia was screaming her name. Pamela gathered up her skirts and ran for the carriage. Marcia was babbling, but Pamela pushed her aboard, unhitched the horse, then hiked up her dress and leaped into the gig.

Pamela was an excellent horsewoman and soon had the carriage turned and was whipping her steed down the hill. She careened past a knot of frock-coated men and heard Wright call her name, but kept going. She saw a tangle of confusion at Cub Run Bridge - an overturned wagon was blocking the escape of the fancy gigs and civilian horseman. But that concerned her not at all, for Pamela was not aiming for escape. She was wild, crazy – for in fear but in awful anger.

The Widow Shannon hit the turnpike just in front of a fleeing mass of blue-clad troops. She wheeled the carriage about to confront them, standing like a madwoman, reins gripped in a small, steel fist, the other hand grabbing for her parasol to wave in their faces.

"Stand and fight!" she shouted. "Stand and fight!"

The men ran past, faces black with gun smoke, and white holes for eyes. Some were cursing and yelling they had been betrayed.

"You cowardly bastards!" Pamela cried. She began laying about her with the parasol - drubbing any head or back within reach. "Fight them, you Yankee cowards! Fight them!"

The parasol broke, but still she kept beating at them with the splintered remains.

Hands reached up and pulled her from the carriage, and she heard Marcia scream as she too was tumbled out. She found herself sprawled in the field, sputtering curses as a knot of soldiers turned

Allan Cole & Chris Bunch

the carriage about and fought each other for a place aboard. Then the carriage was gone and Pamela sobbed in frustration as the blue tide continued to roll back toward Washington.

She had little memory of what happened next, but she found herself huddled, weeping in a wagon. Wright was beside her, patting her shoulder, trying to comfort her. Her dress was wet, and she vaguely recalled the congressman helping her ford the stream past the blocked Cub Run Bridge.

Marcia's face came into view, as white and pinched as ever, but she seemed more worried for Pamela than herself and stroked Pamela's temples with cold fingers. Pamela gathered her wits. Very well. The first fight was lost. There would be others. Meanwhile she must proceed with her own plans.

"I couldn't find your carriage or horse, Mrs. Shannon," Wright said softly. "I'm very sorry, but I fear they are lost."

"What shall I do?" Pamela moaned, letting tears stream from her eyes. "I'm only a poor widow woman."

"Do not concern yourself, Mrs. Shannon," Wright answered, taking the hook. "I'll see everything is put right. Your government will see you suffer no losses. This I promise you."

Pamela mumbled thanks, then sighed and pretended to fall asleep, a round hip pressed firmly against Wright's knee.

"Your cousin, Miss Weatherby, is a most remarkable woman," she heard the congressman tell Marcia.

She didn't hear Marcia's reply, for by then she really was asleep.

CHAPTER FOURTEEN

OUTSIDE VICKSBURG - LATE JULY, 1861

PATRICK SHANNON SAT motionless in the saddle, carefully studying the ruined mansion. Finally he pulled his right boot out of the stirrup, lifted his leg over the saddlehorn and slid to earth, dropping the reins to the ground.

His horse, plains-trained, lowered his head and stayed picketed. Patrick walked to where the porch steps had been. To either side was a now-gone-wild formal garden of roses and poinsettias. Vines grew up the few still-standing charred timbers of the great house. The Mississippi afternoon was hot and still. A dustdevil touched down in the now-caked ashes, then vanished. Patrick guessed the fire had roared through the great house two, maybe three years ago.

Ruin must have come to the Shannon empire for the house to have been abandoned, the grounds never rebuilt. All that his great grandmother had built was gone, Patrick thought hollowly, broken by pride, foolishness and an evil woman's conspiracy. None of us, he thought, not my oh-so-brave cousins, not my father, no one, had understood what was happening.

His fingers reflexively found the old musketball, still hanging on a length of rawhide, around his neck. It was an unconscious gesture he always made whenever he remembered the family he fled and most of all Grandmother Shannon. Old as she was, he firmly believed, if she'd lived just a few more days, somehow, in some way, she could have prevented the tragedy.

But she was dead, wasn't she? Patrick - shaped by six years of living by his wits on the frontiers of law and society - had grown pragmatic.

Templar whickered, and Patrick came back to the present. He remounted, and thought about which path he would take next. In one direction, pushing back through the unpruned fruit trees was the road to Vicksburg and - with luck - a fat purse. In the other, visible more in Patrick's memory than reality, was the track that followed the bluffs for awhile, then curved inland. In for a shilling, in for a pound, he thought, and tapped his heels against Templar's sides. The gelding started forward, onto the abandoned track.

Patrick glanced back and shivered. He'd had to see the mansion once more. But never again. Let it disappear into jungle and wasteland, so it would appear no person had ever built there.

"Don't you have a case of the jollities today," he said aloud, forcing something resembling a smile across his face. Patrick, who'd grown up sort of neutral about horses, had learned one of the animal's virtues was you could talk to yourself and not appear a crack-brained young man who'd spent too much time alone with both eyes on the main chance.

The desolation ended a quarter mile away from the grounds Now there were tidy, hard-worked farms checkerboarding the landscape. The men and women working the fields were black free tenant farmers, not slaves. Patrick's cheeriness became real. It would appear that some good might have come from the disaster. It seemed his great grandmother's old will had been allowed, and these farmers had been given, as promised, the Shannon land they'd worked for shares.

As if sensing his mood change, Templar broke into a trot. "Hang on, you tub of glue," Patrick said. "There'll be time enough to run in Vicksburg."

He barely touched the reins, and the horse slowed. Templar would have pitched Patrick into the bushes if the young man had yanked the reins or if his bit were anything other than a relatively gentle half-breed type. The three-year-old did not respond to any physical usage - or at least not in the manner desired. There were still barely-visible scars on the horse's flanks from its first owner's spurring, treatment that had turned Templar "mean," into a "gravedigger," and part of the reason that he was now owned by an eighteen-year-old trickster.

Near the road, just on the other side of the rail fence, a man was hoeing at the edge of a waist-high cornfield using, Patrick was glad to see, a full-size tool rather than the slave's back-destroying short hoe.

"Afternoon," he said, courteously.

The black looked up, tried to cover surprise, then bobbed his head in instant, total humility. "Good day, young marse."

Allan Cole & Chris Bunch

The man hastily went back to his work. Patrick grimaced. Perhaps this was not a freeman. Perhaps he was a slave. Perhaps Patrick had been dreaming his childish fantasy had, at least in part, been fulfilled. He passed an abandoned farm, its fields grown over, the third one he'd seen this morning. Perhaps there would be no neat white farmhouse with green trim at the end of this lane.

He did not look back and see the black staring in now-complete astonishment. Patrick Shannon was an unusual sight, even in these days of war, when travelers were far more common than before. None of his garments went with their brothers. His new tophat was cocked at a rakish angle, the way a young city swell should wear it. But under the hat Patrick wore a collarless homespun shirt, a red-checked bandanna tied around his neck. The shirt was worn loose. Patrick's corduroy pants were tucked into high-top boots, almost heavy enough to belong to a drover. There was no need to impress anyone out here in the country. Before he got into town and targeted his mark, he'd dig out the frock coat, vest, tailored pants and neck scarf.

His saddle was another bit of strangeness - a large-skirted rig with a high cantle and fork. In Texas this "stock" or "Mexican" saddle was commonplace, but east of the Mississippi it was rather rare. Lashed behind him was what the now-vanished mountain men called "possibles," a rather bulky roll made up of a foul-weather slicker fastened around Patrick's "city" clothes, a change of underclothes, a blanket, a frying pan, a coffeepot, some flour, bacon, coffee beans, salt and a can of baking powder. His toiletries were in one of the four saddlebags hung front and rear from the saddle, a Colt's .31 caliber five-shot pocket pistol, balls, caps and powder was in another.

Patrick, not quite considering himself a gambler, had learned the truth of the caution from his rogue Californian uncle, Michael, that "people tend to take their gambling losses seriously and are prone to violence."

A third bag contained Patrick's continuing self-education - a worn Plays of Shakespeare, Volume Three of Motley's The Rise of the Dutch Republic, and Seth Jones; or the Captives of the Frontier, by one Edward Ellis. In Vicksburg he hoped to have time, and the

172

money, to stop by Clarke's Emporium and replace the dime novel and locate Volume Four of Motley. He was bored orrie-eyed with the endless chronicles of the Dutchers against the Spaniards, but he'd set himself to finishing the work if it killed him.

Slung to one side of the saddle, wrapped in oilcloth, was a long, percussion-fired doublebarreled shotgun, this intended for game instead of protection. Also very unusual were the two jute sacks tied behind Patrick's possibles. They contained grain. Templar was too valuable to be fed on roadside grass, unlike many of the horses that belonged to the men Patrick chose as quarry.

Templar was also a bit strange. The animal was carefully curried - but his mane and tail were long and untrimmed. And the horse was decidedly... not gawky, but certainly gave no hint of purportedly being a direct descendant of the Byerly Turk, the great warhorse of the Battle of the Boyne and one of the three stallions from which all thoroughbred race horses were descended. It was yet another reason Patrick had become his owner. Templar was even more spraddle-gaited on command. But he was a horse that loved to run, as the marks had found out the hard way.

Invisible, but still more unusual was Patrick carried more than five hundred dollars, most of it in gold. The times were inflationary, but sugar was still holding at eight cents a pound, and venison was a dime, so it was curious for anyone, let alone a eighteen-year-old, to carry that much hard currency. However, the world Patrick moved in did not resort to banks, nor keep the hours when banks were open.

Just ahead Patrick spotted Mr. Cuffe's farm, or at least the building and barn, still neat as a Currier & Ives engraving, that'd belonged to the free black man six years before. In the raked, sanded yard was a tall young man. At first, Patrick thought him to be Cuffe, then realized that everyone ages - this must be one of Mr. Cuffe's sons.

"Hello, the house," he called.

"Afternoon, Marse. What c'n I help th' young massah with?"

"You're a Cuffe?"

"That's correct, marse. I'm Abraham."

"I'm Patrick Shannon."

173

"Yes, Marse. Ah think I 'member you."

Patrick dismounted, then really heard what Abraham had said. "Your father never called me marse," he said, a bit sharply.

A voice came from within the house. "I din't. But that was some time past, Mist' Shannon."

"Not for me."

Mr. Cuffe walked out. He was a little fatter, a little balder, a little grayer, but otherwise the same. Patrick found himself across the yard, and holding Cuffe's hand in both of his. "It is good to see you, sir."

"Y'all take note of that, son," Cuffe said. "Th' last white person who called me sir was the late an' truly lamented Missus Shannon. I guess what she taught stuck tight."

Patrick pulled back - this was passing strange. But before he could comment, Cuffe beamed. "An' it's good t' lay eyes on you, boy. Abraham! Put Patrick's horse in the barn, if you would. An' fetch his duffle in. He'll be stayin' for dinner an' th' night."

He glanced at Patrick. "'Less, son, y'all don't think it'd be right, beddin' down in the same house with us."

Again, the slight dig.

"Mr. Cuffe," Patrick answered honestly, "last night I slept near a ditch, and got woke up near dawn when the slicker leaked and some peckerwood's razorback decided I was running a boarding house. I'd be honored, sir."

"Come in then, boy. There's a pitcher of green tea coolin' that'll slip down easy."

Cuffe and Patrick started for the house. Cuffe stopped. "Nice lookin' horse."

"Thank you, sir."

"What's he turn th' mile at?"

"Never timed him, sir. Quick enough."

"Horse like that... 'specially if somebody left him sort of ungroomed an' somebody else didn't have th' eye... horse like that might win some real upset races."

"That right, sir?" Cuffe grinned again - and Patrick smiled back. "I sincerely hope," he said, "that you're the only one in Vicksburg with that kind of eye."

Allan Cole & Chris Bunch

"How'd y'all happen across him, anyway?"

"Well, sir, I was walking along one day, and came across this rope. A nice, new rope it was, lying right in the middle of the road. So I thought I'd best take it with me, before somebody came along and stole it. Which I did. But when I got down the road a piece, I found out there was a horse attached to the other end of it, and so I figured I better not hang on, and try to convince people there'd been an accident, so I stepped up on him and ended up in Texas."

Cuffe chuckled. "You're a Shannon, all right. Now. In. 'Fore th' sun bakes any more of our brains."

Mrs. Cuffe was as tall and curvaceous as Patrick remembered. He asked about their children. "Some farm 'round here," Cuffe told him. "Abraham an' Luke, they're still helping me. Most of th' girls are married up. Some of th' boys moved in town. Ethan took up blacksmithing, Matthew and Ezekial are stevedorin'. Two of the boys went north. Like some other folks around here."

"I saw some of the farms have been given up." Cuffe just nodded. Patrick decided to push a little. "You said... they went north. You mean to the Free States. Why? If they were already free, down here?"

Cuffe was looking for words. Mrs. Cuffe, without turning from the stove, said softly, "Freedom, 'round here, don't hold th' worth it once had."

"What do you mean, ma'am?"

A silence grew uncomfortable, and Patrick was sorry he'd pried.

"Back in January," Mr. Cuffe finally said, "police went an' arrested a freeman by the name of Edgar. Arrested him 'cause he had sixty-some dollars in his britches. An' what they called suspicious documents."

"Abolitionist tracts?"

"I heard no more. They brought him up, front of th' mayor, who tol' Edgar he could either get out of 'Sippi... or get sold as a slave. Edgar put th' chains back on. An' th' state sold him for jus' short of two thousand gold dollars."

"Ah'd die, first," Mrs. Cuffe said.

"That's not right," Patrick said.

175

"Right... these days... seems pretty much made up by folks as they go on. Even here in Vicksburg."

"You mean secession? But Mississippi was the first to leave the Union."

"Th' state was. Vicksburg voted coop'rationist... up to th' last minute. Even a'ter th' vote over to Montgomery, Vicksburg stuck with th' rest. But there weren't fireworks an' celebratin' like I heard there was down in Natchez. But things change. Now there's talk of strangers comin' in town bein' made to take a loyalty oath. Shops are sellin' Jeff Davis letter paper. Pictures of what they're callin' our new pres'dent in most shops."

"We don't go to town much. 'Less we have to," Mrs. Cuffe put in.

"Vicksburg's spooky," Mr. Cuffe said. "Not many young men left. Mos' gone to be sol'jers. And ever' day, trains come through, headed east, carryin' more troops, headed for battle."

"It's pretty dead, then?" Patrick asked, sounding just a bit disappointed.

"It'll be pretty lively for the next week," Cuffe said. "Word just came in 'bout some great victory near Washington. They say the Federal Army was beat on pretty bad. So there'll be celebrations and some people around who'll... be th' kind of folk you prob'ly want to meet. Th' kind who don't have a good eye for horseflesh. But th' kind who think they do, an' keep gold handy for th' event. Assumin' you're thinkin' of some specie of horse business."

"I might be, sir. I might be," Patrick said, relieved.

"That horse y'all came in with, which I'm suspectin' could be a rattler tryin' to appear a bullsnake, how'd you say you come by him again?"

"Well," Patrick began, "it's kind of involved, but the whole thing started back when they asked me to scout for the Texas Rangers, when they went and lost the tracks of the entire Mexican Army—"

"I thought so," Cuffe interrupted. "If you want to wash 'fore supper, I'll get some soap down."

Allan Cole & Chris Bunch

Comfortably full of corn dodgers, okra pancakes and hamhock, Patrick sipped from his coffee cup and set it on the porch steps. He took his stubby pipe and tobacco pouch from a pocket, and held the pouch out to Mr. Cuffe, who was taking his digestive ease in a rickety canebacked chair. "Try some of mine, sir? It's Perique. Bought it downriver in Natchez."

"I thank you, Patrick."

Without being asked, Abraham went into the house and fetched two rather blackened clay pipes, handing one to Mr. Cuffe. The three filled, tamped, lit and blew smoke against the gathering twilight. Mrs. Cuffe finished washing up, and joined them. "Passin' strange," Abraham observed. "Sittin' here, full up, jus' talkin', like all of us're th' same." Patrick understood and didn't say anything.

The silence hung for a spell, then Mr. Cuffe broke it. "So where'd you go adventuring? We all spent time wonderin'. Hopin' you hadn't... you know. Passed over."

"You don't have to say," Mrs. Cuffe said. "Jus' we don't get out much, an' like hearin' about people's travels."

Patrick had several versions of his adventures ready. The version he decided on was the short Christian one that didn't exactly lie, it just avoided some areas that might not suit the current congregation. He'd fled south in the yawl he'd taken from Diana Shannon's dock and that night the red-ribboned will that gave Patrick everything went into the flames of the campfire.

Over the next few days, he'd drifted south, slowly forcing what had happened in Vicksburg from his mind. He'd done some casual wood chopping for a riverside farmer, and convinced one of the shanty-boat stores he knew how to cook better than the store's owner, and so kept himself fed until Natchez. He sold the yawl to a black man he'd spotted on the docks, and considered exploring Natchez-Under-The-Bluff to see if his Cousin Michael's advice on Vicksburg-Under-The Hill applied here, as well. But Natchez was too close to Vicksburg. He'd been reminded of that quite sharp and sudden, when he spotted the broadside nailed to the side of a building:

$200 REWARD
RUNAWAY BOY

177

A SNEAK THIEF WHO BETRAYED HIS FAMILY

There was a drawing that Patrick quick guessed was supposed to look like him. It was pretty poor, but the description wasn't far off. Thief, he read on. Who'd stolen his loving mother's jewels and sold them to spend his Ill-Gotten Gains on Drink, Sport and Even Lust. His Tender Years should Not Deceive the Honest Citizen into Thinking that Patrick Shannon was anything other than a Scalawag and Miscreant. He should be Apprehended On Sight and the Apprehender telegraph, instantly or sooner, his Mourning But Determined To See Justice Take Its Course Parents, Edward and Pamela Shannon, Cherry Valley Plantation, Vicksburg.

Patrick found a riverboat and a story to convince the mate to let him book a cabin. It was less the clever story about how he was running away from his dirt-poor but brutal uncle than the mate's lust for the brass telescope his Cousin Joshua had given him, which he said was the only relic his poor dear Daddy, who'd been killed fighting the pirates, had left. Patrick wasn't sure which pirates would've been around ten years or so ago, but neither was the mate. All he knew was the telescope would make the skipper's plug hat and tailcoat shabby funeral garb. That got Patrick a tiny cabin, and in less than an hour the riverboat's great buckets churned brown water, and the packet was headed for New Orleans.

Patrick's story then became complete fiction. In New Orleans, or so he told the Cuffes, he'd encountered a prosperous businessman, to whom he'd eventually poured out his troubles. The businessman, touched, offered the boy a chance to enter his own home in New Orleans and a place in his business - as if Patrick were his own son. The man's wife and children had also taken the young Shannon to their collective bosom. Patrick spent almost a year with this altruistic family before one of New Orleans' terrible fevers carried off the family, and, in mourning, Patrick went west.

The only truth in Patrick's finely-spun tale was he had met a prosperous-looking man in New Orleans and had gone to work for him. But he'd met the man in a riverside coffee house, where Patrick was nursing the dwindling remains of his money and trying to plan what came next.

Latimer was a rum cove, a swindler - one who practiced Vincent's Law. Latimer was a card cheat. Or with anything else he could figure to painlessly separate the vincent from his termage which would preferably be in gold. He sat alone at a small table, well-dressed and gentlemanly-looking, perhaps fifteen years older than Patrick, a barely-touched cup of chicory coffee at his elbow. Nothing moved except Latimer's eyes and his hands, ceaselessly rolling a small silver ball on the tabletop. In front of him were three silver spoons, turned upside down. If it had been a deck of cards the man could have been the twin to the sleek gambler Patrick had seen deal four aces from a fresh deck when he and his family came upriver.

He introduced himself, and asked Patrick if he considered himself a man with a quick eye. Patrick thought of ignoring him, then remembered what his cousin Michael had said about gamblers - that at first they'd let the mark win. He also remembered what Michael had said about always watching the sharper's hands. Maybe he felt confident, maybe he felt desperate, maybe he was just the world's most lonely twelve year old boy. But he allowed himself to be convinced to bet a dollar, and he won, then two dollars, then five, then ten. When the stake was thirty dollars, there was a crowd of men standing around. Latimer asked if he could have one more chance to get even, but Patrick suddenly knew this would be the last round, the round when that silver pea Patrick had no trouble seeing being placed under whichever spoon would suddenly vanish from the ken of man.

He picked up the money, and stood up. "No, thank you, sir." Latimer had been about to say something more, when a bluff man pushed past Patrick. "If y'all are through playin' with infants, I allow I'd appreciate my chance, sir. You git, stripling." Patrick – now thirty dollars richer - got.

Three days later, he was wandering the Quarter. He figured the less time he spent in the minuscule room he'd rented with Latimer's money the longer he could stand its four stained walls. He was trying to build up his courage to find either find a recruiting officer who might think Patrick was older than he looked, or else start haunting the docks and importuning ship's officers, when Latimer saw him, and approached.

"Young man," he said, without preamble, "I wish to thank you. That suidae who was so rude to you, and his equally boorish friends contributed mightily to my purse, largely due to his disbelief that a mere boy could see what he could not. I pocketed four thousand dollars from yesterday's recreation. You did well, although I should tell you that you withdrew a trifle early from our game. With all of those flies swarming to my honeypot, I would have allowed you to walk with up to a hundred dollars, since a mighty sweetener serves my cause well, or, as they might say, in aurus veritas or at least credulity."

Patrick said he had no idea what Mr. Latimer was talking about. Latimer smiled, and offered to buy Patrick a sarsaparilla, or whatever he chose to drink. A chill ran up Patrick's spine. He'd heard of men like Latimer - even seen a couple of them in New Orleans, ankling past the hotel he and his parents were staying in. The gambler evidently guessed what Patrick was thinking. "Not that at all," he said. "I chase the cloven game. Disabuse yourself of that notion. I desire to discuss a matter of business, and of a potential partnership."

Patrick, thinking no harm could come in broad daylight, accompanied Latimer to a cafe. He'd tried a story about how he was at loose ends in this city because his enormously rich father had gone to Vera Cruz on business, and his mother had run away with a senator, and... and Latimer, though smiling politely, was listening to none of it.

When Patrick finished, Latimer nodded in total disbelief, and said, without preamble, "You know, boy, the two of us could make a raft of money together."

That was how Patrick became a gambler's shill. Latimer worked many swindles, but essentially Patrick's role remained the same, to be the credulous young boy, either a city fool or a country bumpkin who always managed to take the smooth gambler, whether at cards, side bets at the dice table, or whatever. Once Patrick provided the setup, and the mark closed in on Latimer, thinking he was a sheep for the shearing, the wolf's fangs would flash. They worked mainly out of New Orleans, although sometimes traveled as far as Baton Rouge and twice to Natchez. They were never exposed, although there were several times they left a hotel or bar by a back window rather than through the main entrance.

Latimer found Patrick a small apartment in the same building he lived in, near The Gem on Royal Street, where New Orleans' finest rum punch was concocted. Patrick, age fourteen, was beginning to wonder why he'd waited so long to run away. Here he was, dressed like a gentleman, living in hotels with maids to clean up after him, eating at fancy restaurants, and all he had to do, once a week or so, was pretend arrant stupidity and greed. The hell with being a clipper ship captain or a brave dragoon. Like his Uncle Michael, he'd settle for this gambling life.

Then someone slashed Latimer's throat.

Patrick had gone to his mentor's apartment to find out how a high-stakes game with other gamblers had turned out. There was no answer to the knock, but the door opened when he tried the handle. Latimer was sprawled in a caneback chair, fully dressed. On the table was a decanter of claret and two clean glasses. A fly buzzed loudly. Latimer's throat had been neatly and, Patrick later learned, professionally, slashed from windpipe to carotid. Blood soaked Latimer's scarf and silk shirt. There was a single card on the table in front of him. The deuce of spades. There were no other cards in sight. Patrick heard shouts from outside. He went to the latticed window. Patrick knew the two men below to be policemen. They were shouting to a patrolling constable further down the street, and pointing up at Patrick's window. The boy didn't stay to see what their specific interest was. He went back to his own room, grabbed the always-packed valise, a coat, his hat and went out the back at the fastest calm, unhurried walk a fourteen-year-old had ever managed.

He was out of New Orleans that night, on a cattleboat heading for Galveston. If the law had questions about the late Mr. Latimer they hadn't pursued him. When sharper or crook vanished from New Orleans, the most that would happen is the local constabulary would log him by name, by alias, and with the inscription: GTT. Gone To Texas. If the villain returned, the matter might be reopened. But not very probably.

Mr. Cuffe, after hearing the sanitized version of Patrick's progress to Texas even the late Doctor Bowdler would have been proud of, asked just what Patrick had done when he got to Texas. Patrick made a business of relighting his pipe. "A little of this, a little of that," he finally said. "All honest work, of course."

"Did y'all ever," Mr. Cuffe's son Abraham, who'd listened in fascinated silence, "run into any of th' freemen from these parts? Whole passel of 'em went to Texas, allowin' things might be freer out there."

Before Patrick could answer, Mr. Cuffe said, somewhat dryly, "Mos' unlikely Patrick'd run int' any of our friends, son. Most folk doin' a little o' this, a little o' that don't truck with other folk who spend time farmin' or goin' to church wi'out much in th' way of money."

Patrick was again reminded of his elaborate charades - played as much for his own amusement as anything else - fooled only a certain percentage of his listeners. A little of this, a little of that had included helping a sutler, cooking again, helping a teamster run supplies to miners working a salted claim, clerking, and a ghastly three days turning bulls into steers.

Patrick, like most other refugees in the new state, spent as little time as he could at honest work, preferring to live by his wits as best he could. Sometimes he used the name Shannon, sometimes other names, depending on what felt right to him. One thing he stayed away from, though, was cards and rigged games. Besides, there was more money to be made, and people didn't usually get so hostile, racing horses. Patrick allowed to Mr. Cuffe he'd been known to accept a friendly wager on which horse might run a furlong or a mile or even four miles fastest.

"Is that where you got that animal you'd prefer everybody think splayfooted?"

"Nossir," Patrick said. "Templar was a gift to me, from a minister I ran across - Ten Gallon Baptist by my recollection - who was up to his... uh, midsection in Mexican bandits, and after I ran the first twenty of them off, firin' high of course so as not to hurt no one, the others retreated across the Rio Grande, and he was so pleased

Allan Cole & Chris Bunch

with me savin' him that he gave me his own Bible, which unfortunately I went and lost just last week crossin' a river, plus this fine horse, which—"

"I just thought I'd try again," Mr. Cuffe said, and they talked of other things for awhile. Patrick was just as happy to not be giving too many details of his adventures. Texas had been... rough. He'd seen whites wanting to kill Mexicans wanting to kill Indians and Indians wanting to kill tejanos, Mexicans and each other. He'd even - he thought - killed a man himself. Patrick had been riding back from a match race below Waco, having taken almost seventy five dollars, mostly in Mexican silver, from a rancher, after a long dry spell of racing horse proud vaqueros for five dollars here, ten dollars there.

It was dark on the brush-hung trail and Patrick, feeling a bit foolish, became apprehensive. A prickling on the back of his neck – not on his thumbs, as the Bard said. He'd unwrapped, loaded and capped his shotgun, and rode on with it across his knees.

Three horsemen burst out of a thicket, shouting. The shotgun came up, Patrick's mind still gasping in shock, and both barrels fired. Horses reared, screamed, and men shouted. Patrick slapped reins across Templar's neck, and the horse exploded through and past the melee. As he rounded a bend, Patrick chanced a look back. He thought he saw, sprawled in the trail's center, a motionless figure. He never reined in, nor went back to make sure, but rode on through the night and never went returned to Waco.

Texas was a bloody land, but there was something out there that held him. Seeing a winter storm blow straight toward him, coming across miles and miles of empty prairie, and him the only rider on that prairie. Seeing a world that went on and on until the eye hurt, wanting relief, wanting to see comfortable horizons, but at the same time not wanting them. The frontier drew - and scared him.

He still wasn't sure what'd brought him back to Mississippi. Maybe it was the war. More likely, it was the ripping pain of the murder had lessened, and he had to pick at the scab. Had to know what, if anything, had happened to the legacy of the Shannons. Or maybe not. Maybe he was just looking for a good horserace.

Allan Cole & Chris Bunch

He came out of his thoughts, aware the Cuffes were also silent.

Finally, Mr. Cuffe cleared his throat, embarrassed. "Guess I best 'fess up, boy," Mr. Cuffe said. 'Cause it won't get easier." It was full dark now.

"To what?"

"Th' letter you sent me? Sayin' you'd be passin' through Vicksburg? I passed word of your arrival up North - the mail appears to be still movin' - to your cousin, Susan." Patrick's comfortable feeling vanished. "Did I do wrong, Patrick?"

Patrick started up, almost the way a yearling buck does, having heard something but not knowing what, ready to bolt but not sure why, then recovered. For over six years now, he'd avoided any contact with any other Shannon, north or south. "Why," he said, voice harsh.

"It 'pears I done wrong," Cuffe said sadly. "An' I do beg forgiveness. But your cousin sent five, maybe six letters down from Phil'delphia over th' years, askin' if we'd heard aught about you."

"We di'n't think," Mrs. Cuffe said, "there'd be harm in it. Not like havin' bus'ness with that other woman."

Patrick knew who she meant - Pamela, his stepmother. He forced calmness - Cuffe was right. There could be no harm from Susan Dolan, nee Shannon. And hadn't he deliberately come back to Vicksburg to get the lay of the land - and of the Shannons?

"You didn't do wrong," Patrick said, not knowing if that was entirely the truth. "I just took a start from the surprise. How is Susan?"

"All well," Cuffe said. "Or, at leas' nothin' bad enough to let on in a letter. Other'n they're bein' troubled by th' Young Widow Shannon. Your stepma? You know, she's up North, and gone to law over that will? Even been plaguin' us with—"

He broke off, confused when he saw how pale Patrick's face had become, and the tears welling up in his eyes. "Patrick? Are you—"

"Shush up, Daniel." That was Mrs. Cuffe. She was suddenly beside Patrick, arm around his shoulders. "You didn't know 'bout your father?" Patrick shook his head. Mr. Cuffe muttered to himself.

"How, uh—"

Allan Cole & Chris Bunch

"Nobody told us, exact. Guess it was some sort of accident."

Patrick found himself on his feet, and walked across the yard to the well. He had never thought he would see his father again. But Edward still was... had been... .his father. Hell. He stood there for a long time. When he came back to himself, the Cuffes had gone to bed.

They'd left a candlestub burning on the porch. He found his way to the pallet laid out in the room Abraham slept in. But he didn't remember getting much sleep that night.

Patrick was planning to get into Vicksburg the next morning, but for some reason he couldn't get himself started. It was sort of like the time he'd taken a bad fall off Templar, and spent some hours walking around and talking to people, or so he was told later, without remembering any part of it. He curried Templar carefully, a job he liked no more now than he had when he was a boy on his father's plantation. The Cuffes left him alone.

Now he was the end of the direct line. Or that was what, he guessed, Grandmother Shannon would have thought. So? So there were other Shannons. A name's a name, and a cousin's as good as blood kin. Hell, Philadelphia was chock full of them, weren't they? Plus there was Michael out in San Francisco, and Joshua up in Massachusetts somewhere. As far as he could tell, with the exception of meeting Diana, being a Shannon had brought him not much more than grief and pain. The hell with it... and with them, as well.

He came back to himself in the late afternoon, and apologized profusely to his hosts. They told him not to behave like a fool. A man was entitled to mourn, wasn't he? He helped Mr. Cuffe with the evening milking, the old man laughing a lot and observing that it was pretty evident that whatever a little of this, a little of that meant in Texas, it more'n obviously didn't include pulling a cow's teats. He'd seen citified Yankees do a better job.

Patrick thought he'd reached some sort of decision - or, at any rate, postponement, on the whole thing about being a Shannon. But his tongue seemed to have a life of its own. "After... after I left," he said, "what happened?"

Mr. Cuffe told him, in a tone as elaborately offhand as Patrick's question, all he knew, which surprisingly enough included Pamela's success with the change of venue, "There wasn't anybody who'd challenge it, with no Shannons, at least none related, left here in Vicksburg. Mr. Levy, the lawyer's heart went on him 'bout then, just after the fire at Missus Shannon's house."

"What about that?"

"Nobody knows. It was mid-winter, an' stormin'. Th' house'd been all boarded up for some time. Maybe tramps. Maybe lightnin'. All us coloreds, when we saw th' flames, run to see if there was anything to do. Way, way too late then. Terrible shame. Th' gates of the river were opened, and that great palace was dissolved." Patrick waited, but Mr. Cuffe said no more.

"You goin' to join up, Patrick?" Mrs. Cuffe asked, elaborately casual, over the coffee.

"No ma'am, I don't have much truck with politics."

"You will, Patrick," Mr. Cuffe put in softly. "You will have to. Because like it says, through the wrath of the Lord the land's darkened, an' the people shall be as the wrath of the fire. No man shall spare his brother."

"No. Not me," Patrick said. "Besides, it'll be over right quick, I expect."

"An' who d' you expect'll be winning?"

"Why... us. I mean... the South. Ain't no way I can see Yankee factory workers can stand up to men who already come to battle knowing how to ride and shoot."

Mr. Cuffe's wife answered. "No, Mr. Shannon. That's not what'll come to pass. Because like th' Book promises, there'll come th' Year of Jubilee. It took fifty times fifty... but it's comin'. An' I mind it mos' clear in my heart."

The room was silent, except for a crackle of wood from inside the stove. "P'raps we'd best talk 'bout other things," Mr. Cuffe said, finally.

Patrick was up before dawn. He drew water from the well and, shivering, bathed. Then he put on his city finery, not forgetting to

186

load his pocket pistol and cap four of the five cylinders. Patrick saddled Templar, and packed his duffle. "You know," he said, quietly, "you run 'em under in Vicksburg, we'll think about getting a packhorse for you. Let somebody else do the hauling, hey?"

Templar nuzzled his shoulder. Patrick was ready. He tied Templar to the porch railing, and sat down to wait. One thing he liked was rising early, and seeing the sun come up, although there'd been times he'd seen it through eyes redder than any sunrise. As light flooded across the yard, Mr. Cuffe came out, yawning. "Good morrow, Patrick."

"Mornin' sir."

"You're not staying for breakfast?"

"Nossir. Like to get my traveling in before it gets too hot. Also give me a chance to spy out the land early." He stood up, and stuck out his hand. Cuffe took it.

"You ride careful," he advised. "An' be wary. As I said last night, there's terrible times comin'. We'll all need th' wiles God give us to see us through."

"I plan on trying to stay out of the line of fire, sir. But thanks for the warning."

"I was givin' it to me as much as you, son. Now, you come back. Anytime." Patrick swung up into the saddle. "You want t' say how you really got that horse?"

"Surely, sir. Not many people know it, but General Sam Houston has a truly beautiful granddaughter. Seems she was out ridin' outside Austin one day, on Templar here, which was her most prized mount. She hadn't heard there was a Comanche war party out. Just as a matter of chance, it happened that I was passing—"

A laugh. "Go with God, boy."

Patrick turned Templar, and headed him out the gate. Daniel Cuffe watched until the young man was but a dot on the dusty track toward Vicksburg.

CHAPTER FIFTEEN

VICKSBURG - LATE JULY, 1861

PATRICK HEARD THE thunder before he saw anything. Then the horse rounded the bend ahead of him at full gallop. Its rider was a small black, and he rode near-standing in the stirrups of the tiny saddle. The horse was brown, with a blaze face.

A smile flashed across Patrick's lips as quickly as his hand went inside his vest and his gold hunter came out, its cover snapped open. He glanced behind him... estimated the stretch of the open road behind... just over a mile... counting... as the horse galloped toward him and past. Patrick spun in his saddle, still counting. About... there should be a mile, he thought, waiting, counting seconds.

Now, he thought, as the horse crossed the imaginary marking point. Oh mercy, he thought. Just under two minutes. What a gorgeous horse. But the rider was using a crop, which suggested Patrick was seeing a time close to the animal's best.

Patrick cantered off after the racing mare. It was almost another mile before he came up on the horse, now being walked after its workout by the jockey. "Mornin'," Patrick said, cordially. The black - and Patrick now saw he was not young, just very small - knuckled his forehead.

"Mornin, massah."

"You ride well."

"Thanks, massah."

"Who's the mare belong to?"

"Her... an' me... we belongs Marse Thomas. Marse Hami'ton Thomas. F'm Vicksburg. Marse Thomas' named her S'ciety."

"You know the mare's bloodlines, by chance?"

"Marse tol' me she's pure lineage f'm Peytona, horse f'm th' ol'en days, down outen Mobile, he tol' me."

"How interestin'," Patrick said. He dug a coin from his pocket, and tossed it to the slave. "I assume your master's a sportin' man?"

"Oh yassah, yassah. Nothin' he likes better'n wagerin' an' all."

"A true gentleman," Patrick said, mostly to himself. Then, to the jockey: "If a man wished converse with the good Mister Thomas, where'd he find him?"

"Right now... in town. He'll be at th' Washington, that's one th'—"

"I know the hotel," Patrick said. It was where Fitz Maguire had stayed when he conspired with Pamela and his father to destroy the Shannons. "I'll find him there. Thanks."

The black ducked his head once more, and Patrick turned back toward Vicksburg. The settlement hung like the Golden City, full of promise.

Patrick rode into Vicksburg, following the track that became Washington Street, the city's main thoroughfare. Vicksburg had grown since he'd seen it six years ago - or maybe his eye was better now. No, he decided, it was a lot bigger: new houses, businesses, a long line of new warehouses along the river. Everything looked new and prosperous. Even the street was graveled. He hailed a man lounging against a storefront. "Pardon, sir?"

"Yeah." Disinterest.

"Did they redo the Courthouse since I was here last?"

"Redo it? Whole damn' thing's new, four years ago."

"You can see the tower clock from way out here."

"Three more of 'em," the loiterer said. "One t'each side of th' thing. An' it's got col'ms like some kinda Greek temple."

"Impressive."

"Some say." The idler grunted, spat, and muttered something remarkably like 'shee-yit.'

"What's the matter with it?" Patrick wondered. "I ain't seen nothin' near as pretty in all Texas. Have to go to New Orleans to find an equal."

"You still feel that, knowin' a nigger built it?"

"What?"

"City went an' hired th' goddamned Weldon niggerlovers to put it up. They went an' let one a' their slaves draw th' plans. Slap in th' face f'r anybody white. Should'a run 'em out f'r abolitionists. A'ter burnin' that uppity nigger." The man spat once more, evidently concluded the conversation was over, and stalked off, up a dirt alley.

A yellowed handbill, or maybe a newspaper clipping tacked to a hoarding caught Patrick's eye. He leaned over from the saddle, and

189

read from the weathered fragments: "the duty of patriots at this crisis... follow the destiny of the State... abide its fate... for weal or woe... We are Mississippians... not for any citizen of the State... to set himself against the ACT of the State... we too take our position... .ready to defend her rights and to share her fate..."

Patrick noticed a handwritten poster in the window of the shop the idler been leaning against:

Our Stock of Mourning Goods Has Never
Been So Complete. We Feature Black Organdie,
Black Silk Grenadine, Black Mosambique, Black
Silk Mitts, Black Kid Gloves, Black Lace Veils.
Patrick tapped Templar's reins, and rode on.

A freight wagon had overturned just above the City Landing, so Patrick dismounted to let the shouts, curses and whinnyings sort themselves out.

"Help the cause, sir?" A young woman stood on the board pavement. She wore lace, crinoline, gloves and a bonnet, neatly framing her froth of brown curls. She carried, over one shoulder, a rather redundant parasol to keep what little of the sun's rays that could get close from daring to darken her pure white skin. She was, Patrick thought, about sixteen. And beautiful.

He immediately swept off his top hat and bowed deeply. "Of course, ma'am. I stand ready to help any cause, especially one held dear by such a beautiful example of Vicksburg's womanhood as you. But as a newcomer to the city, one who has traveled far and is weary with the dust of the road, I must ask: what cause? The Home For Wayward Banshees, perhaps? Or The Society To Protect Alligators From Steamboats? The Vicksburg Association To Help Heal Suddenly Broken Hearts Who've Fallen In Love At First Sight? Not that I mark the difference, having an equal love for them all."

She giggled. "I mean the Cause."

"Ah yes. The Cause." Patrick dug into his pocket, and took out a few pieces of change. "Now which of the Coins does the Cause merit? Being a stranger in these parts."

The small gloved hand scooped all the coins up. "How bold," Patrick said, pretending shock. "Young miss, does your mother

190

know you are out and about, confronting strange men on public streets? I mean, you have no idea who I am. I might be a river pirate. A rakehelly gambler. Even, dare I whisper it, a spy? No. Not a spy. Spies wear black. That's why they only come out at night. They'd fry in this heat."

"Of course my mother knows I do this. She's in the Ladies Military Association, too."

"Of course! That is the Cause. Now I know everything. Except your name. I, highting like they do in Walter Scott, hight Patrick Shannon." He bowed again.

"I'm not supposed to be this informal," the young woman announced. "But I'm Lucy Baldwin."

"A delightful hight," Patrick said. "And what do you do, besides jeopardize your health, beauty and sanity by accosting strangers?"

"I go to school."

"School. Where they stand up and recite things like..." and here Patrick began talking through his nose, trying to sound as much like a Yankee as possible, quoting from vague memory, "'... republicans must find/In manners simple, and in speech sincere/In meet endeavors to...' oh blazes, I forgot what you're supposed to endeavor to. Great endeavors, I guess."

Patrick realized he was babbling a bit, but also realized talking to a horse can only go so far to alleviate loneliness. And Lucy was very beautiful.

"Of course not," she said. "I go to Warren Female Academy. We study Geography, Grammar, Rhetoric, Botany, Pure Mathematics and Ancient and Modern Languages."

"Ay, caramba," Patrick said in his best - fairly poor - border Spanish. "la senorita es un grande cerebro, y es muy, muy hermosa tambien."

"I don't know what you said," Lucy said, a little suspiciously, "but I hope you aren't making fun of me."

"Miss Lucy," Patrick said, solemn-faced, "I never, ever make fun when I've just fallen in love."

She looked him over carefully, then smiled. "Are you going to enlist?"

Allan Cole & Chris Bunch

Patrick thought quite rapidly. "Well, I have considered it, but I want to make sure I join the proper regiment. I mean, it'd be awful to take the colors and then spend the whole war in some barracks somewhere. To dream of sabers and end up with a mop? A true Southerner would have to kill himself if that happened. Maybe by falling on his mop? I want to be where I do the most good for the Cause."Again, Lucy's smile vanished. "You have been making fun of me. And that's not nice. You're just another of those, aren't you? Good day, sir."

She swept off, her exit marred a bit by almost stepping in a horseturd as she made her way across Grove Street. Patrick stared after her. Lucy Baldwin was, he decided, incredibly, amazingly beautiful. The question was, who or what were those? Oh well.

As he turned to mount a rather round passerby wearing astonishing sidewhiskers, a terrible checked vest, and baggy brown pants and coat addressed him: "Y'all shall find, good sir, around Vicksburg that question'll be asked you a lot, by others than Miss Baldwin."

"Guess I better find a better answer than the one I came up with," Patrick said, determined not to lose his temper at the eavesdropper - especially since he seemed to know something about the gorgeous Miss Lucy.

"You could just go ahead an' join up. The South needs men like you. And horses like yours."

Patrick, having heard tales of the army requisitioning mounts, shook his head. "This fleabag? Sir, I admire you as a gentleman, but you have no eye for horseflesh. Damn' beast's one step away from the knacker's yard. Show you." He clucked quietly twice, then led the horse forward. Obediently, Templar went lame, but kept moving bravely, as if used to the affliction.

The man laughed loudly, as if he'd just witnessed the most amazing circus act. "Congratulations, sir. My heartiest congratulations, if for no other reason than you have proven my powers of observation to still be potent. If you have a moment, sir, I'd be pleased to make your acquaintance. Here. Care for a cigar? Cuban, they are. Name's Kelly, sir. David C. Kelly. Captain now, by

Allan Cole & Chris Bunch

the grace of the Lord Jesus Christ, Colonel Nathan Bedford Forrest, and the Confederate States of America."

Patrick hesitated, then, curious, followed the man over to the covered sidewalk. He tied Templar to a post, and sat down on one of the few unoccupied benches along the walk. He accepted the cigar, bit the end off, and lit it from the wooden Lucifer Kelly was holding out.

"Thank you, Captain Kelly. Am I correct in believing you know that angel who's found me a craven knave?"

"I do. Her father's a merchant. The family's got a big house, up on the hill. But she... and the family... are no better than they ought to be. Don't hold with slaves, they don't. Use white folks for servants. Some thought, back some months, Baldwin was Secesh. But he's given handsome to the Artillery Company. Guess it takes all kinds."

Patrick again held his tongue. He was smoking the man's cigar, after all, and it was a very good one. "Yes, indeed, I've only seen but one other horse that could mock a limp that clever," Kelly went on. "Man who owned him made passels of money, yes I say passels, letting other horsemen find out a sleek coat and strong features do not make an equally strong time when the trumpet's blown."

"Is that right, sir?"

"It is, indeed. His camouflage of that four-legged fireship was not impaired by the fact he most deliberately failed to curry either his horse's mane or tail. Something which you, no doubt, have merely neglected, in your journeying from..."

"Texas, sir. Patrick Shannon, at your service."

"A state I have never been fortunate enough to visit. And now, with my duties, one which it shall be equally unvisited for another long spell."

"Your duties, sir?"

"I am a fisher for men. Formerly in the service of the Lord Jesus Christ, but now, during this Emergency, for the honorable Colonel Forrest. Once a pastor, now a recruiter, sir, and one especially interested in signing a fellow Hibernian to the Cause, the South needing more warriors in the tradition of Finn and Ossian. Are you related to the newspaper Shannons?"

Allan Cole & Chris Bunch

"I do not have that honor."

"That's as well. Even though the man's sons have enlisted, I still suspect him of being co-operationist, in spite of his now-fiery editorials. But to the subject at hand. First, though, to satisfy my curiosity. Did you happen to acquire that fine mount from a gentleman named Herron?"

"Nossir," Patrick said. "He was a gift from my late father."

"Thank you for satisfying my curiosity. Now, my question: have you ever considered enlistment? I could offer you quite a bargain. Colonel Forrest is a fire eater. A man who's determined to take those bluebellies by the throat, and shake them into pieces. He promises a chance to fight a real war, assuming you were telling a bit of the truth to the young lady, about not wanting to languish in some rear area when better men go out onto the field of battle. Best of all, you'd be joining the cavalry. I've already raised five companies, nearly five hundred men, with the prospects of three more. All of them are brave boys from Alabama, Kentucky, Texas or Tennessee, none waverers, sir. Colonel Forrest promises a heap of fun, and a chance to kill as many Yankees as you can." Patrick considered his prospective answer, while Kelly kept talking.

"The battalion will have the best of food, the best of weapons, supplies and uniforms. Colonel Forrest has made over a million dollars as a trader and planter. I cannot promise you a band or dance on Saturday night as some battalions boast, but I can promise you will be in the forefront of the fight to save our beloved South. Plus, sir, plus, and I must lower my voice, I can offer you good hard specie. In U.S. dollars, if you wish. The city of Vicksburg will provide three hundred dollars. I'll add another hundred on top of that. Now, you must admit that is handsome. Don't you, sir?"

"That's most generous, Captain," Patrick said, picking his words carefully. "But I could not take advantage of the offer. Three hundred dollars, it was? I do have business to contract here in Vicksburg, however."

Kelly looked at him shrewdly. "The first time the Lord called onto Jonah to go unto Ninevah and preach a warning it was in a gentle tongue, my boy. The next summons was a great tempest. Once Jonah was called, there could be no turning away. I do not

194

know whether you are religious, Patrick Shannon. But you must hear the holy call of the South against the Canaanites of the north. They mean to come on us with fire and the sword, and it is our sacred duty to stand against them, to protect our women, our children, and our way of life against them. Consider my parable, and here, take my card. I'm currently residing across the river, in Louisiana, with Doctor Young. I shall be there for the remainder of the week. I would be delighted to welcome you to the colors, Mister Shannon. Good day."

Captain Kelly strode away, or rather waddled with the rather satisfied air of a minister who's fed quite well on someone else's fresh-butchered hog. Patrick admired his simile, then realized it was his belly being creative. Perhaps he could take care of two kinds of business at once.

He started to toss Kelly's card away, then thought better. If anyone accused him of being somewhat less than willing to become a Knight of the Confederacy - he could swear that he'd already had dealings with Captain Kelly and this Forrest Bedford or whoever he was.

Perhaps he might run into Miss Baldwin and try that on her. He tucked the card into his vest pocket.

"Oyster-pie... there's never been a better oyster-pie in all Vicksburg!" Mister MacMeehan's appearance, rather than his spiel on this sweaty July noon, was the best advertisement for his hotel's wares. He oozed fat in all directions. Not aimless poundage gained from eating anything and everything that wandered within range, but dedicated fat that the Washington Hotel's owner knew not only how to eat, but when to eat, and you were a perfect damned fool if you didn't follow him through at least three helpings.

"Now, here's a goose that any woman would be proud to serve for Christmas," he went on. "Look at it, sitting there sizzling. How could anyone not want to sink his teeth into it? Goose, roast goose, with wild rice stuffing. Won't see that again until we've beat the Yanks, I vow. And the dressing! Applesauce, by Harry. You can't find a better morsel than a slice of goose with applesauce!"

Allan Cole & Chris Bunch

Patrick marveled anyone could shout that loudly, that clearly, and that lengthily. He caught a waiter's arm. "I'm looking for a gentleman named Thomas? Hamilton Thomas, I believe it is."

"O'er theah. By th' winder." Patrick noted the table, then wended his way toward it. The dining room of the Washington Hotel was packed, so evidently Mister MacMeehan's boasts were believed by the well-to-do of Vicksburg. About half of men at the tables were wearing uniform, some wearing officers' livery, others privates' garb. Others wore planters' linen or businessmen's suits. The women were as finely dressed as their companions.

Mister Hamilton Thomas was sitting at a table with six other men. There were two seats unoccupied. Patrick had deliberately waited outside the dining room until he'd seen, through the cut-glass windows in the doors, there were no completely empty tables.

"Your pardon, sir," Patrick said. "But all tables appear occupied. Would my presence here at yours be objectionable?"

Thomas gave Patrick a quick glance. Frock coat, vest, fine shirt, a little rumpled, but certainly a gentleman. "Be welcome, sir." Patrick nodded thanks, and slipped into a seat.

Hamilton Thomas wore fawn trousers and vest, a fine broadcloth shirt, a neckcloth that appeared to be silk, and a short jacket. He was about thirty years old. Thomas and his friends continued their chatter. They were drinking cobblers - two jiggers of brandy over shaved ice, a little sugar water and three orange slices - and from their flush and the volume they were not on their first round.

Patrick, pretending interest in the room around him and Mister MacMeehan's ballyhooing, listened closely. His expression suggested mild amusement and even more mild interest in the world about him. In five minutes, Patrick knew his prey as if he'd hunted him half a lifetime. The world of these men was circumscribed by horses, dogs, hunting, lesser beings and women. In that order. Not that they had any real knowledge of the five, but that had little to do with their ability to hold forth, hour after hour, on the subjects.

He mentally added a sixth category that would be part of their culture in the future: soldiering. For colloquy they substituted humorless laughter; for repartee, catchphrases; for original thought, consensus; and for cleverness alcohol. In short, they were the Flower of the South.

Patrick got a waiter's ear, ordered a slice of the goose, dressing, coleslaw and coffee, then went back to listening to Thomas and his friends:

"... held his point, and as I'm damned, up came two brace of..."

"... out of Virginia, a veritable stallion I was assured, and I paid in gold, but damned if all the wenches I've bred him to don't birth nigger tiny tims. Until we open up the trade to Africa once more, we'll all have these wretched, sickly..."

"... after all, she is a widow, and used to being serviced. I had no choice, since they burnt Mollie Bunch and her girls out of town. So I left my carriage back of the stables, not wanting the embarrassment, and..."

"... of course they ran at Manassas, Alfred. How can you hope to build an army out of the gutterscrapings of Europe to stand against our boys who've been raised since birth as..."

Patrick noted none of Mister Thomas' friends wore uniform. Then his direct target spoke: "... Oats, chaff, mash, preferably spent mash from your still, sir, and salt. No carrots, no sugar, no bread, and you have a horse that would leave Lexington in the dust. I would put my land, my birthright and all the gold I have on that. That's why Society is what she is, sir..."

That was Patrick's opening but he said nothing, merely ostentatiously raised an eyebrow, then turned to accept his plate as the waiter arrived. Thomas, as intended, caught Patrick's look.

"Excuse me, sir? For some reason you seem to feel what I just said to be wrong, or foolish. Am I correct?"

Patrick knew he'd best walk carefully. The man was an instant hothead. "I think nothing of the kind, sir," he answered. "But you used the word Society? Are you the owner of that fine animal?"

"Clever man," Thomas said. "Only all of Mississippi knows that. Of course I am."

"Forgive me," Patrick said. "I did not know that... I only arrived in this great city two hours ago. But I saw a horse this morning on the road below the city, and stopped its rider to enquire about the

197

animal. One of the... well, not most, but more impressive beasts I've seen.

Thomas grudged thanks, then said "I do not see what my ownership of Society and your look have in common."

"Merely," Patrick said, "that I wondered how a horse that ran as quickly as Society could manage on such a diet. My poor animal, which of course doesn't have nearly the lineage of yours, would wither away. Or else founder much beyond a mile. Is Society just a sprinter, then?"

"By the Lord Harry," one of Thomas' friends near-shouted. "Society'll run the length and never think she's warmed up."

"Most curious," Patrick said, and cut a bite of goose. "It must be in the breeding."

"You said you have a horse, sir. May I inquire as to particulars?"

"I do. A four year old. I have no knowledge of his bloodline, unfortunately. I acquired him as payment from a bankrupt debtor, who was certainly no gentleman. But for some reason the damned animal loves to run. I feed him on oats, as do you. But I add mash soaked in wine. And, a few hours after the race, a toothsome morsel or such. He seems to relish such rewards, and runs all the harder."

"What times?"

"The best thus far, over four miles, was just at 7:45. But I suspect my watch needed repair."

"Seven-forty-five," Thomas grunted in complete disbelief. "That time rivals Boston!"

"I know," Patrick said, nodding. "As I said, my watch needed repair."

Thomas knocked back his cobbler and motioned for another round. "What brings you to Vicksburg, sir? You said you were not a native."

"Pleasure," Patrick said. "I intend, eventually, to return to my parent's plantation in Virginia. But I am in no hurry. Why do you ask?"

"I would dearly love to see this wonder bullet of yours run. Are you planning any matches?"

"I had not. I have only just arrived in the city. Are you suggesting you might wish to try Society against my poor halfbreed?"

"Not for pleasure, sir. Nor for glory."

"I see," Patrick said. "What sort of stakes do you have in mind?"

"Hard specie only. I disbelieve in notes or promises."

"Since I only deal with men of honor," Patrick said, "I have no such qualms. But such an arrangement is quite acceptable to me. To repeat - what sort of stakes?"

He was enjoying himself, as was Thomas in a grinding, malevolent sort of way. From here, each question and response was as formal as if it were part of a code duello, which, in a way, it was.

"I think," Thomas said, "that I am capable of matching any stake you could name."

Patrick reddened a little, but caught himself. "Perhaps... five hundred dollars," he said.

Thomas blinked. "I, uh... very well. But I shall have to visit my bank, first."

Patrick kept from smiling - Southern gentleman sounded rich and looked the same. But almost without exception they were land-poor, beggared by their debts for seed and slaves, and what little cash they could come upon would go to buy luxuries from England. "Very well," he said.

"Would you accept my friend, Farley, here, as stakes holder?"

Patrick didn't like this, but knowing no one in the city but a free black, and having a passing idea neither Miss Baldwin nor the recently-unfrocked Captain Kelly would volunteer, had little choice. "I accept."

"Play or pay," Thomas said.

Patrick considered. That meant that if there was a forfeiture, for any reason, the other party would automatically win. Thomas was not only a Southerner, but a plunger, to boot. "Agreed," Patrick said once more. "To keep it simple - one heat and a distance of four miles, since that is the distance discussed. Acceptable?" Thomas nodded. "When shall we meet? Dusk, perhaps, after the heat settles?"

Allan Cole & Chris Bunch

"Good," Thomas approved. "I like to run in the open. Milldale Road, north of Vicksburg, is tolerable straight and unrutted. Do you know it?"

"I can find it," Patrick said. And so it went, bargaining from weights to the start, each of them trying to secure the slightest advantage, but finally the fencing was over. Five hundred dollars would become a thousand dollars... Patrick's dream of Vicksburg as a Golden City appeared a true vision.

Patrick sensed trouble as the sun inched its way out of sight, and the heat grew bearable along the dusty road. There were at least fifty bloods waiting for the race, and all of them seemed to have spent the afternoon lubricating themselves against the weather. The starter, who'd been introduced to him as a Captain Travis, was no more sober than the rest. It would be Us against Them. Correction, Him. But this sort of trouble was hardly new. Patrick determined he'd collect his winnings as rapidly as possible, offer to buy drinks at, perhaps, the Prentiss or Commercial Hotels, then somehow lose his way.

He tentatively thought his next target would be Jackson - state capitals normally collected fools with money. He caught himself. Yes. All he had to do was catch the bear, and then a fine stew would certainly be his. A minor point.

There was a cheer as three horses came down the country lane. One of them was Society, and was ridden by the small black man. Patrick smiled - this wasn't unexpected, since he'd noted Mister Thomas clearly avoided saying whether he would be riding his own horse or not. The other two riders were Thomas and his friend, the stakeholder, Farley. They dismounted and walked up to Patrick.

"Good evening," Thomas said, cordially enough. "Are we ready to have a go?"

Patrick nodded. He took the wallet containing his five hundred dollars, leaving him with the sum of $23.75, of which almost all was in script, and passed it to Farley.

"I need not count it," that man said. "Assuming that everyone here is a gentleman."

Allan Cole & Chris Bunch

How courtly, Patrick thought. He never ceased to be amazed at how easily terms like honor and civility came off these men's tongues, and how little it was in fact honored.

Someone in Laredo - a transplanted Irisher, of course - had told him these gentlemen learned their manners from the British, who also paid no real heed to etiquette, let alone true courtesy. He said nothing.

Farley eyed him. "You're satisfied with the arrangements," Farley continued.

"I am, sir."

"Unusual," Farley said, "there are some who might object to riding against a blackamoor."

Patrick once more chose not to comment, but made a final check on Templar's cinch, ensured his stirrups were properly shortened, then mounted. There was another cheer. Captain Travis moved to the center of the lane. Patrick walked Templar back a couple of dozen yards, and turned his horse. Society was just behind him.

"Name's Patrick," he said cordially to the jockey.

The slave gaped, astonished a white man had volunteered anything other than an order, then painted on a smile. "Ah'm Neptune. A'ter th' packet, marse." Some slaveholders thought it clever to name their possessions after steamboats, horses, or even geographical features.

The horses walked toward the line slowly. Captain Travis held his hat overhead. Lap and tap... assuming the two horses were even at the line, the starter would "tap" them away, by dropping his hat.

Now there was no courtesy - both Neptune and Patrick maneuvered for a slight advantage. Slight was the word, because if one horse was too much in front, the start would not be allowed. In a long race like this one, getting the break was not as important - but Society was too fast a mare to take any chances.

A foot from the line, Neptune dug his heels into Society's flanks and rose in his stirrups. The horse went off like a cannon, nearly bounding past Travis as the hat came down...

Bad start, should be disqualified, but to be expected... and Patrick was up in his stirrups, leaning forward over Templar's neck, muttering, words not thought, not hearing the bellows and the cheers as they were past the knot of spectators, dust boiling up, Neptune pulling away by a length.

Coming up on first mile, give it just under two minutes, Society two lengths ahead of him......Closing in on second mile, Patrick seeing Neptune now working the bat... a length away... call it well under two minutes......Up on him now, trying to pass, Neptune moving Society over, blocking, Templar changing direction in mid drive, going to the left of Thomas' mare, pulling up... crop coming back, catching Templar on the cheek, Patrick feeling the flinch, flinching himself, foul but never to be called...

"Come on, horse, come on," a steady mutter, never saw the three mile, horses even, and Templar caught his stride and took it on home, hooves crashing cannonfire, dust cascading like a packet's wash... ahead... one length, two, two and a half, and... Dimly seen someone waving a kerchief and it was four miles.

Patrick let Templar run himself out, then gently brought him back. He met Neptune and Society, and the black would not meet his eyes. So, the slash had not been an accident. A excited man at roadside was shouting, "by Christ, but your animal is a goer, sir! I have it at under eight, sir! Under eight! I'd be proud to buy you a drink back in town."

"And I'd be pleased to accept."

He tapped Templar into a trot - the horse seemed as unfazed by the run as always. Patrick may have had a friend at the finish, but there were none at the start. Thomas and his angry companions were in a growling knot in the middle of the road. Patrick dismounted, and walked Templar toward them.

"That's a ringer, God damn it!"

"I beg your pardon, sir?" Patrick, trying to stay calm, picked up his possibles and saddlebags from where he'd left them and lashed them back on Templar.

"That horse of yours is a champion, a full breed," Thomas snarled. "And you used deceit, sir, deceit to cozen me into this race."

"I did not know cleverness in racing could ever be termed deceit," Patrick retorted. "And I also thought Vicksburg gentlemen knew how to lose with grace."

"Not when we're cheated." That was Farley.

Allan Cole & Chris Bunch

"You owe me five hundred dollars."

"Try and collect it."

Patrick should have shut up, and asked for his stake back. Instead, the Shannon temper flared: "Then you are the cheat, sir. You and your flapping-mouth friend. A pig, a liar and a cheat."

"You will meet me for that."

A cold shiver went through Patrick. The joke was that meant pistols for two and coffee for one, over on DeSoto Peninsula. But it was not a joke at all, as Patrick remembered six years ago on that same ground and the lives of the entire Shannon family exploding with the gunshots.

"I shall not," he said firmly. "You will return my money, or I shall ride into Vicksburg and swear charges against you as a common thief."

Thomas' open hand came back, then forward, meeting Patrick's blocking arm and Patrick's hard-driven fist slammed out, sending the older and heavier man sprawling. That was it. The South tolerated all blood and violence - but the laying on of hands put him down as a commoner, beyond the pale. Now any and all retributive measures would be acceptable, even to a court of law.

Before Thomas could pick himself up, Patrick swung up into the saddle, and shouted "Go!," sending Templar leaping forward, through the men. "Come on, my friend," he said, burying his face in Templar's shaggy mane. "You've had to do it before... you'll have to do it-" LASH-CRACK. It was a pistol ball, going past, somewhere overhead. Christ, the bastards were serious. He chanced a glance behind him, and saw men mounting, and horses galloping after him.

A side road led to the left, back toward the city and the river, and Patrick guided Templar into it. They wouldn't - couldn't - catch him. Not now. Patrick knew this matter would not be forgotten even after these "gentlemen" sobered up and cooled off. He ran through his choices as quickly as Templar pelted down the dark, twisting near-path: keep moving for another city - with no stake, and not enough to feed himself and Templar for more than a day or two. Go to ground at Mister Cuffe's. That was an excellent thought, he jeered to himself. Here you are, a man of violence, for so they'll name you, going to a free black man. That could well produce a mob, if you're seen in the passage. Patrick shivered, knowing that in these times of trouble, he would be seen.

Perhaps... and his hand flashed from the reins to his vest pocket, and felt the reassurance of that calling card. Captain Kelly? That was an interesting option. He had mentioned hard currency - three hundred dollars, it was.

The ferry across into Louisiana ran every half hour. Patrick determined to seek out Captain Kelly. Not that he had any intention of enlisting in any army. But any man who could so lightly speak of handing out three hundred dollars might well be someone to befriend.

Allan Cole & Chris Bunch

CHAPTER SIXTEEN

PHILADELPHIA - AUGUST 4, 1861

MARY NODDED AS the priest spoke, although his words were a jumble of nonsense in her ears. She smelled the sacramental wine on his breath and it made her nervous stomach tremble. His face wavered and she quickly moved her eyes to the tabernacle on the altar behind him. This is stupid, she thought. I am not the fainting type.

The tabernacle seemed to tilt forward and Mary shut her eyes, hoping the priest wouldn't notice them behind the gauze veil. She took a firm hold of her nerves. I will not, she thought, be remembered as the bride who got sick on the floor of Saint Patrick's Church. I am Mary Cassidy, she thought. A graduate of Mount Saint Joseph's Academy. A teacher and model of behavior for many impressionable young ladies. Soon I will be Mary Dolan, Mrs. Hugh Dolan, to be exact. The newest member of the Shannon clan.

She felt the comfort of Hugh's hand clasping her own and opened her eyes. Hugh's fingers tightened - as if to offer strength. Mary noted with surprise his hand was moist and quivering with fear and the tightening of his grip was to borrow strength from her. Mary had to bite her lip to keep from giggling.

If her brave soldier was as frightened as she, they were both doomed to embarrassment before this ceremony was over. Somehow this notion calmed her. Very well, if responsibility had to be taken - she would take it. The ceremony had already been a long one and if the priest had any sense at all, it was only going to get longer.

The priest made blessing motions and took three steps to the side. Again a jumble of Latin spewed forth as he began praying for the soon to be entwined souls of the second couple.

It was a double wedding. Mary found a part of herself watching the unusual event along with the rest of the crowd. Saint Patrick's was crammed with the Shannon clan, here on the first Sunday of the month to see the sons of Ian and Susan Dolan marry before setting off to fight the rebels. Hugh Dolan and his younger brother Kerry, were resplendent in their uniforms of the Hibernian Target Shooters. Both young men were ramrod straight: Hugh with his tall, dark good looks; and Kerry, smaller, but quick and wiry, with fine pale hair. They both sported clean-shaven chins, but luxurious side whiskers.

On Kerry's arm, in white velvet and lace picked out in pinprick white buds, was his bride, Nancy O'Neil. Golden hair peeked from under the veil. Woven into her coiffure was a wreath of orange blossoms. She was a factory girl and from a poor family, but they were respectable people and didn't Nancy have a fine, parish education - the equal of any woman in the room excepting Mary?

And there was Mary Cassidy, herself - dark as Hugh, but slender and willowy (she'd despaired of ever being able to gain the weight necessary to be truly fashionable) in a gown that was the lovely twin of Nancy's. They'd agreed on this to not compete with the other and Susan had employed the swiftest and most skilled dress makers in Kensington.

Ian and Susan were paying for the double wedding - paying handsomely if the sincerity of the priest's tone and richness of the incense were any hint. In a way it was a triple wedding for them. Mary was a foundling, taken in and raised by Susan as if she were her own daughter; and since Mary had no father Ian was giving her away.

The priest moved to a spot between the two couples, his hands came up, his eyes lifted to the ceiling, and he began yet another prayer. Parish school training took over and Mary locked her knees into that old position schoolgirls learned would be comfortable, but not invite the bite of a switch from a patrolling nun.

Joshua Shannon watched Ian wipe away a tear. This was a happier occasion than the last time the family had come together. But a little of the Vicksburg pall remained, for the militia uniforms of the Dolan lads made him wonder what his grandmother would have made of these times. After all war had cost her, would she say this one was worth fighting? Joshua knew the answer as soon as he'd thought the question: She would have said worth had nothing to do with the argument. That this was tragic and stupid because the whole thing could have been avoided if men weren't so greedy, and cowards as well.

Ian coughed loudly to cover emotion and Joshua saw tears flooding down Susan's cheeks into a sodden kerchief. Joshua imagined well their feelings, especially with his own son Donald, beside him. It was the shock of awareness that their sons were full men now, and shouldering the burdens of the world. Not just marriage - he looked at Donald, who would soon trade the frock coat and crisp breeches he was wearing for a midshipman's uniform.

A bit of panic tugged his heart when he plainly saw how young Donald was. Just seventeen with a long pony's face, eyes wide and pale blue, frame strong, but gangly because it was not filled in. He had a smudge on his upper lip where he was attempting to grow a mustache. At least Ian's boys were in their twenties - Hugh, was oldest at twenty two, and Kerry was just turned twenty. Joshua thought Donald was too young to fight, but the boy had made his mind up. Joshua was too aware of the wild Shannon go-to-hell streak to deny him. Donald would have just run off - like Patrick, Joshua's own father Luke, and many another Shannon lad, all the way back to Emmett.

Fortunately Joshua was a man who commanded great respect in Marblehead. He'd made a tidy bundle in steamships, traveled to England and done even better there. Now he was retired, a man local politicians fawned over. Joshua didn't like any member of that crew, but realized they were a necessity to navigate the dangerous shoals of a life on land. So Joshua had traded a few favors, and won Donald appointment as a midshipman.

Prudence had not been pleased. In fact, his wife was a most unhappy woman. She had every reason to be so. Besides her son, the war had also roped in her husband. Joshua was off to Washington, determined not to sit this one out. His grandmother had been right - the whole thing could have been avoided. But that had not happened. If there was anything in life worth fighting for, Joshua had reluctantly concluded, this was it.

He looked at Susan, arm about Ian, weeping in pride... and no little fear for her own sons.

Colonel Michael Shannon eased his bones on the hard church pew. For not the first time, he congratulated himself for having no

Allan Cole & Chris Bunch

wife and children. If he fell in battle there was no one who would be harmed; no penniless widow left behind; no little ones destined for a poorhouse upbringing; no grown sons to haunt his sleep with that greatest of all parental nightmares - outliving one's own children. He'd seen men distracted by worries of home. He'd watched them pore over old letters the night before battle - huddled by the campfire out in the cold Mexican badlands. Some of them got a look in their eye - suddenly certain of their own foul luck. Men like that rarely survived the fight. But that must be nothing, he thought, compared to the fears of those who waited at home. It would be particularly hard on for Susan.

She was already overloaded with responsibility managing what was left of Diana's estate. She'd seen each Shannon had his or her fair share and handed over some of the businesses to help out the poorer relatives. She'd been hard-pressed to stay atop the financial insanities of the late 1850's, trimming expenses after the crash of '57, consolidating some enterprises, selling off others, and gingerly treading across the great money swamp.

The whole time she'd been bedeviled by Pamela Shannon. The woman had slowly but surely spun a legal web that threatened to entangle all of the Shannons. Susan said she was in Washington now, and had seemed to find some powerful friends in the Federal courts. It was a pity, he thought, society frowned on shooting women.

Susan's work had been made doubly difficult by her ardent views on abolition. She'd returned from Vicksburg more convinced than ever of the evils in the South. These views were unpopular among many Irish Catholics, who saw the hand of the hated British aristocracy in the anti-slavery movement. This was especially the belief of recent immigrants who'd fled the hunger and oppression of the Emerald Isle. They charged that the same Brits who became weepy eyed over the plight of the black, earned fortunes as rack rent landlords in Ireland. Didn't the Irish deserve the same consideration as the abolitionists wanted for the black man in the South?

Michael had to grudgingly admit there was some truth to these charges. Still... Still... To be another man's slave? Michael had always gone in any direction the wind blew him, and out in the empty places, the mountains and dry creek trails, and in the gold fields, he'd met black men who thought as he did. There was no hunger they would not suffer if they could still call themselves free. Susan didn't need example to know this truth. She was born to it, the family said. As a child, she even despaired of seeing a bird in a cage, and would buy them from the market stalls with her spending money - and then set them free.

Then the choir' voices lifted in a sweet wedding song that rang against the good stone and brick of Saint Patrick's church, which reigned over the Irish neighborhood at 19th and Spruce. Ian had helped rebuild the church after it was destroyed by fire some years back. Much of the brick came from the brickyard Susan had bought as a complement to Ian's construction business. The very row of pews Michael sat in was donated by the family. Most of the Irish contractors in Philadelphia depended on parish school and church construction projects, just as business people depended on their fellow Irish to buy many of their goods. So as Susan became more active as an abolitionist, the controversy among her Irish cousins forced her to take more of a behind the curtain role in business.

Ian trotted her bids around to potential customers, while Hugh managed the brickyard. Young Kerry fronted the lucrative enterprise she'd discovered, installing gas fixtures in homes that brought affordable, clean light to many a neighborhood.

Michael wondered how she'd manage things now her boys were off to war. Of course, that would be the least of her worries, and she would have strong, steady Ian to lean on. This should bring some comfort.

What about you, Michael, he thought - sitting here judging the fortunes of others as if you had no stake in the game? How do you come to find yourself taking soldier's pay again, and wearing a colonel's uniform to boot? You had it made in California, my boy. Had a run of good luck - which you'd like to lay to your skills as a businessman, but know better. You were an El Patron, amigo, taking your ease on the verandah at the Rancho Shannon or sipping vino with the glittering senoritas of San Francisco. What could he say? It seemed like a good idea at the time. The right thing to do, somehow.

He also suspected Diana's ghost would haunt him to his grave if he didn't do something.

Michael fumbled at his pockets, wishing he could have a smoke. He could use the acrid bite of the cigarro to cut away the confusion in his mind. He'd joined a volunteer regiment of cavalry after hearing about Fort Sumter. Just as common sense was returning and he was even thinking fondly of the rattlesnake hills outside of Pueblo Los Angeles, the colonel up and died from a surfeit of bad oysters. To his complete surprise, his fellow soldiers elected Michael Shannon to take the colonel's place. He'd toyed with lighting out right then.

But he saw all the glad young faces around him, and remembered other young faces - just as green and eager as these. None among them had fought a war before, or heard horses and men screaming, shot and shell falling all around, smelled the gore from fallen comrades and the stink of one's own fear.

He'd suckered himself, that was all there was to it. The great California gambler had met his match. He'd been sitting on aces and kings. Guilt made him throw in the hand and draw another.

The choir hit a final high note, and the priest began to pray again. Jesus, Michael thought, I wish I could have a smoke.

Nancy O'Neil thought it a glorious wedding - a wedding beyond anything she'd of dreamed in her family's cramped row home. They called them "Father, Son and Holy Ghost" homes: three rooms per family, with the households stacked three stories high.

Her father and mother were so proud to see their oldest child marry into such fine clan as the Shannons. "You've caught yourself a lovely man in Kerry Dolan," her mother kept saying.

"I didn't catch him, mother," Nancy always argued. "He caught me. And I didn't fall into those arms of his so easily, either. I had other young men sniffing after my-"

"Here, now, none of that talk!" Her father had protested. But he'd grinned - for it was true. Everyone agreed Nancy was a great beauty, although she couldn't see why and had always thought of herself as rather plain. She'd made up for this imagined plainness with high spirits and a saucy tongue.

Allan Cole & Chris Bunch

Nancy's mother was a seamstress, which is how Nancy came to meet Kerry. She'd taken a repaired dress to Susan's house on her way to work at the mill. He'd answered the door and been stricken by a fit of stuttering when he saw her. She'd thought him rather stupid and had ignored him and joked with Susan until her mother's work had been examined, praised, and money fetched. As she was leaving, Kerry had jumped up from his seat so quickly he toppled over a vase of flowers. He's not only stupid, she'd thought, but clumsy as well.

She'd seen him frequently after that - or, at least thought she had. Several times after work, as she streamed out of the factory with the other girls she'd spied a fine carriage at the corner and a face staring out the window she could have sworn belonged to the tongue-tied youth she'd met at Susan Dolan's house. She even thought she'd seen him mooning about under the gas light at the end of the block down from her home.

One market day, when she was minding her young brothers and sisters while her mother bargained with a fat-faced farm woman, Nancy saw Kerry at the edge of the crowd. He was pretending to watch a juggler toss colored balls and dishes to the delight of the market audience and Nancy's small brood of four. Her suspicions were confirmed - he was following her.

She was irritated. Who did he think she was? She hadn't asked for this attention. Did he think she was a trollop because she was poor and forced to work? She saw him slide up to the juggler and whisper. The man nodded, stopped his juggling and took something from Kerry's hand. Now, he's spoiling our fun, Nancy thought. Paying the man to stop. What gall!

Then Kerry grabbed some dishes and begun flinging them into the air. Nancy gasped, thinking the clumsy fool had gone mad and was about to shower them all with broken crockery. But the plates hadn't fallen, and the crowd was crowing and applauding the feats of this rank amateur, who was tossing first three... then four plates into the air. Kerry started walking forward, juggling as he came. With alarm, Nancy saw he was moving toward her. She wanted to flee, but the crowd had begun to catch onto Kerry's act, and hooted at the bright red flush on the pretty girl's face.

211

He stopped directly in front of her. The plates flew faster and faster. Then he stopped abruptly and caught the plates as they fell one by one. He tucked them under his arm and bowed low with an exaggerated flourish.

"If you'll only let me come calling, Nancy O'Neil," he said, "I'll prove I can talk as well as juggle."

Her fury built to a boil. To be humiliated, like this—

"What a sweet young man," Nancy heard an old woman say. The crone wiped a tear at such a romantic display. "And handsome, too," said another.

Nancy had looked into Kerry's face and saw this was true. Not only was he handsome, but she could see the trembling behind that bright, wide Irish smile. All of his courage had been invested in this display. Her heart melted.

"Who is he, Nancy?" her little brother asked. "Can we take him home with us? All that juggling... it would be great fun."

"You see, Nancy O'Neil," Kerry said. "Even children love me. How can you resist?"

Nancy's pulse was suddenly hammering, but she pretended great indifference. "Oh, you'll not find me lacking in resistance, Kerry Dolan," she responded.

His face fell and she'd gathered up her brood and started away. It lit again as she turned for the final word. "But, if it will stop you from lurking about, I suppose it will be all right. I'll ask my father and mother." She couldn't help but laugh, his face was so full of hope. "It was a lovely show, Mister Dolan," she added. "I'll get the neighbors over when you come and we'll all make a pretty penny."

That was six months ago. Over that time Kerry proved to be the kindest and gentlest of men. Although she pretended to argue, Nancy agreed with her mother - Kerry was a wonderful catch. She could barely imagine the foolish girl she'd been when Kerry had embarrassed himself at their first meeting. She should have seen then who he really was. She looked to the side, and saw Kerry's handsome profile. He had a small smile at the corner of his lips. Tonight, she promised herself, she would make that smile grow and grow.

Allan Cole & Chris Bunch

Ah, will this priest ever be done, she thought. I have a great longing for a husband in my bed.

Mary tried to focus on the ceremony, but it was difficult. For some reason, although she was a prime participant, she couldn't yet place herself in the event. It was as if she were witnessing the actions of another person. I should be remembering every detail, she thought. I should be swooning with romantic notions imagining a storybook future for myself and my prince. But how can you imagine a future, she thought, when there is a war between you and whatever that future might hold? Have faith in the Sacred Heart of Jesus, the nuns would have advised. And the sweet mercy of his mother, Mary, your namesake. But Mary Cassidy knew this was a leap in faith she was not able to make. Then she thought: we have tonight. And two other nights. This will be our future.

"Do, you, Mary Cassidy," priest said, "take Hugh Dolan as your lawful wedded husband, until death do you part?"

For Hugh's sake, she banished fear and said as firmly and calmly as she could: "I do."

Thomas Shannon Ryan watched the wedding party troop into his father's tavern. There were loud cheers and a few salty jests from those who'd already run afoul of the jug. The loudest was his father. "There'll be two fillies to tame tonight," he shouted. He clapped Hugh on the back and pawed Kerry's shoulder. "At 'em lads, at 'em," he cried.

Thomas saw the pained look on Susan's face, which she quickly covered with a laugh. She pushed the brides past his father into the big main room of the tavern.

"She's the salt of the earth," his father said in his loud, drunken voice. "And I'll fight the man who calls me a liar. You just see if I don't. I'll put the boot to that great slanderer of the Shannons, or my name isn't Dan Ryan."

He sang a different tune in private - "I've never trusted woman or man who loves a nigger more than Irishmen. I'm not fooled by that breed. Susan with her queenly ways, acting like she was the Blessed Virgin, giving us the gift of this tavern. Why, if the truth be

Allan Cole & Chris Bunch

known, I work harder than a nigger, and when the day is done... there's no profits for naught but Queen Susan and her kin."

Thomas curled a lip. Sure the old man was right about the niggers and stuff. But where would he be without the charity of the Dolans' and the Shannons'? He'd be nothing but a red nosed sot, dancing jigs for drinks and tips. His father caught him looking his way and gave Thomas a foul glare. He rolled heavy shoulders and took a step in Thomas' direction. Thomas clutched the brass knuckle-duster in his pocket.

He was in a bad mood himself and wouldn't mind settling a few ancient scores. Come on you old shit, he thought. I'll knock every tooth from your mouth. His father spotted the hand in the pocket and turned away. Thomas laughed loudly, hoping his father would hear. Dan Ryan hadn't laid a hand on his son for more than a year - ever since Thomas had started running with the Schuylkill Rangers and learned how to handle himself in dozens of gang fights. Dan Ryan might be a hulking brute and a bully, but Thomas had soon set him running when he took a club to him for mistreating his mother. And well he should - by now Thomas had thumped bargemen bigger and meaner than his father for failing to pay the toll his gang exacted on the river trade.

A red-faced middle-aged man lurched toward him, a big, friendly drunken grin on his mush. "What's this," he joked, "I thought only the Irish were invited to this party?" He stuck his face close to Thomas, who tried not to draw away as the whiskey punch breath washed over him. "Aye, you're a Shannon, all right," he finally said. "I knew your grandmother well, back when she was September Shannon... and a right pretty thing she was, Irish as the rainbow over Paddy's pig pen."

"Thank you for remembering her... Cousin," Thomas said, forcing politeness. He wasn't sure who the man was, but he wouldn't be at the wedding reception if he wasn't somehow related to the Shannon clan.

"Cousin is right," the old man said. "Which is why I'm wonderin' at the great lack of drink in your hand. Come on, lad. Don't shame the Irish. Let's put a mug of punch in your gullet." He

Allan Cole & Chris Bunch

put a friendly paw on Thomas' elbow to tug him toward one of the big punch bowls scattered about the tavern.

Thomas shook the hand off. "I ain't a drinkin' man, if it's all the same to you, sir."

The beefy drunk took offense. "What's this? You won't have a drink with the likes of me? Is that how your story goes?"

Thomas saw the drunk was working himself into a fighting mood. He stepped in quick, grabbing flab between two fingers and twisted hard. At the same time he ground a bootheel into the man's foot.

"Listen, you old drunk," Thomas hissed. "You keep up the blather and I'll be followin' you home tonight. Maybe you won't be so fond of whiskey if I cut your liver out."

The man gasped in pain, shocked into sobriety. "Ssss... orry, lad. I didn't mean to-"

Thomas twisted harder. "Shut your mush," he said.

The man shut it, but a whine of pain escaped his lips. Thomas pushed him away before fury overtook him. He calmed himself. The only thing Thomas hated more than a drunk was drink itself. He'd hated the taste of the stuff ever since he could remember, and he despised people who let spirits get the better of them. Like his father and the misery he had made of their lives.

Pity for his mother - and Shannon money - was all that had kept Thomas coming around the tavern since he joined the gang. "I was a fool to marry a Ryan," his mother Clare, had said repeatedly when Thomas was growing up. "But that was God's will and I won't question my Savior's decision. I pray every day he has higher plans for you, Thomas," she'd say. "Isn't that why I gave you Shannon for a middle name? People should know you come from better stock and you are meant for finer things."

Wasn't that a right privy-load? Meant for finer things. Sure, he was. Waiting for a handout from his Great Aunt Susan, more likely. What did his mother know? Always had her head bowed over a rosary - when it wasn't being thumped by Dan Ryan.

His father was mostly right about the Shannons, although Thomas couldn't bring himself to actually hate Susan. She was okay, he supposed, even if she was funny in the head about niggers.

Besides, whenever Thomas got himself stuck good in the Schuylkill mud, what his middle name didn't get him out of, Susan's money did. But she'd been showing her disapproval more of late, so he might not be able to tap the source for long.

Resentment flared. Bugger the old bitch, she was bad as his mother, with all her blather of what's right 'n what's crook. It wasn't fair. He looked at her sleek sons, with their fine uniforms and pretty women for brides. Everybody treatin' them like they was royalty, and heroes as well. He'd like to give that smug Hugh Dolan a blow to the pearlies, show him Thomas Shannon Ryan was just as much as man as he, even if he wasn't la-te-da rich, and born with lace curtains in his nursery window.

He felt the room close in on him, all the bright chatter and fine clothes of the Shannon crowd getting under his skin although he was as flashily dressed as any man in the room in dove gray breeches and long-tailed coat, with a crisp white shirt and silk waistcoat cut tight to show off his narrow waist and broad shoulders. He'd stolen it along with a great crate of ready-to-wear gents' clothes off the Schuylkill docks.

Thomas felt he was suffocating and wanted badly to escape the tavern and find himself a bit of fun. There was nothing much around the tavern - it was on a court off the Delaware River, just down from where Walnut intersected with the docks. On the other end of the court was the Shannon Brickyard, where he'd worked under Hugh for a month or so, last time he got in trouble with his gang. Susan had made him work off the money she'd given him to get out of that trouble.

"Hello, there, if it isn't my young friend, Tom Ryan," came a deep voice. Thomas turned to see the friendly face of his uncle Ian. "You're not leavin' so soon, are you lad?"

Ian winked and put a heavy arm about his shoulders. "You haven't even gone up to kiss the brides," he said.

Thomas flushed, suddenly feeling shy. He'd always admired Ian, and the man seemed to genuinely like him. In fact, if it wasn't for Ian, he doubted his Aunt Susan would have always been so forthcoming when he got into a scrape. "I... just wanted to get some air, Uncle Ian," he said, a little weak.

Allan Cole & Chris Bunch

Ian glanced around. Everyone was drinkin' and jawin' and having a fine old time. Around the edges of the room, old men and women perched on chairs, soaking in a little life that wasn't routine. But among all the cheery faces, he also saw the loud drunks; the fights that were brewing; wives glaring at husbands; husbands getting their backs up at the glares.

"Don't mind them, young Thomas," he said. "Takes all kinds to make a family."

A fiddle started playing. There were shouts and a clapping of hands and stomping of feet. A pipe joined in, then a drum. "Come and dance with the brides, Thomas," Ian laughed. "It's a rare chance a man has to do a jig with two such pretty ladies."

Thomas hesitated, then shook his head. "If you don't mind, Uncle Ian," he said, "I'm still needin' that air."

He made a few more polite sounds, then slipped through the crowd for the door.

Ian watched, feeling sorry for him. Susan came up as the music shifted and a singer joined in: "While I was up a ridin'\on the far fam'd Kerry mountain\I spied Colonel Parker and his money he was countin',\I first produced my pistol,'\and rattled on my saber,' Sayin': stand and deliver,\for I am a bold deceiver..."

Susan shook her head at the departing Thomas. "A perfect tune for the likes of him," she said. "I'm glad to see the back of him this night."

Ian grimaced. "I know you don't like the lad, darlin'," he said. "But he's really not all that bad a sort."

Susan snorted. "You've a blind spot for the boy," she said. "He's out doing Lord knows what with the gangs, and you're saying he's not that sort. What sort exactly is he then, my dear sweet Ian?"

Ian laughed. "Oh, don't go on like that. It's just that I was a wild one when I was his age. And what with his father and all, who could blame him for gettin' into the wrong crowd? He'll wake up one day, mark my words."

Susan patted her husband, a fond smile on her face. "You're a hopeless romantic, Ian Dolan," she said. "But don't you dare change a bit of it. It's why I love you."

217

Ian turned suddenly somber. He looked deep into Susan's eyes. I'd better tell her now, he thought. I've been delayin' this too long. He opened his mouth to speak - to pour out the news of the decision he'd made. "An old mate of mine stopped by for a talk the other day," he said. "And I got to thinkin'-"

Susan gave him a push. "Save your thinking for later, Ian Dolan. You're looking at an Irish lass who wants to dance."

Before he could say another word she grabbed his arm and pulled him amongst the dancers. I should insist she hear me out, he thought. But then he saw the happiness on her face, and the fear for her soldier sons just behind that happiness. I'll tell her later, Ian thought. He grabbed her still slender waist and whirled away with her.

Little Robert Conners was only thirteen, but everyone said he was a wonder already with pipe and drum and he had a high, sweet singing voice his mother prayed would never change as he grew older.

Kerry and Nancy danced together as Robert sang a lovely old tune: "Her eyes they did shine like the diamonds\Her cheeks like the red rose in June,\Her skin was as white as the lily,\And her breath had the rarest perfume...\The maid with the bonny brown hair."

"It's the wrong woman the song is praising," Kerry said. "Young Robert should be singing about the girl in my arms with bonny golden hair."

Nancy gave him a poke in the arm. "You just keep talking like that, Kerry Dolan, and see what you get." Kerry laughed and when he looked into her shining eyes he fell in love all over again. "It's a good thing you made an honest woman of me, Mr. Dolan," Nancy said with a giggle. "And just in time, too. For it's not a maid you got for a bride, as you well know."

Kerry had no idea what she was talking about. Probably another one of her jokes, he thought. The girl was full of them. "Just in time for what?" he asked.

"I'm with child, you silly man," Nancy said with another laugh.

Kerry was startled. Almost overwhelmed. "But how-"

Allan Cole & Chris Bunch

Nancy gave him another sharp whack on the arm. "What do you mean - how? You know very well how, Kerry Dolan. You didn't want to wait, remember? Of course... I must admit I didn't protest too loudly, did I?"

Kerry stopped in mid dance and tried to draw Nancy away from the throng of dancers. But she just shook her bright curls and kept dancing until he did the same.

"What do we do?" Kerry asked, still bewildered. He was worried about his decision to join the Army. He feared he was abandoning her when she was at her most vulnerable.

"We don't do anything, in case you're missing some vital information of how these matters work," Nancy said. She patted her belly. "I'll take good care of the new Dolan. Don't you worry a bit about us." She leaned close and he could smell a perfume that had to be even rarer than the one in the song. He felt a hot stirring in his groin. "You just wait, my bonny Kerry," she whispered to him, her breath tingling in his ear. "There's no reason to be careful anymore. As if that did us a lot of good."

She kissed his earlobe and he felt as if he had been lit by a match. "Wait 'til you see how good I can be when I don't have to be careful."

Nancy gave him a wonderful leer. "I've not much experience, as you know," she giggled. "But I've been practicing... in my imagination."

Hugh watched Joshua escort his Mary off the dance floor. He delivered her to him with a flourish. "I'd keep her close for bit, Hugh," he said. "After dancing with me she'll be limping like a barefoot cabin boy on a hot deck."

"Don't believe a word," Mary said. "Our cousin, the captain, has wings for feet."

"I wish I could say the same," Hugh mourned. "The dance floor empties whenever I do the jig. It's either that or broken bones. So much for the myth all Irishmen are natural born dancers."

The musicians struck up a new tune. Robert pounded a tricky rhythm on the drum head, while an older man took up the song: "... No wonder people grumble at the taxes more and more,\There never

219

was such taxes in this fair land before;\ They're going to tax the farmers, and their horses, carts and ploughs;\They're going to tax the billygoats, the donkeys, pigs and cows;\They'll tax the ladies' flouncy gowns, their high-heeled boots and stays;\And before the sun begins to shine, they'll tax the bugs and fleas..."

Hugh was busy filling Joshua's hand with a cup of punch. He grimaced when he heard the song. "My mother must have requested it," he said.

"Oh she did, indeed," Mary said. "I saw her myself. She gave Robert a few coins to reward the man who could remember that old tune."

Joshua looked so puzzled, Hugh thought he'd better explain. "My mother's been muttering about taxes for weeks. Ever since she learned that Mr. Lincoln is going to approve the income tax."

"I don't like it, either," Joshua said. "But it is difficult to argue against the need. It costs a deal of money to fight a war."

"She realizes that," Mary said. "She just thinks the government is squandering what they've already collected. Feathering the nests of scoundrels and thieves, is the way she puts it."

"No one would argue that," Joshua said.

Robert's high voice piped in, rising above the other singer's: "They're going to tax all bachelors as heavy as they can,\ And they'll double tax the maidens who are over forty one;\They'll tax the ground we walk on and the clothes that keep us warm,\And they're going to tax the children on the night before they're born..."

Hugh smiled. "Sometimes my mother takes it personally," he said. Then he turned serious - "It's been hard on her since... Vicksburg."

"I know it," Joshua said, soft.

"She's taken all the worries of the family on her shoulders," Hugh said. "Now she'll have even more to worry about with me and Kerry gone."

"And isn't it that Pamela Shannon who's making things so hard for her?" Mary said, hot. "The lawyers are eating up all the money just to stay even in the fight. I swear, if I ever meet that woman, I'll... Well, it wouldn't be right to say what I have in mind in polite company."

220

Allan Cole & Chris Bunch

"You'll take care of her, won't you, Mary?" Hugh asked. "She depends on you more than any other."

"No one will get the best of her if I can help it," she answered. "Or my name's not Mary Ca-" She laughed. "I almost forgot. It's Mary Dolan now. So you can be sure that's a promise."

The crowd was clapping loudly and singing along as young Robert and the other musicians neared the end of the tax song: "They're going to tax the farmers' boys that work along the ditches,\And they'll double tax old drunken wives that try to wear the britches;\ Then they'll double tax the hobble skirts and table up some laws,\But the devil says he'll tax THEM if he gets them in his claws."

Hugh listened to the night sounds of the river outside the window: the gentle creaking of boats tugging at their ropes; the rush of water under the bow of a solitary barge; the far away voices of crabbers working their traps. They were honeymooning in a summer cabin the family shared that sat along the cool banks of Gray's Ferry.

Mary lay next to him, quiet... expectant? He wasn't sure what was in her mind. They were both naked under a light coverlet, but lay apart, the few inches separating them an oddly wide gulf. Hugh felt cold, although the summer night was sultry and close.

He looked into Mary's eyes and saw the familiar face he'd known half his life, ever since his mother brought her home from the nuns. They'd been so impressed by the brightness of the orphan child, they'd sought Susan out to help find a family to take her in, and his mother ended up doing so herself. Mary'd always been quiet - not a shy, mousy quiet - but the quiet of a thinker, contemplating deeper things. She wasn't a jokester or prankster like Nancy with her merry laugh. But she always had a smile on her face and her eyes shone with inner humor at life. He saw that glint of humor even now, recognized every dimple and one small mole on her cheek. Familiar... but somehow mysterious.

"What are you thinking, my darling husband?" she suddenly asked. The question startled him.

221

"I was wondering the same thing, myself," Hugh answered. "I was thinking how I'd known you most of my life, and yet I don't think I really know you at all."

"What can there be to know?" Mary asked. "I'm not such a mysterious woman. It's only me... Mary Cassidy... Now, Mary Dolan... Your wife."

She laughed, but there was an edge to the laugh, and he looked into her eyes again and saw a little fear. She shivered under the coverlet, as cold as he.

Hugh gave himself a mental thwack between the eyes. Here he was, the experienced one, the young blade about town. A soldier about to shoulder his country's burdens and march off to war. Quaking as if he were the virginal bride. He was probably scaring holy hell out of her. All silent and tense without a tender word or glance. What should he say, what should he do, to set her at ease?

"The truth of the matter, my sweetness," he said, "is I'm as nervous as a... well, a bride, in fact. And now that I think of it, why shouldn't I be? I've never been a husband before. I've never had a wedding night."

"Oh, dear," Mary said, "don't tell me you're a virgin too. One of us has to know how to start. " She laughed again, but this time Hugh heard no touch of fear.

He sputtered, deliberately falling for her trap. "Virgin? Of course I'm not- Uh... I mean... You're the only one for me, Mary my love, but... uh... Sometimes... Uh... In the past..."

Mary was gasping with laughter. He stopped his stammering and laughed with her. He put out an arm and she snuggled close, sliding into the crook of his arm as if she'd been born to it. The last dregs of nervousness fled when he felt the hot touch of her flesh and the naked breast against him. He felt a hard surge between his thighs. Mary shivered again, but he knew it wasn't from imagined cold. She was silent.

"Let me show you how to begin, my love," he said, husky. He pulled her to him and she pressed against him, eager, wanting to respond, but not knowing how. Hugh thought his heart would burst from wanting to take her, but forced himself to be calm, tender. First he taught her about her own body. Soft places where a brush of his

222

lip could make her quiver. Secret places, that only a lover can find. Then he taught her about his, made her laugh at his odd equipment, so eager... so mindlessly seeking... so easily hurt that it must be a joke God played on men, sticking it on the outside of their body.

She tensed when he entered her... gently... and he paused when he felt the virginal barrier. Then she cried out and it gave way, and he was flowing into her and they were moving with each other as if they had been lovers for a century or more... And he drifted away, Mary calling his name into his ear... and he never thought his name could sound so fine... like it was being cried out by a choir of angels...

Nancy knelt on the bed, naked except for her bridal veil which she had fashioned into a short skirt wound about her round hips. The bedclothes were heaped and molded in what she had declared to be a rocky spring. Nancy made dipping motions among them, then rubbed her hands over her body as if taking a bath.

"Oh, la," she said brightly, "here is the beautiful Indian princess, bathing alone in the wooded pool, as bare as God made her." She looked down at the flesh gleaming through the sheer material of the veil and giggled. "If God made her draped in lace, that is."

There was a cough on the other side of the room. Nancy looked in the direction of the cough and pouted. "Now, don't you spoil this, Kerry Dolan," she scolded. "You're supposed to be the handsome Prince Hiawatha, peering stealthily through the forest glen at the helpless Indian princess."

Kerry stood up from behind the big stuffed chair. "I was being stealthy, dammit! It's your fault. You made me laugh."

Nancy peered at him, then curled a lip and pointed a finger. "Another thing," she said, "if you're to be a handsome Indian prince we simply must do something about your drawers."

Kerry looked down. "What's wrong with my drawers?"

"People named Hiawatha," Nancy said scornfully, "especially people named Hiawatha who have any hope of making love to a beautiful Indian princess, do not wear drop seat flannel drawers cut off at the knees."

"Oh, now it's my knees you're maligning is it, my pretty?" Kerry said, stroking his chin.

"No, your knees are fine, " Nancy said, giving a saucy toss of her blonde curls. "But I was hoping to see more than knees. After all, this is our wedding night."

"Shall I take them off then, you naughty lass?" Kerry put his hands to the waistband.

Nancy shrugged. "You do as you like. I'm an Indian princess, bathing in a pool, remember? But let me warn you, Mister Hiawatha, if you come jumping out of the bushes with those drawers on, well you can just forget the whole game and I'm sorry I made it up."

Kerry bounded across the room, leaped into the bed and flung himself on Nancy. She squealed in pretended alarm. "Not with those drop seated drawers!"

Kerry made a few fast motions, then grabbed one of her hands and pulled it toward him. She pretended to fight. "No! No! A thousand times, no!" she cried.

The cries stopped when the hand finally touched him. "Oh, my goodness," she said, with a great wide smile. A small fist closed around him. "Or should I say... Oh, your goodness."

"You were right," Kerry said as his hand slipped beneath the veil and smoothed along her belly.

"Right... about... what..?" His fingers were stroking silkiness, as she caressed him in return.

"It's much better without the drawers."

A single gas light hissed in the corner of Susan's bedroom. She wept quietly, knotted up in her bed like a child in pain. Ian knelt over her, his shadow bulking huge on the wall above the bed. "Please, lass," he begged. "Please stop. I'm the sorriest man in the world to be the cause of your tears."

Susan was inconsolable. She groaned at his words as if he'd struck her. He touched her shoulder, trying to give comfort, but she flinched at his touch and he snatched his hand away.

"I've wounded you sore, my lass, but can't you-"

She whirled violently, face furious beneath the tears. "Don't call me your lass," she spat. "I'm a woman of nearly fifty years and my

224

sons are grown men who could be dead in a week. Now you're saying I could be widowed as well in just a week more."

"It won't be like that, la- ... Susan, dear. I'll be in the artillery... not down on the line fighting. Besides, the war won't go on very long, and I promise I'll be careful."

Susan's tears stopped as if a water cock had been suddenly closed. She dragged an angry hand across wet cheeks. "What do you take me for, Ian Dolan? You cannot promise a rifle ball won't take your life. Only God can pledge just a thing, and I believe he's abandoned us all for being such fools."

"But how could I refuse?" Ian pleaded. "The friend who came to me knows I have a head for figures. I've built schools and churches and many a brick home and I carry more factoring about in my brain than old Benjamin Franklin himself. Doesn't the Union have great need for men like me in such desperate times? As my friend said, our factories can produce cannons by the thousands, but not the men to aim them."

Susan tears flowed again. Ian's hand reached... then fell. "Oh, darlin' Susan, you must understand. I cannot let my sons go, and hide here like a coward."

"You're a fool, Ian," Susan cried. "It's manly conceit guiding your reason. Nothing more. You might as well be poor Russell Conners, going to his doom before Edward's pistol... knowing he had not a chance in heaven...but fearing a slight against his manhood more than death. I tell you, Ian Dolan, since time began your sex has been responsible for more misery than all the demons let loose on this Earth by Satan himself."

Ian's head dropped. He had no answer.

"What's worse," Susan continued, "you do all these things without a thought for women. You didn't even ask me, Ian, you just ran where your rooster's heart led, without ever asking my view."

"I knew you'd object, lass," Ian said quietly.

"Of course I would. There's no sense in this decision. I'm to stay here and carry on alone. Keep the family from poverty, if I can. Worry every hour of the day over the fate of my men. I had no choice. I have no choice. By, God, Ian Dolan, I can't buy a stool for

Allan Cole & Chris Bunch

the drawing room without consulting you. I'd suffer your angry silence for a week, if I did so."

"That's so," was all Ian could say.

Susan rose higher in the bed. "That's so. That's so." she mocked. "And here's another you can't deny. When you decide a thing, the matter is settled... as if it were the law of the land. You can catch the train tomorrow to the battlefields and certain doom, and I cannot stop you. But, if I made some such foolish decision... You could send a policeman to fetch me back."

Ian sat on the edge of the bed, his head bowed so low from her punishment that even in her fury Susan could not help but feel for him. Ah, Dear Heavenly Father, she thought. What if this our end? What if he dies and his last thoughts are of my hatred? For hate him I do, and Holy Mother forgive me, but how could he do such a thing? I must forgive him. But why must it be women who are always doing the forgiving? We trot back and forth from that bitter well so much, we might as well be laboring beasts with no will of our own... And Holy Mary, Mother of God, I must stop thinking these thoughts, or I shall go mad. Susan began to cry again. She leaned against his strong back, crushed her cheek against the rough night shirt. "Oh, Ian," she said, "I wish this hadn't happened... but it has. And I will do whatever must be done."

Ian stirred, but he didn't turn. In the dim light Susan saw the shine of tears on his face. "Come and love me, then," she said. "Love me with all your might."

He turned and took her into his arms. She crushed her lips to his and fell back - pulling them both down with her weight, dragging up her gown to help him find his way.

One of his hands went to her breasts and anger rose up again... along with a violent rutting passion... and she impatiently pushed the hand away. She reached for his cock and pulled him into her, her legs splaying wide and her hips thrusting up and slamming against him.

She bucked and screamed and bit him on the shoulder, thrusting her hips faster and faster, as if she were the master... desperately wanting to shut out the world through force of will...

Allan Cole & Chris Bunch

Later, as Ian slept peacefully in her arms, she watched the dawn rise in her window. She wept again, softly so as not to wake him.

Then she dried her tears. And swore they would be the last she would shed... until Ian returned... safe in her arms again.

CHAPTER SEVENTEEN

CANTON, KY. - SEPTEMBER, 1861

'Y'ALL FIXIN' TO have a go, Patrick?"

"I don't believe so, Billy," Patrick said, listening closely to his own voice, and hoping there wasn't a quaver to it. "Shotguns don't have the reach of cannon. Or so I've been told."

Both of them were talking in a murmur, even though there was no way anyone on the USS Conestoga could hear them. But why take chances? Because damned if the gunboat wasn't near the most frightening thing Patrick had ever seen. The Federals had timbered the river tug from the waterline to its upper deck. Both sidewheels were "armored" with planking as well. But what caught real attention were the four monstrous cannon sticking out to either side of the ship's bow. Cannon a hell of a lot bigger, Patrick thought, than the six Confederate guns Colonel Forrest had brought up. Patrick fingered the musketball amulet around his chest, and hoped it'd give him as much gumption as Grandfather Emmett must've had at Saratoga.

"Tell you what," Billy said, tapping the stock of his musket, an old, percussion-converted Tower, which his father'd brought back from the Mexican War. "I'll take first shot, then you go to load, an' y'all can have a turn."

"Thanks," Patrick managed. His throat was suddenly a little dry, and he didn't feel like talking a whole lot.

"I bet," Billy went on, seeming to have no trouble talking, in fact, quite the opposite, "Johnny's back there kickin' hisself blue it was his turn to be aholdin' the horses."

Patrick wasn't sure Johnny Evans might not be the happiest of the trio. Colonel Forrest had ordered one in three when they dismounted - one trooper to remain to the rear with the horses. That put about four hundred men on line along the river.

Forrest had taken his battalion out yesterday after hearing one of the three much-feared Yankee warships was marauding. He'd led them on an all night march, partially cross-country, partially along the narrow, rutted lanes of Southwestern Kentucky, to the Cumberland River.

There'd been murmurs from the men about the whole idea, but not loud ones. Everybody'd seen Colonel Forrest swell up, turn turkeycock red, and open up on whoever'd made him mad. He didn't use much in the way of profanity, and didn't need to. Everybody had heard he'd killed more than a couple of men in a storefront shootout, some said with a gun, some said with a knife; and supposedly once faced down a lynch mob in Memphis - single-handed.

There were other stories as well - stories from back when Forrest and his brothers owned a slave market in Memphis in the '50's, stories that any black who didn't crawl on request wouldn't show up on the block. Supposedly they'd had a back corner used for a midnight buryin' for any mouthy nigger, man, woman or child. So nobody complained within range of Forrest, Kelly or any of the officers. But they wondered - where the blazes were the Confederate gunboats that were supposed to turn the Mississippi and its tributaries into Secessionist canals?

After a month in the service of the Confederate States of America, Patrick had yet to see much war. Captain Kelly's promise that Forrest would provide the best of food, weapons or anything else hadn't been fulfilled. So far the guns, the uniforms, the remounts and the rest were undelivered. Patrick still wore the corduroy and homespun he'd used for his traveling garb and was armed with nothing better than the long barreled shotgun and the pocket pistol he'd joined up with. And nobody who hadn't brought one with him had been given that supposedly essential arm of the horse soldier, a saber.

At least Kelly had followed up on the bounty. Patrick had $250 in gold of the $300 promised money. It wasn't he had become suddenly frugal - so far, there hadn't been much to buy. What little he'd spent had gone for grain for Templar. Everybody thought Patrick foolish - an army horse couldn't be babied, any more than a soldier. It'd have to learn to live on corn and forage, pretty much like its master was.

Patrick slept in Doctor Young's barn for three days, while other volunteers trickled in. Then they'd gone back across the river, Patrick keeping his head low and staying in the middle of the throng, and boarded a sorry little huffer pulling too many overcrowded

229

boxcars. The train had creaked to Jackson, and then north. Eventually, after only three or four centuries of travel, Patrick and the others reached the roiling chaos that was the cavalry camp outside Bowling Green. They were sworn in by a half-drunk politician... and there they met Nathan Bedford Forrest.

He'd walked out in front of the civilian official and just stood there, watching the men in his new command. He was tall - Patrick guessed over six feet - and built like a bull. Dark hair. Mustache and chinbeard. Clean, hard features.

Suddenly he spoke: "I'm not much for speeches. Words don't kill Yankees. Bullets do. I aim to take you into a fight. Anybody who don't like the idea had best slink on home now. Stick with me, and we'll win this damned war." There'd been cheers, and hats thrown in the air, and that was when the war began.

The first thing, Patrick learned, was to find a bunkmate. Two men would share blankets and, if they were lucky, a tarpaulin on the march. He had not the foggiest idea what a proper bunkmate should be, except he knew he wanted one who knew what a bar of soap was. Beyond that... nada.

The bunkmate found him. "Y'all from Vicksburg? Saw you when you boarded."

Patrick saw a gangly young man, about his age. He shook his head. "Nossir. I am not. Virginia and Texas, sir."

"You a city boy?" Suspicion.

"Sometimes," Patrick said. "And sometimes I've slept in a swamp."

The young man grinned. "Ain't never been that lowdown, but I 'spect this war might make it so. Maybe need somebody to teach me how to stay clear of the gators. Name's Jeter. Billy Jeter. Come from Al'bama. Over to Colbert County. M' people farm along there."

Billy became his bunkmate. The next step was to form a mess. Technically that was four men, but most commonly it would be eight to ten when they were campaigning. Each mess drew its own rations, sometimes cooked, sometimes raw; and other supplies were also divided up. The other two were: Johnny Evans, another Alabaman from near Huntsville, and Dack Noble, whose parents had a farm not too far from Yazoo City in Mississippi.

Allan Cole & Chris Bunch

The surprises began for Patrick. First was that he'd somehow expected the Army to be made up of older people. It wasn't. Two of his messmates were Patrick's age, and Evans was an elderly nineteen. Their sergeant, Reed, was six months shy of twenty; and Fairfax, the officer eventually put in charge was also nineteen. Fairfax was a former school master.

Billy was completely illiterate, Noble read about as well as a child in his second year of schooling, and only Johnny could write - after a fashion. His spelling proved constantly marvelous: "A brim ham lilkern" was the current and despised president of the United States; "ashpottatoh" was an Irish potato; and "lew tennante" was Fairfax's rank.

Johnny, however, was a born artist. Patrick could sit for hours watching the bit of charcoal or pencil flash across paper or even bark he'd cozened, and see the swift motions emerge as a picture. One time he drew a sketch of Patrick, and Shannon felt flattered as all hell, and then desolated, realizing he had nobody to send it to. He thought for a wistful minute of Lucy, the young girl in Vicksburg, but decided that would be presumptuous. Johnny got drunk once, on some triple-run that had found its way into camp, and drew up the girl he would marry, "when we've won the war."

To Patrick's eye, the sketch made her out to look like any other farm girl he'd ridden past with a grin, and a tip of his hat - and sometimes tumbled in a haymow. But to Johnny she was beautiful, and so she was in Patrick's eyes. Most of army training, he was realizing, was learning to wear off your own sharp edges and put up with the ones other people hadn't as yet honed away.

The second surprise was Patrick was considered the most experienced one in the company. This was as far from home as any of his messmates had ever gotten, and even Lieutenant Fairfax had only been once from his home outside Natchez down to New Orleans. "Patrick, jus' how d'you keep this doggoned blanket roll from unravelin'?" "Irish, which end of this saddle goes for'rd?" "Pat, y'all sure you can't make johnnycake 'thout sugar?" "What in th' name of the Lord are they lookin' for when they go to holler Slope Arms, anyway?"

Allan Cole & Chris Bunch

At first, he thought they were dumb, but it slowly sunk through that all of them had grown up doing the same thing over and over and over, and so they had no more appreciation for novelty than a plow mule. They would instinctively know how long after a workout before you watered your horse, how to run a ruler-straight furrow all the way across a field without ever checking behind, and just when the stars and moon said to plant the corn or the cotton. None of them needed sights on a rifle or musket - the few in the camp that had arms - to know where to aim to tuck a ball the size of a squirrel's head just between his eyes. So even though they were slowly armed with archaic muskets or even sporting rifles and shotguns from their fathers' father's day, it wouldn't do for any Yank to stick up his skull and expect to not get a fairly serious headache.

All of them were riders, even if they'd never been on an animal as fancy as Templar. In fact, the mounts the quartermasters eventually came up with were better suited for these farmboy-warriors than a high-spirited breed, being mostly saddle- or carriage-horses bought, donated or requisitioned from the surrounding country, although there were a few rangehorses that came in from Texas that threw everybody before they gentled down.

But none of the recruits had ever cooked or sewn. That was women's work. Bathing was also sort of a sometime affair, probably happening most often back on the farm when it rained or when somebody kicked them in the creek. This thing called drill was completely beyond them. None of them could see the slightest purpose in learning to march up and down, since they'd joined the cavalry where a man wasn't supposed to walk. As for guard duty - there could be no military purpose whatever to roust a tired soldier out of his sleep, make him pick up a musket, and walk back and forth for two hours or so, guarding something like Forrest's tent when the Colonel was off to Points South for the week. It was either dumb, or harassment or ignorance, and when the officers caught you asleep, and started shouting a man could get himself shot for sleeping on guard duty - why, that was all bullroar, just like everything else called drill.

Patrick absolutely agreed, particularly when he was on guard duty one night, and found Lieutenant Fairfax in his tent, earnestly

Allan Cole & Chris Bunch

studying a volume by somebody named Hardee, titled Rifle and Light Infantry Tactics. He remembered one of his tutors, who'd taught by staying one chapter ahead of what he was teaching the next day. He bagged the book a day or so later when Fairfax went into Bowling Green, and memorized and practiced a few of the rituals they were supposed to be learning. That almost proved his undoing. Patrick so shone in the next few days of the thrice-daily School of the Soldier (individual drill graduating up through School of the Company to School of the Battalion) his company commander, Captain Blackstone, singled him out for praise. Fairfax had suggested Patrick might be suited for promotion. Patrick started stammering, no, no, he didn't think he would- it wasn't right, or suitable - but thanks very kindly for the offer... p'raps another time, and so on and so forth.

He knew men were going to die, and he also knew he wasn't going to be responsible for their going. Until he got a whole lot more comfortable with this whole thing of being a soldier, he'd stick with taking care of nobody but Patrick Shannon, thank you.

People were already dying around him. Some stupidly. One private, tired of his mount's dislike for the currycomb, lashed the animal's flank with a knotted rope. The horse kicked his skull in, and the man took an hour of choking gurgles to die. Another, on the firing range, had the habit - perhaps he thought he looked soldierly - of resting both hands on his musket's muzzle while he talked and while the musket was loaded. One day the musket went off, nobody knew why, blew both the man's hands off, and he bled to death in a few minutes. Three men drowned trying to swim across a river. Patrick was told none of them had ever seen a body of water that couldn't be waded. But mostly they died of sickness. Camp fever it was called. Sergeant Reed said it came from rotten air.

Patrick didn't know anything about that. But he knew from his time out on the trail that you had to keep yourself clean, even if it meant bathing in a horse trough. You changed into clean clothes when you could, and you washed the dirty ones out. You didn't drink water downstream from a dead horse, and you didn't piss in the stream, either. When you went to the jakes, you dug it under.

Patrick didn't think any of this was special knowledge, it was just what you did. But a lot of the soldiers didn't and a lot of them died.

In less than a month, eleven men in his approximately 80-man Company - B Company, it'd been named - died. One of them was Dack Noble. His messmates had done what they could after Dack collapsed one morning at drill, getting him back to their tent, and into his blankets. One minute he was freezing, the next frying. They got cool water from a nearby farmer's well for him to drink. Someone had sat beside him night and day. He'd died just before dawn of the third day, and been buried before noon. There'd only been a handful of men at the ceremony in the new graveyard. Captain Kelly had said the words and, recognizing Patrick, had tried to make it sound like this wasn't the second, third or even fifth burial he'd done this week, and had other duties far more important - duties for the living.

The drill and the training continued - on foot and then on horseback. "At the walk... forward!" "Close it up, dirt farmers! Y'all look like a passel of Yanks!" "At the gallop... Charge! Charge!" Bugles blasting away, and Patrick slowly learning to tell which tootle meant what. Men died in these drills, too, falling from horses and being trampled, or breaking their necks. But that was somehow acceptable - they were learning how to kill and that was a harsh school.

They saw little of Colonel Forrest - he was spending most of his time cajoling or shouting for long-promised supplies, or using his own fortune to buy what they would need. But every now and then a trooper would turn and see the big grim-faced man just behind him, watching and listening, his face showing neither approval or scorn. Every now and then there'd be a snap of advice: "Always gallop toward the enemy. Never away." Or: "Remember, the only difference between you and the infantry is you get to the battle quicker. You kill the Yankee same way he does." Or: "The way we will win this war is to always hit the Yankee where his soldiers don't think we will." Or, one time when Patrick caught him bent over a grindstone, sharpening his saber like he was a common butcher, something that Shannon had heard was not a gentlemanly thing to do: "War means fighting, and fighting means killing."

Allan Cole & Chris Bunch

Patrick had words with him just once, and that really didn't count. He, Johnny and Billy had been ordered out on a pretend picket, in front of friendly lines that didn't exist, waiting to give early warning of an enemy that didn't exist either. No one came to relieve them and pretty soon it got dark and started drizzling. Only Patrick had tucked some grub - salt pork and cold cornbread - in his saddlebags. He shared it with the others, not forgetting to rub in how much they owed him. Johnny and Billy started complaining. Hell, this wasn't right. Everybody else was back in camp, and had steak for supper, and most likely the band would've set up, and what kind of Army was this, anyway?

Normally, Patrick would have joined in, and probably been the loudest of the complainers. But maybe he was wetter, sleepier or just generally more riled up than the other two. "You two are talkin' trash," he said, flatly, slipping into the careless peckerwood style of talking the Army seemed to issue when a man took the oath. "There ain't but four things y'all really got to have. First, is nobody chasin' you around. Second, is a full belly. Full of what don't count. Third is dry clothes. Four is a place to sleep. That's all you need, and you can manage on just the first two. All the rest's nothin' but gravy on your biscuits." He heard a noise and spun.

Colonel Nathan Bedford Forrest stood there. He had two pistols and a saber slung on his belt. He wore a slouch hat, and rain dripped from it and his beard. Patrick swore he could see Forrest's eyes gleam in the darkness. There was nothing but the sound of rain dripping from the trees around them. Forrest stared long and hard at Patrick. "You'll do," he said, finally, turned and vanished into the night.

One day Forrest decided they were ready and so they rode to war. Now they were crouched on a rain-drenched riverbank, hidden like so many footpads, about to ambush a warship. "Y'all got any thoughts on what to be aimin' at?" Billy inquired.

"You see any heads look like they need shooting?"

"Naw... naw... wait. There's one, he's abobbin' up an' down like a coon duckin' a dog. What kindy hat sailor officers wear?"

"I'll be damned... sorry, Billy... if I know that. Somethin' impressive, I'd guess."

Allan Cole & Chris Bunch

Billy Jeter, like many Confederate soldiers, didn't hold with swearing, and had Patrick read to him by the hour from either a Bible he'd talked Kelly out of or from one of the many religious tracts that drenched the camp. Patrick sometimes wondered if they were supposed to kill Yankees or convert them. He didn't tell Billy that, not even when Jeter got on him for his "intemperate language;" not even when Billy said they should kneel and pray together for this literal curse of Patrick's to be lifted. Patrick declined.

He also didn't mention having been raised sort of Catholic. That would have made his messmates check him for cloven hooves and a forked tail, at the very least.

The command whispered down the line. "Get ready. Fasten down on your targets." Then there was a shout: "FIRE!" The treeline rippled flame, then smoke. Patrick jerked from the smash of Billy's musket next to him, but he thought he saw that head with the hat disappear.

"You got him!" Billy was slithering back, handing the musket over to Patrick. Patrick, all thumbs, fumbled out a paper cartridge, tore it open a bit, poured some powder into the muzzle, pulled out the ramrod, not wanting to get up on his knees, pushed ball, paper wad and musket home, fumbled for a percussion cap... and the world exploded.

Patrick swore that great cannon out there in the river, hell it wasn't but a few yards, maybe even feet, was aimed straight at him and then it bellowed, and he knew he could see that great iron ball blast out, toward him... over him... gunblast echo... he must've heard it WHIRRING... gunboat cannon recoiling back into darkness... ears ringing as he dropped the tiny cap in the dirt, and dug out another one.

A shout from behind - Captain Kelly, he thought, "they're shootin' high, like Bedford said!" Shoved the new cap onto the nipple, and scooted forward, up the ridge now staring straight at the gunboat... holy Lord, he wasn't afraid! Or anyway didn't think he was...

"Y'all go'n aim straight past that cannon," Billy shouted, "y' kin mebbe bounce th' ball inside, like you was at a turkeyshoot."

Allan Cole & Chris Bunch

Patrick aimed... hearing down the line the SNAPCRACK ripple of other muskets going off, and the holler came with it, the high-pitched ululation some said came from hogcalling but nobody knew for sure, and all Patrick knew was it scared him to the marrow, so he knew it'd have to set a Yankee back.

The musket surged against his shoulder, and he realized he'd fired, no idea if he'd put the ball into the gunport as Billy had suggested or maybe let it go at the moon. He couldn't have missed, could he?

The damned gunboat was even closer now. He couldn't hear much, and was fumbling to reload, and Billy was pulling the musket away, shouting about givin' somebody else a chance, and he slid back down the slope as the cannon muzzle came back out the port, fresh-loaded, and again the gates of hell opened. He heard screams, and they weren't battle cries.

Smoke from the cannon fire rose around the gunboat, and down Forrest's battleline. Patrick saw men muscle the little sixpounders up, and they cracked/cracked/cracked and Patrick saw wood splinter and fly, and saw men shout and fall on the Conestoga.

Then Billy had shot and it was his turn, and he loaded, and aimed, and was hollering as loud as anybody, and by heaven this time his musketball did go through the port, he knew it did, and Billy was shouting as loud as he was, a shriek of "damnyoudamnyoudamnyou... " He couldn't have heard, his eyes must have told his ears to respond to something, but he thought he heard the Conestoga's engines chuffing louder. Certainly he saw one side-wheel churn water, and the Federal gunboat was turning, back the way it had come.

They'd won! A handful of men with muskets, and a few little cannon had driven off the Terror of the Cumberland. Why hell. He heard cheers. Damn.

He automatically reached over to Billy's pouch, to begin reloading, like they'd been taught, and found it empty. Impossible. Must've spilled, somewhere. He looked up at the sun, which'd gone and moved on him.

They'd been fighting, confirmed by checking his hunter watch, for over an hour.

Patrick suddenly felt how cramped his legs were, and got to his feet, having to use a nearby branch for a cane. Billy came up. Twenty feet away, a man was leaning against a tree, sort of smiling. Patrick realized he couldn't have much to smile about, since his left arm was gone and his butternut-dyed homespun shirt was solid dark. He started over to see if he could help, and then stopped. Nobody, not even Reverend Kelly, could've done anything.

Captain Blackstone was shouting. "Pull back! Back to the horses! Form up!"

Fairfax and Reed were giving orders as well, and the soldiers half-slid, half-stumbled back from the river. They found their horses just where they'd left them, tethered to a low tree, uninjured, if spooked. Only Templar was behaving like he was perfectly used to cannonfire, a true descendent of the Byerly Turk. But there was no sign of Johnny. Patrick, hoping his friend hadn't cut and run, shouted to Sergeant Reed, who scowled, and ordered them to scout for tracks. Neither of them were Natty Bumpos, but they didn't have to look far.

Johnny Evans lay sprawled next to a thicket about thirty yards from where he'd been ordered to stay. There wasn't a mark on his body, but he was very dead. What happened, how or why he'd left the horses, no one could figure. Patrick guessed they'd take him back to their camp, and give him, and the other dead, proper burial there. But different orders came down.

Forrest ordered the dead buried where they fell. Neither Patrick nor Billy had dug a grave before, but they did the best they could. It was still pretty shallow, though, when they were told that was enough. They tried not to look at Johnny's face, suddenly sallow and vacant, as they laid him in the ground, sort of wrapped in his sleeping tarp. Patrick wished he could cry.

They covered the grave over, tied a cross together from a couple of branches and stuck it in the ground, and Billy said some kind of prayer. Then the cavalry mounted and rode off.

Patrick stared back at the hillside that looked like any Kentucky riverbank. He'd have to write Johnny's people and tell them what happened, and where he was buried. He wondered if anyone would be able to find it again.

238

CHAPTER EIGHTEEN

PHILADELPHIA - LATE MARCH, 1862

IN HER DREAM Nancy was as light as a bird, tripping down the street in her brightest work frock, chattering gaily with her factory mates and coyly ignoring the lustful swains who gathered each day to ogle the girls streaming out of the great smoking mills of Kensington. She had not a care in the world, or a serious thought in her head as she gossiped about beaus, both ardent and wayward, and speculated about the parish dance Saturday night. Then her old enemy pain knotted in her bowel and slashed from groin to toe and she groaned awake.

To her despair, she found herself once again in Susan's big guest room in the old sprawling house off Chestnut. She noted in relief that no one was about; with shaking hands she drew the bottle of laudanum from its hiding place. She gasped down a dram, and gritted her teeth against the pain as the potion did its work.

She looked about the room, wondering how she'd once found it so lovely and comfortable. Months before, when the pregnancy had started to go wrong, Susan had brought her here from the crowded clutter of her parents' humble red brick row home. The room had been a wonder then, with its rich gleaming furniture, bright farm paintings, and big soft feather bed. But now it had become her prison, where she had been locked up with the pain.

Nancy felt the child in her belly give a weak kick and she knew the laudanum was affecting it as well. She realized it was wrong, but once she'd discovered the release it offered she could not muster the willpower to resist. One of her friends kept her supplied and thus far Nancy was sure neither Susan or Mary suspected her shameful weakness.

She desperately wished she had their strength; quiet stolid Mary, and Susan, a veritable rock in this awful storm, always chirruping brightly about the positive things in life. Why couldn't she bear up as they did? There must be something wrong with her. Other women had difficult pregnancies; other women had husbands gone to war. But ever since that night when the pain first struck and blood burst from her loins, Nancy had been fearful of the smallest things. And what would her darling Kerry think of her of now? Here she was, legs permanently raised by the pillows the midwife had ordered put there to dam the flowing blood. Food and drink was fetched and people fussed over her as if she were a grand woman instead of a lowly factory lass.

Only a small bit of the pain lingered; but the full terror and shame of her situation raged within. She reached for the laudanum to flee to brighter days when she had no cares or worries. She heard footsteps on the stairs - someone was coming. She quickly hid the bottle. There was a knock: it was Susan and Mary. The pain flared, although not as bad as before. She tried to make her voice light as she called for them to come in.

When Susan opened the door and saw the poor pale child curled in the bed, her heart gave a wrench. Nancy was so thin. Her skin stretched tight over her bones, making the sheet-covered hump of her belly an obscene thing. Her eyes were bruised tunnels of misery. Susan forced her brightest smile. "How do you feel, dear?"

Nancy did her best to smile back. "I had a lovely sleep," she answered.

Susan decided to ignore this evasion, saying instead: "I am so glad to hear that, dear. With the child so near, you'll need all the rest you can get."

"We've come to give you a nice bath and rubdown," Mary said, unrolling the bundle she carried and shaking out the towels. She thought her sister-in-law looked like death itself, but covered her feelings by smoothing out the towels with elaborate care.

"Thank you just the same," Nancy said, "but I'd just as soon go back to sleep."

"Nonsense," Susan said. "You'll sleep better after a bit of a bath."

Nancy wished they'd just go away. All she could think of was the flicker of pain in her gut and the laudanum in its hiding place. If only she could have just a bit more, she could drive that beast back before it became enraged. But the women were bustling about, pulling at the bed clothes and fetching hot water and a washing stand. "If you think it's best," she managed.

Allan Cole & Chris Bunch

"Of course it is, Nancy," Mary said. "It'll relax you and afterwards we'll put you in a fresh gown and splash you with something sweet-smelling I found at the market."

"You're both so very kind," Nancy said.

"Perhaps we'd better change the bedding while we're at it," Susan said, fingering the limp sheets.

Nancy was in a sudden panic, fearing discovery of the laudanum. A hand involuntarily shot out to clutch the sheets. "Wait!" she cried, voice hoarse.

The women were taken back by her tone. But before they could respond, Nancy saw the housekeeper in the door with something in her hand. She pointed, drawing their attention away. "It's Mrs. Fawcett," she said. Susan and Mary turned.

"A letter's come for you, Mrs. Dolan," the housekeeper said.

The women hesitated for a long moment. Even Nancy in her torment felt trepidation whenever the post came. Philadelphia prided itself on the efficiency and frequency of its mail delivery; but since the outbreak of the war the women of the city were not certain whether it was a blessing or a curse. No one knew these days what manner of tidings the mail would bring.

Please, dear Lord, Susan thought. Don't let it be what I've been fearing all these months.

Mother of God, Mary prayed, if it's about my Hugh I will surely die.

I can't go on like this, Nancy thought - one agony driving away the other. I won't. I won't.

Susan gathered her strength. "Thank you, Mrs. Fawcett," she said, taking the letter and willing her fingers to not betray her with a coward's trembling.

Nancy saw her study it. "It's from Washington." Susan's voice was flat, noncommittal. Nancy's fingers crept to the place where she hid the bottle. If something has happened to Kerry, she thought, I'll drink all of it... and that will be the end.

Mary watched her mother-in-law turn the envelope about. "It's only just been posted," she heard her say. Mary wanted to scream for her to open it and get it over with. Finally, with worry creasing her brow, she did. Her brow cleared, to the vast relief of both young women.

"It's only from my cousin Michael," Susan said, not quite suppressing a wild laugh. "He's been in Washington on Army business." She quickly scanned first one page, then another. "Wait. He's seen Ian and the boys! Oh, what good news."

"Read it to us, please," Mary begged. Nancy nodded, urging her to read as well. And so Susan did:

My Dearest Cousin Susan

I suspect you are surprised at hearing from me after only a seven-month absence. I have been such a poor correspondent in the past I imagine you feared you wouldn't hear from your favorite Californio for a Mexican year at the least. I even failed to send along a thank you for your many kindnesses during my visit to your fair city, much less to ask after the health of those two lovely brides, Mary and Nancy.

Susan paused to enjoy the giggles Michael's praise drew from her two charges. It was a lovely sound, rare in this house for much too long. Then she continued:

But I must warn you, my fairest of all cousins, this missive is not a sudden conversion on my part. I'm afraid that at my time in life my bad habits are as worn in as my favorite saddle and your misplaced affection in me will soon be tested anew.

"Isn't he a devil?" Mary laughed.

"Yes, he is," Susan agreed, feeling very warm about her black sheep cousin, whose letters over the years - while infrequent - were always a joy. She went on:

The Army sent me to Washington on business. While I was there I had the good fortune to bump into some family members I am sure you are all eager to hear news of. Cousin Joshua was one, and he's as hale and hard-headed as when you last laid eyes on him. A little later the business took me across the river to Virginia, where I saw your handsome Ian, and those two strapping young bulls you call your sons.

First, to put all your fears to rest, Ian and the boys have been pulled back for garrison duty. The politicos here are awful cowards and have a great fear of Johnny Reb sneaking around Gen.

McClellan's advance to knock on their door. Your brave men have had the good fortune to be among those to guard the city. The duty is as safe as my favorite old boots I forgot at home when I joined the boys of the 13th California.

There was chorus of "thank gods" in the room, and with a great smile wreathing her face, Susan plunged on:

They've made a good camp, and although I'll not lie and say they aren't short a few luxuries - your charming company most of all - they're eating well and catching up on some much deserved sleep. You should hear from them personally in a few days, for they have all said they had letters just about written and were planning to finish when their officers allowed them the time. I pulled a few strings to get them a few hours off last night, and took them out for some drinks and a good meal.

Ian is just as you saw him last, Susan, except he's brown as a coffee bean from all the healthy outdoor life. He looked smart in his uniform with his sergeant's stripes and twice as strong as any of the horses that haul those guns about he is so proud of. I promised him I would send along his love, and I would suspect that when you get his letter that he'll have a few more things to say that only married eyes are fit to read.

Susan felt sudden warmth bloom between her legs, and had to stop and laugh at herself for acting like a love-struck maiden. Mary and Nancy wanted to know what was so funny, but she shook her head and continued:

I swear Hugh looks taller every time I see him. He cuts such a dashing figure Mary would fall in love with him all over again if she saw him now. He was his usual quiet self, but except for missing Mary, he's in good cheer. He drew me aside when our too-short night was ended and said it would be a great favor to him if I mentioned in my letter that his thoughts were always with his dear wife.

Mary wiped away tears, savoring those few words. She was Hugh's "dear wife." How lovely to hear that phrase, even voiced through Michael's pen and Susan's lips.

I must say, my dear cousin, your son Kerry is the most amusing company a fellow could wish for. He's not only as handsome as any in our family - I except myself in this observation, for I alone was not graced with that Shannon blessing - but as humorous and full of good-natured antics as they come. He had us all laughing the entire evening. But he also has a good head on his shoulders and I know he'll make us proud in the years to come. I will say that he pestered me all night about Nancy; telling me to say this and say that until my brain was so full that everything he said fell out. The gist of it was he loves her more than life itself, and doesn't care if she blesses him with a girl or a boy, so long as the child resembles its mother - from her fair features to sweet nature.

Nancy clutched at those words for dear life. They drove away self-doubt and soothed better than any potion from a bottle. She realized Susan had stopped and she looked up to see her mother-in-law and Mary looking at her. They were smiling, but she could see held-back tears in their eyes, and she realized to her great terror they wondering if she would even be with them much longer. She must not let that happen. She must not let them think that. Nancy felt the child in her give a lazy kick, and she grappled for strength. What was it Kerry had said? Ah, yes - he loved her more than life itself. Her darling, darling Kerry, with his juggling and jokes. She smiled back at the two women, and nodded at Susan. "Go on, please," she said. Susan did:

We had a grand evening of it, talking over old times and lying about our new adventures. I saw them safely back to camp and we were all in such fine Irish voice that we tarried with the sentries a bit just to cheer them up. I wouldn't have any worries about your men, Susan. They're as good as any soldiers I have ever seen, and full of such uncommon good sense I'd bet all my holdings the three of them will soon be safely home.

Now for our good cousin Joshua. As I said, he's in robust health and that wily old sea dog has managed to get himself a fine frigate to command. You might not know what a feat that is, for there are few ships available just now. But our persistent cousin kept after those Navy fellows, until the end they could not resist him. His ship is named the Oregon, and it is a lovely thing even to my uneducated eyes. Joshua took me on a tour of it that lasted half-a-day, and although I didn't understand much of what he had to say, it was

Allan Cole & Chris Bunch

plain the craft met his demanding approval. His boy Donald, is at sea with the blockaders, off the Carolinas now, and Joshua had word only a few days before our meeting that all was well with him.

As you can see from this letter, my Philadelphia senora, the luck of the Shannons is still with us all. And I look forward to the day when we can all gather in your grand house again to celebrate the end of this war, and victory for the Union.

Now for the last part of this missive. As I was completing my business today, I happened to see-

Susan abruptly stopped. Mary saw that her lips were tight and her face had paled. "What is it?" she asked.

Her mother-in-law shook her head, but managed a smile. "Nothing. Only business that needs seeing to. I'll deal with it later." She put the letter in her apron pocket. "Now, for that bath," she said, her voice light again.

At that moment Nancy cried out in pain. "Oh, my god, I think-" Another wave struck and Nancy's words turned into a deep groan. Susan and Mary rushed to her, and saw the sheets were wet from her water breaking. The baby was coming. "Help me," Nancy moaned. "Please... help me."

Her fingers scrabbled for something under her pillow, but the pain cut deeper and she shrieked. A small green bottle fell out and burst on the floor. A sweet, heady odor arose. Susan and Mary ignored it, kicking aside the glass as they struggled to keep Nancy in the bed.

Susan shouted for Mrs. Fawcett to fetch the doctor and midwife, then took a hard grip on her daughter-in-law's shoulders. "It'll be over soon, poor darling," she crooned. "I promise it will."

Three days later Susan dragged herself into her little office just off the parlor. She slumped into the chair, every bone and muscle aching from weariness. The house was silent. She heard the infant give a faint cry, then the cooing of the wet nurse. The crying stopped as little Keith Shannon Dolan began to suckle. Outside she heard the church bells calling the last mass. She supposed she ought to go and give thanks the lives of the mother and child had been spared. But she could not dredge up gratefulness for God's kindness. Not after

Allan Cole & Chris Bunch

all the awful hours He'd seen fit to make Nancy suffer. Susan had given birth to two children of her own and had assisted in the birth of many others, but never had she seen a woman forced to undergo such an ordeal.

For awhile she'd thought death would have been a blessing. Not only had the labor been three days long, but accompanied by unrelenting agony. In the end, the doctor said Nancy's hips were too small to let the child pass. While Susan and Mary held the young woman, the doctor and the midwife had dislocated her hips. A few awful hours more, and the child was born.

Nancy was asleep now, her immediate ordeal over. But Susan doubted the girl would ever be the same again. Susan and Mary had been too overcome by what they were witnessing to be shocked when they realized what that shattered bottle had contained. Now, in her weariness, Susan thought she really couldn't blame the poor girl. Despite the danger to both mother and child, other women had fled to opium during difficult pregnancies. She did not think Nancy a coward, but only wished she had been alert enough to see what had been going on.

Susan dragged her mind back to the immediate tasks at hand. She saw Michael's letter on her desk, and remembered those last few pages. Michael had written he had seen Pamela exiting the court building in Washington with an important-appearing man at her side. Michael said the man proved to be an Ohio congressman, who had apparently become Pamela's protector. This congressman had made it his personal business to help wage the woman's legal war against Susan and the other Shannons.

Susan sighed. If it wasn't one trouble, it was another. In her desk drawer she had a document from a federal court notifying her it was investigating Pamela's claims. Susan's lawyer was still contemplating how to deal with it. She was certain his sage advice would prove to be costly.

God forgive me for imagining such a thing, Susan thought, but I wish that woman would walk into the path of a freight wagon. Pamela Shannon was the most conniving, evil woman she had ever encountered. What made the matter almost ludicrous, was there was not nearly as much to fight over as Pamela believed. Diana's estate

246

had been divided just as the will required. With all the Shannon hands it was shared with, there was little hard cash left over. As for properties and business contracts, the other members of the family had asked Susan to oversee them. Some she had sold, for she was not fool enough to think she could deal with all the intricate things her grandmother did as a matter of course.

That money had been divided as well, and she had been scrupulous seeing her cousin Edward and his wife received their fair share. But they had spent it as fast as she sent it. What was left of the estate had not weathered the war well. In many places trade had been blocked or abandoned and contracts were worth less than their fancy paper and seals. What remained was certainly not enough to make even one person rich.

Even the Philadelphia holdings were suffering. This was one of Susan's greatest frustrations, for all about her other people were making money off the conflict. Old businesses were expanding and new ones being formed. Susan had been coldly cut out of many of these opportunities. It was not just her abolitionist views that caused it. With Ian and her sons gone the fact that women were unwelcome in business was made plainer ever day.

She fingered Michael's letter, wishing she had her grandmother's abilities. Diana would have put all of those men into flight. How had she done it? What secret strength and knowledge had she drawn upon? Diana's accomplishments were even more amazing when you considered that her times were certainly no easier than Susan's.

Feeling overwhelmed, Susan opened the desk drawer and put the letter on top of the document from the court. Then she assembled fresh paper and pen and ink. She had a letter of her own to write. She must inform Kerry he was a father and that his dear wife was... Ah, God help me, what shall I say? How shall I phrase it? How would news of his wife's ordeal and present condition affect him?

She thought of her grandmother again and how she had shouldered the troubles of the family for all those long years. Very well, Susan decided, if sin was necessary then she would take it on her own soul. If lies needed to be told, Susan would be the one to tell them. She supposed that when Kerry returned he would hate her for it. But that was a burden - like all those Diana had accepted - that she would just have to bear.

She began to write:

My dear son... I have the most wonderful news...

CHAPTER NINETEEN

SHILOH CHURCH, TENN. - APRIL 7, 1862

CORPORAL PATRICK SHANNON looked every inch the hardbitten Secesh soldier: from his battered, rain-soaked slouch hat to the ripped butternut-died homespun that passed for a uniform in the Army of the Confederacy. to the pair of .44 Colt's Army revolvers in his belt to the .52 caliber Sharps carbine ready in his hands. But he knew down deep he must be as green as Grady Tolliver, the Kentucky boy who'd replaced Johnny Evans and was now hugging a tree about ten feet away. Or, come to think, as most of the Yankees they'd been fighting for the last two days. No one, not Mister Poe, not Monk Lewis, could have known just how bloody the world could become.

He was still carrying, wrapped in an oilcloth pouch, The Letter. He'd written it two days earlier - before the bloodbath started. It had taken him about six tries to get the courage. It was addressed to MISS, for such was Patrick's desperate hope she still remained, LUCY BALDWIN, GENERAL DELIVERY, VICKSBURG, MISSISSIPPI. Patrick had felt a fool writing to somebody he'd met on a street for about a minute, and who more than evidently hadn't thought the world of him. But...there was no one else.

Occasionally he'd thought about writing to one of his cousins, most likely Susan and Ian, in Philadelphia. After all, they'd invited him to visit, and it was no great bother to mail a letter north, particularly when your unit spent most of its time raiding behind Union lines like Bedford Forrest's Tennessee Cavalry did. But that invitation had been a long time ago, and surely they wouldn't want to remember Patrick, given they were sure-fire abolitionists and Patrick was a sure-fire Johnny Reb, no matter how he'd ended up wearing gray.

At least, his wandering thoughts consoled him, fighting out here in the west he wouldn't be likely to find any Shannons in his gunsights. If they'd joined up they'd be serving somewhere on the east, probably under that new general they called Little Mac. Or so he hoped anyway, not wanting to think about the Shannon's proclivity for wandering, nor his cousin Michael from California.

So he'd written the letter to Lucy, on the backside of five pages carefully slit from the Family Genealogy of Billy Jeter's Bible. He didn't talk about how damned lonely he was. He'd attempted to sound cheery, and put in some colorful details about a soldier's life, jolly, and how much everyone in his company appreciated getting letters from folks at home, and how he really didn't have anybody, since his family had died years ago. He finished the letter, but hadn't found anyone who looked like he was going anywhere near a village to mail it. So he'd carried it into battle. A battle where more men had died, just in front of Patrick's eyes, than existed in the whole world. A black part of his mind grinned, and said, well, perhaps they might find it on the Field of Honor, afterward, and somebody would mail it... and he closed off that thought right smartly.

He'd finished the letter on the fifth, while the Confederate Army had been marching back and forth aimlessly in front of the Union lines and Bedford Forrest had been screaming like he was a gutshot horse they were losing every God Damned Chance of Surprise They Could Have Had. But they'd still stunned the Yanks when they attacked, since it looked like the bluebellies were - as Billy put it - blind in one eye and couldn't see out the other.

"Here they come again," somebody hollered, and Patrick forgot about the letter. His fingers touched the musketball amulet for luck, and he peered into the haze that hung thick over shattered country that had once been thickets and farmland. Some of the haze was from the remnants of last night's driving rain and this morning's occasional showers, but more was blue-white gunsmoke. Patrick saw movement to his front and strained to make it out. Thunder - cannonfire - rumbled, and every now and then he could make out the SIZZT of a musketball overhead. Somebody out there was shooting at the scattered rearguard Patrick was part of; but the shots were fired from a good long safe distance, and real high.

"Y'all think," he called to Billy Jeter, who knelt behind a tree stump a couple-three yards away, "that this time it'll be the daughters of Shiloh come out to dance, like the Good Book promised Samuel?"

Billy managed a wan smile, having learned to take joshing about his religion with a bit of salt, but didn't answer. The movement

Allan Cole & Chris Bunch

formed into a man on a horse trotting at them. He carried a banner on a staff. There was nobody behind him, at least nobody Patrick could see. Maybe a line of skirmishers or even a full-on attack would materialize. Or maybe not - this horseman, most likely an officer, wouldn't be the first who'd started out leading a charge that became a solitary turn. The question was, to which army did he belong, and then a bit of wind blew the haze away, and the banner rippled out, and it was blue and gold. Union.

"Shoot him!" bellowed Sergeant Reed from somewhere down the line and the muskets were up and aimed. Patrick held the rider's chest in the center of his notched sight, aimed off a little bit to allow for the breeze and then took his finger off the trigger. Damned brave fool didn't deserve to die. Patrick could be magnanimous, since there was only the one attacker. But the rest of the line didn't agree and white smoke billowed along the torn-down fenceline, and the rider, just yards away, screamed, threw his arms high, pitching the banner away, and crumpled. His horse whinnied surprise, reared, and galloped off. Grady Tolliver got up and ran forward before Patrick could shout to stay down and stop being a damned glory-hunting fool like the man they'd just killed. He'd learn, soon enough. Or die.

Grady grabbed the banner and started to run back. Then he stopped, frozen. "Corp'ral Shannon," Patrick heard him shout over the cannon-roar. "Corp' Shannon!"

The hell... but nobody seemed to be shooting close, and there was still no sign of whatever attackers the man had thought he was leading, so Patrick chanced going to see what Grady's problem was. If they'd just wounded the Federal, he didn't see what Grady expected to do about it. The whole damned battlefield was covered with wounded men, some crying aloud for water, some for the wife and children left hapless behind or however the quote went, and nobody had time for one more bloody mess. That part of the battleground, his mind corrected, not littered with those who'd already gone from the army militant to the Army Triumphant, as Patrick had heard it put.

The man they'd shot lay sprawled, the last of his breath wheezing through his sieved lung. He wore gray and the shoulder boards of a Captain, Confederate States Army. Patrick guessed he'd

251

ridden out on some kind of glory raid and grabbed some Union brigade's colors as a trophy.

"What'll we do," Grady wanted to know. "We went an' killed us'ns one of our own officers!"

Patrick shrugged. "Get our butts back under cover," he said, "before somebody stacks two more fools next to this one." But Patrick, his mind as powder-blackened as his face after the last two days, still found a bit of wonderment at another part of war that didn't show up very often in Currier & Ives.

Patrick thought he'd already seen real battle. Not the skirmish with the Conestoga, but at Fort Donelson, where Bedford Forrest and seven hundred of his troopers had been trapped, along with about seventeen thousand other Rebs, by a hellhound of a Yankee general named Grant. The only reason Patrick wasn't in a Yankee prison camp, which word already said was an unspoken death sentence, was because Forrest had led his men out of Donelson in the heart of a winter night, cross-country through frozen streams to freedom. The other Confederate generals had ended up whining, getting drunk, and surrendering.

But even that or the raids and the skirmishes since, hadn't been anything like the last twenty four hours around this church called Shiloh, not far from a place on the Tennessee River named Pittsburg Landing, where half or maybe more of all of the Yankees in the West were waiting. Captain Blackstone said the Confederate march north had been intended as a surprise attack before the bluebellies could form up and march south, a surprise planned by Confederate General Albert Johnston. But Johnston was dead, just at the beginning of battle, or so Patrick had heard, and if the Union seemed to be making up for their surprise handily.

Patrick had known they were expecting a real fight - back in Corinth they'd been issued a hundred rounds of ammunition per man, when the normal ration was forty. Not that the ordered amount had anything to do with what Forrest's brigands carried - they were battle wise enough to know they'd need as much as their horses could carry and ten more rounds besides.

Forrest and his cavalrymen had ridden onto the battleground on the midmorning of the sixth. Patrick knew better by now than to think anybody could make sense of a battlefield, but this had been worse than most. Here were a group of men serving three cannon, firing in one direction. Here was another group of cannoneers, blasting away in another direction entirely. Here were men marching forward, bayonets fixed, faces pale. There were others, arms abandoned, looting bell-shaped white canvas tents abandoned by the Yanks when the battle began. Men streamed forward, some singly, some marching in tight order like they were on a parade ground. Some of these formations were dripping stragglers, who for their own reasons weren't intent on heroism. Sometimes these stragglers were ignored, sometimes they were threatened, and twice Patrick saw mounted officers slashing at them with the flat of their sabers.

Coming back, stumbling, streaming, faces broken by pain and shock, were the wounded. Sometimes their wounds were dressed, sometimes they still gaped open. Other, less fortunate men sprawled on the ground, some silent, gray-faced, some screaming, some begging for water or a bullet to let them sleep forever. And there were the others, the ones who would never make nor hear a sound again. Sometimes they were whole men, if bloodied or torn, and sometimes there was nothing but pieces. Patrick saw, leaning against a tree, half of a man, just belly and legs, as if its invisible upper half had paused for a pipe before marching on.

The officers were shouting, and the men were dismounting, forming up - column of fours - and moving, now dismounted infantry, walking over somebody's cotton field. The yelling began, that high, wailing yip-yip-yip the Southerners hollered without knowing why or how, when they went into battle. Ahead thunder and more than thunder, and smoke closed off the sun, and there were splintered peach trees and thick brush and Yankees. Patrick was firing, no time to shoulder the carbine and take aim, and what looked to be blue a few feet away and the Sharps bucking in his hands, and blue vanished and time blurred as he levered another round into the chamber, shot, ran, screamed, hid, crashed through brush and Yanks were running away. Time came back to normal, and he looked about and counted heads... Billy... Grady... nobody wounded... smoky

Allan Cole & Chris Bunch

faces, and Patrick was shouting, along with the officers and sergeants, to reload for another attack.

But the brush was too thick, and then another charge wasn't necessary, as Patrick heard cheering, and saw white, or anyway as close as white could be in this spring mire, white rags tied to the ends of bayonets. Somebody told him that night, when things calmed down, the Tennessee Cavalry had gone in near the center of the line, which the teller had said reminded him of a hornet's nest when you whacked it with a stick, and they'd made the sixth attack that day, and the first one that wasn't beat back.

Back that afternoon, when Patrick had come to himself, somebody said they had the bluebellies on the run, and they were breaking like they did at Bull Run, damn' cowards. Patrick saw a couple of Union regimental flags torn up, and trampled, but he had his own feeling about cowardice. He found three dead men, all shot; two of them still held their Springfields ready. But none of the three had either ball or powder in their pouches. There were other unarmed corpses nearby. Patrick thought anybody who'd go on a battlefield, let alone stand up to Bedford Forrest with nary a bullet to shoot, was hardly yellow.

The cannonade renewed, shattering blasts from the Union gunboats over on the river, and the scream of exploding shells around him. Patrick was curling up close to a stump in a dip he wished to be a dugout when he felt something moving next to him. He opened his eyes - he hadn't known they were closed - and saw a tiny rabbit, eyes as clenched shut as his had been, nose twitching more than his body, pressing close, and then Patrick was that rabbit as more thunder rolled.

At nightfall Patrick was detailed to take one other man and work forward to see if he could tell what the Yanks were doing. He picked Billy, without any discussions of volunteering - it was Jeter's turn - and nobody was going scouting with a new boy like Grady. They left most of their gear, except for a pistol, knife, and a canteen each, and slipped into the night. The battle ground was hardly dark - shells exploded in red gouts, and torches flared as Confederate soldiers, discipline forgotten, looted Union riches. For the most part the looters were left alone - no one in the army had drawn rations for days, and raw bacon, stale bread and chewed coffee grounds only went so far.

Patrick and Billy wormed forward, not having much trouble slipping past the skittery and thin-spaced Yankee pickets, down a ravine that'd been fought over that day, trying not to think what that softness was they stepped or crawled across from time to time, and not listening to the moans in the blackness until they could see the river. There were steamers and gunboats aplenty. In the light of many torches Patrick could see Union soldiers streaming off the transports and forming up for battle. That had been enough. They'd made their way back and reported to Captain Blackstone. They hadn't, of course, been the only scouts sent out that night. Blackstone told them others had seen the same massive reinforcements arriving, like so many blue ants swarming.

Blackstone told Patrick to hang on for a minute. After Billy was out of earshot Patrick's company commander stroked his beard for a minute, then said, without preamble, "Colonel Forrest told me, when I reported what the first scouts come back with, to stand ready for a night attack. He went lookin' for Gen'ral Beauregard to tell him. Said, before he left, if we didn't hit the bluebellies tonight, we'd be whipped like hell in the morning."

Patrick waited, but Blackstone didn't say anything else. Patrick left, wondering why, of late, some of these people with shoulderstraps or stripes had started telling him things that went beyond the stretch of Patrick's guns, currycomb or line of sight.

Patrick had done a bit of looting for himself - half a smoked ham, some canned Cove Oysters and a sack of oats. He'd fed Templar, who seemed astonished there was actually fodder in the world beyond roadside grass or half-dried hay, stroked him for awhile, and then went looking for his squad and shelter. They were holed up in a Union tent, which Patrick was most grateful for when, around midnight, rain came sheeting down like a waterfall. He didn't allow himself to do more than drowse, remembering what Forrest had told his Captain. The Colonel may have been a brutal slaver, and was surely homicidal - Patrick had seen him, on a raid, shoot a

255

fleeing, unarmed Yank in the back - but, especially after Donelson, he was as brilliant a warrior as any Xenophon or Ney Patrick had read about.

Every ten minutes a monstrous shell crashed down, harassing fire from some great cannon on a gunboat, firing at random. At three, there'd been another crash, and then screams. About fifty yards away, one of the gunboat's random shots had found a target, impacting almost on a tent full of soldiers. There wasn't anything that could be done. There were four men sprawled in the remains of the canvas, murdered by the shockwave without a mark, dead in the ruins of their card game.

Billy had picked up two of the playing cards, showed them to Patrick in the light of the candle he held, and nodded, moral lesson obvious. Patrick did not say anything about the fifth man, who lay, minus a head, a few feet away, one hand still clutching his prayer book.

There'd been no attack ordered, and at dawn they'd been told to withdraw. The men shouted protest and grumbled. Patrick and Billy may have seen the blue swarm, but they complained as loudly as anyone, even though Patrick had done a fast ammunition check with Billy and Grady, plus the four others Sergeant Reed had told him to corporal for - and come up with about twenty rounds per gun per man. Not much, but hell, they'd gone and won yesterday, hadn't they? But no one consulted Patrick's squad, not Captain Blackstone, not Colonel Forrest, and surely not General Beauregard. The dawn had been gray and rainy, not that brilliant red sunrise of the sixth, which everyone had cheered at, but Patrick remembered, from years ago, a phrase of his Cousin Joshua's: "red sky at morning/sailor take warning..."

The withdrawal turned into full-scale retreat about noon. So far Patrick hadn't seen any soldiers dropping their weapons and running. The Army of the Mississippi was leaving the battlefield with dignity. Now it was mid-afternoon, and about half the company was holding a dirt road not too far from some crossroads. There weren't any officers around, and no one knew where the rest of the company had

256

disappeared to. They were starting to get a little nervous, feeling like maybe they'd been forgotten. And the drumfire was getting closer.

Patrick saw a rider pelting toward the line. It was some lieutenant Patrick vaguely knew from some other company. The man was shouting: "Th' Colonel's down! Led a charge an' was hit! Shot off his horse! Forrest's been hit! He's not dead, but—" and the rider was out of earshot.

Patrick found himself on his feet. The rest of the company was up as well. No one said anything, no one looked around, but all of them were walking away, slowly, back to where the horses waited in a copse. It was just then two cannonballs spattered mud high in the air a dozen yards in front of them, musketfire started, and shouts began.

A skirmish line of Yankees came out of the haze and behind them a solid line of advancing infantry.

Somebody - it was that damned Carruthers, who never was worth a penny whistle, yowped, tossed his carbine aside, and broke into a run. Patrick came out of his own haze and was after him. He caught him in a dozen steps, smashed his Sharps into the man's back, sent him sprawling and turned, thumb pulling hammer back to full cock, and firing, around throwing muck just in front of a man who'd begun to break into a run - the man was Reed, his sergeant, part of Patrick's mind said, and why aren't you running like a sensible person, since there's a whole passel of Yanks coming on, but Patrick was shouting: "Stop! We ain't runnin'! Stand and fight, dammit! Kill one for the Colonel!"

The panic broke before it started, and men were turning, muskets or carbines coming up, fire spattering toward the oncoming Union soldiers. The skirmishers went flat and returned the fire.

"First Section," Patrick shouted. "To your horses! And walk, damn you!," not thinking how stupid a nineteen year old was bellowing commands like a grizzled old sergeant. "Reload! Pick your targets. You can't hit any if you don't hit one! Third Section, on your feet..."

And so it went, fire and withdrawal, the Yankees stopping, not knowing if the cavalry was picketing for an infantry regiment, brigade or even a division, and slowly the half-company pulled back,

257

mounted, fired a final volley, and, at the walk, just as Forrest had drilled them time and again, broke contact and continued the withdrawal.

They were ten miles and more beyond the battlefield, still headed away, when they were told Forrest hadn't been killed, but wounded, a musketball in his hip, charging a full skirmish line of infantry with a handful of men. Now he was on his way to a hospital, promising not just to live, but to be back inside a month.

Patrick was starting to think he'd get a chance to mail The Letter when Billy pulled his horse up beside Templar. "I got a question, Patrick. I mean, Corp'ral."

"Don't be asking me," Shannon managed. "Corp'rals don't get issued brains."

"We kilt a whole bunch of Yanks, right? Broke their best like they was sticks for kindlin' right? And we took their tents an' supplies? They ain't gone be comin' South for awhile, will they?"

"Sounds to me like you're right on everything."

"Then we won, right?" Billy looked closely at Patrick.

Patrick began to say something, but instead smiled broadly. "Hell yes, Private Jeter. Who you think won?" Billy yipped with glee, and pulled his horse back to pass along that his ever-wise corporal had confirmed victory.

Patrick had discarded his first response - that the Yankees still held Pittsburg Landing, and it was the South that was retreating, not them. But he had not. Corporal Patrick Shannon was learning how to lead.

CHAPTER TWENTY

WASHINGTON - EARLY JULY, 1862

"WOULD YOU CARE for a little more nice cold punch, Mrs. Brady," Pamela asked, lifting the frosty pitcher from its bed of ice.

"I don't mind if I do," Mrs. Brady replied in her genteel Virginia drawl. She laughed as Pamela refilled her glass. "My late husband would have a fit... brandy punch in the middle of the afternoon."

"It's only a little brandy," Pamela said. "A taste for health's sake."

"Just the same," Mrs. Brady said, "Walter was opposed to it. He did not think it seemly for women to imbibe during the daylight hours."

"I do not think he would be so opposed if he were with us now," Pamela said. "In these terrible times women are doing all sorts of things that would have been unthinkable of before. My dear Edward also held stern views where our sex was concerned. But I like to think he would be proud of me. In my way, I'm fighting the battle he would have waged if he had lived."

Mrs. Brady sighed and took an unladylike pull on the punch. "It's true, patriotism demands that we do some of the most distasteful things. But whenever I despair, I think of our poor boys in gray and press on."

Outside Pamela's luxuriously furnished and decorated rooms they could hear the steady hammer of drums and the shrill of brass. There were so many military bands playing at all hours in Washington the strains of their music were constantly in the air.

"You are an example to all who love the South," Pamela said. "I give thanks to our Lord each night that you have granted me an opportunity to strike a blow for our dear homeland."

Mrs. Brady took another drink. "No second thoughts, dear, about joining our little band of spies?"

"None at all," Pamela said firmly. "As a matter of fact, I have a few documents that might interest you." She dug a hand under the pillow of the chair beside her and pulled out a thick envelope. "Congressman Wright was kind enough to lead Marcia and I on a tour of the War Office the other day. I managed to slip some Army telegrams under my petticoats."

Mrs. Brady straightened in her chair, impressed. She opened the envelope and sifted through the papers, her smile growing broader as she saw their worth. "Very good, indeed, Mrs. Shannon," she said. "And to think some of our sisters feared you could not be trusted."

Pamela dimpled sweetly, playing the precocious daughter to the older woman. "I hope they trust me now."

"I had no worries from the very beginning, dear," Mrs. Brady said. "Oh, I know the word was about that you had changed sides. But I could see the instant we met that you were only pretending... and biding your time."

Pamela smiled, and topped up the woman's glass. "I assume my long friendship with Mr. Fitz Maguire helped convince you of my true motives," she said.

"Well, of course it did, dear," Mrs. Brady said. "He's such an important man in Richmond, and so close to our beloved President Davis, how could anyone doubt your patriotism?" Mrs. Brady tucked the papers back into the envelope and put them away in her purse. She drained her glass. "These telegrams are so important," she said, "I'd best cut short this delightful visit." She rose, and Pamela came to her feet with her. "I must see they get to Richmond immediately."

"This is so exciting," Pamela said. "To think I found something worthy my very first time."

She escorted the woman to the door. "Shall I send along your best wishes to Mr. Maguire?" Mrs. Brady asked.

"By all means," Pamela said. "And tell him he's been a great inspiration to me."

Mrs. Brady nodded, said her good-byes, and exited. As soon as the door closed Pamela whirled, lifted up her skirts and ran to the window. She pulled aside the shade and signaled to a frock-coated man leaning against a post across the street. He got the signal. Mrs. Brady came out of the building and started down the street. The man followed.

Pamela laughed aloud and clapped her hands in delight. In an hour or two the Pinkerton agents would have Mrs. Brady and her whole group of petticoat spies under close arrest. Humming a light tune to herself, Pamela waltzed about the floor, clutching an invisible partner. The most delightful thing about her small victory, was that once word leaked out Fitz Maguire would get the blame for setting them up with a traitor. And he didn't even know that Pamela was alive.

She called out. "Hercules!" When the child didn't immediately appear she shouted again. "Hercules!"

The servants' door opened and he poked his small black face through. "Yes'm."

"Draw my bath. Make it good and hot this time. And put out those salts Mr. Wright gave me." Hercules frowned, unhappy. "Well. What's holding you up?"

"How come you still got me drawin' the bath, missus? You got other folks to do that now. Mrs. Taylor ain't doin' nothin'. And I got to wash the buggy yet."

Pamela stamped her foot. "I didn't ask other people, Hercules. And I certainly don't intend to bother my housekeeper with such a lowly chore. Now you get, hear me? And if you give me any more of your sass, I swear I'll hand you over to Mr. Lincoln, himself. You'll be toting bricks down at the yard along with those runaway niggers before the day is through."

Fear replaced the frown. "Yes'm," Hercules said. And he was gone.

Her mood spoiled, Pamela stalked across the room and opened another door. Marcia was on her knees in front of a dress mannequin, her mouth full of pins, her hands busy with the hem. "Aren't you done with that yet, Marcia?" Pamela snapped.

Marcia removed the pins from her mouth. "I'm doing my best," she whined.

"Well that just isn't good enough," Pamela said. "You know very well I must have it ready for the dinner tomorrow night."

"I wish you would stop treating me like a servant," Marcia said. But she got busy with the dress again.

Pamela advanced deeper into the sewing room. "Don't be so cranky, Marcia," she said. "Haven't I done everything I could for you? Why, I've been working my fingers to the very bone in your behalf ever since I came to Washington." She pointed around at the fashionable quarters they now resided in. "You're living in the very lap of luxury. With no more worries where the next penny will come from to pay the rent."

"Mr. Wright certainly has been generous," Marcia said.

Pamela found her tone offensive. "What do you mean by that?"

Marcia lowered her head, blushing. "Nothing," she said.

"I asked you a question, cousin," Pamela pressed. "You weren't impugning my honor by any chance?"

Marcia gave a hard shake of her head. "I'd never dream of it, Pamela," she said.

"Every single thing that Mr. Wright has done for us," Pamela said hotly, "was out of pure friendship, and nothing more. I won't have people thinking differently."

"You have never given them cause to," Marcia said in a rush. "Please. I didn't meant anything by it. I'm just hot and tired."

"Am I not always in your company when Mr. Wright is about?"

"Yes. Yes, of course, you are," Marcia said. "Really, Pamela. There's no need to go on. I really do apologize if I gave the slightest hint of disrespect."

"Very well," Pamela said. "I'll forgive you."

She heard a knock on the main door, then Hercules' brisk, small steps. A moment later he appeared at the sewing room door. "It's Mr. Wright, missus," he said.

"Tell him I'll be right there," Pamela answered. She turned to Marcia. "I need a private word with him, if you don't mind."

Marcia shrugged. "I'll stay here," she said.

Pamela gave her a look. "The door, however, will remain open. So you needn't worry."

"I never do," Marcia said, and went back to her work.

Pamela snorted in disgust. She pinched her cheeks, wet her lips, and tugged her bodice into a more enticing display. Then she curled her lips into a dazzling smile, hoisted the hem of her dress up between two lovely fingers, and made a grand sweeping entrance into the parlor.

The instant Wright saw her, he threw his arms open and advanced. "My God," he said, huskily, "You are the most beautiful woman that-"

Allan Cole & Chris Bunch

Pamela cut him off with a soft hand across his lips. "My cousin," she whispered, warning eyes darting toward the open sewing room door." Then as Wright's arms began to encircle her narrow waist, she ducked under them and danced away. She took up position by the pitcher of punch. "Would you care for a glass, my dear Mr. Wright?" she asked loudly.

Wright glanced at the open door, frustrated. He gave an sigh of resignation. "No thank you, Mrs. Shannon," he said. "I can only stay a moment." He came closer and whispered: "Later tonight?"

"Ten o'clock," was Pamela's whispered reply. "And mind that loose board on the backstairs."

Wright chuckled. "I know it well. The fifth step is my mortal enemy."

Pamela shushed him. Then in a normal voice: "Mrs. Brady was here."

Wright nodded, and winked. "I'm sorry I missed her," he boomed. "Delightful woman. Delightful." He leaned closer to whisper. "We'll both be thanked for this day's work."

"It's nice to make new friends," Pamela said.

"Making friends is what life is all about, Mrs. Shannon," Wright laughed. "And while I'm at it, did I tell you we have a new friend at the federal court? He's promised to give your case special consideration."

"Lovely," Pamela said. "How can I ever thank you for your many kindnesses, Mr. Wright?"

Wright leered and mouthed "ten o'clock." But what he said aloud, was: "Think nothing of it. If your government cannot assist a patriotic widow in need, then what use is it, I ask you?"

A volley of cannon fire rattled the windows. Pamela cursed under her breath. The constant practice was an even greater annoyance than all that martial music. "Before I forget," Pamela said, "I have that list I promised you." She went to her sewing basket and removed a small notebook. "I went through my papers and wrote down the name and value of every slave my husband and I owned that snake, Maguire stole from me." She handed him the book. "As soon as you bring me the emancipation papers, I'll sign them. Then every blessed black soul will be freed. Aren't you proud of me?"

263

"Well, I most certainly am, Mrs. Shannon," Wright said. "This is a marvelous gesture. I think our friends will look mostly kindly on this. Most kindly indeed." He was referring to several noted Radical Republicans who were constantly pressing the Abolitionist cause, urging President Lincoln to abandon his piecemeal approach and to free all the slaves.

"Are you sure it isn't any more than that?" Pamela said. "After all, I don't really own them. Mr. Maguire does."

"Actually, our case is becoming better than I had hoped," Wright said, "Even with that fool McClellan making a mess of things in Virginia, what were once your lands are now under Army control. And as we speak our Radical friends are drawing up a new bill that demands a grim future for the South once it loses. Under Reconstruction, all property ownership will be up for grabs, I tell you." He tapped the notebook. "This gesture will endear you even more to our friends. Believe me, they will support your suit to regain your other properties with a fervor."

The more she thought about it, the more Pamela approved of Wright's plan. The fact her fortunes were absolutely pinned to those of the North gave her little concern. Even with McClellan's retreat - the latest in many other Union failures - she had no doubt as to the outcome of the war. She was so certain she nearly ignored all battlefront news and the recent alarms over threats to the city. She had seen soon enough that no matter how many Yankees were killed, there were plenty more to sacrifice, and the factories of the North poured out materials without cease.

Wright waved the notebook. "I'll have a clerk draw up the appropriate forms. Now, I must beg your forgiveness and end our visit. I only stopped by to ask after your health." He looked at the open door. "And your charming cousin's, of course."

"I'll be sure to tell her, Mr. Wright," Pamela said, walking with him to the door. "She'll be most grateful."

She let him steal a kiss and a squeeze of her breast, then shooed him away and shut the door.

Pamela marched to the drinks table and poured herself a small cognac. She would only allow herself this one more; liquor was bad for one's complexion and figure. But a little would do no harm. All in all, this was turning out to be a most remarkable day.

CHAPTER TWENTY-ONE

ANTIETAM CREEK - SEPTEMBER 16-17, 1862

IT WAS WELL after ten o'clock, but neither army slept. Cannon grumbled, and occasionally a picket thought he saw something and opened fire. Men were chattering, shouting, restive, awaiting the next day. Columns of soldiers still packed the dirt lanes, dust thankfully damped by an occasional rain shower. First Sergeant Ian Dolan guided his horse along one column, trying not to hurry, trying not to bull his way, remembering what it had been like to be afoot in Ireland and be brushed aside by a mounted British "gentleman."

The two great armies had found each other again. They curled across the half-cleared rolling countryside of Maryland, waiting for the morning and battle. In their center was the tiny hamlet of farmers, ironworkers and canal men named Sharpsburg; about a mile from where the Potomac River wound, shallowing but still a formidable obstacle. Not far from the village was steep-banked Antietam Creek, crossed by several arching stone bridges. The only significance Sharpsburg had was as a crossroads, and that was enough to make it a battlefield... just as Manassas Junction - fought over twice now - just as Winchester, just as Port Republic, had been.

Gen. Robert E. Lee - after driving out both the Army of Virginia, which Ian and his sons had been serving with, and McClellan's Army of the Potomac - marched north, crossing from Virginia into Union territory for the first time. Ian had not talked to anyone who could do more than guess Lee's intent, but theories ran from sacking Philadelphia - Ian shrank from the thought, even though he doubted even a general as good as Lee could strike a blow that spectacular - to attacking Washington, to just raising general hell with the Union. The Army of the Potomac, now combined with the disgraced Army of Virginia, stirred its bones and ambled off in pursuit. Now, Ian thought, we've hunted the lion to his den, and all that remains is the easy task of skinning him. Or so they say.

He shuddered, even though the night was far from cold. The cavalryman acting as provost back where the lane forked had told him his goal was about a mile away, but his tone had been doubtful. He'd said it was not far beyond the copse Ian had just passed - if, indeed, those trees were the grove the man had meant. A stone fence ran beside the lane, and then there was an opening, where a gate had been torn away. In the field on the other side a few meager campfires glowed. Ian dismounted and led his horse into the field, figuring at least he would be able to ask further directions.

A sentry challenged him. "What unit are you, now?" Ian asked after answering the challenge.

"Eighty-sixth Pennsylvania."

"And am I not the Great Navigator himself," Ian marveled, and slowly worked his way through the camp, looking for his sons.

He found them still awake, not far from where one of the banned but ignored campfires burnt. He'd brought presents - a Copperhead chicken had attacked him earlier that day and been duly sentenced, executed and pan-fried by the battery's cook. He also had a flask of applejack.

"You see, boys," Ian said, feeling very much the paterfamilias, "how it is when you're artillery. Not like you poor sharpshooters, forced to carry the whole world on your backs. Most of which, I note, you abandoned coming north."

Kerry grinned. "Not us, Dad. Most likely the 118th. Our Corn Exchange Brokers wanted to make sure they'd fight the war in comfort. Marched 'em off with patent writing desks, paper collars and Jamaica ginger so they won't smell bad."

Ian smiled - any army on the march could be followed by what it abandoned, and the greener the unit the more there was to dump. He declined chicken, and barely tasted the applejack. "I'll never find my way back fuddled, and tomorrow looks to be... busy."

Hugh was very serious. "How bad will it get?"

Ian considered his words carefully. "It'll be bloody, and more, is my call. Even Little Mac won't be able to find a way around this one. And we know the Rebels won't turn away from a fight. It's my thought Bobbie Lee came north looking for a place, and now he's drawn his line in the dirt and put the woodchip on his shoulder."

Hugh nodded somberly. "Such was my feeling as well." He sighed. "And I'm the one who never thought he'd be called on to fight. At least it's a cause better than taking land away from Mexicans or filibustering in the Caribbean."

267

Allan Cole & Chris Bunch

"We can do without that," Kerry broke in. "And any cause worth dying for is worth living for, isn't it? Don't be so damned gloomy, brother. Would I ever let them harm your curly locks, even though they're getting a bit thin, considering how you're getting on in years?"

Hugh, just 23, smiled a bit. "You see how it is, father? The steady abuse I get from this little one keeps me from ever having time to fret." He put an arm around Kerry's shoulders, and let the subject change. "Have you heard from Mother?"

"Not for a week or more," Ian said. "But no one in the battery's had a letter either. Our mail's still somewhere in Washington, I'll wager. Last I heard, though, all was well. Mary sent her love, Hugh. And Kerry, your Keith is putting on weight like he was going to be the Christmas goose."

They talked of this and that as the night wore on, of Philadelphia, the past, the Shannons and their kin and friends. Pointedly, none of the three talked about the morrow, nor the future.

The changing of the guard broke their soft conversation, and Ian stood. "Time for me to be off. I've got guards of my own walking the rounds, not that I think any of them will be nodding from anything but nerves."

He started to shake hands, then clasped Hugh and Kerry each in a bone-cracking hug. "Be wary on the morrow," he said. "And we'll all pray for the other and furlough this winter for all. Home for Christmas is my intent."

Hugh followed him to his horse. "You know, Father, if... something does happen, I've thought that there's only a few would mourn me, but if we lose this war... there'll be millions wearing black."

Ian didn't answer, but led his horse away into the night. At the gate, he turned back and saw the two, still standing, outlined in the last embers of the fire. Coming from my loins, he thought, and how did God allow me to produce two such fine ones. Surely what they are now is less my doing, me being not much more than a man lugging the hod, than Susan's, so I'll not be over-boastful about things. Lord, if you are up there, hold them close on the morrow. He thought for a moment of what Hugh had just said, then shook his

Allan Cole & Chris Bunch

head violently. No, he was wrong. There'd be many that would mourn either of them. He remembered what Kerry had said about a cause worth living for. As he rode off, back down the line, a stray thought crossed his mind, that is it not just like a man to be wondering about his own death, when all problems come to an end, whether or not you believe - and no one sorrows for the poor ones, the poor women, left behind to manage as best they can?

Colonel Michael Shannon also slept little that night, but where the Dolans attempted to construct a small world of peace, he carried white rage wherever he went. His orders had been clear: the 13th California was assigned to Third Brigade of the Army of the Potomac's Cavalry Division. The Brigade included two volunteer Pennsylvania cavalry regiments and was commanded by Colonel Richard Rush, whom Michael mildly respected even though he'd begun the war insisting his troops be armed with lances like they were Arthurian knights. What Michael had not respected was the unit's orders. The 13th, like all of the Union cavalry units, had been ordered to take position just in the center of the Union lines, not far from the house McClellan had commandeered for his headquarters. "And then?" Michael had asked, and then grown steadily more pale with anger as he was told McClellan planned to hold the cavalry in reserve until the proper moment when they would make a grand, final charge and smash Lee's center, leaving nothing more of the Confederacy and its dreams than scatters of panicked, running men.

Michael sought words, and found them... eventually. In an Army that was becoming very proud of how far it could distance itself from the Second Commandment, the trim-mustached, close-bearded Californian was already amassing a legend: "I would assume, Colonel, that coyote-chewed order comes directly from the fountainhead of all god damned wisdom, Little Mac his very own syphilitic bat-brained self, am I correct? Sir, may I inform you that this imbecile, this maricon sin cojones, this remnant of a whore's nightmare, who had what little brains a devious Deity blessed him with sneezed out in the Crimea, has not the sense God gave a dead goat.

Allan Cole & Chris Bunch

"The bandy-legged son of a bitch wants a charge, is it? Just because that nit is no larger than Napoleon he thinks this is Austerlitz perhaps? And that monte de mierda Pleasanton to be Murat? Has no one informed that reject of a pimp's hangover that the Army of Northern Frigging Virginia carries guns, sir? And, the last time I bothered to inquire, had passing familiarity in how to use them! Sir, does anyone realize it will leave this beloved numbwitted Army of Mac's Pot with no flank security, no ability for reconnoitering, and no mounted units able to provide close support when all of McClellan's laurel-haunted wet dreams blow up in his face? Unlike the custom in every other goddamned army since Sir Francis Goddamned Bacon learned how to make gunpowder go off!"

The tirade had gone on for a bit, and finally Michael had demanded permission to see Gen. Pleasanton himself. That interview had gone no better, which did not surprise Michael, since he thought the West Pointer nothing better than an uninspired timeserver.

He came back to where the 13th waited, its horses curried and fed, its weapons loaded and ready. This latest idiocy fit right in with everything else that had happened - or, more correctly, not happened - to the cavalry since the Army had gone after Lee.

The Confederate general had kept his armies moving, spearheaded by the foot cavalry of Stonewall Jackson, moving up to thirty miles a day, frequently barefooted and living off the green corn they stripped from the countryside as they went. McClellan's infantrymen strolled along at a pace of five miles a day or so.

The cavalry had been sent out again and again to learn just what the hell Lee's intentions were, and every time they tried to break through the screen J.E.B. Stuart's centaurs maintained they were hammered. Not that this stopped Gen. Pleasanton from making the most wildly inflated estimates of how many men Lee had. Perhaps the Colonel kept a board in his tent, and tossed a dart to see how many Rebels had been seen before he sought out McClellan. Hell, Michael's thoughts went on, we stumble around, and Lee dances around us like he was with the Ballet Francais, even after he beats up old Pope down at Bull Run again and loses ten thousand or so effectives.

Shannon paced, while the sky hinted light, enough to show the country below and around him dark hung in dank mist. "How simply God Damned marvelous," he snarled to his adjutant, Major John McCorkle, "here we shall piss around, for the entire saints-abandoned day, no doubt, watching the struggles of puny man as if we were on Mount Olympus. And while we watch, we may mutely contemplate our fate... which will most likely be that we shall simply sit and stew here while that cabron Little Mac blows the most gorgeous chance to win the war he'll ever have."

The Major smiled sardonically. "Sir, he could win. He is popular with the men. He did turn us into an army."

"So he did," Shannon grudged. "But a blacksmith who forges and tempers his ax, and then hangs it on the wall of his smithy in fear its blade might be chipped or blunted is laughable. Such a man, such a general, is not. Because far more of his soldiers will die - I can say from personal experience - because of this caution, squeamishness or care. Call it what you will, I don't give a damn."

He took out a cigar, bit the end off and spat viciously. "You know, Mac, I don't believe the South can win this war. But I sure as hell know the North can lose it."

"Ready," the Number Four man shouted. Ian wanted a final check through the nubbin sight, to make sure they had that damned Rebel battery to rights this time, but knew he had no more rights behind that gun than the gunner in the First Sergeant's position, standing back of the battery, arms folded in watchful readiness.

"Fire!" Lieutenant Maxwell shouted, and the twelve-pounder bucked and recoiled, smoke boiling from its muzzle. Number One man instantly swabbed the barrel out with his water-dripping ramrod. "Load," Ian bellowed, as Maxwell paced to the next gun, just as its Four man shouted "Ready."

Ian saw long lines of blue moving forward, and could hear the beginning of musket volleys over the cannon duel. He wished, or perhaps he did not, the terrain would allow him to peer far down the Union lines, back of Antietam Creek, to where the 86th Pennsylvania, and his sons waited. Perhaps, Ian thought, they'll not be used today, or the Rebels will break before they're needed.

271

"First Sarn't!" Maxwell shouted. "Put another man preparing charges. We will be firing volleys next!"

"Yes! Sir! Brooks! LaCoutre!..."

Michael peered through the long telescope, held steady in a notched tree branch. The fog was lifting, and the sun glared, but he did not feel the building heat. His mind was held by what he could see, down around the two wooded areas. Line after line of blue had marched into battle, but nothing but stragglers were coming out. Bastard, he thought. God damned McClellan's feeding them into the grinder a company here, and a brigade there instead of screwing what little goddamned courage he's got to some kind of sticking point and sending in the whole line.

He looked down the valley, and while it was hard to determine much through the haze from the artillery and musket fire, it appeared to him only this right flank was engaged. Piece it away, and throw it away, he thought.

A man stumbled up the rise toward Michael. He was wet to the waist from having waded Antietam Creek below. His face was quite blank. "It is the cannon fire, sir," he said in a very calm voice. "I cannot abide cannon fire."

Having made his point, he went on further to the rear. The man wore the insignia of a Union Colonel.

The horses trotted forward, seemingly paying no mind to the shells bursting to either side, the growl of gunfire ahead, nor the continual shouting. Ian saw the line of blue near the turnpike he and Lieutenant Butscher had been ordered to reinforce with two guns. There was a mad chaos of intermingled units, men from New York, Michigan, Pennsylvania, Wisconsin. Ian barely noted the bodies sprawled around, some in gray or butternut, sprawled over the turnpike fences. Quite smoothly the horses pirouetted as if on a parade ground, cannon mouths pointed toward the enemy, gun trails dropped from the limbers, and the two-wheeled carts pulled some yards back. Further to the rear, the caisson and second limbers were already positioned, their crews ready.

"Load double canister," Butscher shouted, and the smooth, well-drilled machinery went into motion.

Ian slid off his horse, and ran back to the caisson. "Don't be forgetting to knock away the extra cartridge," he reminded. "We're not in the business of proof testing, and I have no desire to be blown into the clouds."

The Number Five man from each gun was at the caisson, got cartridge and shot, ran back to the gun, where Number Two man waited. First cartridge, then shot, then the second shot. Number One rammed the cartridge... one gunner sagging down, hit before he could finish his task... another man taking his place, Number Three man lifting his thumbstall away from the vent, shoving a wire down piercing the cartridge, moving away, as Number Four shoved the lanyard-ready primer into the gun, and shouted "Ready" and...

...and the Texans came out of the smoke, John Hood's twenty three hundred men, terrible behind their colors, screaming high and fierce, and the Yankee infantry crouched behind the remnants of the fenceline aimed low and...

..."Fire!"...

...as the riflemen pulled triggers, muskets aimed low, through the bottom rails of the fenceline, some smoothbores loaded with buck and ball - three buckshot, one round bullet...

...and the invisible hand swept red across the field, and men shouted, screamed, died, regimental banners fell were picked up by another brave man, fell once more as he was killed, and...

"...Load double—"

...Lieutenant Fugate took a ball full in the mouth, and fell, and Ian was crying out: "Double canister! On my command! Number Six man forward to the guns!"

"One volley, lads," someone shouted. "Then we'll be among 'em with the cold steel!"

Kerry's world narrowed to the long bayonet attached to the end of his musket. He licked dry lips. Could he? He glanced over his shoulder at Hugh, just behind him, and hoped he didn't look as pale as his brother.

Unordered, the column broke into a shambling run toward the bridge over Antietam Creek named after the farmer Rohrbach.

It was somewhere else on the battlefield, and Ian did not remember how he, nor his cannon, had arrived there. There should have been thirty or forty artillerymen to man the two bronze 12-pounders dubbed Napoleons, because Napoleon III had supposedly designed them. But there were less than twenty, Ian noted, and half of them were infantrymen who must've sprung to help when a cannoneer went down. Just in front of the position a road ran across their front, a road that'd been worn down a few feet, a road that was now heaped with bodies. Again his guns had been sent in at point blank range to plug a sagging line, and again the cannon roared and spat about three hundred round bullets like huge sawed-off shotguns. But now there were other guns out there, manned by men in gray, and Rebs with muskets and keen eyes and they were shooting and it was the Union's turn to be swept down.

A man screamed just in front of Ian, a man whose legs had been shattered by grapeshot. "For the Love of Mother Mary," he moaned, looking Ian straight in the eye, "for Christ's own sake, man, shoot me, shoot me!"

And then he screamed, and begged again, this time in a foreign tongue, a tongue Ian realized with a shock was the Gaelic he'd never learned in Dublin because no one but back country boys spoke it, and then he saw, lying nearby, the emerald-green banner, and he guessed the troops fighting - and dying - around him were the Irish Brigade from New York.

The man begged yet again, and very slowly Ian Dolan unholstered his revolver.

A man pelted down the cavalry's picket line, shouting, "Charge, boys! Mount up and we'll charge 'em. Save the Union, lads!" There was a hesitant stir from the cavalrymen, and then the horse broke stride, and the man was pitched from the saddle. Michael ran to see if he could help, and from ten feet could smell the brandy fumes. The battle had been going on for seven hours.

Allan Cole & Chris Bunch

Shouting they knew not what, Hugh and Kerry charged over the top of the crest, over the bodies of those who'd tried before, feeling the ground roil in shock from the supporting cannon behind them, ears deaf that everyone else in the double line was shouting as well, and they went down the road toward the bridge.

A country lane wound through a meadow, following the calm creek with its soft brush-covered sides, then turned sharply to cross, over a stone bridge whose curve was pleasing to the eye, climbed the steep bank on the other side. A few days earlier, it would have been ideal for a carriage ride on a quiet morning, a peaceful picnic along the bank with a lover, and who could tell how the afternoon might pass, far away from the prying eyes of parents? But peace was gone from the world, and now the 86th Pennsylvania ran down the road, bayonets gleaming, and the Rebels, safe behind a stone fence and in a disused quarry, rose up, firing point blank down at the Yankees.

Men spun, collapsed, and other men ran over them into the gunfire, bending forward, as if they were forcing themselves into a winter storm, and Kerry's foot was on the bridge, and he thought he saw, over the parapet, the water, but the creek should have been brown or clear, not dark red and, he felt the solid blow at his chest, but no pain, and then red wildfire flashed and there was nothing.

Hugh saw his brother contort, tossing his musket high and away, and then sag sideways over the parapet down into the water, and the hell with orders as Hugh went over the rail. He landed, expecting to be swimming, but the water was but chest high. His brother's body floated up, but inches away from him, and Hugh did not need to touch him to know.

He dragged his brother's body across the creek, part of his mind screaming wonder at why, why did they charge this bridge, why did they charge here at all? Somehow he reached the cover of a sheltering high bank, and dragged Kerry's corpse onto dry land, his lungs gasping, chest heaving, eyes dry.

His musket was gone, but there was another one near the edge of the bank, and a bullet pouch hung on a corpse he could reach without exposing himself. Carefully Hugh loaded the musket, keeping his mind just on what lay in front and the Rebels and not

Allan Cole & Chris Bunch

seeing the empty-eyed horror that lay beside him, half in and half out of Antietam Creek.

There was a colonel above him on the bridge, rasping, croaking, "Come on, boys, I can't holler anymore," and Hugh was up over the bank.

Going up the hill above him, scuttling like grayback lice were the retreating Confederates. He found gray in his sights, and touched the trigger and the man fell face down into the leaf mulch. Hugh reloaded, then panted up endless hills after the men who'd killed Kerry.

A man carrying regimental colors spun, leg shot from underneath him, falling, the flag going down, and Hugh had the colors, and was waving them, shouting, and a bullet clipped the flagstaff, but the flag never touched the ground, Hugh scooping it up as a bullet clipped through the brim of his forage cap, and men charged past and he was running with them.

Ian had managed to pull both guns back, even though half his horses were shot down, and returned to the battery, which was in a nice safe place - only five men had been hit in the last half hour and those by the increasingly feeble Confederate counter battery fire. Shells still shot turf high in the air, or exploded in the sky, but Ian felt there was just a slight possibility, if they didn't get sent forward again, he might see the end of this day.

It was then he saw the carriage. It was a newly-painted buggy, cheery in red and green, drawn by four matched horses. The man driving it was expensively, if conservatively dressed. Paying no heed to either the cannon fire coming in, nor the crash as Battery H fired back, he rode where Ian and Lieutenant Maxwell were trying to bring order out of blood. The battery commander, Captain Waller, had been hit earlier and Maxwell had taken command. "Good afternoon, gentlemen," the civilian said, as calmly as if the two were chance-met on a country ride. "I hope I am not obstructing your duties by stopping here. I believed, though I know nothing by experience, you folks might not have time to worry about dinner, and thought I could bring some victuals out."

Maxwell goggled, unable to find words. Ian stepped in. "Sir, all of us're thankful for the thought... but you're in danger, and not gettin' paid for the joys of it. If you'd—"

The man seemed not to hear, and climbed down. He took a hamper from the carriage, and Ian saw two more behind it. "I have ham and biscuits, sir. The biscuits may be not as hot as desirable, but the ham's the best my smokehouse can offer. There's a few jugs of sweet milk back there, but you boys will have to provide your own cups."

Without waiting for a response, he took slices of ham and biscuits about the size of Ian's paw out, and gave one to each man. Carrying his hamper he started toward the battery, not even flinching as a gun fired, and, seconds later, a Secesh cannonball ricocheted across the landscape in response.

There were fewer men than before, but they were still advancing, still on line, stretching to either side of Hugh. Some were wounded, all were filthy and gunsmoke blackened. Hugh didn't know any of them, none were from the 86th, but that was all right. They were attacking. They were killing Rebels.

Someone had taken the flag from him, and now he was carrying a bayoneted musket. Just ahead and to the right were the outbuildings of Sharpsburg, and Hugh could see men running, running away from the attacking Union forces through the streets, and caissons and wagons forcing themselves down the dirt streets. "We've got 'em on the run," somebody shouted, and there was a ragged cheer.

From nowhere, came a long gray snake, its head reflecting sparks in the lowering sun, its body reaching back endlessly to the south. "Hell," someone cried, "More damn' Rebs!"

The oncoming soldiers - a division or more - deployed smoothly, calmly, into line. Hugh's musket was up, aimed, focused really since it was impossible to miss, and he fired. He thought he saw a man fall. Hugh reloaded, and aimed and fired once more, and loaded and started forward, bayonet out.

Someone had him by the arm, shaking him. "Come on, man! You can't win the war by yourself!"

277

Hugh knocked the hand away, and the man didn't wait, but started running. Hugh began walking, marching really toward the gray lines, and a voice told him of course he couldn't win the war, but he could take at least one more with him.

He heard another voice, a soft lilt from the night before, a voice that told him any cause worth dying for is worth living for, and he came back to himself, as the first line of A.P. Hill's three thousand Light Infantryman opened fire.

Before dusk the soldiers filtering past the cavalry's position changed from stragglers to units still armed, still keeping some kind of unit coherence. Shouts went back and forth, yeah, the Rebs had stopped the attack, but we still held the field, and damn, there'd never another day like this one, and thank hell it was over. There came another, derisive shout as a platoon moved past the last of the cavalrymen, still picketed neatly waiting for some high officer to inspect their splendor: "Whole damn' day, and I never did see me a dead cav'lryman!"

No response came back. Michael still was near his observation post. Someone had laid out a meal for him on a cartridge box, and he'd never noticed. Michael's face was cold. Major McCorkle stood nearby. He'd never seen the Colonel like this.

"God damn McClellan," Michael finally hissed. "God damn his soul to hell. He let good men go down that valley and kept us, and how many guns and what, ten thousand infantrymen out of battle? For what? For fear some imaginary rebels would come out of there?"

His arm waved across the mile of open ground and the narrow bridge across the Antietam impossible for any army to cross to turn the Army of the Potomac's flanks. "God damn him to hell!"

Michael turned away from his adjutant. He was damned if he'd let anyone see him cry, but the profanity just had run out.

It was nearly full dark before Ian Dolan found his sons. He'd gone to where the 86th had bivouacked the night before, and inquired his way forward, following the path of their attack. It had been simple - wounded men from the unit were spattered across the

278

countryside as if the army was playing a bloody game of hare and hounds.

Hugh was slowly, laboriously digging a grave, just on the near side of Antietam Creek. One arm was bandaged. Kerry's body was wrapped in a tent section.

"Odd, isn't it," Hugh began in a very casual voice that held knives below it. "I was the one who thought I'd die. And all that happened was this little graze of shrapnel." He looked down at the body. "Aren't big brothers supposed to take care of... of..." and then Hugh Dolan found he could cry.

His father held him close, trying to keep himself from shatter. After awhile Hugh pulled away, and walked to the creek and splashed water on his face. By now it was too dark to see what color the water was, nor did Hugh care.

Hugh walked back toward Ian. "Well, Father? Did we at least win? Or is it like the other times? Not that it matters either way if we could have Kerry back."

Ian thought of a poem he'd once read the boys, and some lines that ran, "'But what good came of it at last'/Quoth little Peterkin./'Why that I cannot tell,' said he;/'But twas a famous victory.'"

But that was not what Hugh wanted to hear. Ian told him the truth. "We're sore hurt ourselves, but the Rebels are cut near to death. And they can ill afford to spare the men. We beat them, son."

CHAPTER TWENTY-TWO

PHILADELPHIA - SEPTEMBER 23, 1862

THOMAS WAS CERTAIN it was going to be his lucky day
when he saw the recruiting sergeant was drunk. The fellow had a big
bloated Dutchie's face purple from all the drink he'd taken since
morning. He bleared at Thomas through piggy eyes. "You a goot
kinder, you," the sergeant said solemnly. "Der kinder lissen't ta ol'
sergeant, yah? Comen back der Union't Army ta join."

He had never laid eyes on the sergeant in his life, but if the sot
wanted to believe otherwise the better for Thomas Shannon Ryan.
"Yessir. Thought a lot 'bout what you said. Talked it over with me
dear dad, too, 'n I'm here to raise me hand 'n go down to fight
Johnny Reb."

He scratched at the rags he'd rolled a drunk for not a half hour
ago. Thomas had almost given the guy two bits instead of just taking
them; now he was glad he hadn't. The shit had been flea ridden.
Probably wouldn't of said nothin' either.

The sergeant belched loudly and grinned. "You in time, just.
Gottdamn niggers free now, der president he say. Soon alla blackies
der army join. Get alla gottdamn bonus money. All der white kinders
shit outta der luck. Wait, you see it happen like I say. You t'ank der
ol' sergeant, yah?"

"I'll thank you now, sir," Thomas said. "'N if you'll get out the
papers I'll be signin' me name."

The sergeant's eyes widened. "You can der name, write?"

Thomas gritted his teeth. All Shannons could write; and read as
well. Thomas even read a book now and again, holding back any
volumes looted by his gang pals until he'd perused them. But he
buried his temper as he remembered the role he was playing: a poor,
but honest Irish lad, with an ignorant tongue and nary a copper to his
name. In a few minutes he'd be out of these rags and back into his
finery, with plenty of money to turn a pretty girl's head.

"Yessir, I can write," he said. "I got the good nuns to thank for
knockin' it into me noggin."

"An officer, you'll be," the sergeant laughed. "Der private ta der
officer in der week."

A moment later Thomas was hunched over the documents, considering what name to use. Kelly? No, he'd already been a Kelly. Sullivan, the same. And Duggan and O'Neil as well. How about Faherty? He knew a Faherty, and a right shit he was. What was his given name? Bill, that's it! Bill Faherty it is. He signed it with a flourish, curling the tail of the Y in Faherty back under the whole signature. He'd show him a Shannon could fuckin' write, even if he was a Faherty today, and dressed in some bum's rags.

"Hey, kid? Don't I know you?" came a voice from behind.

Thomas forced himself to be casual as he turned to see another sergeant. He was big and mean and sober as a judge. Thomas instantly recognized him: he'd collected an enlistment bonus of a hundred dollars off the man not a week ago. Thomas had lost count of the number of times he'd enlisted under fraudulent names; it was at least a half-dozen, maybe as many as ten.

He studied his accuser, scratching his head. Then he shook it... slowly. "Nossir. I don't remember you from nowheres."

The drunken sergeant was befuddled, looking back and forth from his colleague to Thomas. The sober sergeant advanced closer, peering at Thomas. His eyes became certain, his look angry. "Shit yes, I know you," he said. "You skinned the taxpayer out of a hundred dollars and me out of a nice commission only last week."

Before Thomas could bolt, a heavy hand fell on his shoulder. "Well, I gotcha now, you little son of a bitch," he snarled. "And you'll either live up to your bargain, or it's jail, you little shit ass."

Thomas, thinking quick, turned shocked and innocent eyes on the drunken sergeant, who was just now seeing that his own commission was in danger. "Please, sir," Thomas begged, "I don't know what this man's sayin'. I'm here to join up with you, and now he comes along 'n tries to take me off somewheres. What did I do? What's he tryin' to say?"

The drunk lurched to his feet, furious. "Der thief, he is, that's what he's up ta. After mein money, he is. Yah." He lumbered around the table and grabbed the thick arm that held Thomas. "Offen der hands, you," he snarled. "Der kinder is mein."

"You're drunk, sergeant," Thomas's captor growled.

"Der drunk, is it? Der names you call? Offen der hands, I'm sayin'. Or der head I punch."

He ripped the imprisoning hand away. As the two men grappled, Thomas whirled and bolted out of the recruiting office. The shouts of the two combatants turned to the rage of wounded suckers by the time he reached the corner. He heard bootsteps thundering after him, but within a few seconds he'd disappeared into the heavy traffic with much-practiced ease.

Two hours later he was sitting in a quiet cellar restaurant, scrubbed and in one of his most stylish suits. He nursed a cup of strong black coffee as he considered his future. It was apparent the enlistment bonus game was at an end - his face was too well known. This was the price of success, and Thomas was willing to accept it. Also, the federals would be hot on his trail. The law would kick his arse good to make an example for all the other lads playing at the same sport.

For an idle moment Thomas considered escaping by joining up for real in some other city. He could confound his pursuers by using his given name, and he'd soon be lost in a sea of blue uniforms. He quickly dismissed this as a sucker's plan.

Thomas knew very well what the state of the Union was. The odds were that he'd be killed or maimed by Johnny Reb, just like what had happened down at Antietam. Oh, they couldn't fool him with their lies of a great victory. He knew what was what in this old world. Little Mac was trumpeting his claims all over the land, but Thomas knew it was a crook soon as the news of the terrible casualties began to leak out. Sure, the southern lads had suffered as well, but that was their hard luck. From the word on the street and the newspapers, it becoming more obvious each day an enormous number of men in blue uniforms would not be coming home. And Jesus Christ, wasn't the President, himself, calling for more civilians to join up so his generals could hurl them against the enemy? There was even talk of conscription! Fuckin' hell! Forcing a man to take up the gun was as barbaric and undemocratic a practice as Thomas could imagine. He certainly had no desire to chance his luck on some other bloody battlefield. A hero's fate was a mug's game.

Allan Cole & Chris Bunch

Thomas prided himself on his knowledge of current affairs. He did not just read newspapers, he devoured them, skimming every column for items that might enhance his career as a thief and swindler. It wasn't just the big score he was after, but long term knowledge he dreamed would someday lead to him rising to the very top of his chosen profession, whatever that was to be. Hell, someday he might even be mayor of Philadelphia. Now, wouldn't that be something? Mayor Thomas Shannon Ryan. Except maybe he'd drop the old man's name and make it Thomas Shannon.

He pressed his mind away from the escape of day dreams, and focused on his problem. His options were few indeed. He'd have to leave Philadelphia for awhile - until things cooled down. New York seemed the best place to disappear, and also to meet other bright lads like himself. The trouble was he was temporarily embarrassed when it came to funds.

Thomas was a big spender when he was flush, buying gifts for his girls, treating his friends, and adding to his wardrobe. He had no idea where all the enlistment bonus money went. Somehow money seemed to flow into his pockets and then flow out again without his conscious knowledge. He'd have to work on that habit. It was a bad one and would hamper his plans for a bright future.

Swearing new parsimony, Thomas turned his attention on how to raise the necessary funds to depart. There was no time to work up another game. He could sell some things - his clothes and what all - but that would take too long.

Thomas felt a familiar chill down his spine. It was a warning sign he'd rarely ignored in the past; when he'd had, it was to his great sorrow. The law was close - there was no question about it. It'd be best if he left on the earliest possible train. But where to get the money?

He thought of his great aunt Susan. He'd mostly stayed away since Ian had gone off to war, and he wondered if she'd be so easy with her funds without the old man about to prod her. Oh, well, what did he have to lose? All she could say was no. Having made his decision, Thomas finished his coffee and rose. Already the words he'd use were forming in his mind.

Allan Cole & Chris Bunch

He squared his shoulders, smoothed his clothes and marched out of the restaurant.

Susan drew the curtain aside and watched Thomas bounce down the steps and walk briskly away. He hesitated at the corner, peering about for signs of danger and, finding none, strolled out of sight. She let the curtain drop and returned to her small desk, wondering if she had done the right thing. Thomas had confessed he'd run afoul of the law again, although at first he hadn't said exactly what it was he'd done. He'd only assured her that he'd done nothing to injure anyone, but badly needed to flee the city for awhile.

Susan had pressed him hard, and when he finally, stumblingly, admitted what he had been up to, she'd surprised him by giving him the funds he needed and foregoing a lecture on his evil ways. She wasn't sure herself why she hadn't shown him the door without a penny. Of course what he'd done was wrong, but after so many months of warfare, Susan had become hardened to the constant thievery committed by public officials and business leaders. Perhaps she'd relented because Ian would have urged her to help Thomas if he had been here. Or maybe she just wanted him gone from her sight.

Although she hadn't answered him when he asked if she thought he was a coward for not joining up like Hugh and Kerry, she'd only meant her silence as a bit of punishment for his many sins. If she had answered she would have said that of course he wasn't a coward. Although in this instance the cause was noble, there was enough of Diana in her to distrust all wars. What was the use of another Shannon risking his life to correct evils that should have been fixed long ago?

She'd grimly noted this morning, when the news had finally sunk in President Lincoln had signed a preliminary emancipation proclamation, there was little joy in her city. There were no pealing bells announcing human beings would be freed from the yoke of slavery on January First. If anything, from the grumblings at the market she'd heard, there was real danger some rowdies might celebrate by attacking black men and women in their homes and jobs. Susan shuddered - there was obviously much more to this freedom business than the stroke of a pen could solve.

She shook her head, dismissing these problems as best she could so she could attend to her own troubles. Susan picked up the documents her lawyer had sent over. They were in response to the latest actions taken by Pamela. The federal court in Washington had announced it had completed its investigation into the Widow Shannon's claims and found them worthy enough to proceed.

Now Susan was required to file an answer to the suit so a hearing could be set. At a meeting last week the lawyer had advised Susan to seek some kind of settlement, which Susan rejected because she knew Pamela would never accept such a thing. Failing that, he'd advised her to delay the proceedings as long as possible in hopes a more favorable climate might prevail in the future. This advice she had taken.

Susan dipped her pen into the inkwell and signed her name to put the plan into motion. As she started to call for Mrs. Fawcett to send for a runner, she heard plodding feet mount her steps. It was the postman with his second delivery of the day. Susan decided to fetch the mail herself, and give the postman the letter for her lawyer.

As she made the exchange, Susan recognized Ian's handwriting on one of the envelopes. Her heart leaped as she snatched the letter from the postman.

She ran back to her office and closed the door so she could savor Ian's words alone. It had been many long weeks since he'd written. She ripped open the envelope and eagerly began to read:

My Darling Wife Susan

I never in my life dreamed I'd be the one to bear such terrible news to your door. But our Kerry was killed this day and may God forgive me for there is nothing I can say or do to make his mother's suffering less...

Mary heard a loud crash from Susan's office. Alarmed, she raced to the door, the housekeeper at her heels, and pushed it open. She saw Susan lying on the floor next to the fallen chair. Mrs. Fawcett gave a small cry, and Mary rushed to Susan and knelt. Her mother-in-law's face was ghastly white, and when Mary touched her

285

face she thought the skin seemed as cold as death itself. But Susan was alive, thank God, although her breathing was as ragged as if she had suffered an awful wound.

"I think she's fainted," Mary said, and she began to vigorously rub life into Susan's hands. "Fetch some spirits."

She saw the letter lying on the floor. Mary picked it up, wondering if this was the cause of Susan's collapse. She read Ian's opening words and felt the knife cut into her heart. Her second thought was gratefulness that it was Kerry and not her Hugh. Then the knife cut deeper as she realized another letter might come someday announcing the same fate for her husband.

The room swirled as she was set adrift from all that was familiar. She heard Nancy's tired, shuffling feet on the upstairs landing, and as Mrs. Fawcett ran into room with the spirits, Mary pulled herself back from the brink.

As the housekeeper yanked the top off the bottle, Mary began rubbing Susan's hands again, calling: "Susan... Susan, dear... Open your eyes, Susan..."

Nancy shuffled back to her room. She was a bit disgusted no one had come to tell her what was going on. But that's the way things were in this house since little Keith was born. They all treated her as if she were the child, keeping things from her, constantly fussing over her and making her feel... useless.

She heard Keith stir in the nursery, and swerved to that door. She straightened herself up, tugged her robe belt tighter... she'd show them she could care for her own child. But as her hand reached for the latch, she suddenly felt very tired. A bubble of self-pity welled up and she had to fight to hold back the sobs. She sagged and turned back to her room, feeling like an old woman with barely the strength to lift her legs as she shuffled her slippers along the carpet.

In her room she slumped on the bed, wishing she had some laudanum to ease the aches. No one had said a word to her about the habit she'd formed during her pregnancy; but guilt and shame drove her to stop asking her friend to bring a bottle by. At that moment she decided the next time her friend came, she'd ask her to resume the deliveries - and to hell with what Mary and Susan might think.

Allan Cole & Chris Bunch

There was a knock; Nancy flushed, heart thudding as if she'd been caught in a guilty act. She recovered. "I'm awake. You may come in."

Susan and Mary entered. Nancy was startled at their appearance. Susan's eyes were red-rimmed and she looked much older than her years, face haggard, wrinkles deeply etched. Mary was as pale as her mother-in-law, her eyes wide and glistening.

"What's wrong?" Nancy asked. "Is it something to do with all that noise downstairs?"

The two women sat on either side of her bed. Nancy turned her head this way and that, wondering who was going to speak. "Nancy, dear," Susan said, chin trembling, "I have some awful-" She broke down, crying, unable to go on.

Mary took Nancy's hand and squeezed it hard. "It's Kerry," Mary said. "He's been... killed. And I'm so sorry-"

She threw her arms around Nancy, to hold her close for the expected explosion of tears. To Mary's surprise, Nancy seemed to accept the news calmly and... coldly.

She gave Mary a quick kiss, removed her arms and turned to Susan. She patted her mother-in-law. "Poorness," she said. She rose from the bed and assumed an attitude of great purpose. "I'll go tell little Keith," she said and exited the room.

Susan and Mary looked at one another, bewildered at Nancy's reaction. They rushed into the hallway. They heard Nancy crooning in the nursery. They looked in the door and saw Nancy was holding Keith in her arms, rocking him back and forth.

The child cooed and plucked at her face as she sang: "Hush little baby, don't you cry/ Poppa's gonna buy you a diamond ring..."

Mary went to her and put an comforting arm on her shoulder; she was startled when Nancy glared, eyes full of hatred. Then her sister-in-law turned back to the child, eyes just as angry, but with an odd gentle smile on her lips.

She began to rock the child with hard, jerking motions; and as she sang, her words came with staccatoed force: "... And if that diamond ring don't shine/ "Poppa's gonna sing you a lullaby..."

Allan Cole & Chris Bunch

Little Keith began to cry. Nancy ignored this, pressing on - jerking him harder. "...And if that lullaby don't rhyme/ Poppa's gonna-"

She abruptly stopped as the child's cries turned to loud squalls. The smile turned to thin-drawn lips and she shoved the baby at Mary so hard she nearly fell.

"He doesn't like my singing," she said.

And stalked out of the room.

CHAPTER TWENTY-THREE

VICKSBURG, MISS. - DECEMBER 24-25, 1862

"OH THE MINSTRELS SING," Patrick brayed happily, "Of an English King/Of many years ago/Who ruled his land/With an iron hand/But his morals were weak and low.

"He was dirty and lousy and full of fleas/But he had his women by two's and threes/God bless the Bastard King of Eng-Uh-Land."

Templar seemed to catch a bit of his owner's mood, and broke into a canter. Patrick leaned forward and patted his neck. "Maybe some oats in hot wine for your Christmas dinner, old friend. Our Miss Lucy swears she loves animals, 'specially horses."

Templar nickered, and they continued down the road from Jackson to Vicksburg. Patrick thought they were no more than six or eight miles beyond the city, and should reach Vicksburg by midmorning. The road, too wide to be a track but sloppily muddy all the same, was deserted - not many travelers out on this cold, soggy Christmas Eve day. Patrick didn't mind the weather at all: he was pretty close to dry under his slicker, and he was quite warm in the heavy blanket coat a Confederate supporter had donated to the cause.

This was shaping to be some Christmas, he thought. Two weeks ago he'd figured he'd be in the field on the Lord's Day looking for trouble with Forrest - who was out just now ripping up General Grant's supply lines somewhere in Tennessee. Instead, here he was, headed for Vicksburg, for a Christmas maybe spent indoors and... his eyes flickered back on one saddlebag where all those letters were safely weather-proofed in oilskin... Lucy.

He'd gotten a response to that cautious first letter two weeks after he'd posted it; it was just time enough for him to feel like a Romantic Kid, instead of a grown man, nineteen going on twenty and a full sergeant, given his stripes by Old Forrest himself. There'd been five letters in the first set, then five more a few days later. They began quite formally. Evidently Lucy felt corresponding with a soldier was part of her Duty to the Cause.

Patrick replied, and found words coming easily. He wrote of his day, and the people around him, trying to give little sketches of what it was like to be a soldier. He naturally chose only the colorful and humorous, and made no mention of the ghastly ambulance trains on the retreat to Corinth, or the cold shock that ran through him when Forrest's Tennessee Cavalry Regiment had its first complete muster, and there'd been not more than three companies of ragged men in line in front of their horses.

The letters grew warmer, and one day Patrick received a package. It contained a daguerreotype of the girl in all her finery, which the enclosed letter said she'd convinced her father to pay for as a sixteenth birthday present. She was even more beautiful than Patrick remembered - hair in ringlets that cascaded down her shoulders, and she wore what had to be an expensive gown.

She had even managed to smile, although it had started to wear a little during the long minutes while the photographer was exposing the plate. She also enclosed a shadow portrait done by one of the other girls at the Academy. Finally, there was a lock of her hair, tied with a blue ribbon.

The lock of hair went into that pouch hanging around his neck, next to the musket ball great grandmother had given him. The two portraits were oilskin-protected in the dispatch case he carried. Patrick was now an important man. Forrest, the soldier of iron, had returned to duty within a couple of weeks of his severe wounding after Shiloh, the ball still lodged near his spine. He collapsed a few days later, and had to take leave for surgery. But where the wound might have crippled a less savage and determined man, Forrest had come back for good in June.

He'd called twenty men to his tent - Patrick being one of them and wondering what the hell he'd done this time - and announced he was being detached, together with his brother and Captain Kelley, to organize another cavalry regiment. The twenty men had just volunteered to go with Forrest as cadre. Nobody dared to argue with the cold-eyed man.

It was hell leaving Billy and the others. They promised to stay in touch, and maybe they'd all fight together one day when Forrest was given a whole division to command. Patrick mounted up - his few possessions lashed to a scrounged packhorse - touched his hat, and rode off. He was starting to learn the way of the army - make a friend or enemy you swear is for life, serve with him for a time, and then he was gone forever.

Allan Cole & Chris Bunch

The new regiment had been formed and trained. Patrick was sure there was no way he, Billy and the others had been that stupid, back a whole year ago. Maybe he was old-soldiering, but maybe he was right. The new recruits were different - not as eager, not as patriotic. Or maybe, Patrick thought, not as foolish. Also, from his lowly viewpoint, the war wasn't going well. His opinion was formed from poring over every newspaper, Yank or Reb, he could get his hands on. Lee'd just whipped some idiot named Burnside at Fredericksburg, and it sounded pretty bloody, all right. But this time the South was fighting in Virginia, not in the North - like Antietam.

Here in the west, Forrest and Morgan and the guerrillas were giving the bluebellies conniptions, but that seemed to Patrick like they were poking pins in a blindfolded Samson, whose wild swings every now and then connected - hard. New Orleans was now occupied by the Yanks under Beast Butler, and Forts Henry, Donelsen, Island No. 10 and Fort Pillow were in Union hands. Vicksburg itself had been attacked earlier, the city half-evacuated and shelled after Mayor Lindsay rejected a surrender demand.

The Union retreated - but only for the moment. Everybody knew they'd be back - at least everybody in uniform. From Lucy's letters, after the Yankees had been driven away, it seemed as if all the civilians in the city thought that some sort of final victory had been won. But the North now held the whole damned Mississippi except for a hundred or so miles, and Patrick knew they weren't about to leave matters as they were.

Patrick had sweated bullets when he'd heard of the cannonading - civilians had no damned place in the middle of a battlefield. Lucy had written that Mr. Baldwin believed civilians had a duty, too. She, and most of the girls from the Academy had volunteered to help nurse at City Hospital. Patrick had flinched when he'd read that. Hell, Lucy was still... well, not a kid, but surely too young to be listening to a gutshot man die. But he was smart enough not to say anything in his return letter.

About then Forrest had taken the new regiment a-raiding. This Patrick enjoyed. It was pretty close to a chess game - figure out where the Union outposts or garrisons were, and hit somewhere else, burning and, well you weren't supposed to call it looting but rather raiding U.S. supply lines; or else attacking the soldiers who liked to sleep till noon and who could be counted on to flee like so many chickens with a fox in the yard. There wasn't a better master than Forrest on this great board of Kentucky and Tennessee.

The only part Patrick didn't like was the killing. It was a pity, he often thought, there wasn't some kind of way war could be bloodless, maybe like the way the Indians out west counted coup, or even single warriors fighting hand to hand. Patrick may have disliked the slaughter, but that was the part Forrest gloried in. Still... that was better than being in a battle like Shiloh. Patrick guessed that raiding, or cutting-out parties or reconnaissance patrols was about as close a body could get to Walter Scott and the Romance of the Cavalry everyone was always prattling on about.

Not that Patrick looked like any sort of cavalryman in a painting. He remembered his cousin Michael's description of what he'd looked like during the Mexican War, and grinned. Patrick was a cavalry sergeant, but carried neither lance nor saber. Instead, he had a single Colt's revolver holstered crossdraw at his belt, and on his right hip a razor-edged butcher's knife in a handmade sheath, much better suited for camp chores or close-in fighting than any exotic Jim-Bowie-short sword or Arkansas toothpick. Two more revolvers were holstered on his saddle, and, when the troops went a-raiding, pre-loaded revolver cylinders hung like a garland around his neck. On one side of his saddle, scabbarded butt-up, Patrick carried a brand new repeating Spencer carbine, recently acquired in a political discussion with a Yankee cavalryman that the Yank had lost; and, just in front, very close at hand, a double-barreled shotgun, its butt sawed off at the grip, and barrels cut just in front of the hand guard. In the rearing, screaming melee of a cavalry skirmish, that brutal murder's tool was a deal better than any saber, even one as long as the sort Charles XII had lugged in Russia.

Patrick was also well-shod and -clothed, and his saddlebags held gifts for Lucy, her two sisters and Mr. Baldwin. He also had just under a hundred dollars in real gold specie, and as much more in Confederate dollars of his own money. Maybe he couldn't run quite as wide-open a deception as he did in civilian days, but there were still officers and civilians around who thought they had a fast horse and were willing to put some coins on their thinking.

Patrick ran out of Bastard King lyrics, and searched for another song as Templar clopped out on a great long bridge that led across a slough. He was happy - even if he couldn't manage to shake the damned cold that was giving him a case of the sweats every few hours. But a little cold was no never-mind. Vicksburg would heal everything. Vicksburg and Lucy Baldwin.

Everybody in Patrick's company got a case of the sulks when they found out Forrest had no intention of spending Christmas in garrison - everyone except Patrick. Yes, he would have preferred to be in his tent out of the wet and cold... but there'd been worse Christmas's, and a lot of them. He remembered that first Christmas in New Orleans. Even though Latimer had tried to help the boy, and taken him to a lavish oyster-and-wild-turkey dinner along with a couple of fancy women, that had still been the first time away from family, even though his father hadn't known how to provide the merriest Yule. But the one after it had been worse.

He'd been walking - which in Texas meant you were slightly lower in the social order than a coyote - between some farm somewhere and some settlement somewhere else, not sure if he was lost or on the right track. He'd made a frozen camp with nothing to eat except frijoles some Mexican herders had given him, when he realized what day it was. Patrick had flopped down right there, and busted into tears. Yes, he thought, he'd had worse times than even Nathan Bedford Forrest had planned, riding out with blood the intent on the day the Savior was born.

Forrest had called him to his tent. It'd taken a minute for Patrick to pay heed to what his superior was saying, marveling that Forrest now wore general's insignia. Then he caught the drift. From somewhere - Patrick didn't know where, since he didn't exactly broadcast his past - Forrest had learned that Patrick had spent time in Vicksburg. Plus, he said dryly, the sergeant had shown some talent in... finding his way about.

He gave Patrick his orders. In Vicksburg the General "just happened" to have been told about a certain warehouse not far from the shantytown below the city. In it were two, perhaps three, cases of

293

percussion caps, the vital and always-scarce means of firing a weapon. They were owned by a certain merchant, Forrest went on, handing Patrick a slip of paper with a man's name and address on it, who was an old friend.

Patrick was to make sure these caps existed, and arrange for a wagon to transport them back, or else get them on a train, if the trains were running. Forrest gave Patrick an envelope with a hundred dollars in Yankee greenbacks, and a pass that looked as if it'd been written by a six year old just learning to cipher - Forrest being famous for having said he never saw a pen without thinking of a snake.

"That, Sergeant, should ensure the provost won't be thinking evil thoughts about why you aren't with your unit." Forrest had smiled a bit, or at least his mouth had reshaped itself a little behind the bushy beard. "Ride hard, son, and you could be in Vicksburg by Christmas. And there'll be no cause for you to start on my business until after the 25th."

"Thank you, sir."

"Not pryin', sergeant, but I've been hearing some wondrous stories about that horse of yours. Supposed to be able to outrun a spring flood, they say. Mind if I ask where you got him?"

"Nossir. Not at all, sir. It was in Texas, back before the war started. I ran into this abolitionist, sir, just outside Austin. Evil man. Looked like that Simon Legree Mrs. Stowe wrote about. He had this poor beast all loaded up with tracts, so Templar could hardly stagger, and—"

"You're dismissed, soldier."

Patrick grinned at the memory then recalled another fine song: "Good King Wenceslas looked out/On his feet uneven," he caroled. "Drunker than a Englishman/Or a Baptist deacon..."

Ahead of schedule, and feeling cold, he pulled off the road when he spotted a plantation house up a winding lane. Now this, he thought, is the way all the Yankees think us Southerners live. Pretty grand, he thought, admiring the white-painted colonnaded house, the neatly-kept outbuildings and stables. Pretty grand indeed. I would hope, assuming my fine brother soldiers haven't milked the cow dry,

294

these kindly folk could spare a cup of coffee and perhaps a bit of ham for a brave soldier fighting for the Cause.

Quite suddenly Patrick felt the skin just over his spine crawl like a snake, and his hair prickled. Without thinking, his left thumb unsnapped his holster catch, and his revolver was half-drawn, fast glance down to make sure no water'd gotten to the powder, all five of the six cylinders were still capped, and a fully-loaded cylinder would lie under the hammer when he cocked it.

As his hands flashed through their automatic drill, his expression went unchanged, still holding the mildly friendly smile he'd pinned on. The weapon went back in the holster, but the flap stayed unsnapped. He tucked the reins over the saddle horn, and both hands slid out, lifted the Spencer enough to snap the lever back and forward, chambering a round.

As Templar turned onto the drive that half-circled the house, he heard a bang... bang... bang... eyes flickering, noise identified, an outbuilding door banging in the cold wind. The place looks abandoned, he thought, as he pulled Templar up. But he didn't dismount immediately, still looking for more clues. Maybe they'd all panicked some months back... not hardly. The winter shutters were up, and the whitewashed stones lining the drive were clean, not mud spattered from the winter rains.

Whoever lived here had packed up and skedaddled no more'n a day or so ago, at most, he thought. He peered through a window - yes indeed, the house still held furniture and everything. Perhaps, he thought, if the door's not locked, or if there's a kitchen window not well bolted, perhaps the fine people who live here wouldn't object to a hungry man's foraging. Not looting, of course. Just something to eat, perhaps something to drink if the sideboard's untouched, and then on into Vicksburg. Nobody, not even a suspicious provost could call that looting, especially if they were all inside in front of a fire somewhere else on this raw day.

Patrick slid from the saddle, loose-tethered Templar to a low railing, and strolled, most casual, around his horse. He stretched widely, and no one would realize how close his left hand was to that scabbarded carbine. Nothing. He started to look for his unlocked door or unbarred window, but decided to wait. He took coffee beans, pot and nearly-full flask that held some fairly superior 40-rod Kentucky whisky out of his saddlebags. Not far away was a rack, about half-filled with wood kindling, as if somebody'd run off in mid-task.

He built a small fire, just out of the wind in front of the main entrance. He crushed the beans with his small frying pan, dumped them into the pot with water from a pump in the yard, and put the coffee on to boil. He squatted on his haunches, watching the flames and smoke curl up. You could, you know, have just kicked a door open and lit some kindling in the fireplace, couldn't you? Of course a big bold dragoon like yourself isn't hesitating about a little polite burglary, even for food, now are you? Hell of a proper soldier you are. Bet you aren't worth a damn at pillaging and rapine, either.

"Templar," Patrick said, as his coffeepot began to boil, "how would you like to end up living in a place like this after the war? Maybe up in Kentucky where there's that bluegrass everybody's going on about? Get you a half-dozen brood mares, nice stable to keep you out of the cold? You think you could get comfortable with an arrangement like that?"

Patrick was reaching for the coffeepot when Templar whickered, and the pot went skittering into the fire as Patrick spun, one knee down for a pivot, right hand lofting the Colt's out of its holster, web of the thumb over the hammer, barrel dropping, piece cocked by its own weight, pistol up, leveled and pointed, not aimed, left hand cupping the revolver frame... and the woman screamed.

She stood a few feet away. She'd come out of the house without him hearing the sound of the door. Maybe she'd intended on saying boo or something. The scream seemed to echo on and on, but it was only in Patrick's mind. He noted both her hands were empty, and there was no one behind her. Even women fought, or helped others fight, these days.

"Lady! Come on! It's all right!" The woman swayed. Patrick, knowing he wasn't supposed to do this, caught her before she fell. But his right hand still held the pistol ready.

"Come on," he said, trying to sound calm, but really scared now. Nobody left a woman unattended, especially not these days, and all he needed was her goddamned brother or husband or father to come out the door and see him and there would be gunplay if he couldn't find some real fast words.

"Ma'am... it's all right. I just stopped here to get out of the wind. Make myself some coffee. It's all right. I'm a soldier. Sergeant Shannon. I'm with Colonel... I mean General Forrest. Up in Tennessee," he babbled. But it seemed to work. The woman's limpness became firm, and she found her footing.

"I'm... all right now," she said. "It was just that y'all startled me."

"I'm right sorry, but you startled me more'n somewhat," he said.

"I saw you ride up... and didn't know what to do, since I'm all alone. But the coffee smelled real good, and I listened, and heard you talking to your horse, and... well, I guess I thought you wouldn't come to do a body harm, sounding like that."

"I hope not," Patrick said sincerely. "I'm not in the business of hurting women and children. I mean, I guess, you're part of the reason people are fighting? Aren't you?" That made not a lick of sense, but for some reason it made the woman burst into tears.

"They... they ran off on me," she wailed.

Patrick decided nobody was going to come out of the house with a shotgun and evil intent, so he uncocked and holstered the pistol. The woman wept on, and Patrick, rather awkwardly, patted her. She fell in his arms again, sobbing harder, and Patrick was too aware of curves under her dress.

She was, he thought, pretty. Real pretty, even if not beautiful like Lucy. Maybe she'd been beautiful, when she was Lucy's age. But now she was some older. Patrick guessed her to be twenty two, or twenty three, or so. Fix her hair up, let her fix herself up - Patrick was suddenly conscious the woman must not have bathed in a few days; but neither had he - and she could be some kind of belle at a cotillion.

Eventually the woman stopped bawling, and Patrick got an explanation of sorts. The woman, Mrs. Green, but Patrick could call her Mahala, was a widow, or so she feared. She'd married her planter/cavalier just when the war started and he'd joined up. They'd had only a week together before he rode off to war. She had not heard anything from him, nor from anyone in his company, for a

297

long time. "And I heard there were some terrible battles back in summer over to Virginia, around Richmond, which is where Oliver said he was, in the last... last... letter that..." and the tears came again. What about her family? All her folks were over in Alabama, and she hadn't dared leave the plantation in the hands of the slaves, not that she was even sure it would be safe to travel all that way without an escort.

Patrick asked what had happened to the slaves.

"The niggers ran off!" and Mahala out-dissolved Niobe once more. They'd heard the Union soldiers were coming back, and they'd deserted her four days ago, even though she'd babied them and took care of them like they were blood stock, and they ran off to join the abolitionists. "They just... just abandoned me. I know," she hissed, "what my... my poor dear husband would have called such heartless animals. But such language isn't polite. As if they'd get treated any better by Yankees! They'll learn... they'll learn... and then..." she let her thought trail off.

Patrick escorted her inside, found kindling and wood for the kitchen stove and made coffee. There was brandy in the front room, and Patrick added a dollop to each cup. Mrs. Green - Mahala - drank thirstily and said she hadn't eaten anything except some potatoes she'd found. Even the milk had gone bad. Patrick looked around and blinked - the kitchen and nearby larder was so crammed with food it looked like Harvest Home.

"Why didn't you cook something?"

She couldn't. She didn't know how. She certainly didn't know how to milk the cattle, nor what field they were in, if they were still even there. "I'll bet the niggers ran off with them, too." There were canned goods, including oysters. Mahala didn't know how to open the tins. She had no idea whatsoever on how to light the kitchen stove, nor even a fireplace, so every time she tried to light a fire, all that she'd gotten was sparks and choking smoke. She'd brought quilts out, and huddled in them. She had the hatchet used for the kindling ready "in case... in case, you know." She would have loaded one of her husband's guns, but again, she didn't know how.

Patrick sighed, checked his hunter - there was more than time enough to reach Vicksburg before dusk - and started making a meal for both of them. Mahala wolfed the eggs, smokehouse ham, fried potatoes and grits like she was a starving infantry private. She had more coffee - and, if Patrick didn't mind, just a little bit more of that brandy, even though a real lady doesn't indulge that much, but these are exceptional times, and she did just meet a brave knight.

Patrick waited for her to clear up her dishes, but she made no move. Another "talent" somebody never taught this fine Southern woman. He heated water, found soap, and washed up. Mahala made no move to help him, any more than she'd help set the table or fix the meal. After he finished, he allowed himself a brandy in reward, and sat back down across from her. She was, he decided, quite a bit prettier than he'd thought at first. He smiled, and she smiled back.

"Perhaps," he said, realizing time was slipping away, "you should be changing into some traveling clothes. I'll be happy to escort you into the city, or to a friend's house, if you'd rather. If they left any horses—"

"Those damned niggers left nothing!"

"Then you can ride with me on Templar. He's used to carrying double-up."

Even before he finished, Mahala was shaking her head, No. Of course she couldn't leave. She had a duty to her... her late husband. Perhaps, even, he would return for Christmas, it would be a miracle, and not know how to find her. Very well, Patrick said. But he couldn't just leave her here by herself. These were parlous times.

Mahala looked down at the table, then up at him. Perhaps... perhaps Patrick could stay here? At least for a few days. She was sure the Army could do without him for a week or so - no matter that he was the bravest sergeant in the entire Army she didn't doubt.

"And it is Christmas Eve or shall be. I think I kept track of the days. And I'm sure I remember how my father used to make Christmas punch, and we could... well, forget all the miseries of the world."

Patrick said he couldn't do that. He had his orders. For some reason, he didn't mention Lucy. There was a long silence. Then Mahala said, nearly in a whisper, that she would do anything if he could stay. Just for a little while.

Allan Cole & Chris Bunch

"It's so cold now," she said. "And this house makes... noises when I'm alone. And... and I'm afraid." Again, silence. "You know," she said then, "Oliver and I were only man and wife for a few days. It's hard, being by yourself, for so long. Especially at night. And... there were things he showed me..."

She let her voice trail off, and looked at Patrick under her eyebrows. Then she gazed at him directly, and it seemed her eyes glittered. "Besides," she said, in an entirely different tone, "the niggers will be crawling back. And this time... you have a gun."

Once more, Patrick felt the chill along his backbone.

It was fortunate for Patrick's turn of mind that Vicksburg was a shouting, laughing crowd as he rode into the city. The city was full of soldiers, and there were encampments all around the outskirts. By now a garrisoned city was so familiar to Patrick he barely noticed it. But the throng kept him from dwelling on that plantation, and also how long it had taken him to stand up, back in that kitchen, and say he'd best be on his way before nightfall.

The Jesus-shouters are surely right in one way, he thought, when they say that Man seems hell-bent to fall into sin. That damned cold had come back on him some, enough so he'd had a short, but violent case of the sweats half an hour ago. He'd need to find some quinine, assuming there was any available in the city, and dose himself good.

He saw the cross-street he'd been directed to and, a few doors up, what must be the Baldwin house. It was quite a place, he thought as he dismounted. He slung the saddlebags over his shoulder, almost ran up the steps and hammered at the great knocker hung in the center of the door.

The door opened, and a middle-aged, pleasant-appearing white woman stood there. She possibly asked if she could be of service, but Patrick did not hear. All he was aware of was Lucy, standing behind the woman. In that instant, he forgot everything that had happened that day and forgave himself for what, after all, had not happened.

"Sir," the maid or whoever she was saying. "May I help you?"

"I'm Patrick," he managed. "Patrick Shannon."

Lucy put a hand to her mouth and then it appeared her turn to float into the ether, and they were both lost.

Patrick was instantly and firmly taken in hand by the Baldwin family. Mr. Baldwin was summoned from his office, and he decided Patrick must stay with them - there'd be no question of his finding lodgings elsewhere or, worse, having to sleep under canvas like other poor soldiers.

A servant was sent to the city provost marshal's office to sign him in, so he didn't have to go back out in the cold. Templar was taken into the stables behind the house and unsaddled, where, indeed, warm mash in wine and a thorough currying waited.

Yet another servant took charge of Patrick's gear - after he'd sorted out the various guns, knives, bullets, spare revolver cylinders, powder, percussion caps, as well as the presents he'd brought for the family.

A bath was drawn, and his clothes brushed down. When the laundry he'd brought was washed and dried (one very unwashed shirt, a pair of badly holed socks, unspeakable undergarments and a pair of Union-blue breeches with the knees out), his present garb would be cleaned.

Patrick stood bemused, as much by the bustle as by Lucy's presence. She was here and there, giving orders, always smiling, very much the mistress of a great household. All the servants seemed to think the world of her and the Baldwins. He finally came back to himself and asked why the furor.

"Why," Lucy said, "because this is Christmas Eve. We have bare enough time to get ready for the ball, after dinner, as it is."

Ball? What ball?

Patrick learned that a grand occasion had been planned, as much to celebrate the defeat of the Yankees a couple of months ago as for Christmas itself. Of course Patrick must come as their guest, and the guest of the city.

"It is a pity," Lucy said, "we cannot invite all of our soldiers. But at least there will be room enough for generals and their colonels, or however you men call your leaders. And," she giggled,

Allan Cole & Chris Bunch

"some of the more... handsome young officers have been asked. Or so," she added hastily, "some of my friends have told me."

Patrick turned a bit green. Go to a ball? Dance? With generals as witnesses? He'd rather make another charge into the Hornet's Nest. Mr. Baldwin, who seemed all business, and was intently studying some account books and paying little heed to the bustle, caught Patrick's expression and found it amusing. Lucy's father was an amiable, balding man. The remnants of his hair winged on either side of his head, and an extremely luxurious and well-tended beard hung almost below his cravat.

"Lucy," Baldwin suggested. "Will you excuse yourself? And then show Mr. Shannon to his quarters?"

The two walked into another room for a few minutes, and then he heard Lucy giggle again. It was a sound he was becoming very fond of. She returned with the air of someone who's just been given a secret, and wants more than anything else to share it. Instead, she took Patrick and his gear to his rooms. They were two comfortable chambers above the stables that had been used by the Baldwin's carriage driver, who was now off at war. The rooms looked across a spacious courtyard that, in summer, would be a palette of roses. Now it was cold, bleak and bare.

Lucy pointed. "Over there," she said, "is my bedroom." Patrick noted its location, then looked at Lucy. She was blushing furiously. "Come on, you sluggard," she said. "Put those silly saddlebags down. We have to go out."

"But I thought you said—"

"Come on!"

Mr. Baldwin was kind enough to loan Patrick one of his own coats, so Patrick didn't have to wear the warm but filthy blanket. A cold wind whipped down the streets, but most people seemed not to notice. Be damned, Patrick thought, if it doesn't look a bit like what I imagine Mr. Dickens' Christmas in London might appear. You only wanted some snow, and you needed to ignore the occasional building with its roof blown off, or a great gape in its walls where an eleven-inch naval cannon had torn through.

Allan Cole & Chris Bunch

Nor did London, Patrick thought, have as many soldiers milling around. Nor... and he lagged behind Lucy and unobtrusively dropped a ten dollar bill - Confederate, so it was hardly the benefice it might have appeared - into the ragged forage cap beside a legless man huddled against a wall; not a beggar, because he said never a word, he just looked.

As Patrick hurried to catch up with Lucy, another dizzy spell caught him. He had to stop a moment, and steady himself against a building. No, by damnation. You're just tired from the long ride. Directly, he felt better, and went after the girl. She appeared not to have noticed.

"Where are we going?" Patrick wanted to know.

"You'll see, you'll see," she said gaily, skirting a not-yet-filled-in shell hole that'd shattered the wooden pavement. Patrick shrugged. He'd find out. Besides, he had a question that was important as the blazes to him.

"Lucy," he said, choosing his words with care, "I know you wrote that your father said civilians have duty like soldiers do. But... you know, the Yankees are going to come back, sooner or later. Have you made any... provisions for something like that? Such as, maybe, digging a really deep hole? Or a railway ticket to someplace else?" he finished rather awkwardly, realizing he sounded like an old lady school teacher.

"They won't be back," Lucy said. "They're just going to sit out there in the swamps until General Lee takes Washington and then the war will be over. Besides, even if they come, there isn't much they can do. You know," she went on, "I used to go up on our roof, back in August, and watch the gunboats out on the river. Boom... boom... boom... and the cannonballs would come in. Sometimes you could hear them whistle, but they never seemed to hurt anyone. Or not usually, anyway."

Patrick murmured something about luck not liking to be chanced promiscuously. "No, Patrick," Lucy said, vehemently. "I saw them! You know, they tried to dig a canal all the way across Swampy Toe, so the river would pass us by, and couldn't do it?"

Patrick gaped - Swampy Toe?

Allan Cole & Chris Bunch

"Oh," the girl said. "I forgot. You're not a native. That's what we call DeSoto Peninsula."

Patrick knew it by that name very well, and an image flashed of two men with pistols on a foggy summer morning. Lucy didn't catch his expression and chattered on. "All their gunboats, and digging, and here we still are. And here we'll be. And here we really are."

She took him by the elbow, and led him into a shop. From that moment, everything became a great, odd blur, with only Lucy's presence keeping him tied to any kind reality. He nodded, numb and feeling like a fool, as she introduced him to the small, intense man with a tape around his neck. This is Sergeant Shannon, she said. She chattered on at top speed, piling up detail at an incredible rate... Sergeant Shannon's staying with us. He's with General Forrest's Cavalry, and is here on an important mission. He was at Shiloh. He'll be going to the ball with us tonight. Mr. Carnahan the tailor said he was very sorry, but he could hardly make up a proper set of formal wear in less than six hours, could he? Of course not, Lucy retorted. But didn't he have something that could be... well, re stitched in time? Carnahan shook his head, then rethought. Not coat and tails, but if the gentleman didn't mind going in uniform, and he disappeared into the back and came out with a very ornate high-collared coat, with gleaming buttons in a single row down its front, and great epaulettes, long bullion fringe dangling.

Perhaps this? Lucy loved it. Patrick pointed out it was intended for an officer, probably one of high rank, maybe even a general. What did that matter, Lucy wanted to know. None of us can distinguish rank. That gold really sets off your eyes. Patrick shuddered at the thought of General Pemberton, military commander of the city, coming over at the ball and asking to have a few words with the sergeant about his... interesting attire. He started to say this was ridiculous, but Mr. Carnahan was ahead of him. The fringe... and the epaulettes... could be removed in a moment. It would take no work at all for him to cut a set of three stripes, perhaps of red, no, you are a cavalryman, so they shall be gold. Perhaps Mr. Shannon would consent to try the coat on?

Patrick asked if whoever had ordered the coat might not get a little irate if he learned some itinerant horseman had bought it out

304

from under him. Mr. Carnahan coughed discreetly, and said the gentleman in question would not be back to pick it up, or at least so he dearly hoped, since that gentleman had the misfortune to have led his troops from the front in the counterattack at Baton Rouge, and, well...

Patrick tried the coat on. It did not quite fit like a glove, but close. Carnahan said there was more than enough material to let it out a bit in the shoulders, and perhaps a tuck at the hips, sir, since my late customer had a long-standing love affair with his victuals, and the pants, mm, well, I'll let them down some, and have it delivered within two hours. Patrick was caught by circumstances, and besides, when had he had the chance to preen like a peacock since New Orleans when he was just a child anyway? He reached for his pocketbook, fairly sure Mr. Carnahan would prefer specie. Lucy and the tailor looked aghast. Good Lord, sir, pardon me, Miss Baldwin, but put your money away. This is being done on account. Whose?

"This is Christmas," Lucy said. "Since we didn't know you were coming, we hardly had time to find a nice present, and these days there isn't much to be had, anyway. Don't argue with me, Patrick Shannon, or I shall lose my temper."

That was the last thing Patrick wanted. Leaving the shop, Lucy took him by the arm, and beamed up at him. "I am sure, Patrick, you'll be the very handsomest man at the ball tonight." And the bitter winter wind was a summer breeze.

Patrick, as he went in to supper, paused to admire himself in his new regalia. He thought, look more than passable.

Lucy poked him. "I'm sorry Daddy bought you that outfit," she said. "Now you're going to be nothing more than a proper popinjay!"

Patrick flushed, and followed her into the dining room. Supper was a marvel, fully worth of the holiday. There was a good piece of bacon for each of them, a saddle of mutton, mashed potatoes, turnips, egg bread, a bottle of claret for each and pound cake and walnuts to finish the meal. Patrick noted after the servants brought the food out, they also sat at the long table like they, too, were family. Best of all, Patrick saw none of the Baldwins drew attention

305

to this charity, just as it had been the stable hand, Stevenson, who'd told him when the cannonading started the family had insisted all the servants shelter in the courtyard where they would likely be safer.

Patrick tried to eat like a gentleman, but failed fairly seriously. He didn't quite make a hog of himself, but managed to clean every plate near him for several yards. He hadn't eaten like this since... since before the war.

Mr. Baldwin saw him looking around at the magnificence, and misunderstood. "You understand, sir, we hardly eat this well under normal conditions. It would be a sin against the Cause."

"We even," one of Lucy's sisters put in, "have starvation parties." She tried to look patriotic, but a slight moue of distaste crossed her face.

Patrick had read of these in a Richmond paper - there would be music and dancing and water to drink, but nothing more. He guessed that was all right, it maybe reminded civilians of what the soldiers were going through. But he knew damned well nobody in uniform who'd ever known a day or two on the march without bacon or bread would consider attending such an event, and his fellows at the front would know him to be demented if he did. Besides, a rather cynical thought touched him: how many of those public penitents went home afterward and stuffed themselves silly. But he said nothing.

Whatever lay beyond splendor was Lucy Baldwin. She wore a corn-colored silk gown, trimmed with black lace. Her hair was curled in a single coil hanging over one shoulder. Patrick just stood there for several lifetimes. "Well?"

The phrases reached his lips before he could stop them: "She walks in beauty like the night/" he whispered. "And all that's best of dark and bright/Meet in her aspect and her eyes." Patrick realized he was in love, and thought he didn't give a damn who knew it.

"And don't you two make a perfect pair," Mrs. Baldwin said from behind them, and both of them turned red.

The Baldwins and Patrick walked to the ball, which was held at a house not far away. These days it would not look proper, Mr. Baldwin noted, to be lording it in a carriage like some nobleman. A

Allan Cole & Chris Bunch

smile sped across his face. Have you noticed, he asked slyly, how easy that sort of self-sacrifice becomes when the streets look like they've been plowed, and all but two of our horses have been requisitioned by the army? Patrick was starting to like Mr. Baldwin.

There was a gaggle of carriages and saddled horses in the courtyard - evidently many of the guests weren't concerned about what people thought, and that the army hadn't been all that rigorous when it combed the city for remounts. The Baldwins gave their heavy coats to liveried slaves, and were instantly separated in the throng. The mansion was enormous. Patrick thought the Baldwin's house, big as it was, would have fit quite comfortably in the domed ballroom that rose two full stories in the center of the house.

There was a great chandelier, crystal punch bowls, an orchestra and everything such an affair was supposed to have. The guests wore formal wear or uniform, and Patrick noted there were at least three real generals in attendance. The women were all lovely in their silk, he decided, even if none were near as pretty as Lucy. He remembered reading about the great ball for Wellington's officers, in Quatre Bras, the night before Waterloo, but decided that was not a cheerful image for the season. Besides, Lucy was standing very close, no doubt due to the press of the crowd.

Music began, and she looked up at him shyly. "It's a waltz." Patrick nodded vaguely, having never pretended to be an expert. "You're not supposed to dance a waltz," she went on, "except with someone... special."

Patrick had not the slightest idea about how to waltz, but was unconcerned. He'd gone with Latimer to one of the great quadroon balls at Pontchartrain and marveled. Later, there'd been the fandangos in Texas where you didn't even think about dancing until you had at least one jug of cactus liquor salted down. He studied the dancers for a moment, and was pretty sure he had matters in hand.

He bowed to Lucy, took her hand, and led her onto the dance floor. The waltz, he guessed, was considered risqué because you were allowed to take your partner in your arms. In Pontchartrain, on the other hand, any dance in which you retained most of your clothes was considered decorous. Contrary to what might have happened in one of Mr. Dickens' less gloomy works, Patrick neither stumbled,

307

fell, nor trod on Diana's feet. Not that he was surprised - he'd always found dancing easy, if not exactly the most interesting pastime for an evening.

Then there wasn't anything but the music, and Lucy's hand, soft in his, his other hand touching just at the curve of her hip, and since there were many other dancers on the floor it was natural to move closer. Lucy was looking up at him, her lips slightly parted.

The thought touched his mind, and he bent his head... and caught sight of Mrs. Baldwin, standing at the edge of the dance floor. Watching. Not upset or anything. Just... watching. Patrick moved back - just a trifle.

The evening became a great swirling kaleidoscope: music, people, the punch drunk sparingly, but the center was Lucy. He could not remember a Christmas like this. In fact, he had not been this happy since... since ever?

It was almost midnight, and Patrick wondered if the ball would come to an end, and they would attend mass. He didn't know what religion the Baldwins had, but if they were Catholic... Patrick had noted the cathedral when he'd ridden through the city looking for the Baldwins' house. Whatever they wanted, and whatever happened, he decided, a great deep joy filling him like he'd read the saints had. But he knew where the happiness was coming from, and it was hardly from Heaven.

They'd just refreshed themselves with a shared glass of champagne punch, when the room gently turned a few degrees around Patrick. Very suddenly he felt awful.

"I think..." he said, bracing himself against a table, "I'd best get some air. A little... woolly-headed."

"What's the matter," Lucy asked. "You only had two cups of punch and... Patrick, you're sweating. Come on."

She took him by the hand, and led him out of the ballroom. She led him to a glassed-in porch, just off the main room that looked out on the carriage-filled driveway below.

Patrick breathed deeply, and the house stopped attempting its own waltz. Better. It was cool... no, cold out here. He shook his head. "Sorry," he said. "Just a bit of... I don't know what."

308

"Are you all right now?"

"I... think so," he said. As Lucy shivered, he realized it was cold out here. Patrick saw a shawl on a chair, and wrapped it around her shoulders.

"You're sure you're feeling well?" Lucy asked again.

"Never better," Patrick said. It was almost true.

She looked at him closely in the light that shone through the half-open glass door from the ballroom.

"You do look a little better."

"Um-hmh."

"Patrick Shannon, if I hadn't been writing to you for so long, and if I didn't know better, I would swear that..."

"You'd swear what?"

"That you just did that to get me out here and—"

And Patrick kissed her. She mmphed in surprise, then, to his utter astonishment, kissed him back, her arms going around him very, very tight. About the turn of the century, Patrick came up for air. Now his head was truly swimming. He looked down at her. Her eyes were closed, lips half-parted.

"I think," he began.

"Ssh," Lucy ssshed, and they kissed once more. Patrick's hand crept around her side, moving gently up her ribcage, and Lucy's hands made never a move to stop him, and... and hooves thundered up the driveway. They broke apart.

Patrick saw the horseman - a uniformed dispatch rider - slide from his saddle and run up the steps into the ballroom. Trouble, no doubt, but man was born to trouble and what did he care. He was about to resume kissing Lucy when, inside, the music squawked to a discordant halt. Lucy went to the doorway to see what was going on.

A gaudily-uniformed man leapt onto the bandstand, wildly waving for silence. "I have just been told," he shouted, "the Enemy is coming down the river! We are to be attacked! This ball is at an end."

The hush exploded. Lucy turned back to see what had happened

Patrick Shannon lay sprawled, face-down, on the floor. As far as she could tell, he was not breathing.

Allan Cole & Chris Bunch

Part Three

"Vicksburg is the key. The war can never be brought to a close until the key is in our pocket." ... *President Abraham Lincoln*

"Vicksburg is the nail head that holds the South's two halves together." ...*Jefferson Davis.*

CHAPTER TWENTY-FOUR

VICKSBURG, MISS. - APRIL 16, 1863

PATRICK'S EYES SNAPPED open to the sound of thunder. He lay perfectly still, trying to figure where he was. He was in a bed. A large bed, with smooth cotton sheets that smelled of lavender. There was another sweet odor in the air - lilacs. He was naked - no, he wore a cotton flannel nightshirt. He felt... he felt good. Weak, but good. It was night. He was in a room lit by two oil lamps, one on either side of his bed. At the end of the room were glass doors leading out onto a gallery. One door was half-open. The thunder was louder. Patrick turned his head. Beside him, bolt upright in a chair, was Lucy. She, too was dressed for bed. Her gaze was rigidly fixed out those doors, and she looked frightened.

"Lucy?" Patrick didn't mean for his voice to be a croak, but that was how it came out. She jumped, and turned, forgetting her apparent fright over the building storm outside... if that was what it was.

"Patrick! You are awake."

"I think... yes," Patrick said.

"How do you feel?"

"Like... like I've been beat up by kittens." He tried to sit, but collapsed back on the pillows. "What time is it?"

Lucy started crying. "Patrick, you're going to be all right. Oh, we prayed, and we did everything we could, and it's been so long."

Patrick stretched out a hand and she flung herself across him. Then she was laughing through her tears. "You are such a fool, Patrick. You kept trying to get up and go get something called caps for the General. We had to tie you to the bed a couple of times."

His mind rocked... and the warmth of the night and the lilac smell slipped through. He moved Lucy away and forced himself up. "Lucy! How long have I been sick?"

"It's... it's April now. Thursday. The sixteenth. You've been sick since Christmas, and the Yankees are trying to capture the city. That's them, that's their ships out there," she said, and Patrick realized it wasn't thunder he was hearing, but artillery.

"They're shooting at us with their damned cannons," Lucy went on, "and I didn't know what to do. I was frightened, and I should have gone down to the cellar like Daddy told me, but I couldn't leave you."

"Christ!" Patrick had only half-heard what she'd said beyond the date. "What happened to me?"

"We had doctors... and they said it could be any kind of fever that soldiers are afflicted with. You'd get better, then you'd get sick again. One doctor said you were worn down, and that every fever in the army was lining up to get at you. We gave you quinine, and calomel, and even tincture of opium and things like that... and soup. One of us, or one of the maids, always sat with you and somebody slept in this room every night in case you woke up. You'd eat, but you'd never come to full consciousness all the way. Except this morning, when you opened your eyes up, and looked at me and said something very clear."

Lucy giggled. "Mother was in the room, too."

"What did I say?" Patrick was trying to assemble his thoughts, but kept veering to the fact he'd just lost a third of a year in his life. Hell, he felt like a junior version of Mr. Irving's snoring dutchman.

Lucy did not answer, nor did she look at him. "Just... something." Thunder slammed, and Lucy jumped. "Patrick, this isn't like the other time when they shot at us! This is... terrible."

"You better get into the cellar," Patrick said. "I'll be fine. Where's your family?"

"They're all at the Grand Ball. At Major Watts' house. Daddy said it's being held because everybody'd heard that awful General Grant is taking his army away, all the way back to Memphis. I didn't go because of the way you sounded this morning, and I was praying you'd wake up. Somebody must have heard about the ball, and told the ships they could sneak by!" Lucy's eyes widened. "There must be... a spy in the city!"

"I wouldn't doubt it." Patrick was starting to think clearly. He blew out both lamps - he doubted the artillery was aiming at little dots of light, but who could tell? He lowered his feet down to the floor.

"What are you doing? You can't—"

Allan Cole & Chris Bunch

"Trying to find out what's happening out there." Patrick tried to take a step, damned near fell, and steadied himself on the bedpost. "Lucy. Help me over to the window."

"You shouldn't be out of bed!" Patrick didn't argue, but hobbled a step, almost fell once more, then had a bit of balance. Lucy was close beside him. "You are a fool," but she lifted his arm around her shoulders and he used her as a crutch to get to the windows.

Now the crashing would never be taken for any storm, no matter how violent. Flames roared across the Mississippi. It looked like someone had fired DeSoto City for a torch. Out on the water monsters glided down river, leviathans of the night, great dragons of the river. Their mouths were fire and flame, and their tongues steel and iron. Flaming tar barrels lined the Vicksburg's waterfront and, every now and then, Confederate cannon roared a response.

Patrick thought he could see cannonfall, high waterspouts against the blackness. A ship exploded into flames, but the monsters paid no heed, their voices howling against man and his city. It was hell, and it was magnificent, and a man could get himself dead or full of glass just being a bystander. Or, worse, a young girl.

"Lucy! Get downstairs!"

"No! Not without you!"

"I'm not... all right." Patrick moved away from the window, and collapsed. Fortunately the bed was close, and he managed to collapse on it. "Damn!" he swore, and Lucy did not pretend false shock. "I can't get down those stairs... and you surely can't carry me. I'll be all right."

"No!" Lucy's voice was firm. "I am staying with you."

"I'm not going to argue." It seemed the ships were passing now, and the cannon fire wasn't as intense. There wasn't much chance of the Baldwin's house being struck anyway, except by the purest misfortune - about that of getting hit by lightning; although Patrick remembered a bibleshouter in Texas who'd been struck down preaching under a tree on a rainy day, not long after he'd bellowed the hand of the lord could reach out and smite him if he was lying. His thoughts swirled away from that.

"Sit with me," he asked. "Tell me what has happened since... since I got sick."

313

Lucy told him as best she knew, and none of it was good. Just as Patrick had predicted, the Yankees had begun another assault that Christmas night. But this time they hadn't been driven off by counterattack, flooding, winter, or even meager rations. The city was under siege, and supplies of every kind were already running short. There were many more soldiers in Vicksburg, and it had changed from a garrison city into a fortress. It was surrounded by the Union - General Grant and his army were below them, General Sherman was to the North, there were Yankees to the west in Louisiana so no supplies from Texas could get through.

The Yankee cannon were already shelling the city. The road, and the rail line east to Jackson were still open, but Lucy had heard there were Union cavalrymen out there. People from the surrounding countryside had flocked into the city, fled south to relatives, or friends - hoping the Yankees would let them pass through the lines. Some held firm, praying somehow the war would pass them by.

Patrick suddenly thought of another problem - this one most personal. Four months. Shit! General Forrest must have me down as a deserter! I could be shot first time I stick my head out the door!

"Lucy," he demanded. "Did anyone tell the army about me?"

"Of course, silly silly," she said. "Even though none of us have ever served, we're not complete ninnies. Daddy and Doctor Alison went to General Pemberton, and one of his aides was nice enough to write a letter to your General Forrest. He even wrote back, and said... we think at least, did you know that man has the worst hand I've ever seen?... you were to remain where you were until fully recuperated, then report to the local military district, I think it was. Anyway, he said when you were better, you could come back to him if you wanted. But if you didn't get better, he wanted everyone to know you were... I'm sorry, Patrick, that's what he wrote... one of his best men."

Were, Patrick mused, remembering Forrest crawlling back to duty with a minie ball inside him. If he'd written that, Patrick must have been a whole lot more than just sick. He blew out hard, then realized his breath was sweet. That made him curious. "Lucy? Did someone brush my teeth?"

"Every morning."

Allan Cole & Chris Bunch

"I must have had the best treatment of any patient in all Christendom," Patrick said. "I only wish I'd been around to enjoy it." Another thought struck him. "Where's my horse? Where's Templar?"

"Out in the stables. He's disgusting and fat, because he wouldn't let anyone ride him. He kicked poor Mr. Stevenson when he tried, and—" There was a monstrous crash and a whistling filled the cosmos, and Patrick pulled Lucy down and threw himself across her. He realized the whistling was going away, damn fool, and Lucy was laughing. "Some soldier you are. That's the gun they call Whistling Dick. It's one of ours! Now get off! You're crushing me!"

Patrick started to, then considered - and decided he was feeling somewhat stronger. He didn't move.

"If I recollect, Miss Baldwin, before I decided to go sing with the angels for a spell, weren't you and I doing something interesting?"

"Get off me! You're taking advantage!" But she didn't push at him, nor move. "And besides, you're too sick to be doing anything like..."

"Let's see now," Patrick said, starting to breathe a little hard. "We were doing something like... " and he kissed her, and she kissed him back, hard. There was nothing wrong with his memory, she could indeed make the world walk widdershins.

"What would happen if Daddy walked in right now," she whispered, when they'd come up for air.

"I surely wouldn't kiss him. Besides, I thought you said he was at the ball."

"They are... all of them, except the servants, who are asleep."

"Don't you think... when they come home... they'll make a ruckus? And turn on some lights?"

"I suppose," Lucy said, and this time it was she who kissed him, arms tight around him. "Oh, Patrick, I was so afraid that you were going to... to... and there's so many soldiers these days and so much sickness."

"Ah," Patrick said, "but they didn't have the love of a good woman to sustain them."

"That's what you said this morning," Lucy breathed. "That... that you loved me."

Patrick didn't say anything. He thought of making a joke, but that would not have been right. But he couldn't just out and say... he settled for just nodding in the darkness. Lucy must have felt the motion, because she pulled him down to her, and this time the kiss didn't seem to ever end.

His hand fumbled at the hem of her nightclothes, found it, and slid up, along the smooth of her leg, nightdress lifting with his hand, and his hand found a small breast, nipple hardening between his fingers. Somehow, some way her garment was around her shoulders, neither one of them having time to take it off, and his nightshirt was on the floor.

Their bodies touched, slid together, hardness found wet warmth and Lucy sighed, and her legs closed around him.

They lay together afterward, still joined, Lucy's legs behind his knees. "I could go to sleep like this," she whispered.

"That would give everybody something to talk about," Patrick said.

"Who cares." Lucy nipped at his shoulder. "I thought... that was supposed to hurt. It didn't, not at all. And I thought I saw stars on the ceiling."

"Just call me the Demon Lover," Patrick said. "I did see stars. And comets. And suns."

"If... if you're of a mind," she said, her voice becoming throaty, "I'd guess we'd have time to look for them again. I was pretty good at Astronomy, you know, even if Mrs. Warren didn't exactly teach it this way."

And her hips began moving under him.

Allan Cole & Chris Bunch

CHAPTER TWENTY-FIVE

OFF CAPE FEAR, N.C. - APRIL 18, 1863

"**SHIP HO! THREE** points off the starboard bow."

"Boy! My respects to the captain, and he's needed on deck."

Joshua was pulling on his boots before the Officer of the Watch on the quarterdeck above finished his order. He already wore undergarments and breeches. He hurriedly buttoned his uniform coat, grabbed his cap and glass, and was out of his cabin as a pair of legs came down the companionway.

"I heard, and am coming" he said calmly. "Return to your post, and give my thanks to Mister Colston."

The legs went back up the ladder, and Joshua started after them. A great weakness caught him, and then the pain. It was as if a great invisible being was squeezing his chest, and he could not draw breath. The pain shifted to his shoulder, ran like liquid fire down into his left hand and was gone. Joshua took a deep breath. This was not the first nor the tenth time it had struck over the past few weeks, and he had no idea what was causing it. At first he'd thought diet, but no matter how he modified or eliminated the limited rations available, or stuck to the savories that were somehow acquired by his mess cook, the pain would return. At least, he thought, it was gone quickly, and had not interfered with his duties. I shall be damned, he'd told himself, if I shall let this body of mine turn traitor. It is but a passing thing, anyway. I am far too young to be worrying about my health.

Feeling quite normal, he went up the companionway onto the Oregon's maindeck, then to the quarterdeck. Around him, the frigate was coming alive, more than six hundred men hurrying to their fighting stations. They were moving without shouted commands, drumrolls, bosun's pipes or the trumpet blasts other ships used for command evolutions. Joshua had carefully schooled his officers and men, even convincing the bosun and master-at-arms to lower their customary enraged bellows. The mission was hard enough without silver trumpets to go before proclaiming their presence.

The ship was surging forward, screw thrashing the Atlantic, seemingly as eager, if Joshua permitted himself or anyone else to romanticize rolled iron, as its crew.

His first officer was at the starboard railing, peering into the darkness through his glass. Joshua noted the direction, and followed suit. Nothing... .nothing... no. Something was out there. A shoal?... a school of porgies? "I have it," he said aloud, and the startled Mister Colston jumped, then reported. "Sir, we have full steam, and as per your standing instructions I ordered full speed in pursuit."

"Very well that," Joshua said, his attention on the indistinct shape in the darkness. Even identified, the blockade runner's paint made it hellishly hard to keep the ship in view. It was either light gray or dull white, to camouflage the sleek craft against the sand dunes, when it laid up close inshore, waiting for night and full darkness before making the dash into Wilmington. Even at sea the color helped disguise the craft as it skirted close to the terrible shoals collectively known as the Frying Pan.

"Mister Colston," Joshua said, not lowering his telescope. "The lookout who spotted that craft is to have an extra tot of rum tomorrow, and I shall note his vigilance to the crew at Sunday Quarters.""Aye, sir."

"Guns closed up, sir."

"Thank you, Mister Stewart."

"Shall we try a ranging shot, sir?"

"I admire your eagerness, sir. But no. It would only waste powder. I would estimate the range to be far greater than a mile at present."

"Even with the pivot gun, sir?" The great cannon the gunnery officer was referring to was the Oregon's prize, recently installed on a turning mount amidships on the forward foc'sle. It fired a monstrous shell, weighing well over one hundred pounds. A solid shot would hole any craft at sea, including even an ironclad or monitor if it struck solidly, and the shell would shatter the fragile blockade runner like a balsawood model.

"Even with the pivot gun, sir. It may be the eighth wonder of the world, but it does not quite have the reach of the Lord's vengeance, contrary to your dreams."

Joshua's ship, the steam frigate Oregon, was part of the North Atlantic Blockading Squadron, endlessly patrolling the North Carolina coast. The large ships, frigates, sloops stayed well offshore,

318

and consequently saw action infrequently. No matter how many times Joshua reassured the crew that little by little just their presence was strangling the Confederacy, allowing no guns or war supplies in, and just as importantly keeping the South's cotton from going out to be exchanged for gold in England, the long, dull drone of their duties ground away at everyone's spirit.

Even when a blockade runner was sighted, the contest was far from even, no matter how many tons of explosives a warship could hurl at the barely-armed thin-hulled runners. The three hundred feet of the Oregon, with its crew and 48 cannon of various calibers was still not guaranteed victory. The problem was—

"—The bastard's going to run away from us," Lieutenant Commander Colston said gloomily. Joshua tried to find a mark to estimate the ship's speed, could not, but realized the light shape in his glass was smaller. "It must be turning fifteen, no sixteen knots," Colston continued.

That was indeed the problem. The Oregon, fresh from a shipyard overhaul and with a clean bottom, both of which were some time in the past, was capable of ten knots at the most, and that was with a prayer and the chief engineer hanging lead weights from the safety release valves of all four boilers. This made the blockade a chess match - the runners tried to out-think the blockaders, using weather, phases of the moon, local pilots who knew the mazelike waters of the North Carolina Coast, speed... and luck. The prize was great riches and honor in Wilmington, the penalty capture, death in battle or by drowning in any of the myriad clever ways God had provided on the coast of Carolina.

If it had not been a near flat calm this night, Joshua knew, the ship ahead would never have been seen. Even so, it had only been spotted by one lynx-eyed seaman. Yes, Joshua decided. The Secesh was showing the Oregon her heels.

"Mister Stewart," he said. "I shall be turning a bit further to starboard. If you can avoid removing our bowsprit with that great Moloch of yours, you may try your skill."

"Thank you, sir," the young man said eagerly and darted forward, shouting commands as he went.

Allan Cole & Chris Bunch

"For the sake of morale, sir?" Joshua's first officer guessed. "And at least it will give the men something else to clean on the morrow besides what they holystoned this day."

"You, mister, are far too clever," Joshua said obliquely, "and would be well advised to keep your candle under a bushel basket, if for no other reason than to allow an old man to deceive himself as to his cunning."

Colston chuckled. Less than five minutes later the 150-pounder bellowed, sending a great cone of fire and its immense shell into the night, gunblast sounding through the shrouds like a momentary gale wind, and then there was nothing as the offshore wind blew the smoke away.

"Damn it," Colston swore, blinking wildly, momentarily blinded by the flash.

"As I suggested moments ago," Joshua said, "you wear your cleverness on your sleeve. One of us, at least, had sense enough to close one eye when he heard the firing order."

It was Joshua's turn to mutter something. "Short. Far short. And I will wager the piece is at full elevation " he said, having spotted the climbing white column of water. "Continue Firing. Three rounds!" he roared in a voice near as loud as the huge rifle, a voice trained on clipper ships and Cape Horn storms, a voice that easily carried forward without need of the trumpet beside the helmsman.

"As you noted, we need the training," he said in a normal voice to Commander Colston. "But fire the rockets now."

"Aye, aye, Captain." Colston issued commands, then turned back to the rail, and stared through his glass at the escaping Confederate ship. "Goodbye to all that prize money." he said sadly as two great rockets exploded up into the night, sending out the alert.

"Mister," Joshua said, now completely formal. "None of us came to war, or so I hope, with the intent of becoming rich."

"Nossir. Sorry, sir. You're right. But he did." Colston said, nodding at the dot in the night.

"No doubt," Joshua said. "That is yet another reason why the Secessionists have doomed themselves. I said a long time ago," he went on, thoughtfully, remembering a tiny old woman lying in bed, on a hot Vicksburg afternoon, "these Southerners would destroy

Allan Cole & Chris Bunch

themselves. And so it is becoming. When this war has finished, I may rent myself out as a somewhat waterlogged Cassandra."

"The problem is," Colston said, "they're taking too many of us with them."

Joshua did not reply. Instead, he, too, lifted his glass once more. But he did not focus it on the blockade runner, but swept the horizon. Somewhere beyond was the coast, the waiting guns of the Confederate forts, the treacherous shoals, the inshore element of the Blockading Squadron aboard tiny shorehugging gunboats... and his son, Donald.

Now it is your turn, son, he thought, if your ship is within range. But do not become too eager. There is always another day and another battle.

To Joshua, miles out at sea and yards above the water on his great frigate, the Atlantic may have been calm. But to his son, close inshore in shoaling water, aboard the spitkit Pocono - one hundred and ninety feet long, a bit more than a hundred men for its crew, and seven cannon - it was middling rough. The gunboat was built for speed and shallow draft, not for comfort, and it was an item of pride among the crew the Pocono would roll on wet grass.

It was fortunate Donald McKay Shannon had a cast iron stomach. To him, the ship's pitching was only an indicator of how close to the shallows the gunboat was, and the state of the weather. Midshipman Shannon had the deck, and perhaps should have made his rounds quickly and then returned to his post aft. But Tucker had the wheel and Mister Munro was the quartermaster on watch, and that guaranteed no surprises.

Donald was leaning against the ship's foremast, not exactly hiding, but not advertising his presence, and listening to a seaman proudly read a letter aloud to his mates, who were sitting around the one hundred pound main gun amidships in the bows:

"Mother, if you truly wish to experience the adventures of a jolly tar, go down to the hotel, and climb up on its roof. Then talk to half a dozen hotel hallboys, who are far more intelligent, agreeable and educated than the average officer. Then descend to the attic and drink some warm water, full of iron rust, and eat a meal as tasty as that beef Aunt Jane pickles and attempts to foist off at Christmas. Then go on the roof once more, and do this half a dozen times until you are tired. Then go to bed, with everything shut so as to be unbearably close, so as not to show a light, and you will truly know adventure."

There was laughter, and Donald stepped from behind the mast, clearing his throat loudly. There was a scurry of movement, and a gasp or two.

"Carry on," he said. "You're off watch, aren't you? Although you might be better advised to keep your eyes sharp. It is nights like these the runners come in or go out." He started back toward the stern, and said, quietly over his shoulder: "Hotel hallboys, eh? I would have said stablehands."

Laughter grew once more behind him, and grinning, Donald went back down the deck toward the binnacle. By Navy Regulations, common tradition and certainly his Commanding Officer Lieutenant Peabody's wishes, Shannon should have jacked them all up for disrespect and skylarking on deck. But he'd never found it easy to play Dutch Uncle to a sailor who might be his father or grandfather. Not, anyway, until his own beard grew out and thus far it wasn't cooperating well, although his sidewhiskers were impressive enough, fluffing beyond his ears.

It was hard enough learning war and the sea without alienating those who could not only help him, but very likely keep him alive. Paying attention to those with more experience, at least until they've proven themselves utter fools, was a commandment preached by Joshua from the first moment Donald had thought of being a sailor. Preached by Joshua, and graven in stone by the battle at Drewry's Bluff.

Donald McKay Shannon, not far beyond his nineteenth birthday, had, as the phrase went, seen the elephant, and it was a damned huge beast. His first post had been aboard the U.S.S. Galena, one of the most unlikely ships ever launched in a day when ugly not infrequently ruled the waves. In 1861, Congress had ordered three ironclad ships to be built. Donald, remembering his father's conviction that the day of the wooden ships was done, had agitated, as best the most junior midshipman in the Navy could, for a posting on one of them.

For some reason, his application was speedily and joyously accepted. The three ships were the U.S.S. New Ironsides, which unlike its namesake the Constitution had armored sides, had all the beauty of a floating row house block... and a maximum speed slightly faster than a healthy man could walk in an hour. The second was the U.S.S. Monitor. And the third was the Galena.

From a distance, the ironclad Galena looked like a not unhandsome sloop, all of whose masts except a stubby foremast had been cut away. Amidships was a single funnel for its twin boilers, and the rest of the deck was clean. It was from aboard, or alongside, the Galena showed her real gawkiness. Two layers of one inch thick plates, with iron bars between them, were laid horizontally to look like ship's timbers. The sides curved in and up from the waterline at a ridiculous 45 degrees, what naval builders called tumblehome. The iron plates would supposedly be impervious to a direct hit from any cannon up to a six incher. Not only was the Galena ugly, but nearly as slow as the New Ironsides, and just as unhandy in any sort of a seaway, either under sail or power.

The Galena, with Midshipman Shannon aboard, arrived in Hampton Roads, Virginia, just days after its sister, or niece at any rate, the Monitor, had sent the wallowing pig named the C.S.S. Virginia, formerly the United States frigate Merrimack, lumbering back upriver to Richmond after the two ships had spent four hours hammering at each other rather inconclusively. They weren't there for the grand event, but Donald realized very quickly that would not be the way the story was told on a seaman's next commission.

Two months later the great Confederate ironclad, with nowhere to go, trapped by land forces around the James River, and the United States fleet downriver, blew herself up. Now the way was open for the Navy to show the Army how to fight the war. Four days after the Virginia's rather inglorious suicide, five Federal warships, including the Monitor and the Galena, went up the James River. The Navy had things well in hand. They would shell, and force the surrender of Richmond, the Confederate capital.

Allan Cole & Chris Bunch

The passage upriver was marked by the near-ramming of the Monitor by the Galena, and the near-ramming of the state of Virginia by the Monitor. Ironclads may have become the instant darling of everyone from President Lincoln on down, but they maneuvered with all the grace, or so the Galena's quartermaster put it, "of a hog on roller skates."

The Confederates were waiting seven miles below Richmond. The Union Navy hove into view and the battle began. The Confederate artillery was entrenched on a bluff, high above the river - the guns of the Union ships could not elevate enough to target them. That was the first discovery. The second discovery, for the men of the Galena, was the armor they'd spent so many hours oiling and chipping rust from was approximately as shellproof as a canvas sail. Shell that bounced off the Monitor sieved the Galena. Some said it was hit eighteen times, some said more. The funnel was so shot up that steam boiled and screamed in all directions, and the ship reeled, iron shards and wooden splinters whistling, its hull shattered almost beyond repair.

Three hours and twenty minutes later the Federal Navy went downriver a deal faster than it had come up, after its own miniature version of the Battle of Bull Run. If thirteen men hadn't been killed, and almost as many wounded, it might have been a laughable farce. When the day was over the Galena was ordered to return to a Northern shipyard to have its iron plating stripped away, and a slightly wounded Donald Shannon transferred to a new ship. The only reason he'd survived the day, was an old seaman, who swore he'd been on Lake Erie with Perry, had knocked Donald down and sat on him when the young middie was intent on jumping on a cannon's mount and shouting heroic slogans.

The last irony was the best - many of the land-mounted guns that shot up the United States Navy had been taken from the Virginia before she was blown up, and her flag flew over the Confederate battlements at Fort Darling. Donald wrote home, after he'd learned those two facts, that sometimes wars and victories weren't as neat as the history books made out.

At least this new post wasn't on a ship made of boilerplate. Donald wasn't entirely convinced his father was wrong in predicting

Allan Cole & Chris Bunch

the future as steam and iron, but he wanted to give reality a chance to catch up before he gave ironclads another chance. Not only was the Galena now a conventional sloop of war, but four months ago, just after Christmas, the Monitor had gone down in a storm, ordered to sea by someone who'd never heard of winter weather.

Oh well, Donald thought. Father said the interesting thing about being a sailor was just how many ways there were of being bored and killed. His current commanding officer, Lieutenant Peabody, seemed intent, through inexperience and bone-deep stupidity, in exploring all of them.

Donald reflexively checked the ship's bearing, and estimated the Pocono's position as being just clear of Drunken Dick Shoals as it slowly worked its way back and forth, up and down just off the shoals. He then took his own advice and glassed the horizon shoreward and to sea. This was a night for blockade runners. His father, Donald knew, despised prize money on principal, but Donald did not. Joshua, already not a poor man, received $4,200 a year, his son $1,000 when he was at sea, $800 when not. The skipper of a blockade runner, Donald knew, with a bit of envy, also received a thousand dollars.

Per voyage, plus the profit if he also owned a share of the cargo when it was sold in Wilmington. Now, if the Pocono happened to seize such a runner, it and its cargo would be auctioned off. Twenty shares of the benefits would go to the prize vessel and from that Peabody would get 15%, the Pocono's officers divide 20%, and the crew 35%. Thus far in the war, the Pocono had taken two runners, both before Donald was assigned to the gunboat. The crew still grew misty-eyed on the fine liberties the Confederate treasure had funded.

Mister Munro, the ship's quartermaster, which meant pilot and navigator, came up beside him, but did not speak. Lieutenant Peabody would no doubt have said the man "knew his position." Lieutenant Peabody had also, earlier that day, called Munro "boy." Donald had to hide his angry and embarrassed flush. But even though Donald would no more have called the dignified black a boy any more than he would have used some of the other words too many people used, Munro was a bit of a conundrum to him.

325

Allan Cole & Chris Bunch

Growing up in Marblehead, Donald hadn't seen many blacks, let alone become friends with them. There hadn't been more than a handful, all free, and mostly laborers or farmers, with a couple of shopkeepers. None of them were anything like the long-bearded patriarch beside him. But neither were the other eight black men in the Pocono's crew like Munro.

The Navy, early on, had taken the lead of the merchant marine and accepted blacks into service, either free or escaped slaves, what everyone except Donald called "contraband." Donald knew if he ever allowed the term to cross his lips in the presence of his father, he would be the target for A Look - the one that could quell a mutiny or even a boiler explosion.

The other blacks aboard the Pocono, like those on the Galena, were firemen, water tenders or stewards. Mister Munro was a pilot. Before the war, he'd been a slave - and the de facto master of a small fishing boat. When the blockade began, he and two other men had cold-cocked their owner and sailed his schooner out to greet the Union ships.

No one quite knew what to do with him, but no one was foolish enough to want to waste his fathom-by-fathom knowledge of the Carolina coast. Mister Munro could read and cipher not just books but charts as well, the latter well beyond a high percentage of the whites. But his color was all some people could see. By rights, as a quartermaster, particularly on a ship as small as the Pocono, he should mess with the officers. But Mister Munro chose to eat with the other blacks, even though they held far lower rank, rather than make an issue of the matter.

The ship was, in theory, color-blind, as was the entire Navy. But in practice it wasn't that simple. If the Pocono had been Donald's command, the black would have been treated as his rank and authority warranted. But although midshipmen might imagine wearing Captain's epaulettes, dreams did not produce instant promotion.

Donald knew he should leave the issue of color alone, but it still bothered him, and so, on solitary night watches like this, he kept picking at the scab. He also got a chance to listen to Mister Munro talk. He had a voice like the timpani of the gods, and could have

Allan Cole & Chris Bunch

made an earth-shaking preacher. Donald thought he could listen to the man say or read anything down to a muster list in fascination, and wished he himself had a voice like that, instead of a nasal Massachusetts near-whine. Mister Munro seemed amused by Donald's persistence, but not offended.

"What will you do," Donald began, "after the war?"

"I am not sure," the quartermaster said. "Firstly, I must assume I shall live through this apocalypse, which at times seems rather laughable. Perhaps return to fishing, although that now appears a bit mundane, once one has fished for men as we are doing. If I had any sense, I'd be planning to go to Canada."

Donald remembered the family tale about the near-legendary Diana Shannon and the two runaway slaves who'd fought Indians with her during the Revolution, and then headed north when peace came. He even remembered what one had told her when he left, words that sent a chill down the back of everyone who heard them, second or third or fifth hand, which was why they capped that part of the tale of Cherry Valley: "Perhaps," one of the blacks had said, and the teller always said the man spoke gently, "we shall return. When America fights the rest of its Revolution."

"Canada, sir?" Donald asked, bringing himself back to the present. "You've told me you would hate Massachusetts for its weather and Canada's a bit closer to the Pole than Marblehead."

"I could learn to accept that, I imagine. It cannot be much worse than a storm off the Cape here in February. Because once across the border the colored man is safe."

"Sir, don't you consider yourself... and the others, uh, like you, safe now?"

"Hardly. Look at those of us who've run away from our masters, and enlisted. All of us expected to be treated like white men. Instead?" Munro shrugged. "Instead, they put us to work shoveling coal and working in front of a hot fire, and don't even give us good hog and hominy, let alone some other things not quite so material a Christian might appreciate."

Donald shifted, uncomfortably. "But... isn't this a beginning? It'll be better, by and by."

Allan Cole & Chris Bunch

"So it is claimed. In the meantime we are to be purified with fire and water. I've heard some of your sailors tell my people that if they save the Union they'll come out some day in Congress." Mister Munro snorted. "If they do, they'll be brushing the white man's coat, I fear, just as they've been doing all their lives."

Donald's retort was forgotten as white rockets to seaward shattered the night. "A runner! Turn out!" he shouted, and, following orders, stamped hard on the deck, just above where his useless captain slept. "All hands! We've got a Runner! Cap'n to the quarterdeck!"

The orders came in smoothly, as they should. Peabody may have been an imbecile, but he believed in drill, over and over and over again. It may have been the only thing he did know.

"Mister Munro, take the deck. We shall require full power for maneuvering. I am going forward to the main gun. Inform the Captain, if you would, sir."

"Do you wish rockets, sir?"

Donald started to say yes, then thought. No, he didn't. If there was a runner close, he did not need to advertise his presence. Nor did he need to alert the monstrous guns of Fort Fisher, just inland. "I do not."

Five minutes later, hanging in the bows of the Pocono, he spotted the runner as it sped, toward the safety of New Inlet. The lookout yelled the sighting to the Captain, who was pacing near the helm. "Mister Shannon," came the return. "Challenge that ship when we are in range."

"Aye, sir," Donald shouted.

Closer... closer... No one on the Confederate ship had seen the gunboat yet. Donald heard voices, commands from the vessel: "Are you ready to take her in, Pilot?" Another voice: "Ready, sir. Port, port, hard-aport."

That was close enough. "Rockets," he ordered, and white light bloomed. He lifted the speaking trumpet. "Ship ahoy! Heave to or I'll sink you!"

The runner's paddles churned faster. A bit of Donald's mind had the leisure to admire the craft. Her sole purpose, from design to launch, was intended for just what she was doing now. The ship

328

looked to be made of iron, painted off-white. It was a third longer than the Pocono, but ten feet more slender in the beam. There were three short, back-canted stacks that could be collapsed to make the ship even harder to spot. Up forward was a smooth shield, a turtleback, covering the forward part of the ship, a midship house, two raked and stubby masts and a low poopdeck. The deck sat just a few feet above the waterline, and to further lower the profile the ship's boats were hung even with the gunwales.

Now the excitement of the chase overwhelmed Donald: "Strike, sir, or we fire." Again, no response from the Confederate ship. "Captain! Request permission to fire!"

"Granted! One shot - across her bows," and even before Donald could give the proper command the gun captain pulled the lanyard, and the 100-pounder blasted.

"Damn you," Donald snarled, "Wait for the command or I'll have you disrated and scrubbing the jakes! Reload!" All these orders came without lowering the glass.

The solid shot sent white spray cascading not twenty yards in front of the plunging Rebel steamer. "Sir! She's not obeying! May I fire into her!"

"You may fire when... no!" came the shout from Peabody. "She's striking her colors!" Indeed, a white flag fluttered up the runner's mizzenmast. "Stop engines," Peabody shouted. "Prepare to send across boarders."

"Belay that! Belay that, goddamit," Donald was shouting, sure what would come next, and just as the bells clanged and steam came off the Pocono the surrender flag disappeared, the runner's paddles churned white, and she began pulling away into the darkness, in a not uncommon if frowned on ruse de guerre.

"Full power! Full power! After that ship! Mister Shannon! I'll speak to you about countermanding my orders when we capture the Rebel! You may fire into her, sir, when opportunity presents."

Shit! I'll be for it afterward, Donald thought absently, but didn't worry about the future, intent on ordering the guncrews. Peabody, or more likely Mister Munro, had enough sense to let off a bit of way, so one of the nine inch smoothbore cannon could be brought to bear in addition to the pivot gun. The Pocono's guns spat flame once,

329

then once again. The question was, Donald thought, whether the runner was still trying for—

"Breakers!" came the cry from a lookout. "Breakers ahead, breakers to port and starboard!" That answered Donald's question. The runner wasn't trying to reach the usual channel. Instead, he either planned to go close inshore in the hopes the Pocono would back off; or else to beach his the craft under the guns of Fort Fisher and save as much cargo he could, once the Union gunboat was driven off. Maybe. Or maybe he knew of a secret or newly-tide-washed channel.

At that moment a juggernaut roared overhead, a monstrous scream in the night that vanished into the blackness.

"Fort Fisher in sight, sir! They've opened fire," came the quite unnecessary report.

If the guns of the Pocono could shatter the Confederate ship like paper, the monster cannon of the earthworks fort, only one of the Confederate coastal defenses, could do the same to the gunboat. The largest gun on the Pocono was a 100-pounder, the smallest Confederate cannon over there a 150-pounder.

"Leadsman to the bows!" Donald commanded, paying no attention. "Gunner, damn you! Sink me that ship!"

Another shot, another miss, and then a sailor was in the chains, paying no attention to the guns behind or in front, chanting as he cast the lead-bottomed line. "By the quarter less four"... 22 ½ feet under the Pocono's keel and she drew twelve feet whereas the runner probably needed only ten to remain afloat..."Quarter tyree"... 19 ½ feet... "Quarter less tyree"... 16 ½ feet... "She's shoaling fast, Cap'n," Donald yelled.

"All engines, back full," Peabody shouted. "Stand by to come about! Mister Munro! Is there a channel we can use?" Not boy, Donald's mind pointed out bemusedly.

Then the 100 pounder fired once more, simultaneous with the trainblast as another salvo from Fort Fisher went overhead, and the runner was hit, square on the port paddle box.

"We've hit her!" a gunner shouted, just as the lookout screamed, "She's struck!"

Allan Cole & Chris Bunch

All luck had run out for the Confederate, as one of its paddlewheels disintegrated, and sent the ship careening to the side, crashing hard aground onto a shoal. Again the thunderblast as Fort Fisher fired, still high.

"They're abandoning ship!" and Donald, through his own glass could the minuscule dots of men dive into the boats, the boats lower, almost overturning as surf crashed against the blockade runner, surf that would likely destroy the wreck within days or even hours.

The boats pulled hard through the cresting surf toward shore. The tide was on the turn and Donald's developing weather sense told him the weather was worsening. It was a long pull to the beach for them - over a mile or more on a gradually shelving shoreline. The beach itself was long and flat, ending in great dunes. Donald thought he could already see riders and soldiers coming down the beach to help in the rescue.

"Mister Shannon!"

"Coming!" and Donald ran back to where his captain waited. "Sir?"

"Take two boats, Mister, and board the wreck. Recover what you can, but leave nothing for the Rebels. I'll take the ship back out, and wait for your signal to recover. Do well, and we'll forget your lack of discipline earlier."

Aye aye sir, and I note you aren't going, but then the captain isn't supposed to leave his ship, no matter what you may privately think the reason for his order. The hell with that, anyway, Donald thought happily. This was, finally, like one of Captain Marryat's adventures and he was in charge.

"Twenty volunteers!" and there were twice twenty clamoring for the end of boredom and perhaps a little loot. "Master-at-Arms! Issue cutlasses and revolvers. All weapons are to be loaded, but none capped until we close with the Rebel!"

Hoping for a boarding party, the curved swords had already been laid ready. Long, oil-gleaming Colt's .36 Navy revolvers were taken from arms chests, shoved into holsters, the holsters belted around seamen's waists while Donald found two of his own, and a long dirk that might be handier than a cutlass. The boats, already laden with the needed gear, from jugs of coal oil to axes and prybars,

Allan Cole & Chris Bunch

were hoisted out and lowered. Again, Peabody's drilling took effect, and the stroke oars set the pace on each boat, and they pulled away from the Pocono's side like they were clockwork mice, requiring but a single order from Donald to begin their repertoire.

Down in the boats it was more than middling rough, and Donald's boat shipped water over the stern. He paid no mind whatsoever. There'd never been a wave that could wash a Marblehead man from infant to graybeard, out of a small boat, whether he was a fisherman on the Banks, a whaler, a merchant on a Sunday's punting or a midshipman commanding a boarding party.

"Bailey," Donald ordered. "Lay us alongside the starboard side, if the surf permits. We'll go up the falls."

The stroke oar acknowledged his command, and Donald worked his way to the bows of the boat, trying not to be hit by, or throw off-stroke, the rowers as the waterbeetle skittered over the waves toward the wrecked Confederate ship. There was a man already in the bows, next to the small gun they would hopefully not need. Mister Munro held a gleaming cutlass, and there was a revolver thrust in his waistband.

"It appeared I would not be needed aboard ship, since the Captain proposed no more than backwatering and holding his position," he explained calmly. "I thought you might appreciate the company."

Donald grinned. "Aren't you, well, a bit... senior to be playing pirate?"

Teeth bared, in what was probably intended for a smile. "I merely thought it might be... interesting to pay a chat on my Southern cousins. Perhaps there will be someone left aboard, and we might reminisce over old times."

The guns of Fort Fisher were still firing, but at what, Donald had no idea. The Pocono had disappeared into the night, and certainly the fort wouldn't fire on its own ship, at least not until someone realized it was falling into hostile hands. The bow oar shouted a warning, and the boat was amid a horde of small, floating crates. There was enough light in the sky to see the crates were marked. Donald could make out the letters LC inside a triangle, and the figure 18.

Allan Cole & Chris Bunch

"Aw, shit in my hat," someone complained. "Cannonballs! Fuckin' military crap!"

There were other moans - if the blockade runner carried rifles, powder and such the prize money would be far less than if the ship carried what everyone hoped.

"Quiet in the boat," Donald snapped. "You're all a bunch of fools! Whoever heard of floating cannonballs? Bow oar! Let's take a look!"

A boathook snaked one of the crates close, and it was lifted inboard, and marlinspiked open. Donald chanced opening a panel of his lantern as they did. Even in the dark, under the guns of a Confederate fort, even with the Confederate army not two miles away on the beach, there was a muted cheer as the men saw what was inside.

"Brandy, by the lord," someone said. "Bottles and bottles of brandy."

"Which you'll not to be drinking," Donald snapped. "Not until you get back to the ship, at any rate. We'll rescue what we can on the way back. Push the crate back over. Dammit, that's an order! Now, put me alongside the runner."

The boat, its fellow just behind, slid under the stern of the blockade runner. Donald caught the name on the stern: Duchess of London. The falls that had lowered one of the boats still dangled, but there was an even better entryway - a ladder dangled close at hand.

"Mister Munro... Zeigler... Field, and you other four. Follow me. Bailey, hold the boat clear." He shouted similar orders to the other boat, and twelve men swarmed up the ladder onto the blockade runner.

The ship was as tidy as its lines, Donald thought. This must be no more than its first or second voyage. He felt a flicker of fairly irrational pain. Six months ago maybe, this ship would have been launched by its Glasgow builder, would have made a swift passage to Nassau, where it loaded cargo, then perhaps one run through the blockade, and now it would be utterly destroyed, either this night by Donald Shannon or within a day or so by the killing surf. Nothing so beautiful should die like this.

Allan Cole & Chris Bunch

Donald stood, alone with his thoughts, as his crew went to work like the experienced despoilers they were. Boxes and barrels were dragged up from the hold and axed open, contents revealed in the careful opening and swift closure of a lantern. Donald saw the runner's cargo without surprise. He remembered one of his father's basic tenets about the South, that it was not only doomed as a culture, damned as a society, but would cheerfully accede in its own destruction.

Donald had never seen a Confederate soldier, but was more than familiar with the way journals like Frank Leslie's Illustrated News pictured them: ragged, carrying a rifle completely unlike by caliber and manufacture than that borne by the next ranker, marching with rags wrapped around their feet instead of boots, frequently without hard rations and forced to subsist off the countryside. He'd even read a description of what one captured soldier's haversack contained, the man's only worldly possessions: a jack knife, a plug of twisted tobacco, a tin cup, two cups of coarsely cracked corn, and a bit of salt tied in a rag. It was a pure wonderment to Donald, as it was to others in the Union, the Rebels fought as tenaciously and effectively as they did.

Given the conditions of the hard-pressed Confederate armies, and given that the South still had little manufacturing capability, the Duchess of London should have been laden with uniforms, rifles, powder, shot and shell. Instead, there on the deck, were bales of silk. Gowns made in London. More brandy. Tinned delicacies, from goose liver to sturgeon's eggs. All these delights would be auctioned off to the rich in Wilmington, the fighting soldiers never apprised of what cargo the latest brave blockade runner carried as cargo, and the auctioneer would never accept Confederate currency. What made things still less savory were all those crates floating around the Duchess. If someone had gone to all the trouble to acquire boxes fraudulently marked as containing ammunition, that someone could only be a member of either the Confederate government or military, not merely an amoral profiteer.

Donald ordered his boats loaded with pillage to the gunwales - the stroke oars would know how much could be taken aboard without swamping the craft. He did specify what items were to be taken: victuals and valuables usable by the ship or its crew, or for trading stock with the other gunboats of the squadron. He paid no mind to any of his seamen's stuffed pockets, bulging tied-off pantslegs or jerseys. A bottle of brandy or two would hardly be the ruination of the Pocono, and the silk shift he saw a sailor hastily wrap around his middle might as well go to the man's wife, sister or doxie as up in flames. A little caught up by his men's example, he went to the ship's bridge, and did a little acquiring of his own: a pair of sextants, an octant, a barometer, an artificial horizon, a salinometer that could be very useful navigating close inshore when the charts either lied or offered blankness. For himself, he lifted a beautiful chronometer, all gleaming brass and walnut. Whoever had outfitted this craft had not stinted in any way.

His larceny was broken by two events: the lookout posted in the bows shouted the Confederates were bringing boats on horse-drawn carts out from behind the dunes, and soldiers were forming up just at the water, intending a counterattack. Rockets and lights outlined the beach.

The second was Mister Munro: "Sir," he said quietly. "Would you accompany me? There is something below of great note."

Donald started to protest, then realized the counterboarders were a long way from being ready to push off through the surf and followed the quartermaster below. Now, under shelter, both men could open their lanterns completely.

"I would estimate," Mister Munro said, ushering Donald through a doorway, "this to be either the master's or owner's cabin, from its Babylonian splendor." The compartment was richly decorated. Waxed and varnished furnishings gleamed, and the pillows and hangings were of silk and brocade. But the luxury was not Mister Munro's interest.

A man was sprawled on the deck. There was a long dagger thrust through his chest.

"Damnation," Donald swore. "Why the hell didn't he surrender to you instead of fighting?" In the back of his mind he was setting up a way for Munro to conveniently alibi his actions.

"I did not slay him," Mister Munro said, his voice showing nothing but surprise and shock, and Donald knew he was telling the

335

truth. "First, I carried no dirk, second, look at what is on the haft of that knife."

Donald knelt. A piece of foolscap had been impaled on the handle. Donald did not need to hold his lantern close to read the word scrawled on it: TRAITOR. He gaped, not having the foggiest about what had happened. Guessing a proper naval officer shouldn't look completely bewildered in front of a subordinate and hence stalling, he attempted to emulate Mister Poe's Monsieur Dupin and find clues to the mystery. The man was middle-aged, Donald guessed, which made him archaic. His complexion would have been florid, to complement his luxurious and perfectly-trimmed beard. His clothes were of the very finest, European cut, with nothing nautical about them. It was evident he had never refused a meal if a banquet could be arranged. Given the opulence of the cabin, the man was almost certainly the owner of the Duchess.

Donald slid his hand through the still-sticky mass of blood into the man's inside coat pocket. He found a notecase and took it out, reflexively wiping his gory hand on the carpet beside the body. With Mister Munro hanging on his shoulder, he took the leather wallet to a table, and opened it. Donald whistled. Whoever the murderer had been, he certainly had not committed the crime with avarice as the purpose. The notecase was stuffed with money: Federal gold certificates, some odd notes Donald recognized as English pounds but not a solitary Confederate bill.

"Three... four thousand dollars here," he estimated.

"Well, that will give everyone aboard some prize money," Mister Munro said.

Neither man considered pocketing the cash for an instant. Donald found calling cards and a letter which he unfolded, read and became even more perplexed. It was written on official Confederate stationary, government stationary, and directed anyone reading the document to give the named bearer the fullest cooperation. The signature was that of Jefferson Davis.

"Now I am truly at sea," Donald said. "If he was a traitor, then why would Jeff Davis... " his voice trailed away.

"Who is he?"

"Somebody named Fitz Maguire. That mean anything to you?"

Allan Cole & Chris Bunch

"Fitz Maguire?" the quartermaster repeated. Then shook his head. "Not one of the Wilmington swells," he said. "Not anyway up until I took my congee from the city."

Donald looked over at the body, and nothing suggested itself. There was a shout from above: "Mister Shannon, sir! They're putin' out their boats."

He had no more time to play Ratiocinator. He and Mister Munro hurried toward the doorway. Donald glanced back at the corpse. Most likely, he thought, this would be a great mystery, if anybody ever read about it anywhere but in the report I'm going to file.

Pity Mister Poe has passed on, or I'd send him a letter and ask for his thoughts. All he could figure was the evident fact the corpulent magnate's cleverness had run out at a very critical moment.

He shoved the notecase in a pocket, and, pulling out the pouch that contained fuzees for his incendiarism, Donald hurried on deck, intent on burning the blockade runner to the waterline before the Confederates could rescue her. As for getting back on the boats, as for finding the Pocono in the night and building storm, that was nothing. He was a Shannon, was he not?

But his mind kept returning to the deck below, even as the flames built: Fitz Maguire. Now, dammit, that name did mean something to him, or should, anyway.

Shouldn't it?

Allan Cole & Chris Bunch

CHAPTER TWENTY-SIX

PHILADELPHIA - LATE APRIL, 1863

IAN DOLAN WAS going home. He'd felt the hard tug of it as soon as the train cleared Baltimore. Now, as they tunneled through pre-dawn darkness, wheel and rail conspired to make a homesick song - Phil-a-del-phia... Phil-a-del-phia... Phil-a-del-phia - until all thoughts of war vanished along the track.

As others in the crowded coach hacked and coughed in the smoky air, the sharp scent of the Delaware tingled in Ian's memory. He did not hear the snores and chattering of his companions, or see the sweat-stained uniforms and frocked cloaks jammed against him. Instead he became caught up in his own recollections of the rhythms and people of his city.

Just now the common folk would be yawning awake in the rowhomes and shantytowns that surrounded the factories at Southwark, Moyamensing and Gray's Ferry. In a few minutes the first whistles would shrill and out would come the counting clerks in their identical dark suits. The second blast would draw the laborers who would quickly fill, then empty the streets. The third hoot of the whistle would draw the final and startlingly glorious wave. Thousands upon thousands of young, single girls would exit the boarding homes and the air would sparkle with the sound of their cheerful chatter.

There would be whole platoons of sun bonnets and long capes hanging almost to the ground. These women were the skilled spinners and weavers, who would troop into the factory and make it come alive with laughter and small talk. Then the big machines would shriek into being and the factory would be transformed into a moving forest of spindles and pulleys and whirling gears.

Outside, the streets would be filling with freight wagons and carriages. Children bound for school would be dashing in and out of traffic, and storekeepers would be laying out their wares under the unrolled awnings. Down at the main market early shoppers would be testing the freshness of the produce and meat, all the while keeping their purses clutched close to keep them from the nimble fingers of young market thieves.

At the parks old people would be taking their daily constitutional, or gathering in groups to discuss current events. Housewives would be washing down the porches, and newsboys would already be out, shouting the day's headlines.

As warm familiarity made its timid approach - like a long banished pet - Ian finally dared the rest. He saw his own wide, clean street; the scrubbed porch and the big door with its polished brass knocker. He hesitated before that door, wondering if he should just fling it open... or knock. Would he be a stranger in his own house? What would be his welcome... his position?

How was a soldier on leave supposed to behave? Susan was his wife, the house his home. But in a few days he'd have to abandon it all again. What right did he have to do more than sympathize with any problems the family faced? If anything needed fixing - unless it was no more than a sprung latch - Ian wouldn't be around long enough to see it through.

A dream-like image of Susan's smiling face blew through his confusion, and Ian shed the last remaining doubts. It was early morning when the train chuffed into the station. He shook Hugh awake and rose, stiff in knee, but completely home.

"Ye say yer with Hooker's lads?" the woman asked. She held the hackney's reins tight, eyeing the narrow gap between a freight wagon and a streetcar.

"Yes, ma'am," Hugh answered. "We're just up from Virginia for our leave."

"Maybe yer know my Johnny, then," the woman said. She flicked the reins and the hackney jounced toward the gap. She looked back over her shoulder at Hugh and Ian. "John Murray's his name. Private John Murray."

Hugh gulped as the hackney scraped the freight wagon. "Uh, no. Can't say as I-"

"Get outter me way," the woman shouted as the streetcar veered across her path. She cracked her whip, yanked the reins to the left, and whiskered through - ignoring the curses from the other drivers. "Mary, Mother of God," she muttered. "They thinks they own the road, they do." Another flip on the reins and they were bearing down on a railroad car waiting in the middle of Market Street.

She turned her head to continue the conversation and Hugh had a sudden vision of meeting his maker only a few blocks from home. "Yer sure ye don't know him?" she pressed. "He's not so tall as yerself, and much fairer. And he's got one eye that's green, while the other's bright blue."

Keeping panic at bay, Hugh pointed vigorously at the railroad car. "Look out," he croaked.

The woman looked, sighed, then skillfully steered the hackney around the vehicle. "Loaders are runnin' late today," she sniffed. Then: "If ye run inta my Johnny, be sure ye say his missus was askin' for him."

Hugh swore on the head of Pope Pius himself if he should ever meet the odd-eyed John Murray, he'd be sure to pass on the message. Satisfied, the woman settled down to concentrate on the traffic. Hugh glanced at his father and saw Ian was dead to the world, eyes closed, lips trembling in a gentle snore.

Hugh gritted his teeth as the hackney dodged a coal cart, bumped wheels with a hay wagon, and skinned the heels of a boy who darted past carrying a bundle of firewood. A woman burdened with a basket of cotton yarn and a jug of rug loom oil stood stubbornly in their path, daring the hackney to hit her. Once again, tragedy was avoided at the last instant.

As they made their way through the turmoil that was Market Street, Hugh was thinking fondly of a nice, safe bayonet charge. It wasn't the woman was a bad driver; on the contrary, she was a skilled practitioner of that art, threading the chaotic streets with ease. Hugh imagined that her Johnny would be as amazed as he was at the confusion that had greeted them since they left the station in the chaos that was a war time city.

Everywhere Hugh looked the commerce of war was spilling its goods and noise into the streets. Carts and wagons and streetcars pointed every which way; people leaped in and out of the spaces between the vehicles, only to be confronted by more confusion on the sidewalks where hawkers manned wooden-barreled counters in competition with the overflowing shops, and pushcart immigrants.

340

There were bargains advertised everywhere: ladies' shoes for 35 cents, petticoats for 25, and gold rings for a dollar. Awning signs boasted full meals for 15 cents, hair cuts for ten, and rooms for six dollars a month - including gas service. Every other shop seemed to have cigars for sale, and he caught glimpses of women behind those windows hard at work rolling more.

Even more impressive were all the building sites. Lumber and brick were stacked everywhere, and workers were scrambling about in a fury to get new homes up. He'd heard from his mother nearly two thousand had been built the past year, and from the activity he was sure there would be another two thousand built before this year was done.

There was something odd about the whole scene, however - an oddness not fully explained by the vigor of a city producing for war. As he saw an old man hefting a pallet of bricks across a catwalk, he realized what it was - there was a great absence of men his own age. Old men and striplings manned the building sites, and as he took closer note, he saw there were more women laboring than he'd seen in his entire life.

Big women muscled crates into wagons, smaller women strained at block and tackle, and he saw a young girl in a shoemaker's window spitting nails into her fist to hammer into the sole of a boot. The scene was even odder because so many of them wore widow's black. Old women, middle-aged women, young women, hard at their tasks, all dressed in the common uniform of grief.

Hugh had a small inkling of the life his wife and sister were living. He looked at the hackney driver. She'd seemed to be a woman in her forties or more. Her eyes were weary, forehead lined, and the wisps of hair peeking out of her cap were streaked with gray. But when he looked closer, he could see the youth beneath those marks of hard work and worry. Why, she couldn't be more than thirty, he thought - most probably less.

Poor Mary, he thought. Poor mother. Then he saw a beggar in a tattered blue uniform. He was legless, and pulling himself along on a wheeled cart.

Poor all of us.

Allan Cole & Chris Bunch

Nancy slowly stroked the brush through her hair. In the mirror her flowing locks glowed with health; under the bristles her scalp was tingling after its hour-long massage. She critically eyed her image: a bit pale, if one looked close, but the lotion she'd coaxed into her skin mostly hid that. Nancy gathered her hair up and pinned it back - the better to display her décolletage. She'd powdered her bosom to cover the rash that had plagued her since... since... she couldn't remember when it began. Nancy batted her eyes in the mirror, giggling at the sultry image she made.

How could Kerry resist her? Even if she was a little skinny. Nancy promised herself she'd keep Kerry so busy in their bed that he'd never notice. She pulled her bridal veil from the drawer. As she fingered the lace she giggled again and blushed, recalling the fun they'd both had with the veil on their wedding night. She shook it out and draped it over her pillow, promising herself that she'd make good use of it when she got Kerry up here.

Downstairs Nancy heard Susan call out a glad greeting, and the deep boom of male voices - a warm sound she hadn't heard in ages. Finally. They were here! Ian. And Hugh. And... and...

From the nursery came the sound of little Keith awakening. He was crying for his mommy. Nancy laughed - Keith was just in time to meet his daddy. She could hardly wait to see Kerry's proud face when he saw his son.

Nancy gave herself one more look over before she leaped up and raced downstairs. Suddenly, the bright image was shattered. Her hair seemed brittle and greasy now. Her eyes those of a crone. Her face pinched, her breasts sagging dugs that made a mockery of the dress.

Oh, God, she mourned, Kerry will think I'm... ugly. I was beautiful before... Keith was born. Everyone said so. Kerry won't come now, I just know it. He'll stay away when he hears he has such an ugly, worthless wife. And it'll be all Keith's fault. All his fault that I'll never hold my Kerry in my arms again.

Tears began streaming down her cheeks. She unpinned her hair and went to the bed. She laid down on it, curling into a small ball, and clutched the veil tightly in her fingers.

342

Allan Cole & Chris Bunch

Hugh felt a bit of a fool, standing there with a big grin on his face, shifting from foot to foot as his mother and father hugged and sobbed with joy. Mrs. Fawcett came shyly up to him, tears streaming down her round face, and gave him a quick squeeze. She balanced her tubby little body on her toes and gave him a wet peck on the cheek. Then he was pumping old Mr. Pollack's hand, not hearing a word the handyman was saying, but grinning even more hugely to cover his complete confusion.

His mother broke free from his father and whirled. She looked at him with enormous, tear-streaked eyes, then ran into his arms crying: "Hugh! Oh, my darling little boy." He hugged her tentatively, and patted her awkwardly on the shoulder, saying: "There. there. It'll be all right," and other meaningless phrases. Then, he couldn't help himself, but he just had to know. "Where's Mary?"

His mother pulled away, laughing and crying at the same time. "Why, she's at school, Hugh. Teaching her class. We didn't know what train you were coming in on. We only just got the telegram saying you'd be on the way. I know your Mary will be kicking herself when she learns she wasn't here to greet you."

"Then I'll go to her," Hugh said. The world suddenly fell into place and he gave his mother a kiss and headed for the door. "I'll surprise her." And he was gone.

Ian saw Susan was somewhat befuddled. He gave her a squeeze. "Never mind the boy. He's not forgotten his mother. But he does have another woman in his life now."

Upstairs a child squalled. "Oh, my goodness," Mrs. Fawcett said. "It's young Keith." As she ran up the stairs she called back, "I'll fetch him to meet grandfather."

Ian's face clouded. He coughed, as if to clear his throat, then said: "How's his mother?" Susan couldn't speak. She just shook her head. And Ian asked: "Isn't our Nancy well?"

Susan firmed herself. "No, Ian. She's not well at all."

"Annabelle, stop that fidgeting. I saw that, Bridget! Keep your hands to yourself, young lady. And you... Patricia! Tongues are to

343

speak with, not to taunt your schoolmates." Mary Dolan sighed. "I don't know what has gotten into you today, girls. But if doesn't stop - this instant - I'll keep the whole lot of you after school."

Momentary obedience reigned. Mary looked out over the scrubbed faces of her thirteen-year-old charges. Forty pairs of oh so innocent eyes gazed back. But Mary could still see deviltry lurking in the young ladies of Mount Saint Joseph's College For Girls. She was young enough herself to remember her own mischief when she sat out there, pigtails prickling, petticoats sticking, and mind on the fun being missed in the warm spring sun outside. Actually, the misbehavior was more her fault then theirs. Her thoughts were on Hugh, whom she prayed was at this moment aboard a train steaming for Philadelphia. Her emotions jumped back and forth from aching joy to fear she would do or say something that would disappoint him.

The noise level in room rose again; she forced her mind back to the task at hand. "Patricia. If you are determined to use that tongue of yours, please remind the rest of us what we were just discussing."

Patricia reluctantly came to her feet, long pony legs gawky under her school dress. "West Virginia, Mrs. Dolan," she said.

"Correct." Patricia grinned and sat.

Mary heard someone's whispered protest: "Stop that!"

"Bridget," Mary snapped, for it was she who was the tormentor again. "Tell us exactly what West Virginia is."

Bridget came slowly up, unconsciously sultry with her smoky eyes and maturing figure. "A place near Virginia, Mrs. Dolan?" Bridget rolled her eyes, drawing a chorus of giggles.

Mary merely pointed for her to sit. "Anyone else? ... Clara?"

Clara bounced up, eager to answer. "President Lincoln has just made it a state," she said.

"Very good, Clara," Mary said. "At least some of you are listening."

Someone raised their hand. "Yes, Margaret?"

"What if the Rebels don't let Mr. Lincoln keep it, Mrs. Dolan? My mother says they're already invading West Virginia. She says my father's camp is near the railroad where that dirty old General Jones is attacking."

344

As she cautiously considered her reply, the door opened behind her. All the girls were suddenly staring at the visitor who had just come in. Mary didn't need to look - that visitor was most certainly Sister Hortense, here to see what all the disturbance was about.

Mary rapped her knuckles against the desk. "Ladies, if you please. Margaret has just asked a question. Margaret, would you repeat it please."

Margaret, however, was gaping along with the others. "Margaret!" Mary said, sharper still.

The girl pointed behind her. "But Mrs. Dolan," she pleaded. "It's your husband come home."

In a daze, Mary turned to see Hugh towering in the doorway. Beside him was Sister Hortense, a smile wreathing her ancient features. Mary thought her heart had stopped. She couldn't breathe. Then she was in his arms and the girls were all laughing and shouting. Later, she would be mortified at such an unseemly display of public emotion – and in a Catholic school at that. At the moment she didn't care, but unconsciously, shamelessly crushed the whole length of her body against his. She dimly heard Sister Hortense's own girlish giggles as the old nun pushed them out of the room and murmured for Mary to go home - that she would take over the class.

Moments later they were outside the academy, traffic rumbling all around, and curious people stopping to stare and smile at their long embrace. In another time – not that long ago – they would have been hisses and cold glares at such a public display.

"Thank God you've come home," Mary whispered. But even as she said it she knew it was only a reprieve she had to thank God for. In a few days Hugh would be gone again. She pulled him tighter, then heard an old, disapproving woman hiss. She pushed away, laughing. "We'd better stop this," she said. "Or you'll next be visiting me at the Good Shepherd's Home for Penitent Women."

"Then we'd best find some place quick," Hugh said, "so you'll have something to repent."

The old house shifted in its sleep. Nancy was wide-eyed in her bed, listening to the settling timbers tick away the night. A frog croaked in the courtyard outside, its voice resonating in the gutter pipe. In her room, darkness was a damp cloying blanket that made her feel unwashed. The room itself was musty with her own scent, and every breath she took was drawn consciously and with distaste.

She felt as trapped as any inmate of the Fairmont Avenue Prison. A prisoner was better off, she thought: he was confined by others for good cause, and there was a term set to his suffering. Nancy's sentencing, however, was undeserved and seemed to stretch endlessly before her. She could not imagine ever being able to take a carefree breath of fresh air, or enjoy something so simple as sunlight on her face.

Worse still, she was well aware that she was her own jailer, but was helpless to correct the situation. She refused to see her family; barring the door to her own mother and father when they came to beg her to return home to their loving care. But she wept when they departed, angry at herself and them for not battering down the door.

Nancy's skin crawled when she thought she heard a child whimper. Was it Keith? If it was, she determined to let him cry - one of the other women would eventually go to him. With great relief she realized the sound came from outside, and was only a cat after the croaking frog. She'd tended to little Keith's needs - if grudgingly - since his birth. She'd forced herself into believing she loved him, and was frequently wracked by guilt for her miserly attentions. But now Ian and Hugh had returned, she couldn't even bring herself to touch the child; and the guilt had soured into resentment.

She suddenly thought that it was Keith who made her a prisoner. If he were gone she could open that door and walk out without fear some clutching little monster would confront her, demanding a display of emotion she did not have to give. With the child gone, Kerry was certain to return. It was the damned baby that was making him stay away.

Honestly, there was something evil about that child. The way he'd tormented her during her pregnancy, and nearly ripped her apart being born. He was a devil, is what he was. And Kerry, her wise and good Kerry, knew that.

Another sound drifted down the hallway - low voices. It was Ian and Susan in whispered conversation. She painfully recalled the little time she had spent with Kerry in her own marriage bed; making love for an hour or so, then snuggling and talking deep into the night.

Shut up, she thought. Shut your faces! Some of us are trying to sleep, if you don't mind. I'll scream, she thought. I really will. I'll scream for them to shut up and let a body alone.

Instead, she fought back the poison welling up. She forced her body to relax, and laid staring at shadows on the ceiling, listening to the ticking of the timbers as the old house counted the minutes of another night.

"She's gone quite mad," Susan said. "I keep hoping she'll suddenly come out of it, but she seems to get worse with each passing day. I feel sorry for her, but I don't know what to do. It's certainly no fault of her own. She was a good girl, a strong girl, but... Ian if you had seen how much she suffered when she was with child. And my God, the birthing itself would have tested a martyr. I don't know how she survived it. But we had hope for her. Mary and I kept telling one another that she'd improve, once she got her health back.

But then..." Susan's voice trembled, and Ian tightened his arms about her... "our Kerry... was killed... and I suppose she just didn't see any reason to try anymore."

"What can be done?" Ian asked.

"I don't know. I've talked to the doctor again and again. I even spoke to Father Quinn. You know what a favorite of his our Nancy was. But she wouldn't see him anymore than she would see her own mother and father, bless them. And when they come, she only gets worse. Quite... violent. Breaking things in her room. Screaming all sorts of mad things.

"She's in such a helpless state that her father and mother have let me make Nancy our ward so I can care for her and little Keith."

"Now I see why you didn't take Hugh and myself up to visit with her," Ian said.

Susan nodded. "I've been worried how she'd behave when you came home without Kerry. It must be hurting her very deeply. Both the doctor and Father Quinn say I should... put her away. In a home for the insane."

Ian stroked her head, soothing. "I know that would be very difficult for you to do, lass. But... Perhaps they're right."

"If they are not," Susan replied, "then the situation really would become hopeless. You hear it whispered when someone goes into a madhouse, but you never hear of anyone coming out. And little Keith needs his mother, even if she is... not well. Besides, Nancy is no harm to anyone but herself. Mary and I can manage."

Ian kissed her. "I'm sure you can," he said. "I've yet to meet anything that is your match. Your grandmother would be quite proud of you."

Susan laughed, but without humor. "Oh, I don't know about that. Diana was a mountain of strength. There was nothing that woman couldn't do with ease. Take this nonsense I'm embroiled in with Pamela. She'd have sent that woman and her fancy congressman packing before breakfast, and managed an Indian raid before dinner."

"Diana Shannon was a woman of genius, I'll not quarrel with that," Ian said. "But she was only human. She made errors. Grievous ones, if the truth be told. And it is no dishonor to her memory to say so. As a woman of business, she had no peers - of either sex. And it cannot be denied that without her, the Shannons would not have survived, much less prospered."

"It's unlikely I would have even been born," Susan said.

"Yes. I agree. But she didn't do so well when it came to her own sons, did she?"

"No. I think she would be the first to admit that as a mother... well... mothering was not her strength."

"If she'd been able accomplish half as much with them," Ian said, "you would not be suffering the slings and arrows of Pamela Shannon."

"I suppose you are right," Susan said. "And I have managed to stave the woman off. With the help of the lawyer, I have her tangled up in court delays. But I cannot promise the outcome in the long run. I fear for it, if you must know."

"And if you fail," Ian said, "what will it matter? It's only property and money you'll be losing, and the loss will be shared by

Allan Cole & Chris Bunch

the whole family, not just you. So it would not be that great a burden."

"But my grandmother worked her whole life for it," Susan said.

"Did she, now?" Ian said. "Is that what you think Diana Shannon worked for? Property and money? What did she tell us all that night in Vicksburg? Did she say - 'This is my monument... remember me for my riches?'"

"Of course, not," Susan protested. "But-"

Ian put a finger to her lips to shush her. "The family was her monument, was it not? And the boy, Patrick. Why do you think she spent all those hours with him - the last hours of her life? To make certain that he was a worthy heir? Or to give him a bit of her knowledge, to ease the way in his own life? Even though we've heard naught of the boy, I've always believed Diana Shannon gave Patrick enough of her own talents, just in the tale-telling, for him to be well-armed against the awful shocks life brings."

Susan laughed and this time it was unforced. "You'd think your were a lawyer yourself, Ian Dolan," she said. "Where did you get all those smooth words? Have you been saving them up?"

"I'm a bricklayer, lass," Ian laughed back. "We're a patient breed, and we go at things with great care. That's why I admired your grandmother. It was a lovely wall she built, even if it did lean a bit at the beginning... and the end."

Then he pulled her to him, hungrily. "And as for what I've been savin' up," he whispered, "there's plenty more in the bank, and if you'll only help me spend it..."

Susan chortled, and curled her fist around him. "Come put it in this bank, sir," she said. "For our special customers, we remain open all night." She lifted a leg and pushed him deep inside.

"Welcome home, Ian. Welcome home."

Breakfast was late the next day, and quiet. Ian and Hugh cut into thick steaks and ate like starving men, and the looks they gave their wives showed other appetites had yet to be satiated. In between forking more food on the plates of their men, Susan and Mary exchanged shy glances with one another, blushing and smiling every time their eyes met.

Allan Cole & Chris Bunch

Ian tore off a hunk of crusty white bread to dip up the gravy on his plate, but first sniffed deeply at the bread. "Heaven," he enthused. He dunked the bread into the juice and took a bite. "When the Good Lord divided up the loaves and fishes," he said through a thick mouthful, "he could have stopped with the bread."

"Don't blaspheme," Susan laughed.

"Oh, you've become the Pope, have you? Pope Susan the First. Next you'll be sayin' every word you speak is direct from God himself. Just like old Pius the Ninth."

After the laughter, Hugh turned to Mary, mildly serious. "You don't think that papal infallibility business will be approved, do you?"

"There's a good chance," Mary replied. "Everyone in the parish is nervous about it. There's already enough distrust of Catholics in this country. Even Father Quinn is worried. He says it might undo all the gains we've made in this war... proving our loyalty."

Hugh's face darkened. "I'm certainly not fighting to prove my loyalty. And it displeases me to hear such a thing from a priest."

Mary patted his hand. "I don't think that's how Father Quinn meant it. He's only frustrated - like the rest of us - that our pope is so political."

Susan snorted. "With all the monarchs in Europe in trouble," she said, "I guess the Pope has seen his chance to be a real king. In my view, that's what this ex cathedra thing is about. Pius wants to be lord of the earth, as well as our souls, and he certainly doesn't seem to care how his posturing injures his flock in America."

"I'm no firebrand radical," Hugh said, "but I don't like how our church has been behaving in this war. When it comes to slavery, Rome has let the locals interpret religion anyway they like. There's priests serving as chaplains on both sides, and I know for fact the Southern fathers speak out against the black race as much as their Protestant brothers."

"Welcome to the world of racial politics, dear," Susan said. "I wish you had been with us in Vicksburg when your great grandmother went on about how cowardly everyone has been since the country began. The theologians were the worst of the lot, in her view, because they should know better. But they twist their thoughts

Allan Cole & Chris Bunch

to meet the fancy of the men whose boots they lick. Remember, it was a bishop who said that while a Christian must treat his slaves decently, slaves should heed the words of Peter: 'Servants, obey your masters.'

"And here in our city of brotherly love, when the Irish politicians exhort the wavering to join the cause of the Union, they sing a very telling jingle." She singsonged the verses for her son's edification:

"To the tenets of Douglas we tenderly cling,/ warm hearts to the cause of our country we bring;/ to the flag we are pledged - all its foes we abhor-/ And we ain't for the nigger but we are for the war.'"

Susan's temper was running high. There was a host of church sins she wanted to rail on about. The Jesuits in Maryland owned slaves, for instance, as did the Ursulan nuns in New Orleans. She got a grip on herself. It was not the time to preach, especially among the long converted. "Enough of that," she said. "But I promise you they'll be hearing from the likes Susan Shannon Dolan once this war-"

A scream pierced the air. And a woman wailed: Get away from me!"

"Nancy!" Mary gasped.

They rushed out of the kitchen to the big main room. Another scream and sounds of struggle drew their eyes upward to the third story landing.

Just by the banister, Mrs. Fawcett was desperately wrestling with Nancy, who was fending her off with one hand, while holding little Kerry with the other. The baby was still - too frightened to cry.

"Please, Nancy," Mrs. Fawcett was begging. "You can't do this!"

"I said, get away," Nancy shrieked.

Then, so quickly they could not believe what they were witnessing, Nancy put the child on the floor, and grabbed Mrs. Fawcett by her ample waist. She lifted the housekeeper off her feet and flung her down the stairs. Mrs. Fawcett howled, and tumbled down and down, until she finally came to rest against the second landing's banisters.

Allan Cole & Chris Bunch

Hugh raced up the stairs, his father behind him. But he had barely reached Mrs. Fawcett's side when Mary shouted for him to stop. Nancy had the child held over the rail, about to hurl him down the three story drop. The sight turned his blood to ice.

"He's my son," Nancy screamed. "I'll do what I like with him!"

"Please, Nancy, dear," Susan begged. "He's only a baby. Don't hurt him."

"I hate him," Nancy shrieked. "I hate all of you!"

"Let him be," Mary pleaded. "Little Keith's not the blame for your troubles."

Hugh was only half listening to the mad exchange. He crept slowly upward, one careful step at a time.

Nancy laughed, wild. "Oh, you think you're so smart, Mary Dolan. I know you've all been talking about me. I know you've all been to see Kerry. And you've turned him against me." She tipped the child forward until he was dangling close to the rail.

"My God, Nancy," Susan shouted. "Kerry is dead. My son is dead."

"Liar," Nancy shrieked. "You're all liars!"

And she gathered her strength to throw the child, lifting him high over her head. Hugh scrambled up the last steps and hurled himself at the banister just as Nancy threw. He didn't hear the screams, but only concentrated on the baby's hurtling form. He flat dove across the rail, his body plummeting after the child.

He hooked a finger into its nightgown, felt cloth tear, then hold. But it was no good, because he was falling too and he could see his mother's frightened face looking up at him from a great distance. Then his boots caught the rail, and his slide stopped.

The nightgown ripped again, and he prayed pleasegod, pleasegod, as he reached with his other hand and grabbed the child by the arm. He was just getting a good grip, digging in harder with his toes, when Nancy attacked him - hammering on his legs with surprising strength.

"I'll kill you both," she shrieked. "You're supposed to be dead, damn you! Not Kerry!"The battering suddenly stopped and Nancy screamed again as Ian muscled her away. But it was no good, he could feel himself slipping. Keith was staring at him, eyes as wide as dinner plates. It was as if the child knew they were both going down.

Then firm hands grabbed his legs. "I've got you, Hugh," he heard Mary say. "Hold on!"

Other hands joined hers and he was pulled back to the landing, Keith safe in his arms. Mary and his father were supporting him. Nancy was sprawled unconscious on the floor. His mother was crouched over her.

"I had to strike her," his father said. He looked as if he were about to burst into tears. "Like I was striking a man."

"She's all right, Ian," his mother said.

Ian looked at his meaty fist as if it were his enemy. "I didn't mean to hurt her," he said." But... she..."

"I said she'll be all right," Susan said. "She's breathing fine, and there's nothing broken."

Hugh was as dazed as his father. Through the haze of his confusion, he saw Mrs. Fawcett limping toward him. She'd not been badly injured.

She reached for the baby. Numbly, Hugh handed his nephew over. "Poor little thing," Mrs. Fawcett cooed. "Come to your Auntie Fawcett. We'll go have a nice warm bath... and then a big piece of sugar candy..."

Finally, just as she reached the steps and was clambering down, Keith began to cry. Hugh found the sound oddly comforting.

Mary hugged him, and he suddenly felt queasy. He gently plucked her away. "I'm sorry," he said. "But I think I'm going to be sick."

A few days later, Ian sat in Susan's office listening to the doctor and Father Quinn plead with his wife. A document waited on the desk for her signature.

"It's really the best thing for her, Mrs. Dolan," the doctor was saying. "And for your family as well. You can't stay with her every minute."

"Saint Bartholomew's is a lovely place, Susan," Father Quinn said. "There's a garden for Nancy to walk in. And the nuns will take excellent care of her."

Allan Cole & Chris Bunch

"I can't put my own son's wife in a cell," Susan said. "He would never forgive me."

"There are no cells," the doctor said. "The rooms are quite spacious, the meals nourishing. Beyond that, there's nothing much else that modern science can do for her."

"Will she... recover?" Susan asked.

The doctor shrugged. Father Quinn patted Susan's hand. "It's in God's hands, Susan," he said. "Not science."

Ian felt as if he were watching and listening from a great distance. He saw his wife come to a decision. She pulled herself together; her back became ramrod straight, her chin jutted like the prow of an ironclad. For just a moment he could see Diana's strong features in her.

Susan pushed the document away. "Nancy will not leave this house," she said. "I'll take care of her myself."

Outside, Ian heard a newsboy hawking the headlines. Hooker was crossing the Rappahannock.

The Army of the Potomac was on the move again.

CHAPTER TWENTY-SEVEN

VICKSBURG, MISS. – MAY-JUNE, 1863

THE AIR FLUTTERED and shrieked, and Patrick flattened against the dirt. He kept his head up and spotted the shell as it flew overhead, leaving a trail of smoke from its sputtering fuse. The shriek ran down the scale, and about a block away came the dull thud as another Yankee cannonball struck Vicksburg.

Patrick got up and dusted himself off. A few yards away was a very small, very elderly old lady, wearing, in spite of the heat and dirt, gloves and shawl.

She looked at him critically. "Young man, you need to listen more closely. I knew that shell would land nowhere near."

"Yes ma'am. It's a skill I'm still developing." He touched his slouch hat, and walked on.

He had to stop every now and then to recover his wind. He guessed, in spite of his hopes to the contrary, that the surgeon who'd snarled at him to get the hell out of his tent had been right. You are no more fit for duty on the lines than a kitten and do not bother me for another month. And this time, God Damn it, sir, I mean a month, not twice a week.

In spite of the best care possible from the Baldwins and their personal doctors, Patrick couldn't seem to shake his "camp fever." Privately he wondered if he wasn't getting over one brand of sickness only to get hammered with its bigger brother, but none of the doctors thought that made sense, so he kept his mouth shut.

His progress to the Baldwin house was in an unusual manner, as was that of the old woman proceeding at a good clip in the opposite direction. He was doing the Vicksburg Shuffle - walk slowly in the middle of the street, talking to no one if in company but keeping ears pricked for the sound of an arriving shell. If heard, eyes went skyward and the shuffler considered his next move - to flatten, to run, or to pray. If the shell was spotted just overhead it was perfectly safe to proceed, since nothing fell straight down, or not generally anyhow. Sighting the shells was made easier because of their smoking fuses by day, and trails of sparks by night as the cannonading went on around the clock.

There was a song: "Listen to the Parrott shells/ Listen to the Parrott shells/ The Parrott shells are whistling through the air.../ Listen to the Minnie balls/ Listen to the Minnie balls/ The Minnie balls are whistling through the air..." and so on.

The streets and houses were mostly deserted because everyone had gone underground. Great and small caves had been cut into the sides of Vicksburg's hills and bluffs. The Baldwins had not thought this necessary until a cannonball - fortunately solid shot - had shattered one of the verandah's wooden Doric columns Mr. Baldwin was so proud of. Then excavation began on the open hill below the mansion, facing away from the Union lines. It still wouldn't be safe when ships shelled the city, nor would it be proof against the Union mortars that sent monstrous shells arcing high over the city then falling in a near-vertical drop.

The Baldwins had to pay a team of free blacks two hundred dollars to dig their cave. One of Lucy's sisters murmured that if Father had only believed in holding slaves, it would have been simple to just order the work done. Patrick pretended he didn't hear. Two neighboring families - the Gehmans and the Longs - either paid, or did order their blacks to help in the digging. They went in with the Baldwins because one family's house had been burnt to the ground, and the other, next to the Baldwin house, had become a hospital. A yellow flag indicated its neutrality, but the house had still suffered three hits since the siege began.

The cave was dug into the clay hillside about ten feet, and was six feet high and four feet wide. Then it branched off into a large central room, about twenty feet in diameter, and a ceiling almost seven feet from the dirt floor. Around it individual chambers and even two-room suites were dug for each person or couple. Small furniture was brought from the houses. Beds were made of planking nailed together and laid on the ground, mattresses on top. The blacks and the servants slept in the central room. Cooking was either done all at once in a house's kitchen when the shelling slowed, or in the open at the cave's entrance with the chef keeping one eye on his pots and fire, one on the sky, and feet ready for a sudden leap for safety.

Patrick could never sleep underground. It was dank, buzzed with mosquitoes, and reeked of sweat, dirty clothes, and fear. He wished, though, he had been able to dig an underground stable for Templar. At least the Baldwin stables were partially shielded by another house, and he'd paid two of the blacks to bank dirt against its walls. Templar was the only horse remaining, and both of the blacks looked at the animal thoughtfully. By this time horses were far more valuable as food than transportation. Patrick ostentatiously displayed one of his Colt's, and lied that he always slept next to his mount, and their hungry interest waned.

With every cannonball blast Vicksburg crumbled a little more. Street signs had been blown down. The almost-deserted avenues were frequently barricaded with earth works. The few open stores had little for sale. Ornamental gardens and shrubs grew rank and unattended, except for the fruit trees, which were watched hungrily and sometimes looted green - three soldiers had gone after a man's peach tree, and he had killed two of them and the third was not expected to live. The civilian had not been arrested. Everyone tried to find a few square feet for their own vegetable garden.

Fences had been ripped down for firewood, as were sheds and even unoccupied houses. Cannonballs tore wooden houses apart, leaving their secrets gaping, naked to the passerby. Brick houses were more resilient - the shell would make a small hole entering, then utterly destroy the inside of the room. There wasn't any glass to be seen - those panes unshattered by shellfire had been carefully removed, and packed in a safe place until "better times would prevail."

All cemetery enclosures had gone - wooden ones for firewood, iron ones to be cut up and used in place of cannonballs as ammunition for the Confederate artillery grew more and more scarce. The tombstones themselves were not infrequently carried off and used for tables. There were wild dogs in the street, and at night, the yowling of abandoned cats resounded as they stalked the growing rat population. Almost everyone was lousy, and it was common to see a stately beauty, when she thought she was unwatched, scrape angrily at an armpit or waist. Clothes - if there was water to spare - would be boiled and reboiled, which merely kept the louse population a little intimidated.

Allan Cole & Chris Bunch

Vicksburg was, to use the cant of military engineers, "fully invested." The city, now stuffed with what Patrick had heard to be thirty thousand soldiers plus residents and refugees who'd fled the oncoming Yankee armies, was under siege. Thirty four thousand Federals surrounded the city on the land, more Union soldiers were across the river, and occasionally a Federal gunboat would add to the merriment by shelling Vicksburg from the river.

The forces were commanded by General Grant, whose reduction of Fort Donelson earlier in the war had sent his reputation soaring, and a General Sherman, who was reputed a far more stern killer than even Grant. There were, or so Patrick had heard, at least two hundred U.S. cannon positioned around the city, which he didn't believe, knowing there were not that many cannon in the Christian world. But he lost his agnosticism at night, when the darkness howled and the ground roiled and the air bellowed fire.

At night it was all a man or woman could do to keep from screaming for silence and peace. Some had given in, but their mad howls or remote stares had no effect, as the shelling went on and on.

The Union forces slowly drove zig-zagging trenches closer to the Confederate lines. The CSA fought from great trenches ten feet deep, carefully dug with ramparts, parapets and firesteps to shoot from, and protected in front with entanglements of telegraph wire or abatis of sharpened tree limbs. Every once in awhile, the Union would mount an assault, and the cannonading and the rap of musketfire, like the clatter of iron balls on a tin shed, would grow louder. So far all attacks had been driven back, but after each battle a wave of wounded men would stumble or be carried from the trenches.

The dead - if they could be reached safely - would be buried near where they fell. More were left unburied, and the smell covered the city like a nauseous blanket. Patrick had smelled rotting corpses before, but always on a battlefield, and the stench was doubly obscene hanging over a city where women and children still lived - and died - cannonballs hardly discriminated between a five year old girl and a wolf in butternut.

Nothing came into Vicksburg, except cannon fire and, every once in awhile, items smuggled by night - luxuries too expensive

Allan Cole & Chris Bunch

even for Mr. Baldwin. But the battle continued. Patrick recollected an editorial, in a four-month-old copy of the Whig: "All the information we receive from the North, through the abolition journals, indicates that the backbone of invasion has been broken, and that the South is fast getting into position from which it can descry the dawn of independence on the horizon. Common sense is beginning to teach the Northern people the utter hopelessness of the task they have undertaken..."

Patrick having read that shortly after another Union attack, resolved to never, ever pay attention to what a newspaper writer said about anything until after it happened and he could see for himself - and maybe not then.

As for the "position" of the South - there were men fighting and dying out in those trenches, and it ripped Patrick's guts he wasn't able to join them, even though he would be just another unsteady musket on line. Too many of the moaning or silent soldiers he'd seen being carried toward a hospital were men he knew damned well stood to gain nothing from the war.

If the Confederacy won, they'd still be dirt-poor farmers or laborers. Meanwhile, all too many of their "betters," their masters, the ones who'd agitated for war and who would be the only ones to profit by victory, still lounged around Vicksburg in silk and tailored suits styled like pre-war London fashions. The South had grudgingly passed a conscription act, but all that meant was a rich man had to come up with $5,000 in specie or whatever the latest negotiable price was to avoid serving. Or else be on the seemingly-endless list of exempt professions, from railroad employee to druggist to government official - of course - to college president to factory owner to newspaper editor - also of course.

In short, no one but a barefoot cotton-hoer with no slaves, money or common sense would be carrying a musket into battle. Or, Patrick thought ruefully, a damned fool named Patrick Shannon.

He thanked God, although he wasn't quite sure if he still believed or if he ever really had, for Lucy. Their passion had not been a single night's flame, but built and grew to a wildfire. They were besotted with love and its pain-sharp pleasures as their sweat-slick bodies touched, clung, and separated. Both of them were insatiable, making love whenever and wherever they could. Lucy swore she could not, any more than Patrick, sleep in the cave. No matter how he argued, she refused the safety of the underground. Patrick was learning when her full lips compressed and her brows furrowed there would be no arguing, merely battle. He noted even her father avoided Lucy when she was set on a course.

Patrick thought Lucy's temperament wonderful - all too many of the women - girls, more correctly - he'd known simpered and coquetted and swore they were almighty pleased to do whatever a man wanted, whenever he wanted... assuming of course it didn't conflict with their current plans or prejudices. Pamela was the high priestess in that temple of Southern womanhood.

With their love, and the bodies' fire slaked slowly at night in one or another of the Baldwin's mansion bedrooms; or hastily, nearly being found out half a dozen times, in the stable the garden or even once in the cave itself, came a problem Patrick was attempting to grapple with. That was - what next? By rights marriage plans should be looming. But... but there was a war on. Patrick had served with too many soldiers who'd married their sweethearts and ridden off to battle, just like in the ballads. And, just like in the ballads, they'd gotten themselves killed. Patrick had written the letters home - or, on request, written letters for others if they were illiterate - and knew there was nothing romantic about that pain. Especially if there were children or worse sometimes, a child yet to be born. He pondered further. Logically, if this war continued as the bloody threshing machine it had become, the odds were greatly against his survival.

Worse yet, he could be maimed or blinded, and what sort of husband would he make as a cripple? No one had the right to put a girl just shy of eighteen through that for the rest of her life. His mind flinched away, swearing he would rather be killed. Logic aside, he held a surging knowledge that he would survive unscathed, an absolute belief as certain as any shouted by a tent-meeting Methodist. Indeed, his mind jeered. You are the first to hold that belief, no doubt. You've never sat around a fire in camp, when somebody has gotten a bottle or two from the sutler, and heard anyone else make that quiet confession? And helped dig a shallow grave a few days later when he was proven apostate?

He must think more on this, and with some degree of celerity. The day before, after he'd sought out Mr. Baldwin at his office intending once more to try his best to convince the man to write a letter to the surgeon swearing Patrick was competent to serve, and once again been rejected, Mr. Baldwin had asked Patrick to sit down. He had a question, and shifted uncomfortably, as uneasy as Patrick, who'd somehow sensed the subject. It was, of course, about Lucy. Mr. Baldwin had noted there seemed to be a certain amount of... attraction between them. Or at least an attraction he might be tempted to call it infatuation, on Lucy's part.

Patrick hastened to assure him the... attraction was quite mutual, and he held Mr. Baldwin's daughter in the highest possible regard and respect. Mr. Baldwin nodded, and a very long silence was knitted between them.

"In normal times," the man eventually said, "I might now consider myself entitled to ask about other matters concerning one Patrick Shannon."

Patrick flushed, and the man's gentle tones nearly drew a youthful confession of unworthiness. But Mr. Baldwin stopped him before he could embarrass them both.

"I've heard what gossip there is about your family and yourself. But I make it a rule to ignore gossip, and I would certainly never judge a man by it. Besides, you have lived under my roof long enough for me to size you up myself. And I like what I see."

Patrick nodded his thanks, although he still felt like a fraud.

"I never had the fortune to know your late great-grandmother," Mr. Baldwin continued. "We moved from Memphis the year after her unfortunate death, you see. But certainly she was what I might call legendary, and I do not think I am over speaking her regard by some elements of Vicksburg's society. Elements, I might add, I was always in the fullest agreement with on political matters as well."

Patrick knew Mr. Baldwin had been quite outspoken against Secession, one of the so-called Co-operationists until war had been declared, when he threw himself completely into helping his beloved - if newly-adopted - state. He also thought Mr. Baldwin was hinting those citizens of Vicksburg who believed in slavery had thought Diana Shannon as evil as Harriet Beecher Stowe.

"Thank you, sir," Patrick said. "If I'm anything, if there's any weight to me at all, it's because of her." He wondered where the hell that phrase had come from - it sounded far too pompous for a man coming up on twenty one.

"That was well spoken," Mr. Baldwin said. "To continue - were these normal times, I might inquire about your other relatives. I know you are an orphan, as you say, but I also have heard, at that great reunion before the war there were many Shannons gathered. Most, I have been told, from the North. Not," he added hastily, "that is the curse it might be thought by some others here in Vicksburg. I would also inquire about your plans for the future, as regards a career or a profession. Were our conversation to proceed as amicably as I should hope," and here Mr. Baldwin's choice of words became marked, "I might offer some suggestions or options beneficent to not only you, but... to other citizens of Vicksburg as well."

Translated, that meant if Patrick said the right things, but admitted his financial future was no better than a quick tongue, a fast horse and a knowledge of all the roads out of town, Mr. Baldwin would suggest a job opening. Perhaps clerking in his own firm, or studying under another merchant or lawyer. All of this, of course, contingent on what his eventual intent was regarding Lucy Baldwin.

"As you said, sir," Patrick ventured, determined to not let this conversation slide into an unexplored and uncomfortable direction, "these are not usual times. I have expressed my deep feelings for your daughter, and can't say too strongly that I intend neither her nor her reputation the slightest damage. If there is concern in that quarter, perhaps I should arrange to find living arrangements elsewhere? I should hope that is not the case, since I credit the care you and your family have given me from... well, let's say I wonder if I'd be sitting here talking to you, otherwise."

Mr. Baldwin grinned. "Pshaw. I should never have complimented you on your pretty speech. Now we are both sounding as stuffed-up as any of Mr. Thackeray's characters. If you will go to that shelf over there, yes, the one with those dusty ledgers that look not to have been touched since the Second Crusade, and reach far behind them, hoping none of my clerks have an arm as long as you do, ah, sir, yes. That decanter contains the remnants of a very excellent brandy I had the foresight to acquire some years ago. A true Napoleon, I was told. Here are two glasses, and I shall pour.

"Now, sit down once more, and allow me to finish this conversation, which is becoming uncomfortable to us both. I shall finish with... call it a parable. I, too, once served in a war. It was that utterly obscene land grab against the Sauks and the Foxes, long before you were born. When I returned from the slaughter, and slaughter is what it was, no matter what President Lincoln has allowed it to be labeled, since he served as well, and had burnt my uniform, and was wondering what would happen next, I happened to meet Leona one day, as she walked out with her aunt as chaperone. There was this, there was that, there were words, there was anger, there was concern, her family knew I was a doomed rakehelly... but that was thirty years ago, and our good times have outweighed the bad times. Those, too, were... unusual times, and required unusual responses.

"What I am attempting to say, Mr. Shannon, is I desperately hope I can remember myself as a young ex-Captain of militia, and how no one seemed to believe in my honesty, sincerity or future. I shall attempt not to behave as stupidly as my elders did in 1833, if... if circumstances require some response on my part. No, no sir," Mr. Baldwin held up his hand. "Do not answer me, nor even speak. Savor your brandy. We can speak on this another time."

Yes, Patrick thought, his steps quickening as he approached the Baldwin house. The future would require some very immediate and intense consideration.

He found Lucy in the kitchen. She was stirring a great pot of corn meal mush, which was intended for a meal for the wounded and sick soldiers in the improvised hospital next door. It wasn't much - but there wasn't a great deal of food in Vicksburg for anyone. Lucy spent most of her waking hours at the hospital, doing what she could, when she could. He remembered his shock, months ago, when she'd written to say she and the other girls in the Academy were helping nurse at City Hospital, and how he thought no one as sweet as she should face such a charnel house. Now he felt foolish - these were, indeed, unusual times, and anyone who didn't find it in himself or herself to do a bit more would most likely be pulled under by the current.

He crept up behind her, and slipped his arms around her waist, sliding them up to cup her breasts. As her nipples hardened under his hands, she leaned back against him, moving her buttocks across his groin.

"Now how," he demanded, just a bit outraged, "did you know it was me, and not some lust-crazed surgeon from next door?"

"Stupid," she said, turning her head so he could nuzzle his neck. "Don't you think I can tell what your footsteps are like? Actually, I saw you through the window coming up the steps. If I hadn't known it was you, you might be wearing all this mush for a cravat, and I'll bet you never thought about that, did you?"

Patrick hadn't... and was rapidly becoming incapable of thinking about anything. Lucy turned in his embrace, and put her arms around him, and they kissed, her tongue flickering in and out of his mouth. Eventually the kiss ended and she stepped away, to lean back against a low table near the stove.

She held her head to the side, with as coquettish an expression as Patrick had seen from any New Orleans demimonde. She slid one hand down to her knee, and then back up her leg and thigh, bringing up her dress as she did, as if by accident. She was barefoot, and, as far as Patrick could see, was wearing nothing under the gown.

"I hoped," she said, voice throaty, "you'd come back, before I finished... before anyone else returned. Now," she went on. "Come here… as quickly as you can..."

Patrick paced toward her, a somnambulist. She slowly unfastened his belt, and then her fingers moved down the buttons of his breeches. They fell, and she ran fingers up the base of his hardness, gently moving around its tip.

"Come here," she said once more. This time her hands lifted her gown above her waist. As he moved toward her Lucy's legs lifted, bare heels digging into the backs of his thighs, pulling him to her, and she bit her lips to keep from shouting as she let herself fall back on the table and he drove into softness.

Allan Cole & Chris Bunch

Dinner that night was cold rice and milk. The milk was from one of the few cows that hadn't been frightened dry by the shelling - or been butchered out. Patrick thought about the meals he'd eaten back when.

Food was just about the main topic of conversation in Vicksburg, second only to when the siege would somehow be miraculously lifted. Prices were astronomical - five pigs for $430, a barrel of flour for $400 or a turkey for $50 - when there was anything to be bought. Patrick wondered why the army didn't raid the warehouses, seize the foodstuffs and jail the profiteers.

Mr. Baldwin scowled, and said rather severely that would be dictatorial - and the very thing the South was fighting against. Patrick remembered tales of his great grandmother's raids – backed by Dolly Madison - to get food for refugees in the War of 1812, but didn't say anything. The civilians ate what supplies they'd been able to purchase before the siege began, and what staples were occasionally sold.

In late May, the Baldwins' larder consisted of a hogshead of sugar, five sacks of wheat flour, ten sacks of corn meal, twenty pounds of bacon, a barrel of cane syrup, some spices. Cooking became most creative - corn cobs were ground and used as a substitute for baking soda, raspberry or blackberry leaves or sassafras were used to make tea, ground okra seed or sweet potatoes for "coffee."

Patrick came back to the shelter one day, and found Lucy and her sisters in tears. At first he thought someone had been hit by the shelling, but then found the vegetable garden, which consisted of nothing but onions and radishes, had been discovered and stripped by marauding soldiers.

"Our own kind," one of them said, woefully. "If it weren't for The Cause..."

When the siege began the soldiers in the trenches were given adequate supplies of hardtack and brined beef, generally eaten uncooked. But now their rations had dwindled. In theory they were given a daily issue of four ounces daily of bacon, the same in meal, and ten ounces of peas, rice and sugar. But this was on paper, only.

365

Allan Cole & Chris Bunch

The real ration was half, and even then wasn't given out every day. The cowpeas were ground, and baked as bread. But it didn't work - the outside turned black and hard as a cannonball, and the inside remained raw.

Patrick heard, with a thrill of romantic horror, that soldiers were eating rats, and impromptu markets just behind the lines had hung and dressed rodents on sale. He determined to see for himself, grand visions of Mr. Dumas' and Mr. Lewis' gothics vivid in his memory. He was terribly disappointed when he found that the "rats" were muskrats, and about the only soldiers hungry enough to eat them were hard cases from a Louisiana regiment, and even they called them "marsh rabbits."

He came away thinking, though, that when the histories were written about this siege, there wouldn't be any qualifiers on the nature of the chubby little rodents being eaten. Similarly, tales started about people eating cats but Patrick as a boy having once sniffed a rancid feline carcass knew that tale to be false. But there were unusual items on the menu. Dogs were killed and eaten. Patrick, on one of his forays trying to get back on active service had been asked to a meal by an acquaintance.

Dog, he'd found, wasn't bad. It was a little fatty and greasy; but boiled, the fat skimmed and accompanied by a few sweet potatoes and onions it proved to be quite palatable. He did not tell the Baldwins of his gastronomic adventure. Nor did he tell them the story he heard from one of Mr. Baldwin's clerks. It seemed that a soldier had managed to capture and partially tame a songbird - the clerk said it was a "jaybird," and Patrick thought this more likely. He made a present of the bird to a little girl in a family that'd been especially kind to him. After the soldier had left, the little girl laughed at the bird, keeping careful hold on the string around the finch's leg, and then looked up at her mother and said, "Can we have him for supper?" The bird was in fact served in soup that night. Once again, that story might have been apocryphal.

What was available was mule- or horsemeat. It cost five dollars or more a steak. Patrick used his rapidly dwindling cash to buy meat for the family, and whatever could pass for fodder for Templar. That was another worry, particularly when he gnawed at the sweet-tasting stews that had been four-legged a few hours or days ago. Mule and horse were so common that no one, not even the most fastidious, complained any more, but expressed joy when meat, any meat, was on the menu.

Some wag even composed a Grand Menu for a prospective siege restaurant:

SOUP
Mule Tail
BOILED
Mule Bacon with Poke Greens
Mule Ham Canvassed
ROASTS
Mule Sirloin
Mule Rump Stuffed with Rice
VEGETABLES
Boiled Peas and Rice
ENTREES
Mule Head stuffed a la Mode
Mule Beef Jerked a la Mexicana
Mule Ears fricasseed a la Gotch
Mule Hide Stewed New Style Laid On
Mule Spare Ribs Plain
Mule Liver Hashed
SIDE DISHES:
Mule Salad
Mule Hoof Soused
Mule Tongue Cold a la Bray
JELLIES
Mule foot
PASTRY
Pea Meal Pudding With Blackberry Sauce
Cotton Seed Pies
Chinaberry Tarts
DESSERT
White Oak Acorns
Beech Nuts
Blackberry Leaf Tea

Allan Cole & Chris Bunch

Genuine Confederate Coffee
LIQUORS
Mississippi Water vintage 1492 Superior... $3.00
Lime Stone Water late importation Very Fine - 2.75
Spring Water Vicksburg Brand 1.50

Everyone, including Patrick, thought the jest a capital one. But it was also close enough to reality so no one laughed that hard.

Sometimes he wondered just what his cousins in the North would think of this war if they saw not just the way soldiers suffered, but women and children as well. Unfortunately Patrick's caustic view - which he was starting to think had been Grandmother Shannon's real legacy - reminded him of who had seceded, and who had stood and cheered and waved banners and sung songs about killing Yankees. That part of him suggested the only real innocents in Vicksburg might be the children.

Returning from a futile attempt to find real feed for Templar, Patrick glanced at the yard in front of a small, neat house, and froze. Sitting in the middle of the carefully raked gravel was a small black boy, no more than four or five. He had a block of scrap iron he was using as a hammer, and was banging cheerfully on the tip of a large shell, Patrick's mind spot-identified it as being from a rifled cannon of some sort, maybe a three-incher. The shell contained about a pound of gunpowder.

Before Patrick could scream at the boy, run to him and try to save him - before he could even duck for safety - the shell exploded.

The blast sent Patrick staggering back and down. By the time he got up there was nothing in the yard except a small indentation and red splatter across the scattered white gravel. A woman came out of the porch, and Patrick was glad, very glad that the shock ringing and ringing his ears kept him from hearing the screams.

At the end of May the rains stopped, and the wells started drying up...

...If a body wasn't in the trenches, time passed slowly. Women knitted, talked and read, sometimes aloud. A new Dickens novel, Great Expectations had been smuggled into the city, and was most

368

popular, as were Mr. Bulwer-Lytton's works. Another popular book was something called Love Me Little, Love Me Long, which Patrick, who'd been known to read the back of a liniment bottle if bored enough, couldn't manage to wade through.

The other big pastime was starting or anyway passing rumors. Joe Johnston was on his way to relieve the city, and would arrive with a great army tomorrow or the day after at the latest. Patrick even spread this one himself once, but the third time it came around, he became skeptical. There were also the atrocity stories. Union soldiers had invaded some plantation somewhere, and after shooting the master to death - because he was nobly attempting to save his women - committed Horrid Deeds: swording pregnant women, impaling babies, and all the rest; the ghastliness limited only by the dark depths of the inventor's mind. Patrick imagined there were probably equally horrific tales being told in the Yankee lines of slaves being crucified or fed into gristmills or something of that order.

Of course evil - terribly evil - things happened in war. He'd even encountered the aftermath of some, and refused to think about them. But as a general rule? He figured the ancient Assyrians must've had terrible stories about how those evil Jews sacrificed their enemies by tossing great numbered stone tablets from mountain tops onto their heads. And then there were tales in Rome about Egyptians burying legionaries alive under their pyramids and so it would go, war by war, up to the present, and no doubt into the future, as long as there were men enough to pick up the sword.

Another song came around: "Oh! A life on the Vicksburg hills/A home in the trenches deep./A dodge from the Yankee shells/And the old pea-bread won't keep."

Patrick was sure some of the balderdash he'd heard trilled at the start of the war wasn't popular these days. Songs like "Adieu to the Star-Spangled Banner Forever," "The Banner of the South," "Our First President's Quickstep," and even worse. On the other hand, he doubted if many Yankees were bellowing the lyrics to "We're Gonna Hang Jeff Davis to a Sour Apple Tree," either.

Patrick found a pair of swallows nesting under the eaves of the main house. Every time a shell exploded nearby, bits of the nest would be knocked away. Tenaciously, the swallows would rebuild. Patrick sat staring at them by the hour.

He remembered other swallows, hundreds of them he thought, flashing at dusk around a ruined springhouse. That'd been where he'd met Russell. He realized with a shock that his cousin - who'd appeared to his 12-year-old eyes as a mature man - couldn't have been more than a year or two older than Patrick was right now.

Achingly, he wondered what might have happened if not for Pamela's evil, and pistols on the DeSoto Peninsula. It was all there, for one moment, and then it all vanished, he mourned. Poor Russell. Poor everyone.

The thought intruded that if he survived this war he must go to Philadelphia. Why, and on what grounds, and with what unfinished business to take care of with the Shannon family he did not know. But the thought would not leave him.

Patrick stepped out of the rider's path, and idly noted as the officer reined in his horse in front of the blacksmith's shop. The man dismounted and entered. Patrick's horseman's eye noted the animal's sore-pocked hide and protruding ribs.

The officer had not been gone an instant when a shell screamed in, exploded, and the animal reared and fell. Patrick gaped as two ragged men, wearing the remnants of uniforms, came out of an alley, brandishing great knives. In seconds steaks were cut from the horse's exposed flank, and the men were gone.

Other men, and Patrick thought he saw a woman or two, followed. By the time the officer came out of the smithy, the carcass was half-butchered as neatly as any slaughterhouse would have done.

Templar whickered, marring the unnatural stillness of the night.

"Damn it," Patrick whispered. "Shut up, Templar. There nothing else I can do."

The animal started to wicker once more, and Patrick thought he sounded puzzled. He clamped his hand on Templar's muzzle, and stroked it. "Now, come on."

370

He was just at the Confederate front lines, at a place he'd scouted in daylight. The ground wasn't as shattered with shellfire as other parts of the lines, and he could make out the remnants of a road. He thought it might be the ferry road, or perhaps the one that led down to Warrenton, toward where Grandmother Shannon's plantation had been. There'd be less than nothing there now, he'd been told. The Union fortifications had devoured farms, roads and plantations. Now it was war's ruined pavilion. Patrick hoped the Cuffe family had gotten out of the line of fire before things got too bad.

He stopped behind the last cover before the Yankee lines, where a shell had thrown up a parapet of muck tall enough to conceal Templar. Now was the moment. Patrick couldn't swallow, and had to keep wiping his eyes with a sleeve. He could not afford to get blurry-eyed and dead. Out in the night he thought he saw movement. A Yankee picket. Do it now, Patrick, he thought. While you still can.

"Go on, now," he pleaded with the horse. Templar just stood there. "Dammit horse, go!" Templar did not move. Patrick took off his hat, and swatted Templar's flank. The animal jumped sideways - Patrick never struck him. "Horse, please! Templar, you're going to be steaks if you don't."

The animal shifted from side to side. Patrick took a deep breath, and drew one of his pistols. He cocked it, keeping it hidden behind him, then fired it, straight up, just behind Templar's flank. Templar reared, startled, neighed, and leaped forward, Patrick slashing at his flanks with his hat. He turned and ran back, doubling for cover, as he heard the shout of the Union pickets coming to alert.

Thirty yards back into the Confederate positions, he stopped. Templar was standing in the middle of the battlefield. He took a few tentative steps back, and Patrick hissed. A figure came out of the night... two figures. They took Templar's reins and led him away. Templar reared once more, then went along.

It didn't look, or so Patrick's mind insisted his eyes had seen, that anybody was yanking on the bridle or anything. Maybe it was somebody who knew horses, or maybe Templar would end up with a new owner who did. Patrick had put the last of his gold - a twenty dollar piece in an envelope made of wallpaper, together with a note

Allan Cole & Chris Bunch

explaining what the horse meant to him, and begging whoever found Templar to take care of him. The saddlebags contained what fodder he'd been able to buy.

Templar was gone. There was nothing out there but the night and the shell-ploughed ground.

Patrick went back into the city and found an abandoned house. His teeth were buried in his lower lip to keep himself under control, but he never tasted the blood. He made sure no one was within hearing, and then he cried. Cried hard, cried about what he'd done, cried because there was nothing else that could have been done, cried the way he hadn't since... since the night Grandmother Shannon died. Patrick Shannon had driven off his only friend.

Except for Lucy, he thought. But that would be for later, when he was able to stop crying. God Damn It, he thought forlornly, running that old musket ball back and forth through his fingers. I was right, way back then. All life is a series of leavings. He tried a prayer for Templar, even though every time he looked up at the sky all he saw was black emptiness.

The words never did come. It was dawn before he managed to find his way back to the Baldwin house.

On June 4 the army finally ordered the seizure and central disbursal of all rations in the city. By then most people were hungry enough not to object to the immorality of it all. But it was very late, and most hoarders had more than enough warning to hide their best.

The night before the thunder came, Lucy had been playful. Patrick, after a dinner of nothing but cold cornbread and water, made his good nights and left the cave. It had been very still, with almost no cannonading coming from the Union lines, but even so, no one seemed interested in sleeping outside the shelter. He'd seen the look from Lucy, and knew she would be along shortly. He'd casually made reference to the great bureau in Lucy's bedroom, hoping she'd use that as a clue to where he could be found.

In the room he'd taken the sheet away he'd used to cover the bed against the plaster that rained down when the artillery was firing, fluffed pillows, had a towel and basin of water at hand, and two

372

candles on either side of the bedstead - feeling more than a little like one of Mr. Congreve's seducers... but liking the feeling. He'd been staring out the window, wondering why the Yankees were so quiet, when it suddenly became darker, and there was a giggle. He spun, and Lucy was in the room. She'd crept in, blown out one of the candles and held the other in her hand. She wore a long skirt, blouse tied with a sash, and a kerchief around her hair.

"Patrick Shannon," she said, in a note of shock, her mind evidently in the same channel as his. "I declare you are a foul scoundrel! This appears to be a trap set to lure a fair damsel to a fate worse than death."

Patrick started toward her, and she blew the candle out, and he heard footsteps going away.

"Lucy!"

"Sshh!" A clatter. Then... "Catch me if you can."

Patrick, naturally, went in pursuit. At the bedroom door, he stumbled and almost fell on something. He picked it up. It was one of Lucy's slippers. He listened. He thought he heard her going downstairs, and followed. At the landing he found another slipper. So it was to be hare and hounds. He went on, picking up other bits of the trail - the kerchief, the blouse, the dress, and, eventually, Lucy. She was in the great front room, glassless windows wide open toward the river below.

Lucy was naked, lying on her back, flat on the carpet, smiling up at him. Patrick dissolved out of his own clothes, and began to kneel beside her.

"No," she whispered. "Show me... like you do. With your mouth. I want to learn how."

Patrick realized he was blushing and was grateful for the darkness, and part of his brain snickered that maybe the great traveler wasn't quite as unshockable as he wished. He obeyed, though, turned as he knelt, and his lips and tongue began moving slowly, softly, in circles, steadily up from her inner thigh as Lucy's mouth took him in, and Vicksburg, the occasional shellblast, the dusty smell of the carpet they lay on and the planet went somewhere else.

Allan Cole & Chris Bunch

Sometime later they returned, slowly. The carpet was prickly against their skins. Patrick's head was pillowed on Lucy's thigh, and they were lying on their sides. He wondered if he was making her uncomfortable, and took a while to remember what words were so he could ask. But before he could, the night exploded.

For an instant Patrick thought the house had been hit by a shell, and damned himself for ever allowing Lucy to endanger herself, and then thought no, it was a sudden storm, lightning flashing, but it was not that either. As he rolled to his feet he realized all of the Union guns had opened up.

A night attack, he thought, hands finding Lucy's clothes, and helping her put at least some of them on; but it wasn't that, as above them shells crashed, incendiaries exploding in amber or blue flashes. A full bombardment, targeting the Confederate batteries on the hills above them. More or less clothed, they hurried for the shelter, having to dive for shelter twice as the darkness flamed and the ground roiled and shook. Christ, he thought, this was worse than Shiloh!

They slipped through the two blankets hung at the cave's entrance to block the light within. Patrick had time for a bit of guilt and a hope no one would ask, but no one even seemed to have noticed Lucy had been out of her own chamber. There were maybe twenty people, black and white, in the cave's central room. There were only two fat lamps going in the room, and each time a shell landed outside they sent shadows racing across the dirt walls. He led Lucy to a seat beside a wall, not far from the cave's entrance, and helped her down.

He sat, keeping an arm around her. The cave was mostly quiet, except for one slave who was saying something - maybe a prayer? - under her breath over and over. Mrs. Baldwin was praying aloud, her shoulders shaking. Someone - one of the white servants - was keening, until Mr. Baldwin, forcing his voice to near-calm, ordered her to be still. Again and again the shelter rocked - Patrick guessed the Union cannon were firing short without realizing it.

He held Lucy closer. "It'll be all right," he said. "It'll be all right." He felt her head nodding and then the world came to an end.

Allan Cole & Chris Bunch

All was shock and blast and darkness, and there were screams, and rumbles, and Patrick smelt gunpowder and a blast of stale air and a smell like a freshly-dug grave. The screams grew louder.

"Stop," he found himself shouting. "We're not dead! Find a light, someone!"

A match scraped, and flared. Mr. Baldwin relit the fat lamp, and then shock - silent and gasped - ran through the room. The cave's only entrance was gone, and dirt spilled into the chamber about a foot from where Patrick was. That last shell must have landed almost on the cave, and blocked the entrance.

"We're buried alive," one of Lucy's sisters breathed.

"No, we're not. Does anybody have a shovel?" Patrick demanded.

Someone was bawling, and someone else saying something about being trapped. "Come on," he said. "It's just a little dirt." But inside he knew it was dense clay and there might be ten feet of it between them and open air.

Someone lit the other lamp, and Patrick, remembering what he'd read in Frank Leslie's about mining disasters, was about to order it to be put out to save air, but bethought himself. The darker it was, the more likely that hysteria might strike. Now, where the hell were those shovels?

He didn't realize he'd spoken aloud, until he saw one of the Long's slaves shaking his head. "Outside, Marse," the man said mournfully. "We was told not to clutter up in here."

Hell. "Get some plates. Dinner plates. We'll use those."

In a few minutes, Patrick, and the other eighteen people in the cave, realized the worst. Evidently the blast had blocked the tunnel's entrance, and seemed to have packed the clay very firmly. There was only room enough for one man to dig and one to shovel the clay back into the central room. Patrick had taken first turn, but had weakened and someone else had taken his place. He sat beside Lucy now, listening to the scrape, scrape, scrape, and feeling the air get thicker and thicker. He was trying to keep from panic, trying to tell himself the air wasn't that bad, it was just his fear of being

Allan Cole & Chris Bunch

underground, and then he saw one of the lamps' flames start to shimmer.

He looked at Lucy. She tried to smile. What a stupid way to die, he thought, and red anger blazed through him - not for himself, but for everyone else in the cave, who surely weren't soldiers. Five men, the only white one of serving age being Patrick, the rest women and children. Patrick told himself if he survived he'd somehow arrange to get an artilleryman in his sights one day.

He wondered what it would be like, suffocating here. Would it hurt, or would they just sort of drift off to sleep, like the penny dreadfuls said happened? Or would someone panic and start clawing at the earth, ripping away his or her nails like he'd read happened when some poor soul did get entombed and then came out of his fit? Damn, damn, damn, he thought.

Then: "Lucy," he whispered. "I love you."

Her eyes glistened. "I love you, too, Patrick."

"When we get out... will you marry me?"

"I shall, Patrick. Of course I shall." He kissed her, not giving a damn whether it was propitious.

A few minutes later they heard the sound of shovels, digging toward them from the outside.

The Baldwin house was a shambles. At least three shells had smashed into it. The upper floor where Patrick's sickroom had been was gutted. The front living room, where he and Lucy had made love, was shattered, walls peeled away like the skin on a dried-up orange. Mrs. Baldwin was in shock. Lucy, her sisters and the servants mourned loudly.

"Never mind," Mr. Baldwin said. "Wood is wood and stone is stone. We can rebuild. At least none of us were touched. And what we'll make will be better than what we had before."

Patrick wondered - if this ever ended, not just the siege but the war and the inevitable aftermath of a confrontation between two completely different peoples - would things indeed be better? He was hardly naive enough to think they could not get worse.

That was one thing he had learned from the Army: things could always be worse.

376

Mr. Baldwin was true to his promise about remembering his own youth. When Patrick haltingly asked for the hand of his daughter, all the while feeling like the prize fool in a farce, the man reacted with laughter and joy. Patrick almost broke into tears, since it had taken him three days to prepare for the worst if Mr. Baldwin told him to get the blazes away from his daughter. Similarly, Mrs. Baldwin was enraptured, and preparing for the wedding seemed to keep her from brooding about her destroyed home.

Surprisingly, Lucy's two older sisters seemed to become a little standoffish. Patrick wondered why, then shrugged. He was having enough trouble trying to understand one Baldwin. And, come to think, one Shannon.

The cave was redug and enlarged and given several exits. The barrage now seemed continuous and heavy, and almost everyone spent most of their time either underground or close to shelter.

There were more Union soldiers around the city now, and their saps were closer and closer, moving like great carnivore worms toward Vicksburg.

Both Patrick and Mr. Baldwin had mourned about not being able to give Lucy a proper trousseau. Patrick would wear that uniform Mr. Carnahan had made so long ago, that he'd worn but once. But there was no need to fret about Lucy. Clothes were offered from everywhere. A widow whose husband had been killed at Murfreesboro volunteered her gown, and helped Lucy, her sisters and Mr. Carnahan the tailor repaired the garment until it looked - or so Patrick was told, being forbidden to see her in the dress before the ceremony - like it had been custom-made for Lucy.

She even had new shoes, which almost no one in Vicksburg owned. She'd made them herself. In the cleanup after the shelling, she'd found a huge old trunk belonging to her mother that had been forgotten about for years. In it was a leather coat. Lucy carefully disassembled her worn-out shoes, used them as a pattern and cut new material from the coat sleeves. The soles weren't as heavy as they should have been, but what of that? It was still summer. Patrick was

Allan Cole & Chris Bunch

completely enchanted, and told her when the war was over they must have the shoes put into a glass case, and she could tell, uh well, other people about her heirloom.

"Other people, Patrick? Such as," she asked, trying to look innocent.

"Yes. Like, uh, well, you know, uh, little people?" Lucy giggled.

Patrick didn't hear much of the ceremony. He kept looking sidelong at Lucy. She was gorgeous, easily the most beautiful creature God or Buddha or Allah or the Universe had created. The minister - Patrick kept reminding himself to not call him a priest - went through the ceremony with all stops pulled, as he should have, the Baldwins being important members of the congregation. Mr. Baldwin delicately inquired as to Patrick's religion, and what were his thoughts on the upcoming ceremony.

Patrick answered honestly that, although he'd been born a Catholic his father hadn't been much of a church-goer and he himself was fairly lapsed in the faith. It didn't seem necessary to mention his own growing agnosticism. Plus Patrick was pretty sure if he'd held out for a Catholic marriage there'd be some kind of training or something Lucy would have to go through, even if it was wartime, and neither one of them wanted to waste time. And so the ceremony was High Episcopalian.

There was a reception afterward, with a hundred contributed delicacies that people had held out for some kind of happy event, and catawba wine, and someone even brought a case of champagne they'd had hidden in a cellar, awaiting the day of victory. No one seemed to notice it had gone flat, and wouldn't have said anything if they did.

Patrick lifted Lucy over the "threshold" of their honeymoon "cottage." Perhaps in another time, another place, he might have been a little saddened. The cottage was, in fact, a smallish cave. It had an open walk, with a parapet in front to keep the shells off, which made a sort of patio. It was overhung with creeping vines and shaded with pawpaw trees. It ran about twenty feet underground, and had another wing that opened to let air freely circulate. Just outside the door was a table, with an arbor of branches. Shelves were cut into the dirt, and on them were tin cups with wild flowers in them. The "cottage" had been loaned by a friend of the Baldwins for their honeymoon.

Patrick let Lucy slip down. She looked about. "I do love it, Mr. Shannon."

"Thank you, Mrs. Shannon. I picked it out with you in mind."

Lucy walked to one wall, where the bed was - a mattress hung on ropes tied to a wooden frame. "This will be very different," she said.

"In what way, my love?"

"I don't know if... when we finish... I'll be able to keep from looking over my shoulder to see if we're about to get caught."

As she spoke, her fingers were moving over the stays and buttons of the gown. The gown dropped in a pool around her feet, and she slipped out of her chemise.

Patrick's uniform was off and tossed into a corner.

Lucy stood there, smiling, her small breasts arched. "You're even more beautiful," Patrick managed, "then the first time I saw you, on the streets of Vicksburg."

He went to her, and stood close, the hard tips of her nipples just touching his chest.

His hands moved gently down her back to cup her buttocks, moving, moving and caressing.

Lucy sighed, deep in her throat, and her legs went limp.

Patrick laid her down, ever so gently, on the flower-patterned sheets as her legs came up against his chest and parted.

Allan Cole & Chris Bunch

CHAPTER TWENTY-EIGHT

WASHINGTON – JUNE 21, 1863

THE CAPITAL WAS sweltering through another "Rumor Sunday." It was a day of skirmishes along the Potomac and oppressive heat. There were wild tales of Rebel barricades thrown up on city streets. A small panic erupted on G Street when a hole dug for a new flag pole was mistaken for evidence of an artillery attack. At Willard's Hotel, men fought the heat with tall, frosty glasses of whiskey punch and sherry cobbler, and perked their ears at the rumble of big guns beyond the Bull Run Mountains.

The specter of two disasters at Manassas echoed in that distant thunder. The word was that General Lee was marching north and no one could find Hooker to stop him. It was as if his army had suddenly vanished. The governor of Pennsylvania and mayor of Philadelphia burned up the telegraph wires with pleas for help. General Pleasonton's cavalry clashed with Stuart in the Blue Ridge gaps, and hopes were roused as Rebel prisoners began arriving from the mountains. But they were quickly dashed when the first ambulance trains hauled the wounded and dead across the Long Bridge.

Little of this was on Pamela Shannon's mind as she slipped out of the drab little building just off Pennsylvania Avenue. She gave a sour look at the small sign that read: Madame Roberval's Clinic For Female Weaknesses. Female weaknesses, indeed, she thought. In her view, male weaknesses would be a more apt description. She stuffed a small, fat package into her purse, popped open a rather colorless parasol to shade her features from any curious stares, and hurried to catch the streetcar.

She was dressed in one of Marcia's poorest costumes - shapeless and drab to match the borrowed parasol - and was the object of only the most casual interest as she boarded. She found an empty seat and sank into it. The other passengers were discussing the latest news and fearful gossip. Lincoln was/was not calling out one hundred thousand militia. Hooker had/had not been ousted from command. The Rebels were/were not mounting the latest British cannon within range of the capitol.

What an indignity that place was, Pamela thought. Despite Madame Roberval's advertised boasts she had treated women of royalty in Vienna and Paris, in Pamela's view the woman was nothing more than an expensively dressed middle-aged tart whose only talent was discretion - and a reliable supply of the vaginal syringes and thin leather condoms that Pamela now carried in her purse.

Since that ingrate Hercules had run away to join the black troops over on Analostan Island, Pamela had run dangerously low in safeguards against Congressman Howard Wright's occasional bouts with virility. In the past, it was Hercules who'd fetched what she needed, sparing her the company of the common trollops and wayward wives who frequented Madame Roberval's. The woman did a booming war time business in pills, potions and questionable surgical procedures to cure a caught out woman of what ailed her.

With Hercules gone, Pamela was temporarily forced to make the trip herself. She'd decided to travel incognito, and sans carriage, to avoid answering any embarrassing questions if she were recognized. Of course, she could always claim she was afflicted with painful monthlies and was seeking treatment: female weaknesses covered a broad canvas of innocent, if delicate, possibilities. But where her reputation was concerned, she would just as soon avoid situations that might demand an explanation.

Loud argument filtered through her ruminations. Someone was branding the fearful talk among the other passengers as nothing but low lies. Pamela was quite used to it. In heaven, the Lord may have rested on the seventh day. But in Washington his lumps of clay went wild in the silence, speculating on all sorts of disasters; which is why the wags dubbed them "Rumor Sundays."

Pamela snorted - for her, today was to be more of a "dirty Sunday." Marcia was off on a planned visit with Maryland relatives in Silver Springs. As soon as Howard had learned of her intent, he'd launched a few plans of his own. Pamela had been pressured into giving the servants the day off, so that Howard could bed her in vigorous comfort.

She patted the packet in her purse, relaxing now that she didn't have that worry on her mind. Actually, it wasn't going to be that much of a bother. Howard was reasonably clean, grunted only a little, and despite his heated promises of a day of monumental amour, he was unlikely to test the endurance of even a poor quality condom. Still, Pamela wasn't one to take chances when it came to that sort of thing: the vaginal syringes alnd their contents would provide her with double protection.

The streetcar gave a jolt as the driver reined in his horses to let a wagon load of wounded soldiers pass. Pamela gritted her teeth and tapped an impatient foot. She wanted badly to get out of Marcia's loathsome dress. And if the delays were few, she had just enough time for a hot bath before her anxious lover arrived.

Fresh from her bath, Pamela dusted her body with scented powder and slipped a thin French shift over her naked body. It was a wonderful silky thing that showed off her figure in a tantalizing shadow show. She daubed on a hint of makeup to aid nature, and tied her long tresses with a ribbon. She made the knot simple so Howard could easily undo it, then anointed herself with a light, fruity perfume. She turned for a final check of her preparations. Her boudoir had been dusted, scoured, and thoroughly waxed by the maid. The big bed was dressed in her best linens, and she'd hauled in extra pillows in case Howard had a notion for something tricky.

There were some tasty snacks laid out on a side table, and several bottles of wine and a jug of punch set to chill in an enamel tub. It was really quite nice, Pamela thought. She shut the window so the sounds of their lovemaking would not be heard by the daytime crowd on the street, then sprinkled a little cologne on the bed to sweeten it. She'd decided to give Howard a really good show. She'd keep him stoked and hard for as much of the day as she could, and put on such a pretty display of amazement at his prowess he'd have something to bloat up about for months to come.

Yes, it was time Howard had a bit more of a reward than usual. Despite the legal snarl Susan Dolan had tried to ensnare her in, Howard had kept Pamela's case inching along in the courts. He'd called in many favors and bent more than a few arms to keep her suit alive and well. Victory was all but assured; now she only needed the gift of patience to weather the long months that still remained in her war against the Shannons.

Pamela had no trouble waiting, especially with Howard paying all her bills and giving her a generous allowance as well. He'd even been hinting broadly of marriage of late. With Pamela's subtle prodding, Howard had become totally disgusted with his always-complaining, always-ailing wife and was ready to divorce her and plead for Pamela's pretty hand. But she'd held off this final landing of her fish; she was not certain marriage with Howard Wright was the future she most desired. He was wealthy and well-connected, to be sure; and for an otherwise strong-willed fellow for Pamela he was as malleable a man as she'd encountered. At the moment, however, she thought it'd be best to wait until the case was settled. Of course, there was talk that Howard would make an ideal Senator.

But Pamela feared tying herself to the fortunes of a divorced politician. No, she was right to hold off; although she really ought to hurry along his separation from his wife: he'd be even more pliable after marinating in guilt for a time. As she took one more look in the mirror, she heard the apartment's outer door open, then light footsteps on the carpet. She frowned: that couldn't be Howard!

Marcia's voice echoed through the empty rooms: "Hello? ... Pamela? ... Is anyone home?"

Pamela cursed: what the hell was she doing home? That damned girl was going to ruin everything.

She calmed herself, then called out: "Just a minute, Marcia dear. I'll be out in a moment."

She hastily pulled on a wrap and exited the room, firmly closing the door behind her to hide the tell-tale preparations.

"Why, Marcia," she said in tones of concern, "what in the world are you doing home? Did the carriage break down, poor thing?"

"Didn't you hear?" Marcia answered. "The Rebels are on their way to Silver Springs!"

Pamela bit back anger. "Oh, that's nonsense, Marcia. You really shouldn't let those silly rumors spoil your good time."

"But what if isn't a rumor?" Marcia said, still visibly shaken by her imagined ordeal. "I saw people... in wagons... fleeing... with everything they owned!"

Allan Cole & Chris Bunch

Pamela desperately tried to think of something to overcome the girl's groundless fears. Then she shrugged... Howard would just have to be inconvenienced. She caught Marcia staring at her, and remembered the makeup and perfume. Especially revealing were the silver slippers she wore, and the necklace and earrings. She tugged the wrap closer to hide the naughty French shift.

"Expecting someone, cousin?" Marcia said, with barely disguised contempt.

Pamela laughed. "Why, who could I possibly be expecting dressed like this?" she answered. She feigned a blush, and giggled. "Although I must confess to a bit of play-acting in private. Pampering myself... and trying on jewelry and makeup and what all."

As she turned back toward her room, intent on removing any evidence of her real plans, there came a knock at the door. Oh, God! Howard! The son of a bitch was early.

"I wonder who that could be," Marcia said, giving her a knowing look. And before Pamela could react her cousin flung open the door, saying: "Why, Mr. Howard, what a pleasant sur-" The word stuck in her throat when she saw a uniformed stranger. The man was young, quite handsome, and blushing furiously.

"Excuse me," he stammered, "I'm Lieutenant... uh ... Glas. Uh... John Glas, that is. Uh... Are you... uh... Mrs. Shannon?"

Marcia shook her head, too embarrassed to speak. Pamela was as amazed as her cousin, and so relieved she forgot she was hardly dressed to receive. She stepped forward. "I am Mrs. Shannon," she said. "How may I help you, lieutenant?" The young officer gaped at her, thunderstruck in the presence of such under dressed beauty. "I said: how may I help you?"

Lt. Glas caught himself, blushed even deeper, and fumbled an envelope out of his pocket. "Oh! I... uh... have a message. Uh... Yes, that's it! A message! Here!" He thrust the envelope at Pamela. As she took the envelope, she idly noted the breadth of his shoulders, the pleasing shape of the muscles under his jacket, and that he was exceptionally long-limbed. About twenty two, she surmised, with the looks of a German god. Then she glanced at the envelope and saw it was from Howard.

384

"Marcia," she said quickly. "Why don't you fetch the lieutenant a nice cold glass of punch?" Her cousin only gaped at her, still mired in her error of assumption. "Please, Marcia," she pressed. "We mustn't forget our manners."

"Oh!" Marcia gasped. "Yes. I mean, no. We mustn't!"

To Pamela's relief, Marcia rushed off just in time to miss what the lieutenant had to say next: "Congressman Howard... uh... sends his regrets, Missus. But... Uh... Duty has called him away." Glas finally found his voice, and a modicum of composure. "It's rather tragic, Mrs. Shannon," he said. "There are quite a few Ohio boys coming in with the wounded. Congressman Howard simply had to make sure they're being properly taken care off. He'll be at the hospital all night."

Pamela nodded: she'd opened the envelope and the message within confirmed the young lieutenant's words. "Don't mention any of this to my cousin," Pamela said. "She is a woman of decidedly delicate nature."

"Oh, I wouldn't... uh... No, I'd never... uh..."

Pamela laughed. "Oh, do sit down, sir. Marcia will be along with the punch in a moment." She indicated a small divan. He did as he was told. Pamela sat across from him, primly tucking the wrap about her. "You will forgive my dress, won't you?" she said. "You've caught me quite unawares with this important news."

"Oh, no... not at all... I mean... yes, I forgive... uh... Oh! Here's the punch!" Marcia had re-entered the room and Glas grabbed at the tumbler to untangle his tongue and drank deeply. Marcia perched on the edge of a straight-backed chair, as nervous as the lieutenant. Both of them sat in uncomfortable silence as Pamela picked up reading where she had left off:

...I beg your understanding for this unforgivable rudeness. And I promise you, my little Virginia Sweetmeat, that your loving Howard will be your Humble Servant to the end of Time if only you overlook this Unavoidable, but still Inexcusable, Failure to attend our Rendezvous. I have a bit of News, however, that may allow you to see Your Faithful Lover in a more favorable light. I was saving this for our meeting, but realized it would be grossly unfair to hold it back, now that I am being so Tragically Delayed.

385

Allan Cole & Chris Bunch

"I was speaking with friends in the Naval Department last night, and one of them told me a curious tale. It was a tale of apparent Murder, and no little Intrigue. The story itself is unsuitable for your lovely, innocent ears, but its outcome, I am sure, contains news that should give you Great Pleasure. It seems that a man - a Rebel, no less - whose name matches that of the Evil Fellow who Robbed you of Your Fortune, was found Dead Under Dishonorable Circumstances.

"And that name - I shall withhold it no longer - is Fitz Maguire! He was found Murdered, with a note pinned to his breast that Branded him a Traitor to the South. They have his papers at the Naval Office, and I shall fetch them with me when next we meet. If this news bears out, I cannot begin to tell you how much this Helps Our Cause in the courts as far as your property is concerned. With that, I must take my leave, My Darling, My-

The note fell from Pamela's fingers. She looked up... seeing nothing. "What is it?" Marcia asked, alarmed.

Pamela ignored her, and snatched up the message again. This was no dream. Maguire was dead! Murdered! Vilified as a traitor to boot! Pamela smiled, remembering her conversation with Mrs. Brady, the amateur spy she had roped in. A great bubble of joy rose filling her until she was about to burst.

"Are you well, Mrs. Shannon?" Glas asked, his voice anxious.

Pamela laughed aloud. "Am I well? My dear, sir, I am as well as I have ever been in my life!"

She felt powerful, able to bend legions to her will: she was Queen Cleopatra; she was Catherine The Great; she was the Empress of Constantinople. At her word, a man had died - no... two men! Russell Conners was the first; and now, most satisfyingly, Fitz Maguire was the latest victim of her merest whim. She wanted to shout victory to the world. She was suddenly shaken by the most marvelous and violent orgasm she'd ever experienced. It was all she could do to keep from plunging her hand between her thighs to coax it on and on and on.

A shadow fell over her. She looked up and saw Lieutenant Glas' handsome face peering down at her. Once again she noted those broad shoulders and muscular arms. She saw for the first time that his eyes were deep blue, and his hair was fine spun gold. "Shall I fetch a doctor, Mrs. Shannon?" he was asking.

She looked into his clear, innocent eyes. There was not a brain in that head of his: in fact, he quite reminded her of the gorgeous stallion Edward had ridden to his doom. Pamela shook her head, voice husky when she spoke. "Really, there's no need. It's only the weather, I'm sure."

She pulled at her wrap, delighting as Glas' eyes plummeted down, then widened when he saw her naked breasts and long, hard nipples heaving under that thin French shift. "Marcia, dear," Pamela murmured. "You wouldn't fetch a little of that punch? There's a love." Marcia rushed to do her bidding.

Pamela smiled sweetly at the concerned young officer. A delicious idea bloomed in her mind; she squeezed her thighs together in delight, and grinned when she saw his gaze fall on the shadow of her sex. "Tell me... Lieutenant... Is it true that Silver Springs is in difficulty?"

He frowned, puzzling at this sudden shift in topics. Pamela thought she'd never seen such a sweet look of utter stupidity. "Difficulty? Why... what do you mean?"

"Well, my cousin was expected to visit with relatives today," Pamela answered. "But she heard the Rebels were running amok in Maryland, and turned back."

Glas shook his head. "No. There's no danger. I had heard the rumor, and there is nothing to it."

Pamela clapped her hands in delight. "Marcia," she cried. "Did you hear? Silver Springs is quite safe after all." Marcia came back with her drink. Pamela took the glass from her, saying: "Now, there's no need for you to miss your visit."

"I don't know..." Marcia said, quite nervous at the prospect.

"Don't argue," Pamela said, firm but loving. The feeling of power was such she could be denied nothing. "I am sure your family is worried sick about you. Run along now, dear." She waved a pretty hand at the door. "And be sure to give everyone my love."

She turned back to the lieutenant, feeling so strong, so sure of herself. His face had a stunned look; he seemed only dimly aware of

387

Allan Cole & Chris Bunch

what was going on. She heard Marcia's slow steps to the door; heard it open... then close.

Pamela moved slightly and let the wrap do as it pleased. Glas' eyes fed on her briefly, then turned guiltily away. She touched his hand, and he quivered like an unbroken colt. How charming!

"Could you stay a bit longer?" she asked. She stroked the hand, gentling him. "In case I should feel... faint?" He couldn't answer, but only nodded. "What was your name, again, lieutenant?"

"John," he croaked. "John Glas."

"John," Pamela purred. "Such a strong name, too. But... would you object if I called you... Johnny?"

Johnny said he'd take no offense at all.

Lieutenant John Glas might not have been the brightest man in Mr. Lincoln's army, but he proved an eager student in bed. Pamela commanded him as if she were his general, and he willingly obeyed her every whim. She was insatiable, ordering him to do this and do that; but his energy and his glorious cock never seemed to flag.

She rode him like Edward's stallion, bounding up and down, rocking her hips, impaling herself until that leather-sheathed tool fairly hammered at the gates of her womb. She had one orgasm after another, until they all seemed to run together in a heavenly, never-ending sensation.

Each time he came, she pulled away and slipped off the condom. She washed him with wine and licked and sucked him clean, marveling at the length and girth of him; glorying in the golden nest his fine pubic hairs made. Then she slipped on a fresh sheath and rode him some more.

When she tired of that, she poured wine down her breasts and let him suckle and sip. She put sweetmeats between her thighs and got him to lap at her like a dog, and then taught him to dive into her with his tongue and wriggle it around like a fish.

She humped a pillow under her belly and bade him to mount her, and he slung away wildly, his balls rapping deliciously against her thighs; she taught him to pleasure her with his hand at the same time, and came so hard that her shouts rattled the window glass.

They made love until nightfall, then she made him rip off the sheets and turn the mattress over so they could do it all over again.

388

Finally, his cock lay limp against his thigh and could rise no more. She nestled in his arms, as satisfied as she'd been since Maguire last bedded her.

"I love you," Johnny hoarsed.

"Hush, dear," Pamela said. She hoped he wouldn't spoil it all by being silly.

"What shall we tell the Congressman?" He asked.

"Nothing at all," Pamela said.

"But... We must," Glas said. "After all that has... happened... between us. And I know that he and you are... " He didn't complete the sentence.

Pamela pulled away and perched on an elbow, smiling at him from the vast distance of her superiority. She had no fear, no worry. After all, she was a woman who could command death itself. "You're some kind of an assistant to the congressman, correct?"

"Yes. I was attached as a congressional liaison."

"Then I expect people think you are a man who is going places, otherwise you'd be off chasing the Rebels... A wealthy family, perhaps?"

"My family isn't rich," Johnny said. "But they do command respect in Ohio. And I'm not ashamed to say that's how I got the appointment. There's many ways to serve your country in wartime, my father always says."

Pamela laughed. "Well, Mr. Respect From Ohio, if you desire a future of any brightness, I'd advise against speaking up. Because, I promise you, if Howard finds out you'll be off chasing Lee by morning."

"But... what about us?" the young man agonized.

Pamela came up on her knees and let her breasts dangle over him. "You just let me worry about us, dear," she said. "And if you do exactly as I say... I promise, you'll go very far indeed."

He started to speak, and Pamela lowered herself until her nipple filled his mouth. He grabbed her breast and began to suckle and moan like a child. Pamela giggled as she felt him stiffen against her leg.

What a lovely young man, this Johnny was. She definitely planned to take a hand in his future.

Allan Cole & Chris Bunch

"You'll mind me, Johnny dear?" she whispered. He nodded, still lapping away.

She patted his golden curls. "Good boy," she said. "Good boy."

CHAPTER TWENTY-NINE

GETTYSBURG, PA. - JULY 2-3, 1863

THE PEALING OF church bells woke Lieutenant Hugh Shannon, and his hand crept out for Mary, to tickle her awake and suggest a pleasant pastime while others thought of morning mass. His hand ran over wet grass and muck, and his eyes reluctantly peeled open. He'd fallen asleep slumped against an ambulance wheel, and didn't really remember when he'd allowed himself the moment's rest. It would've been no more than an hour or two ago, at the latest. Lord God but he was tired, and it had barely begun.

Once more Robert Lee had taken his army north, and this was no feint, no skirmish, no bluff. This was invasion. The Army of Northern Virginia spread across more than a hundred miles as it swept up the Shenandoah Valley, using the Blue Ridge Mountains as a screen. Joe Hooker had taken the Army of the Potomac after it, but had been relieved and replaced by somebody named Meade, who only a few people knew as a competent, methodical engineer, and hardly a fiery-eyed leader.

Not that it mattered to the army who marched in front with the banners. They'd all come to realize generals came and went, winning or losing battles, but the man who'd actually win or lose the war was in the front rank, wore tatters, carried a bayoneted Springfield musket and was in need of a bath, a solid meal and a week's sleep without dreams.

Hugh had no idea of just what the latest Grand Strategy was, even though the 86th Pennsylvania's commander, Colonel Dennigan, had shown Hugh where they were on a map a day or so ago. All he knew was Lee was somewhere out there to the West, and Meade was dancing the army north, trying to keep it between the Rebels and Washington, then Philadelphia, then Harrisburg. The Army was looking for a fight - hoping for once the Union could fight on its terms and not Bobby Lee's. For once the Army wasn't moving like it was wading through molasses. Maybe they didn't have the racetrack pace of the late Stonewall Jackson's well-named "foot cavalry," but the Army didn't drag along mistresses, dress uniforms, china dinnerware and visiting senators like it'd done in the past.

The Army had changed in other ways. On the forced march north Private Butscher, whose very German presence no one in the almost-entirely-Irish regiment could explain, including Butscher, had drawn Hugh aside.

"This Lee, once again, he comes north, like before, ja?"

"Ja," Hugh had agreed, with a bit of a smile.

"This is quite enough," Butscher said firmly. "Once before, he tries, back at Antietam, and we send him home all bloody. You think he learn from that. But he did not. Very well. Very well. Sometimes, when you are dealing with a real scheisskopf dummer, you have to hurt him bad before he learns. Good. Very good. If that is what Mister Lee wants, that is what he shall have." He spat into the roadside weeds and marched on stolidly.

The biggest change, at least from Hugh's perspective, was the offer of a brevet commission when he and his father had returned to camp. Probably he would have been proffered an epaulette anyway, if he had survived long enough - the Army favored competent men who took life sometimes a bit too seriously. But Kerry's death had ensured the offer, just as his brother's dying had also guaranteed Hugh would accept. Hugh hadn't become a gloom-and-doom crier, but he kept more to himself after Antietam.

He spent more time making sure his messmates had everything they needed, both in camp and on the march. He'd lost the blind rage that burnt through him on the bridge, but there was a balance still due for Kerry, and always would be. Perhaps he would die in settling the account, but that was an acceptable price. He still meant what he'd told his father before Antietam that if necessary this cause was one worth dying for, even though he hoped with every breath to live through the war, agreeing with Kerry's dictum that something worth the dying was worth the living.

Hugh, neither slow nor impulsive, was a canny, crafty soldier, and his skills and caution had been noticed. He'd hesitated when Captain Gooley offered the promotion, considered all the ramifications, then soberly accepted. On the one hand, an officer, required to lead from the front, was more likely to die in battle. But on the other, a sufficiently cunning officer would never lead his men into that deathtrap if there was an open flank. Hugh knew he could

392

take better care of the soldiers in his charge than anyone else, and at least he'd had a few days to organize his company before the order came to march north.

The two armies had stumbled together yesterday, outside the farming town of Gettysburg. The battle grew like a cancer - cavalry stopped foot skirmishers, fell back as Rebel infantry came up, Union lines formed and the attack and counterattacks began. There'd been too many rebels, and once more the Union Army had broken - but the present was different from what had gone before. The retreat had been slow and stubborn, frequently broken by improvised counterattacks as brave as they were futile, and the beaten soldiers hadn't turned retreat into a route. Other divisions formed up and attacked through the defeated ruins of their brothers. But the rebels kept coming and coming. Both sides bled and died as if this were to be the war's Ragnarok.

By dusk the Federals had a ragged line on Cemetery Hill, south of Gettysburg. Ragged, but it held. For some reason neither Hugh nor anyone else could fathom, the South did not continue the assault. Perhaps because it was night, and neither Army fought comfortably after dark. Perhaps it was because Stonewall Jackson had been killed, and a bit of the fire had gone out of the Southrons. No one knew, but everyone thanked their gods they would have time to regroup.

The 86th Pennsylvania was especially grateful, since they didn't arrive at Gettysburg until nearly nine, and its stragglers from the long hot march took the rest of the night to find their companies. Colonel Dennigan had gone back to division headquarters, and returned, grim but not displeased with what he'd heard. General Meade was on the battlefield and had taken personal charge. The order for the next day was not to retreat, nor to attack. Meade evidently liked this ground well enough to fight from it. Let General Lee come to him. The engineer now saw the problem clearly, just in front of him, and would methodically solve it.

Hugh, fully awake, grunted, and pulled himself to his feet, clenching his teeth as his sore muscles - everyone in his body - shrieked at having to do something so soon. There was a soldier five feet away, whistling merrily, and shaving in a tin basin set on the stretcher hung from the wagon's side.

"Mornin'," the man said cordially. "Want to fresh up? I'm 'bout finished here."

Hugh blinked - not because the soldier was casual about using the word "sir" - most of the Army of the Potomac didn't allow rank to get overly in the way of anything - but because he was behaving as if he were on some peacetime militia maneuver. Realizing he did have some sort of duty to look a bit soldierly, he used the man's metal mirror and only partially filthy water to wash. He even accepted the offer of the man's cut-throat, not having shaved for four days and seriously thinking about saying the hell with it and growing the bush.

Looking a little more like an officer than a vagrant, Hugh found his first sergeant, an Ulsterman named Ingram, and got a muster - forty three men of D Company present, two sick, one malingering, and the bastard would soon be regretting it, only three still unaccounted for from the march. Hugh felt some pride - that was a hell of a lot better than most units would be reporting, not bad at all since he was currently the only officer Company D had.

Sergeant Ingram had already arranged to acquire breakfast for the company from three devout pigs who'd wandered into the lines wishing to be martyred, and would the lieutenant like a bacon sandwich? And fresh bread. That artillery unit over there brought their baker and oven with them. Lieutenant Shannon would indeed.

Time passed. There was the constant clatter and roar of gunfire to their front, just over the hills, and dispatch riders pelted down the roads, dust boiling in their wake. Long columns of soldiers went down those country lanes, the only thing clean about them the gleam of their muskets and the shine of their bayonets. No one in the 86th objected to being ignored - most everybody felt the call would come sooner or later, and if it didn't, hell, they'd done their share of war-winning and deserved a breather.

Around noon a story came around. True, happened not more'n an hour before. Some general or other had decided to scout the lines. He'd asked for only one orderly to accompany him, and the orderly that came forward turned out to be a rogue from either Cork or

Tipperary, depending on the tale-teller; in any event, given the way he talked, the orderly was certainly from the West. The general asked the Taidh if he was brave, and the man grinned saucily. The general by the Lord demanded a response, and the private had scratched, and then said, "Gin'ral, if you'll be goin' forward, an' gettin' y'r arse shot off, an' endin' in hell, it'll not be an instant before I'm tappin' on the window m'self."

Hugh was thinking about being hungry again when the shouting began. Sergeants bellowed men to form up, and the hell with your coffee on the boil - no breadbags, no knapsacks, no blankets, just canteens and cartridge boxes, officers shouted at the sergeants, other officers shouted at everyone and no one, and eventually the 86th Pennsylvania was in formation, almost three hundred and fifty strong. The regiment should have had nearly six hundred men on the rolls, but replacements always ran behind the casualty lists. Its strength, until a new draft had arrived only a week earlier, had been only two hundred men.

Colonel Dennigan snapped orders. Somebody had noted there was a big hole near the left of the Union lines that was an open invitation for the Confederates. At the double, no time to worry about whether your canteen's full, no time to worry about rations, just make damned sure you have the "forty dead men" in your cartridge box and sufficient percussion caps. The 86th went out of the field and down the dusty lane toward battle.

Cannon shells lofted dirt high to the right and left, and Hugh saw new men flinching. He, Sergeant Ingram and the other noncoms chanted reassurance: Can't hurt you if you see it go off... they're blind as brickbats... faster we get where we're going the quicker we can start putting up breastworks. Musketballs spat overhead. They were very close now.

The rolling countryside had grown rougher, unlogged. Some of the men felt a thrill of fear as they realized there was nothing at all between their right and the entire Confederate army, over there, out of sight under the haze of dust and gunsmoke. Now there were corpses, and the stunned wounded, and men stammering back, and a gasp became a cheer as the 86th saw a great column of gray-clad

Allan Cole & Chris Bunch

men come across the fields and realized the Rebs were all prisoners, guarded by a handful of Yanks.

"Well I'll be dipped in shit," came a voice from the ranks. "I'll not be believin' we're winnin', f'r once."

There was laughter, chopped suddenly as men in blue burst from the woods around the hill nearby, men running away, and a groan of anger and pain went through the regiment. Down the lane galloped a long-bearded man, a general, whose name Hugh did not know.

He pulled his horse up by Colonel Dennigan's. "Colonel! The Rebs have driven us back. I want your regiment up that hill. We must hold this line!" Dennigan began to protest - he'd been given other orders. The general cut through. "Sir, I take full responsibility. Get up that hill, and hold it firm!"

Dennigan, who'd never hesitated to march toward the guns, did not falter. "You heard him," he shouted. "I want a few licks in for Pennsylvania! Forward!"

And the 86th obeyed.

They crested the hill whose name no one knew as Confederate skirmishers came up the other side, and behind them three solid lines of infantry. The 86th Pennsylvania, not in battle line, bayonets unfixed, no orders given, charged. Soldiers smashed together, without tactics, without plan, but without mercy.

Hugh was shouting at the top of his lungs, waving the saber Gooley had given him in one hand, revolver in the other. And out of the gunsmoke there was a long bayonet coming at his chest and Hugh shot the Reb down, and cut at another one, and he saw someone aiming at him from far, too far, and another pistol sounded nearly beside his head, and the rifleman gave a shout and fell back.

There was another Rebel firing at someone, not looking at Hugh, and Hugh snap-shot, weapon clicked on a fired cap, empty, he not remembering shooting but once, and he hurled the heavy pistol against the Confederate's skull and he was down. The fight swirled around trees, over stumps, across boulders, through brush, men sometimes shooting, sometimes stabbing, sometimes fighting with clubbed muskets, knives or fists.

Smoke cleared, and Hugh spotted one of his men, new, and dammit I should know his name, the way this day is going I shall be writing his family this night, and he stopped, fascinated. The man was methodically loading his musket as if he were a drill demonstrator on a range. He readied a cartridge, loaded it down the muzzle, rammed it home, capped the musket's nipple, cocked the piece, and aimed. Then he lowered the musket from his shoulder, and began reloading. At no time did he pull the trigger. It wouldn't be long before the musket exploded in his hands.

The smoke obscured, and when it blew away, Hugh did not see him. Men were shouting, and the 86th was falling back, and he dimly heard Dennigan yelling and just before they went all the way back down the hill like that other regiment everyone was screaming, Hugh louder than the rest, and once more they charged.

Again the Confederates sent them reeling, and there were more shouts - "Dennigan's hit! He's down," and Hugh saw Major Ardiff next to the colors, bellowing for the charge and the 86th obeyed, staggering forward over the bodies of their own and the Rebel dead and wounded. He saw no more of Ardiff, and now it was Captain Gooley screaming orders. Gooley was in front of the line, now an irregular weave of Yankees, but they were still attacking. Hugh heard cannonblast from beside him, glanced over, and somehow, someone had wrestled a battery of small guns to the crest of this hill, and he turned back in time to see a Confederate rise from behind a rock, and shoot Captain Gooley down before being bayonetted.

There were four men beside their fallen Captain, bending to carry him back out of the fray and musket fire volleyed and the four went down as well.

Someone was yelling in Hugh's ear: "Sir! Sir! You've got the regiment!"

Hugh nodded automatically and now it was his turn to shout the charge. Yet again, the 86th obeyed, and this time the Confederates broke, turning, walking, then running, throwing their muskets away, running as far as they could from the carnage. Hugh and Sergeant Ingram, who was bleeding but still fighting, were crying for the regiment to stop, to hold, don't follow them, and reluctantly, like

Allan Cole & Chris Bunch

hounds pulled back just as the rabbit breaks cover, the 86th quivered to a halt.

Hugh stood panting, allowing himself one moment's breath. His sleeve was blood-soaked, but it was other men's blood, he realized, looking at his gore-streaked saber. He recovered his wits, the realization he'd gone from company officer to Regimental commander within a few minutes slowly sinking through. Now he must consolidate the hilltop against the inevitable counterattack with whatever remained of the regiment. It was still smoky, but he saw blue uniforms here and there. There were not many of them. But there'd been enough, he thought. The small cannon were still firing.

His hearing was starting to return. Sergeant Ingram was shouting for the men to drag up wood for fortifications, and to send for stretcher-bearers and surgeons. Other men - privates all - were also giving commands - practical, live-saving ones. Butscher was one, and Hugh noted, actually able to feel some amusement, he seemed to have completely forgotten his English if not his volume.

Hugh saw a horse climbing slowly up the hill, ridden by that general, whatever his name was. He saw Hugh next to the regimental standard, still on its staff if shot-riddled, and the standard-bearer leaning on it for support, blood seeping down one leg, and made his way over.

"You are now in command of the regiment, sir?"

"I suppose." Hugh started to salute, realized he still held the saber but was too tired to change hands. "Lieutenant Shannon, sir. Company D."

"A brave fight, sir," the general said. "And a close-run one as well. I would wager you have but..." and his eyes swept the hilltop, "... a hundred, perhaps a few more, men still able to fight. I saw that last charge you ordered, sir, from just below the top of the hill. Most brave, most brave. I would, if not being rude, ask what you would have done if it had been repulsed as were the others?"

Hugh took a minute to think. When he answered, it was no more than the truth. "Why, sir, we would have attacked once more. You gave us our orders."

...The battle roared on all that day, and again groaned to a stop when night fell. Once more, the North stubbornly held, as did the

Allan Cole & Chris Bunch

South. Men did what they could for food, for water, and for the wounded, for the dying. There was not much that could be done until the matter was settled. And everyone on the field knew there could be but one more day of this savagery.

The Confederate line was lit at dawn, not by sunlight, but cannon fire. It appeared to Ian the Confederates must have their guns drawn up wheel to wheel along their entire front. The ridge that was named after a Seminary was lined in white and gray, with red flaming through, and then there would come the scream of incoming shells, their blast and, as often as not, the echoing screams of horses and men. Smoke like an evening fog came down from that hill across the valley between the two armies, and Ian had a memory of someone - Michael it was, calling something or other out in California the Valley of Smokes.

At least, he thought grimly, no one in his battery was worried about being flanked by Confederates. The guns were in the very center of the Union line, and First Sergeant Dolan would have traded every bit of that supposed security for one minute's lifting of the barrage. It looked as if every gun over there was shooting counterbattery fire directly at the 2nd Pennsylvania Light. And most of it seemed to be striking home around Battery H. One gun had already been blown off its carriage, and one sat uselessly after its entire crew had been cut down. At least one of his caissons had exploded, and a limber lay shattered nearby.

Ian wasn't sure where the steady stream of ammunition bearers were getting their shot and powder from. He was not even sure who was serving the guns. The battery's blacksmiths, buglers, wagonmasters and saddler were out there, and just as at Antietam, infantrymen and even some rear-rank file closers had come out of nowhere to help as best they could.

Ian had no idea where the battery's officers were - if they had been killed, wounded or translated directly into Heaven. Nor did he care - it was his goddamned battery now, and his goddamned war and the commands came automatically, and were just as automatically obeyed by the gunners, none of whom could hear Ian's screamed orders any more than he really heard instead of felt the blast of shells exploding around him.

Half of the battery's horses had been hit, and Ian no longer felt sorrow as he shot an animal with his revolver. Just minutes ago he'd ordered the few remaining horses taken off to some kind of safety, maybe to the back slope of this ridge correctly if chillingly named Cemetery. At least, Ian thought, humor most grim, they wouldn't be abandoning their guns if attacked, which regulars had said was the greatest sin an artilleryman could commit. Not unless they wanted to carry them away on their backs.

The commands went on, as he saw a man wave readiness: "Number One... Fire!" and his officer's sword slashed down, and the gun belched smoke... "Load"... another signal... "Number Three... Fire!..." By Heaven, he thought, it seems as if we're hurting them, and taking less fire or mayhap I'm getting used to it, how in the Lord's name can anyone get used to this... but nobody told First Sergeant Dolan to cease fire, so the square Irish automaton continued, and his equally mechanical artillerymen kept shooting and sometimes falling.

Someone had him by the elbow, damned if he knew who the man was, except that his teeth were gleaming through his powder-black face, the man was laughing, holding his mouth close to Ian's ear and shouting, and then was gone. It took a minute to decipher - something about the Confederates had made a terrible mistake and changed their point of aim, and now all the cannon fire was going over the crest of the hill and landing in the midst of all those behind the line slackers.

Bandsmen and clerks and quartermasters and sutlers were dying, and honest men out here unharmed. Ian managed a grin - it wasn't right, but it surely was understandable, and yes, the cannon fire on their position was diminishing.

He chanced a look at the Confederate lines as the cannon smoke lifted, and his spine chilled on this burning July afternoon. From the trees and brush and rocks over there, down across the valley, came the lines of men, divisions and divisions of them. They were arrayed for a grand review, banners and standards neatly demarking each file, officers holding their swords up as fuglemen. They came at the

Allan Cole & Chris Bunch

walk, bayonets shining, and their lines stretched out of sight. There were... Ian had no idea how many... thousands, for certain. Lee must have gone insane, and ordered his entire army into the attack, against massed cannons firing across open ground, in a last futile grasp for victory.

He heard them above the cannons and the musket-raps and the screams of dying horses and men. This was not the keening Rebel yell. These men were roaring, in a great single voice like the gray winter seas off Kinsale Head from Ian's boyhood or the storms he'd seen in winter crash against Cape May. But they were not the sea, not the storm, but only men, and already he saw tiny figures spin and fall as the rifled guns found the range. This was the end. This was the madness. Ian, seeing those solid lines, not hurrying, not slowing, bayonets like dancing sparks, moving inexorably toward him, felt no fear, just a great pity. Ah, the poor bastards, he thought. The poor, sad, weary bastards.

He turned to the battery. "All guns!... Load triple canister!... Full depression!... Fire!"

The 13th California Volunteer Cavalry sat on a hilltop three miles away from the crashing finale to the battle. But they weren't being held out of battle without reason, and none of them, including Michael Shannon, felt the impotence and blind rage of Antietam. Things had changed as much for the Cavalry as for the rest of the Army of the Potomac. Now they were doing one of the cavalry's intended tasks, keeping the right flank of Meade's army from being surprised by a Confederate attack. Not that anyone believed there was one grayback available for anything beyond the main battle area - but there had been surprises before. Michael personally hoped there would be a surprise this day - but for the Confederacy.

Two weeks earlier, George Armstrong Custer, he of the flowing dirty blonde locks and overweening ambition, had been promoted brigadier general and specifically asked for Michael's regiment for his brigade. Michael had no idea why - he was hardly friends with Custer, and wondered if he himself had been that big a pain in the ass when he was twenty four years old. Probably, he decided, but at least he'd never been a gloryhound, someone who would definitely

Allan Cole & Chris Bunch

not live out this war and probably take half his command with him. Perhaps, Michael thought, he chose us because he's truly feeling immortal and is making plans for post-war investments in San Francisco real estate. Or maybe he thinks Californios add to his glamour, like Jeb Stuart likes twittering Southern belles. Not that Custer's reasons were worth worrying about, since the transfer got the Californians under the direct command of General Gregg, who may have looked like an Old Testament prophet but was a deadly fighter.

Nowadays the cavalry wasn't pieced-out here and there as bodyguards and provosts and river-crossing lifeguards and dispatch riders any longer. Instead of a single division, there was now a Corps, with their own infantry and artillery, under the overall command of Old Lady Pleasanton, who surprisingly was a bit more aggressive than he'd been running a single division. The Corps was now fought the way Lee used Stuart, either as pinprick raiders or as fast-moving shock troops, committed in force rather than piece-meal or not at all. They were still used to ride guard on the lines of communication and railways - but mobile, not as infantrymen walking their posts with horses tethered nearby.

There was a price. The joke Michael heard at Antietam about no one ever having seen a dead cavalryman wasn't heard any more. The yellow-legs had left their dead scattered across Virginia and Maryland in a hundred savage skirmishes and even some battles. Brandy Station, even though it'd been technically a defeat for the North, marked the turning point. The Union Cavalry had crossed the Rappahannock River trying to find out what was on Bobbie Lee's mind, but not minding the idea of locking horns with Jeb Stuart at all. They found him, and played a murderous game of King of the Mountain in charge after charge. At day's end, the Union forces were forced to retreat - but Stuart's cavalry had been unable to pursue.

For the first time the Union horsemen had fought on Stuart's ground, by Stuart's rules, and left the South staggering. Jeb Stuart claimed victory - but had to move his tents off Fleetwood Heights. There were too many bodies wearing gray scattered around to let him sleep comfortably.

That was once. And there might be a repeat engagement this day, Michael thought suddenly. Down below him was a thin line of cavalry spread out across the field. Michael spotted an outrider galloping back in one hell of a hurry. He looked down a country lane and saw clouds of dust boiling. So there were some spare Secesh around. Michael thought a minute, and made a bit of sense out of what appeared to be the South's strategy to still win the battle of Gettysburg. Lee was bashing hell out of the Union center, or trying to, and had sent the cavalry to turn the flank, figuring it would be unguarded as it had been so many times in the past, and then rip hell out of the bluebellies when his main assault broke through.

Not bad, General Lee, Michael thought. But you can't play odd without occasionally varying it to evens once in awhile. Even us dumb Yankees get the idea once in awhile, and sure as hell there's never been an engineer ignore something as basic as securing the wings of your formation. Michael thought Meade probably sent out flankers every time he dropped his drawers and squatted. Come on, you Secesh heroes. Dance right on in this nice cave and meet Senor Tigre, and we'll see who's really smiling.

"Major McCorkle," Michael drawled casually. "You might want to wake the boys up. Life might get a bit interesting in un poquito." McCorkle saluted, and the orders went down the line...

"...The Thirteenth is ready, sir."

"Very fine, Mac. Now we'll see if we get our Beau Sabreur today. You think he'll be warbling Kathleen Mavourneen as he comes?"

It was a legend when Jeb Stuart rode to battle he and his aide, a banjo-playing minstrel who'd been stranded in Richmond before the war, would sing, and the ranks would join in the chorus: "Kathleen, Mavourneen, the gray dawn is breaking/The horn of the hunter is heard on the hill..."

Stuart just might hear another horn this day, or maybe find out who was hunter, who was prey. The thin line out there, maybe a hundred men or so that blocked the Hanover road, was a deception. There were more than five thousand cavalrymen up here in the woodland, the hidden mailed fist.

Allan Cole & Chris Bunch

"Don't get impatient, companeros," Michael called. "We'll let the stew bubble awhile before we jump in."

He paid no attention to the grumbles. His people would do as they told - or get transferred to Company Q, which was Michael's purgatorio: cavalry denied their horses until comprehension dawned.

Down below, the battle built. Michael watched closely. Over there - where the flags were - would be Stuart and his staff. The man was not a total fool. The thin line of skirmishers looked too good, and so he dismounted a battalion, and sent them forward on foot. The Union horsemen fell back, as ordered. Musketfire shattered from the woodline, as the infantrymen in front of the waiting horsemen opened up.

"Don't be firing, gentlemen. Keep your powder for when you'll need it."

Michael followed his own orders, and checked the loads on his two revolvers. He wished he could carry a cut-off shotgun, but leadership had its requirements, and a double took too long to reload when his other arm would be all tied up waving a silly saber for people to rally around.

"Colonel?"Michael turned his attention to the front. A wall of horsemen came rolling over the hill, onto the field. Now Stuart's forces were committed, and he'd play hell disengaging them."Thank you, Major."

Michael was about to issue orders, when he heard a grand halloo down the ranks, and a strange-looking rider galloped past. He wore a black velvet jacket with gold braid, black hat and black velvet pants with a gold stripe. Custer, of course, who was proud of his getup, saying he wanted his men to recognize him in the field. The general was shrieking at his Michigan Wolverines and they spurred after him.

"Draw sabers," Michael shouted, a little unnecessarily since those who'd chosen to keep the unwieldy chunks of steel already held them ready. "Trot!" The 13th came out of the gloom into the sunlight, men and horses blinking at the glare. "Gallop!" And: "Charge! Come on, boys!"

Two inexorable forces... the two columns slammed together in a shockwave. Michael saw horses spin through the air, end over end,

404

other horses pulling away, trying to leap downed animals, and the melee began, a swirling, crashing battle, face to face, shots, yells, horses screaming agony, men impaling others as they themselves were stabbed to death, dazzling blades dulled by blood, some fool shouting for surrender.

Michael ducked a saber-cut, shot sideways, didn't know if he hit his assailant, cut at another rider, broke into the open and saw an officer in gray slash down a wounded Yank who'd dropped his sword and was reeling in the saddle, and shot the man off his horse. Another rider cut at him, and he parried, struck back, felt the blade slice home, and he pulled the saber free.

Now where's that sunnovabitch Stuart, I'd pay a pretty to get a shot at him, and someone shouted and he saw a rider in braid and gray jump his horse over a fence, trying to get away, and something hit the man and knocked him from his saddle, no, it couldn't be Stuart because his rollickers would have fallen apart but we sure as hell got somebody important.

Then they were pulling back, regrouping, and charging, and the Confederates were reforming and the two sides closed again, metal clashing like a huge open foundry under the scorching afternoon sun.

By nightfall it had ended. Stuart's cavalry had been driven from the field. It would take the Laughing Cavalier a great deal of imagination to convince the adulatory swarm of ladies that he'd carried the field this day. But there were too many empty saddles for anyone in blue to think about cheering or looking for champagne. Besides, they weren't through, yet.

The 13th had barely reassembled - and begun worrying about food, fodder, resupply, the minor wounds and hurts for man and horse and mourning or trying to forget their dead when Custer sent for Colonel Shannon. His orders were brief - put a scouting party out after dark, when you think the time is opportune. Detail your most reliable officer. General Meade has to know Lee's intent, and has to know it before dawn. Michael saluted, and withdrew. His entire body ached, and he dreamed of building and then falling into a horse trough filled to the brim with liniment. Hell, he wasn't a young dragoon any more.

Allan Cole & Chris Bunch

By rights he should have stayed in San Francisco and become a Cavalry Expert, holding forth from his club's bar on how the war should be fought, and how none of those young plowboys on horseback could hold a candle to a real Cavalryman like the ones back in St. George Cooke's day. But he'd been a damned fool, and jined once more, and now was stuck.

Just before midnight, Michael, two privates and one sergeant, all volunteers, rode toward the battlefield. There'd been a minor mutiny when Michael announced he was the reliable officer, and he had to suggest to Major McCorkle he'd get a pop alongside his head if he didn't shut up and take charge while his Colonel went a-riding.

Michael swung wide, through Gettysburg itself, before cutting back toward the battleground. The town had been ripped up badly, streets blocked with furniture, wagons or logs. The tidy brick buildings were pocked with holes from cannon balls and musketballs. There'd been some looting, Michael noted, seeing scattered clothes and broken bottles in the street. But not much. Nobody'd had that sort of free time over the last three days.

On the town's outskirts was a barn, and Michael heard the screaming before he reached it. Lamplight gleamed, from the barn's gaping doors. He glanced inside as they passed, then quickly away, having seen more than enough of the busy, bloodsoaked surgeons and orderlies and gore solidly painting the barn's wooden floor.

There were soldiers about, but no one seemed interested in fighting any more, with one exception. Michael encountered an old, fiercely-bearded and -tempered Pennsylvania Dutch farmer, herding five scared boys in tattered gray with a pitchfork. Caught them in his corn, trampling it, ja, just like the others in their Kompanie had but this time their guns they did not have, and would the Herr Offizer want them shooted?

Michael's sergeant directed the farmer to take his charges to an assembly area, and warned him all five had better arrive safely, or else... and they rode on, amid babbled assurances that the farmer was not ein Morder, not like these Rebels, ja, ein gute American.

They went into the valley Lee had sent Pickett's and Heth's and Pender's divisions across. They kept their horses at the walk, and stayed spread out. But no one challenged or fired on them. This was horror. This was beyond nightmare, beyond Goya's worst etchings. There were bodies scattered. There were bodies on line, platoons and perhaps companies who lay drawn up for some bizarre prone inspection, dead where volleyed musketfire or canister had taken them. Here was a regimental standard, buried in the blood-soaked ground, abandoned when its bearer fled or was killed, and not recovered. Perhaps, Michael thought, there was no one left alive in that regiment to recover it. There were bodies and parts of bodies, ripped apart and flung away. There were four horses dead in their traces, still harnessed to the riddled caisson they'd drawn that somehow had not exploded.

At least the dead were silent. The battlefield was not. They rode past a horse whose guts trailed, whose screams had died to a whimpering whistle. A private half-drew his pistol, but Michael shook his head. They could not chance mercy's noise. It was not just horses, but men. Groaning. Shouting. A dark lump beside Michael dully repeated a prayer that had gone unanswered for hours and would never be answered. A plea from the darkness - "Mister, whoever y'all are, f'r the love of Jesus... kill me, Mister..."

They rode on, up Seminary Ridge. Michael cursed as he saw, looming out of the blackness, a Confederate outpost. Three men were there, muskets ready. They looked at the Yankee cavalrymen, and Shannon's men looked back. No one lifted a weapon. After awhile, Michael tapped his horse's neck with his reins, and they rode past.

There was light now, light from fires, from torches, from lanterns. A mist crept low over the ground, but never grew heavy enough to be a merciful shroud. Men moved through it as if sleep walking. Men who'd lost their friends, lost their regiments, lost everything except their lives. One man, stark naked, wandered by, still carrying an ornate sword in his hand. Michael thought he could see his eyes gleam in the darkness.

Sound drew them, a low murmur that became groans that became screams, and they pulled up and dismounted in a small copse overlooking a glen. In and around it were surgeon's tents and wagons. The ground was covered with wounded, dying or dead men. Michael could have walked through the entire clearing without touching the ground. The arena was a horrible assembly line. Orderlies would bring men, sometimes shouting in agony, sometimes still, out of the tents or just lifted up from where they lay, and load them into a wagon until it could hold no more. The wagonmaster would gee his team, and the wagon would disappear into darkness.

Another wagon would pull up and be filled, and then another and another. Michael, who'd seen oceans of blood and never showed signs of bother, was violently sick. He finished retching, and his sergeant handed him an uncorked canteen. The man's face was dead white in the firelight from the clearing station below. Michael rinsed his mouth with the whiskey, spat, rinsed once more and gave the canteen back. He could have drained the entire vessel without it affecting him.

He motioned, and they remounted and turned their horses back toward their own lines. Meade would have his answer. Lee might hold position after the sun came up, but only to allow the ambulances a clear start on their via doloroso back to Virginia.

The battle was over. No army, not even the Army of Northern Virginia, could fight on the morrow after paying this day's butcher's bill.

Michael knew, without finding rationale for his thinking, Lee would never come north again.

The wolf had gotten his death wound today. Now all that remained was for his hunters to keep themselves alive and fighting until the brute drowned in his own blood.

Allan Cole & Chris Bunch

CHAPTER THIRTY

VICKSBURG, MISS. - JULY 4, 1863

IT WAS NOT long after midnight when Patrick forced himself out of Lucy's arms and went out through the streets of Vicksburg. It was deathly silent, and Patrick remembered his anguished hopes for quiet just a few weeks ago. But this was the silence of death, not tranquility.

Independence Day it was now, and Patrick was sure it would be deliriously celebrated in the north. But not in Mississippi. Maybe not ever more. In a few hours, General John C. Pemberton would surrender Vicksburg to the Army of the United States of America under General U.S. Grant. The -"Gibraltar of America" would cease to threaten, and the Mississippi would become a Union highway, splitting the South in two.

There was still one Confederate fort downriver from Vicksburg, but that could not hold for more than a day or so. There would be no more pork or beef or flour or salt coming into the Confederacy from Texas, and worse yet no more of the hard-faced men of the frontier who if they couldn't kill a Mexican would settle for a Yankee. Finally, the last link to Europe was cut off. The South was being strangled, slowly, not by a thug's silken cord but by the iron of the Union Navy's blockade at sea and now the steel of the Army's bayonets.

Word flashed through Vicksburg the previous day that a flag of truce had been raised, and Pemberton went through the lines to confer with Grant. The rumor engine went full throttle, and there were instant tales Pemberton was a coward, was secretly in league with the North, or even that he had taken gold to throw open the gates of the city. Patrick knew better. The battle had been lost weeks ago. He'd seen children's bellies starting to bulge from hunger, just as he'd seen them in poor barrios in Texas. The soldiers were hollow-cheeked and empty-eyed, and some regiments were only able to issue the horrible peaflour once a week. There was no corn, no meat, no rice, not even for the hoarders. Lucy had said nursing women were coming to the hospital, asking why their milk was drying up.

Vicksburg had not fallen by storm, was still able to repel attacks. The city could hold out for a few more days or possibly even weeks. But what ultimate good would that do? People would soon start dying, not of shot, shell or disease - but starvation. Fighting to the last bullet might not sound noble, but not when the fate of a baby might depend on stopping the meaningless slaughter.

There was no relief, no rescuing army on the horizon. Even the wildest optimists now knew that. Pemberton could hold in the trenches if he wished, but the cold-eyed Grant would hurl attack after frontal attack at them, and eventually breach the line. Enough people had died in and outside Vicksburg. Everyone said there would be a general surrender tomorrow, most likely by noon.

Patrick Shannon, for the most confused of reasons, would not be present when the barred starry flag came down for the white one, the arms were stacked and the regimental banners burnt. He'd known he would not give up as soon as he realized the city was about to fall. There would be three options, he tried to explain to Lucy. The first was captivity. He'd heard about the prison camps up north. The fevers, neglect and brutality killed Rebels as fast as Union grapeshot. He'd already come close enough to death by fever. Lucy had mentioned parole. Patrick shook his head - there was never any guarantee a prisoner would be paroled, especially if he wasn't an officer. He could not afford the chance.

The second option, and Lucy had brought this up, without looking at Patrick, was, well, if they burnt Patrick's uniform, maybe no one would know, and said he had always been an invalid and...

"Desert?" Patrick forced gentleness. "No."

Lucy managed a forlorn smile, and said she hadn't known Patrick Believed in the Cause that much. Patrick felt a surge of admiration - there were women, he knew, who could send a lover out to certain death glorying in their "patriotism." He started to lie - it would have been simpler - but caught himself. Not to Lucy.

He tried to explain, and completely confused not only his wife, but himself as well. Yes, he'd sort of been forced into service by circumstances, and no, he wasn't exactly a rabid believer in state's rights and surely not in slavery nor secession, but he'd given his word, even though a court would probably say it was given under

410

some sort of duress. No, he didn't like killing, and he certainly was scared a lot of the time, but he felt a strange sort of still-owed debt to the men still in gray or butternut. Men like Billy and his other his messmates, even though he didn't know if any of them were still alive, nor how the hell his carrying on the war might help them he had not the foggiest.

"I don't understand," Lucy said. "Maybe you had best talk to Father."

Patrick shook his head - this was what he was going to do, and it was probably pretty damn-foolish and could well get him killed. But logic and reason, if that's what they were, need not apply to the Shannon brain at that moment.

Lucy had started to get angry, then started to cry, and then fought control. "What will you do?" she asked, a strange note of calmness in her voice.

Patrick explained. As soon as he'd realized he would not surrender a plan had come to him. It wasn't very good, but it seemed that it would work. He figured the truce would last until the surrender, and most likely the Union pickets would be a little relaxed. He would slip through the lines and head north-east, and maybe start looking for Bedford Forrest or anyway the Confederate Army.

What about later, Lucy wanted to know. When would they see each other? Patrick shook his head, not knowing. It could be as long as when the war's over. Maybe, she said, maybe when... and she stumbled over saying it... when Vicksburg surrenders, I can come through the lines and—

Patrick cut that one off short. No. He'd be serving again, and it was more dangerous for the few civilians, whether camp followers or wives, who chanced trying to follow the army than for the soldiers themselves. He could hardly afford to find quarters for her, not knowing where the hell the Army might send him. It was best if she stayed with the family. The war would sweep past, and they'd be safe. The Yankees weren't monsters, weren't Huns or Tartars, and there'd be some kind of Federal army administration with orders to get things back to normal.

Allan Cole & Chris Bunch

Lucy reluctantly agreed. After all, she said, at least she'd gotten to see him and... and all the rest. Her friend Adela had gone and gotten engaged to her beau, and they'd done, well, just what she and Patrick had before he went off, and all she ever got was letters now. So, if Patrick was determined, and she was very certain she would never understand men, she wanted to know what he would need in the way of supplies - there were still some emergency foodstuffs in the cave, and certainly the Baldwins would willingly part with them.

Patrick would take only a small knapsack, soap, a toothbrush, some corn bread and bacon well-wrapped, and his pistols, plus powder, caps, and bullets. First he had to snake through the lines, and someone staggering along under a Yankee peddler's pack wouldn't get far. Lucy thought maybe he should wear civilian clothes for fear of the Union cavalrymen patrolling behind the Yankee positions. Patrick instantly refused - anyone caught by the Yanks who was armed and out of uniform would be either hanged as a guerrilla or partisan or shot as a spy. Then he rethought. On consideration, he would take civilian clothes, rolled in his pack. Once through the lines, he could change clothes and pretend to be either a deserter or a noncombatant, if necessary getting rid of his pistols if he thought them a hazard. That would still another role he could choose to play.

"When will you go?"

"Tonight," Patrick said. "After midnight, just before they'll change their guard." He started to get up, to ready his gear for travel.

"No," Lucy said. "My sisters can get your clothes and things ready."

As she spoke, her fingers were untying the string that held the top of her blouse up. She let it fall, and undid the buttons of her skirt. She did not need to say more, and they fell together in savage hunger, a hunger as fierce as the one that had consumed them eons ago, in a sickroom under cannonfire. Again and again they coupled frantically, bodies twisting, squirming, pounding, trying to meld, trying to become one, trying to force all memories into the few hours of daylight and early night, trying to stop the sun itself in its course and never cause the rising of the moon.

Some hours later Patrick washed, and pulled on his clothes. His knapsack lay outside their cave, already packed. He checked its contents, then loaded and primed both pistols. One went inside the top of his pack, the other in his belt - he did not need the added weight of holsters to bear him down.

The Baldwins were nearby in a forlorn group. Lucy's sisters were crying, as was Mrs. Baldwin. Mr. Baldwin started to say something, then just handed Patrick a small pouch. By feel Patrick could tell it held coins, gold most likely. He started to protest, but caught himself. He nodded his thanks.

Lucy was in front of him. Once more, words were lacking, and maybe they hadn't been coined. "I love you," was the best he could manage. Lucy held him very tightly, and he could feel her jaw working against his shoulder. She stepped back. Patrick turned and went down the street as fast as he could walk. He could not let himself look back.

The streets of Vicksburg weren't as deserted as usual. There were a scattering of uniformed and civilian drunks, but they were quiet in their befuddlement. Other men in uniform were quite sober, and moved swiftly, intent on private purpose. Two men passed, and he heard them muttering something about finding a skiff at the waterfront and floating downstream, trying for Port Hudson. He wished them Godspeed.

He left the ruined outskirts of the city, and came upon the trenches. There were guards posted, but Patrick went unchallenged. He must not be the only one who'd determined to fight on, or anyway to not fall into the hands of the Union.

Beyond the last trench, Patrick moved close to the bluffs and the river. He inched his way across the barrenness between the lines, then found his way across the Union trenches. Christ, he thought, marveling at all the cannon, and all the guns and supplies. How the hell did we hold out this long, against all this? He intended to follow the brushy maze of ravines north, until he was well beyond the Yankee rear echelons before striking inland.

He moved slowly, carefully, feeling the night and the silence as if he were a mouse caught out from his burrow - a mouse who knew overhead were the great silent hunting wings of an owl. He never took a step without knowing what his foot would land on, never went down the side of a ravine without first being certain he could slither up its far side, and that no armed man lurked, waiting.

It took him two hours or more to move less than half a mile. He was just starting to feel a bit of confidence, that perhaps, just like his great grandfather, Emmett Shannon, he would make good his escape, when a soft voice came from behind.

"Johnny Reb, best you freeze like you was an icicle." The voice was very calm. "That's right. That's good. Now, I want to see both your hands come up, real slow, fingers spread, headin' straight for the clouds. If your paws come up holdin' anything whatsoever there's fixing to be a real loud noise in your right short future."

Patrick did as ordered, very slowly.

"Congratulations, Secesh. Your war just come to an end."

Part Four

With its cloud of skirmishers in advance,
With now the sound of a single shot snapping like a whip,
And now an irregular volley,
The swarming ranks press on and on, the dense brigades
press on,
Glittering dimly, toiling under the sun- the dust-cover'd
men,
In columns rise and fall to the undulations of the ground,
With artillery interspers'd- the wheels rumble, the horses
sweat,
As the army corps advances.
- Any Army Corps On The March – Walt Whitman

"Civil War?" What does that mean? Is there any foreign
war? Isn't every war fought between men, between
brothers? *- Victor Hugo*

CHAPTER THIRTY-ONE

NEW YORK - JULY 11-16, 1863

THOMAS SHANNON RYAN strolled along the sunny side of Broadway, twirling his cane and humming a merry show tune. He tipped his hat to the ladies and exchanged winks with the swells; but all the while his eyes darted here and there looking for a chance to change his luck. It was a sweet day for fortune: a fresh breeze swept away the city's damp, barnyard smell; and down an alley he could hear tinkling music and soaring voices coming from a rehearsal hall.

He was resplendent in his dove gray suit; his hair and mustache neatly clipped by the little dancer he'd been bedding these past few months. Thomas caught a girl staring as she went by on a streetcar. She was clutching a pair of roller skates - obviously bound for the new rink uptown. Thomas smiled and she blushed and turned her head; but he could see the ghost of a returned smile on her lips and almost hopped aboard for a bit of a flirt now and who knows what later. He decided to pass up the opportunity: it was not a lack of female companionship he was suffering, but a chronic shortage of the means to keep his wallet fat.

Thomas paused to glance at the scrap of paper in his hand: the address was 444 Broadway, the site of Tony Pastor's new variety theater. It was here he was to meet his mark, a scion of New York society who'd been sniffing after Thomas's sweet little dancer and been caught in Thomas's badger trap.

He'd arranged to catch the fellow struggling to get Sheila's dress up, then played the old outraged husband game. After a minor beating and an hour of friendly threats, the scion had agreed on a reasonable price to soothe Thomas's wounded pride. The man did not have the required sum on him, so a meeting had been set for Saturday at noon, outside Tony Pastor's place. The theater had been chosen because, the man said, it was near his home.

A block or so later, Thomas found the theater and took position beneath the posters advertising the evening's fare, which seemed to consist of the usual assortment of patriotic singers, dancers, jugglers, comics and prestidigitators. He noted with casual interest, however, Mr. Pastor seemed intent on convincing the public his show was uniquely different from the racier amusements that were scandalizing the city. Elaborate posters hailed: ENTERTAINMENT FOR THE ENTIRE FAMILY... LADIES ESPECIALLY WELCOME... FREE KITCHENWARE... DRESS PATTERNS... DOOR PRIZES FOR EVERY LADY WHO ATTENDS!

Thomas pulled his watch from his vest pocket to check the time: it was just coming up noon.

"Well, if it ain't me old chum, Thomas Ryan," came a voice. Thomas looked up to see a mountain of a man, dressed in an expensive, tight-fitting suit. His thick fingers were covered with big-stoned rings; a fat diamond pin locked his collar around a massive neck that rose into a triple-tiered chin; and above those chins was a broad, ruddy ham of a face, nose clubbed flat and a permanent grin, thanks to a knife scar clipping one corner of his mouth.

Thomas nodded. "Good to see you, Tim." Of course, he was lying through his teeth: Big Tim Carey was important in these parts; and even if he did owe Thomas a favor, it was unlikely Carey just happened to be strolling by 444 Broadway at Saturday, noon.

Big Tim turned to the two plug uglies accompanying him. "Didn't I tell yer it was a good mornin' fer a walk, boys?" He inhaled deeply and drummed his chest. "Air fresh as a field of daisies, 'n th' chance to meet a pal to enjoy it with."

The men didn't say anything, but only mean-eyed Thomas. He slipped his hand in his pocket to finger the clasp knife. Big Tim would have no qualms about putting the boot into him, even with all that traffic rumbling down the street and the market crowd streaming past.

Big Tim saw the gesture and lifted the unsmiling corner of his lip, to display real humor. "Aw, yer needn't get yer collar hot, Thomas," he laughed. "I'm here to save yer, lad... not to cause yer any worry."

"I'm pleased as hell to hear that, Tim," Thomas said. "But what could cause me worry on such a lovely Saturday?"

Big Tim clapped him on the shoulder: it was a friendly blow, but heavy enough to numb the muscle in case Thomas decided to go for the knife. "Aw, we shouldn't be funnin' one another, chums like us," he said. "We both know yer supposed to meet a feller. 'N that feller ain't comin'... today, or any t'other day."

Thomas sighed. "I didn't know he was a friend of yours, Tim. He never said."

"Oh, he ain't rightly a friend a mine, exactly," Big Tim said. "A friend of a friend, is more like it. 'N if yer think on it, old Thomas, you'll see right off yer little business with that feller makes a real small pile a shit fer th' likes a me."

Thomas took his hand out of his pocket: he'd have to run; out of the corner of his eye, he saw the two plug uglies move closer, boxing him into the theater foyer. Shit and double shit!

"Ease off, lads," Big Tim barked, to Thomas's surprise. They stepped back. "See, it's like this," Big Tim resumed. "Yer sucker ran downtown to whine to th' boys at the Hall. 'N I heard they was comin' down to see yer, with some real unfriendly ideas in their knuckly heads. But I says: 'Hold on! That lad's 's fine an Irish boy ye'll ever meet. Saved me bacon, he did.' 'N when a feller sticks out his neck fer Tim Carey, why he's his friend for life."

Thomas laughed in huge relief. "So you came down to put me straight, instead?"

Big Tim nodded. "Least I could do." He shook his head. "Course, that little rich bastard wanted more'n a bit a thumpin' and a warnin' off. Set his fine, princely hat on - if you'll beg me pardon - fuckin' yer little Sheila to boot. But I put that bit a business out of his head."

"Thanks for speaking up for me, Tim," Thomas said, meaning it.

"Nothin' to thank," Big Tim replied. "Least I could do a'ter yer cracked that feller's head fer me down at the Bull Horn."

The "feller" Big Tim was referring to was the proprietor of the Bull Horn Hotel. A few weeks before he'd taken offense to Big Tim's entirely truthful charge that the whiskey was watered. He'd blindsided Tim with a gnarly club and was coming over the bar to finish him off, when Thomas stepped in and shattered a bottle over the innkeeper's head.

Big Tim gave Thomas another blow on the arm, but this one was lighter, friendly like. "Lookee here, lad, I feel bad that yer outter pocket on my account," he said. "Suckers is hard to come by, these days."

"I'll manage," Thomas said.

Allan Cole & Chris Bunch

"Sure you will," Big Tim said. "A smart lad like yerself always ends up on th' top of th' pile. But how about if I grease th' mill for yer? Why'nt you come with me, and meet some of th' lads?"

This was the chance Thomas had been looking for since he came to New York. Despite all his efforts the Tammany crowd had remained cool to him, and he'd been forced to make his living on their leavings.

"Where you headed?" Thomas asked.

"Over to Third and 46th," Big Tim said. "There's a to do at th' draft office. Drawin' names to feed the war with our boys, they are. Maybe we can find yer a better sucker to skin."

With dollar signs chorusing in his head, Thomas heartily agreed. A few minutes later they boarded a street car at 14th Street and were headed up town.

"There's a lot of hard feelin' 'bout this draft business," Big Tim said after they had rousted a few people from some prize seats. "They're hittin' us real hard this go 'round. Thirty thousand men, is what th' government wants from th' town. 'N I don't have to tell yer that lads like that shit who was a'ter yer Sheila ain't gonna be th' ones to go."

Thomas immediately raised his mental price. By law, a rich young man could buy his way out of the draft by paying someone else $300 to take his place. But if the quota was 30,000 draftees, Thomas figured he could demand at least $600, and maybe more; and with so much confusion sure to surround the lottery, he could make the same deal six or seven times without anyone being the wiser. Then he had another thought.

The draft, as Big Tim had indicated, was highly controversial. Most of the Tammany politicians had opposed it - charging that it was a plot by big business to replace whites at their jobs with all the cheap black labor fleeing the south. "Will there be any trouble?" he asked.

Big Tim just shrugged. "Maybe," he said. Then he grinned. "Or maybe not. In either case, are yer with me, lad?"

"Absolutely," Thomas said.

"That's the spirit!" Big Tim cried. "Yer just stick with me, my boy, and fore yer know it, ye'll be fartin' through drawers a silk."

Allan Cole & Chris Bunch

Despite the heavy presence of police, the large crowd gathered outside the draft office was remarkably good humored. Through the big glass windows, Thomas and the others could see uniformed men - working under Capt. Jenkins, marshal of the district - dumping the names of candidates for the draft into a large revolving drum. Every minute or two, they'd give the wheel a turn, then draw a sheaf of names for Capt. Jenkins to call out. Most of the new conscripts took it good naturedly when they heard their name.

Thomas noted they all seemed to be working class fellows from the factories and yards in the area. Mingled among them, however, were some richly dressed young men, who glowered, or jumped nervously when their names were called.

Big Tim pointed out one richly dressed draftee to Thomas and gave him a nudge. "Looks just like a maid, beggin' to have it put to her," he said. "Go to it, lad. Take any yer like, 'n as many as yer like."

Thomas hesitated: his immediate prospects looked good; but Big Tim had also mentioned introductions to some important men. Tim caught the reason for his hesitation and indicated a small group gathered at a hire hydrant. They were all tough-looking, expensively dressed, and the crowd was giving them a wide berth. "I'll be over there," he said, "jawin' with me mates. Come say hello when yer done."

By the time the drawing was half over, Thomas had $1,200 in his pocket, and prospects for $2,400 more. He decided to quit when the crowd began to thin: much more, and he'd begin to stand out - both to the police and the suckers. He wandered over to the hydrant, where Big Tim was deep in conversation with his cronies. Their talk was dark, however, in marked contrast to the jokes the crowd was hurling at the unlucky men whose names were drawn.

"It h'ain't fair to th' workin' lads," one man was saying. "Those rich sons of bitches oughter have to take their chances 'long with ever'un else."

"They're gonner turn this inta niggertown afore the war's over," said another. "Alla whites'll be shot full of minie-balls by Johnny Reb."

Allan Cole & Chris Bunch

"Fuck th' niggers," said a third, "me whole district's gone to feed th' cannons. They'll be puttin' me in prison with th' paupers, along with me dear wife 'n darlin' children."

Big Tim nodded sympathetically as each man spoke, but was keeping his own counsel, concentrating, Thomas noticed, on a small wiry man with gray sideburns and cold eyes. Thomas recognized him - Joe Flynn, an important fellow at Tammany. Flynn was as silent as Big Tim; but as proof of his importance, when he finally spoke, in a high soft voice, the other men fell silent.

"What's your view, Tim?" Flynn asked. "You have your ear to the ground, as everyone knows."

Thomas was surprised how refined Flynn seemed: despite his size and age, it was his reputation for brutality that had marked his rise through the ranks.

Big Tim shrugged. "Feelin's runnin' high in th' neighborhoods, Joe," he said. "But yer know that 's well as any of us." He indicated a group of newly conscripted young men talking calmly to the draft officers. "Those lads just don't understan' what's happenin' to 'em yet."

One of the other men broke in. "There's gonner be another drawin' Monday, Joe. Want we should put a stop to her?"

It was Flynn's turn to shrug. "Washington is putting a lot of pressure on the authorities, gentlemen," he said. "Mayor Opdyke and Colonel Nugent had no choice but to go along with this evil business."

"That may be so," Big Tim said. "But I gotter tell yer, Joe, I just can't get it out a me noggin' that there's money to be made."

Flynn raised bushy eyebrows. "There are others who have been thinking along the same lines," he said. "Why don't we go up town and have a few words with them?"

Big Tim nodded. "I'd like that just fine." As they started to go, Tim spotted Thomas at the edge of the group. He waved to him. "Come see me tomorrow," he bellowed. "Maybe I'll have a job a work for yer."

Thomas didn't connect with Big Tim until late Sunday. He didn't worry: word was out certain Tammany Hall politicians and gang leaders were having a helluva powwow over the conscription

421

crisis. He later learned the participants roughly broke down into four groups: (1) those who thought President Lincoln's callup, with its $300 loophole for the wealthy, was grossly unfair to their poor and working class constituents; (2) those who believed it was a conspiracy of Radical Republicans and other "nigger lovers"; (3) those who were convinced it was a wider plot concocted by the British to wipe out all the Irish who had fled their homeland; and (4) those who believed the blood bath of the war must end, and a treaty should be negotiated with an independent Republic of the South.

But the unspoken agreement among all four was that Big Tim was right - there was money to be made in the discontent raised by the draft order. Finally, it was agreed - the lottery must be stopped.

While he waited, Thomas decided to celebrate his newly won entry into the New York gangs by spending some of the money he'd earned on Sheila and her family. Sheila Davitt was one of nine children. Her father had been killed recently in a freight accident, and it was up to Sheila and her brother, Bill, to earn enough to keep the family together. Thomas and Sheila descended on the family ladened with presents and food. In a short time, Sheila and her mother had whipped up a great feast and all the children gathered at the table with the adults to praise Thomas's good fortune. But he noticed despite the good cheer, Bill was silent and withdrawn.

"What's his trouble?" Thomas asked Sheila when they had a moment alone.

"You won't get a straight answer from me, Thomas Shannon Ryan," Sheila laughed. "I'm his sister, remember? I doubt you'll find a sister in the land who'll admit their brother has a pinch of worth." She looked over at her brother, who was staring out the window, gloomily watching the Sunday traffic. "But one thing I'll say about our Billy, he's usually a cheerful sort. He ain't one to let the world get to him."

She called to her brother: "Why the sorrowful face, Bill Davitt? Your girl finally get smart and send you packing?"

Bill turned from the window, his eyes unglazing. "I'm sorry," he said. "Didn't mean to spoil everyone's good time." He gave Thomas a weak smile. "Thanks for bein' so nice to my family, Thomas. They could use a bit of cheerin' up."

Allan Cole & Chris Bunch

Thomas quite liked Bill. He was about his age, and worked like the devil down at the iron works. "You look like a lad weighted down with a big problem, Bill," he said. "Anything I can do to help?"

Bill shook his head. "No, but thanks just the same." He grimaced. "Seems I was one of the lucky boys whose name was drawn yesterday."

Sheila breathed in, sharp. She ran to her brother. "Oh, no, Billy. You're not going off to war, are you?"

Bill shrugged. "I'm afraid that's what the Good Lord has in mind for me."

Thomas knew this was a double blow to the family. Not only was the oldest male being hauled off to fight, but there was no way they could make up the income. "Don't be so quick about giving up the ghost, Bill," he said. "I'll stand the $300 for you. Then you won't have to go."

He felt good when he said this; and was especially pleased at the look of immense relief on Sheila's face. "There you go, Bill," she said. "You can thumb your nose at the Army now."

Bill shook his head. "Thanks just the same," he said. "But I couldn't do that."

"Don't be so proud," Thomas said. "It ain't charity. We're like mates, right? And you know I think the world of your sister."

"It ain't that," Bill said. "I just wouldn't feel right about it. To have some other poor sod take my place... and my chances... No. I couldn't do that." He looked up at Thomas. "You probably think I'm a fool."

Thomas thought he was twice that, but he liked Bill too much to say so. "If you change your mind," he said, "the offer will be good... anytime."

"I thank you again," Bill said. "But I won't be doin' that. I ain't no hero, mind you. I sure as hell don't want to get shot. If there were another way - an honest way - I'd grab it like a drownin' man."

Big Tim came through. Thomas met him late that night and was thoroughly filled in on his duties. "We want the lads roused up good," he said. "We're gonner hit every yard and shop in th' city, and call 'em out to put a stop to this business."

Thomas raised an eyebrow: Big Tim was talking about putting together a mob. "I hear there's going to be twice as many police at the draft office. You're askin' for some broken heads... or worse."

Big Tim snorted. "Worse is what we want. And we're countin' on broken heads - especially police broken heads. When th' shit starts, yer stick with me 'n the boys. 'Cause that's when we do our real work."

Thomas was too anxious to make a good impression to consider what doubts he might have. When Monday morning dawned, he was on the streets with a whole legion of other rabble rousers. He hit every place where draft age men were known to work to call them out for the rally, and got them good and angry at the injustice of the system - pushing hard, as he had been ordered, on the race issue. "Jobs 'n niggers," Big Tim had told his crew. "Stick to that and we got a sure thing, lads. Nice 'n simple. Jobs 'n niggers. Jobs 'n niggers. Hammer it into their thick paddy skulls."

To Thomas's amazement, it worked. Now, he disliked niggers as much as the next fellow, but certainly not enough to charge a police line. Also he thought the whole thing was plainly transparent: it was the bosses who were clearly to blame for the high prices and low wages afflicting the country. It was legalized thievery as far as Thomas was concerned, although he was more jealous than angry at the system. But to the working types he encountered, it was "all the niggers' fault." Or, "shoulda let 'em stay slaves." And, "oughta send 'em back to Africa where they belong." It took little persuasion to convince the men to leave their jobs and march on the draft office.

At the appointed hour he met Big Tim and the other boys in front of the two-story building. Upstairs residents were leaning out the windows, watching the commotion as the young working men paraded up. Through the office's window, Thomas could see the officials blithely filling the drum with names, while outside Tammany shills worked the quickly mushrooming crowd. "They're killin' the Irish for a bunch a niggers," someone shouted. "They're takin' our jobs, lads. It'll be our women, next," cried another.

The crowd was getting fired up, screaming its own epithets and obscenities in return. It spilled down 34th Street in both directions and Third Avenue was a sea of angry men, pushing forward to get closer. Thomas spotted a group of policemen trying to break up the mass, but they were quickly put into retreat; stopping in a nearby alley to regroup. Then he found himself catching the spark - this was power, dammit! - authority cringing before the wrath of common men; and those common men were driven by the words and deeds of clever fellows like Thomas Shannon Ryan.

He felt Big Tim's hand grip his shoulder in excitement. "It'll be any minute now, Thomas," he chortled. "All's we need's a bit of a jog to get it goin' the rest a the way."

Thomas suddenly wanted to provide that "bit of a jog." Then he'd really shine in the eyes of his new pals. They'd be toasting him in all the taverns of New York. He ran to a clear space near the draft office, where the pavement was broken, making dangerous footing for the mob. He caught up a huge piece of pavement, then, with a wild, joyous cry, hurled it through the glass windows. Thomas saw the startled draft officials dive away from the shower of glass. The crowd roared approval, and reached for their own missiles. A fusillade of rocks hammered the office. As Thomas dodged out of the mob's way, he saw a uniformed man with a bleeding face being led away by two companions. The blood on the officer's face stirred him to greater madness, and when Big Tim shouted for someone to fire the place, he eagerly grabbed a tub of pitch brought along for just that purpose, and set it alight.

Men ducked out of his way as he again ran toward the draft office and hurled the tub inside. It spilled over the upturned drum of names and quickly caught and roared up and up and up. The heat made him feel like a towering genie, laughing at the tremendous magic he had unleashed.

Somehow he found himself back in Big Tim's company, watching as the fire grew until first one block and then the second went up. They all howled in amusement at the people streaming out of the buildings to escape the flames; others were dangling from upstairs windows, then crashing to the ground. Men broke into a tavern just before it went up, and kegs and bottles were grabbed and

Allan Cole & Chris Bunch

passed around. Thomas plucked a jug of rum from someone's fist and upended it, choking as the fiery liquid - the first he'd drunk in his life - poured down his throat. He split into two men - one full of blood lust and piss and fury; the other, his rational self, appalled at the fury he'd helped unleash.

The firemen came with engines and pumps, but Big Tim directed the mob to beat them away from the hydrants. The police fought against overwhelming odds, driving a wedge through long enough for Police Superintendent Kennedy to mount a wagon and beg for the mob to desist. But there were no pleas for peace that would go answered that day, or those to follow. He was attacked and nearly killed before his officers rescued him. they ran down the street with club-wielding men at their heels.

Someone shouted, "let's get the niggers," and the crowd broke into massive chunks and roared off to hunt victims. Big Tim and his men trotted behind them, urging them on as shop windows were smashed and more buildings and homes were set on fire.

Thomas the Mad giggled when he saw the wagons and burrows being piled with loot by gang members. Thomas the Appalled moaned as he saw the awful destruction. Thomas the Mad laughed until he was sick when they came to the Bull Horn Hotel and he saw Big Tim revenge himself on his enemy, the proprietor.

The fool barred the way, refusing to hand out the spirits the mob demanded. He went down under a shower of rocks and pummeling fists. In moments the hotel was stripped of anything drinkable and then set on fire. He heard guns cracking and saw men streaming past with weapons looted from the armory to battle police reinforcements, who quickly melted away under the onslaught. But he paid no mind, as he hastily bent to the task of helping fellow gang members fill up a cart with goods from jewelry stores and furniture shops.

He watched with superior amusement as the Tribune office was attacked. A flying wedge of policemen saved it from destruction, and the mob moved on for easier game.

Thomas the Appalled was shocked when he saw a small crowd chase down a black man, then hang him from a post by his own belt. The shock turned to gut puking when they went by the smoking ruins of the Colored Orphan Asylum, and he saw the weeping children and teachers cringing in the rubble. But the queasiness was quickly soothed when Big Tim shoved more rum into his fist and called him a "right good lad." Once more he banished Thomas the Appalled, and upended the bottle.

He remained gloriously drunk all that night and far into the next. The police were helpless as the rioting spread across the city. There was no militia to stop them, for they were off chasing General Lee.

Mayor Opdyke issued a plea for peace. Governor Seymour did the same, standing on the steps of city hall, until he was driven inside by the mob. Black men, women and children were attacked whenever they showed their faces; many were killed. Block after brownstone block was set on fire, until more than 1,200 homes were turned into ashes, as were many more businesses and plants. Big Tim and the other gangsters filled warehouses with their loot, and cried for more. They hired themselves out to revenge seekers, and coined huge sums as arsonists. The word came down federal troops were on their way, but they were all too far gone to pay any mind.

On Wednesday morning, Thomas stood before an untouched jewelry store, directing a group of thugs as they broke the door down and rifled through the shelves and cases. In a few short days he had become a man to be reckoned with - one of Big Tim's lieutenants. But he was less than mighty that morning: he was hung over; his eyes blood shot, his breath foul, and he badly needed another drink.

He was feeling so poorly it took him a long moment to react to the loud shouts of alarm, and the rush of a small mob around the corner. "It's the soldiers," somebody cried, and Thomas and his men finally had the presence of mind to slink into a dark alley mouth.

There came the tramp of feet, the sharp clatter of horses, and the shriek of heavily-burdened wheels. Thomas peered out and saw the troops march around the corner and head down the street toward them. Horsemen cantered in front of the marchers, and the dismal parade was pocked with horse-drawn cannon. A limp, dirty banner fluttered in front of the soldiers - it was the 77th New York. The last Thomas had heard, the 77th had been fighting down at Gettysburg. The men were dusty, their uniforms ragged, but Thomas had never seen such grim purpose. They gripped their weapons as if they meant to use them, and their hard eyes swept the streets for signs of resistance.

It came to him these men would be angrier than any mob Tammany could whip up, and their fury would have come honestly: they had been fighting the war, dying in droves, only to be been recalled to pacify the very souls they'd been engaged to protect.

Drums rattled, orders were shouted, and the 77th broke out of its marching formation into a battle-line that looked like the drawings Thomas had seen in magazines, "from our artist on the battlefield." Bayonets gleamed as muskets came off men's shoulders and he heard the snap as weapons were cocked and caps pressed onto nipples. In the middle of the line the cannon were pirouetted as men darted around their brass masters, and then the trails were down and the guns aimed down the long street.

He thought he saw a familiar face in that bleak group of killers. An older man moved from gun to gun, giving quiet orders. The man looked Thomas's way for just moment.

It was Uncle Ian!

He was sure of it.

What the hell was he doing with the New York regiment? The man turned away and he became uncertain his alcohol-pummeled brain hadn't been imagining things. But, imagination or not, he felt ashamed of himself. Thomas the Appalled gripped him by the throat. "A right good lad," he mocked. "Coward's what you are. A mean-spirited common thief, who lets 'em hang innocent men and women to get what you're after. And you're drinkin', now. Drunk as your father ever was, and doin' deeds more worthless than any crawl he ever made through the gutter."

He stood, motionless, his ears registering more orders from the soldiery: "Load canister!" "Stand by your guns!" "Fire only on command!"

He saw a knot of looters stumble forward into the open space between the crowd and the 77th, all of them drunk. "You'll not be firin' on good Americans like yourselves," one of them shouted, confidently. Thomas knew better - he'd seen the faces. But still neither side moved.

Allan Cole & Chris Bunch

A musket-crack broke the tableau, and a man in blue cried out and crumpled. There were shouts from the mob of surprise and shock, but none from the soldiers. Instead: "Full elevation, lads! The bastard's on a rooftop, and there's more of 'em up there!"

A man wearing gold braid stepped out of the formation. "You are ordered to disperse immediately.. or be fired on!"

There was another gunshot, but no one saw who fired or where the ball went. The muskets of the soldiers were shouldered and aimed.

"What'll we do, Thomas?" one of his men asked.

Thomas turned, wondering what he should say, that inner voice still louder than anything he heard or saw. But before he could answer the muskets volleyed, the cannon thundered and the street was a welter of blood and screams as the mob broke and fled. It was a terrible sound to hear in a city's streets, for some unknown reason more terrible to him than any of the rioting before. The sound shocked him out of his hesitation.

"Go tell Big Tim," he said. "I'll stick around and see what's what." His men did as ordered, dashing back down the alley, away from the army lines.

Thomas waited a long time before he followed, while the soldiers reformed and swept on further into the city, and the sound of more gunfire shattered. His mind shrilled with many voices, giving conflicting advice. Then Ian's face rose up in his mind; his eyes were not accusing, but were full of hurt and shame that Thomas Shannon Ryan had fallen to such a state. When the sound of guns and cannon faded, Thomas quietly made his way home.

The place above the cigar shop was empty; Sheila was with her family. Thomas heated water and took a long bath. He scrubbed his flesh until it was pink and raw and scoured imagined alcohol slime from his teeth. Then he fell on his bed and slept. He did not dream and when he awoke he was stiff from being in one position the whole night through. He heated more water and took another bath. By the time he'd finished and dressed he had made up his mind.

The door opened and Sheila entered. When she saw him, she gave a glad cry and rushed into his arms. "I'm so glad you're safe," she said.

"Not so glad as I," Thomas said, forcing lightness.

"It's awful out there," she said. "The soldiers have been fighting the mob. Billy says they're using grapeshot, and putting men on the roof to shoot the leaders."

"I'm not surprised," was all Thomas said.

"They're huntin' the ones they haven't caught," she continued. "Billy says they're trackin' them down to their homes and kicking down the doors to arrest them." She looked up at him, eyes frightened, and tear filled. "I thought they might of come for you."

"I'd have deserved it if they did," Thomas said.

Sheila hugged him hard. "But you're safe, now," she said. "And it's almost all over."

Gently, Thomas pried her arms away. "I'd like you to do something for me, darlin'," he said.

"Anything," Sheila answered.

"Got fetch Billy for me," Thomas said. "Tell him I figured a way out of his mess."

"He won't come. You know how stubborn he is."

"Tell him the idea I've got is as honest as they come."

Sheila stepped away from him. "What're you thinkin' of Thomas Ryan?"

"Thomas Shannon Ryan," he corrected. "And what I'm thinkin' of is this... Tell me, Sheila, darlin', will you still love me if I put on a uniform?"

Sheila immediately took his meaning. Tears streamed down her cheeks. "Ah, God help us, Thomas. Is that the only way?"

He took her in his arms. "Maybe not," he said. "But it's the way I want to do it, Sheila. The way I have to do it."

CHAPTER THIRTY-TWO

CAMP DOUGLAS, ILL. - APRIL 21, 1864

"STAND Y'AL A fill a' 'baccy, Sarn't?

Patrick gaped at his fellow prisoner, then managed - "Well damn a horse if I won't," as he scrabbled for his battered nosewarmer and thumbed tobacco from the extended oilskin pouch. "This is about the first good thing, let alone kindness, anyone's done me this week. Who died and mentioned you in his will, Mr. Whatley?"

The frail private grinned through gap teeth. "'Member m' set a' checkers?" Patrick did, indeed. The pieces had been carved from bone, and then stained with walnut and berry juice the man had gotten a guard to bring in to the camp. The board had been made of a shell crate, inlaid with stained wood for the squares. "'Reck'lect that passel of Yanks th' screws let in yestiday fer us t' prance our lightlies fer? One a' them wanted a whichmacallit for a soovenwhar, an' took fancy t' th' board. Cost him ten dollars gold, an' his pipe, an' his 'baccy."

Patrick pulled a long splinter from the wooden wall, stuck it in the stove and puffed his pipe to life. He sighed in momentary contentment - tobacco did indeed cut hunger pangs when you were famished - then remembered his duty and stirred the great pot simmering on the stove. He and Private Whatley, late of Morgan's raiders, were taking their turn at mess duty.

In the pot, amalgamating into something that would be called stew, was about twelve pounds of beans, some hominy, one hacked-up side of barely-cured bacon from an emaciated hog, a handful of salt and a cup of vinegar, plus some onions one of the other prisoners in the hut had contributed that'd been carried into camp by a sympathetic guard. That, plus the cornbread Patrick's less than skilled baking had produced, and the finest water the swampy land could provide, would feed a hundred prisoners for one full day.

Tea or coffee hadn't been seen for some time, since the Federals who ran the camp had decided that the sutler, who'd been permitted to sell a few items for those lucky enough to have a few coins, had been ordered away from Camp Douglas as another reminder for the

Southrons they weren't to think they were living in the lap of decadence.

Even the always-creative Johnny Rebs had run out of bark or herbal substitutes to drink. If a prisoner wanted something hot to drink to wake him up, he could boil some water on the stove. The kitchen was identical to the others in Camp Douglas - the walled-off last twenty feet of a wooden 90 x 24 foot single-story barracks with a stove at each end. A Sanitary Commission had inspected the camp earlier in the war and pronounced "nothing but fire can cleanse this place."

"You heard they're plannin' to cut the rations again?" Patrick growled.

With Whatley he didn't have to worry about keeping his upper lip or the troops' morale firm. This was not another of the rumors that flowed through the prison camp with even more regularity than they had in besieged Vicksburg, but had been confirmed by one of the guards.

"First they chase the sutlers off, now this. Guess that frigging General Hoffman will be able to give even more money back to Congress claiming it ain't needed for us overfed lardbutts."

"Ain't no cause to fret," Whatley said, undisturbed. "They ain't no way even a damyank kin kill us more'n once, an' they a'ready went an' took their best shot at both of us."

Whatley had been wounded and captured in some minor skirmish and for awhile his captors had wanted to hang the bandy-legged man as a guerrilla. This was one reason why he and Patrick were friends. Patrick, too, had faced a death sentence after he'd been captured: those damned civilian clothes tucked in his pack had nearly been cause for his being hanged from the nearest bridge stringer - especially after the Federal soldiers holding him learned he was one of Forrest's men.

But even after less bloody-minded people had prevailed, that eliminated any possibility of Patrick being paroled as he'd heard some Confederates had been after Vicksburg's surrender suddenly made over 29,000 rebels the Union's responsibility.

"I know you're immortal," Patrick grumped. "But none of the rest of us are."

The smile vanished from Whatley's face - this was a little too close a reminder of what was around them. The camp, in Chicago, held about four thousand prisoners at any one time, depending on how the war was going. The number constantly changed, but not because of parole or prisoner exchange. General Grant had ordered a halt to that nonsense a few days ago; not that it ever happened frequently, reasoning all a Reb would do, once exchanged, was re-enlist and fight on.

The grim Ohioan's grand strategy was obvious to Patrick - he intended to kill every Secessionist that held a musket any way it took, and talk peace at the graveside. Men died in Camp Douglas of everything from wounds, to neglect, to the myriad diseases, to lack of medical attention, to malnutrition, to scurvy, to a guard's bullet if a prisoner got too close to the well-named "dead line" just before the outer fence.

Sometimes a prisoner just had as much as he could take. That was one reason for Patrick's black mood. The day before yesterday, when word filtered down about the banning of exchanges, he'd seen one of the prisoners - one of those compulsive athletes who spent all his waking hours walking around and around the camp's perimeter - come out of his hut in tears. No one came after him. The man wiped his eyes with a ragged sleeve, looked straight at the fence, with a guard nearby on the far side, and started toward it. It had been a minute or two before Patrick realized his intent, but it was too late. The man walked directly toward the low wire that marked the dead line. The guard saw him, and brought his musket up, shouting a warning. The man seemed not to hear. He stepped over the wire and marched toward the fence.

Patrick, running as hard as he could, clearly heard the guard's musket being cocked. The prisoner was just at the unclimbable fence when the shot went off. The minie ball struck him full in the chest, and he staggered back and fell. Patrick leaped over the dead line, and knelt beside the prisoner, paying no attention to the warnings shouted at him. The prisoner was dead. There was a quiet, thoughtful smile on his face.

Sometimes prisoners just gave up. One such man had gotten Patrick in his present position of undefined but very real authority.

Allan Cole & Chris Bunch

He was in charge of the entire hut, even though there were several sergeants older than he was, and three holding higher non-commissioned rank. The man had been sickly, captured after he fell out on the hurried retreat from Chattanooga. He didn't seem to want to eat, not the issued rations nor even some proffered "treats" - bits of dried beef or fruit secreted by prisoners for especially depressing days. He didn't speak unless he was spoken to, and only with as few words as necessary. As far as Patrick could tell the man didn't sleep. He sat or lay near one of the windows, staring out at nothing in particular. Like most of the other prisoners, he had nothing but the clothes he'd been captured in, but with one interesting exception: a prisoner was thoroughly robbed after capture, not so much by the front line troops that caught him, but by the rear area sorts whose hands he passed through on his way to a camp.

Patrick, for instance, still had the pouch containing the musket ball and lock of Lucy's hair because he'd hidden it in his crotch not long after he'd been taken to the nearest collection point - plus his boots, which made him a rich man considering the number of Confederates who arrived barefoot in this frigid swamp.

The apathetic prisoner's only valuable was a mouth harp. Once or twice he took it out, started a tune, then let the note die into silence. He paid no attention to the shouts from other prisoners for some music, any music.

There weren't any Confederate officers and damn-all in the way of leadership in Camp Douglas. The officers were in their own camp, an island stuck out in the middle of one of the Great Lakes. Military discipline hadn't broken down in the camp - it never existed beyond what the guards imposed. They were either raw recruits detailed off while they were being trained in the huge camp, only part of which was a prison, old soldiers too canny to get near a battlefield, or wounded veterans not quite shot up enough to be paid off.

The other prisoners in Patrick's hut didn't seem to care whether the apathetic prisoner lived or died. Patrick did. He made sure the man ate, shouting at him when he didn't. He ordered a couple of the other prisoners to take his charge to the shed they used as a chilly bath-house, and have his lice-ridden clothes banged against a wall until he was no lousier than everyone else. But Patrick didn't feel he was accomplishing anything - the man seemed determined to let himself just fade away.

Patrick tried talking to him - what was the matter? Didn't he have family? A girl? Friends? Come on, man. You've got to fight, even if it's only for yourself. He never got an answer.

One night, he heard a struggle, and rolled off his straw pallet to investigate. There was a scuffle at the end of the hut. In the moonlight coming through the window Patrick recognized both men - one was his charge, the other a beefy bully from Georgia from the next hut who stayed fat on rations he'd browbeat from weaker prisoners. They were scrabbling over the harmonica - the apathetic man was moaning "Don't... don't... .don't..." and the Georgian muttering by Christ if he wasn't gonna play it, someone would, or use it for tradin' stock.

Patrick, knowing how weak he was, and not being a back alley brawler in the first place, didn't attempt to play hero. He grabbed the hut broom, and thumped its butt square into the Georgian's temple, sending him reeling away. Before he could recover Patrick landed on the man's back with both knees, driving the wind from him. As he lay wheezing Patrick shoved the broomstick under the man's throat. He pulled back, and the Georgian gargled in pain.

Patrick leaned down and whispered in his ear: "Y'know," he said, trying to sound as country-roughneck as he could, "this is th' way I useter kill chickens growin' up. One pull, an' y'could hear th' neck snap. I useter like doin' that a lot. Ol' Forrest, he never let me do it to a Yank, but I allus wanted. Mebbe now's m' chance."

The Georgian, eyes bulging, began a wordless keening for mercy, believing, as it seemed most of the camp did, anyone who rode with Forrest would do anything to anyone. Patrick kept the pressure up for another few seconds, then jumped up and back - waiting for the bully to rush him. But the man scuttled away like a Borneo orang-utan, not getting all the way up until he was out of danger.

Nobody said anything, but all of a sudden Patrick found when he had an idea, or a suggestion about how maybe it was time certain duties got shared out more equally, he was obeyed. It seemed as if

Allan Cole & Chris Bunch

fewer men in ex-Sergeant Shannon's hut died than in other, less controlled barracks; but maybe that was Patrick wanting to find something to feel proud of as the days dragged past and the fall became winter turned into spring.

The apathetic man had died two weeks after the attempted theft. The mouth organ wasn't in his pockets, nor stuck in his mattress. No one ever found it. The bully didn't seem to learn his lesson, and kept stealing. Eventually enough was enough, and he was waylaid one night, trussed and gagged with strips torn from a mattress, and tried by twelve of his peers. The verdict was guilty, and there were only four sentences possible. The lightest three were a beating, sending him to Coventry, or deprivation of rations for a specified time.

The bully made the mistake of swearing revenge on the kangaroo court if they did anything other than untie him, including hollering for the guards. The next morning his body was found by a guard. It appeared he'd fallen and broken his neck on his way out of the jakes. He'd in fact been strangled. He was not the first, nor the last who faced this never-spoken-of prison justice.

Patrick wished he had a better eye for observation, because just as the army created its own customs and culture, so did this prison camp. There was nothing at all to do, day in, day out, other than keep your assigned area clean, do whatever you thought, or your hut leader decided needed doing, and try to make the time pass. Those somnolent sorts who could happily sleep for twelve or sixteen hours a day would've been stock for jokes in normal times but now were greatly envied. Some men kept diaries, or wrote endless letters home - at least mail got through occasionally. That was one of the few bright spots in Patrick's life - Lucy was an inveterate writer, even though the mail system lost about a third of her letters. Patrick wondered how accidental those losses were, since they were addressed to an unredeemable captured Reb and came from one of the South's most despised former bastions.

The letters gave him something to cling to. Lucy was as much in love with him as he was her, and constantly wrote about how she couldn't wait until Patrick was paroled or - and this was new - the war would end so he could return to her arms. One minor thing was a bit worrisome of late - Lucy was sounding increasingly hateful about the North and the Yankees.

He hardly expected her to become a Black Republican, but he'd learned when you lose you smile, tip your hat, cut your losses and move on. Not so with Lucy or, evidently, all too many of Vicksburg's women. But he was bright enough to not comment in his letters back. Parts of each of her letters were wild tales of the atrocities that'd gone on before the city fell, always witnessed by a friend of a friend of hers, or shrill denunciations about the Federal soldiers still occupying Vicksburg. They were rude, ill-mannered, loud, rough-jesting, dishonest, tobacco-smoking and -spitting, godless, lewd, drunken, and so on and so forth, which made them sound to Patrick not much different from an average Southern regiment.

The most recent missive reported the greatest horror of all. Lucy's oldest sister had not only fallen in love with a Yankee captain, but was going to marry him! Patrick thought of writing back that at least she'd gotten better pickings than someone he could think of who was stuck with a penniless wandering buck-sergeant jailbird, but decided that didn't sound real right, either.

Patrick had thought about writing a letter to Susan in Philadelphia. But he couldn't. What would he say? Former Confederate cavalryman now repents, especially after he's being slowly starved in a prison camp. He'd changed some, he realized now, since he'd decided to slip out of Vicksburg before the surrender. Now he wished to hell he'd run up the white flag with the others, and the hell with whatever secret oath he'd felt toward his absent messmates. There'd been enough people die around him in this camp, with hardly a bullet fired.

He believed, deep in his bones, that it was over now, and wished the war had never come; or that he'd had brains enough to head back for Texas or maybe California or even the Sandwich Islands after Mrs. Cuffee, way back when, had prophesied true about the war swallowing everything and everyone. But you didn't complain when life dealt the wrong cards and you lost, not if you were trying to be honest with yourself and remember you might still be cheering the

Allan Cole & Chris Bunch

horses if yours was running in front. So the letter to Philadelphia was still unwritten.

Men in the camp who couldn't write or didn't want to found other pastimes. There was a thriving theater group, acting out plays from books brought in by friendly guards. There were gamblers - for money, food, duties or gimcracks. Some fools actually used the single thin blanket they'd been given for a stake, and promptly lost it. Other men taught classes in everything from French to sonnet-writing to better ways to farm a small spread.

Patrick found himself teaching one, to his amusement, trying to remember all Michael had said about shifty gambling and warning the naifs what to look out for. That wasn't the only subject Patrick taught, nor the most popular. The number of soldiers who'd never learned to read nor write was astonishing, not only because their parents wanted them in the fields, but also because there simply wasn't a school within traveling distance. Patrick sometimes wondered if the rich and influential men of the South preferred it that way, remembering his readings in medieval times about the church and nobility's fear of an educated peasantry.

In Camp Douglas men seized the opportunity. Patrick wondered if some of the artists who drew Johnny Reb as an iron-fanged descendant of Tamerlane would recognize a dead-silent barracks-room half-full of warriors listening intently as Patrick intoned from a primer a guard had given him: "F. The idle Fool is whipt at school. G. As runs the Glass Our life doth pass," marking each letter on the wall with charcoal as he spoke.

Patrick wished that he was more mercenary, but he found it impossible to charge any of his students, other than accepting the occasional favor.

Other men became craftsmen, working anything and everything that could be sold or traded for food or cash to the guards or the Chicago citizens who were occasionally admitted to the camp at so much a head, just as if they were visitors at the zoo. There were jewelers working with bone. For awhile it became the fashion to make rings by using a spoon to carefully flatten the edges of coins, turning them and gently beating them into a circle. The center was drilled out and the coin, hopefully with some of the legend still intact

438

if the maker was skillful enough, became a ring. Patrick nearly went insane from the endless tap-tap-tapping before another pastime became popular.

Private Whatley, with his incredible talents as a whittler sans compere, was actually making money out of being a prisoner of war - every bit of which went straight into food, tobacco or even once or twice completely forbidden flasks of whiskey for his hut mates.

"Sarn't," he now said thoughtfully, "y'all know a bit about chess, don't you?"

"A bit 'bout marks it," Patrick said honestly. "I surely ain't Paul Morphy." He'd found, to his amusement, that sooner or later every soldier, no matter his education or home, started talking like the worst backwoods cracker.

"Ain't concerned with your playin', but I needs help with th' namin'. Since I took that fat Yank for ten dollars, an' someone said chess is played by th' rich, I bethought m'self I might be makin' a chessboard next. Those little guys... pawns, I heard 'em dubbed, I'll carve 'em like sojers, Johnny Reb, Billy Yank. Th' pieces at th' end, whatever they're named... cannon, maybe. Th' rest of th' pieces I'll whittle outer life."

"I don't get you."

"I been goin' through th' ill'strated papers out'n th' jakes, an' savin' pictures of famous people t' use as m' models. Th' South'll be white, an' Marse Lee th' king, f'r instance."

"Why not Jeff Davis? He's our president."

"Th' day I start carvin' pol'ticians' faces is th' day they're th' ones payin' direct f'r my time. 'Sides, we ain't got no sour apple wood around f'r th' shapin'."

Patrick snickered -Whatley was a great deal more clever than his accent or demeanor appeared. "Who'll be queen?"

"I kinda thought that spy-woman. Greenhup, or somethin' like was her name?"

"Greenhow, I think," Patrick said. "How do you know what she looks like?"

"Don't. Don't need to. Make her purty. Lady spies is allus purty. Anyway, th' problem I got, is who'd be th' white queen? You got any idea what Miz Lincoln looks like?"

Allan Cole & Chris Bunch

Patrick thought about the matter. Who, indeed should be queen? Not the President's wife, surely. It was as good a thing to ponder and pass the time as any to let the day come to an end. His cogitating was broken as one of his hut mates, LaCoutre, entered. He held a folded newspaper, and looked worried. Patrick noted the paper must've just been published, since it wasn't yellow like the old ones handed around and around the camp for something, anything to read until they fell apart or somebody grabbed them for an emergency visit to the outhouse. He handed the paper to Patrick, his grimy thumb indicating the subject of interest.

Patrick scanned the story, his stomach turning: NEGROES MASSACRED BY REBELS... Helpless Black Soldiers Shot After Surrendering... Notorious Outlaw General and Slaver Nathan Bedford Forrest Ordered Slaughter... Deeds Of Outrage Unparalleled in Modern Warfare... 300 Perhaps More Brave Ex-Slaves Who Volunteered To End Slavery Murdered... Men, Women, Children Shot Down While Rebels Laugh as They Do The Devil's Work...

"Shit," he said not realizing he'd spoken aloud.

Fort Pillow, Kentucky was garrisoned by about seven hundred Union soldiers, including, the paper said, about two hundred and fifty black artillery men. Forrest, now a major general, led five thousand men against the fort. He'd surrounded the post, and ordered it to surrender. The fort's commander had refused. Forrest had then said, "if you surrender, you shall be treated as prisoners of war, but if I have to storm your works you may expect no quarter." The paper said he also told his men there was no need to take Negroes prisoner.

Brave though the Union soldiers may have been, they were hardly a match for Forrest's veterans. The fort fell quickly, and the Confederates marched inside, and the murders began. Confederate soldiers opened fire indiscriminately on white and black men, women and children. People tried to flee down the steep banks to the Mississippi and were slaughtered like coyotes took down lambs. "Some of the children, not more than ten years old, were forced to stand up and face their murderers while being shot... sick and wounded... butchered without mercy... all around were heard cries of 'no quarter,' 'kill the niggers,'... all who asked for mercy were answered by the most cruel taunts and sneers... deeds of murder and

440

cruelty closed when night came on, only to be renewed the next morning, when the demons carefully sought among the dead for other wounded and those they found were deliberately shot... heart-sickening details..."

Patrick, able to read no more, gave the paper back to the Louisiana soldier. "You believe what it says?" LaCoutre wanted to know. "The papers, they always lie about what soldiers do."

Patrick wished he could console himself with that belief. But he couldn't. Maybe there hadn't been women and children at Fort Pillow - it was pretty rare when they were up in the front lines unless it was a city or town being attacked. But that wasn't important. He knew Forrest, the slaver and killer. He also knew what he'd heard other soldiers say about the idea of a black, any black, allowed to pick up a gun, let alone serve with the north. Perhaps the officers had lost control when their blood-savage men rushed the fort. Perhaps. Certainly they would not have tried too hard to regain authority when the shooting started, since most Confederate officers believed about the same as their men, only being a little more cautious about how they phrased it.

Whatley had taken the paper, and puzzled the words out. "I ain't hardly no nigger-lover," he said slowly. "An' there surely ought t' be prison in fate f'r any nigger tryin' t' jine th' army if'n we catch him. But shootin' folks? Women? Children? Naw." He gave the paper back to LaCoutre. "Naw. I jes' don't b'lieve it. Sojers don't do things like that. That Yankee rag's lyin'."

Patrick shook his head. "No, Albert," he said heavily. "I suspect it's the truth, or leastways most of it is. Shit."

"If you are right, Patrick," the Louisianan said, now looking even more concerned, "then you have some mos' serious troubles yourself."

"What?"

"This paper was give me by Corporal Campbell. You know him?"

Patrick did. He was a firm abolitionist, and felt the most extreme measures should be applied against the South after the inevitable Northern victory. But he was fair in his judgments and allowed no casual brutality from the guards under him, unlike some others.

441

"He told me to take it to you, direct. He said, he knows you were one of Forrest's men. He said clear for me to warn you, when he is walking the post, and if he comes to see you, if you are ver' close, or even not so close to the deadline..." LaCoutre drew his thumb across his throat and made a tzzzk noise. "He said this was a warning. He said... anyone who rode with Forrest, maybe deserve trial. Or maybe just a rope or bullet, and save all the bother."

The three soldiers stared at each other, and Patrick felt ice along his spine.

Allan Cole & Chris Bunch

CHAPTER THIRTY-THREE

PHILADELPHIA - APRIL 30-MAY 2, 1864

THE BIG CALICO prowled restlessly before the cellar door. Every so often Montmorency would stop to sniff at the bottom of the door, then scratch at the kitchen tile and mew a warning to whatever was on the other side. Mary tried to ignore him as she sat at the kitchen table wading through a stack of student essays. Concentration was difficult: Mrs. Fawcett was clattering about the hot stove, and Nancy sat across from her picking apart a piece of buttered toast. She hummed a tuneless song as she broke up the bread and made meticulous little piles of crumbs.

Outside, the morning sun fought a feeble battle with the musty chill that permeated the old house. Mary thought that every year it took longer for the house to shake off the winter's gloom. The thought aroused the beasts of loneliness and fear as she recalled Hugh's visit last spring. She wondered what he was doing this moment, and whether he was thinking of her as he went about what she prayed was a dull and routine task.

The cat scratched and mewed again. "What's gotten into him?" Mary burst out - the heat of her annoyance surprised her.

Mrs. Fawcett studied the calico's antics. "Maybe a rat's gotten into the cellar," she finally said. "I'll fetch Mr. Pollack to go down and see."

Mary pushed the papers away. She needed activity - vigorous activity. "I have a better thought," she said. "Let's clean this place from bottom to top. We'll surprise Susan when she gets home from the market."

"I don't like rats," Nancy said. She got up from her seat, crossed to the cellar door and opened it. The cat mewed in glee and dashed down the stairs. "Montmorency will fix him," she said with unnerving relish.

There was an ungodly ruckus downstairs that came to a sudden, obviously victorious, halt. "Better get Mr. Pollack to fetch a shovel to scoop it up," Mary said to Mrs. Fawcett. "Montmorency is too finicky to eat the poor thing." She rolled up her sleeves and started tying back her hair. "And ask him, please, if he's got time to help us clean out the cellar. We might as well start with the dirtiest job, then everything else will seem like play."

Mrs. Fawcett laughed. "There's nothing like knocking down a few cobwebs," she said, "to cure the ailments of spring." And she went off to do Mary's bidding.

Her mood vastly lightened, Mary gathered up a broom and pail and other scullery items and marched to the cellar. Mrs. Fawcett was right - the prospect of grimy activity cheered her immensely. At the landing she twisted the valve that fired the gas lights, then began to descend the stairs.

Nancy called before she had gone far: "Do you mind if I help?" Mary turned, her astonishment barely disguised. This was the first interest in anything Nancy had shown since... well, it seemed like forever. Mostly, she did nothing at but ghost about the house, silent except for that tuneless humming. When her mother and father came, she refused to acknowledge them, but stared pointedly away, to their great torment. Worse still, when they brought little Keith to visit - he was chattering and toddling about now, and knew he had a mother someplace in this house - she disappeared into her room and barred the door until his visit was over and he was carried away in tears. "Please," Nancy pressed, mistaking Mary's musings for hesitation. "I want to feel useful." She had a spark in her normally vacant eyes.

Mary smiled and nodded. "I'd love the help," she said. The two of them trooped down the stairs. Although Nancy had taken up the tuneless humming again, Mary felt as if it were old times - the two daughters-in-law combining forces to tackle a tedious chore. This was turning out to be a most amazing morning.

An hour or so later the cellar had been nearly cleared out: Mr. Pollack had removed the dead rat Montmorency proudly displayed, and was stacking the coal in its bin; Mrs. Fawcett and Mary were nearly done attacking the floors and walls and ceiling with brooms and buckets of water and strong soap, while Nancy sorted obvious rubbish from items that still promised some future usefulness. As Mary wrung out the mop for what she hoped was the final time, Nancy called to her, excited: "Look what I found."

She was struggling with an old rug that covered a large, bulky object. As Mary went to help the rug fell away to reveal an odd, box-

Allan Cole & Chris Bunch

like object so old and dirty that its wood was quite black. "I don't know what that is, exactly," Mary said, eyeing it with some distaste. "But no one will quarrel with you if it goes into the trash heap."

"Oh, no, we can't do that," Nancy said with some heat. Mary was once again surprised at her... involvement was the only word that came to mind. "Can't you see... it's a loom!"

Mary studied the machine, for that is what it definitely was now that she picked out the parts. She noted the beam and the treadle and the distinctive frame. "You're right," she said. "But it's so old - at least fifty or sixty years, is my guess - I doubt it's good for anything... except firewood."

Nancy clutched one of the upright bars in obvious distress. "It's perfectly good," she said. "Just because it's old, doesn't mean it's useless." She took a rag from her apron pocket and began brushing away some of the grime. "Let me have it," she said. "I can fix it. I know I can."

Mary remembered Nancy had once made a living among modern machines that performed the same function. "Of course you can have it," Mary said. "As if I'd had the right to say no." She got out her own rag and began helping Nancy clean the loom. "This looks like it came from Susan's grandmother's time," she said. "Perhaps it belonged to one of her weavers."

"You mean, Diana Shannon?" Nancy asked, growing even more enthused. Mary nodded, marveling at how firm and alive the wood felt as she dusted it. The grain practically leaped up as the dirt fell away. Nancy gripped her arm. "Don't tell Susan about this," she pleaded.

"Why ever not?" Mary asked.

Nancy struggled for an answer, then shook her head. "I don't know. Just don't say anything... Please?"

"I won't breathe a word," Mary said. "And that's a promise."

As Father Quinn droned through the mass, Nancy ran the loom's treadle mechanism around in her mind. She could visualize its connection to the heddles, but was having difficulty with the arrangement of the small cords that made it operate. She became mildly aware of a stir in the church when the priest came forward to address the faithful. He was saying something about someone's child dying. She listened closer.

"It is written," the priest said, "the sins of the fathers must be visited upon the sons. Jefferson Davis is the enemy of our nation, but all of us must contemplate, and then mourn the news that his child - who was only five innocent years of age - should die so tragically. The news accounts tell us he fell from a balcony while witnessing a parade. It is tempting to see a lesson in this. I overheard some of you rejoicing over Mr. Davis's obvious sorrow. But if this is so, then Mr. Davis would have been quite correct to have behaved the same two years ago when President Lincoln's own son died. Willie Lincoln was only twelve when typhoid struck him down. Was that dread disease a repayment from our Lord for Mr. Lincoln's sins? I think not. Just as I think..."

The rest of his words blurred out. She was sorry for this Mr. Davis, whoever he was, and equally sorry for the Lincoln family. But she thought it was unlucky to dwell upon it - after all, when Kerry returned from his business trip, they'd be wanting to start a family of their own. She patted her flat tummy, and buried a giggle as she wondered what it would be like to swell up with child. She and Kerry would have to find another way to do it. She giggled again, sure that their imaginations would not fail them when the time came.

Someone hushed her. Nancy quieted her impulse to hush the person back and returned to her loom repair. Instantly she saw the solution to the treadle problem. Very good, Nancy Dolan. Now, on to the warp. A complicated harness arrangement jumped up in her imagination, and as the priest went on about this and that and other fine things, she concentrated on the pattern so she could quickly reconstruct it when Mass was over and they returned home.

Mr. Burstell's small office was abustle with Monday morning litigants. Susan slid into the chair and smoothed her dress, trying to force a posture of casual ease. Internally she was aboil - wondering what news her lawyer had that would cause him to send for her so abruptly. She feared to pray that the news was good; God didn't need tests in a world of such madness.

Allan Cole & Chris Bunch

The other people in the office were engaged in the usual gossip about the war and politics. "I don't think Mr. Lincoln has a hope to be re-nominated, much less re-elected," an elderly gentleman was saying. "And I must confess that I believe he fully deserves his current unpopularity with the populace."

"Who'd you pick, then," snorted a younger man. "That damned McClellen, I suppose."

"At least he's a Democrat," the older man replied. "More importantly, he's an experienced warrior. And that is what this nation needs now."

"Oh, come on," scoffed the other. "Little Mac had his chance to end the war, and he sat on his cowardly rump instead."

"I take issue, sir, with your calling the general a coward," the old man shot back. "And no man of reason can deny that General McClellen is the best fellow to sue for peace and win back unity."

"I've heard him talk a lot about unity," the younger man said, "but I sure haven't heard any details on how it's supposed to be done. I mean, that's what we're fighting the war for, isn't it?"

"No, sir," the older man said. "The war is over the Negro race. And if there was ever such a lowly banner to parade the troops before, I have not seen it yet in my readings of history."

"You got the right to think as you please," the young man replied. "But I'm with the President all the way. And I'm with General Grant. And I pray to God old Grant whips those Rebels until there's not flesh enough left to cover their bones. And when the war's over, I've got a second prayer for Mr. Lincoln to see the light and strip those Southern bastards of everything they've got and give it all to our boys in blue in payment for their suffering."

The older gentleman was blowing himself up for a counter-attack when the door opened and Mr. Burstell poked his thin patrician nose out. "Mrs. Dolan," he said. "Please do come in."

As Susan rose and entered his office Mr. Burstell eyed the two quarreling clients. "Gentlemen," he said, "my own opinion is this: I agree with the fellow who supports the President; but admonish him for the use of rough language in the presence of a lady. In the future, sirs, please confine your debate to the streets and the taverns. Thank you."

447

Amusement lightened Susan's worry as Mr. Burstell fussed with papers and his specs. He was an old-fashioned fellow in many ways, but somewhat ahead of his times in others. On one hand, he'd scold a man for using a word Susan had used herself - in private; on the other, he treated her with the same respect he would any male client, and listened closely to her opinions on business. She returned the compliment, taking his advice whenever possible. She'd rarely had cause to regret it.

Finally, he got things in order. He looked up at Susan with sad eyes and her heart fell. "I am so very sorry to inform you, Mrs. Dolan, that our pleas have fallen on deaf ears."

"I'm ready for whatever you have to say, Mr. Burstell," Susan said. "Tell me the worst of it."

"All of our avenues are now closed," he said. "There can be no more delays. The court has set a date to hear Shannon vs. Shannon."d

"And when will that be, sir?

"October. Five short months from now, Mrs. Dolan."

Susan reacted in shock. "So soon?"

Mr. Burstell nodded, somber. "I fear so. And, as you might suspect, the hearing will be in Washington, so we must be prepared for the worst. Pamela Shannon has very powerful allies."

Susan sighed. "What do you suggest I do, sir?' she asked.

Mr. Burstell took off his spectacles, wiped them, and replaced them. "I once suggested the offer of a settlement," he said. I again urge you to consider that remedy."

Susan knew she had no other choice but to attempt to buy Pamela out. "How much should I offer?"

Mr. Burstell considered, then scratched a figure on paper. He turned it for Susan to see. Her eyebrows shot up. "That much?"

"Can you raise it?"

"I don't know. A hundred thousand dollars is a great deal of money."

"Obviously you would want to start much lower, but I fear you must be prepared to go at least that high. I've gone over the books, and I believe the sum can be managed if you sold a few properties, and sought assistance from your bankers." Mr. Burstell gave her one

448

of his miserly smiles. "Would you like me to approach them in your behalf?"

Susan realized she had no other choice. She nodded, then gathered up her things and rose, stretching out her hand for Mr. Burstell to shake. "I'll do as you advise," she said. "Thank you, sir, for all your trouble."

Susan rode the street car home, as depressed as she had ever been in her life. It seemed as if God himself were conspiring against the Shannons. A rare wave of self pity rose up and tears spilled. It seemed grossly unfair she would fail after coming so far and struggling alone for so long. The unfairness was especially hard to bear because she had lost to a woman as despicable as Pamela Shannon. If there was a person ever born and bred for the hellfires, it was Pamela. And yet it was she who was being rewarded. What kind of justice was it when a woman of such low morals carried the day? How had her grandmother managed all those years? It was a mystery to Susan that she shared the same blood of a woman so strong and fiercely determined.

As the driver slowed the horses for the Chestnut stop, she got out her hanky to wipe her eyes and blow her nose. Someone offered assistance as she stepped down, but pride returned and she politely refused it. She walked to the familiar old house with the iron fence. She paused outside to gather her strength. Whatever had to be done, she would do. People were counting on her. Some of them were helpless to care for themselves, so she would have to carry on, no matter what her personal failings. Susan pasted a cheery smile on her face and climbed the steps. She opened the door, listening to its familiar creak, and stepped inside. As she did so, she heard an odd mechanical clatter coming from the living room. What in the world could that be?

She walked to the living room entrance and looked in. Sitting in the center of the room, was the most remarkable machine. It was wondrous old loom made of rich wood, and threaded with a rainbow of colored yarn. Sitting before the machine was Nancy. As Susan watched, Nancy skillfully threw a shuttle loaded with yarn across the race. She quickly pressed the yarn down with a wooden comb, kicked the treadle forward, then threw another shuttle -loaded with a different colored yarn - back in the other direction. Nancy laughed in sheer joy at the pattern she'd formed. Susan stepped into the room, stunned.

Mary called from the other side of the room. "See what Nancy's done?"

Nancy turned to see her standing in the doorway. She looked so proud sitting before the loom and she had a smile on her face that brought back memories of the girl who was. She pointed to a wonderful shawl rising out of the loom. The shawl was rose-colored and bore the beginnings of a marvelous blossomed tree. "Do you like it, Susan?" she asked.

"It's lovely, dear," Susan said.

Nancy nodded, she knew it was, and only wanted confirmation. She shifted the treadle and threw another shuttle across. Her fingers flew, her feet danced on the bars. "See?" she cried. "I'm just like Diana Shannon."

Susan cried for the second time that day; but this time happy tears. In Nancy's madness, Susan had found new strength to face the world.

Allan Cole & Chris Bunch

CHAPTER THIRTY-FOUR

THE WILDERNESS - MAY 5, 1864

THE UNION ARMY marched into a land of ghosts. It was known only as The Wilderness, which suggested James Fenimore Cooper's Forest Primeval. It was far worse. The Wilderness was a strip of woods about six miles by twelve miles. It'd been logged years ago, and piddling attempts to turn it into farmland had been made. They hadn't succeeded, and the land grew rank with tangled vines and brush between the pines, scrub-oaks, chinkapins and hazels. There was no breeze, and the morning was desperately hot.

The men of D Company made little sound other than the scuffle of their boots and low murmurs as they, and the rest of the two hundred and five men that made up the decimated/rebuilt/decimated yet again 86th Pennsylvania filed down the narrow, still-rutted abandoned farming road. Hugh Shannon heard birdsongs from their front, and the flutter of wings. He tensed, but it was nothing. It was possible for birds to take flight without it being a warning.

Here and there he'd seen abandoned or ruined farmhouses, built like old New England saltboxes, but of peeled and shoddily-planed logs. There'd been a small church that'd been commandeered by the surgeons, and the foundations of a devastated stage stop tavern. But this was not what made The Wilderness haunted. A year earlier, the two Armies had collided on this ground. The names of the tiny crossroads and hamlets were all too familiar to the scattering of soldiers who'd been skilled or lucky enough to stay alive since then: Chancellorsville, Hazel Grove, Banks Ford, Guiney Station. This was where Stonewall Jackson had been shot by his own men in a ghastly but all-too-common accident, and where, in some desolate field, where they'd buried his amputated arm.

The country may have been shadowed by the past, but it seemed to only bother the newest recruits. One of Hugh's dedicated privates spotted a skull near the side of the track, and held it up with a guffaw. "Corp'ral Butscher?" he hollered. In spite of a certain language problem, Hugh had deemed him more than worthy of promotion after Gettysburg, and if he survived much longer, and would make just a bit more effort to speak something resembling English when rattled, he would wear sergeant's stripes.

"Ja?"

"Now, wasn't it I who told you, last summer, that you forgot to relieve one of our outposts?"

Laughter from the ranks. Butscher just stuck his jaw out. "A joke, hein? I find it almost funny as the digging of the garbage pit will be for you, Kieley, when next we camp."

More laughter. The one consistent thing about the Army was it'd somehow managed to keep its sense of humor. D Company was still smiling about First Sergeant Ingram's bellow when they had formed up this morning: "God damn and blast you, Private Muloney in th' rear rank, don't be standin' with yer one foot in Virginia an' th' other in Moyamensing!"

But there wasn't much else the same, and not just because of the constant stream of replacements as the Army renewed itself like Antaeus. Lincoln had brought the hero of Vicksburg, General Grant east, and put him in charge of the entire Army. It was a little confusing, because while Grant was wise enough to stay out of Washington and with the troops of the Army of the Potomac, General Meade was still, technically in charge of those Union forces. No one below the rank of brigadier general gave a damn about the technicalities, since they'd decided the bearded man who evidently liked a nip as much as they did was the one who'd win the war in the field and, most likely, kill them in the process. But at least it would be over.

Hugh wasn't sure if Grant had changed the army, or if it'd changed on its own, part of a strange transmutation that happened to include the Ohioan. Grant had made big changes - he'd told all the fat-assed artillery and cavalry regiments, that'd spent their war getting fatter guarding Washington from who knew what, to leave their cannons and horses. He had handed them muskets and told them to start thinking like the infantry they now were. The consensus among D Company was Grant was a fighter, and he'd take them where there'd be a fight, and from all reports stay with the battle no matter how many men died if he sensed victory or even advantage. Hugh had never seen the man, not even in the now-frequent reviews before the Army marched south this latest time.

He'd heard he'd been questioned as to his grand plan, had chewed his ever-present cigar for a moment, then growled "Continuous hammering." Subject closed.

This was what the 86th, and the Army, seemed to want to hear, from what Hugh saw. They no longer gave a damn for pretty uniforms with sashes, Zouave's turbans, shiny brass bands or regiments who paraded with their men carefully sized from left to right by height. Hugh had seen a perfect illustration of that the day before on the march South. Colonel Gooley, formerly Captain, still nursing his wounded arm from Little Round Top, had ridden down the files of the 86th with some pompous and richly-dressed Philadelphia civilian. Hugh thought he recognized him as some politician he'd seen making a vote-getting appearance at St. Patrick's Church, but wasn't sure.

The man had been praising the virtues of the 86th - how manly they appeared, how well they marched, how the fire of battle was in their eye, how he would have known these were Philadelphia men from afar and so on, his voice loud, intended to be appreciated by the men in the ranks. Colonel Gooley, embarrassed, had called for the obligatory cheer... and received nothing but some ragged catcalls and mostly silence.

The Army had no interest any more in who they impressed or didn't impress. They knew what they were: the most smoothly oiled killing machine as had ever marched on this continent, and as good as any soldiers, anytime, anywhere, from Alexander's hoplites to Napoleon's Guardsmen. They'd heard a newspaper writer call them "the perfect instrument for war," and they accepted the accolade as merely an acknowledgment of truth. There were only two exceptions to that insular certainty: themselves, which was why replacement regiments assigned to an old guard division would fight like berserkers to prove they belonged under the same colors as the veterans.

The other exception was the Army of Northern Virginia. It might have appeared there wasn't much hatred any more between the two armies. Certainly when the lines were close pickets would send coffee and tobacco back and forth, flags of truce were always honored when it was time to pause in mid-battle to pick up the

Allan Cole & Chris Bunch

wounded, and even, on rare occasion, they might join in the same songs. But that did not mean there was any particle of mercy on the battlefield. No one had time for hatred, not for the dangerous luxury of an emotion that could make you brave, crazy, careless and dead. Both sides accepted the war could continue until there were only two privates, armed with clubs, on a bare desolation of smoke and brimstone to settle the matter.

This spring Grant had taken the Army south once more, and this, men were told, would be the beginning of the end. New replacements, officers and correspondents were sure the new general with his ability to move fast and unexpectedly, would catch the Rebels by surprise. The veterans just grinned and said nothing. They'd heard that far too often to hold the comforting thought even for a moment.

Hugh was as cynical as the others. After Gettysburg, Captain Gooley, who'd left the hospital tent he'd been fortunate enough to end up in after only two days, had been given the regiment and carte blanche. He'd wanted to promote Hugh to Major and make him adjutant. Hugh shook his head. Even though he'd had only seventeen men left after Little Round Top, which made any thought of a coherent unit called Company D somewhat of a joke, he'd said he would stay with his unit. For the same reasons First Sergeant Ingram had refused a battlefield commission, and once more the two of them had made raw recruits, more of them draftees than volunteers now, into something resembling soldiers.

Resembling was the correct word. No matter how much drilling, how much mock skirmishing and charging, how many hours of School of the Soldier, a recruit only became a soldier in battle. No matter how carefully and lovingly they were taught by the veterans, all too many of them did not live to be awarded that bloody baccalaureate.

Hugh was snapped back to the present as he heard a new sound over the shuffle of the march as the long columns snaked into the forest: the pop-pop-pop of musketry. Hugh and Ingram exchanged glances. Once again, Reynard had been smarter than the hounds allowed. Hell. Hugh had hoped the Army would have at least cleared this jungle before the battle began. He could barely see ten yards to either side of the path they marched on. But it wasn't in the nature of the Rebs to wait until the battle could be fought on ground preferred by the North.

Gooley shouted to Hugh and the other company commanders for a hasty trailside conference. The orders were simple - somewhere in front of them was a crossroads that the Rebs could not be allowed to take. Where was it? Gooley wasn't sure - their division commander had the only map, and he had only a few moments to make his sketch the night before. Put your companies on line, gentleman, and move them out, as skirmishers.

The book said men moving through heavy growth should never have their muskets loaded for fear of shooting themselves or their comrade. Hugh wasn't about to let his company go into battle with empty weapons.

He snapped commands: "Comp'ny D! Halt! Order Arms! Fix bayonets! Load at will! Load!"

After the clatter and the ramrod pumpings ceased, he ordered his company out on line as ordered, to the west of the path. He tramped into the brush with them, and within seconds, was alone. No, not quite. He saw a blue uniform over there... and one over there. He heard shouts to move forward from unseen sergeant and corporals, and Hugh started on in the direction he sort of guessed was south, although he couldn't see the sun or anything else above the trees. I am, he thought disconsolately, the only man in the Federal Army who'll be courtmartialed for losing a company, and by losing I mean just that. But he trudged on, hearing querulous yells to either side, the clunk of musketbutts against trees, curses, and heart-felt obscenities as a soldier sprawled full-length, tripped by a vine. Next came gunfire - carbine fire, which meant it wasn't from his musket-armed infantrymen - from where he felt/hoped his flanks were. Company D was in contact with the Rebels. Hugh smelt gunpowder through the dry woodsy smell, and hastily drew his revolver, not cocking it, however, since he, at least, felt fully capable of shooting himself in the leg.

The thickets weren't as dense, and there was a clearing. The path was no longer to be seen, but here and there, along the fringes of the clearing, his company began raggedly coming into sight. Just

455

Allan Cole & Chris Bunch

as Hugh began to heave a sigh of relief, a great wall of sound blasted, and the brush across the tiny clearing sheeted red fire, and musketballs spattered, sending dirt plumes up as if a spring torrent had begun, and more minie balls thudded into the trees.

Hugh was shouting for his men to drop and pull back into the trees, and men were going down, only some of them by choice as the screaming began, and Hugh was flat, crawling hastily backwards into cover.

As he did, his mind produced a wonderment: the battle had begun, men were dead and dying, and none of the Federals had seen a single Confederate soldier thus far.

"Come on, boyos," Ian panted, feet planted in swampy mire, his back against the cannon's carriage, pushing with all his strength against the Napoleon. "Come on now! It's Saturday night, and we've found this great keg of porter lonely on the corner, and all we needs do is roll it inside before the coppers show. Come on, lads! I've a thirst on me like Pantagruel, the giant!"

His cannoneers redoubled their work, but to no use. The 12-pounder was well and truly stuck. What made it worse was the cannon blocked the pathway to battle and it looked like half the Union Army was behind the detail from Battery H. There was no diverting through the brush, either. The track Ian was attempting to move at least one of his cannon into battle on was long-ago-laid corduroy - logs laid side to side for a trail - through the swamp on either side. They'd run out of room for the horses to pull the guns a quarter mile back, and Ian had ordered ropes and his men to start thinking like mules.

"Once more," Ian shouted. "Once more, for the love of Mary!" Again he leaned into it, until the veins on his forehead stood out and red tinged his half-closed eyes. "It's moving," he lied. "Come on with you, now!"

"Sergeant!" Ian came back to himself. In front of him, a glower permanently graven on his thin-lipped, glowering face, was a Union brigadier. Ian levered himself upright, and stood, panting. "Where's your battery commander?" the man snapped.

"B'dam if I know, sir. P'raps somewhere back there, where you come from, fondlin' his fundament." Ian's temper was as short as his breath.

The brigadier shrugged. "It doesn't matter. Get that gun out of the way. I'm taking two regiments through here, and we have no time to spare."

"Sir, and that's what we've been burstin' our pricks trying to do, and with little success."

"Then stand aside," the general snapped. "I'll have my men tip it into the swamp."

Ian went scarlet. "Meanin' no offense, but you'll piss through your ears first, now. Th' boys up front need cannons as much as they do your muskets!"

"I said, stand aside!" The brigadier's hand swooped to his holster, and came out with a pistol. To Ian it looked as great a weapon as ever he'd been threatened with by any tough when he was a rum boy along the Liffey's quays. "That is an order." The pistol was cocked and aimed, full at Ian's chest.

He began a building growl, and then someone had him by the arm, and was tugging him away. The brigadier seemed to dismiss him from the universe, and snapped orders. Infantrymen - more than enough to have freed the cannon and helped take it forward - swarmed over the gun, and tipped it into the swamp. Without a sideways glance, the brigadier, followed by his command, went past at the double.

Ian sagged. "That pox-begotten sister-fucking pimp! I hope his wife takes a lover, and he's a great black with a cock as long as that pimple's arm, and pleasures her so much she'll never remember his name when he comes home! That ha-penny slut of a—"

"Sarn't," one of his men interrupted. "That ain't doin' us no good a-tall." Ian, whose wrath never lasted for but a moment unless there was good reason, calmed himself.

"'Sides," the artillerymen went on, logically, "ain't as though we would have done much good, even if they hadn't tipped us int' th' shit! If we can't see but a yard, how can we fire further? Or were you plannin' us t' use th' guns for woodchoppin', now? "

Allan Cole & Chris Bunch

Ian did look around, and indeed the jungle was heavy around them. He nodded jerkily. "Back to the others, then," he ordered. "We'll collect a party, see if we can drag our gun out, and see if th' brawl's still continuing."

The men followed him to the rear. They thought, seeing his slumped shoulders, he was brooding on the disgrace the infantry general had brought. He was, but not as a worry of the moment - it was still promising to be a very long war, and Ian was a very good shot, even with the vee-sights on a Napoleon, and he had a very long memory for generals' faces.

His real depression came as he realized the truth of the gunner's observation - this would be a battle fought between men, musket against musket, bayonet against bayonet. In such a struggle, he knew who the victor would most likely be.

Thomas Shannon Ryan heard the shrieking before he saw the Confederate battle line. Then it came out of the brush and the smoke in a gray rush, and he swore each of them was coming straight at him, long needle of their bayonets about to pincushion his chest. He was shouting, and he heard the rest of the 76th New York hollering as well, and the musket he'd had but little training with came up, and he aimed - not really sure how the sights worked yet, wishing he had a pistol, because at least he'd learned how to handle one of those when he was running with the Schuylkill Rangers.

But hell, it couldn't be that hard, considering the shitpots around him who'd made it through other battles... and.... and how very odd it became, almost as if Thomas the Mad had returned to him, even though he'd touched not a drop since New York, and his mind was working very clearly, noticing each second precisely and memorializing it, time becoming a fly fallen into amber. There was a gray chest above his musket barrel, and he pulled the trigger. The chest was gone.

He lowered the musket, one hand opening his shellbox for another cartridge, but there was not time, another man was lunging at him, and son of a bitch but it looked as if he had a long Swiss pike, such as Thomas had seen in a bored visit to a museum, attempting to impress some slut who evidently thought she was a

458

bastard of the Twivills. Thomas had more than enough to time to step aside, spin a knee into the Rebel's groin exactly as if this were a streetcorner melee, and as the man fell to smash his gunbutt against the back of the soldier's neck as if he was carrying a shillelagh, and the man was not to worry about any more.

Thomas brought the musket back up, bayonet ready, but there was no one coming at him, and he leisurely lowered and reloaded it, seeing the Confederate line fall back through the dense smoke.

His fingers "remembered" what the corporal had been teaching him, and they fed the cartridge into the barrel, took out the ramrod, pushed the cartridge home, as his eyes swept around. No one to worry about to his front... beside him was the dead Confederate, not far from him was Ellis, that earnest fool the corporal had told him to watch once the fighting began. On the other side was a man he didn't recognize. He stared at him in some fascination, never having seen such a sight.

The Yank had been bayoneted clean through the chest, his attacker, who was nowhere to be seen, striking with such force the bayonet had pinned him, like a butterfly in a collection, to a small oak. The man was screaming, eyes closed, both hands pushing at the rifle imbedded in his chest. Thomas was considering what to do when the man pulled the bayonet out, Thomas marveling at such strength, blood spurted, and he fell dead.

Thomas' musket was loaded, and he realized he was standing in the open, which was very foolish. He moved toward a tree that looked to be thick enough to stop a minie ball, before the next charge came, and was almost behind it when something struck the tree and it exploded and sent him spinning.

He did not know if he was knocked out or no, but realized he was flat on his back, his eyes pressed closed, wetness, but ah god, ah god, at least there's no pain, wetness across his face, oh christ, I'll even pray if I'm not blind, and he forced his eyes open, blurry forest around, dirty sleeve wiping blood off his face, feeling splinters grate against bone, and he could see, THANK FUCKING GOD HE COULD SEE, and the pain sledged him in a wave, and was gone.

But the pain wasn't from his face, not surprisingly, since he'd learned years ago most blows to the face looked ghastly but weren't

Allan Cole & Chris Bunch

incapacitating unless the hitter knew just where to strike as Thomas did, and wasn't he going on, and his head turned and he looked in mild curiosity at his upper arm. What he saw was almost as interesting as the impaled man had been. He'd heard of all sorts of wounds and even, in his short time in the Army, seen a great number of them. But this was new. Evidently some sort of cannonball or something had splintered that tree, sending bits of wood like shotgun pellets into his face. But that burst of pain had come from the splinter in his arm. It was almost eight inches long and two inches wide, Thomas estimated calmly, and his arm was neatly brochetted in the middle.

Curiosity vanished and the agony came back and stayed. He moved his arm, and felt bone grate. But there was not that much blood, at least not yet, and he did not think he was doomed.

Thomas shouted for help, but none came. There was no one around but the dead and dying, and the one soldier he thought he saw through the smoke ran past without stopping. No more than what he expected, Thomas thought. He wouldn't have stopped for some strange teague, either.

Even though the gunfire seemed to be getting farther away, and he hoped he was not blacking out, the smoke was thicker now. Wisps of smoke rose from the dry forest floor, from the years of piled needles and leaves, so much tinder. Smoke, and he could see flame flicker, and the forest fire blossomed into full life.

Thomas shouted for help... but again, no one answered.

The battle was now chaos. Hugh, with what remained of his company, was advancing in the middle of some Rhode Island regiment, and how they'd gotten there, he had no idea. Sometime later, he saw the sun through the smoke for a moment as he staggered through a clearing, and how the blazes did it get to be so far overhead, since it was still morning? They went forward, and they fell back. Hugh killed men, and saw Southerners kill Yanks. He had no idea whether they were winning or losing.

There was a lull, and Hugh found himself crouched in a depression. There was another man prone five feet away. He wore a tattered gray uniform, and held a loaded musket.

Allan Cole & Chris Bunch

The two stared at each other. Hugh cocked and lifted his revolver, and the man's fingers were at the haft of the long bowie stuck through his belt.

Then the pistol was lowered, and the Confederate's fingers went back to his musket butt. "Tell you what, Yank. If'n we do this right, we'll both of us have a tale for our grandkids," the man offered.

Hugh managed a trace of a smile, and, no other words being exchanged, each of them backed out of the hollow into the fight.

Muskets thundered, and men shouted and fell, and Hugh realized the fire was coming from behind them. Hugh fought his way through the undergrowth, shouting, "Cease fire, goddamit! You're shooting your own men! Stop firing!" and he came into an open space and had only a moment to realize the soldiers on line wore gray, not blue, and they'd been outflanked by the Rebs when redness rippled, and something smashed into his thigh and Hugh spun and fell, just as he'd seen so many others before, feeling flash-agony like when that damned mule he and Kerry had been trying to ride when it lost patience and kicked him so long, long ago.

He started to sit up, then thought better, and let himself sag back down. Christ almighty, he could be hard hit. A ball in the thigh? Amputation, perhaps, or perhaps not possible if it was too high up, and even if the surgeon was skilled and he did not die under the saw there could come the slow rotting from gangrene.

He realized there was someone kneeling over him, and he opened his clenched-shut eyes. It was Sergeant Ingram, and just behind him Corporal Butscher. Ingram's hands moved quickly over the wound, and Hugh gasped, and then Ingram was ripping Hugh's uniform open and tearing his undershirt off, forming it into a hasty bandage.

"Y're nae hit i' th' bone, sir. Th' ball went through an' through clean, an' there's no great goutin' of the blood," he said, seeing Hugh was conscious. "But I'm a-feared you'll be never-more singin' 'Tentin' T'night' wi' th' army, y' lucky bastard. Sir."

Hugh winced as the bandage was tied tightly and the throbbing reached up through his chest. "Thanks, sergeant for the diagnosis," he managed. "At least you're making me feel better."

"Nein," Butscher protested. "the Ober-Feldwebel is not tale-making. I saw, too. You are no more for this war, mein Hauptmann, but for home and der kinder." Not waiting for a response, he was shouting for stretcher-bearers to raus fucking schnell or there would be to pay hell of the darkest kind.

Hugh started to give final orders to Ingram, but realized he had no idea where the rest of his company was, nor what it should be doing nor even how many if any men were left.

He made himself relax. If he was not hit by shellfire on the way to the surgeons, and if they didn't butcher him, there was just a vague possibility his damned duty or responsibility or whatever it was he'd felt was fulfilled and he would see Mary again.

Ian found a glade wide enough for two of Battery H's cannon, and managed to move them forward and into line. He missed but one thing - powder and shot. Somehow, he'd lost the rest of the battery and all the officers in his struggle to get the guns up. The hell with them, he thought. Two guns, with his men, were more than enough to hold the position, wherever the hell it was in this jungle.

None of the runners he sent back looking for the caissons returned. The battle-sound roared closer, and Ian ordered his men to take up fighting positions in front of the guns. They'd fight as infantry, then.

But in all that long day they saw nothing. Not a Rebel, not the rest of the battery, not even another Union soldier.

Hugh heard voices, and, without opening his eyes, tried to force his mind to make sense of them. He had been husbanding his strength since the stretcher bearers had brought him back to lie outside this charnel house they called a hospital in the long rows of wounded, dying and already-dead until the surgeons reached him.

"Sir," the first voice had said. "It appears General Lee is driving us back."

"So it seems," came the flat drawl, and Hugh opened his eyes a crack and peered at the two standing not five feet away. One, with his back to Hugh, was as unkempt a private as he'd ever seen, from his tramp's hat to the long coat he wore despite the heat to his filthy and baggy pants. The other man was a resplendent general, with epaulettes and stars.

"To pry, sir," the major general said, "might I inquire as to our response?"

The shabby man looked around, thoughtfully. His eyes swept over Hugh and the other casualties, and saw them without seeing, or so Hugh thought, feeling them chill as a winter wind from off the Schuylkill. He took a cigar from a breast pocket and lit it with a flint attached to about a foot of rope for tinder. He took two deep puffs, then examined the tip of the cigar, ensuring it was properly lit. "If we manage to cling to tenable positions through the night," he said, "then we shall attack once more tomorrow morning."

"And if that fails as well, sir?" Hugh could not understand why the general was forcing the inquiry, especially as he now suspected, through his pain-haze, who was being questioned. "Do we then retreat, back across the Rappahannock, as we've done before and return to our quarters?"

Again, there was a pause. "I think not," Grant said, still conversationally. "I would compare the positions of our armies to two terriers in the pit who have found each others' throats. Since we are in contact with General Lee, I see no reason to give up the advantage."

"No matter the price, sir?" and Hugh saw a tight, satisfied smile on the general's face.

"No matter the price," and the statement was flat, ending the conversation, just as a team of bearers hurried to Hugh's stretcher and bore him away to the operating tent.

The night roared like an immense falls, like Thomas imagined Niagara to sound. The roar was not water, nor battle, but fire. The Wilderness was a sea of flame and stifling smoke as each ember became a flame and each flame a holocaust. Thomas staggered through the night, awash in his sea of agony, coughing as if he were a lunger, and kept remembering a song... or was it poem... he'd read once, about lying down to bleed awhile, and then rising up to fight again. He could not stop, could not sit, could not even let himself

Allan Cole & Chris Bunch

lean for a moment's breather against a tree, as the fire bellowed at his heels.

He'd seen men who did. There were other wounded men stumbling or crawling through the tangles, hoping they were headed toward the rear and not deeper into the battlefield. Sometimes they stopped for just a moment, and the fire swept over them, taking them in silence or screaming. Sometimes they just vanished in the strangling smoke, and Thomas wondered if that was a kindly death.

Just moments ago he had seen another soldier leaning, head down, on a branch that'd been cut from a larger tree, not aware the branch was searing into fire. Thomas had pulled air into his lungs, about to shout warning, but there wasn't the time as the man's clothing caught and then, as Thomas felt himself beyond horror but learning differently, the flames set off the man's cartridge box. The exploding gunpowder nearly tore the soldier in half.

And' bad cess to you, he thought, moving on, for being weak and giving in, because I'll not let myself weaken, and we'll do this five steps and rest, no man, you can make it ten, and then fifteen, and feel the heat coming after you, getting closer is it not? It is not, he forced himself to think... and I am gaining on the blaze.

He heard the low whine, and saw, not far away, another man. Not a man, but a boy, one of the drummers maybe the Army disgraceful bastard that it is would allow to serve with grown men, trying to pull himself along with just an arm, his legs shot through and dangling behind him useless, aware of no one nor anything. You poor dumb fucker, he thought. Let go and lie there, because there's no way you can escape that red and yellow beast that's closing on us all, and I'm sorry there's no one to say the words if you don't remember the prayers but there's no question they'll be no damned good.

And he staggered over to the boy, and bent, grabbing his outstretched arm, and pulling him along, pulling, pulling, saying not a word as he did so, having not the breath nor the thought but I shall not let this happen, it shall not be allowed as hell grew closer about him and the night flowered into scarlet day.

Allan Cole & Chris Bunch

CHAPTER THIRTY-FIVE

WASHINGTON - MAY 21, 1864

DEATH AND MISERY shambled through the streets of the Capitol. Ambulance trains carried the wounded off the steamers crowding the Sixth Street Wharf. At Long Bridge, wagons hauled coffins made of pine and rosewood across to Arlington where hundreds of freshly dug graves waited to receive them in the green fields surrounding Gen. Robert E. Lee's commandeered mansion.

All over the city residents and visitors were reacting in horror as the grim tide rolled in from the battlefields of Virginia. For three days the dead and wounded had poured in without cease, and it seemed as if General Grant's entire army was being sent back for burial. At night people gathered at the docks on the Potomac, torches flaring across black waters, to receive the still-living victims of the fierce fighting.

Women set up refreshment tables for the walking wounded. Men knotted by the ambulance trains, waiting to help load the maimed, the sick and the dying. By day, residents turned out to greet the grim parade with makeshift booths serving hot drinks and sandwiches, while small boys - white and black - ran beside the wagons offering dippers of cool water to fevered men.

Susan and Mary sat in shock as their hired carriage skirted scenes of carnage spread out under blooming tulip trees and silvery poplars shedding their plumes on blood-spattered avenues. One whole street was lined with stretchers filled with the groaning surplus of overflowing hospitals. They saw women going from stretcher to stretcher to peer at the occupants, searching for - and fearing they would find - a familiar face.

Soldiers too able-bodied to merit a stretcher, but too injured to walk more than a few steps at a time, sprawled exhausted on green lawns, edged with blossoming daffodils. A newsboy trotted beside their carriage for half-a-block, pressing them to buy the Courier, which he boasted had the latest casualty count - eighteen thousand dead.

Mary gripped Susan's hand harder, feeling like a small child buffeted by an evil wind. Susan squeezed a reply. Mary wanted to leap off the carriage and run back to help, but everything was in such chaos all she would do was add to the terrible confusion. Still, every wounded man they passed made her feel as if she were abandoning him. Finally, she withdrew her hand from Susan's, got out her rosary and began to pray.

Susan heard the clicking of the beads and whispered her own prayers: for those men and their families; and for the souls of the leaders responsible for such misery. She wanted to pray for Ian and Hugh as well - wherever they might be; but dared not even think their names, for fear of bursting into tears. She had to keep telling herself she was here for the sake of the Shannons. It was up to her to face Pamela and salvage the family's future. But as she looked about, she wondered if this war was not the end of history - and when the last shot was fired, if only graves would mark the place where the United States of America had once stood.

"Do come in Susan," Pamela said. "It's good to see you after so many years."

Susan, followed by Mary, stepped into the room. As they entered, three men rose. One was a middle-aged civilian, next to him was a handsome youth in uniform; the third was an elderly gentleman with a small pointed beard. In one corner, a plain young woman looked up from her seat.

"This is my advisor, Congressman Wright," Pamela said. "His assistant, Lieutenant Glas. And my attorney, Judge Roland." She added emphasis when she said "Judge." The plain woman coughed for attention. Pamela smiled apologetically. "Oh, I'm very sorry... this is my cousin, Marcia," she said.

As Susan introduced Mary, and polite greetings were exchanged, she glanced about Pamela's quarters. They were spacious and expensively decorated. Just how expensively was surprising, even though Susan knew that with all her powerful friends Pamela did not lack money. As she and Mary took their offered seats, she noted the fine fabric of Pamela's tea dress. It was soft pink, with a chaste neckline, and decorated with innocent ruffles and bows. But on Pamela the virginal look was spoiled by the way the soft material clung to her sultry figure. As Pamela sat, Susan caught the lustful look the congressman gave her as the fabric

466

tightened. The young lieutenant also let his gaze linger familiarly on her rounded form.

Susan's instincts quickly and correctly summed up the situation.

"Forgive me if I appear impolite," Susan said, "but it was my understanding this meeting was to be private. Otherwise I would have brought along my own attorney."

Pamela blushed prettily. "They aren't staying, Susan, dear. They've only come by to collect Marcia for a nice supper at Willard's. I asked them to wait a moment so you could meet a few of my dearest friends."

"How thoughtful of you," Susan said, chilly.

The judge smiled benignly. Lt. Glas tore his eyes away from Pamela long enough to nod. The congressman allowed his features to grow solemn and concerned. "You have my word, my good Mrs. Dolan, no interference was intended. It is unfortunate mere business should cause such divisiveness in a family. Pam- I mean, Mrs. Shannon, has always spoken well of you. So well, in fact, that I predict that once this matter is settled, the wounds will quickly heal and the family will be rejoined."

"Here, here," the judge barked. "Well put sir. Family should always come first over money. As I told the President the other day-"

"I beg your pardon, sir," Susan broke in. "At any other time I'd be honored to hear your words to the President, and his remarks in return. However, my attorney was quite firm in his instructions. He said if there was any departure from the agreed upon ground rules, I was to leave immediately... and telegraph him for advice on how to proceed."

She rose. Mary quickly took the cue and followed suit. Pamela jumped up to stop them.

"There's no need to get upset, Susan, dear," she said. "They're leaving, now... just as I promised. Make yourselves comfortable, while I see my friends out."

Susan and Mary sank back into their seats. A few moments later, after good-byes and well-wishes were exchanged, Pamela led the men and Marcia out. They lingered in the hallway for a long time and Susan could hear mumbles of final advice being given. Mary

Allan Cole & Chris Bunch

leaned close. "She certainly likes to be in control," she whispered. "Thank God you saw through her."

Susan grimaced. "I didn't see through anything," she whispered back. "She did this to rattle my wits. I'm only hoping this act was staged because she's seriously ready to consider an offer to settle."

"But, why else would she have us here if she weren't serious?" Mary asked.

Pamela's return prevented an answer. "Everyone's off to Willard's," she said, quite gaily. "It's really unfortunate we can't go with them. Willard's does a lovely supper."

"After what Mary and I just witnessed in the street," Susan said, "I don't mind foregoing supper."

Pamela crossed to an open window. "You mean all those poor soldiers, I suppose. Well, as awful as it seems, you do get used to it. Life must go on, and all." She sniffed the breeze blowing through the window, and wrinkled her nose. "But there's no excuse for that awful smell. It can really spoil your appetite if you think on it."

She closed the window, shutting out the offending odor. "It's the fault of the city's embalmers," she said. "They're a lazy lot, and let the bodies of those poor boys stack up until they get quite ripe in the heat. I keep telling Howard there ought to be a law to at least control where they put their businesses. There are certain things quality people shouldn't have to endure - even if there is a war on."

"Yes. I'm sure," was all Susan could manage in the face of such coldness.

She felt Mary tense beside her. After the horror of the streets, the conversation seemed... well... quite mad. She fought hard to maintain control and present a bland face to her enemy.

"Oh, well," Pamela sighed. "I guess there's certain sacrifices all of us must make, and inconveniences we must endure for the good of the cause."

Susan merely nodded. Mary barely covered a snort of disgust.

Pamela strode to her chair and sat. She arched her brows, eyes twinkling. "I suppose it must surprise you to see me in such solid Yankee company."

"When we last met, you certainly were of a different... mind," Susan said.

Allan Cole & Chris Bunch

Pamela laughed. "I was so young, then," she said. "But my views, you'll be pleased to know, have changed. I remember how shocked I was when I overheard you lecturing Patrick on the evils of slavery." Another laugh. "How ignorant I was. But, how could I help it, considering my upbringing?"

"Yes. How could you, indeed?" Susan said.

"Mind you, I'm still a woman of the South," Pamela continued. "Although I certainly don't hold with slavery. Now that I have been freed from the confines people of our sex suffer on the plantations, my view in that regard has changed greatly."

She took a dainty sip of tea, then added with a pretty frown, "But that doesn't mean I encourage the company of Negroes. Socially, that is. They're good servants, if you keep a firm hand on them. Some of them can even read and write. A few, I am told, are nearly as smart as normal folks."

Pamela leaned forward in her chair, a great smile of amusement on her face. Deliberately taunting: "But just between us ladies at tea, I suspect that somebody white snuck into their momma's bed. It's the only thing that could explain it."

Susan's temper soared to the flash point. But she knew Pamela was trying to get that reaction out of her. She clamped a lid on her emotions and tried to shift topics.

"That's a lovely dress, you're wearing," she attempted.

Pamela clapped her hands in delight. "Oh, thank you for noticing. I swear, I was in a terrible state before you arrived - hoping I wouldn't make a fool of myself in front of ladies of taste coming all the way from Philadelphia."

She plucked at the dress. "I relied on a local seamstress, who swore it was the latest in fashions. And I'm glad to hear my confidence in Mrs. Keckley was not misplaced. Of course, she is Mrs. Lincoln's seamstress as well, so I suppose I shouldn't have worried about being in good hands."

"Indeed not," Susan said.

"If any woman knows about good clothes, it's Mrs. Lincoln," Pamela chattered on. "Actually, her habits in that area are in danger of becoming quite a scandal. Why did you know that she bought

Allan Cole & Chris Bunch

three hundred pairs of gloves in less than four months? Now, tell me, what could a body do with three hundred pairs of gloves?"

Susan shook her head - an answer was not expected.

"Mrs. Keckley says the president's wife just got back from a shopping trip to New York," Pamela continued. "And she can't imagine what Mrs. Lincoln is going to do with all the furs and silks and laces she bought. Why, she spent three thousand dollars alone for a set of earrings and a pin. Only last week she confessed to Mrs. Keckley that she owed twenty seven thousand dollars for her clothes. When Mrs. Keckley asked her if the President knew, she said 'God no!' and begged her not to tell."

Pamela frowned and shook her head in disapproval. "I'll bet she's on her knees right now praying that Mr. Lincoln wins a second term. Because if he doesn't, why with none of their rich Republican friends around to pay her bills, they'll be bankrupt."

"I'm sorry for Mrs. Lincoln," Susan said. "And at any other time I'd be delighted to continue this fascinating discussion. However, don't you think it's time we got down to business?"

"To the point as always," Pamela murmured. Then she grinned. "What's your offer?"

"Fifty thousand dollars," Susan said, just as quickly.

"Oh, pooh. That's no offer, Susan dear. Be serious, now. It's the entire Shannon fortune we're discussing."

"It isn't nearly as much as you think," Susan said. "It's a big family. And the war has not been kind to many of our investments."

"I'm as sorry for you as you are for Mary Lincoln," Pamela said. "But that's neither here, nor there. Come, now. You didn't travel all the way to Washington to play silly games."

Susan sighed. "Very well. I'll skip the preliminaries, if you like."

"I like," Pamela purred.

Susan motioned to Mary, who pulled out a sheaf of documents from her large purse and handed them to Pamela. "It's all there. What I can sell, and what the bankers are willing to loan. A hundred thousand dollars is the highest I can possibly go."

Pamela just laughed. "You must think I'm a fool, Susan. Don't you think it's unkind to treat a country cousin so shabbily?"

470

Allan Cole & Chris Bunch

Susan pointed at the documents impatiently. "Read for yourself," she said. "You'll see that every I'm saying is true."

Pamela let the documents spill to the floor. "I don't think so," she said.

Mary leaped to her feet and gathered up the papers. "Come on, Susan," she said. "This woman has brought us here under false pretenses."

"My, my," Pamela said. "You have such a... spunky... daughter-in-law. You must be proud."

"Pamela, you really must listen to reason," Susan said. "A hundred thousand is the most I can raise."

Pamela made an elaborate show of stifling a yawn. "Then we'll just have to wait to see what the court says," she replied. "As the widow of Diana Shannon's only true blood-relative, I just might end up with the whole thing."

"Or, nothing at all," Susan snapped.

Pamela laughed. "I'm tempted to offer a wager," she said. "But when Judge Roland is through with you, I doubt you'll have enough left over to pay my winnings."

Susan rose from her chair. Mary was right - it was time to go. "I only want to know one thing, Pamela Shannon," she said. "If you had no intention of honestly considering a settlement offer, why did you go through this elaborate charade?"

Pamela lolled back in her chair, displaying an enormous and quite voracious grin. "I only wanted you to feel the way you made me feel back in Vicksburg. All you Shannons think you're so superior to the rest of us mere mortals. Well, now the shoe's on the other foot, Susan, dear. And I hope it's good and God damned tight!"

Susan stormed out, Pamela's gales of laughter billowing after her. At the door, Mary paused and turned back. "I think you've just made a big mistake," she said.

"Who cares what you think?" Pamela laughed. "Now, run along and play, little girl."

Mary rushed out, furious for giving Pamela an opportunity for a final shot.

Still laughing, Pamela got up from her chair and walked over to the door to shut it. This had gone even better than imagined. She

471

hugged herself - revenge was so much sweeter with the passage of time. It made a fine and heady wine.

She went to the window and saw Susan and Mary climb into their rented carriage. The driver stroked the horse with his whip and the carriage rolled away.

A moment later, she saw a tall uniformed figure dash across the street toward her apartment house. It was Lt. Glas, her own Johnny. He'd obviously done as she'd suggested and made excuses to leave Willard's early. He was just in time to help Pamela celebrate her little victory.

CHAPTER THIRTY-SIX

MOBILE BAY, ALA. - AUG. 1, 4, 1864

"SIGNAL FROM THE Chickasaw, sir," the quartermaster reported. "Sending a boat. Nothing else. You want me to find out why?"

"No need, Mister," Joshua said.

"Prob'ly," the midshipman said to his companion, "the poor bastard's looking to bum a handout, 'r else to breathe some air that don't stink of coal."

The middie thought he couldn't be overheard from behind the binnacle where he had orders to produce corrected compass readings for the three Confederate forts guarding Mobile Bay. He jolted, however when he saw Captain Shannon gazing at him, and turned a bit verdigris.

"Sir," Captain Shannon said quietly, "your language does not become either your age nor your uniform. As to your Nostradamus-like predictions, I can only express my awe. Lay below, give my compliments to the Chief Engineer, and tell him I think anyone of your prognosticative abilities should be most competent at sketching every water line that runs from all four boilers to both engines. And I would appreciate seeing such a masterful sketch before you retire this evening."

"Uh... yessir." The midshipman saluted, and started his hasty retreat.

"Two more things for your edification, young sir," Joshua said. "If you plan on remaining afloat, you would be advised to convince yourself the smell of coal is ambergris, or your career will be very short. There will be a paucity of wooden ships and iron men to serve in them when this conflict is resolved. Commander Fields will be able to assist you in developing that interest as well. Finally, if you will allow me my turn with the seer's ball, I would guess that boat will contain my son, freshly arrived to join the fleet."

"Yessir. Sorry, sir. Thank you, sir." The boy, not quite seventeen, was gone.

Joshua shook his head. "When we were young, gentlemen, did we assume our superiors were that deaf? Or were we so busy being cocks-of-the-walk it didn't matter if they overheard?"

His first officer, Mister Colston, nodded. "I must answer yes to both, sir. But I was always an arrogant pup. Thank God I never had a skipper familiar with the practice of keelhauling."

"Hell if I know, Captain," the quartermaster, Mister Glendenning, added in his turn. "I never spoke to an officer until I was twenty five." Joshua laughed, and his long-bearded navigator went on: "As far as that snotty, he's more than dense - he's got to be the only soul aboard who hasn't heard who's on that river monitor."

Joshua's smile vanished. While it would be wonderful to see Donald and congratulate him on his promotion to lieutenant, Captain Shannon was not entirely pleased at having learned his son was a firebrand.

Three months ago, the Pocono was lying hove-to off the Carolina coast when a shore battery blew most of the gunboat's stern away and sent her limping north for the repair yards, leaving Donald looking for new berth. Joshua had dispatched a quiet note that he might wish to come South. But he'd intended Donald would find service on a ship somewhat out of the line of fire, instead of immediately volunteering for what would be the very forefront of the fray.

The Confederacy only had three ports left, and two of them, Charleston and Wilmington, would be shortly taken by the army, with the navy having no more to do with it than provide artillery support and shuttles to the beach. Mobile promised greater interest. David Farragut, who was very nearly as heroic as his arrogance and self-promotion suggested, was looking to fight the great fleet action of the war. At first he intended only to reduce the forts guarding Mobile Bay's entrance, but then, hearing of the Confederacy's Great Lurking Monster, planned even greater feats. It was the ironclad ram Tennessee - under the command of Admiral Franklin Buchanan, hero of the battle between the Virginia and the Monitor. Union spies reported it as having twin screws and engines, six inch armor plating, two seven inch rifles, and four six inch or thereabouts rifles for its secondary armament. It was intended to sink either by ramming or cannonading any Union ship afloat.

Joshua had listened to the hushed agents' reports in a special council of all the Gulf Blockading Squadron's captains aboard

474

Allan Cole & Chris Bunch

Farragut's flagship, the Hartford, with great interest and skepticism. He noted all of the spies but one were landsmen. He'd taken that one exception aside and asked him his personal opinion of the Secessionist's secret weapon. The man had considered, spat on the deck, realized the blasphemy of what he'd done, rubbed the stain away with a bare foot and told Joshua: "In m'own humble 'pinion, which hain't nobody asked about, th' goddam thing's rotten as punk, usin' pisspot engines pirated from a ol' steamboat, and 'bout as seaworthy as a mud turkle. Th' pig hadda be buoyed up, just gettin' over the bar comin' downriver, an' it'll never clear the main bar off'n th' forts."

Not that the Tennessee couldn't be lethal, but no more so than the bulls Joshua teased when he was a boy - stay the blazes out of their pastures and there wasn't any problem. Were Joshua in Farragut's position he would continue the blockade until Sherman or some other general went looking for new glory and seized on Mobile. No ships were coming in or going out of Mobile, even though the Federal blockade was hardly airtight, and there was no likelihood of that situation changing. He'd let the Tennessee posture up and down the harbor all it wished to keep the civilians in Mobile happy. But Joshua wasn't Admiral Farragut, and so the assault would be mounted just three days from now. There weren't enough soldiers available to attack the city proper, but Farragut had been able to cozen enough infantrymen to storm the forts at the harbor's mouth while he Wreaked Havoc on the warships inside.

When Joshua heard Farragut's plan, he had not been pleased. He wasn't worried about the Tennessee, or the other Confederate ships. It was those forts, and their monstrous guns that could utterly destroy a warship in minutes, that concerned him. There were also torpedoes - explosive-filled containers hidden just below the surface - that could be set off either from shore by electricity, or when any ship happened to collide with them. But neither of those gave Farragut more than momentary pause. He, after all, had great experience at reducing forts - from New Orleans to Vicksburg. Joshua thought that he, himself, had fair experience at falling overboard, but that didn't mean he went out of his way to practice the skill.

Allan Cole & Chris Bunch

Farragut disliked ironclads, feeling them to be ugly, barely sea-worthy and surely never to be the subject for a Currier & Ives engraving or a Romantic painting by one of Turner's successors. But he grudged them necessary, particularly after he determined to go toe-to-toe with the Tennessee. And so four cheese-boxes-on-shingles were assigned to him, two from the north, and two from the Mississippi River fleet. No one expected these latter two to make it all the way from South Pass without turning turtle or vanishing, but both of them now rode uneasily in the nearly nonexistent swells a couple of miles from Joshua's, ship, the Oregon. On one of them, the Chickasaw, was his son - newly-assigned as the gunnery officer. Joshua was curious as to just how Donald had arranged things so neatly, so quickly. There was more than a sufficiency of naval officers itching for any combat post to relieve the endless ennui of the blockade.

The boat, hopefully carrying his son, was no more than two hundred yards off. Joshua realized he was very happy, happy in the same way as when he returned to Marblehead after a long voyage. He recognized he was fulfilling a dream that he never knew he'd had - to have a son carry on a Shannon tradition of sorts - one that had begun with Isaac Connors back before the Revolution, had moved across the family line to Luke Shannon, then linearly to Joshua Barney Shannon. It wasn't exactly like the dream should have gone - in a normal time it would have been two officers of the merchant marine or possibly two ship owners meeting at sea. But this would do, he thought.

This would do. He started toward the companionway, to welcome Donald aboard, and as he did, the world became silent, then roared like the wind he remembered from rounding Cape Horn in a norther, and it was if he were looking across the deck at the sea and the boat bobbing toward the Oregon through the wrong end of a telescope, but a telescope that was being collapsed.

The world and all in it receded to a pinpoint, and the pinpoint became darkness.

Lieutenant Donald McKay Shannon couldn't believe what was happening. He'd hailed the deck twice and no one paid the slightest

476

attention. This was untoward, and he would have to rag his father for not running a taut ship.

"Stay in the boat, you men. I'll have you up in a trice," he ordered.

He stepped deftly, as precisely as if he were on a dance floor - without ever swaying nor missing a step - from the boat's thwart to the ship's ladder - and swarmed up and through the gangway.

On deck, there were no sideboys, no bosun, no Marines, not even the officer of the deck to greet him. Donald, even more puzzled, saluted the colors, then spotted, aft, a knot of men on the quarterdeck. There were sailors on the main deck, but none of them paid him the slightest attention. Their attention was instead held by whatever was going on abaft the wheel. Donald hurried across the deck, and up the companionway.

His father lay sprawled on the deck, surrounded by what the entire bridge watch. Even the wheel was unattended. A man with a long gray beard stood crying, unashamedly. Donald pushed through the throng and knelt over his father. He was quite motionless, his face pale. Donald held his ear close to Joshua's mouth. He heard not a whisper of breath. He stripped back a sleeve on his father's coat, and felt for a pulse. Again, there was nothing.

Donald stood, trying to keep his own eyes from blinding. "What happened?"

The older man - obvious from his uniform the Oregon's quartermaster, shook his head. "I don't know, sir. We were... just talking... about you... I guess you're his son... and... he just dropped. I don't know," the man repeated. "I don't know what happened."

Joshua stared down at his father's face. It looked calm, but unrevealing, the expression, he thought - and hoped - of a man who'd had time to make his peace with his God before he was summoned.

Then the tears came.

At dusk the body of Captain Joshua Shannon was committed to the deep. Commander Colston, who'd taken over the Oregon, had asked Donald if the family would object - there were ways, especially when it was a high-ranking officer, for a body to be preserved until it could be buried on land or even shipped home. Donald told him no – his father had always said he would never be buried in dirt.

Each ship in the squadron had sent a representative, and for most, it was the ship's captain. Donald felt glad, as much as he could feel anything, that his father was not only popular, but respected. Admiral Farragut himself came across from the flagship, and made a brief speech before Joshua's body, cased in a new sail with a cannonball sewn at the feet, slid out from under the flag covering it and sank beneath the Gulf waters.

Donald's own skipper, George Perkins, a damned decent man, far different from the Pocono's Lieutenant Peabody, took Donald aside when they'd returned to the ironclad and asked if he wished to be assigned... lighter duties for the attack. Perkins said he did not want Donald to think he was being a milksop, but he wished no one serving his guns whose mind was not fully riveted to the matter at hand. Donald managed a weak smile - the captain would go to any extreme to avoid being thought anything but an ironjawed martinet.

"Nossir," he said. "I'll be fine. When my father took the colors he told my mother he'd most likely not be home until the end. He felt…" and Donald was embarrassed, because Marblehead folk didn't talk about things this directly, but he had to explain… "this whole war was... important, and had to be fought. So I guess I've got a pretty good idea about things, too."

Captain Perkins, nearly as discomfited as Donald, just nodded, and left Shannon's small stateroom.

The world was silent except for the lap of waves on the Chickasaw's low deck and the low hum of the monitor's machinery. Donald's bootheels clanged on the iron deck, but he didn't hear them.

The watch on deck and atop the for'ard turret spoke softly when they had to speak at all. Every now and then one of them would glance back at the young man pacing back and forth near the stern, shake his head, and shake their head in sympathy.

Donald's eyes held on the lights of Mobile to port, but he did not see them. All he saw was emptiness, now and to come. He knew

Allan Cole & Chris Bunch

men died in war - he'd seen enough of them go down already. He also knew, even if he didn't believe, that he himself was mortal.

But not his father. Fathers, even if they were naval officers in command of a steam frigate in wartime, died in bed, when they were very, very old.

Hell. He'd tried to write to his mother, and tell her, even though he knew Admiral Farragut had already dispatched a letter by that day's courier boat that would be hand-delivered to Marblehead.

Hell.

He wondered, numbly, what would come next, and decided he did not much care, one way or another.

But he was glad he'd refused Captain Perkins' offer.

The morning of the fourth was overcast, hot and still, as the fourteen wooden and four ironclad ships of the United States Navy sailed to battle. Farragut had lashed his conventional ships together, keeping the more vulnerable craft on the far side of the Confederate fort the channel and the mines dictated they must come closest to. One of these was the Galena, which Donald noted with great surprise was actually a good-looking ship, now that all the boiler plate had been stripped away and she'd been given decent-sized masts. Just the same, if he had the con at any point in the battle, he would stay as far clear as possible.

The four monitors sailed in line just ahead of the main group and closer inshore. Their orders were simple - to engage Fort Morgan and, when she appeared, to destroy the Tennessee. If it was already hot at six in the morning on a warship's deck, inside a monitor it was an oven. This was another constant that made ironclad sailors, when asked about what it was like, scrabble for words and finally come up with something as unsatisfactory as "different."

Different it certainly was. The Chickasaw, for instance, was about two hundred and thirty feet long and fifty six feet wide. But she drew only six feet of water - less than half the draught of the shallow-water Pocono. But she rolled considerably less, both because of her width, but more because so little of the ship was above the ocean's surface. From the waterline to the deck was only a

479

few feet, which meant the Chickasaw could actually take green water over the deck while anchored in a harbor.

The deck itself was barren except for the turrets fore and aft, a single stack that rose aft of the raised cylindrical pilothouse that sat just a few feet higher than the turrets. Below, there was but a single deck - fairly low for the accommodations for the one hundred and thirty eight sailors and officers with storage spaces, but occupying all the room from the top deck to the bilges for the engine spaces.

The ironclad's sole reason for existence were the turrets, each of which held two enormous eleven-inch Dahlgren cannon. For some illogical reason the designer of this class of monitor had little faith in his own work, so each turret was different. One was an Ericsson, named and styled after the gunnery on the original Monitor, the other the clever invention of the ship's own builder, James Eades. The Ericsson, which Lieutenant Shannon had been placed in charge of, was the simpler - the turret was all of a piece, deck and cylindrical bulkheads. After firing the muzzle-loaders were permitted to recoil back into the turret, hopefully shell-proof shutters were closed and the guns reloaded.

With the Eades turret, the inner decking was independent of the turret, and, after firing, the entire platform with the guns was lowered by steam into the bowels of the ship, out of harm's way, for loading. The argument between the two guncrews of course, was constant. Safety... speed of firing... ease of aiming... and so on and so forth.

But now no one was talking as the four screws of the Chickasaw churned them forward toward the forts and the bay's mouth. It was eerie in the iron cylinder, with sunlight flashing in from the gratings in the turret's roof and the open gunports. Donald heard shouts from Captain Perkins - he'd chosen to navigate the ship from atop the other turret - and knew he was dancing around the grating like a cricket on a hot stove.

He managed a smile through the dullness that hung over his mind, and caught an equal grin from one of the gunners. Frequently Donald, at twenty, felt positively patriarchal around his slightly-older skipper. Someone murmured "... and a little child shall lead them," but there was no maliciousness in the words. At least Captain

Perkins was over his sulk after being told the Chickasaw was not being given precedence of line in the ironclads, no matter how loudly he volunteered. In fact, they were bringing up the rear, the more heavily-gunned, if single-turreted Tecumsah and its sister ship Manhattan in front, and the Chickasaw's own mate, the Winnebago, third.

There came a whistle from the pipe to the pilothouse. "Guns," Donald answered.

"Cap'n says th' fort's in range... You may fire when ready. But don't waste a shot."

"Aye aye, sir," Donald replied, peering over one of the guns, out through the port.

He saw the shore and the low bulk of the fort, just as white smoke blossomed from its ramparts. "Run the guns out," and the trucks squealed on the iron. "If you will bear right a bit more," he ordered Neilsen, one of the ship's masters who in battle controlled the big iron wheel that turned the turret. "Very well... very well... Gun captains! Aim for the embrasures or any cannon you see! Fire when you bear!"

The guns crashed, and smoke boiled back into the turret and battle was joined.

The two lines of warships bore down the channel into the bay. Donald paid no mind to anything other than his guns as they hammered at Fort Morgan. Every now and then, when the turret traversed, he could see the other ironclads in line ahead, blasting at the shoreline. It seemed to him the return fire from Fort Morgan was lessening, but that wasn't too likely - warships weren't normally very successful at knocking out land-based cannon. They were damned close inshore, he thought, and wondered if they'd strayed off the channel they'd been ordered to keep.

Not a minute later came a shout down the pipe: "The Tecumsah's been torpedoed."

And Lord it was so. Donald chanced a look out a deck hatchway, and through the gun-fog he saw the leading ironclad drifting out of line, white steam clouding above its stack. The ship was listing and before his mind properly took it in the Tecumsah was gone, vanished below the surface. Donald shuddered - the monitor

481

must have struck barely a moment ago, and had already sunk. What were the chances of anyone in the engine room - or even the turret - getting out in time? Fearful reason told him what it was like aboard the Tecumsah as it turned and rolled - cold water dashing against the fiery boilers; iron exploding. cannon crushing anything in their fall; redhot metal being quenched as if in a blacksmith's tempering bath; lungs no longer screaming but gasping for air... and finding nothing but saltwater and then silence.

The Chickasaw pulled even with where the Tecumsah had gone down. Donald saw a few heads struggling in the water, and from somewhere, a boat pulling to the rescue. But that was all he had time for. There were orders to give and guns to feed.

Now the battle line was past the forts guarding the mouth of the bay, and into Mobile Bay itself. The powder smoke in the turret had become too thick to see, and Donald took his Captain's lead - even though he knew it foolhardy - and was ordering his guns from atop the turret, shouting commands through the grating.

Then the Tennessee came down the bay - black angles of iron - its ram cutting a wake in front of the long casemate; guns long fingers protruding through the ports... moving slowly... ponderously... like some fabled beast. There was no sign of its crew, nor was there anything about the ship that suggested human hands had aught to do with its forming, except possibly the Stars and Bars fluttering from its flagstaff. Donald knew it for what it was - a great dragon in the sea; and that it must be killed this day. The ironclad was bearing directly on the first warship in the main column - Farragut's flagship, the Hartford.

"Can you bear on it?" came the shout from Captain Perkins on the other turret.

Donald estimated range, and whether he had an open field of fire. "I cannot, sir. She'll need to be closer, and I'm afraid I'll strike the flagship."

The Tennessee tried to close the Hartford, but was easily evaded, and then it was past and gone - into the powdermists before time began - toward the mouth of the bay and the Confederate forts.

Allan Cole & Chris Bunch

The squadron now held Mobile Bay, and was preparing to anchor. The battle appeared almost over - there was little fire coming from the forts, and the Confederate ships still afloat were declining battle. Donald had chanced taking half his men off the guns to help the mates down in the magazine ready more charges, when the shouting began once more, and the Tennessee returned.

The 175 pound shells were rammed down the mouths of the Chickasaw's guns, and they were run out. There was no shouting, no panic. Donald needed to issue almost no orders as the turret traversed on the black bulk of the Confederate ram. Orders and signals came in a flurry... signal from the Hartford... close with and ram... four bells... full power... steer for the Tennessee, and Mobile Bay became a melee.

Donald saw the Hartford, with some fool who had to be Admiral Farragut standing in the rigging, reverse the expected events and ram the Confederate ship. He thought he saw two other ships do the same, but the world to him was the slam of his cannon as the Chickasaw closed on the Rebel ship.

Surely Captain Perkins wasn't lunatic enough to try and ram, and hell, they were about the same length, but it sure didn't look like it, and someone was on the grating beside Donald, shouting at him to get below for shit's sake, and he came back to himself as both turrets of the Chickasaw fired. And now there was no bay, no wooden ships, and no humans in the world as he dropped down the ladder and slammed the deck hatch to, and the hammering began. The Chickasaw rode barely thirty feet off the Confederate's flank... hammering, hammering, and Donald had a flashing vision of this battle being all wars to come - when men would not matter, save how cleverly they positioned their iron masters for battle; how quickly they served the guns; and how quietly and unobtrusively they died when hit.

He could hear nothing but the ringing of the cannon and the cacophony, and saw nothing but the occasional flash of dark plate that was the Tennessee so close, so close, and the battle went on and on and on, although the calm part of his nature that his father had taught made some sense of what was happening: you are striking the Confederate hard... look, now, in that flash, see how her gunports are jammed shut, or perhaps not opening because the guncrews have been killed where they stood... and there is a timber sticking through the casemate... now their smokestack's fallen... and what did that roiling chain on the afterdeck connect to before the last salvo ripped it asunder? The rudder? Is their steering crippled?

"Aim fair for the end of the casemate," he shouted to a gunlayer, mouth inches from the man's ear.

The man nodded, sign-languaged to his crew, and the guns slammed yet again, and the smoke was so heavy Donald could not even see the other gun in his turret, and everyone's face was as dark as minstrels.

There were more shouts then, loud ones, even over the guns that were no longer firing except in his mind and eardrums: "She's struck! She's surrendered!"

Donald peered through the port and saw a white flag waved from the Tennessee's battery grating. It was over.

After a time he went on deck, marveling that while there were great dents in the Chickasaw's armor, the ship or its turrets had not been holed.

The Tennessee lay, a smoking hulk, dead in the water. Now there were more white flags, and some enterprising sorts from another ship boarding to take its surrender. The battle was fought and won.

Donald wondered at its worth for a moment, his mind seeing that white canvas vanish in the green depths of the Gulf; the men buried full fathom five on the broken Tecumsah with never a ceremony; or the seamen killed on the other ships.

A curious thought came - perhaps the best you could hope for was to fight and die in a battle of your own choosing, whether it was fought by men or women, blood or words, for land or an idea or simply to be allowed to live a life of your own choosing.

That rang true, and he no longer felt rudderless in a world made empty by Joshua's death.

CHAPTER THIRTY-SEVEN

NEAR BERRYVILLE, VA. - SEPT. 4, 1864

THE HORSEMEN WENT through the great Shenandoah
Valley with fire and sword. Their task was simple: destroy the
South's granary. The Shenandoah Valley was to become a
wasteland.

There were various rationales. The partisan John Singleton
Mosby rode from the Shenandoah, and his forces were irregulars -
waging war as brutally as the Spanish guerrilleros against Napoleon;
neither Mosby or his supporters were subject to the customary
usages of war, and therefor must be brought to bay. Another reason
given was the savaging would be revenge the Confederate's burning
of the city of Chambersburg in Pennsylvania - which was in turn a
reprisal for the North's depredations in the Valley that summer.

The real reason was simple: war still raged. To anyone of sense,
it had been clearly lost for a long time. Editorialists could pick any
one of many times the South should have surrendered - Antietam
when it was proven no amount of blood would make the North
bargain for peace; New Orleans, Vicksburg or the blockade, as the
South was sealed off from the rest of the world; Gettysburg, when it
became plain no cleverness of Bobbie Lee's would turn the tide; or
even the savage hammering earlier in the year, from The Wilderness
to Cold Harbor. The South could not replace their dead, but the war
dragged on. Jeff Davis sat in Richmond, surrounded by sycophants
and warhawks, or so they said. No communiqués came from him
other than fight on, fight on.

The conflict grew in frightfulness. Lincoln and Grant replaced
generals who were incompetent, hesitant or merely of too kindly a
nature. Sherman was given an army, and the vague goal of Atlanta
plus instructions to rend the countryside as he went. He cut a swath
through Georgia and now held Atlanta. Lincoln had named Sept. 5 a
holiday in celebration, although no one who'd seen that wasteland, if
he still had bowels, would find anything to revel in.

The Shenandoah Valley had not only been an invasion route for
Southern armies, but contained the Confederacy's richest farmland.
Very well. An army, or a nation, that cannot eat, cannot fight. An
Army that cannot find barns for shelter nor straw for fodder, loses its

heart for battle. An Army that relishes the clean country air, would breathe smoke from burning farmhouses and the stench of the slaughtered. An Army that needs clear water to drink would fill its canteens from wells rotting corpses had been dumped in. An Army that marches through a desert marches without spies, without scouts, without friendly warnings... without even the moment's lift a young maid cheering by her gate provides.

Phil Sheridan was put in charge. The short, bullet-headed cavalryman whose parents had come from County Cavan knew what he was supposed to do. "When we are finished," he said, "a crow flying over the Shenandoah will have to bring its own rations."

A minister with the Rhode Island cavalry put it more plainly: "The time has fully come to peel this land." He was not condemned for bloody-mindedness but praised for clarity of thought.

Sheridan took a bit of time evaluating his command and commanders, and then, following Grant and Lincoln's lead, cut away what little dross and panoply the Army still carried, dismissed subordinates he thought too soft for the task, and promoted others.

Michael Shannon was now a Brigadier General, commanding a full division of cavalry, almost three thousand hardened young hellions, which included his "own" 13th California.

Knowing well how the Shenandoah campaign, and the war itself, would be fought, he did not find his new stars that great a compliment. Michael did not, however, ask to be relieved nor did he resign his commission, and sometimes wondered why, finding only the vaguest of answers. In an earlier day he might have quit cold and gone back to California. When he considered his own history - from his adventurous days during the Mexican War, to the roguish sometimes-gambler, sometimes-politician, sometimes-speculator in San Francisco, or even the wryly cynical colonel of cavalry he'd been in 1862 - it was if he was studying the biography of another man.

At one time he'd been fond of chamber music and literature. But while he still carried Shakespeare, a volume of Gibbons's, and Childe Harold in his saddlebags, they went unread. Now he could laugh uproariously at and was highly entertained by the crudest minstrel show or barracks jest, and when he could concentrate on

486

reading it was the most tawdry of illustrated weeklies. But perhaps it would all return, once they had convinced this great beast of the Confederacy it was dead and must lie down. Perhaps.

He sat considering what he'd become, and what the world around him was, staring but not seeing the holocaust roaring up a hundred yards away that had been a plantation rich enough to raise blood mares for a sideline. This was not the first farm torched that day, nor the fifth.

The cavalry rode "up" (directions in the Shenandoah followed the terrain, and therefore reversed compass directions) the Valley in a great arc on the flanks and to the front of the infantry. Cattle were shot in the fields and, if there was time, choice cuts butchered for the evening's meal - but not to worry about carrying the scraps, since there'd be another fat heifer on the morrow. Houses that held any suggestion they belonged to Confederates or sympathizers were looted and burnt.

If there was a quartermaster's wagon handy, something comfortable but unwieldy such as a feather mattress or fine china might be taken, and used as a bit of a jest for a few days before being discarded. If not... the fire took all. This was against orders, but no officer ever enforced the edict more than casually.

Fields roared into flame, no matter who they belonged to. Pot-shotting the heads off fowl, or beheading them with the seldom-used sabers gave great sport. The carcasses were left where they fell - most soldiers were bored with chicken by now. No one bothered with ration bacon when every mile's march provided fresh porkchops. Tobacco? Well, it might not be Turkish or sugar-cured, but there was enough for a man's pipe to be always smoking like a winter chimney, and even enough to send home in a parcel if a man found access to the post.

A private from the Sixth Ward of New York, who'd perhaps eaten mutton a dozen times in his life, was heard to complain wistfully he wished they'd "have a breather, an' somebody'd show him how that mint sauce th' swells went on about was made, because sheep's tastin' wearisome an' flat of late."

What little commerce the Valley'd had - all agricultural, from woolen to flour to saw mills, tanneries, charcoal furnaces - was razed. Special treatment was reserved for the rail lines. The rails were ripped from the tracks by horses, the ties pulled up, stacked and fired. The rails were then laid over the burning creosote-soaked wood until they grew hot enough to bend, were twisted around the nearest large tree, and the Army moved on.

As for the men and women of the Valley, the day before Michael had ridden past another pillaged farm. A woman and her two sons stood wailing beside the road. Sitting easily in his saddle next to them was one of Michael's captains. The woman had sobbed something about what should she do, where should she go? The officer shrugged and said "Go north, or go to hell, madam. It matters little to me," and rode away. Michael thought of reprimanding him - but the captain was one of Michael's most efficient officers, and therefore he said nothing.

As for the poor bastard carrying a gun or worse yet defending his land with it, he was deemed a partisan and a Union general put their fate succinctly when he said "I have instructed my command not to bring any of them to my headquarters except for interment."

Mosby's rangers, in turn, gave no mercy. No cavalryman rode unaccompanied, and any single wagon would be heavily guarded. At night around the encampments, pickets went out, never less than five to a group, and sleeping areas were constantly patrolled by alert sentries. There'd been Union soldiers found at dawn, curled in their blankets, their throats as neatly slit as any Virginia farmer ever butchered a hog.

The South should not have been shocked. Michael remembered one of the stories the Shannons told, of how in the Revolution - after New York's Wyoming Valley and his own Grandmother Shannon's home in Cherry Valley had been razed by Indians and renegades - soldiers, under the personal direction of George Washington, marched into another valley, the Susquehanna, and burnt and slaughtered in retaliation until there was nothing but the silence of the graveyard. It did not matter that the targets had been Indians for the principle to appeal to America's war leaders. By 1864, to many people a still-fighting Rebel was a greater barbarian than any savage with a scalping knife.

Jeff Davis, when the leveling began, sent Jubal Early out with more than ten thousand soldiers. He was dancing around somewhere in the Shenandoah, but Sheridan didn't pay him much mind. Sooner or later they'd meet, and that would be the end of that. Meantime, there was more important work.

An aide galloped up, and pulled in his horse. "Sir. Colonel McCorkle's compliments, and you're needed to the rear. He said it's urgent."

"What's the problem, companero? Did somebody steal the aguardiente again?"

"Nossir. Sir, it's pretty ugly. It's rape, sir. Rape and murder."

There'd been five civilians huddled in the barn: a woman, her just-adolescent daughter, two toddlers and a nursing babe. The barn, hidden in a hollow some distance from a farmhouse, wasn't easy to spot from the road, and evidently the five had hoped they wouldn't be found out. They had been wrong.

When their discoverers finished with the women, they'd tried to cover their tracks. They used knives, probably fearing gunshots would attract attention, then fired the barn. But the curling smoke had been seen by an outrider, and a patrol swept down before the blaze could destroy evidence of the evil.

There were three of them. They stood in front of Michael, guarded by two grim young cavalrymen who held their Spencers ready, looking as if they'd be delighted to use them. The three, judging from the blood and bruises had already been badly used after capture.

Michael looked them over, his expression calmly curious. "It would appear we have a motley selection," he said. "Judging from appearances."

One of the men started to say something, and got a carbine butt in the kidneys that sent him to his knees.

"What you see, sir, is what they claim they are," McCorkle said, trying to appear as under control as Michael looked. He sat behind a tiny field desk.

Michael walked to the first man, who wore homespun. "You, sir. Are you one of Mosby's men?"

"Nossir. I ain't in no Army. I'm from 'round here. I'm jes'—"

"But you were armed. That's all."

He went to the man in ragged gray. "And you are one of Colonel Lee's soldiers, eh? I guess he would be almighty proud of one of his men." The man stared sullenly at Shannon, but did not answer.

"The best for last," Michael murmured, looking the man in blue uniform up and down.

"He said he was with the 34th Massachusetts." McCorkle said.

"A fine unit," Michael said. "How did they so err as to allow scum like you in their ranks before you deserted?"

The man glowered. "Th' three of us di'n't do that. We was jus'... jus' lookin' f'r shelter, an' come upon... upon th' bodies. We ain't guilty a' naught, none a' us."

Michael, his expression still deceptively mild, looked at McCorkle who did not speak, but picked up a long Arkansas bowie from the ground, and put it on the desk. Michael lifted it up, and examined the blade.

"No doubt the blood on this knife is from a chicken?"

"It ain't from them folks."

"Of course not... Colonel McCorkle, I do not wish to hear all the details, but is it possible these three might be unlucky innocents who wandered into the middle of someone else's carnage?"

"Not goddamned likely, sir. One of the kids was... was still moving, according to the patrol sergeant. He had his men quarter the area, just to make sure he hadn't missed anybody."

"Thank you, Colonel."

Michael took out a cigar he'd handrolled out of the local tobacco, and rolled it between his fingers. There were many like these three - they called them bummers. Sometimes they were stragglers, sometimes deserters. Mostly all they wanted was loot and freedom enough to consume it; and they were ignored, since in a peculiar way the bummers were carrying out the same task the army had been given. But this was certainly different.

"Very well. Since we are not planned to bivouac any time soon, and must continue the march to keep the army's flanks covered... Hang them."

490

The man in homespun's eyes rolled, and he sagged to the ground in a faint. The man who might have been a Confederate soldier paled. But the man from Massachusetts was of firmer stock.

He growled what might have been a laugh. "That don't stand, Gin'ral. Ain't no single man, ev'n if he's a gin'ral, got th' right t' string a body up. I know I got rights, an' one of 'em's a proper trial, not this joke."

"A joke, eh?"

"Damn' straight. An' even if'n y' round up a court-martial board, ain't no way we'uns'll hang. Honest Abe don't hold with hangin' his soldiers, no matter what, so we'll be reprieved. An' it'll be our word 'gainst that pussy sergeant as to what happened, an' there's nothin' but Confeds in there anyways."

Michael looked thoughtful. "An interesting brief. I've always held barracks lawyers in a certain regard. But there are two errors in your case. The first is this matter will not be reported to General Sheridan before, oh, perhaps tomorrow or the next day, if at all. I doubt President Lincoln, though I respect his powers enormously and admire him greatly, is empowered by any Constitution to raise the dead.

"Sergeant! Three ropes, tied to that oak limb across the way. Borrow that ambulance if you will for a gallows. Tie some sandbags to their ankles. Even though they don't deserve it, we'll give them the mercy of a clean drop.

"You three. Five minutes to pray to any God of your choosing. And may He have mercy on your souls."

The three bodies hung limply, their necks cocked at impossible angles. Michael considered his work. No, not quite.

"Mac, before we ride on, find somebody who can carve, and secure three boards. Letter all three of them the same: I KILL WOMEN and hang them from the chests of these carrion."

"Yessir." McCorkle, who'd been staring at the corpses as if looking at his first casualty, swallowed hard, and hastened away.

Michael continued pondering on the unpleasant, but necessary task that had been efficiently carried out. He wondered what the

Allan Cole & Chris Bunch

Michael Shannon of old might have thought. He, himself, felt not much of anything...

CHAPTER THIRTY-EIGHT

CAMP DOUGLAS, ILL. - SEPT. 23, 1864

THEY BURIED PRIVATE Albert Whatley on a gray and blustery Friday. That marked the end for Patrick.

He'd been hammered from outside and inside, and knew exactly what the poor bastard they were burying had felt. Patrick had been sick for nearly four weeks that summer and Whatley had been his nurse. Sometime in July, LaCoutre had died of some nameless fever, and by the time Patrick was on his feet the hut was full of strangers. Men came to Camp Douglas only for one thing - to die. Die soon, die late, it didn't matter.

Then Whatley got sick, and sicker. Nothing anyone could do seemed to help. Patrick even implored a Yankee medical orderly, whose duties were confined to caring for the guards, to see if he could do anything. The man shook his head, but gave Patrick a pack of sassafras tea, and, as he left, slipped Shannon an opium tablet.

"Sometimes," the Yank said, "that helps... either way."

Patrick dosed the little cavalryman immediately, but it didn't do any good. It seemed as if the man's skin had been built for someone else, and then stretched. His complexion grew sallow, and then more sallow. His eyes burned like a madman's, and he raved in and out of delirium.

The last he came back, and grinned at Patrick, "Ain't this 'bout the dumbest dam' way to pass time you ever thought of?"

His eyes roamed to the side of his pallet, where his tools, scraps of wood and that never-to-be-finished chess set lay.

"An' we never did figger out who was gonna go an' be the Queen of the North." His eyes closed then, and never opened.

After the burial, Patrick came back to the hut and slumped down on its steps. No matter how he tried, no matter how he said he was being a weak-livered fool, he knew, knew to the bottom of his guts he would not live out the coming winter. He didn't have the strength, didn't have the will, and didn't know where he could get either. Camp Douglas, this fourth year of the war, was a little short of joi de vivre, as LaCoutre might have put it.

Not that things were any better anywhere else. The war raged on, even though it was obvious to Patrick that it should have ended months, even years, ago. Atlanta had fallen to Sherman earlier in the month, but Lee and his Army fought on in Virginia... fought like a bear Patrick had seen, roped and gutshot by vaqueros but still trying to reach his tormentors before he died.

But that wasn't the real reason for his depression. It was Lucy. Two weeks ago, a despairing letter had reached him. Times were still hard in Vicksburg - there was not enough food, other than the relief supplies that had poured down from the North. No one, including the Baldwins, had the money to rebuild yet, and construction materials were coming down-river in a trickle.

Then the worst - Mr. Baldwin was dead. He'd been working long hours, trying to figure some way for his firm to fight its way back to profit - in a time when there seemed to be no business but war and no capital for anything beyond what the battlefield needed. He'd left his office late one evening and was on his way home when a freight wagon lurched around a corner, and its six horses trampled him down. The wagon master had been drunk.

Patrick mourned - he'd honestly liked the man, the little time he'd been able to know him.

Now the family was shattered. There didn't seem to be any money in the Baldwin firm, at least none that wouldn't be tied up until the war ended. In July, Lucy's sister had married her captain - against the wishes of every member of the family except Mr. Baldwin. She'd "gone north." Lucy thought they would close the house in Vicksburg. Not that there was anything to close up - the glassless windows were covered with oilcloth; the holes in the walls were sealed with planking from the rubble of cannon-blasted buildings; and the old broken doors could not be replaced at the present time.

Lucy said they might go to Memphis, where Mrs. Baldwin's married sister lived. Lucy doubted they would find much of a welcome, since her aunt and uncle were strong Unionists, who'd been overjoyed when the city was returned to the Federals early in the war.

Patrick had to do something, anything. Such as? Such as escape from this camp, journey the how many hundred miles south - hoping no one noticed his drawl - without a coin nor a gun, and feeling but

494

half-healthy? Absurd. Maybe he should write that long-thought-of letter to Philadelphia, and throw himself, or rather Lucy, on what mercy remained in the breast of the Shannons. He'd have to do something like that. But as yet, he didn't know how.

So much, he thought, for that feeling, that certainty that he would, indeed, live out this war. There was not a chance he'd be anything other than another low mound, in that rapidly-growing burial ground in a few months. He'd have to make sure somebody would carve his name on a cross, so if anybody came looking they'd know for sure. All too many of the headstones in the graveyard were blank, or just said what regiment a soldier had belonged to. He felt too bleak to even feel sorry for himself any longer. Poor Lucy. Poor South. Poor Yankees. Poor goddamned everybody.

Someone called his name, and he glanced up. It was Corporal Campbell, he of the fervent abolitionist beliefs and the death-promise of five months ago, standing just at the perimeter, a carbine cradled in his arms. Patrick had stayed well clear of the corporal and the fence itself since the warning, ducking out of sight whenever he saw Campbell near the dead line with a gun. But now he didn't give a rat's ass.

"You! Shanahan, or Shannon, or whatever it is. C'mere."

Bullshit. Patrick didn't get up. "No, Corporal," he called. "This ain't a shootin' gallery and I ain't your wooden duck. You'll have to draw your bead from where you stand."

It wouldn't be the first nor the fifth time a Union guard had shot a prisoner well inside the compound with no provocation whatsoever.

"God damn it, man, would you... " Campbell stopped. He walked a few feet away, set the carbine down, then came back. "All right? Dammit, I'm not going to kill you."

Not believing a word, and expecting Campbell had a pistol hidden, but what of that - it might be quicker and hurt less than letting a plague boil your lungs out - Patrick walked across the open ground to just short of the dead line.

"You'll notice," he said, "that even if you pot me from there I'll still not fall off sacred ground."

Campbell's face reddened. He started to snarl, then forced calm. "Jesus Christ on a busted crutch but you Rebs are stubborn," he said. "Look. I went an' said something back a few months ago when I was pissed, all right? I went and made a damned fool of myself out of the heat of anger and 'cause of what some general did, as if you'd ever have a way of stopping him even if you was there, unless maybe shooting him in the back, just because I knew you was with Forrest. And I was wrong. Shitfire, I might as well of been a Copperhead Democrat, sayin' one thing an' practicin' another, like you Rebs do, goin' on about th' law an' justice, but doin' just as you damn please when it pleases you, which is one reason this war is bein' fought."

"If you're runnin' for office, Corporal, even though I'm admiring your little speech, I've got to remind you Rebs don't have the vote."

Campbell ground his teeth. "All right, Shannon. God blast the day they let you hard-headed teagues come over anyway, slave lovers like you are. I hunted you up to make sorta an apology, even though I'm realizing you ain't about to accept it. So I'll make it short. Get your ass, right now, over to the main gate and the camp office. There's a man there I told about you, and he wants to talk."

"About what?" Patrick said, suspiciously.

"Just go, goddamit, or else crawl back in your shack and fucking starve or freeze, I don't care!"

Campbell stamped back to his carbine as Patrick backwatered away from the dead line. The Federal walked down the fence line without another word or looking to see what Patrick did. Shannon had no idea who could be interested in him, but couldn't figure how indulging his curiosity could make matters worse - although he knew he was likely wrong.

After sluicing his face off at a pump, tugging his tatters together and wishing he'd shaved this month, he went to the camp office. A man was waiting for him. He was very young, had a neatly-trimmed Van Dyke, and wore the uniform of a Union colonel of infantry. Patrick wasn't familiar enough with the protocols of war to know whether a prisoner should salute an enemy officer, so he didn't.

The colonel half-smiled, as if not expecting recognition, and shoved a cigar case across the small field desk between them.

496

"You're Shannon, correct? Sergeant? Formerly with Forrest's hellions? Captured outside Vicksburg doing some damn-fool stunt or other that should've gotten you hanged?"

"I'm Shannon. And I was just trying to keep my own war going... if that's a damn-fool-"

"Stop lipping off, and light up. I don't have all day to fuss with a bigmouthed Rebel potato-monger, even if I do need him."

Shannon obeyed. The colonel snapped a lucifer and held it across to light Patrick's cigar. The first puff sent his head spinning. He hadn't had anything much to smoke since... since that pipe Whatley'd given him, way back when. He felt like he'd just had two snifters of French brandy, and decided to hold his tongue until the room settled.

"I'm Colonel Mowat," the colonel said. "I'm raising a regiment of Volunteers. They're going to call us infantry, but we'll be mounted most of the time. I want you to... " and the colonel changed his tone, mockingly, "... jine up with me."

Patrick's jaw dropped. Hell, maybe the cigar was doped, and the colonel'd been on the pipe himself before Shannon arrived. "Uh... sir... I don't know if you noticed, but... " and his fingers ran over his tattered but still visibly gray uniform, "we aren't exactly in the same army."

Mowat didn't respond to that. "They're calling us Galvanized Yankees, hell if I know why. By us, I mean you. I'm from New Hampshire, and think we should have started licking you folks back about Dred Scott time... when I was wearing knee pants. There'll be four, maybe more regiments raised out of the prison camps."

Patrick regretfully set the cigar back down and stood up. "Sorry. But I'm not a traitor. I ain't fixing to become one, either, no matter how bad it is out there."

"Traitor isn't what I'm asking," Mowat said impatiently. "Although there are those who think traitoring started back about Secession time. What's your views on that one, Sergeant?"

Patrick looked at the wood floor. That self-same thought had been known to cross his mind, as well. Mowat noticed the silence, and indicated Patrick should pick up his cheroot, and then the colonel relit it.

Allan Cole & Chris Bunch

"So let's have no more of that dung," he said briskly. "Here is the proposition. I take you, and some others I've been talking to, out of this goddamned camp... which whoever laid out ought to be made to live in. This sty's even worse than that hellhole you Secesh have down in Georgia. I take you out, give you a bath, clean uniforms, and you'll have to cuss and put it on even if it's blue, and fill your belly full of Army beans and bacon til it's round. Then I'll drill your eyeballs off until I'm satisfied you, and the rest of you, are the kind of soldiers I need. You, Sergeant, will have a section to begin with, and I'll promote you if you deserve it. You'll be paid like any other Federal soldier, and treated the same by us Yanks or I'll remember some old punishments I read somebody named Torquemada tried some years ago and see how they fit on fatlipped bluebellies. In return, you'll fight, and maybe die for me."

"That's where it sticks," Patrick said. "Traitor or not... there's no way I'll pull a trigger on anyone who's wearing gray."

"You won't ever see any Johnny Rebs. We're going west," Mowat said. "When you Secesh started your conniptions, the whole damned frontier blew up - all the way from Texas to Michigan. Every Indian out there decided to seize the moment, for which you can't exactly blame them, and rode out with scalping knives. The War Department's had about enough of their ways, and, since there aren't any proper soldiers to spare, we'll do with what we can.

"Since you might be a sensible man, I'll but mention that this war's lost for you people in every way but name, and come peace there's a whole land out there that we'll be settling, north and south."

Again, the world swam in front of Patrick's eyes, but this was not nicotine-induced. He remembered the great sweeping plains and prairies he'd seen in Texas, and how they drew him, a vastness broader than anyone knew of here in the East, with skies that stretched beyond all knowing.

"You don't know anything about the West, but—"

"Sir, I came back from Texas when the war started."

Now it was Mowat's turn to look surprised. "Your friend Corporal Campbell steered me better than he realized. Can you read and figure?"

Allan Cole & Chris Bunch

"I can. Sir," Patrick said. "I've got a question, now. I've got no particular reason to trust you, or anybody else wearing blue. Come to think, I'm not exactly trusting anybody wearing any uniform. So how do I know you'll keep your word, and we won't end up, say, running through Virginia with Grant looking for General Lee?"

"You don't. Hell, I don't, either. The War Department's been known to lie, or anyway change their mind as I'm sure they'd rather have it put, to colonels as well as sergeants. But if that happens... you can always cut and run. I'll wager you'd have a better chance on showing your heels outside this camp than inside, even though I'd be coming after you with a court-martial and a noose."

Patrick sat considering.

"That's a great deal I've spoke of," Mowat said. "You hardly need answer today. I'll be back in two days time, and I'll have to know then. I'll say but one thing more, Sergeant. Speaking personally, if I was in your boots, I would a damned sight rather die of an Indian arrow or bullet than rot in this fucking hole. Go on, now. Take another cigar with you. I'd give you a box if I had it, and you can tell your fellows I am going to report the conditions I've seen in these camps when I get back to Washington. Not that I expect it will do any real good. That's all."

Patrick stood up, and smartly saluted. Mowat returned it, and Shannon started out. With his hand on the door, he caught himself, then turned back.

"Colonel, I don't have to do any thinking, sir. I'll take you up on your offer. Not for the beans, not for the bacon, not even for the pay and the chance out of this shitheap, but for my own reasons I've been thinking about for some time. I'll serve, and, if you hold up your word, I'll never run, either."

They shook hands. Patrick walked out of the office, not feeling the cold as night came down across the camp, nor the wind rip through his thin clothes. Now he could do it. Now he'd be able to keep that oath he made in the Vicksburg church to his wife.

Damn. Maybe he had been right. Maybe he would live out the war. He hurried away through the dusk.

He had a letter to write to Philadelphia.

CHAPTER THIRTY-NINE

PHILADELPHIA - NOVEMBER 9, 1864

THE SOUND OF many bells intruded on Mary's dream. In it, she was sprinting barefoot through a deserted glen near the cottage where she and Hugh had honeymooned. Hugh was in close pursuit, grabbing at her frock, while she squealed in mock alarm. A few more steps would take her to a soft, shaded bower where she could let him catch her and tumble her onto the moss. But the bells were persistent, hammering away at the dream until it began to shatter. A bright morning sun conspired to ruin the rest of it, piercing a gap in the curtains to play upon her face. Then, as she became more aware, the late autumn chill crept through the edge of the blankets, making her shiver.

She groaned and pulled the covers over her head - was it Sunday already? If so, she was late to church. She thought about pretending she was sick, and going back to sleep to recapture her dream. Why was she so tired? She remembered that she'd stayed up late last night. And last night wasn't a Saturday, it was a Tuesday. Therefore, she wasn't late to church, but late to work. And to heck with her girls, they could tear up the classroom for all she cared. Let Sister Hortense deal with the terrors of budding adulthood. But, wait! Sister Hortense was already taking care of her class, wasn't she? Hadn't Mary had taken the remainder of the semester off for a very good reason?

There was a stir in the bed beside her. Mary, fully awake now, grinned as she also remembered why she had stayed up so late the previous night. She peeked out of the covers and saw Hugh's sleeping face. No dream was necessary - she had her husband home. He'd been out of the Army for a little over two months thanks to the wound in his thigh, which was healing - although slowly and it still gave him some pain. His face was still thin, and tired looking, but she was determined to get him filled out and rested. That part wouldn't be difficult; it was the inner man that had her worried.

Hugh had returned as stolid and resourceful as when he'd stood beside her at the altar three years ago. My god, was it only three years, she thought? It seemed so much longer, especially when she looked at the deep worry lines in Hugh's face. He suffered from nightmares, which was to be expected, but she ached for him when he woke her with his thrashing about, muttering harsh orders in his sleep. He was still fighting the war, although his wound had taken him out of it permanently.

Outwardly, he was the same old Hugh in many ways. But he seemed disengaged with life, staring off vacantly in mid-conversation. Thinking back on their wedding, she remembered her vow to be strong for both of them. It had been a girl's promise, for there was no way she could have known how much strength would be required. Mary burrowed deep into herself and found that vow again. She renewed it, but this time as a grown woman who knew very well what sudden twists in the cliff-edged path that life could take.

His eyes closed, Hugh listened to the bells, but did not ponder on the possible reasons for the chiming. He let the sound wash over him; let it trickle into long forgotten places where normalcy had once dwelled. Last night, for the first time in what seemed like ages, he had not dreamed of Kerry's death. It did not comfort him: somehow he felt he was betraying his brother's memory, and of the men he had fought beside for so long. He was also troubled by his father's decision to remain with his unit. Considering his age and service, there had been opportunity for Ian to leave. Hugh hadn't argued, for it would have been pointless: his father was as stubborn as the guns he commanded. Hugh hadn't mentioned any of this to his mother. It would have only hurt her, and been impossible to understand. Hugh knew why, although he couldn't put words to it. It was a gut knowing - a fear of betrayal, a confusion of ideals like loyalty, and staying the fight.

You might as well get used to it, he thought. The war is over for you. His colonel had let him know he was welcome back when the wound healed, and, even if he was never fully whole again there were many officers under the colors without an eye, arm or leg, so he might consider serving on, even when the war had ended. But despite his misshapen guilt, Hugh knew once he took his uniform off he'd never wear it again. He was sick of death and sicker still to be a cause of it.

Allan Cole & Chris Bunch

Other guilts nagged, not the least his difficulty in re-entering the world of civilians. In her own way, Mary had suffered as much as he. Not once had she mentioned the troubles at home, or what he knew must have been stark terror during the times the Rebels had threatened Philadelphia. For her sake, he had to dig out the old Hugh - the Hugh she had trusted and married - and rejoin the human race. Now he thought of it, there was responsibility he must take if there was ever any good to come out of this war. Men would be coming home to face an uncertain fate. There were widows and orphans too numerous to contemplate if one cared to retain sanity. Yes, it was time to throw off his own miseries and face the world anew. How he would do this, he wasn't certain; just as he had no idea where to start.

But the decision to do something, anything, lifted a burden. He thought about his wife lying next to him. Just being able to do this, to awaken with her firm body next to him, was a treasure.

Mary saw Hugh was awake, even though his eyes were closed. An impish smile crossed her face. She peered under the covers and saw he was as naked as when they'd torn off their clothes last night. To her delight, she saw the blanket above his groin forming into a little tent. He must have the same thought on his mind that now crossed hers. Feeling deliciously daring, she slipped under the blanket to give it a kiss. Hugh didn't move, so she tried another. Then another.

Finally, he stirred. "Is that a mouse nibbling under there?" he said.

"That's right," she giggled, "only a little mouse after some cheese. You go back to sleep and don't disturb her."

"Nice little mouse," Hugh murmured, as she continued her work.

More bells joined the first group, filling the air with their incessant sound. But Hugh and Mary were determined to ignore them. She returned to her explorations.

Someone hammered on the bedroom door. "Dammit," Hugh muttered.

Mary poked her head out of the covers. "Yes. We're awake."

Allan Cole & Chris Bunch

"Can't you hear all the bells?" Susan called.

"We hear them" Mary said. "What is it? A fire?"

"No. It's about President Lincoln. He's just been re-elected."

Mary looked at Hugh. Both of them laughed. "What great news, mother," Hugh called out. "We'll be there in a minute."

"Breakfast is waiting," Susan cried back, her voice happier than Mary had heard it in a long time. She got out of the bed and searched for her robe. "I think this news is almost more important to your mother," she said, "then it is to the country."

Hugh eased himself up, favoring the leg that pained him. "When I first heard that pounding," he said, "I thought, this had better be damned important." He laughed again. "And it was. So I guess I've got nothing to complain about."

Mary giggled. "Don't worry," she said. "The mouse is still hungry. And now she knows just where to find the cheese."

"Mr. Pinkerton was here this morning," Nancy said.

"That's nice, dear," Susan replied.

"He said Kerry sends his love to all of us," Nancy continued, "and we aren't to worry a bit about his safety. Oh, yes, and he misses us terribly."

"We miss him too," Susan said.

Nancy turned to Hugh. "Did I tell you that Kerry was working for Mr. Pinkerton, and is on a secret mission for the President?"

"Yes, you did," Hugh said, as mild as he could. "But I'm glad to hear the latest news just the same."

Nancy nodded and smiled. "It's a good thing Mr. Pinkerton likes me," she said, "or I'd never know what my Kerry was up to." She leaned closer to Hugh, dropping her voice. "If anyone ever gives you trouble," she said, "you just let me know. And I'll have Mr. Pinkerton take care of them for you."

Hugh didn't know what to say, except, "Thank you very much."

Nancy said he was welcome, then chattered on about this and that, addressing her remarks to no one in particular. Finally she stopped. She looked through the window and saw the bright sun. "My goodness," she said, "how did it get to be so late?" she rose from the table. "I hope no one thinks I'm being rude," she said, "but I really have to get to my weaving."

"That's quite all right, dear," Susan said. "We all know you have work to do."

Nancy tripped out of the room, as gay as a young bird. A moment later they heard the clatter of the loom.

Susan saw Hugh was troubled. "She really is much better," Susan said. "Her interest in weaving has done wonders. But unless the Good Lord takes a hand, I fear this is as good as she'll ever get. I really don't mind her little fantasy about Mr. Pinkerton and Kerry. If it comforts her, well what's the harm in it I say."

Hugh thought for a moment, then nodded. "None at all," he said.

He mulled over the wonderful news of Lincoln's re-election, and how the war was certain to end now the South saw the people's firm resolution. In Philadelphia alone, Lincoln had bested Little Mac by more than ten thousand votes.

Then, quite casually he said: "I'm thinking about going down to the brickyard tomorrow."

Susan and Mary were startled, but did their best to hide the surprise. Since his return Hugh had pointedly avoided any mention of his previous life as manager of the yard.

"I would really welcome any help you could give me," Susan said. "There's buildings going up all over the city, but I haven't done well getting any of the business."

Hugh nodded offhandedly. "I'll soon get it going again," he said. "They'll be coming around as soon as they hear Hugh Dolan's back."

"I've also had to let the gas refitting business languish," Susan said. "On top of everything else, it was just too much. Besides, it takes a man with the bustle and smooth talk of Kerry to make it go. People are afraid of modern things, especially when you're talking about their home. And Kerry had a way of making it all seem... well, as if it were the natural state of things to have a house all lit up at night as if it were the middle of the day."

Hugh considered, then thought of Thomas. His father had always seen something in Thomas Shannon Ryan - as he liked to call

504

himself - others in the family perhaps missed. He wondered if Thomas was well enough yet, or if he'd sworn off his old ways. In Thomas's favor was the fact he'd finally come around enough to fight for something, and suffered grievously for it.

"Let me think on it," Hugh said. "Maybe a fresh view will solve it."

As they were finishing their meal Mrs. Fawcett entered with the mail. There were two letters on the tray: one crisp, white, the other battered and much weathered.

She decided to deal with the bad news first. She held up the pristine envelope for Mary and Hugh to see. "It's from Mr. Burstell," she said. "About Pamela's suit, no doubt. The court was to make a ruling last month."

"That awful woman," Mary exclaimed. "I hope to God the court saw through her."

Susan knew better, but she opened the letter with good cheer. She glanced at the contents. "Well, I'm sorry to say, Mary, you didn't get your wish. They've ruled in her favor. We've lost the case."

Mary was stunned. Hugh looked at her with grave concern. "What will we do?" he asked.

Susan shrugged. "Why, eventually we'll appeal, of course, just as Mr. Burstell suggests. But I refuse to let Pamela Shannon turn our lives into a Bleak House. We don't want to become like those poor people in Mr. Dickens' book." She slipped the letter into her apron pocket. "I have a feeling in my bones" she said, "the luck of the Shannons is returning. To hell with that woman!"

She picked up the weathered envelope and studied it - turning it this way and that. "I don't recognize the handwriting," she said. She opened it and examined the contents.

Her eyebrows shot up. "Thank God," she cried, "it's from Patrick Shannon!" Her fingers trembled with excitement. "I'd feared the worst for the boy," she said. "I don't mind admitting that now."

As she scanned the letter, she thought of the bright young face that had peered at her with such amazement when she'd described the wonders of Philadelphia so long ago. She recalled the boy's intense curiosity and natural good nature, despite the torment Pamela

Allan Cole & Chris Bunch

and Edward Shannon were putting him through. He'd doted on Diana's every word, marveling at her adventures and achievements, listening closely to her advice, even though he was much too young to understand it all. She thought of Patrick's hero worship of dear Joshua who was gone from them now, and especially her dashing cousin, Michael Shannon. But the really close friendship he'd formed was with poor Russell Conners. She could imagine how crushed the boy had been by the twin blows of Diana's death, then Russell's at the hands of Patrick's own father.

She grimaced at the young man's tortured words, written in a prison camp. For some reason it did not surprise her that the boy ended up fighting on the side of the South. Nor could she find it in her heart to judge him harshly, especially after reading his tormented confession of misjudgment. It was a miracle Patrick had even survived, much less had the courage to write to her.

Mary and Hugh were staring at her expectantly. She decided to explain the confused particulars of Patrick's life another time. She was too happy to learn that he was alive and well to soil this moment with elaborate explanations. "We'll be adding a new Shannon to the household," she said. "Patrick's young wife is going to come and live with us until the war's over."

Hugh and Mary were delighted: they'd heard Ian and Susan praise Patrick to the heavens over the years, as well as worry about his fate.

Susan looked across the table to the empty chair where Ian normally sat. "We only need to get one more of us back," she said, "and then we'll be complete."

Allan Cole & Chris Bunch

Part Five

Do not weep, maiden, for war is kind.
Because your lover threw wild hands toward the sky
And the affrighted steed ran on alone,
Do not weep.
War is kind.
Hoarse, booming drums of the regiment,
Little souls who thirst for fight,
These men were born to drill and die.
The unexplained glory flies above them,
Great is the battle-god, great, and his kingdom --
A field where a thousand corpses lie.
Do not weep, babe, for war is kind.
Because your father tumbled in the yellow trenches,
Raged at his breast, gulped and died,
Do not weep.
War is kind.
Swift blazing flag of the regiment,
Eagle with crest of red and gold,
These men were born to drill and die.
Point for them the virtue of slaughter,
Make plain to them the excellence of killing
And a field where a thousand corpses lie.
Mother whose heart hung humble as a button
On the bright splendid shroud of your son,
Do not weep.
War is kind.
War Is Kind - Stephen Crane

CHAPTER FORTY

FORT MCGILVERY, VA. - MARCH 25, 1865

THE CONFEDERATES ATTACKED before dawn, striking just at the center of the Union line. They came across the moonscape between the lines without even an opening round of musketry. Ian had been shouted awake by a sentry, and stumbled out of his dugout - trying to make sense of the recruit's babbling. His eyes translated what was going on before his mind did, as he saw pinpricks of red to the left and even with Battery H's position in "Fort" McGilvery - which was actually nothing but a small, muddy redoubt. Fort Stedman - another misnamed dirt-and-straw position - was being hit hard.

Those pinpricks became a spattering then a solid line of fire, and the Confederate lines just a few hundred yards away flamed as their cannon opened fire. Ian needed no further clue, and even before his battery commander was fully aware of what was occurring, Ian had matters in hand.

Slowly, laboriously, the brass Napoleons were hoisted by main strength out of their dug-in revetments and onto clear ground to the front of the fort. They were shotted with double canister and then the men waited. Darkness became shadows became targets, and the guns bellowed and bucked.

The Confederates were sent reeling back to their trenches. Then the cannon shifted fire and brought their own position onto Fort Stedman itself as the Federals counterattacked - six fresh regiments of strong Pennsylvanians. By eight o'clock the red battle flags and their proud bearers were down in the mire and there were new flags being waved as the Rebels began surrendering. General Lee had sent his gray wolves out too often, spending their lives too lavishly, and now the barrel was dry.

There was no time in Fort McGilvery to cheer a victory nor, at least in Ian's case, the inclination. He was too busy ordering his guns lowered back down into the safety of their revetments before the stretcher-bearers of both Armies finished their tasks; the undeclared but mutual truce ended and the siege guttered on.

It was all quite mechanical to him, he realized, sitting on a full keg of gunpowder and stuffing his pipe - an action that would have given anyone, starting with himself, conniptions when the war began. It also seemed commonplace to the others, even to the replacements who'd only heard about Antietam or Gettysburg around the home fires. The battery had ridden too many miles, unlimbered too many times, fired too many shells, and buried too many of its own to get very excited about much of anything, other than the building certainty the war was over. Now there were some men bold enough to chance the gods and talk about what they'd do when they got home.

Even Ian had allowed himself that luxury, though he still thought it a jinx. He rubbed at a strained muscle and swore - lad, you're not the bucko you were, and you'd best be keeping that in mind the first time you see a hod without a shoulder below it back at the yard.

No, Mister Dolan, from now on, it's a supervisor's task for you. Let Hugh have the glory of the ordering and bossing by example. P'raps it'd be time to fit yourself for button shoes instead of boots and might you look passable in a tophat down Chestnut Street? Ian smiled. It was, indeed, becoming a different world.

But it was a world that had been bought at the highest price. The bull terrier that Grant had turned the Army into had held its grip on Bobby Lee's throat, even after the long bloodbath of the Seven Days. Lee had fallen back and back again, forced into defense positions around Richmond. The Confederate lines now covered a semi-circle - more than fifty miles from point to point - around the city of Petersburg, intended to block Grant from taking Richmond; and a new kind of warfare had been born. The new kings of the battlefield were no longer the artillery, nor even the cavalry. Both branches were more likely to fight with a pick and shovel than cannon or sabers.

They called it the Siege of Petersburg, and it had been going on for nine months. Ian, and some of the other old soldiers thought Lee was trying to break out into the open country where he'd proven mastery and fight on; although that was long ago and there weren't many gray wolves over there to remember those times. Perhaps he wanted to move south against General Sherman, who was chewing

Allan Cole & Chris Bunch

up toward Virginia like the moving jaw of a vise that would inexorably crush the South's final hope against Grant's lines.

Whatever Lee wanted, Ian thought - just a bit drowsy in the first real spring sunshine he'd had time to enjoy of late - didn't matter a tinker's dam. Idly, Ian mulled over his own theories, a bit prideful he had the leisure as he half-listened to his artillerymen get their positions ready with no orders other than the mandatory anti-slacking-off howls from the battery's noncommissioned officers.

What Lee should do - except probably Jeff Davis and his goddamned Virginia/West Point pride wouldn't let him - was to run up the white flag for the whole damned army, instead of in bits and drabs like those poor sods of an hour or so ago; or the regular stream of broken men who crept to the parapets of Fort McGilvery each night after dark, whispering they could fight no more.

Ian yawned, thought about refilling his pipe, but it was too much effort, and he let himself lie back against the parados, and once more began the soft dream of how times would bloom for the Shannons - and specifically the Dolan branch of the family - now all the blood and death had washed away the foulness of slavery and monied arrogance.

It was half an hour before they came looking for him, all of the shouts for First Sergeant Dolan having produced no answer.

Perhaps it had been a long-flying bit of shrapnel from a shell fired at random... a stray round or even a precisely-aimed bullet from a sniper.

Regardless, Ian's face still looked quietly content, his expression hardly disturbed by the slight hole just above his right temple.

Allan Cole & Chris Bunch

CHAPTER FORTY-ONE

WASHINGTON - APRIL 9-11, 1865

PAMELA CAREFULLY PLACED the ladder against the bedroom wall, then pushed her heavy hope chest against the legs for a brace. She paused, out of breath from so much unaccustomed physical effort. Her stomach roiled from the medicine she'd taken and she had to lean against the ladder until the sickness passed. She was dressed in pantaloons and a cotton waistcoat. Both garments were drenched with sweat. Finally, she had strength enough to begin.

She climbed the ladder, rocking back and forth as her grip slid on the rails. She tore a nail, but was too intent on her task to care. When she reached the top step, she turned, wagging her outstretched arms for balance, then leaped off. Pamela oofed as she landed stiff-legged on the floor. God, that hurt. She just knew she was going to be black and blue all over before the night was through. She pressed a hand against her flat belly, testing to see if the jump was going to have its desired effect.

Then she cursed when instead of the sharp pain Madame Roberval had said would be the first glad sign, there was only the sick feeling from the prescribed medicine. Pamela gathered herself, took a deep breath, and climbed the ladder again. Once more she leaped, once more she landed with a hard thud, and once more the sharp pain failed to materialize.

As she tottered over to the ladder for another effort, the door swung open and Marcia appeared. Her plain features were mottled with anger. "What are you doing?" Marcia demanded.

"You know very well what I'm doing," Pamela replied as she started up the ladder. "I told you. I'm pregnant!"

"This is a terrible, sinful thing you're up to, Pamela Shannon," Marcia said. "Trying to kill an innocent child."

"It isn't a child yet," Pamela said. "And if I have anything to say about it, it never shall be."

"You've been in here all week taking all kinds of potions from that awful clinic," Marcia said.

"And I've been sick all damned week," Pamela said. "Isn't that enough penance for my sins?" She teetered on the ladder, getting ready to jump.

"Please, Pamela," Marcia said. "At least have the good grace to stop for today. It's Palm Sunday, after all!"

"Every day this... this... thing sits in my belly, it'll get a firmer grip," Pamela said. She jumped, but this time her ankle turned and she fell heavily to the floor. "Oh, help me, Marcia," she groaned. "I think I've broken my ankle."

Marcia roughly assisted her. The ankle wasn't broken, but hurt like the devil as she hobbled back to the ladder.

"What do you plan if none of this works?" Marcia said. Pamela thought it amazing how snotty the girl had become since she'd confessed her problem. She'd had no other choice. How could she have possibly hidden her condition, while drinking who knows how many vials of foul tasting stuff, and retching her guts into a bucket? She'd even cajoled Marcia into making several trips to Madame Roberval's clinic to fetch more when she'd run out.

Marcia stamped her foot. "Answer me, Pamela! I have a right to know. I live with you. My reputation is at stake as well!"

Pamela bit back an angry retort that it was unlikely anyone would ever have cause to question Marcia's reputation. What man would have her? Instead, she said: "It will work. Madame Roberval guaranteed it."

"But what if it doesn't? Nothing is ever sure. You know that."

Marcia's tone, Pamela noticed, was also curious, as if she were taking notes on a caught-out woman's misery. She sighed. "As a last resort I can always get married."

Marcia snorted. "You don't even know who the father is."

"Of course I know who the father is," Pamela snapped back. "It's that God damned son of a bitch, John Glas."

"You shouldn't curse on Palm Sunday," Marcia scolded.

"If the good Lord wanted me not to curse, he should have told John Glas to watch where he put that thing!" Pamela snapped back.

She remembered quite well the night it happened. She and Lt. Glas - he was no longer her darling Johnny - had finished a particularly heated bit of love making. As he'd rolled off, she'd suddenly noticed he didn't have the condom on. When she confronted him, he'd confessed he'd taken it off in mid act.

"You fool," she'd cried. "You know I'm out of the other stuff." She'd been referring to the vaginal syringes and jells she always tried to have on hand for double protection. But because of the war, Madame Roberval had been having trouble keeping a sufficient supply in stock.

He'd hung his head, a sheepish grin on his face. "It doesn't feel as good with that thing on, Pamela," he'd said. "But don't worry. I've taken it off before and nothing's happened."

She'd been gripped by fear and fury and this final confession. How dare he? But Glas had seemed oddly nonplused. "If you get a baby," he said, "I'll marry you. See? I've got it all figured out."

Her answer had been to banish him from her bed and house. Now, six weeks had passed and there was not even the beginnings of the signs of her monthlies - and she was as regular as the train to Baltimore.

Pamela steeled herself for the jump.

"Well, maybe you better go see him," Marcia said, "and get a date set. Just in case."

"I'd never marry that swine," Pamela said. "Never!" She jumped. This time she landed properly, but gasped as pain from her injured ankle shot up her leg.

Marcia let Pamela lean against her as she sobbed in frustration. "Well, if you don't marry him, who will you marry?"

"Why Howard Wright," Pamela said. "Who else? He's been in my bed often enough. He'll never know the difference."

"That's a terrible trick to play on a man," Marcia said.

Pamela shrugged. "Life isn't fair. So what?"

"But how can he possibly marry you?"

"That's no problem," Pamela said. "You know as well as I do his wife's been dead for nearly four months. And if you've seen the glad smile on his face, you can't really think my lie is so awful."

"But it would be so soon," Marcia said. "He can't possibly marry until at least the year of mourning has passed. And that would be much too late for you." Marcia had a satisfied look on her face.

"He'll do whatever I ask him," Pamela said. "Don't worry. If it comes down to it, I'll figure some way around any scandal."

The windows rattled as a great volley of cannons fired somewhere in the city. Marcia gave a small cry, gripping Pamela's arm. Another volley sounded, then there was the whoosh of rockets and the windows lit an eerie red as fireworks exploded in the night sky.

"What's that?" Marcia said, frightened to the core.

Pamela shook off her arm. "Who knows?" she said. "Probably just General Grant winning another victory."

"Well thank God!" Marcia exclaimed.

Pamela stripped the covers and pillows off her bed and made a pad on the floor. "I've saving my thanks for more important things just now," she said, patting her belly. Pamela pulled Marcia over to the ladder. "Now, this time I want you to hold this thing for me while I climb."

"I couldn't be a party to... to murder!" Marcia said.

"Oh, don't be such a fuss-budget," Pamela said. "Now, help me. Please."

Marcia steadied the ladder. "If things don't work out," she said, "you could always come and stay at my aunt and uncle's house in Maryland."

Pamela stifled a groan. Heaven forbid she should suffer such a fate. She'd be at their mercy, and Marcia's as well. The way the girl was behaving, she didn't think Marcia would make life very pleasant. "Hold it very still," Pamela said.

Marcia tightened her grip. "Of course, you'll have to be much nicer to me," she said. "Much much nicer than you have been."

As Pamela jumped another volley of cannon fire rattled the windows.

The cannon thundered louder the next day as the news of Lee's surrender at Appomattox swept the city. Flags were hoisted an hour early that morning, bright banners of joy fluttering in a steady rain. Children took off from school and charged about Washington, harassing paraders with exploding fire crackers. The crowds went wild at the White House when Lincoln appeared and called for the band to play Dixie, which he said was a fine old song that belonged to the Union now. He declared the following day - Tuesday - a holiday and everyone rushed madly about to get ready.

Pamela listened to the celebration in the solitude of her bedroom. Howard had sent over numerous messages, begging her to join him in all the partying. She'd pleaded illness, but promised she'd do her best to see him Tuesday evening.

Neither the abortion medicine or the ladder jumping seemed to be working. Although she was sick in her stomach, and bruised from several falls, on the whole she felt disgustingly healthy. Madame Roberval had come by to see her in person, and promised a new shipment of "special medicine" was due any day now.

"I've prescribed it to two royal princesses," she'd said, in that maddeningly fake European accent of hers," and it has always worked to expel the child without fail." But before she left she'd echoed Marcia's caution. "If I were you, Mrs. Shannon," she'd said, "I would consider buying a little insurance at the altar."

Then she'd wagged her finger at the look of disgust her remarks had drawn. "You can always change your mind," she'd said. "A dear friend of mine - a Hungarian countess, no less - did so and suffered no permanent harm to her reputation."

Late that night, Pamela made up her mind to do as the two women suggested. After she'd determined how she was going to bend Congressman Wright to her will, she fell into a deep, dreamless sleep.

Tuesday evening, Pamela was her gay old self as she rode beside Howard in his elegant carriage. Skillful makeup hid all signs of her week-long efforts to abort. She wore her most daring gown with a plunging neckline that barely covered her nipples. Howard's eyebrows rocketed as she shed her cloak in the carriage. She giggled like a strumpet and leaned close to him to whisper the confession that under the dress she was naked as the day she was born.

She slapped his hand in jesting admonishment as he tried to investigate, and put on a mask of virginal propriety as Lt. Glas and Marcia joined them. They set off to tour Washington and see all the grand displays before going to the White House to hear President Lincoln speak.

It was still raining, but damp did nothing to quell the city's celebrants. Bands played, paraders marched, cannon roared, and fireworks arced through the sky. All the government buildings were illuminated, turning the mist into shimmering gold. Great transparencies, alive with glowing, gas-lit images of flags, Union soldiers and glorious battle scenes, draped the Treasury and other major buildings. At the Post Office there was an amazing transparency of a courier carrying the mail with the words "Behold, I bring you good tidings of great joy," emblazoned on it.

The windows were lit with hundreds of candles, while several thousand blazed at the Patent Office. There seemed to be not one area of the city untouched by the celebration.

From Rock Creek to the almshouse, from the Northern Liberties to the Arsenal, bands played, singers serenaded, and fireworks burst in the skies. Mansion windows shimmered light, working class homes were draped with homemade transparencies, and expensive candles hailed victory in the black shantytown district.

As the carriage toured the victorious city, Pamela oohed and aahed at everything Howard pointed out. On the ride toward the White House, she listened intently to his sage remarks, and laughed wildly, clapping her hands with huge enthusiasm at all his jests. She ignored John Glas. He was sullen, silent and kept casting pleading puppy looks at her, but she refused to meet his eyes. Pamela had not yet settled on her former beau's fate, but vowed to deal with him quickly and harshly at the earliest opportunity.

At the White House, Wright directed Glas and the uniformed driver and guard to clear a path through the crowd that had gathered in the rain to see Lincoln. Pamela and her congressman beau stood on the White House lawn under a great umbrella - while Marcia and Glas sheltered under another - and cheered the warm-up speeches and applauded the band.

Howard hugged Pamela close, oblivious to the people about them. "I have wonderful news to tell you later," he whispered.

"And I have news for you as well," she said. "But I don't know if it is so wonderful."

516

He hugged her more tightly still. "There are no words that could fall from those beautiful lips that could ever cause me alarm," Howard replied.

Pamela smiled sweetly. She patted her belly under her cloak, thinking if that tongue of his didn't remain as honeyed after she had her say, she'd rip it from its moorings.

Lincoln came out and the crowd's cheers rose to hysteria. They fell silent when he spoke, concentrating and nodding at every word. Pamela didn't hear a thing, to intent on her own problems. Despite her self absorption, an extraordinarily handsome man near Marcia and Glas caught her eye. He was in his mid twenties, with skin like ivory, gleaming white teeth, and silky black hair and mustache. His eyes were heavy-lidded and quite romantic. Adding dash to his dark beauty was an expensive great cloak with a flowing cape collared in fur.

His looks were so striking - and also vaguely familiar - Pamela couldn't help but smile at him, thinking her future would be much more interesting if Howard looked like that. The man didn't see her. He was intent on the President's remarks, although he frowned deeply every time the crowd applauded a particularly remarkable turn of phrase. Actually, he seemed quite angry. Pamela realized who he was and turned away in disgust.

It was the actor, John Booth - a fellow so full of himself only a very foolish woman would consider him for long-term company. But there were plenty of those, Lord knows. Pamela was acquainted with his mistress, Ella Turner, whom he kept in his sister's house over on Ohio Avenue. He was also reportedly engaged to the plump, painfully plain daughter of a Republican senator who had just lost his bid for re-election, but was about to be compensated by Lincoln with an ambassadorship to Spain. It was said Booth was deluged by swooning ladies, who sent him perfumed letters by the bagful whenever he appeared in a play.

As an actor, Pamela quite liked him. He was extremely athletic, and liked to make his entrance onto the stage with powerful bounds. He also cut a lusty figure in tights when he played The bard's works. There was a second, more important reason, why Pamela preferred to keep her distance from Booth. He was a Marylander like Marcia and an outspoken and fiery supporter of the South. Frankly, she wondered why he hadn't been locked up for treason. But she supposed it was because no one ever took an actor seriously.

Really, they were such stupid people. She took one last glance at him, and noted that the hair she'd admired was so perfectly waved - even in the damp - it appeared to have been set with a curling iron. How vain, Pamela thought. She turned away.

"Our President is a man of such charity, such mercy," Howard intoned, "that I truly believe he is a saint walking among us."

The congressman's friends rumbled agreement, and toasted the absent Saint Lincoln with the best brandy punch Willard's Hotel offered. They had gathered in rooms Howard had rented for a party after the speech. The big main room had a wide balcony that looked down on 14th Street. At the moment it was crowded with men and women watching the parade of Navy Yard workers marching past, shooting off boat howitzers and generally raising drunken hell.

"I know there are some who would criticize him for his views on Negro suffrage," Howard continued. "Whilst others will chide him for demanding we deal with the South with honor and mercy. But, my friends, Howard Wright is not one of those narrow-viewed men."

There were loud huzzahs, and much stamping of feet and clapping of hands. Pamela waited patiently as Howard completed his extemporaneous speech. He stepped off the chair he'd used as a make-shift dais and was pounded on the back by his congratulating admirers.

The word was out this night Howard Wright was in great favor with the President. He'd been recently re-elected, but in doing so he'd turned his district out solidly for Lincoln. Now he was about to get his reward. Most said he was certain to be made a senator, and Pamela had no reason to doubt it, although the slightest scandal would dash his hopes.

She watched with some trepidation as he made his way through the well-wishers to her side. He wore a black armband of mourning for his recently deceased wife. Pamela was beginning to fear when she told him what was up, he'd quickly make himself scarce.

Allan Cole & Chris Bunch

"Ah, here you are, m'dear," Howard said. He drained a big glass of punch, and put it on the tray of a passing waiter. "Did you enjoy my little remarks?" he asked.

Pamela saw he was tipsy, which was very much to her good. "Quite cogent, Howard, dear," she said. "Why, I wouldn't doubt that someday you are president yourself."

Howard jolted, then grinned hugely. He looked about, and saw everyone's attention was on eating and drinking and generally partying. "You know," he said, "I've been thinking the same thing myself of late." He motioned to a far door that led into another one of the room's he'd hired. "A quiet word?" he murmured.

It was Pamela's turn to look about. Marcia was on the balcony with some other women and she didn't see Glas anywhere. She nodded, and Howard took her elbow and quickly steered her into the other room. She saw, with some surprise, it was a bedroom. Howard closed the door behind him and locked it. He took off his frock coat and dropped it to the floor.

Pamela was delighted. Confidence flooded back - she couldn't have planned this better than if she had set the trap herself.

She gave a maidenly - if hushed - squeal of alarm as Howard rushed to her, tumbled her on the bed and threw up her skirts. "My goodness," he exclaimed, when he saw that she had not lied when she told him what he could expect under the gown. He ripped open his trousers and started to mount her.

"Wait! she cried - but weakly.

"Oh, pshaw," Howard said, thinking she was worried about protection. "We'll just have to take our chances." And he plunged in.

A few minutes later he was done. As he did up his breeches, Pamela stayed sprawled on the bed, purposefully neglectful with the turned up dress. She made her voice quite meek and fearful when she spoke. "Howard, dear," she began, "you know how you just mentioning about us, uh... taking our chances."

Howard eyed the place where her soft thighs met. He licked his lips, and nodded. "And I meant it, too," he said. "But what do we really have to fear? It was just this once. Odds are against anything... uh... happening."

Allan Cole & Chris Bunch

Pamela coyly pulled the dress down, but only a very little. She blushed and ducked her head. "Well, you see, it really wasn't just this once," she said.

Howard sat down beside her. "What do you mean, my love?"

"It was a little over a month ago," she said. "You came to my house and you were... well, a little drunk. Not that you haven't the right... you work so hard! Well... Do you remember that night?"

Howard frowned, then nodded again. She knew he remembered no such thing, but he was drunk so often he'd take her word for whatever she had to say.

"Anyway," Pamela continued, "you were a pretty randy fellow, if you recall. Just like tonight. And you didn't.... uh... give me time to get out the condom. And... Well, I fear there was a little accident, you see... and..."

She burst into tears. "Oh, my God, Howard. I'm so afraid. I'm pregnant with our child. And it'll be the ruin of both of us!"

Howard took her in his arms and let her weep into his shoulder. "There, there, dear," he said, all clumsy male. "It'll be all right. We'll get married. Then who will ever know?"

Pamela pulled back. She batted eyes she'd let get just wet to give her a helpless look, but without spoiling her looks. "You mean... you're not going to abandon me?"

"Why, of course not, sweetness," Howard said.

"But... aren't you worried that people will talk? I mean... your poor wife only just... died."

"And I hope she's burning in hell," Howard said. He fondled Pamela's bare thigh. "You're so beautiful. And you've given me so much happiness."

He patted her and sat back. "Here's what we'll do," he said. "I can get away easily, now. The war is almost over and Congress is close to recess. We'll go away to the islands and take a holiday for a month or two. We'll get married while we're there. Then, when we return, we'll already be an old married couple and no one will think anything of it."

He stroked his thick gray sideburns. "Besides, I'm an important man, now. Much more important than before."

"Of course, you are, Howard, dear," Pamela said.

Allan Cole & Chris Bunch

"No one will dare question me."

"Absolutely not," Pamela said. She stroked his arm, letting her fingers linger on his flabby muscles as if they excited her. "It'll be such a relief to put myself into the hands of a strong man who knows his mind," she said. "And I do love you dearly. I'll make you a wonderful wife. I promise."

Howard kissed her and got up. "I had better go see to the guests," he said. He grinned. "Wouldn't want them to get suspicious, would we?"

Pamela giggled. He gave her another kiss and left the room. She lay back on the bed, savoring her victory. She thought about Madame Roberval's promised miracle medicine, and decided even if it worked, she'd marry Howard just the same. Of course, she wouldn't tell him what had happened, but tie him closer to her by going into mourning over the loss of their dear infant.

She hated children, and had no intention of ever having any if she could only get rid of this one. A sudden thought came. She remembered trying so hard to get pregnant with Edward. Obviously the hateful creature that now dwelt in her belly was final proof it was his fault they had never been successful. Well, good riddance to him. And good riddance to Fitz Maguire. And good riddance to Patrick Shannon, that little shit, who tried to spoil the whole thing.

She hugged herself in delight. Even if Susan Dolan was fool enough to appeal, Pamela's friends would block it. Howard and Judge Roland had sweetened the court by dispensing many favors. Soon she would be a rich woman. Doubly rich, because she'd be married to a United States Senator. Then, no one, but no one, would ever tell Pamela Shannon what to do again.

The door swung open and she made her best smile, thinking it was Wright returning. But she shot up in the bed, pulling her dress down, when she saw it was Lt. John Glas.

"What the hell are you doing here?" she snapped.

Glas wasn't cowed by her temper. He stepped forward, face dark with fury. "I've just been talking to Wright," he said. "And he let slip that he is soon to marry-" his tone became acid- "the beautiful Widow Shannon."

Pamela jumped to her feet. She stabbed a hard finger into his chest." What of it?" Pamela said. "That's our business, not yours. Now, get out!"

John's fury suddenly melted. He fell to her feet, sobbing. "Oh, please don't do this to me," he wailed. "I love you so. You should be marrying me... not that filthy old man." He gripped her by the knees.

Pamela tried to kick him away, but only succeeded in falling back on the bed. "Get out of here!" she screamed. "You're too stupid for words, you German pig."

Glas leaped up, tears coursing down his cheeks. Pamela's dress was up around her waist, exposing her nakedness. "You can't marry him," he shouted. "You can't."

He stepped toward her and Pamela kicked, aiming for his crotch, but getting him in the thigh instead.

The bedroom door slammed open and she heard Howard's voice boom out. "My God, what are you doing, Glas?"

She sat, dragging down her dress. "He tried to attack me!" she shouted.

"I never did," Glas cried out. "I love her, dammit!"

"How dare you!" Howard railed.

"It's me she loves," Glas babbled. "She wants someone young. Someone who can make her happy. Someone who-"

"Liar!" Pamela shrieked. If Glas said much more, the damage would be beyond repair. "He tried to... rape me!" She began to cry.

Howard whirled and ran out of the room. As she gaped after him, Glas said: "See, he's a coward as well. You'll be better off with me."

Before she could respond, Howard ran back into the room again. To her horror, she saw that he was waving a pistol. "I'll get you, you son of a bitch," Howard shouted.

"Don't!" Pamela screamed.

Howard fired. The gunshot was thunder in her ears. But, miraculously, he missed. Glas raced from the room as Howard raised the pistol again.

"Stop it, Howard!" Pamela shouted.

He paid her no attention, but ran after Glas. Pamela followed, pleading with Howard to stop.

522

In the main room there were howls of terror as Glas bulled through the crowd and Howard fired again. Another miracle as this shot chewed into the ceiling. But then everyone dove to the floor giving him a clearer aim. Glas veered toward the balcony. People desperately rolled out of his way.

"Stop and fight, you coward!" Howard roared.

"No, Howard! Please, Howard!" Pamela cried.

Once more Howard fired. The bullet took John Glas between the shoulder blades and flung him against the balcony rail, where he slumped to the floor.

Howard marched forward. Pamela rushed to him and caught him by the sleeve, trying to pull him away. But he kept going, dragging her along, until he reached Glas. "That'll teach you," he rumbled, and kicked him.

Glas's body flopped over. Empty eyes stared upward. Sudden realization hit Howard.

He turned to Pamela, who stood gaping at him in awful shock. "My God, Pamela," he said. "I think I've killed him!"

Pamela sagged, seeing all hopes of any kind of a future fade into oblivion.

"Yes, Howard," she said, numb. "I believe you did."

CHAPTER FORTY-TWO

WEST OF FORT SULLY, DAKOTA, MAY 3, 1865

"WELL, SERGEANT?"

"Cowshit, sir. Fresh. Maybe an hour or so old," First Sergeant Patrick Shannon said. He rose from his crouch, picked up his horse's reins, and swung back into the saddle.

"Not buffalo?"

"Nossir. Buffalo don't crap grain, sir. This is our beef."

Patrick refrained from reminding the Lieutenant buffalo didn't usually travel in small groups and also weren't generally escorted by unshod ponies. Instead, he turned to the other seven members of the patrol. "Spread out. Skirmishing order. They'll be somewhere ahead of us. I count ten, maybe more."

Lieutenant Gadd started to snap something - probably that he was the one in command of this patrol - but broke off. He glowered as the mounted infantrymen swung into action, fingers reflexively checking to make sure their Spencers' magazine tubes were seated and their Colt's loose in their revolvers. Unlike the others, Patrick carried two Colt's holstered on his saddle, and a third at his hip, as he'd learned with Forrest's raiders. A lever-action Henry was scabbarded, butt up, to the right rear of his saddle. At the walk, the patrol moved after the rustlers.

Patrick and Lieutenant Gadd were already less than friends. Gadd thought Shannon was just too damned wise mouthed for any ex-Reb, and the hell with any implicit forgiveness granted when Patrick had taken Colonel Mowat's offer. He was also not impressed with the extra stripes Mowat had ordered Shannon to put up before assigning him to Gadd's company.

Patrick, on the other hand, wondered what the hell a West Point graduate was doing this far from the fields of glory in the East. Although it'd been two months since they'd had news of the fighting, Patrick was sure there was enough war left for honor to be won. He'd thought perhaps that explained exactly why the lieutenant was out here in Dakota, since honor's laurels not infrequently required some bloodshed, and that most likely wouldn't be desirable for the son of a Chicago alderman. The Lieutenant no doubt had a promising career ahead, whose starting point would be boldly marked by his service in the War Between the States, as some were calling it.

Not that a man couldn't get dead out here in some fairly unique ways. Disease and accidents had taken their share of the ragged ex-prisoners who'd been clothed, fed and drilled hard as Mowat had promised before getting their guidon – their standard - as Company I, 7th U.S. Volunteers. They were all especially fit after the one hundred mile march north from where the steamboat had run out of Missouri River and dumped them off in the heart of winter.

Most soldiers worried less about disease than about the Sioux who haunted the featureless prairies around the earth-roofed stockaded fort. The Sioux were seldom seen, except as dots on the horizon; and rarely heard, other than half-imagined whispers in the night. But they were out there. An incautious sentry would be spitted by a lance, or an arrow would whisper out of an innocent clump of brush to strike a dispatch rider down, or a water-gathering party headed for the river a mile away might be ambushed by a scatter of raiders. It was best to die at once if that happened, and if no one rode to the rescue. The Sioux had unusual ideas of how to treat their prisoners.

But this was a different war, not the crowded slashing butchery Patrick had known in the East. It was a war like chess, horsemen against horsemen, and when the battle was done, it was done.

The land was as different as the fighting. Patrick had remembered true. The west was harsh, unforgiving. But it also promised something, loud in the northers that roared down, winds hurling iceshards into a rider's face, soft when spring opened over the land, and silent in the heat-haze of the desolate brown summer. When the war ended, Patrick thought, this was where he belonged. He could not return to the South and its lies and oppression. Mister Lincoln might have forbidden slavery, but that battle was barely joined and he saw no real peace even after the inevitable surrender. Nor did he see any place in the north, although there'd been several offers from Aunt Susan and the others who'd written from Philadelphia. He'd never seen those great cities and their throngs, but even though he dreamed of them, it was always as an outsider, a visitor.

Allan Cole & Chris Bunch

He knew he would have to offer Lucy a better life than sharing a saddle and a dry camp with a wandering horseman and gambler but thus far wasn't sure what it might be. Soldiering drew him in an odd way. Perhaps it gave him a measure of the security he'd never known, a strange sort of family that reached all the way to poor dead Johnny Evans back on the Cumberland, and included men like Colonel Mowat who kept their promises.

But life as an enlisted man's wife would be intolerable for Lucy. The Army didn't recognize any women other than officers' wives, whores, or the handful of "laundresses" permitted each company. These were women Lucy would have nothing in common with, from morals to upbringing to education. At least, he thought with relief, he had someone to worry about.

Lucy was now in Philadelphia. She seemed to be fitting in - her letters were full of the strangeness of this Yankee world. At times her letters seemed a little odd, though, almost as if she were surveying a strange, and a bit abhorrent, race from afar. But what of that? Patrick was not at all sure what he'd think when his enlistment was up and he, too, was surrounded by Yankees. Perhaps he'd find them even stranger than Keplar's Men in the Moon. Lucy was certainly not spending her time weeping and wailing, any more than she had when Vicksburg was besieged. Aunt Susan said she was helping run the household, as well as helping them care for his poor mad cousin Nancy.

From all reports everyone was as delighted with Lucy as Patrick himself. But the situation was temporary. Once the war was over... Patrick shook his head, and his fingers found the old musketball as always when he pondered a problem. He brought himself back to the present, and the sharp spring prairie.

Two hours ago ten or so Sioux braves had swooped on the cattle-herding detail. The two privates detailed as herders had wisely ridden hard for the fort, hollering as they went. The Indians had sent a scatter of arrows after them, then cut out half of the company's herd and lashed it into a shambling, mooing, shitting stumble north. Patrick had come running out of the orderly room, buckling on his pistol belt - eagerly forgetting the paperwork that was the bane of a first shirt - and shouting for the standby guard detail. Unfortunately

Lieutenant Gadd had been just as bored, and as eager to ride out looking for action.

Not only was Gadd an arrogant little simpleton, but he was as pigheaded as any Irishman fresh from the bogs that Patrick had ever known. The company had already given him a name - "Death or Glory" Gadd. According to the popular press, there were many officers given that sobriquet. But Patrick had never heard of one who'd been so-named in any other way than mocking or fearful. Death or Glory - His Glory, Our Death. Patrick was proud that every patrol he'd led out from the fort came back with all its men. Sometimes there'd been wounded, a few times corpses stretched across their mounts, but he'd never pushed his soldiers or horses until they collapsed or died, or abandoned or lost a man on the vast prairies. But with Gadd riding point he felt no confidence whatsoever.

As he thought, Patrick's eyes swept the horizon. He might as well be a ship's lookout in a maritime romance. As usual, he saw movement before anyone else in the patrol did. "There they are," he called, not loudly. He heard a rifle snap to full cock behind him. Patrick didn't turn. "Ryan! I'll tell you when you'll be needing to shoot somebody."

He heard a mutter of obedience. Gadd was standing in his stirrups, scanning the horizon. "Where? Where?" he demanded.

"Heading toward the river. Perhaps there's a ford."

"Patrol! At the trot! Forward!" Gadd shouted.

The men gigged their horses before Patrick could offer a reasonable objection. He shrugged, and kicked his own mount. It lurched forward with the others. His remount was many, many generations removed from Templar... and Patrick turned his mind off to that, just as he kept it away from a thousand other memories of the past four years, and the nine men rode forward, after the Sioux.

The ground became rolling, more broken, as they came closer to the river. Now they saw their stolen beeves about half a mile away. Patrick counted three, no four warriors, their ponies dashing around the rear of the herd, the Indians shouting, seemingly panic-stricken as they saw the on-rushing soldiers. Now where the hell were the rest of them? Ridden on ahead? Maybe.

527

Gadd had his saber out and was waving it about his head. Serve the bastard right if he falls off and impales himself, Patrick thought, trying to maneuver his horse to the side, out of the dust so he could see more clearly.

"Charge! Charge! Taken no prisoners!" Gadd was bellowing.

Patrick saw the ravine when they were about a hundred yards away, to the side of their path. "Halt!" Patrick shouted. "Patrol—"

"Shut up, Sergeant, or I'll have your stripes," Gadd shouted. "Take them, men! Take them!"

The patrol streamed across the prairie in disorder. Gadd was about thirty yards in front of the others when the Sioux sprung their well-planned ambush. Fifteen braves rode out of that ravine at a hard gallop. The four decoys with the rustled cattle turned back, whooping, to join their brothers. Patrick heard flat cracks and saw white smoke - so some of them had rifles, probably gotten in trade across the Canadian border but most were armed with bows or lances. The soldiers were shouting and firing back.

Arrows whipped past Patrick's head, and the patrol was a rearing confusion, horses screaming protest against the hard-yanked reins. Patrick saw one rider - Ryan it was that goddamned fool - pinwheel over his mount's head, and thud onto the rain-damp sod.

Patrick had his Henry out, levered a round into its chamber. He stuck the reins between his teeth and pumped three rounds off, in the general direction of the oncoming Indians. Hell, maybe I'll get lucky, but no one fell.

Gadd was trying to rein in, but his horse had its bit in its teeth and was going for the river. He was still shouting, obscenities now. The saber was gone. His arms were flailing. Patrick saw an arrow shaft through one waving arm, and a second one thup into Gadd's thigh and on into his mount.

Three Indians came in from the side. Gadd was yanking at the still-fastened flap to his holster when the lance darted like a snake's strike. It drove into his side and sent him tumbling from his saddle.

Patrick was among the patrol madness now, shouting orders. "Dismount, goddamit! Pull them down!" Horses reared, pirouetted, stamping, and the soldiers were sliding down from the saddles, keeping tight hold on the reins.

Allan Cole & Chris Bunch

Gadd lay crumpled not far ahead, the lance standing out of his body. The Indians' yelping was triumphant as they wheeled and came in once more on the knot of men.

Patrick came out of his saddle. His voice was loud, but very calm. "On line, now. One man for two horses. Don't let them get away. It's a long walk home. We've got plenty of time. Rifles. Kneeling position. It's just like on the range. Goddamit, Henissart, put the popgun away! You can't hit shit with it anyway! I said with your rifle! Take aim... hold it... FIRE!"

It was a ragged volley, but three Indians fell forward, and the charge was broken. One brave, more courageous, suicidal or foolhardy than the rest, galloped on, intent on counting coup. Patrick dropped him from the saddle with one round from his Henry, saw the man twitch, and put another bullet into his back.

"Reload!" The men were obeying and the soldiers' horses were calming. One horse screamed, and pulled away from its rider as two arrows hit it in the chest with that flat unmistakable sound.

"Get the horses down!" His men wrestled the mounts to their knees, then forced them to their sides, as the remounts, and their owners, had practiced again and again learning real battle tactics away from Fort Riley's parade-ground-drill.

The Indians charged again, and again rifle fire drove them away. Patrick did a fast count. No one down except Ryan, just behind the patrol, trying to get to his feet and recover his breath.

And Gadd. Patrick saw an Indian rein in, and slip off his horse, scalping knife ready. The Sioux grabbed Gadd's head by its greasy, already-balding hair, and lifted.

Patrick went three paces forward, taking a deep breath as he did. He held his breath as the Henry's butt came into his shoulder, and he put the brave's chest just above his sights and pulled the trigger back, back, and there was a puff of smoke and the Indian flung both hands up, shouted in great surprise and collapsed over Gadd's body.

He lowered the Henry, and saw two other Indians dismount, and run toward the bodies. Patrick, not thinking, for he would've knocked any trooper silly for such foolishness, dropped his rifle and was running forward, hand dragging his pistol free.

Allan Cole & Chris Bunch

An Indian hurled his lance, and it sailed past Patrick's shoulder. Patrick snap-shot, and the man howled, grabbed his stomach, and rolled in the dirt. The second man had some sort of short musket, and was about to fire as Patrick knelt, used his left forearm as a brace and sent two bullets into the Sioux's chest.

He ran to Gadd's body, shoved his pistol in his belt and grabbed an arm. He pulled the lieutenant from under the equally-dead Indian, and began dragging him back toward the patrol. He heard whoops, and the thud of hooves, and saw the Indians vee-charge at him. He stumbled on, trying to run, crouching, and the volley came from the patrol, and he heard an Indian screech in pain, and the horse-thunder was going away.

He did not turn until he had reached the horses. He let the body sag down, and chanced a look. The prairie was again bare, rolling toward the river, high against its banks in spring melt. A hundred yards away Fort Sully's cattle milled, bawling bewilderment. There were eight bodies scattered on the sod. Expensive, Patrick thought. Very, very expensive. It'll be awhile before the lodges stop mourning this day.

Ryan stood beside him, his breath rasping, holding one hand against the pain of his probably-broken ribs.

"Whyinhell'd you go an' do somethin' that shit, Top?"

Patrick took several breaths, reminding himself of how easy the spring air breathed. As a matter of fact, his mind went on, almost any air would taste good right now, wouldn't it? He looked at Gadd's blood- and dirt-covered face. The expression was that of a terrier who'd just locked its teeth for the kill and realized its opponent was a mastiff.

Then he turned to Ryan. "Hell if I know," he said honestly. "It just seemed like a good idea at the time. Enough of that. Horne, there's some canvas in my right saddlebag. Strap Ryan's ribs up. The rest of you, mount up. Let's get those cattle headed back. It'll be dark in a couple of hours."

He looked again at Gadd's body and shook his head. You could get killed doing things like this, Sergeant.

The cannonading started when they were two miles from the fort. Patrick wondered if the whole Sioux nation was attacking. He puzzled - the firing was coming in a regular order. The crashing upset the cattle - they began bellowing a chorus.

Patrick saw a rider debouch from the fort and gallop toward them. The man was shouting as he came: "It's over! The war's over!"

He could make out shouting from the fort. The news appeared to be at least a month old, but that didn't quell the excitement. He thought he heard someone say Lincoln was dead, which hardly seemed possible. Then the hollering of his patrol drowned out the rest.

The rider swept past them, still shouting: "It's over! The war's over!"

Patrick looked over at Henissart and saw tears runnel the dirt. "Now... now we can go home," the Georgian said.

Patrick nodded, and tried to smile as his fingers touched the musket ball Grandmother Shannon had given him.

Home? What was that, anyway?

CHAPTER FORTY-THREE

PHILADELPHIA - LATE JULY, 1865

LIEUTENANT PATRICK SHANNON sat on the top deck of the omnibus, staring at the river of evening traffic. He was on his way to Susan's house, where most of the Shannons who had survived the war were gathering to mark its ending. Waiting among them was his wife, Lucy, whom he ached to see again, but whose manner of welcome he feared. Would she spurn him as a traitor? Would the other Shannons scorn him as well for the same, if reversed, reason?

He'd traded his uniform for civilian clothes to lessen the impact of wearing what Lucy might see as the enemy's colors - although she'd lived in a Yankee city and the kindness of his Yankee cousin for many months. But what would the Shannons think? Patrick had slept badly for days worrying over their reaction. He wiped sweat from his palms and tried to force his mind away from his troubles. As the omnibus lumbered onward, he lost himself to the rhythms of the city.

The street below was a turbulent stream of all sorts of vehicles, bobbing and jostling between the hissing gas lamps that ribboned the roadway. Drivers shouted at one another, frantically waving their whips. Boys carrying lanterns trotted before carriages and waged a war of curses and blows with their freight wagon counterparts. The whole city seemed a frantic chorus of loud voices, barking dogs, bawling animals and rattling machine belts.

Bewildering sights floated past. Glowing shop windows glittered with goods. People streamed in and out of those shops, although dusk was long past. Pushcart immigrants called their wares in a confusion of accents. In the poorer districts he saw pawn shops with three golden balls to mark them, intermingled with countless cigar stores. He heard raucous sounds and music echoing from cellar taverns, and was taken aback on one street that seemed to be filled with nothing but women who exposed their bodies as men passed. Brightly lit signs said they were artists' models for hire.

The two-level horse-drawn bus lumbered out of the traffic and past parks with trees as thick as an old forest, but with summer-scented gardens and well-lit paths that beckoned solitary thinkers, strolling families, and young lovers taking the night air. There were quiet neighborhoods of red brick row homes whose windows were warm hearths of light. Church steeples - he'd never dreamed there could be so many churches - guarded these neighborhoods and soothed them with vespers bells and lilting chorales. The omnibus clattered through a working-class district, where people chatted quietly on the stoops and children ran about at play. He could smell the delights of thick stews bubbling and meat roasting and sausages sputtering on the grills.

The sights, sounds and smells combined to make a heady dish for a young man who had never seen a city near as grand. Philadelphia was all Susan and Ian had promised ten years ago in his great grandmother's parlor.

Lord, had it really been that long? He'd been twelve then, and his greatest dream was to be the pilot of a river boat. Actually, as he thought about that day the Eclipse had steamed up the Mississippi to his great grandmother's house, he recalled his most heart-felt wish had been to rid himself of Pamela Shannon by running away. Well, he'd done that, and mostly made a grand mess of his life as a result. Only the past few months of his twenty two years seemed to have made any sense, although events just after the sudden ambush by the Sioux just had become confusing.

Things had moved very swiftly indeed following the death of Lieutenant Gadd. Less than two weeks after the report had been sent to regimental headquarters about the skirmish with the Sioux, Sergeant Shannon had been ordered to turn over his duties to the next-ranking noncommissioned officer and report, immediately, with all his gear (two saddlebags and one bedroll) to Colonel Mowat at regimental headquarters.

Wondering what the hell betided, Patrick obeyed. Mowat, as usual, got straight to the point. Evidently the late Lieutenant Gadd's father had more influence than even his position as an alderman suggested. There had been a flurry of correspondence back and forth, at first by letter, then by telegraph to the nearest town to the small fort Mowat had selected for his headquarters. All of them concerned First Sergeant Patrick Shannon. Gadd's father wanted the soldier who recovered his son's body to be properly rewarded. The Medal of

Allan Cole & Chris Bunch

Honor had seemed appropriate. The alderman had immediately approached his congressman, and been shocked, nay appalled, to be told Congress would be unlikely to approve any award for an ex-Confederate, no matter how valiant his behavior.

At this point, Patrick interrupted the Colonel, protesting he'd hardly done anything that extraordinary. Mowat waved silence and continued. The Chicago alderman felt he must do something - and did. It seemed, after some high degree of string-pulling, that Patrick Shannon was to be offered a chance to join the Regular Army. Patrick's eyes widened, and then he truly gaped as Mowat gave him the rest. If Patrick accepted, he would join the United States military as an officer - a newly-commissioned second lieutenant.

"There is no justice," Colonel Mowat gloomed. "With the war over, the Army's being cut to the bone, and the bone lathed to a toothpick. Generals will be giving up their brevets and going back to captaincies. Or else being pitched out altogether and forced to actually work for their keep. A cruel world, Sergeant. Further proving to me that God is truly a malignant thug."

Mowat grinned. "No. Don't say anything. I know your tendency to leap to decisions. Get out of my office. Here. Take this bottle. Go for a walk. Get drunk. Take all the time you want. That's all." Patrick had befuddled a salute, and headed for the door.

"One more thing, Sergeant... or is it Lieutenant? Whether you accept or not, you're detached. The Galvanized Yankees will be broken up in the next few months. "You're under orders to go to Chicago. Lieutenant Gadd's father wants to hear the details of his son's death. You can go as an officer, or a civilian, but you are going east in three days, so prepare an appropriate tale of derring-do. Dismissed."

Patrick ignored the bottle and thought hard. He took all three days before announcing his decision to Mowat. He would take the commission. Now he could offer Lucy more than a life on the road. Better still, he could go to Philadelphia as a proud man, not as a bankrupt ex-enemy soldier, and see if he wanted to fit in, to completely become a Shannon. Dependent on no one's charity, he and Lucy of them would have a chance to build a life together. Now he would have the chance to show Lucy there was more than the North and the South.

He hoped - no, came as close to praying as he knew how - that finally, in the west, they would find their place.

The driver's whip cracked and the omnibus rounded a hard bend, jostling Patrick out of his reverie. As the wonders of Philadelphia came flooding back he thought about how Grandmother Shannon must have felt when she first came into the city. He touched the hard musketball that dangled in its sack beneath his shirt, calling her memory close.

When she arrived in Philadelphia, Diana had been a country girl herself - although the term seemed tame when he considered that her great empty spaces had been a dangerous wilderness. Had she been frightened? She'd only had his grandfather and great uncle - small boys then - for company. But he couldn't imagine Diana ever being frightened, although she'd said she had... she'd said she had.

There'd been raiders and Indians and plagues and a city burned about her. When he'd heard those tales he'd been twelve. Now he was twenty two, and knew a thing or two about horror. He'd seen blood by the river, towns ripped by cannon, and the hollow eyes of famine. But his own terrors still seemed small compared to his great grandmother's ordeals.

Why is that, Patrick Shannon? Why is that? Was it because she seemed so certain, so sure of the ways of the world? But she was an old woman, and he was still very young. So how fair was it to compare their lives? Yes, but she'd conquered that wilderness by the time she was his age, and was set for new victories when she'd arrived in Philadelphia.

He gripped the musketball hard, trying to draw her strength. He'd made so many mistakes. If his great grandmother were alive, she'd be much disappointed.

What worth had she'd seen in him? Then he thought, wasn't it enough that she'd seen something? If Diana Shannon believed, than worth must be there, however well-hidden.

He remembered the day he'd confessed his pain and guilt over his treatment of young Nehemiah, the friend who had also been his

Allan Cole & Chris Bunch

slave. What was it she'd answered? Then her words came flooding back to him... as if he were a boy perched on the old woman's bed.

"Keep that pain close to you, Patrick... Hold it tight to the guilt and do not let it go. If you keep it safe, it will protect you from committing the sin again... And I promise someday you will take it out and look at it and see something you had never thought to see before. Remember those people when you do that. And you'll never be the same again..."

Patrick wiped tears from his face, then blew his nose on his hanky. He felt better, more capable of facing at least the near future.

The omnibus rattled to a stop and a kind woman, who'd overheard him tell the driver where he was going, said this was his stop. Patrick threw his bag over his shoulders and went down the stairs to the first level, then pushed his way through the passengers and got off. He stepped up on the sidewalk, then hesitated, looking down the long street, and seeing the big old house Susan had described in her letter. It was ablaze with light. The street was empty, except for a long, shadowy form leaning against a lamppost.

As he looked at the house, fear gripped him again. But this time it was more terrible than any he had felt on a battlefield. His heart hammered and he found it difficult to draw breath. There would be people inside who might judge him hard. Susan had lost Ian and one of her sons. Joshua, the rock of the Shannons, was dead. There would be many others who had suffered as well. And Lucy... God help him if she hated him.

He almost turned back. Nearly ran down the street to catch a carriage that would take him to the safety of the train station. He'd run before, he could do it again, and all of his troubles would soon be left far behind.

Patrick recaptured his courage and walked slowly down the street. As he reached the lamppost, the long shadowy form straightened, and stepped forward. Light pooled down over a familiar face with sardonic eyes.

"Que paso, Patrick?" It was Michael Shannon, a glowing cigarillo dangling from one laconic hand. "This is an odd part of the world to encounter you in."

536

Patrick remembered his cousin had spoken those very words in Vicksburg Under-The-Hill ten years before, keeping him from getting into a jam that would have been very hard to escape.

"I'm glad to see you, Michael," he said, his tones heavy with the relief that flooded through him. There was no way he could tell his cousin just how glad he was.

But Michael knew. He jabbed the cigarillo at the house. "There are some things harder than war, compadre," he said. "Coming home is one of them."

Patrick nodded. This was so, although he'd been without a home and family so long he'd never learned it before.

Michael clapped him on the shoulder. "They're waiting for you, amigo," he said. "I thought I'd just step out... in case you missed your way."

"Thanks," Patrick said. "I nearly did."

Michael just gave that thin, easy grin of his. He took Patrick's bag, and motioned him forward with an elegant wave of his long gambler's fingers.

The door of the house opened and he heard a glad cry and then light feet coming down the steps. Patrick looked up and saw a willowy form running toward him.

It was Lucy and she was calling his name.

The last Shannon was home.

The End

Allan Cole & Chris Bunch

www.ingramcontent.com/pod-product-compliance
Lightning Source LLC
Chambersburg PA
CBHW072010020726
47501CB00006B/1751